To my niece Nadia, who will not be able to read these words for many years. May your journey through the woods be bright, may your trials be overcome, and may you come out stronger than you imagined you could be.

Acknowledgments

I want to thank everyone who waited so long with patience and understanding.

If you lived through 2020, you know how important a good book can be. I hope it was worth the wait.

The Cindra Corrina Chronicles
Book 5

Into the Shadowood

Mark Rude

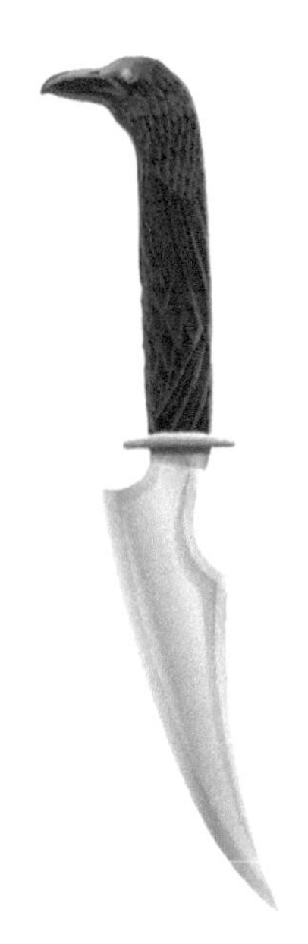

ISBN 978-0-9848275-5-8

Printed in the United States of America.

Contents

Chapter One

Unexpected Company

The Low Road out of Portshia had sprung rows upon rows of makeshift tents and campsites, like mushrooms blooming after a storm. The odors of men, beasts, cook pots, and midden pits all but canceled out the fresh sea air.

"Make way! Make way!" Cindra called.

Faces turned and conversations stopped as the travelers passed by. They were heading in the opposite direction of the war, and the leader seemed to be a lady wearing sword and a shield with the coat of arms of House Corrina. No one knew what to make of it all, so they made light, grinning and chuckling to each other.

Lady Cindra tried not to feel self-conscious as she led her party on their quest, but it was nearly impossible. She had shed her disguise half a year ago; she let her auburn hair grow out and no longer bothered to wrap her breasts to hide them. She was wearing one of the special riding dresses that the king had given her, rather *commanded* her, to wear. Over the bodice of the dress, she wore a quilted arming doublet with mail stitched to the joints, and over that, the king's tabard of dark gray with silver lining, and a black eagle upon the breast. *Vyzeroth*, one of the three Corrina Honor Swords, hung upon her hip.

These details were noticed with wide, incredulous eyes by the soldiers along the road, who made way for them but mocked her just the same. Cindra wished she had donned her plate armor and helmet for the departure so she could hide within a steel shell, safe from questioning stares, but it was packed away in the wagon, awaiting a more dangerous road.

"Don't mind them," Adric said, riding behind her, "Most have never left home before."

Adric Hywahl, her new squire, was a tall lad with a trim build and a handsome face. His boyish looks were giving way to the angular lines of manhood. His blond hair was cut short, for he never intended to wear the bound queue of a knight. He was riding a dapple gray stallion called Smoke.

Adric had been holding a conversation with Padison Pemwreth, the short, round-faced, towheaded boy who drove the wagon. Both had been fellow students and friends of Cindra's at the Freekirk Fighting School, and had remained so after her true identity was revealed. She could not have hoped for better company, except perhaps for Sir Jaron Dunlorden, but he was riding to war with the southern army in the coming month.

Padison called to the men, "What, you don't have lady knights back west?"

Cindra sighed, "Please don't antagonize them, Paddy."

"Twavel bwoadens the mind," Drahn said, "But maybe not *that* much."

The dweedragon sat next to Padison upon the wagon bench, staring back at the soldiers with the same wide-eyed curiosity they gave him. It was his first real journey into adventure since leaving home at the Mystic College of Aldrig over forty years ago. Drahn sat upon a backpack that contained his supplies and personal belongings, and which would serve as a sleeping bag during cold nights. The little creature's scales shimmered between magenta and red, showing his happiness and excitement.

The same colors scintillated upon Cindra's chest, where she wore the gift he had given her. Drahn had made one of his tail scales into a necklace to symbolize their shared experience upon Tirgrim's Bluff, where Cindra had been sentenced to certain death. They had survived, both being marked in different ways. Cindra's arms bore the fractal scars of a lightning strike, while Drahn had taken the lightning into himself, finally discovering the elemental power of his unique heritage.

Bringing up the rear were Nixy and Wenyssaya, two enigmatic figures who were the reason for this strange journey. Nixy DuQuayne, once a street urchin and thief, was in fact the son of the Shadow Lord, an ancient elf who lived within the Shadowood forest. Supposedly, the boy was the repository of powers and a bloodline not seen since the Sorcerer Kings of humankind's earliest days, yet he appeared a nervous child, younger looking than his fourteen years, and uncomfortable in his fine traveling clothes. An ever-present cowlick on his blond head defied the best efforts of brushing.

If Nixy DuQuayne was utterly unimpressive as one of his heritage could be, Wenyssaya was the opposite. She was an elf from the Blackwood Forest to the east, and unusual even by elven standards, as such things were known. Her golden hair was radiant and bounced in curls behind her head, her skin was the color of honey mixed with fresh cream; her amethyst eyes were prominent and almond-shaped, and her delicate ears ended in faerie-points. Her beauty was ethereal, as if the light of the sun became diffused, casting her all aglow. She sat bare-backed upon her white steed, with a black raven perched behind her. The elf maid's presence had the effect of making people forget all of the previous odd sights as the party rode by; *she* was what they would remember.

Cindra had no way of knowing this, because she was too far ahead to hear the murmurings die into awed silence. Besides, she was wrapped up in her own thoughts. She had tried to keep those thoughts practical; this was her first quest after all, and the fate of the kingdom may well depend on its success. Still, her mind fled back to Sir Jaron, her knight, mentor, and lover. He had been an assistant instructor at the fighting school, which gave him access to a private room. She had been his squire, which gave her the right to share that room with him. It had all been necessary to protect her identity of course, but there were so many other benefits.

Now those days were lost. Fate allowed them to spend two long years in each other's company, and fate separated them the moment King Galen III bestowed that knighthood upon her. The secret could no longer be kept, and Jaron instantly became an object of scorn and dishonor once again. Their brief reunions had been bittersweet, made all the more intense by the long stretches of time between them.

I must concentrate on the path before me, Cindra thought, closing her eyes, *We cannot change the past.* She recalled the map of their route, taking them west to the Low Bridge that crossed the Joshian River near its mouth, then to the village of Wellgate, where the Low Road became the Red Coast Road to the west, and the Joshian Way to the north. The latter was their road; it led through the Shadowood Forest, keeping near the west bank of the river.

Wellgate is Jaron's home village, Cindra thought, *He was born there.*

She sighed, reprimanding herself. *The route, the route.* She needed a distraction from her own thoughts.

"Drahn?" she asked, "what do you know about our route?"

He perked up and said, "The Joshian Way was once the main twade woute between Portshia and the gweat city of Wickshome in the far north..."

Padison chuckled, and Drahn frowned, working to pronounce his words more carefully. "*Rickshome,*" he said, "but that was in the days of the Celvestrian Empire's rule, and before the deforesting of Casselvane Pwovence, or construction of the Casselvane Road. Then came the Time of Chaos, and everything changed. The Shadowood became even more dark and mysterious. Woad and wiver became twuly tweacherous in places..." He cleared his throat, glancing sidelong at Padison's grin. "New creatures emerged, like the water oxen that pull barges on the river, but the Joshian Way became little-traveled and overgrown outside the influence of Breega, the only major settlement along the road."

Adric came alongside Cindra, watching her face. It took her a few moments to notice him. Almost as if reading her thoughts, he said, "Breega is Greenfellow territory."

Cindra nodded, her face grim as she remembered her rival in the fighting school. "Rejick Ratham. Do you suppose he'll still be there?"

Adric shrugged, "He might be, but only if he's dodging the king's call to arms. I doubt even Waliss Greenfellow would allow his nephew to ignore a royal decree." He grinned, "For all we know, we passed him on the road already."

"I doubt he would be camped here like a conscript," she said, "If he's in Portshia, he's probably staying at the Drakthorne villa." She said it without scorn or irony, for she too would be housed in luxury if she were waiting with the army. She had lived in the Winter Palace for months in the company of the king and his lords, albeit for reasons of keeping an eye on her, not due to her station or status.

"Still," Adric said, "There's the fighting school in Breega and the old man. They might not give us a warm welcome."

Cindra didn't feel the need to tell her friends about the greeting Jaron had received at the hands of the Greenfellow School when he passed through Breega some four years ago. It would not help morale. "We are on an official mission for the king," she said, "I am sure they will give us safe passage, even if they curse us behind our backs."

"Or to our faces?" Adric asked.

"If so, they can only hurt our feelings," she said with a smile.

The road stretched on and the encampments grew thinner, until all that was left was the trampled grass, dust, and refuse left in the army's wake. Few travelers passed them as they made for Low Bridge, and the sun was now high in the sky. The journey so far had taken longer than expected due to the camped army, but now the way was clear. Five miles out of Portshia, the Low Road forked south to the seaside, where the shipyards and naval base of Casselport made ready for war. The tall masts rose like a thicket of bare trees over the rise.

Considering her last voyage, Cindra didn't care if she ever set foot on a ship's deck again.

Padison had taken up a song, his reedy voice quavering as the wagon hit rough patches. The breeze carried the scent of the sea, and seven miles on, the rushing waters of the river grew in their ears. Cindra hailed the toll-keeper in his little hut and paid several coppers for her retinue. They crossed the long, arched bridge, leaving the province of Casselvane behind.

Beyond the river was the Bridge House, one of the many tea and lodging establishments that seemed to crop up every half-day's ride or so. This place held some memories; long ago, she and her handmaiden had gone riding in the company of Sir Jaron, and Sir Earnold Greenfellow, her bodyguard. Mineth had found the riding difficult and she stayed behind at the teahouse with Sir Earnold, while Cindra and Jaron raced off towards a distant shady tree. They had fallen into a slumber there with Cindra's head upon his shoulder.

She had no intention of stopping here this time.

It was not ten minutes later that Adric joined her again and said, "Looks like we have a new sheep in our flock." He gestured back with a tilt of his head.

Cindra turned in her saddle and looked behind, seeing a distant figure on a black horse, following them from the teahouse. It was not uncommon for travelers to latch on to a larger group for safety's sake. But the lone figure gave Cindra a feeling of unease. She thought, *What if our secret mission was not so secret? What if the new sheep is a wolf?*

She shook off the feeling. "Let them follow if they like," she said, "The more, the merrier."

A mile farther was the crossroad village of Wellgate. Few people marked their coming; save for the odd looks they had grown accustomed to, they were ignored. The shops lining the main square were closed, and the shopkeepers sat out front, murmuring together.

The buildings here were of the same plastered stonework found in most of Portshia, though noticeably more ramshackle and ill-maintained. Shade trees were allowed to grow near the roadside, but farther beyond were cleared fields and scattered farmhouses. Cindra spotted the sign of an inn, and halted her steed. T'ózha snorted, anticipating a rest and a snack.

"We stop here for the night," Cindra said as her retinue caught up.

"There's still plenty of daylight left," Padison said. Drahn nodded in agreement beside him, blinking at the sun.

Adric replied, "There's not much beyond this place according to the map. We'd be camping by the roadside."

Wenyssaya spoke, "I will be glad for what shelter we can get."

Her endorsement seemed good enough for Padison, who climbed off the wagon and began gathering their gear.

"How far is it to the next town with an inn?" Nixy asked. His horse, Nibbler, began looking for food, forcing his rider to turn constantly in his saddle to face his companions.

"Not for another two days," Cindra replied, "Between here and the town of Breega are few comforts, and in a day and a half we'll be in the Shadowood. Take a bed when you can get it." It occurred to her that she didn't know how many beds this small inn had to offer; she hoped there were enough for the five of them, one a-piece. Then she wondered if she and Wenyssaya would be sharing a room, or if the elf maid would want to stay with Nixy? If so, would she have to share a room or bed with Adric or Padison? In all of the logistical planning for her quest, she had never considered something as basic as sleeping arrangements. In her years at the fighting school, living and training with young men, she had always had her own intimate accommodations. She could even kick Jaron from the room when she needed extra privacy. No longer.

I will have to stop thinking like a high-born lady, she realized, *I shared a cramped caravan with a Galindri family for a whole winter without fussing so.*

The innkeeper and stable hand came out to meet them. "Good day to you, s-er, ah..." His confused eyes took in her clothing. "Um, milady? Staying the night, are you?"

Cindra nodded.

He smiled and said, "Well, you're in luck. We've got empty beds for yourself and-" his eyes fell on Wenyssaya, who dismounted her white steed with a hop. "Woodkin!" whispered the man, astonished, "Surely, an elf! As I live and breathe!"

Cindra closed her eyes and sighed, *This will take some getting used to. Good thing I'm not a vain woman.*

The man was still entranced, his mouth agape as the elf maid gave him a warm smile.

Well, not overly vain, she thought. She guided T'ózha over to nudge the man out of his love-struck stupor. "We will take what you have, innkeeper." She said it with authority edging her voice.

The man hopped to it, guiding the wagon towards the barn. The stable hand, probably the innkeeper's son, helped lead the carthorses away. The lad kept stealing glances at the elf maid, ignoring Cindra altogether.

Cindra was a little surprised by the command in her voice. Was it peevish vanity for being so easily ignored? Or was she slipping into her new role as a knight? *Yes, that must be it,* she decided, *I must demand respect.*

And attention, said a tiny voice in her head.

She dismounted, her mouth twisting into a vexed knot.

Adric took the lead of T'ózha and his own horse, Smoke. Padison helped Nixy off of Nibbler, then took the reins, avoiding the beast's teeth. He went to Wenyssaya's white horse, but only then noticed the beast had no tack whatsoever.

The elf maid turned as her horse nickered at the lad. She said to him, "Thank you, Padison, but I will tend her. Thasimé is wary of strangers."

Padison's face turned red as he stammered, "N-no need to be a stranger. We're traveling companions after all." He led Nibbler away with a silly grin on his face.

Wenyssaya patted Thasimé on her muscular neck and said, *"Dimeva, thevethii."* The horse nodded and followed Nibbler. Navithwi the raven left his perch on the horse's rump and went in search of food.

Drahn found himself riding into the barn with the wagon, and squeaked in dismay. He could hardly fly carrying his backpack, and no one had offered to take it for him. *This will not do at all,* he thought, and scrabbled off the back of the wagon towards the inn.

With their belongings unpacked and horses tended to, the party entered the teahouse. Cindra paused to look behind at the traveler who had followed from the Low Bridge; the rider appeared to be a woman wearing a deep blue cloak with a hood, which was currently up and hiding her features. *No wonder she followed us,* Cindra though, *the roads are dangerous for a woman alone.* Feeling a little relieved, she went inside.

The teahouse was nothing special. Like the rest of the village, it saw little travel these days. The walls were cracked and chipped in places, exposing red brick underneath; the ceiling beams were dusty, with little cobwebs in the hard-to-reach corners; the windows had oiled parchment instead of glass, unlike most of the windows in Portshia. Still, the floors were swept and the small tables were clean.

The innkeeper came back inside from the stables and said, "I regret to say that food is scarce. We've some bread and ale to feed you, but little else."

Nixy sounded alarmed, "No food? Why not?"

"Well, young master," said the innkeeper, "we've been picked clean by the army on the march. All the goods they could carry, they took, and for damned cheap too." He grumbled, "King's purveyance laws." It was then that he looked again at Cindra, noticing the black eagle on her gray tabard. "Er, that is, it's not an easy thing to bear, poor as business is here. Begging your pardon, milady."

"Excuse me," came a little voice from the floor. The innkeeper and stable hand looked down in surprise and saw a little purple dragon looking up at them, its scales turning a shade of crimson. "I don't mean to be a bother," Drahn said, "but my belongings are still in the wagon, and I cannot cawwy them myself." He was addressing the innkeeper, but he also glanced accusingly at his companions.

"Oh, I'm sorry, Drahn!" Cindra said, feeling boorish, "Padison, please fetch Drahn's pack?"

Padison nodded and made for the barn, while the innkeeper and stable hand just stared.

Drahn stared back at them and said, "I am a little talking dwagon. Pleased to meet you."

They nodded dumbly.

The stable hand then asked Cindra, "Milady, are you a... a soldier?" He looked to her sword, and went so far as to almost touch the sleeve of her doublet, until his father smacked his hand away.

Cindra turned to him, rather pleased for attention. "I was knighted by King Galen III himself," she said with a little too much pride, "Lady Cindra of House Corrina, at your service." She gave a slight nod to them both.

They made the clumsy bows typical of peasants and freemen. "A lady knight! Gods bless me!" cried the lad.

His father shooed him away and said, "Welcome to the Crossroads Inn, milady knight and company! Pleased to have you all! Such a historic occasion this is!"

"Historic?" Cindra asked.

"It's the first time my house has played host to a lady knight, a little talking dragon, and an elf! Come, come, let me show you to your rooms."

Cindra felt a little satisfaction at that. *Historic.*

As it turned out, the inn had only two private rooms with braziers for warmth, and four beds in total. Sleeping mats were available upon request, all of which had been recently cleaned. Cindra decided that she and Wenyssaya would take one room, and the lads, the other. It was only proper, after all.

Funny how that matters to me now, she thought, *It shouldn't, should it?*

Nixy would have his own bed, since he was a prince, and Adric and Padison flipped a coin for the other one.

"Best of three?" she heard Padison ask.

After the sleeping arrangements had been settled, Cindra walked over to the common room to examine her maps. Spreading them out on a table, she rubbed her eyes and yawned. *Silly to be so tired so soon,* she thought, *I've been in the saddle only a few hours.* But they had been long miles with countless eyes upon her, judging her, laughing, sneering, murmuring.

"Damn them all," she whispered, leaning over her maps.

She heard the voice of the innkeeper, heard his footsteps coming up the porch. He was talking to someone.

"We've room, milady, though you'd have to share with two other ladies already here, if they don't mind. Else there's some lads that may be asked to trade..." He entered the common room, holding the door for the woman in the hooded blue cloak.

The other traveler, Cindra thought, *We might have a new roommate.*

"Ah! Milady knight," said the innkeeper, "We've another lodger of the fairer sex, as it were. Would you and the elf maid be willing to share a room with this young lady?"

The woman seemed perfectly composed, as if she shared rooms with lady knights and elf maids all the time. Cindra thought that rather odd, and her suspicions piqued again.

"I don't see why not, innkeeper," Cindra said, "One of my men can relinquish a bed, I'm sure they wouldn't mind."

"Most kind of you, milady, most kind," he said, and went off to make the arrangements.

"Most kind indeed," said the woman. She turned and drew back the hood. Raven black hair flowed upon her shoulders. Smooth skin like fresh cream glowed in the soft light. Arresting eyes the color of rain clouds beheld Cindra, and she found herself catching her breath.

She is very beautiful, Cindra thought, *there are too many very beautiful women at this inn.*

"Milady knight," said the newcomer, "my name is Deliah. I am pleased to make your acquaintance."

Cindra blinked in mild shock.

Deliah. Cindra's mind was a blur. *Deliah Wyngaard. She could be no other. The way Jaron described her all those years ago, it has to be her!*

The woman had been shown to her lodgings while Adric and Padison carried their erstwhile bed into the ladies' room with curious enthusiasm. Now they joined Cindra at her table, pretending to study the maps while they discussed the new arrival.

"Gods, what a pair they make," Adric said, "Like visions of night and day!"

Deliah, Cindra thought, *What is she doing here?*

"She's a sight, for sure," Padison said, "But her eyes... I dunno, makes me uncomfortable somehow."

"That's what beautiful eyes do," Adric prodded him, "They make you look away, or stare without thinking."

She was a part of Sir Earnold's treachery, she recalled, *She stole the roses from the Selvinian temple's hothouse so Earnold could have them spelled.*

"It's not like that," Padison said, "I mean, it is with Wenyssaya, but this girl's different."

"Different good, or different bad?"

"Different *weird.*"

"She's married," Cindra muttered aloud. She didn't think she meant to; she was too distracted to be sure.

"Married?" gasped the lads in unison.

"How do you know that?" Adric asked.

Cindra looked up, "I think I know her; I think she's the wife of a Casting Guild ward master."

"You think, you think?" Adric said, "Is she or isn't she?"

"If she is the woman I believe her to be," Cindra said, "then she is married, and she is *trouble.*"

"Well, she's out here without her husband or even an escort," Padison said, "That seems pretty weird to me.

The roads are no place for a lady alone, especially with a war coming."

Adric said, "Did you ask where she's going?"

"We only made introductions," Cindra said, "We didn't pry into each other's business."

"Well, you'll have plenty of time to chat her up," Adric said, "since you'll be rooming with her now."

Cindra was annoyed. "You want me to put in a good word for you two while I'm at it? Maybe tell her what charming and virile specimens you are?"

Adric and Padison shared a look. "You'd do that?" Padison asked.

She glared at them. They burst into laughter.

"You're both pigs," Cindra said, smiling despite herself.

"Oink," said Paddy.

As daylight waned, the inn became busier as villagers came in to socialize. Cindra put away her maps in her room, careful not to awaken Drahn, who was snuggled in his backpack atop her bed. Wenyssaya and Deliah were talking quietly by the fire in the common room, seemingly getting on quite well. Adric and Padison were across the room at another table, sipping ale and watching the two women like hungry wolf pups.

People had started coming in for early evening drinks, drawn by rumors of strange guests and great beauty. The common room was filling up, and Cindra didn't want to talk to anyone just now. Her mind was too troubled. She decided to step outside and get a better look at Jaron's home village.

The fields and farm houses looked quiet and peaceful, and she took a deep breath. The breeze had become cold, and a few clouds were gathering to catch the orange fire of sunset. It was easy to imagine a young, carefree farm boy running through the fields, swinging a stick like a sword, playing at being a knight. She smiled at the thought.

A voice came from beside her, "It's nice here, isn't it?"

She started, surprised to find Nixy standing next to her. She hadn't heard him approach. *Little thief prince,* she thought with a grin. "It is nice," she agreed, "Very peaceful and quiet. You grew up in a place like this, didn't you?"

He nodded, "Yeah."

She knew a little about his childhood, and it was not a happy one. His mother had died in childbirth, and her husband had blamed the boy for it. The man Nixy knew as his father was a drunk and broken shell, grieving for a woman who had been special enough to catch the attention of an elf lord.

"Are you scared?" she asked.

"Yeah," he replied.

She put an arm around his shoulders. "I am too," she said.

They stood there for a time, watching the colors of dusk play across the sky.

"What do you think I'm here for?" Nixy asked.

She knew he wasn't talking about the quest, but his life. It was a big question. "I don't know," she said, "I don't know what any of us are here for; the gods don't tell their secrets." She hugged him close, "But I am here to be your friend and protector. You can count on that, Nixy."

"Thanks," he sniffed, wiping his eyes.

The sun sank behind the distant trees, and the sky became pocked with stars. The cold night air turned biting, so Cindra and Nixy decided to go back inside the inn. Conversation was lively as the weary villagers closed yet another day with drink and fellowship, many of them approaching Adric and Padison for news and gossip. The lads were currently entertaining three merchants and their wives, who had clustered around their table.

"That's when she flew at us, right through the air!" Padison was saying, raising his arms like wings, "Most horrible thing I've ever seen! My horse threw me and I got a kick; broke my ribs right here," he pointed to his side.

"A vemlok, for true?" asked one of the women, eyes wide.

Adric nodded somberly, "She attacked our comrade; drained his life away in moments. It took all three of our instructors to stop her."

"No," Padison said, "just the one with the magic sword."

Cindra knew the story; she had been there to drag Padison to safety, and she had watched as Jaron beheaded the undead creature with his honor sword, the companion to the one on her hip. She didn't need to hear the details. Instead, she steered Nixy over to the women by the fire. The beauties were alone, but were still the center of attention for dozens of wandering eyes. None had the courage to approach, but Cindra had no such fears.

"Wenyssaya, Deliah," she nodded to them, "Mind if we join you?"

"Please," said Wenyssaya. Cindra drew up two chairs.

"Milady knight," Deliah said, "I have heard much about you, but I never thought to meet you in person."

"Nor I you, Mistress... Wyngaard, is it?"

Deliah made a slow smile, "It is. I see you have heard of me as well."

"I have heard enough," Cindra said. It sounded rude, but she didn't care.

Nixy even picked up on it. Maybe it was Wenyssaya's training, or maybe he was finally paying attention to conversations. He asked, "So... you know each other?"

"By reputation," Cindra said, "We've never met."

Deliah raised an eyebrow.

Cindra frowned. "Have we?"

"I'm sure I'd remember," Deliah replied, "And how is my reputation these days?"

Cindra paused, "It has not gotten worse, as far as I know."

The elf maid broke in, "I am sorry, I was not aware that there were... difficulties between the two of you. Should we reconsider our arrangements for the night?"

"I hope not," Deliah said, "It is my sincere wish that we can put all of our troubles behind us and share the way ahead in friendship."

Cindra looked at her sidelong. "Share the way? Do you mean that figuratively?"

Deliah smiled. "Literally, Lady Cindra; I am taking the Joshian Way into the Shadowood as well."

Chapter Two

Strange Bedfellows

"You're traveling our road?" Cindra asked flatly, "How do you know where we are headed?"

Deliah smoothed her dress as she stared into the fire. "Your mission may be a state secret, but it is not a well-kept one. My husband has friends in the Order of Astrellaris. The Order knows of your mission, for the king consulted with some of their number. Word gets around."

Cindra was verging on anger now. "So you know our direction *and* our mission? Is *that* what you're saying, Madame Wyngaard?"

Deliah shrugged, "No need to be so formal, Lady Cindra. 'Deliah' will do."

"Answer my question," Cindra demanded, "Do you know our mission?"

Wenyssaya focused a worried look at the woman, awaiting her answer. Nixy shared her concern.

Deliah sighed. "I know you are heading into the Shadowood to introduce this little prince to his elf lord father," she said quietly, "Anyone could figure this out if they have been keeping up with castle gossip these past months. It is my only care that we are heading along the same road at the same time. It is a matter of convenience, nothing more."

She didn't mention seeking the aid of the elves in the war, Cindra thought, *but that doesn't mean she doesn't know.* She asked, "And where are you headed along such a dark and little-traveled road, conveniently at the same time?"

Deliah said, "We all came from somewhere, Lady Cindra. I have important and private business to the north; let us leave it at that."

"How far to the north?"

"As far as Breega," she replied, "Possibly farther. I will not know until I get there."

Nixy asked, "Your husband sounds like he could afford an escort for you. Isn't he worried about you traveling alone?"

Deliah gave the boy a look tinged with sadness, "I wrote him a letter explaining that I am leaving, and shall likely not return. I told him not to look for me."

This news came as a shock to Nixy and Wenyssaya, but Cindra was only mildly surprised that her opinion of the woman could sink even lower.

"You left your husband?" Cindra asked, "Just like that?"

Deliah said, "Things have not been the same for me since Sir Cord Freekirk came knocking on my door those four years ago. I know that my role in your scandal was kept secret to protect the reputation of my husband and the Casting Guild, but he eventually suspected I had a hand in it."

Cindra sat back and smirked, "Such is the price of deception."

"Indeed," Deliah said, glancing at the lady knight's arms, "Deception leaves its mark on all of us, as I am sure you know."

Cindra folded her arms, covering her scars.

Nixy spoke up, "I don't know what this is about, but if you did something to hurt Cindra, I think we should part ways." His lower lip was set firm in a pout of determination.

Deliah fixed him with a look, her storm-gray eyes searching his face, eerie and intense in the firelight. There was a hint of defiance before her face softened, taking on a sad resignation. She spoke to the young man, who had managed to hold her gaze. "I apologize for my manners, and for seeking to impose upon your quest. I did indeed cause much trouble and hurt to the lady and her dear Sir Jaron, and for that I am deeply sorry." She turned bodily in her seat to face him, her hands folded in supplication, "But I beg you, little prince, please allow me to accompany you along the road? I do not wish to travel alone, and I may yet be of some help."

Nixy was taken aback by her sudden sincerity. He asked, "Help how?"

"I know the Joshian Way rather well, for I used to live in the region. It is no place for a woman alone, but I could serve as a guide of sorts. There are many dangers that are known only to those who have lived there."

"Now wait a minute," Cindra began.

"Do you know the way to the Shadow Lord?" Nixy asked, his voice soft and hopeful.

Deliah sighed, "Alas, such paths are open only to those whom he allows. I have never seen his lair, for it is deep in the woods, where the trees themselves drink the light. But I have explored much of the paths of the forest, and can be of use to you. I believe I know where to start."

Cindra did some calculation. Deliah was around Jaron's age of twenty-two, perhaps twenty-five at most, and had lived in Portshia for at least six or seven years, the time when Jaron was still a student at the Freekirk School. That would mean she spent her teen years exploring the dark paths of the Shadowood, a remarkable feat even in Cindra's experience. This woman did not have the look of an explorer, with her perfect skin and soft hands. Even seamstresses had the mark of their work upon their hands. Deliah only had a polished wooden ring on her left hand where her wedding band should be.

Nixy turned to Cindra, "I know you don't like her, but... don't you think we could use a guide? None of us have ever been that far into the wood before, and my father hasn't sent so much as a bird."

Her brow furrowed as she saw the pleading in his eyes. Nixy was uncertain and afraid, and the offer of a guide could only ease his fears. Still, she did not trust this woman.

Cindra turned to the elf maid, "What do you think, Wenyssaya? Will we need a guide, or will the Shadow Lord open the way for us?"

Wenyssaya made the slightest frown and replied, "I do not know that the way is his to open. The forest has a life of its own, and while he is its protector and steward, he does not command it entirely. Honestly, I thought we might have to hire a guide when we need to leave the road."

Cindra sighed. *What good is it having a 'woodkin' that doesn't know the woods? If only the Shadow Lord had an emissary to send from his own lands, instead of calling one from the far Blackwood Forest.* "Very well," she said, "if there is no other option, we could use a guide, assuming your business takes you so far."

Deliah smiled, "I am grateful, milady knight. I shall help all I can until our paths diverge."

Deliah, Wenyssaya, and Nixy went to bed as the moon rose and the night grew late, but Cindra stayed up in the common room with Adric, Padison, and Drahn. The dweedragon had been refreshed from his nap, and wanted to know about the strange woman sleeping in their room.

"Her name is Deliah Wyngaard," Cindra said, as they nursed their last ales by the fire, "She used her husband's secrets to break into the Selvinian temple's hothouse and steal two roses, which were used to place a love spell on me and Sir Jaron."

"A love spell?" Adric exclaimed, "I thought that sort of thing was only in faerie stories."

"Nah," Padison said, "just illegal."

"How do you know that?" Adric asked.

"I asked Filbert Gaddisen about it at the school."

"What for? That barmaid at the Red Eagle you kept mooning over?"

Padison just blushed.

Drahn asked, "Was that love spell the weason for what happened at the festival when Sir Jawon was banished?"

"It is," Cindra said, "It caused quite a scandal, and had my father not been away, it might have gone much worse for Jaron."

"So that's why you keep giving her the stink-eye," Adric said, "I can't say I blame you."

"That's not the only reason," Cindra said, turning her cup in her hands, "She and Jaron... You remember that Jaron killed Sir Earnold Greenfellow at that same festival? It's the main reason that Rejick Ratham gave me such a difficult time at school."

The boys nodded, and Drahn lapped at his ale.

"Well, Sir Earnold had been behind that entire plot," she said, "The theft, the love spell, everything."

This made them all stop and stare.

"It was kept a secret because of the greater scandal it would cause," she said, "Sir Earnold was my father's own knight, sworn to defend me. The fact that he subverted the wife of a ward master to commit a crime, then had some wizard do an illegal love spell... it would have been a terrible admission."

Drahn asked, "So they never knew who cwafted the love spell?"

Cindra shook her head. "No. The reason Sir Earnold went through all this trouble goes back to Deliah again. Earnold and Deliah were engaged to be married."

"Oh, this gets better and better," Adric said.

"Apparently Deliah and Jaron had a bit of a tryst..." she still had a hard time talking about it, and she felt her face color. "This was before we met of course, but Earnold sought revenge and he and Jaron had a duel at the school."

Padison cried, "*That* was the reason for the famous duel! I heard it had something to do with a woman, but I was told not to ask either you or Sir Jaron about it."

"It was *me* who told you not to ask," Adric reminded him.

"Oh yeah," Paddy said.

"So," Drahn said, "Deliah is a womantic wival as well as a tweacherous twaitor. But why did she help Sir Earnold in his wevenge?"

Padison turned to hide his grin from the little dragon.

Cindra said, "She claimed that Sir Earnold intended the charmed roses for another woman, and she owed him for breaking his heart." She scoffed, "It seems like a flimsy reason for committing such an act."

"I'll say," Adric nodded, "A woman who cheats on her intended doesn't seem like the type to risk her marriage and freedom to make it up to him."

"Exactly!" Cindra said, glad someone understood her feelings. She was a snake, this Deliah. 'Womantic wival' or no, she couldn't bring herself to trust her at all.

"So what do you think she's doing out here?" Padison asked, "What's her business, do you suppose?"

"She won't elaborate," Cindra said, "She's been evasive, but she seems very keen on joining us. For all we know, she could be spying for the Dissenter Houses."

"That's a stretch," Adric said, "I mean, I know you don't like or trust her, but a spy?"

Drahn said, "It's possible. Her actions might have been a plot hatched by the Dissenters, and not Sir Earnold at all; or maybe he was an agent as well. Jealousy seems a weak weason to commit tweason."

Cindra had to smile in spite of her mood. Drahn's speech impediment was too adorable sometimes.

"Well," Padison said, "if she's going to be traveling with us, we need a plan in case things go sour. We need to keep an eye on her."

"I'll do it," Adric said, almost too fast.

"No," Cindra said, "I will talk to Wenyssaya about it. They seem to be getting on, so maybe we can take advantage of that. Besides," she grinned at the boys, "sometimes a woman needs her privacy."

Cindra had slept poorly, her mind wandering in an out of dark thoughts. Sharing a bedroom with her rival made it difficult to relax, and she found herself listening for the woman's breathing, just in case she was pretending to sleep. Drahn slept in his backpack at the foot of Cindra's bed, and she kept her *Kos* knife under her pillow; if Deliah tried anything, she would get either a Minozhian blade in her gut, or a taste of the dweedragon's newfound lightning breath.

As it turned out, the woman had not tried to murder them in their sleep, so Cindra felt only a little relieved as they left the village of Wellgate behind.

"So there are no communities between here and Breega?" Padison asked Deliah, who was riding beside the wagon.

"None that have an inn," she said, "If we need shelter, Lady Cindra might demand it of the farmers or trappers who live near the road."

"I'd rather not impose," Cindra said, eavesdropping, "nor would I like the added attention. If there are unfriendly eyes and ears about, I'd not have them knowing about us from the locals."

Adric looked at the distant gray clouds and said, "Well then, I hope it doesn't rain."

The rain came late in the afternoon, much to the company's dismay. It began as a light, almost pleasant sprinkle, but soon grew into a steady beating of fat drops. Hoods were drawn up and cloaks were pulled tighter about the shoulders. Drahn burrowed into his backpack after dragging it under the shelter of the oilskin covering their supplies.

Cindra slowed her mount, letting the party ride past, as if she was seeing to everyone's well-being. Actually, she intended to speak to Wenyssaya about their new guest. She guided T'ózha next to Thasimé, and Wenyssaya gave the lady knight a weak smile from beneath her hood. Navithwi the raven was perched on her knee, unperturbed by the rain.

In fact, upon closer inspection, the rain didn't seem to touch the raven or the elf maid at all. Her hood was lightly spotted, and her traveling clothes barely showed a stain of moisture, except where the rivulets of water ran off from Thasimé's mane and down along the hem of her dress.

"How are you doing that?" Cindra asked in amazement.

Wenyssaya looked at her soaked companion with a touch of guilt. "It is a spell I learned as a child. It is called *Vdamovera.*"

"Between the rain," Cindra said. The elven word had painted a picture in her mind, telling her what it meant even as she heard it for the first time. Whether this amazing quality was a gift of the language, or the speaker, or both, she did not know.

The elf maid nodded. "I dislike rain," she said, "I always have. I hate being wet and cold." Her delicate eyebrows knitted together in dismay, "If I could, I would protect the rest of the party as well, but I fear I do not have the power."

Cindra waved the notion away, "You needn't worry, we all expected there would be hardships." Then she lowered her voice, "But I need to speak to you about things we did not expect."

"Our new friend?" Wenyssaya asked.

"Our new friend," Cindra nodded, "She has a history with my traitorous bodyguard Sir Earnold, my dear Sir Jaron, and much of the trouble that befell them both. I do not trust her motives or intentions, and I would like you to keep a close eye on her."

"I see," the elf maid said, accepting the charge but not liking it, "What do you suspect, if anything? Do you think she is a danger to the young prince?" She looked ahead of her to Nixy, who was holding his face up to the falling rain, catching drops in his mouth and clearly enjoying himself.

She is letting me know where her true concerns are, Cindra thought, *Where my concerns should be as well, I suppose.* "I don't know," she admitted, "but it is no coincidence that she left home to travel north with us, even offering to be our guide. It is all too convenient."

"Perhaps she *is* speaking truthfully," Wenyssaya said, "Convenience and chance make many a companion."

"Is that an elven saying?" Cindra asked.

She smiled, "No, I heard it as I traveled through the lands between my forest home and the Casselvane Mountains."

"The lands of the Dissenter Houses," Cindra said, "I suppose that makes sense."

"My people believe that fate brings us together for either good or ill," the elf maid said, "It is our actions between the meeting and the parting that determine the nature of it."

"Well, I don't trust her actions based on her history," Cindra said, glaring at the woman's back through the curtain of rain, "I want to know what she's up to."

Wenyssaya nodded and said, "She has depth, you know. I have seldom met a human so careful and considered in their speaking."

Cindra frowned, "She's hiding something?"

"She is hiding much," Wenyssaya said, adding quickly, "but this is not necessarily a bad thing. Perhaps you are used to people who speak openly and often, but my people are more reserved. They do not…"

"Babble?" Cindra offered. She glanced up at Adric, who was trying yet again to chat up their guest.

The elf maid smiled, "If you like. Not that the Ilvayiin are a quiet people, but we are used to speaking in words that engage the thoughts and feelings of the listener in a way that no other language can. It is our gift, to be truly understood by human, bird, and beast.

"But this means that we choose what we speak on with care, and do not seek to fill every silence with words, even when we use the tongues of other people." She nodded ahead to Deliah, who was suffering Adric's attentions, "This woman, she is the same."

"So what did the two of you talk about last night by the fire?" Cindra asked, "You seemed to be quite engaged."

"We spoke of tutoring children," she said.

"Really?" Cindra had not expected this, "She doesn't strike me as a tutor."

"Even so," the elf maid said, "she claims to have tutored many children in music, dancing, and reading. It was how she made a living before her marriage to the human spell-weaver." Wenyssaya looked at Cindra through the girl's drenched hair, "Did your Jaron not say anything about her from when they knew each other?"

"He said they kissed in the stables adjoining the fighting school. That's all I really wished to hear, and didn't press him for more."

"Kissed, is that all?" Wenyssaya said, disappointed, "It seems so little to fight a duel over."

"She was engaged to marry Jaron's rival," Cindra said, wanting to change the subject, "The quarrel between those men goes back to their fathers' younger days."

"Indeed?" The elf maid seemed to brighten at the prospect of more gossip. "Was that over a woman as well?"

"A lord," Cindra said, "My grandfather Armon, in fact. Sir Waliss Greenfellow was the old count's champion, but in a time of great need, he fled in fear before an enemy, abandoning my grandfather. It was a peasant conscript named Fedrick Dunlorden who stepped up and defended the count. Sir Waliss was banished, and Fedrick was knighted, eventually becoming the new champion."

"How sad," Wenyssaya said, "That seems rather unfair, but I suppose humans have their own ways."

"You may express your condolences to Sir Waliss when we pass through Breega," Cindra said, "House Greenfellow runs a fighting school there, and they may not be pleased to see us."

The clouds flashed with dramatically-timed lightning, and peals of rolling thunder punctuated Cindra's words like war drums.

That night the party camped just off the road, pitching their tents in the persistent rain. Cindra was happy she made the lads practice setting them up for a few hours after she purchased their gear, else they would all look quite pathetic, shivering in the rain as they fumbled with fabric and tent poles. They had one large pavilion with blue and gold striped fabric, which was too fancy and troublesome to set up quickly, so they pitched the two smaller camp tents; the kind used by soldiers who only needed low shelter for sleeping. Wet clothes were stripped off in the scant privacy of the little tents, and wrung out as well as possible.

This is what a real adventure is like, Cindra thought, recalling her days with the Galindri caravan and her adopted family. *It's sleeping under the stars, out in the weather, with only your own preparations and knowledge to see you though.*

Cindra directed the others as they made camp, handing out bits of wisdom. Collect rainwater for drinking, don't trust streams and pools unless the water is boiled or magically cleansed; camp out of the wind on level, softer ground; don't camp in areas where water might flow in a storm; keep the horses downwind and far enough from your camp so they don't pollute your tents with their smell and inevitable streams of horse piss.

All of these things and more had come back to her as they set up camp, but none of the others had such instincts, save Deliah. The soft, beautiful woman seemed at home in the wild, oddly enough. It made Cindra feel uneasy. Perhaps she *had* spent her early years in the woods, exploring? If so, she must have some interesting beauty secrets.

Wenyssaya, on the other hand, was perfectly miserable. She was cold, a bit wet, and not at all used to roughing it. While she did not openly complain, she did make a variety of unhappy noises. Cindra had always assumed that elves were at home in nature, but then she had never met one before; not a full-blooded one anyway.

It was hard to think of Nixy as an elf, or having elf-blood. He had normal human ears, round features, and seemed a bit small for his age. Yet his blood was of an older and more pure lineage than Wenyssaya's, who could not be mistaken for anything but an elf, even as she huddled shivering in the tent between the other two women.

"Not to pry," Cindra began, "but I thought elves were closer to nature?"

Wenyssaya glanced up through her lashes and said with a childlike pout, "What does that even mean, 'closer to nature?'"

"Uh, well..." Cindra fumbled with the words, "well, you know, more acclimated to it, more at home."

The elf maid sniffed and rubbed her arms for warmth, "I am acclimated to my home, like any creature of nature. My home was not an open field in a rainstorm."

"Fair enough," Cindra said.

"The thing about elves," Deliah said, "is that the stories and legends about them are better known than the people themselves. They prefer it that way. It is part of what keeps them safe and respected."

Cindra looked skeptically at her past the elf maid's golden locks, "What do you know of elves?"

Deliah replied, "I know a great deal. I know they diminish with each generation, so they maintain a shroud of mystery that their fore-bearers did not need."

"Is this true?" Cindra asked the elf. She wasn't going to take Deliah's word for anything.

"It is," Wenyssaya said, "My ancestors were not as reclusive as we are in this age. We discourage outsiders from becoming too familiar."

"Drahn once told me that your people used to be immortal, like this Shadow Lord." Cindra said, "That modern elves were weaker than their ancestors. But he also told me that Nixy is very powerful, basically like a Sorcerer King."

The elf maid nodded.

Deliah looked out of the tent into the flashing clouds.

"What does that mean?" Cindra asked, "Just how powerful were the Sorcerer Kings? How powerful were the first elves?"

Wenyssaya took a shivering breath, "There were many, many stories and legends. Even the elders of my homeland were not alive in that time. But the stories tell of elves able to become one with the elements, able to pass through walls, walk in the air and live in the depths of the sea. No one knows what is truth and what is myth.

"Of the Sorcerer Kings, little more is known," she continued, "Their powers were wild and varied; many were renowned healers, while others used their gifts for great destruction. Some had the power to see the past, the future, or distant places… 'Divination' I believe the human spell weavers call it."

"Some could even govern life and death," Deliah added.

Wenyssaya nodded, "So it is said."

"I've seen Nixy pull on the shadows," Cindra said, "The air gets close and the room gets darker."

"Nixyalderthor's power is like that of his father," Wenyssaya said, "Those first elves and their children delved into the very elements of creation, making them a part of themselves. Nixy can do much, much more, given time and training."

Cindra's eyes grew wide in awe.

Deliah stared out into the night, inhaling the petrichor scent.

Wenyssaya lied down and bundled herself in her blanket. A curious warmth began to emanate from her, like a furnace had been stoked beneath the fabric.

Cindra moved a little closer, enjoying the strange heat while it lasted.

Adric, Padison, Nixy, and Drahn were crowded into the little tent, trying to get comfortable. Adric was officially on watch, so he was sitting up near the entrance flap, but the others were snuggled together for warmth. All they could hear was the rain on the canvas.

"What do you suppose they're talking about?" Padison asked no one in particular.

Adric said, "Probably which one of us is the most attractive, and would make the best lover."

"Really? You think so?" Padison sat up in excitement.

"No," Adric said, "No, I don't."

"Hmph," Padison lay back down, pulling his blanket up to his chin.

Drahn, who was lying on Nixy's stomach, said, "I think I heard Nixy's name, but I can't be sure."

"Probably did," Nixy said, "I been gossiped about by kings and nobles and wizards and knaves. No surprise there."

"What's a knave?" Padison asked.

"You're a knave," Adric said.

"*You* are!" Padison retorted, "So... what is it?"

Drahn said, "It's an older word that means 'dishonest man.' I have been twying to incwease Nixy's vocabulawy."

"What's a vocabulawy?" Padison asked, confused.

"It's all the words you know," Adric said, "Vina's tits, Paddy. Didn't you learn basic stuff like that?"

"Hey, I know plenty of words and stuff! I have a great vocabulawy!" he insisted.

Drahn sighed and shook his head.

"Anyways," Padison said, "Lady Cindra doesn't like it when you blaspheme." He propped himself on an elbow and asked Nixy, "So what's the big story with you, highness? Cindra said you're a prince, but you used to be a- a pickpocket?"

"Paddy!" Adric hissed, "He's a prince *now*, so show some respect!"

"It's alright," Nixy said, "I don't really feel like a prince. Not that I'd know what that felt like."

"Privilege," Adric said, "Special treatment by everyone you meet, feeling like the world owes you something."

"How do you know?" Padison asked his friend, "You're just a cobbler's son."

"A *rich* cobbler," Adric said, "one with wealthy clients. I've even met a prince or two. Not a crown prince, mind you, but a few high lords have been fitted for shoes by my dad."

"Hmph," Paddy hmphed, "Not so many princes have dropped by our leather shop."

"Hah! They don't drop by, you go to them!" Adric laughed, "Privilege, like I said."

"Well," Nixy said as he stared into the close darkness, "I never felt that. Still don't. Sometimes I just feel like there's been a big mistake. Like someone switched me at birth or like I walked into the wrong room."

Drahn said, "There has been no mistake. You have the powers within you." His luminous eyes caught and reflected the distant lightning.

"Yeah," Nixy said, "That's the only thing that makes me know I'm not crazy."

"What kind of powers?" Padison asked, "Show us something!"

"Paddy…" Adric had a warning tone that he had used countless times on his young friend. Padison was far more curious, bold, and mouthy than wise.

"I dunno," Nixy said. He squirmed a bit under his blanket.

"Come on," Padison said, "It doesn't have to be something flashy. Just give us a little something?"

"You don't even know what 'a little something' might be," Adric said, "It might be more than you can handle."

"Nixy," Drahn said, feeling the boy's restlessness beneath him, "You are not a twained wizard. It might not be safe…"

"I don't *have* to be a wizard," Nixy said with a touch of defiance, "It's in my blood, just like with you." He sat up slowly and crossed his legs so Drahn would shift into his lap. Then he said, "Okay, I can show you something."

"Nixyyy," Drahn whined.

"It's alright," the little prince assured him, "I've practiced this a bunch in the castle. Wenyssaya helped me."

"Good!" Padison said, "What should we do?"

Adric shifted nervously as the tent swayed in the wind.

"Just… don't panic," Nixy said. His breathing became deeper and slower, and he stretched out his awareness, pulling on the considerable darkness around them.

Drahn felt the change moments before the boys did. It was a tingling of magic licking about his skin, dancing on nerves that knew the sensation better than most. The little dragon had no hairs, but if he did, they might have stood on end. His scales turned from purple to red as his tension mounted, though it was too dark for anyone to see.

The boys felt it soon after. They became very still, hyper-awareness kicking in as their survival instincts told them something had fundamentally changed. The air grew close and stifling, and the noise of wind changed. Their eyes grew accustomed to the new darkness, impossible though that should have been. There was no new light to see by, but the darkness became like a medium of vision somehow, giving off its own gray radiance. Lightning flashed, and everything snapped back to normal for the briefest second. The shock made everyone gasp.

"What-" Padison started to exclaim, and they were plunged into the smothering twilight once again. Distant thunder rolled across the sky. The odors of soaked cloth and drenched earth became weaker and weaker, and the air turned colder. The walls of the tent became thin, and they could now see the shadows of the nearby horses, the wagon, even the tent beside them. Three figures could be seen huddled within, just a few feet away. The one in the middle had a faint glow, like fog catching moonlight. The figure stirred and twisted, disturbing the other two.

A name came slowly, "Nix-yalder-thor?" They heard Wenyssaya's voice as faint and distant, as if their ears were plugged.

None of them answered.

The darkness became a tangible thing, a fluid pressing on the skin, the lungs. As they turned their heads to look around the tent, no, *through* the tent, their muscles felt sluggish. They saw each other as shimmering ghosts in a gray world; semi-solid specters with all their color leeched away. Padison began to gasp for air, struggling to calm himself in the growing cold. The noise of wind increased, though they felt nothing.

Just don't panic.

The figures in the next tent began to shift and move lazily, their forms gaining clarity and detail as their canvas tent became like a gauzy veil. The middle one, Wenyssaya, was glowing weirdly and beginning to rise. Cindra, the one with shorter hair and a broader back, was reaching for her sword; slowly, a little too slowly.

Adric wanted to tell them they were alright, but he couldn't find his voice. *Were* they alright? He didn't even know.

Drahn looked past them all into the darkness. "What is that?" he asked in a thin, reedy voice.

They all looked where his little claw was pointing; in the vapory distance near the road stood a dark figure. It was tall and cloaked against the slow-falling rain; a wide-brimmed hat obscuring its face.

Adric finally called, "Who goes there?" But his challenge sounded very weak and out-of-breath.

The figure stirred, taking a step towards the campsite. Points of light glowed faintly beneath the hat, little burning embers that resembled eyes. Then the lightning flashed again and the figure vanished.

Nixy shouted in fear, breaking the spell. The cloak of shadows dissipated immediately as everyone gulped the air and stared wildly at the dark fabric around them. They were blind once again. The sound of wind and rain returned; the smell of mud, damp cotton and horse droppings assaulted their noses. They heard Wenyssaya calling again, loudly this time, and Cindra's voice as well. A steady white light pierced the darkness, and the next moment the two women were crouched before the tent entrance; Cindra in a nightshirt, her sword glowing brightly, and the elf maid in her flimsy gown. The rain was dutifully avoiding them both.

"What's going on?" Cindra demanded.

All they could do was point dumbly to the dark, empty road.

Chapter Three

When Next We Meet

"Not the best of times for this fine institution, lad. Not at all," Sir Cord said, as he leaned against a post on the porch of the fighting school. Sir Jaron sat nearby, smoking his father's pipe, one of the few mementos he had kept from the old man's scant possessions.

The Freekirk Daerbrik School had transformed from a place for fighting men in training, to a boarding house for men awaiting war. Sir Cord had received the quartering order a few weeks ago. He had not been pleased at the prospect of using his dormitory and yard to house soldiers who, as a rule, could include any conscript and roughneck their lord could persuade to fight. Conscripts were not like the men he trained; they only had discipline and order when there was a captain about to put a boot up their ass. Left to themselves, they could get up to all kinds of mischief. He'd already had to break up three fights this week.

Jaron puffed fragrant white smoke, which mingled with the steam of his breath in the cold air. "It could be worse," he said amicably, "They could be Greenfellow men."

"True," Cord smiled. He had given his former student, Rejick Ratham, a scathing sendoff back to his uncle, Waliss Greenfellow. He didn't like insulting people's families, but Ratham had made it too tempting. It had not been Cord's proudest moment by far.

Luckily the quartering masters had seen fit to have him house a company of soldiers from his own home province of Cordo. They were some of the last stragglers to be mustered in the wake of the king's main force. Most were conscripted footmen, sixty in number, and they spent their nights on his training floor, sleeping elbow to elbow, head to foot. The trained fighting men were housed in the dormitory upstairs.

Three of his five brothers were among them.

Connor, the eldest, had seen his share of battles, and as the heir to House Freekirk, had been ordered by their mother to stay home; a command he would disobey at his peril. The next-eldest, Caspir, had joined the Eyoronian priesthood. That left the business of fighting to Colin, Carstin, and Ceven, Sir Cord's three younger brothers.

Each had brought a troop of twenty footmen and three or four mounted knights and squires, bringing their contribution up to one company, or eighty men. Sir Cord, as the eldest brother present, would serve as their captain. Jaron would be his adjutant, his right hand. That way he could keep an eye on the lad and make sure he stayed out of trouble.

"I just can't sleep at night knowing my hall is filled with peasants, rapscallions, and ne'er-do-wells." Cord grumbled.

"Always the mother hen," Jaron said, "You should relax more, let your brothers handle their men."

"It's not my brothers' school," Cord said, watching the conscripts play at sparring in the courtyard, "If they break one wooden sword, or chip a mural with their flailing around, I'll have their hides for my camp tent."

"Just when I thought age had mellowed you," Jaron said with a grin, "Besides, when isn't your hall filled with peasants, rapscallions, and ne'er-do-wells?"

Cord was about to make a sharp retort, but didn't want to ruin the lad's good cheer; the Lady Cindra had left on her errantry only this morning, and he had been expecting Jaron to mope about all day. Instead, Cord held his hands behind his back and paced the porch, trying to look thoughtful. "So, how is your new squire coming along?" he asked.

Jaron coughed on his smoke, "Oh. He is doing well enough. I have him training in the kitchens with Celia and Elmore. I'll not have him feeding me the same slop I fed you."

"A good plan," Cord nodded, "But I was referring more to his readiness for war."

"He's as ready as we made them all, I think," Jaron replied, concern in his eyes, "Can one truly be ready for war? When the charge is sounded, when the arrows and cannon balls fly... any man can break."

"What disturbs me," Cord said, "is you are already talking of him breaking. Is he handling the reality of it, or isn't he?" He stopped pacing, facing Jaron with hands on hips.

Jaron sighed, tapping the bowl of his pipe. "He is nervous, perhaps more nervous than he ought to be. His mind is always somewhere else; he sees to his duties, but he's no longer as focused and steady. Did you know he hasn't spouted a piece of wizardly trivia in weeks?"

"I didn't know he did that so frequently," Cord said.

"He used to," Jaron replied, taking another puff, "Sometimes I think he regrets not taking up the family business."

"His regrets are his own problem," Cord said, "All that concerns me is that he performs his duties."

"He'll come around, you'll see," he said, "I did, after all."

"You were different," Cord said, "Your father was an example to aspire to. You spent all those years reading poems and stories about this hero or that; I expect that's where you got your banter with the ladies as well."

"I may have lifted a line or two," Jaron admitted.

"But all the soldiers for hire these days," Cord shook his head, "they've no motivation but treasure and aggression. A man has to fight for something greater than his next meal."

"You think Filbert Gaddisen is the mercenary adventurer type?" Jaron smiled at the thought.

"I don't know what he is," Cord said with a shrug, "How does the son of a wizard family who's built like a scarecrow decide to take up the sword? I've never known what to make of him."

"He's trying to break out of his world," Jaron said, "I can understand that."

"Oh?" Cord asked, "What do you know of it?"

Jaron sighed, "You know I was born a farmer. Besides, I've come to understand it through the struggles of others." He tapped the ash from the pipe bowl and pushed it off the porch with his foot.

Here we go, Cord thought, *I stepped in it again.*

But Jaron said nothing more.

Mealtime was an event at the school, as the kitchens prepared four times the meals they normally would. Cord did not hire additional staff, and old Elmore and Celia would have been overwhelmed without more hands, so he scraped up any of his new guests who could stir a pot or turn a spit. In fact, there was work in the kitchen all the day long, and the stock of firewood was being burned alarmingly fast.

Sir Cord sat at the head table with Sir Jaron and the Freekirk brothers, all of whom were being waited on by their squires. It was crowded at table, since it was intended for fewer seats. Still, it was better than sitting in the dirt with a bowl on your knee.

"...And to make matters worse," Carstin was saying, his gray eyes twinkling, "mother had just come up from a spill accident in the great hall, and she nearly howled like a mad dog when she saw the mess in her chambers! Gods, we were chased about with a switch for the rest of the day, remember that, Cord?"

The brothers' laughter was loud and boisterous, accompanied by thumping fork handles or mugs on the table. Cord joined in the merriment, though he was far more conscious of the marks made on the tabletop. "I was barely involved," Cord said, "but that didn't save me from mother's wrath."

"You were supposed to be keeping us out of trouble," Carstin chuckled, his face now red with mirth. It made his bushy, pale sideburns and receding hairline stand out even more vividly, making him look like some sort of rare bird.

Jaron laughed as well, trying to imagine the large blond men as mischievous little boys. He knew their mother of course; the baroness had always treated him more like a son, rather than merely her son's squire. Yet he could easily picture her chasing those boys about like an avenging Kyraine. The image made him chuckle into his ale.

Colin, a broad man with a thick mustache and a nasty scar on his right cheek, gestured to Jaron. "What of you, Dunlorden? Have you any youthful indiscretions to share, aside from the recent ones everybody's talking about?"

The men all let out mocking hoots and jeers, and Ceven slapped Jaron on the back. Much of his early mischief was in their presence, during his time at Freekirk Villa in Cordo. In different company, Jaron would have taken offense and become immediately guarded. Here, he was just the baby brother.

"Between my time on the farm and my father's posting at Casselvane Keep, there was little time or place for mischief," he said, "That didn't start until I met *you* scoundrels; spawns of Tavenji, all of you."

"Ho ho! Hear that lads?" Colin addressed their squires as well as his brothers, "We're a corrupting force!" They all cheered, and the squires chuckled, happy to be included.

"I hope it wasn't all bad influences," said Ceven, the youngest brother, yet two years Jaron's senior. Ceven was long and tall, though not as broad as his brothers. He was handsome, with chiseled features, blond hair, and blue eyes. "Do you still read those adventure stories and poems, like the ones I loaned you?"

"I think he's taken them too much to heart," Carstin said, "Why read about them when you can live the life of a romantic hero?"

The laughter rang around the table again.

Jaron shook his head, "There is not so much time for reading, but I have grown attached to the theater. There are plays from many lands that feature heroes and adventures, although a good comedy is welcomed."

"I walked by there this morning," Ceven said, "They are preparing to open for the season. The billboard advertised some sort of foolishness called *Mice at Play*."

"It's about *mice?*" Colin asked.

Ceven nodded, "The posters had mice and a cat. Some sort of children's farce, I suppose."

"Foolish nonsense," Colin scoffed.

Filbert Gaddisen said quietly, "Not really. When the cat's away..." As Jaron's squire, he was attending his knight for the meal, and uttered the words before he knew it.

The men and other squires all turned to look at him, the squires with a bit of shock, and the men with a mixture of reproach and amusement. Bradric Hyne, Sir Cord's squire, shook his head at the lad in warning.

"Something to add, squire?" asked Colin.

Filbert realized he'd spoken out of turn, but only offered a contrite nod by way of apology, "The saying. 'When the cat's away, the mice shall play.' I assume it's political."

"I know the saying, lad," Colin said.

"Eh?" Carstin asked, "Political how?" They looked at Jaron, wondering if he had taught his squire the discipline of serving his betters. Jaron was about to rebuke him when Filbert continued, in an almost lecturing tone.

"The cat?" Filbert waited for them to catch on. "The Gold Cat? Count Casselvane?"

Cord made a grunt, but offered nothing. Filbert was Jaron's problem. The brothers looked at each other, bewildered.

"Satire," Filbert said, "Innuendo and allegory."

Ceven, who was more literate, broke in before someone started yelling at the lad, "He means that the cat is the count, and the mice are troublemakers in his house."

"Exactly!" Filbert said, happy to be understood, "If that is the intent of the play, then it couldn't be better timed. It's known that the count intends to ride north to his brother's keep, where he will command the border against incursion. His brother Aren, Baron Syngmore, shall lead Corrina forces into battle." He prattled on, "Of course, if it's too scathing a commentary, it could draw the ire of both the count *and* the king, which would be bad."

Knights and squires alike were flabbergasted. Carstin chuckled, "Cord, do you train fighting men here, or theater critics?"

Cord sighed, "I swear, he came to us this way. Filbert, that will be all. Sir Jaron? Since you and your squire are so theatrically inclined, why don't you both go and see what this play is all about, before it becomes a public scandal."

"Sounds fair," Jaron said. He looked up at Filbert and shook his finger, "Next time, ask permission to speak." Then he gave the lad a wink.

Filbert seemed embarrassed for the first time and nodded, keeping his head low for the duration of the meal.

The next morning, Jaron and his squire set off through the crowded streets to the Grand Portshia Theater. The streets were filthier than usual, due to the addition of thousands of soldiers living in every available space, and hundreds of pack animals moving supplies from one end of the city of another. The pair was on foot, so their eyes were constantly on the flagstones before them, dodging the human and animal waste that had yet to be swept away. Three city blocks farther, they came to the neighborhood surrounding the theater like a protective curtain wall. They found a thruway into the courtyard and soon came to the stage entrance.

"What do we say?" Filbert asked, "It's not as though we are on official business."

"I have no clue," Jaron admitted, "This was your idea."

"It was Master Cord's idea, begging your pardon," he replied.

"Hmmph," Jaron grumped, "I was so eager to come here that I hadn't considered what to say."

The stage entrance was closed and locked, but Jaron knocked a few times until a man answered. He had a flushed face, a baggy gray outfit, and a nose blackened by burnt cork makeup.

"Yes, what is it? Oh! Your pardon, sir knight; can I help you?"

Jaron's mind was racing, trying to come up with something reasonable to say. "Er, good day to you. My squire and I are here on a matter of, um... curiosity. I myself am a patron of your theater, and my squire here is a bit of a literary scholar of sorts..." he glanced at Filbert, wondering if that was actually true. Filbert just nodded in support. "We were wondering if we might sit in on your rehearsal and, um, have a look at the script?"

The man looked them up and down suspiciously. "Just curious, you say? Just want to have a look at the script, you say?"

Jaron fidgeted a bit and smiled. "If it's not too much trouble, please."

The man squinted at them before saying, "A moment. I'll fetch the director." He gave a little bow and closed the door.

Jaron glanced at Filbert, who gave him a look that said 'it was worth a try,' but the lad said nothing.

A moment later, the door opened again and a short, round, puffy-faced man appeared. His hair was a brown wreath about his head, his clothing was loose and unkempt, and he was sweating profusely. Jaron had seen his face before in many a play, but could not put the face to a name. Obviously, he was never the heroic lead.

"What is this about?" asked the man with more than a bit of annoyance. His voice was clear and strong, trained on the stage. "The play opens when it opens, not whenever someone wants to stop by." As he scowled, his bullfrog-like double-chin quivered ominously.

Jaron cleared his throat and gave the man a little bow, perhaps lower than he deserved. "My apologies, master director; my name is Sir Jaron Dunlorden of House Corrina, and this is my squire, Filbert Gaddisen. I was wondering-"

"Bless me," said the director, his face going slack, "*The* Sir Jaron Dunlorden? The Rose Knight?"

It was Jaron's turn to have his face go slack. He wasn't fond of that moniker.

"Oh, forgive my impudence," the man said, holding up a hand, "but the theater has a love of tragic titles. I had come across the name in my inquiries. I did not mean to offend." Before Jaron could think on that, the man beckoned them inside. "Please do come in, do! Welcome to the Portshia Grand Theater, Sir Jaron Dunlorden!"

They were ushered in past racks of colorful clothing, boxes of hats of all kinds, and wood and canvas backdrops smelling of wet paint and sawdust. Before Jaron knew it, he was on the very stage itself, treading the boards upon which so many a story unfolded before his eager eyes. It raised the hairs on his arms and gave him a quiver in his stomach.

There were several actors gathered about, some in the midst of rehearsal, others just lounging on the floorboards or leaning against one of the many support beams that rose to the domed roof. Most were dressed like the man who initially met them at the door, wearing white, gray, or brown baggy costumes and face paint. Two wore hoods with large round ears affixed to them.

Mice, Jaron thought.

"Friends! Colleagues! Allow me to introduce a very special guest to our humble theater, Sir Jaron Dunlorden of House Corrina!" He presented them with a flourish worthy of a play. Jaron felt his face color deeply as he smiled at the actors, some of whom were legends of the Portshia stage. The actors, in turn, regarded him with wide eyes, and applauded him for reasons the knight could not fathom.

"Thank you, thank you," he said, quite unsure of what was going on, "I am a frequent patron here, and am a great admirer of you all. Very pleased to meet you." It was flattery, but had the virtue of being true. The troupe bowed in appreciation.

The director flapped his arms at the assembly and said, "Now, now, back to work, people, back to work! We've much to accomplish and little time to do it in!"

He guided Jaron and Filbert to a cluster of benches that served as his desk and primary workspace, situated center stage and partway back towards the rear of the theater floor.

They took the offered seats as the director cleared away notes, a plate of half-eaten food, and many sheaves of parchment. "Now, to what do we owe the pleasure of this visit, Sir Jaron?"

The knight's brain came back down from the rafters and focused on the matter at hand. "Well, I was wondering... I'm sorry, we have not been properly introduced."

"Ah! Forgive my rudeness," said the director, "You may not have recognized me out of makeup. I am Gillam Kenhallow, master and commander of this fair troupe of mummers." He stood and gave a low bow. "While I am known for portraying kings, wizards, and men of great wisdom, I now play the role of wrangler and herdsman for this flock of peacocks!" He gestured to the stage. "Alas."

Jaron and Filbert smiled at one another, and the knight leaned forward and said, "If I may ask, you said you heard the name 'Rose Knight' in your... inquiries? What do you mean by inquiries? Into me?"

Now it was Gillam's turn to blush a bit. "Oh! Well, you see, the events of the past few years have provided the, eh, bones of a story, as it were. There was some demand for a dramatic retelling of your, ah, *adventures* that might suit the grand stage at some point in the future." Jaron's eyes went wide. "Nothing has been put to parchment, mind you!" Gillam said quickly, "It is a project in the very formative stages, a mulling about of themes and set pieces..."

Jaron asked in a hushed voice, "You want to put our story on stage?" There was no need to elaborate 'our,' since his life alone was not worthy of a dramatic retelling. His and Cindra's however...

Gillam gestured reassuringly, "We would not use your names, of course. Not unless it were found to be favorable to the lord and the crown. Theatrical license, you see. We do not wish to cause undue distress."

For reasons Jaron could not explain, his face broke into an enormous grin. "Brilliant!" he exclaimed, "I mean, well, that's amazing!" He turned excitedly to Filbert, who looked at him like he had lost his mind. This sobered him a bit, and he said, "That's, that's very flattering. I mean, yes, it would have to meet the approval of His Lordship, but yes, very flattering indeed."

"I am glad you approve!" Gillam clapped. "Perhaps we shall work it into the summer schedule."

Jaron smiled, but his heart sank as he realized that he may well be dead and buried by summer. Clearing his head with a deep sigh, he said, "The reason for our visit, actually, was the present play. There has been some concern as to the content, and we were asked to look into it."

It was not exactly a lie; Sir Cord *had* asked them to look into it, but there was no official decree to do so, and they held no authority whatsoever. Still, it felt like an uncomfortable twisting of the truth.

"Indeed?" Gillam seemed taken aback. "I had assumed the story had been cleared with the proper authorities, both religious and secular. Such a trial, gaining the approval of the churches; so many of them, you see. Mention a god, *any* god, and they are all over the script. Mustn't offend! Mustn't contradict! Such a bother." He fanned his face with a page of dialog, "All except Tavenji that is; no church bothers with him."

Filbert asked, "Had you not submitted it yourself?"

Gillam said, "No, dear boy that is for the playwright to trouble with. I am but a simple director in this affair. Although I have written more than my share, mind you. Perhaps you have seen-"

Jaron interrupted, "Pardon me, but who is the writer of *Mice at Play*?"

Gillam's face took on a conspiratorial intensity; he even looked back and forth, as if checking for eavesdroppers. Leaning in close, he whispered, "He is rather new to the game; trying his hand, as it were. I cannot give his name, for he does not wish to be known until the fruit of his efforts have been consumed by the public, and given their approval. This will be his writing debut, you see. Yet his patronage and generosity has given him the, eh, *leverage* to hire this company to perform his rather clever satire."

Jaron raised his eyebrows, looking at Filbert, "He is anonymous?" Jaron asked.

"And rich?" Filbert added.

Nodding, Gillam said, "And he wishes to remain so on both counts. Although, truth be told," he leaned in and whispered, "he is supposed to arrive later this morning to deliver some new pages, and watch the rehearsal."

"Is he?" Jaron asked slyly, "Interesting. In the meantime, might we examine the script? I know it seems irregular, but these are irregular times." That too, was true.

"Of course," Gillam said, gathering pages strewn about him, "We wish nothing but cooperation with the authorities, and I am more than happy to comply... that is, if you are indeed here on official business?" He raised his chin, looking down his nose at them like a professor interrogating wayward students.

Jaron had a brief moment of panic, hoping there was not some badge of office he needed to show, or document he had to sign. He looked to Filbert, who gave him a sheepish glance. Jaron's shoulders slumped and he cast his gaze downward. "Ah, eh, well, w-we don't exactly have *official* authority..." he said, "That is, this is more of an, um, independent inquiry."

"I see," Gillam said, his tone saying he suspected all along, "In that case, I can only help you if you are inclined to help me."

Jaron raised his head. "Oh? In what way?"

"Well," the man leaned in discreetly, "I was hoping that you might fill in some of the gaps in common knowledge, for the sake of dramatic honesty, regarding your relationship with the dear Lady Cindra." Jaron began to balk at the idea, but Gillam said, "Nothing *salacious* need be revealed, mind you! But we wish to do justice to the true feelings that you and the lady might have shared, for the sake of posterity, nay, for the *immortality* that only the theater can grant."

Jaron began to regret his earlier enthusiasm.

Gillam Kenhallow spread his hands in a helpless gesture. "These are irregular times," he said.

Jaron and Filbert spent the next hour reading over the script, trying to make sense of the many footnotes, stage directions and random scribbles that filled the margins. The actual dialog was written by an elegant and practiced hand, with very little thought to performance. Jaron imagined that a more experienced playwright would have given the manuscript a more polished and ready form, and it was likely the director was working on hammering out a finished version before copying it down.

Their attention was divided between the words on the page and the actors on the stage. Two men in mouse costumes, one brown and one gray, were currently refining their performances, trying to get inside the minds of mice.

The brown mouse, apparently named 'Mumfo,' cried,
   "Alas, to scrape for scraps of fallen food
   and scurry under swiftly falling foot,
   that's our lot!"

To which Brio answered defiantly,
   "But ho! There's 'lots' indeed!
   If brave you be, and dash from hole to hall
   betwixt the dreary dusk and rosy dawn;
   a hoard of filth and fancy waits for all,
   a bounty for the bold to feast upon!
   But this requires a mouse of sterner stuff."

Mumfo rounded on him and said,
  "A fool you are if you propose that we
  should make valor a virtue in tiny mice!
  Have you forgotten that our giant host,
  in displeasure with our habitation,
  keeps a cat to curb our propagation?
  Fiorus, the feline hunter, stalks this house!
  His glowing eyes miss nothing in the night,
  and no amount of bravery serves the mouse
  that dares to leave the hole and cross his sight.
  You speak of boldness, bounty, and a feast?
  I fear you are mistaken on this matter.
  Caution's best, but boldness serves you least.
  A feast you'll make, and only make him fatter.
  There is a bounty too, as you have said,
  though not the kind that you might have in mind;
  it's not upon your plate, but on your head.
  The cat collects whene'er he kills our kind."

"It's not bad," Filbert said, his eyes returning to the pages, "Not as sharp as *The Fools of Fallow Farm*, but not bad for an amateur."

Jaron just looked at him. *He* had thought it was rather clever. Perhaps Filbert had been to more plays, at least more comedies. At any rate, he didn't want to seem the bumpkin to his own squire. He said, "The rhymes flowed rather well, I thought."

Filbert muttered as he flipped the pages, "Yes, but rhymes should be used sparingly. They're more appropriate in a poem or limerick, not so much in a three act play."

Jaron decided to keep his mouth shut.

The pages they were able to examine had very little obvious political allegory, unless one stretched the imagination a bit. The story was about a family of mice, obviously, who lived in a house guarded by a cat, Fiorus. The cat made an occasional appearance at the mouse hole, portrayed by a booming-voiced actor using a megaphone just behind the set, and embodied by a large wooden prop of a cat's paw. There was also a painted cat face that could be positioned to look through the 'hole' and onto the stage. It was quite an illusion.

In the first act, the mice were involved in their own petty squabbles about how to best survive, with the two factions led by Mumfo the elder, and Brio the upstart. There were a few funny scenes involving sorting out the chores among the other mice, and a hilarious, bawdy soliloquy to a hunk of cheese.

The second act involved the braver mice venturing out with mixed success, and gaining more approval. The cat, however, made them regret their actions with a show of force, which led to a curious lull in the comedy.

There was still the third act to examine, but according to director Kenhallow, those pages had yet to be delivered.

Jaron was rather enjoying himself, watching the players as they rehearsed different scenes, and the director as he decided how all the action should unfold. It was a rare look behind the curtain, and he found the process fascinating. Filbert, on the other hand, was deep in thought.

"You seem wrapped up in your head," Jaron said, "Did you find something?"

"Rather a lot, sir," he replied, "But it all depends on the author's true intent. It could just be a bit of fun, or it could be something more sinister."

"Sinister?" Jaron sat up, surprised, "I'm not sure 'sinister' is the right word. It's a rather funny play."

Filbert said, "But satire is the best weapon of the subversive. People are too busy laughing to grasp the seriousness of what's underneath. It might take them some time to absorb what the writer had in mind."

"What have you found in this play that's terribly subversive?" he asked. He had an idea or two, but not much more than what Filbert had described at the table yesterday.

"Well," Filbert began, scratching his chin, "Think first of the scale."

"Scale?" Jaron blinked.

Filbert nodded. "The scale of the players. Actors can portray animals of whatever size, and the audience is just expected to go with it. But there is no man in a cat costume on the stage."

Jaron had to admit, "I'm not following you."

"The giant paw, the cat face in the hole, it all puts things in the proper scale," he said, "What's more, it places the audience at the same scale as the mice, in effect, putting them in the hole too."

"So," Jaron began to see his train of thought, "The mice represent the audience?"

"The audience is meant to feel as one with the mice," Filbert said, "They are meant to experience the same level of threat whenever that face appears, and the voice booms out." He folded his arms and sat back. "The cat is someone bigger and stronger than all of *us*."

"So the cat could easily be the count," Jaron said, nodding. *Damned clever squire I have,* he thought.

"Any authority figure or government, really," Filbert replied, "I just assumed it might be the count because his symbol is a cat; this would not have the same meaning if it played in the next province over. But you have one mouse faction that submits, and another that dissents. The dissenters try to get more than they ought, and get punished for it. It's not an uncommon theme, but what matters is the third act. Do the mice win, does the cat, or do things come out even?"

"I see what you mean," Jaron said, "But since there is no third act yet..."

There was a rap on the main theater doors, and the director stopped the rehearsal and went to answer, calling, "Five minutes! Five minutes, everyone! This may well be the new pages!"

Jaron and Filbert sat up in attention. Filbert said, "Should we make ourselves scarce? The writer might not be happy to see outsiders here."

Jaron shook his head and chuckled, "I think not. If he's truly concerned about his anonymity, let him wear a mask."

The doors opened and the portal glowed with the mid-morning light, divided by the silhouette of the new arrival. Jaron squinted as the man strode inside, followed by a bodyguard, greeting the director with a slight nod. As the doors shut, the knight's eyes adjusted enough to see a face under a hood; it had the eyes of a man, but the mouth of a snarling animal, like a wolf or bear. He was, indeed, wearing a mask; the type worn to costume balls. Jaron had once been a guard at a costume ball in Casselvane Keep, but he had not seen any masks that were so gruesome.

"He's got a flair for theatrics, whoever he is," Filbert remarked.

Jaron nodded. A thought was tickling the back of his mind. Something about frightening animal masks...

"Welcome, welcome!" Gillam was saying, sweeping his arm before him, "Always a pleasure, master." He led the man towards where Jaron and his squire were sitting.

Jaron whispered to Filbert as they both stood, "Try not to seem so clever."

Filbert nodded.

Gillam made the introductions, "Master playwright, may I introduce you to Sir Jaron Dunlorden of House Corrina, and his squire... eh..."

"Filbert Gaddisen," Jaron said.

"Just so," Gillam smiled, "Sir Jaron and Filbert Gaddisen, esquire, I present our mysterious master and benefactor."

The masked man gave a slight bow, "Pleased to make your acquaintance, Sir Jaron, master Gaddisen," he said in a silky, refined voice. "Forgive the cryptic titles and theatrics," he motioned to his mask, "but I have decided to remain anonymous. You may call me 'master playwright,' though I assure you the 'master' is simply a formality, and not an implication of competence." He smiled under the mask.

Gillam made a polite laugh, "Modesty, master playwright! It is an excellent work thus far."

"Thus far!" the masked man intoned, "Indeed, a play is either made or broken by its ending. As it happens, I have the first half of the third act here..." He produced a roll of parchment, several pages thick, from beneath his cloak.

"Splendid!" cried Gillam, turning for all to hear, "Our third act has partially arrived, my friends!"

The players applauded and cheered in appreciation, while the masked man gave a flourished bow and saluted the company.

Jaron smiled at the scene, but couldn't help noticing the eyes above the mask. The man's eyes were blue and heavily-lidded, his left eyelid was scarred. Dark brows and a lock of dark, curly hair could be detected under the hood. *I've seen him before*, Jaron thought, *I know this man, I am sure of it.*

Noticing Jaron's gaze, the playwright asked, "So what brings two of our lord's soldiers to this rehearsal? I do hope you're not pressing any of our actors into military service?" There was a smile in his voice, but those eyes gave no trace of mirth.

Jaron found it hard not to flinch at that masked face. He replied, "We were asked by an interested party to examine the direction of this play. It was feared it might cause some offense, times being what they are."

"Oh?" the man said, "And what are they?"

Irregular? he thought. *No.* "Suspicious," Jaron said.

"I see," the playwright said, "Might I ask who these interested parties are, that they send such a deadly theater critic?"

Jaron was a terrible liar, but an excellent fencer, so he made a riposte. "They... wish to remain anonymous."

The man gave a little chuckle, nodded, and turned his attention to the director. "Master Kenhallow, I trust you have shown these fine gentlemen the first two acts already?"

The director gave a helpless sigh, "I have, partly on paper and partly with our rehearsal-"

Filbert interrupted, "If I may, it's a rollicking good play, master playwright! Sir Jaron and I was just saying how it'll lighten people's mood in these hard times, what with a war on and all, if you follow me."

Jaron gave Filbert a surprised look; the lad had managed to sound like a bit of a clod.

The man smiled, but the mask made it look like a snarl. He said, "Such was my design and intent, my young squire. I am glad that its first audience has been so receptive. However," he turned to the director, "I humbly ask that the third act not be shared with unofficial, undeclared parties? It is my first turn as a playwright after all, and I would wish the conclusion of this little farce be revealed only to the most necessary and crucial of audiences? That being the government and churches, of course."

"Of course," Kenhallow said, "and my apologies; there will be no more unofficial inquiries." The director turned to the knight and squire. "I am afraid our benefactor has spoken," he began, showing them to the door with a helpless smile, "I do hope you will return to see our efforts on opening night? Oh, and lest I forget, please feel free to contact me regarding our bargain? I am anxious to hear what more you are willing to share before you depart for the Dissenter lands."

Jaron only smiled and nodded. Before the door could close behind them, he turned to see the playwright watching them, and behind him on stage, the face of the giant cat peering through the mouse hole.

The pair made it back to the school in the early afternoon, weaving their way through the men and baggage in the courtyard. Cord and his brothers were to be found in the Master's Hall, enjoying the relative peace and quiet next to a hot, crackling fire. There were no remaining chairs, so Jaron and Filbert would have to stand to give their report.

"So," Cord asked, "how did your investigation go? Did you get fleas, or cheese?"

The brothers chuckled at each other, and Cord puffed at his pipe, grinning smugly.

Jaron said, "Three hours and *that's* the best you could come up with?"

"Like you could do better," Cord grumbled around his pipe. "What did you find?"

Jaron said, "Filbert and I believe there may be a chance that the play is political, even that it may hold a subversive message, but..."

"But?" Cord asked, "Is it or isn't it?"

"That," Jaron said, "depends on the third act, which we did not see."

Colin's scar twisted with his smirk as he barked, "Ha! I told you, did I not? Complete waste of time."

"At least it got them out of our hair for a few hours," Cord said.

Ceven was a bit more interested. He asked, "What about it made it seem subversive?"

Jaron prepared to drop Filbert's theory on them. "Well," he said, "the cat is really big, and all the mice are really small-"

This astute observation was interrupted by a knock at the door. Filbert went to answer it, and found himself face to face with another former instructor.

"Master Gavadaire!" he exclaimed.

Cord rose to greet him, and his brothers followed suit. The schoolmaster put his pipe aside and clasped the man's hand. "It's good to see you, lad. You've been scarce this last month."

Gavadaire's handsome face was drawn and pale, and his eyes had dark circles under them. In truth, he looked a bit ill. Still, he wore his usual cheerful smile and said, "I regret that I have not visited or sent word, but things have been... difficult. Forgive me."

"Nothing to forgive!" Cord said, "Take what time away you need. This is no longer a school after all, but a boarding house for ruffians." He turned to his brothers, "Brothers Freekirk, allow me to introduce Gavadaire LuVestra, one of my guest instructors this past season. Gavadaire, this is Colin, Carstin, and Ceven, my three younger brothers. They are the ruffians I speak of, along with their men."

The tall blond men shook hands with the newcomer and made formal greetings. Jaron felt completely forgotten, so he spoke up, "Gavadaire, have you been ill? You look rather the worse for wear."

The man gave a weak smile and said, "Alas, I do not know what has come over me, but I feel a longing to return to my order and retreat from the world for a time."

Jaron nodded, "Well, you must do what you feel is best. I admit I'll be sorry to see you go." It was true, and it surprised Jaron to hear himself say it.

Gavadaire smiled and said, "I too shall miss you all, this place, the city. It has been like a second home to me, but I fear I must take my leave. There is a ship waiting to bear me back to Aurilon, and it departs within the hour." As he spoke, he rubbed his chest. Something got pushed aside beneath the fabric as he did so.

Jaron noticed this, and thought it odd. Whatever it was, it looked large and uncomfortable, and Gavadaire was not inclined to wear jewelry. He mused, *Is it a bag of medicine, something to breathe in and sooth a cough?* Then he paid it no more mind.

"We're sorry to see you go," Cord said, "I know you have reasons for not fighting in our civil war, I understand completely. Still, we'll miss your blade on the field."

Jaron said, "But we have a crop of students who will do all the better, thanks to you." He had one particular student in mind, though.

Gavadaire gave a formal bow, clapped his friends on the shoulders, and turned to leave. "Farewell, my friends! Let us renew our bonds when next we meet," he called. Then he was gone.

Only when the men returned to their seats did they notice that the fire had gone completely cold.

Chapter Four

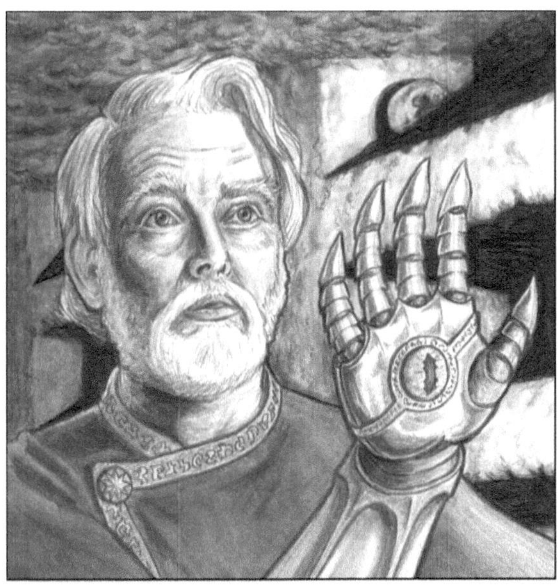

Linchpin

Ildric Finnael absently rubbed at his arm where the flesh met his silver gauntlet as he listened to a report from one of his fellow wizards. He had been at the Tower of the Silver Moon every day for the past week, hearing from masters of several schools of study, each with something vital to share.

Vital in their own minds, perhaps, he thought. His own matters were vital, to his mind, but he was not sure he wanted to make them known just yet.

Currently, Magus Thuumel of the School of Nature was claiming that the snows might not end until the middle of Balmoth at the vernal equinox, perhaps delaying the army's march. Magus Eldram of the Schools of Augmentation and Corruption reported that he would be traveling to advise a contingent of guild wizards to assist the king's army in siege activities.

Arch Mage Ravilus Tage reported that his 'great experiment' might be ready for trials in time for the war. Also, many wealthier lords were having their personal weapons enchanted for the campaign, and the Casting Guild was hard-pressed to keep up with demand. Since only guild wizards were allowed to earn money in the city, any enchanters from the Order of Astrellaris would have to travel with the army if they wished to profit from this new demand.

Vital news, Ildric thought wearily.

It had been only yesterday since he had bid his friend Drahn a safe journey, but he missed the little creature already. For the first time in almost three decades, he was without his dweedragon companion. There was no one else to talk to in his lonely tower, no one to share his troubles and help him focus his thoughts.

Worse perhaps was the lack of focus in his divinations. The Eye of Omithys, his greatest treasure, was revealed only last year to be a dweedragon artifact. It was therefore likely that the arrival of the little dweedragon in the year after Ildric acquired the Eye had allowed the wizard to master it and become the most powerful diviner in the kingdom.

Ildric had journeyed away from Drahn in the past, and his visions had become weaker, but he had always assumed it was the rigors of travel, or being away from his tower's spirit well. Now Drahn had left him, and this was obviously not the case. His recent attempts were like waking from a dream, and he had to grasp for the fading images and context.

This news was vital, yet Ildric was loath to share it. Instead, he had another string of ill news to report. It was going to be a dreary end to a long day.

Grand Master Orellus rose on his spindly legs and took the center podium as Tage took his seat. Orellus stroked his long, white beard to smooth it down, and rubbed a hand over his bald head, perhaps a habit from when he had more hair. "Thank you, Master Tage, for that enlightening news. I would encourage any who wish to travel with the army to make extensive records of each lord's weapon that gets enchanted for future study and reference. Remember, gold is desired, but knowledge is the only coin that enriches all. Now, I open the floor to Arch Mage Ildric Finnael, master of the Divination School."

Ildric sighed and took his place in the center of the chamber, casting a gaze at the bored, preoccupied faces. The week of meetings, debates, and reports had worn on everyone.

"Greetings, my friends," he began, "I first wish to report on an older matter, namely the individual who appeared in this chamber last summer. As many of you know, he identified himself as a denizen of the Void, sent by the gods on a mission to stop the mad wizard from unleashing destruction on us all, in his words. This is a claim for which we have found no real evidence. However, being as our knowledge of the threat is very limited, this claim cannot be discounted.

"His escape and disappearance is the matter I have sought to unravel. Since this tower and all that transpires within it are shielded from divination attempts, I have had to rely on mundane deductions. After thorough research, I have come to the disturbing conclusion that Drahn the dweedragon was responsible for freeing the prisoner and facilitating his escape."

This caused one or two gasps of surprise, but most of the wizards nodded, smirked, or folded their arms, their suspicions confirmed. Ravilus Tage spoke up, "I find it telling, Master Ildric, that it took you so long to determine this, and chose to report it only after the creature had left town." A few others harrumphed in agreement.

"I simply waited my turn," Ildric said, "and an earlier report would have changed nothing. Drahn and the stranger parted ways after the escape, and the dweedragon's whereabouts have been known and accounted for since then. But the stranger has eluded my detection, and that is the more disturbing puzzle."

"Master Ildric," said the grand master, sounding quite exasperated, "This is most unfitting. I hope you do not think to dismiss your pupil's crime so easily?"

"Crime?" Ildric asked, "With respect, grand master, we committed a crime of our own in keeping the stranger a prisoner here for a week. Why, Master Tage even threatened him with torture."

Tage blustered, "I did not- I only-"

"Whether an empty threat or not," Ildric said, "The Order is not a legal authority, and has no power to imprison or pass judgment. Yes, Drahn would have done better to turn him over to the count's authority, or even members of the clergy, but our transgressions were already in bloom, and there would have been consequences."

Incredulous, Tage asked, "Do you expect us to *thank* him for doing what he did? We were keeping the prisoner because of the possible danger he posed, and your foolish dragon released him into the city! Some might even say at your behest!"

Ildric kept his calm, but he gave Tage a glare and said, "Some might indeed say anything that crosses their minds. But if you noticed, since the prisoner escaped, much of the misfortune that has plagued our city has tapered off. The rats have retreated, the contagion they spread has abated, and there have been no more reports of unnatural disturbances. Most importantly, the restless dead have not been seen since winter began."

This caused a few of his critics to pause, but many remained unconvinced. He raised his hands and said, "I understand that this might be coincidental, but as I said before, the real issue is the missing stranger, this little man who gave us many names in many dead languages. Whoever he was, I should have been able to see him these past six months."

Tage sneered, "Perhaps he too is serving some hidden purpose, to be revealed only when it is too late to do anything about it?"

Ildric had endured enough. "Perhaps Master Tage would like to back up his baseless claims with proof? If not, I officially invite him to stuff his beard down his throat until he chokes!"

"That will do, both of you!" cried the grand master, rising to his feet, "Next you'll be throwing down gauntlets and demanding satisfaction; well I won't have it! Your idiotic animosity will no longer be tolerated! If the two of you want to go duel on a mountaintop, be my guest, but there will be no such hostility and- and *childishness* in this tower! Is that clear?" He banged his staff on the floor, causing a deep ringing to echo down the length of the structure.

Abashed, Ildric and Tage muttered apologies to the grand master, who stood there glaring at them like a headmaster at two muddy schoolboys. Ildric was almost afraid Orellus would demand they shake hands and make up, but thankfully the old man had not the energy to milk their embarrassment as once he would have. He sat down, waved his hand and growled, "Continue your report, Master Finnael."

Ildric cleared his throat and tried to regain a little dignity. "As I have said, I have not been able to sense any ripples from this man's presence; not now, nor in the future. I can sense where he has been, and there are some eyewitness reports that have confirmed this. However, I do not believe that he still lives."

This was disturbing news. Many who had been present during the stranger's 'stay' had wrestled with the consequences of interfering in a possible divine event. After all, the man could have been called a living omen, appearing in the midst of a storm that could have been nothing but an omen of doom. Perhaps he had been sent in their darkest of hours? What did it mean that his life was now extinguished? Had he truly accomplished his mission, or were matters worse?

But Ildric was not finished. "There is something worse," he said, "While it is still conjecture, Drahn and I had been puzzling over the identity of our guest for many months. Neither of us have spoken of it to others, but we came to the conclusion that our former hostage was a... a god."

Dead silence fell in the chamber. Mouths dropped open. Eyes went wide. Then someone dropped a pipe, and it made everyone jump, breaking the spell. The room erupted in questions as dozens of learned scholars all spoke at once.

Ildric knew this would be the most controversial statement ever made in the history of the Order, but it was the only theory that made sense. Still, the cacophony would have to die down before he could address it. He raised his silver hand and called for silence.

When everyone had settled down, he continued. "I know this is almost impossible to believe, but consider; he appeared in the midst of a terrible storm, a storm that we believed was caused by the presence of the Dark Heart in our city. The Dark Heart caused the Time of Chaos over a thousand years ago, breaking down the barriers between our world and the realms beyond. If this indeed happened again, then it might allow for a divine being to enter our realm."

A young wizard from Aldrig asked, "Surely you mean a *servant* of the gods, or some kind of spirit creature made manifest?"

Ildric said, "I do not think so, mostly because of the names he gave us. At first, we thought them to be gibberish, but thanks to my little dweedragon apprentice," he glanced sidelong at Tage, "some names were identified as ancient languages no longer spoken. Those we identified seemed to be proper names, names that combined respect with a healthy mistrust. Examples were 'One Who Makes Life Interesting,' or 'The Great Gambler,' or 'Master of Stories and Lies,' and my favorite, 'The Worm in the Fruit.' They all point to one god, a god of the Divine Court who is often associated with Chaos."

He did not say his name. If he needed to, he was speaking to the wrong crowd.

Tage spoke, reining in his usual sarcasm, "Gods above and below, you mean Tavenji."

Ildric said, "It is the only answer that fits."

"I hope you have more than that?" someone asked, talking around their pipe.

"I do," Ildric said, "There was the item found on, er, rather *in* his person. You might recall, those who were present, that he wretched up an acorn after his appearance? I examined it with my considerable powers; I even left the tower in case the warding spells were interfering with my visions. This acorn had no mother tree, no forest of origin, no squirrel hording it away, no natural source or history that I could divine. I could only conclude that it was unnatural, having traveled with the stranger from wherever he came from. As we all know, the oak leaf is a symbol of Eyorona, and acorns are sacred to her. I think this acorn was a favor from the goddess, imparted to our guest."

Another voice called, "But if our guest was a god, why did he need a favor from another god? Surely those were only given to mortals in ancient times?"

Ildric nodded, "If this stranger was indeed a god, I think we can agree that he was quite limited in power; in fact, he only seemed to have his wits and nothing more. Perhaps he needed the help? From what we know of the last commandment of Arathus, the world of mortals was to be forever closed to the gods. But what if a god is no longer a god?"

There was a murmuring as the wizards discussed this among themselves. Then, Master Thuumel spoke up, "But you said you believe that the stranger, whomever you might call him, is no longer alive? Why do you think this? Perhaps he went back to the Void, or the divine realms?"

Ildric said heavily, "I do not think it is within his power. It took a horrible, sky-shattering storm to open a path for him, and unless the Dark Heart is used again to rend the fabric of our world, I do not think he has the power or means to return home. He mentioned that 'the gods have even abandoned their own.' I think he may have been referring to his own predicament."

Reed-thin Master Gaddisen, one of Ildric's frequent supporters, asked, "Are we under any obligation to inform the religious authorities? Might they not need to be involved?"

Master Mattock, a thick and rotund man with a stylized beard said, "Inform them of what? That Tavenji popped out of thin air and we held him prisoner, he escaped, and is presumed dead? Raving lunatics, they'd call us. We have no proof of any of this!"

Gaddisen said, "The evidence is conjectural, but fits the facts. If there is even a chance that it's true-"

Ildric raised his hand, "Masters, please. I agree with both of you. The evidence fits the facts, but it sounds absurd and cannot be proven. Besides, Tavenji is not represented by any of the faiths of the Divine Court, and is no longer officially worshiped by anyone. To whom would we appeal?"

Mattock said, "If it is indeed baseless, as I believe, it would cause undue panic and confusion in the faith communities. There would be inquiries, tribunals, endless meddling in our affairs..."

The murmuring seemed to validate Master Mattock's position. The Order of Astrellaris took pains to avoid such entanglements for a reason. Wizards of the Order mostly revered Lieutrella, goddess of the moon, and the only clergy they tolerated were the Silver Sisters, her mysterious priestesses. The clergy of the Divine Court had their own rules, laws, traditions, and dogma that often ran afoul of the Order's methods and philosophy. Both were made up of elites, and each respected the other, but the clergy had that unwavering moral certainty that *everything was their business*. Wizards followed their curiosity, which could be moderated, but clergy received their directives from on high. It mattered little that the gods no longer seemed to care.

Grand Master Orellus said, "What then is to be done? If he was indeed a god, and is now indeed deceased, it would be of the highest order of importance to know for certain."

"I agree," Ildric said, "That is why I will dedicate the rest of my efforts into getting to the bottom of this mystery. I ask that the Order give me leave to find this individual, be he alive or dead. We must keep this knowledge secret! If word leaks out that I am searching for a fallen god, there is no telling who will be dogging my heels and interfering."

The Order took some time to debate, the vote was taken, and the motion passed. Barely.

Ildric collected his things in the large entrance hall of the tower, donning his cloak and retrieving his staff. Others were already leaving for the night, or on their way down the spiral stairs. Some were sitting by the fireplaces, sunk deep into the upholstered chairs, filling the air with pipe smoke and conjecture. Ildric swept his gaze across the hall, wondering what he had gotten himself into.

The tapping of a staff could be heard, and Ildric turned to see the grand master approaching. Orellus looked frailer than ever, having used up much of his daily strength to rebuke his obstinate underlings.

"Master Finnael?" he asked, "may I have a word?" He took Ildric's arm and walked him towards the doors. He said, "I would not go so far as to ask your plans in council, where they might be open to endless debate, but do you have a plan on where to start your search?"

It was a good question. Ildric thought a moment and said, "The trail runs cold the day after he escaped, or rather, was set loose." He blushed a bit. "The visions before he disappears are dark and confusing, scattered and almost nonsensical. But I might have a lead."

"Oh?" the old grand master asked, "Might you share it?"

Ildric nodded and said, "I think he met a man that day; the meeting created ripples in the future. If there is a trail to follow, it begins with him."

"And who is this man?" Orellus asked.

"I do not know who he is," Ildric said, "but I think I know where he might be found."

The evening was cold but clear, and the walk home would be brisk and bracing. As he walked in the deepening gloom, Ildric wondered how his former pupil's quest into the Shadowood was proceeding. He considered using his powers to look, but thought the better of it. Divination was a tricky thing, as it could not only glimpse the future, but many possible futures. If he saw something dreadful happening, he was hardly in a position to help, and the fear of such a future would worry him sick. Worse, Ildric had a theory that looking too often into a particular future might increase the odds of it being realized. Some things were best left to chance, albeit with a healthy dose of preparation.

Besides, Nixyalderthor had a powerful scrying ward placed on him by his father, so he probably wouldn't see anything anyway.

Drahn was in good company on his journey, he had little doubt of that. He let that be his comfort as he made for the Trade District, commonly known as the Silver District. The guild wizards gave him respectful nods as they lit the wizard lamps along the avenues, and the evening striders parted for him and cast their eyes elsewhere. Some looked to the wizard's feet or back as they passed, and Ildric knew for whom they were searching. His constant companion was not to be found, however.

As he crossed one of the bridges over the canal, he saw the Tower of Sight over the top of the buildings of the Market Square. He imagined his bed, a warm fire, and a meager meal, but it was not to be, not yet. His destination was many blocks farther into the Trade District, almost to the north wall. He felt tempted to hail a cab, but his inner voice told him he needed the exercise. *Do not be lazy, Master Ildwic,* it said. The wizard smiled.

Ildric passed under the district gatehouse and away from the stink of the canal, and walked the main avenue. It ran between the Market Square and the temple of Obamir, and continued all the way to the North Wall Walk. It was named the Golden Path, after the mythical gold-paved road in Obamir's realm that led to the Great Treasury. While nowhere near as impressive as its namesake, it was paved with yellow sandstone imported from the island nation of Ghanael at great expense. Under the midday sun, the road glittered as the light caught countless flecks of quartz. However, the effect was lost at night, and Ildric was not sightseeing.

He was looking for a man he had seen in his visions, a man who had been in the company of the wayward god during his last hours. Their time together had been brief, but it was the only clue he could follow. He knew the man's face, but only as one knows a face from a dream. More importantly, he knew the man's height. He had been a dwarf, and most dwarfs lived in one neighborhood in Portshia.

His staff clicked on the paving stones as he headed for Miner Town.

The ramshackle cluster of buildings had seen better days. Many stood at odd angles, some leaning against each other for support, like drunken sailors. The roofs were shingled with mismatched tiles. Makeshift repairs held many of the old houses together, braced, bound and blocked. Convoluted contraptions sprouted from their surfaces; pulleys and winches, lifts and levers, lines of twine crisscrossing distant windows. Ildric could only guess at their purpose. The moonlight caught the chimney smoke as it rose from cook fires and warm comforts within. The smell was homey and reassuring.

The main distinction of the neighborhood was the proportion of the buildings. They were small, with small doors, low windows, and low fences, except where they corralled livestock. The inhabitants were mostly dwarfs, both the descendants of the old silver miners, and newer blood who needed a place to belong if society rejected them. Some of the residents were normal-sized children of dwarf couples, and the older ones were often tasked with dissuading outsiders from gawking or lingering. A few of these walked about now, shouldering pitchforks like polearms and carrying a hooded lantern.

Ildric rested on a low wall, wondering how to best carry out his search. He did not want to spook anyone or make his job more difficult, but his powers were not what they once were. He might have to go door to door, following the Eye like a man with a lantern in the fog. No one wanted to look out their window at night and see a wizard pointing a glowing light at them, even if they did recognize him by sight or reputation. It just wasn't done.

Neither could he ask after an individual, for he knew not the man's name or profession. What he did know was that chances were better finding him here at night, when most decent people were at home in bed. *Where I would like to be,* he thought, *Well, there's nothing for it.* He stood up and raised his silver gauntlet, muttered a word of command, and closed his eyes.

The dragon-eye stone in the palm of the gauntlet flashed and moved to and fro, taking in its surroundings. The vertical pupil flared, and a faint green light shone from the eye, causing the binding glyphs surrounding it to glow. Ildric moved his silver hand from side to side, sweeping it across the undersized buildings.

Faces appeared in his mind, faces of men and women, children and family pets, goats, pigs, and chickens. He growled with frustration. *It is so difficult to filter what the Eye looks for now.* He searched again and found a cow. *Damn it! People, I need people; male humans, short. Focus!*

More faces appeared, some wrong, some possibly right. He saw pigeons.

"Blast it," he sighed, opening his eyes and lowering his hand, "This is such a nuisance. If Drahn were here..." He did not finish the thought, for it was an unworthy one. Drahn's presence would help him little. Indeed, he had tried to follow this lead many times in the past few months, from the comfort of his tower. This dwarf was the last person the stranger met, as far as Ildric could tell. He had managed to glimpse him many times, but something always interfered with the little man's location in time and space.

In fact, he could only find him by focusing on his meeting with the missing stranger. They had been someplace dark and torch-lit, perhaps underground. The details were murky and veiled, as if the dwarf was protected by some counter-spell, some scrying ward that made him difficult to detect. *But why?* Such wards were expensive, owned by important people who greatly valued their privacy.

Am I even looking in the right place?

With all the other distractions of the past few months, he had not had the time to pursue the mystery of the dwarf. But then, that was before he and Drahn reached the same conclusion about the identity of the missing stranger. That discussion had occurred in early Aramoth, the first month of the New Year.

It had already been decided that Drahn would accompany Lady Cindra on her quest and he was very excited with the prospect. But when he and Ildric agreed that the stranger might be the god Tavenji, Drahn's mind began to change about leaving. Ildric would not hear of it, knowing the little creature would regret choosing to stay behind. He insisted he could handle the matter himself, and directed the dweedragon to go on his adventure. He had told him, "I am not so old and senile that I need your help at every turn, you silly creature."

Perhaps I'd been wrong, he thought grimly.

Now with his faltering powers of divination doing him no favors, Ildric would have to rely on his deductive reasoning skills. Those skills were rusty, to say the least.

"Now," he said aloud to the rising moon, "How do I find an invisible tree in a forest?" He pondered this as the Miner Town patrol wandered by, giving him a wary glance.

They put their heads together and whispered something, then they approached him. One of them, a taller young man of perhaps twenty years, said, "Greetings, grandfather. Are you... 'Talon' Finnael, by chance?"

Ildric smiled and said, "I am. What gave it away?"

The young man smiled back and said, "Lucky guess. Might have been the hand."

"Indeed," Ildric said.

"Have you business here in Miner Town?" he asked, his nervousness showing.

"That, I am trying to decide," Ildric replied, "Tell me, have you seen any odd folk here in the last few months?"

"Odd?" asked the lad, "Depends on what you mean."

The shorter fellow mentioned, "There was a big Maanok merchant here last fall. Had us all worried."

"A Maanok?" Ildric said, "Whatever did he want in Miner Town?"

The lad shrugged and nodded towards a ramshackle row of houses, "I guess he had business with Emen, the bird keeper."

"Hmmm," Ildric said, "Anyone else? Anyone with... pointed ears, perhaps?"

The lads looked at each other with mild surprise. "An elf? We heard tell that the only elf seen in town was staying with you in your tower, begging yer pardon, master."

The taller lad spoke up, saying, "I heard she was living in the keep. Rumor is she's a beauty, like a goddess come back to us."

"I've never met a goddess," Ildric replied, "but Wenyssaya could be mistaken for one, it's true. Alas, but I was referring to a man. He would be about your height," he pointed to the shorter lad, "with light yellow hair and rather long, pointed ears."

"Sounds like old Uncle Tweak," the taller lad said with a chuckle.

"Who?" Ildric asked.

"It's what the people of Miner Town called Tavenji in the old stories. He'd play tricks on our forefathers long, long ago." he said, "Even now, if someone misplaces something, or funny things happen, it's 'Uncle Tweak' that gets the blame."

"Indeed?" Ildric said, "So I assume such a man has not been seen here?"

"No, afraid not, master!" they said, unsure if he was joking or not. They then left him to his pondering and moon gazing, wishing him a good evening.

Good lads, he thought.

Ildric stared at the moon as it rose over the city, and silently prayed to Lieutrella for help. The gods of Nature were a part of the world, and were not closed off like the Divine Court, but the nature gods never spoke to mortals to begin with. Still, one could always hope for a spark of inspiration.

The wizard sat there for some time, his mind spinning. *I cannot find what I cannot see,* he thought, *I could go house to house, knocking on doors. Perhaps I will get lucky?* He rubbed his eyes as he shivered in the cold. *Blast it, think!*

He cleared his mind, letting it drift. His mind sifted over the faces he had seen in his search attempt, even the animals. Dogs, cats, chickens, a cow, pigeons... he meditated on his conversation with the boys on patrol.

He wondered, *Why was a Maanok merchant here last fall? What was he selling in Miner Town? Why go to a bird keeper? Was he just hungry?* He shook his head. *Distracted. I'm getting distracted.*

He looked around, hoping a clue would jump out at him. As he did, he noticed a shadow lurking in a gateway of the quad building across the street. His sense of danger awoke, reminding him that at first glance, he was a tired old man sitting alone on a dark street. Someone might mistake him for easy prey. He lowered his head and cast a spell under his breath, clutching his staff to draw upon the magic around him.

"*Thit runas, aram thimas,*" he said. The spell conjured a dim, spectral eye that floated before him, showing him the street and the building where the shadow lurked. Concentrating, he moved the eye forward towards the gateway. It was an odd sensation; his vision told his mind he was drifting across the street, but he could feel himself sitting firmly on the wall. It was unlike the visions conjured by his more powerful divinations; those were profound and engrossing, like diving through time and space. This was mundane, disembodying, but effective. Better, it was a simple spell that any novice diviner could use. It did not depend on his weakened artifact.

The eye could see slightly better in the dark than his own eyes, and it showed him the face of his stalker. It was a young boy, perhaps eight years old or less. *A street urchin,* Ildric thought. Relaxing his guard, he brought the invisible eye back across the street and guided it down the rows of leaning buildings, seeing what he could see. The spell could be used to look inside a house, but only if there was an open door or window for it to slip through. Strangely, Ildric felt more like a voyeur while using this spell. Regardless, no one in Miner Town had an open window that he could see. Just as well.

He found the dwelling of the bird keeper, with its pigeon coop and hen house. His mind went back to the

Maanok merchant that had visited last fall. *Something is tickling my mind about this,* Ildric thought, *Why can't I let it go?*

He opened his eyes, breaking the spell. Suddenly he was looking at the street in the moonlight once again. "I don't need another mystery," he muttered aloud, but nevertheless, he resolved to find out what he could. Standing, he turned towards the row of houses, and raising his silver hand, he opened the Eye of Omithys.

Winter. Fall. Comings and goings. Many small folk going about their lives. Tall folk. Townsfolk. A Maanok, tall and copper skinned, leading a mule laden with saddlebags. There, he thought, *Focus.*

The large barbarian was dressed warmly, his painted face scanning the houses. Parents herded their children indoors. Neighbors grew alarmed. The Maanok stood before the bird keeper's house, darkening the door. He knocked. The mule brayed. Metal clanked in the saddlebags. The door opened.

Ildric knew the face. "The bird keeper!" he cried, "It's him!" The power of the Eye dimmed as he strode quickly towards the house.

The child in the shadows ran off in alarm.

Ildric stood before the door, trying one more test. He raised the Eye and looked within the house, searching for an inhabitant, any inhabitant. The vision showed an empty house, filled with shadows and meager light. He knocked on the door. A voice came from within.

"Who is it? It's after dark."

Ah, Ildric thought, *I found you, invisible dwarf.* He said, "I am sorry to bother you at this hour, Emen bird-keeper, but might I have a word? It is of the utmost importance."

The door latch clicked and the small door opened, allowing enough space for an eye to peep out. The eye took in the tall visitor and went wide, then a trembling voice said, "A moment, please."

Ildric knew his appearance and reputation often preceded him, but this dwarf's reaction was a bit extreme. *If he means to hide from divinations, I am the last person he wants to see,* the wizard concluded.

The door opened further, and the wizard could see the dwarf properly. The face was the face he had seen in his visions, scant though they might have been. The small man had been eating supper, and was wearing a loose-fitting tunic. He had a mop of dark hair, a prominent brow, and stood about four feet tall. His face was rather pale, though as Ildric had just met him, he could not be sure if this was normal.

The wizard introduced himself. "Greetings, master Emen. My name is Ildric Finnael, Arch Mage of the Order of Astrellaris. I was wondering if you might help me?"

Emen's mouth twitched as he glanced past the wizard, looking into the night. He blinked a few times, his mouth a hard line. Taking a deep breath, he answered, "Of course, I'd be happy to be of assistance. Do you want to buy a chicken?"

Ildric smiled and said gently, "May I come inside? It is a cold night and I am an old man."

Emen blinked some more, a nervous tick perhaps, and nodded, opening the door wide. "Watch your head," the dwarf said.

Ildric thanked him and ducked to enter the house. The ceiling was about six feet high, so Ildric did not have to stoop once inside. The room and furnishings were all scaled to its inhabitant, and all was cozy and lived in. A few feathers twirled into the corners, chased by the draft as the door closed.

"Tea?" Emen asked, "I'm sorry I have little to offer, as my meal is almost finished."

"Yes, please," Ildric said, taking an empty chair by the table. He immediately regretted his decision as a realization struck him. *If this dwarf is in hiding, and as nervous as he seems, he might be dangerous. Best not to drink any tea.* He had spells to detect poisons of course, but using one would be obvious and rather impolite.

Laying his staff across his knees, Ildric watched as the dwarf poured their tea. Nothing suspicious happened, but he held off drinking regardless. He said, "I would like to begin by saying that I respect your privacy, master Emen, but it has come to my attention that you might have met someone I am trying to find."

Emen took a seat opposite the wizard, making a great effort to keep his composure. He cleared his throat and asked, "Who is it you are looking for?"

Ildric said, "It was last summer, towards the end of Hwessmoth, about a week after that great, terrible storm. There was a man, perhaps an elf, who came to town. He had pale yellow hair and rather pronounced pointed ears. Some reports are that he was dressed in motley and silk."

Emen's nose twitched. He took a sip of his own tea, playing for time. He said, "That sounds like quite a character. What makes you think I know this fellow?"

A cautious one indeed, Ildric thought, *Perhaps the truth will shake him out.* "As it happens," the wizard said, "I have been seeking for him since that day. I have been using my considerable powers of divination, and while I cannot find him, the last person I saw him with was you."

Emen sputtered on his tea. "That's not possible!" he said.

Ildric pressed him, subtly griping his staff. "I assure you, it was no easy task gathering this information, but I am not wrong. I care not for your personal dealings, but I must find this person. If you can offer me any help, I beg of you, please aid me."

Emen did not relax, but his expression changed at the sincerity in the wizard's voice. He swirled the remaining tea in his cup, staring at it like he was reading the future in the brown liquid. Finally, he asked, "What is your interest in this fellow? What has he done, exactly?"

Ildric said, "He was a visitor of importance to the Order, and to me. I spoke to him at great length, and we learned much from each other, but before we could reach a true understanding, our ways were parted."

It was the truth, leaving out the whole 'keeping him prisoner' part. Ildric hoped the stray god had not shared that detail with Emen; it might cast things in the wrong light. He asked, "Did he happen to tell you why he was in the city?"

Emen became slightly belligerent. "If you saw us together, as you claim, then you must already know all that transpired, is that not so?" he huffed.

"It is not," Ildric said, "Much was hidden from me. You are carrying some sort of scrying ward, is *that* not so?"

Emen flinched and said, "I don't know what you mean."

At first, Ildric had considered using magic to read Emen's truthfulness, but the dwarf's protection would have clouded the spell. Regardless, his body language was giving the wizard all the information he needed.

Ildric said, "I sense you are a good man, Emen bird-keeper, and an honest one; lying does not come easily to you. However, you have things you wish hidden. For now, my attentions are set on seeking the missing stranger. I do not wish to delve into your business any more than it takes to find him."

Emen pursed his lips, keeping his eyes in his tea. "Silverthumb, if you please."

"Sorry?" Ildric asked.

"It's Emen Silverthumb. I did not introduce myself properly before," he said.

"Emen Silverthumb, I am pleased to meet you." Ildric said, "By chance, did the stranger introduce himself properly?"

The dwarf heaved a sigh, giving up on his weak pretense. Taking a sip of tea, he said, "We did not meet under ideal conditions, but he called himself Tweak."

"Did he indeed?" Ildric chuckled.

"Yes," Emen said, smiling a little, "He was the spitting image of Tavenji, right out of a theater poster.

We call that god 'Uncle Tweak' in our folklore, you know."

"So I have heard," Ildric said.

Emen relaxed a little more, and some of his color had returned. Feeling a bit bolder, he asked, "So who was he really, this important visitor from whom you learned so much?"

Ildric leaned forward and said, "I believe he was sent to us from the Outer Realms, perhaps from the Divine Court itself."

Emen laughed heartily, mistaking Ildric's seriousness for a part of the joke. But when the joke had gone on too long, the dwarf's mirth sobered. "You- you're serious, aren't you?"

"Deadly serious," Ildric said.

"But, but everyone knows such a thing is impossible," Emen muttered.

"Normally, I would agree with you," he said, "but these are not normal times. This fellow appeared in a flash of lightning, in the heart of a fierce and unnatural storm. If I am right, then it is in the best interests of the entire world to find him."

Emen sat there for a moment, absorbing this. Then he said, "Let me get my coat and boots."

The men set out into the night, with Emen in the lead and Ildric following cautiously behind. When Emen had gone upstairs to change, Ildric had prepared a spell for his own protection. *Dwildiis n'shindve* would only serve as a vague warning of impending danger, lasting about an hour. The weakened Eye might enhance that, but then again, it might not. With no way to test it, Ildric would have to be extra alert. Already he felt a sense of impending doom tickling the back of his neck. He wondered, *am I being led into a trap?*

"It's not far, if that's a comfort," Emen said, and he led them to the other end of Miner Town and onto a familiar avenue. *This is Silver Street*, Ildric realized. On the far end, it ran past his home, the Tower of Sight; it ran past the festival grounds, where a portion of the army was encamped; it ran past the Valdakian Temple, where the effigy of the blind god overlooked the gate of the cemetery.

The cemetery, Ildric thought, *This is not a good sign, but it explains a thing or two.* He put his silver hand in his pocket, to avoid unwanted attention. He didn't need to advertise his presence to the guild wizards manning the Dead Watch towers. There were laws governing the magical trades within the city limits, and he didn't want to be accused of stepping on the Casting Guild's toes.

Emen led him to the iron gates of the necropolis, which were currently locked. A single guard stood by, warming himself by a brazier. He watched the odd pair approach.

"Who goes there, and what business have you?" he called, not yet reaching for his halberd. After all, his presence was to keep things in, not out.

Emen smiled at him as he walked up to the fire, saying, "My friend and I have need to visit a dearly departed relative. Do let us in, will you?"

The guard looked at Ildric's robes and silver-inlaid staff. "You're a wizard?" he asked.

"I am," Ildric said, "My business here is personal, not professional."

He said, "Then I expect you know how to handle yourself if you meet someone who should be resting?"

"I do," Ildric said, hoping that was true.

"Very well, then," said the guard, and he unlocked the gate, "If you run into any trouble, I'd recommend getting out into the open where the tower wizards and archers can aid you. It'd be safer in daylight, but it's your hide." As the gates opened, he took a torch from the brazier and waved it to and fro. The light was answered from a tower across the cemetery. The signal was obvious: *don't shoot.*

"Thank you for the warning," Emen said, and he led the wizard into the graveyard.

The cemetery was well-lit by tall pitch-torches, illuminating the walkways and tomb entrances, yet it was still unnerving in the dark of night. Most people had a natural unease in cemeteries, but it was greatly enhanced by the knowledge that the hungry dead were on the loose. At least, they had been.

As Emen led them between the grave markers and effigies, Ildric asked him, "I take it that the person I seek is among the dead?"

Emen shrugged, "I only think I know where he is, and if I am right, then he is dead. I have no real knowledge, but if I were a gambling man, I'd wager that he is."

"How did you happen to meet him here?" Ildric asked.

"Ah now," the dwarf said, wagging a finger, "that is more my business than yours."

"Fair enough," Ildric said. He glanced at the watch towers, seeing the archers with crossbows ready, and the guild wizards peering into the darkness around them. It gave him a little comfort, yet he did not lower his guard. His spell was telling him danger was all around him. *But from where?*

"If this fellow is a divine servant, as you claim," Emen asked, "can he really be killed?"

Ildric shook his head, "I cannot say. Such a thing has never been heard of. But since he is here, he may not be as divine as he once was. Perhaps mortality is the price of his arrival."

Emen stopped and turned, "Does this have anything to do with the tales of the mad wizard from the north? It seems too much to be a coincidence."

Ildric eyed him shrewdly. "It does indeed, master Silverthumb," he said, "I think the one drew the other. For what purpose, I cannot tell. I can only hope it was for the better."

"Some say we are living in the last days," Emen said, turning back to the path.

Ildric sniffed. "Some *always* say that," he replied. *But this time they may be right.*

Emen led the wizard to a mausoleum decorated with the corpulent image of Obamir, sitting cross-legged, with open arms above the door. The carving under his feet read 'House of Generosity.'

"What is this place?" Ildric asked.

"It is a tomb open to all who can pay," Emen said, "Specifically, those of the merchant class who can afford the fee. They can either have their bones entombed here once they rot in the ground, or have their bodies placed in a niche in the catacombs. It has the advantage of being unlocked and open to anyone. No treasures are kept within, so there is no fear of grave robbing."

"You seem to know much about the cemetery, master Silverthumb," Ildric said.

"We all become acquainted at one time or another," the dwarf said. He took a torch from a barrel inside the door, and lit it from the torch outside. "Shall we?" he asked.

Ildric nodded and said, "*Ildas Oridos.*" A soft light appeared on the end of his staff, equaling the torchlight, but giving no heat.

They entered the mausoleum, ignoring the fancy plaques and decorations for the recently deceased, and headed for the dark portal at the back that led down into the catacombs. The air became closer, and the smell of damp earth and grass was replaced with the lingering odors of dust and decay. Impending danger grew in his thoughts with every step, raising the hairs on the back of his neck. His mind told him to sweep the narrow hallways with the Eye of Omithys, but instinct told him to rely on his senses. The smoke from the torch stung his eyes and filled his nostrils, making this difficult. *I am too old to be creeping about in dark tunnels*, he thought.

They descended stairs and sloping hallways, turning here and there, passing many intersections. Ildric could not tell just how far down they had come, but he was sure he could find his way out. That was the good thing about Divination; it gave you a little foresight, but *very* accurate hindsight. If he wished, he could wander blindly in the dark and still find his way out, so long as he had a verge to cast a spell.

What worried him was not getting lost, but getting ambushed. The hallway was so narrow that there was no room to swing his staff if it came to that. He could be grabbed from both sides if people were hiding in the alcoves; people, or things that were once people...

They were not alone in the catacombs; the ground moved before them and behind as a great host of rats scurried in dismay at the intrusion. Some were so bold as to weave between their legs, squeaking horribly when a large foot dared to land on a tail.

"So this is where they all went," Emen muttered, "I don't suppose you can keep them at bay?"

"I could," Ildric said, "If things get worse." He was not willing to cast many more spells outside of a spirit well. He had grown used to the free flow of power, and had forgotten how simple magic could be draining. So they walked with more caution and avoided the rats when possible, kicking the more stubborn ones aside.

"I was wondering," Emen said, "why is a wizard searching for a divine messenger? Why not the religious authorities?"

Ildric replied, "The clergy does not know he is here, else I imagine they would be scouring the city for him."

"They don't know?" Emen asked, incredulous, "You didn't tell them?"

"No," Ildric said, "It would only complicate matters."

"I see," Emen said, "And the king or the count? Did you at least inform them of this world-changing event?"

"The high lords have other things to worry about," the wizard replied, "Besides, why use an army when one man will do?"

"Why indeed..."

"How much farther?" Ildric asked, not liking where the conversation was going.

"Just up ahead," Emen said, reading signs the wizard could not see.

Danger was very close now; the spell he had cast was telling him it was all around, and the wizard took several deep breaths to calm himself. *What have I gotten myself into this time?*

The dwarf lowered his torch, better to illuminate the bottom tier of niches. Old bones and rags could be seen, some of them moving. The men started, but both let out audible sighs as they realized the culprits were merely rats moving among the remains.

Ildric said, "These bones are very old, and I haven't seen any recent arrivals."

Emen said, "You would not. These tunnels are rarely used anymore. That's why it stood out."

"What stood out?" the wizard asked. He feared he knew the answer.

"Up here," Emen said, moving towards a lower niche partway up the corridor. The recessed space was crawling with rats; dark little creatures with thick tails, pulling at scraps of linen and peering at the invaders with bright eyes. Beneath the mass of creatures was a body, wrapped in dusty linens and stained with rat droppings and old blood. It had not yet decayed, judging by the smell. The rodents grew agitated, some rearing up and dashing towards the intruders.

"*Posthe Kiilen,*" Ildric intoned, thumping his staff on the floor. The rodents squeaked and scattered in distress, coming out of every alcove and scampering away from the area. Ildric felt a little wave of dizziness as the magic passed through him, and again he cursed himself for growing dependent on his luxuries. *I suffer a backlash casting a novice warding spell? It must be the nerves, the stress I am under. I must keep a cooler head.*

He forced himself to relax as he stooped to examine the body. "Help me pull him out," he said, leaning his staff against the wall as he bent to take hold of the wrapped shoulders.

Emen placed his torch in another niche, then bent down to grab the feet. Together, they pulled the body out of the alcove and examined the stained wrappings. Ildric had feared that the rats would have eaten into the body by now, but he found no sign of large tears in the fabric. It was as if the rats were only interested in nesting material, and not the meat within.

"Shall we unwrap him?"

The wizard nodded. He removed an herb gathering knife from his belt and began sawing away at the linens. Emen had no knife, so he did the best he could with his hands. As Ildric cut the fabric and exposed the face within, Emen stood and backed up a few steps.

"Is that your... stranger?" the dwarf asked.

Ildric nodded as he examined the sunken, waxy features, "I am too late."

"Far too late," Emen said, "I saw this body in the alcove in mid-Eyoromoth; I think he had been there for a few months already."

Ildric bowed his head. Then the spell that warned him of danger made his spine go stiff and his heart start racing.

"You know," Emen said, stepping back farther, "I had my doubts about you."

Ildric reached for his staff, but it was snatched away. He tried to raise himself from his knees, but he was kicked to the ground before his stiff limbs could react. *Ambushed!* he thought, his mind racing. *Are they vemloks? No! The living!*

Young, strong hands pinned him to the ground. A small boy carried the wizard's staff, a triumphant look on his face as he stood behind Emen. It was the street urchin from the alleyway. *A lookout*, Ildric realized, *Who is this dwarf?*

As the edge of a dagger fell across his throat, Ildric realized he may never know.

Chapter Five

Emen Silverboss

"I don't mean to be rude," Emen said, "but you have put me in a bit of a spot, professionally speaking."

"Should we kill him now?" asked the young man holding the dagger to the wizard's throat, "He's a dangerous diviner."

The second lad gave a pinched laugh, like the chirping of a fox. "But he didn't see *this* coming."

"No, Daymi," Emen said, "you and Cricket bind him well, and search him. The staff may not be his only verge. Look for something made of wood and silver, like a wand or talisman."

He's not a complete fool, Ildric thought.

"What about his silver hand?" Daymi asked, "It's supposed to be powerful magic."

"Tamper with that," Ildric said gravely, "and you could kill us all." He looked up at Emen and warned,

"This gauntlet is bound to my flesh by powerful enchantments. Even in death, it is not safe to remove."

Emen considered for a moment and said, "I'm familiar with your reputation, Ildric Finnael. It is known that your silver hand is a vessel for the source of your power, an artifact from a far-off land that makes you such a formidable seer. The dragon-eye stone! You are feared by many who wish to go unnoticed." He stood, hands on hips. "Imagine how I felt when you appeared on my doorstep, asking after my affairs."

"I told you," the wizard said, coughing in the dust, "I care nothing for what you are hiding."

Emen said, "Surely you have already guessed what I am hiding?" He waited, raising his heavy eyebrows at the wizard.

"The Circle of Gold," Ildric muttered.

The lad pinning him played at his throat with the dagger. The young boy holding his staff giggled and danced about nervously. The other lad tying his hands gave that annoying, pinched snicker. Emen motioned, and the young men hoisted him to his feet, holding the wizard fast.

Ildric felt the tip of the dagger at his lower back, poised to strike his kidney. He wondered suddenly if the visions of his death at Cindra's side on a far-off battlefield could have been overly optimistic. *I didn't think I would die here. Perhaps I won't, but not for lack of my blundering.*

Emen turned to the young boy, who was slightly taller than himself, and said, "Narfi, I want you to go to the Warren and tell Garreth about the body here. Have him bring it to the parlor. Put the staff there too."

"Yes, boss!" Narfi said, and scampered off into the darkness, the wizard's stolen verge lighting his way.

Emen liked Narfi. He was a good valet, a sharp-eyed lookout, and smart as a whip. He was teaching the lad the art of encryption that his own father had passed to him, hoping the boy wouldn't be a pickpocket forever.

Emen retrieved his torch from the grave niche and said, "Master Ildric, if we happen to encounter any vemloks, will you be so kind as to feed them?"

The way to the Warren was a confusing maze of narrow, winding passages lined with long forgotten corpses. There were clever traps and safeguards also, which Emen disarmed and rearmed as they passed. The air was still and stale, except for certain junctures where a cold draft moved, carrying the distant odors of the city. Emen's torch flickered in the dank breath of the tomb.

Ildric asked, "How have you survived down here with the hungry dead on the prowl? You must have taken some loses."

"True, we have," Emen said, "I was almost a victim myself, but they rarely come down this way. It's all the stone, you see. The bodies need to be in contact with loose earth or clay to be infused with the thirsting spirit. Besides, there is far more food up above."

"Do they indeed?" Ildric said, impressed, "I was not aware that the lore of the walking dead was so commonly known."

"There are folktales and superstitions," Emen said, "but many of our modern burial practices come from hard-earned lessons." He paced a few more steps before adding, "Also, our deceased friend passed on that bit of knowledge the day he saved me from one."

"It seems he was poorly rewarded for his valor," the wizard said.

"Yes," agreed the dwarf, "Yes, he was, but not by me. He was taken away for questioning, and it seems his answers were displeasing."

"Yes, that was a shortcoming of his," Ildric nodded, "Who was-"

Emen cut him off, "It is no use asking who, when, or where. You know too much already."

As they went on, the catacombs began to show more signs of use. Dust was disturbed, and footprints crisscrossed the floor. Small objects shared space with the dead; a candle holder here, an iron spade there, a wooden mallet next to an ancient skull. There were torches also, lighting paths for the living. As they passed into a wider area, Ildric saw faces looking at him from the shadows. The small, pale faces of children gazed in wonder as he was marched past, offering nods and salutes to the diminutive leader of the strange parade.

"Children," Ildric said heavily, "You use children, just like he said."

"Like who said?" Emen asked.

"Nixy DuQuayne," said the wizard.

He felt the hands of his escorts tighten on his arms. The eyes of the children grew wide and they whispered, "The pincher prince!"

"I take it you know of him," Ildric said.

"We knows him, the little traitor," said the lad called Daymi.

The one called Cricket sniffed and spit.

"Honestly, he was before my time," Emen said, "but I have heard of him. The boy is a half-elf prince, I understand?" He shook his head and chuckled, "To think my predecessor used him to pick pockets..."

"Is this the same man who attempted to murder him on the castle grounds last year?" The wizard asked, mostly sure it was. Nixy said his attacker, a man called 'Dexer,' was his teacher, mentor, and boss in the Circle of Gold. What he couldn't explain was what had happened to the man that night.

"Let's not speak of the dead right now," Emen said, leading them up a flight of stairs lined with candles, "It's bad luck, you know?"

The lads handled him a bit more roughly after that.

They reached their final destination through a narrow passage that ended in a heavy wooden door. The passage and the masonry around the door seemed newer and improvised, as though they were not part of the original catacombs. Likely they connected the tombs to a basement or chamber that was never meant to share a door. Ildric reasoned that they were nearer to street level than they had been. He could still not feel the spirit well upon which his tower sat, and that was depressing.

The chamber beyond was lit with many candles in fancy stands, and draped with fabric and rugs to cover the cold, bare stone. An arched ceiling gave the room a feel of greater space, and the white plaster caught and reflected the candlelight. Large wine casks stood against one wall, and a fireplace was built into another, next to an expensive-looking desk. The boy who had run off with his staff was lighting the fireplace with a wick.

Ildric's eyes swept the room for his staff, remembering the boy's instructions. There it was, lying across the desk, its glowing light covered by a cloth. *If I can get my hands on it,* Ildric thought, *things will be very different.*

Emen took a seat behind the desk as the young boy poured him a goblet of wine from one of the casks. "Welcome to my parlor," said the dwarf, gesturing grandly.

"Quoth the spider to the fly," Ildric muttered.

Daymi asked, "You want 'im thrown to the floor, boss?"

"Oh yes," Emen said, waving his hand, "by all means, throw him to the floor."

They did so, and Ildric huffed as the wind was knocked out of him. The two lads stood behind him to either side, sneering at his back. Ildric managed to struggle to his knees, which was difficult with his hands bound. He was sorer than he had been in ages, and that was saying something.

He turned to gaze at the two lads. Daymi was about twenty, with dark, curly hair and a permanent sneer.

Cricket was about the same age and build, though he slouched and hung his head, looking up through his long, greasy bangs. The lads were not large or intimidating, but looked hardened and quick.

Emen winced and said, "Oh dear, that looked painful. My apologies, master mage. I don't entertain strangers in the parlor very often, and I haven't quite established my routine."

Ildric peered up at him past his eyebrows. "I hope you didn't bring me here to gloat," he said, "If that's the case, I'd rather you just cut my throat now, and spare me your inevitable monologue."

Emen laughed. "Ha-hah! I like it, I like it. I should really have one prepared for these occasions, shouldn't I? A nefarious speech or mocking lecture, telling you how weak and foolish you are... maybe one where I tell you my plans, before having you killed in some convoluted way," he chuckled into his cup, "after I leave the room, of course."

Ildric snorted, "You have seen your share of theater dramas, I see," he said.

"I have, I have, though I never pictured *myself* as the villain. Ah well." He set down the cup and placed his hand on the wizard's staff, rolling it with his fingertips. "You have spoiled my evening, arch mage. I am now faced with a decision to make, and I don't like decisions. They all lead to consequences and responsibility. So tiresome."

Ildric said, "Not what I'd expect from the leader of a guild of thieves."

"*A* leader, not *the* leader," Emen said, "The real leader is- Oh! You almost made me say it! See how clever you are? I must be on my guard." The boys all chuckled at that.

"Gloating it is, then," The wizard sighed, "Kill me now."

"No, no, not yet," Emen wagged his finger. "It's not that simple, I'm afraid. If you were any other wizard, maybe you could go missing and no one would much care. But you are the great Ildric Finnael, supreme oracle and a damned national treasure! That pretty tower you live in, that's a notable property to suddenly go vacant. Why, I'd have every diviner in the city scouring your last known location."

"He was seen in Miner Town by the night watch," said the young boy, fidgeting against the wall. "Not the proper watch, but the lads that live there."

Emen gestured to the boy. "You see? Some of my neighbors would have to be silenced, and that would break my heart. We could pay them off to keep quiet, but it would eventually become a game of dueling rewards. Someone would talk, and the trail would lead to my front door once again."

"You could help me," Ildric said. The boys laughed at that, but Emen did not.

"I could," the dwarf said, "but to what end? What happens if I let you leave with knowledge of my identity, the location of our lair, and all that you have seen? What have we to gain?"

There was a knock at the door, and Daymi went to answer it. Two men came in bearing the body of the missing god, and a rat or two managed to scamper in behind them before the door closed again. They set the body off to the side, then stood by the door, wiping their hands on their breeches.

Ildric sized them up. They were both older, burlier, and more dangerous-looking than Daymi and Cricket, and their daggers were bright and cared for. *Well, I always enjoy a challenge*, he thought grimly.

"Ah, Garreth," Emen said to one of the newcomers, "You knew Dexer better than most. What would he do if a famous wizard stumbled into our little hideout?"

"Kill him and sort it out later."

"Kill him and sort it out later," Emen repeated, "That's the kind of man he was. Quick to violence, but not a thinker. He left the thinking to his betters, and a trail of bodies behind him."

"And what are you?" Ildric asked.

"A pragmatist," Emen said, "Fortunately, I don't have to make the final decision. Something like this is far above my head, if you pardon the expression, and I'd rather not bear the burden."

Ildric lowered his head, closing his eyes in seeming despair.

"Do you think the Boss is awake this late?" Emen asked the newcomers.

"Maybe," Garreth said, "But the couriers will take time to get a message to him... unless you want to risk contacting him directly?"

"I'd rather not," Emen said, "but it might not do to wait until morning. The sooner we handle this, the better."

Ildric sat like a man awaiting the headman's blow, but he was not in despair; he was in deep concentration. He stretched out his thoughts and feelings, searching for the tug of magic through his metal hand. Its inner construction was Shadowood and brass clockwork, covered with silver plated steel. Engraved spells of silver inlay were traced into the wood and metal, locking the enchantments that allowed him to move it like a natural limb. They also bound the hand to his arm, and bound the power of the Eye to his will. In short, the hand was an elaborate verge, and a powerful one at that.

It was also dangerous to use in this manner, and he rarely did so. A verge was necessary to pull magic into the mind and body, but this verge contained a powerful artifact, and the silver of the hand was in direct contact with his flesh. If his mind and body were not in perfect balance, if his spell was not framed perfectly in his thoughts, the rush of pure, amplified magic could stop his heart or burn his brain.

He built a mental diagram in his mind, line by line, and drew on the magic around him, feeling the skin under the silver gauntlet grow warm, then hot. He balanced that power, letting it flow through the mental architecture and out into the ropes that bound him. He tried not to move his lips or speak as he invoked the spell; most wizards had trouble with this as they grew older, and it annoyed him greatly when he found himself doing it.

Vydavim r'miith.

He felt a minor wave of fatigue wash over him, but then it passed. The next one would be the real challenge.

"Waiting on your word, Silverboss," Garreth said.

Daymi shifted next to Ildric, stropping the blade of his dagger on his pant leg.

Emen hopped down from his chair and said, "Very well. I shall go and see the Boss tonight, and hope he is in a pleasant mood. Arrange a carriage and-"

The wizard pulled on his bonds and they snapped, raining dry, brittle fibers on the rug. He raised his hands before him and cast his unspoken spell, grimacing as the metal burned his arm. His staff flew from the desk and into his waiting hands, the cloth coming free to expose the light on its tip. Ildric's head swam with a wave of dizziness, but he was now pulling magic through a proper verge, and already invoking his next spell; so focused was he that the shouts of alarm and shuffling of feet could not distract him.

"He's loose!" Daymi cursed, and he and Cricket rushed to subdue the wizard.

But Ildric drew his staff back, knocking each end into the boys' hips as they reached for him. The staff had a few useful spells carved into its length, making them far easier to cast. The one Ildric just activated was a combat spell known as "fell blow." It sent the lads flying backwards as if kicked by a mule.

I really like that spell, he thought as their bodies hit the floor, *So satisfying.*

The other two men drew their weapons with blinding speed, rushing towards him. Garreth flipped his dagger to hurl it. The Eye of Omithys flashed and Ildric saw the path of the thrown blade before it left the man's hand. He raised his staff just as Garreth flung the dagger, and the point sunk harmlessly into the wood.

"Doshae cuam, thldii vyniith!" he cried, sweeping the staff. His spell lifted the wrapped corpse of Tavenji and pulled it with force into the men, knocking them across the room. It hovered over them for a moment, wrappings and limbs slipping free as Ildric sought the dwarf. Emen was rushing for the door as fast as he could, his eyes alight with terror. The wizard gestured with his staff, and the body flew into Emen, slamming him against the wall.

"Have *me* trussed up and manhandled, will you?" the wizard fumed.

Then he forced himself to be calm, lest he suffer another magical backlash. It wouldn't do to overpower his captors, only to faint.

The last opponent left standing was the young boy, who was cowering in the corner, an angry wizard between him and the door. The boy shook his head and whimpered, raising his arms defensively as Ildric leveled a silver finger at him.

"Vothii," said the wizard. The boy collapsed, sliding down the wall to the floor.

Ildric strode to loom over Emen, who was struggling to get out from under the body.

"What did you do that for?" Emen groaned, "There was no need to kill him!"

"He is only sleeping, my dear dwarf," Ildric said in disgust, "*I* am not the murderer here."

"Nor am I," the dwarf pleaded.

"No," Ildric admonished, "you just command them. Do not expect me to absolve you so easily, *Silverboss.*"

Emen stopped struggling, for he had nowhere to go. "What are you going to do to us?"

'To us,' Ildric noted, *not 'to me.'* He had judged this fellow correctly. "I have not yet decided," he said, "but we can start by having a little privacy." He raised his staff to the door and cast a ward against it, barring it shut. He then turned to the thieves strewn about the

floor, who were beginning to regain their wits, and placed a deep sleeping spell upon each of them. Finally, he raised his silver hand and examined the room through the power of the Eye. *As I suspected,* he thought, *Powerful scrying wards. This place is made for privacy.*

"Now, with apologies to the gods, and the dead," he raised his staff and lifted the body of Tavenji off the dwarf, floating it to gently rest on the desk. "I fear my need was greater than my respect."

Emen stood up with difficulty and shied away from the door, as if it would burn him to touch it. He trusted nothing in this room now; even his chair didn't seem safe to sit in. He leaned against the wall behind his desk, focusing on the face revealed through the torn wrappings.

Ildric said, "You have put me in a bit of a spot, professionally speaking."

Emen gulped. "So it's to be gloating? Well, that's your right, I suppose."

"No," the wizard said, "Gloating is for the weak and insecure mind. I am deciding how to resolve this without shedding blood, mostly mine." He leaned heavily on his staff, now feeling his bruises and weariness more than ever. "Your urchin pickpockets saw me as a prisoner, and these," he motioned to the sleeping thieves, "they will know what happened here; I cannot remove the memory. Whether I walk out of here, or fight my way out, it's a surety the Circle of Gold will place a bounty on my head."

"Likely," Emen muttered.

"I don't enjoy watching my back constantly; it's exhausting, even with this." He held up the metal limb, making Emen flinch. "My safest option would be to report this to the Order, the count, and the king." He shook his head. "I think we both know what will happen if I do. His Majesty will charge his army to seek out your brotherhood and put them to the sword. The streets will run red with blood, some of it innocent, no doubt."

Emen's mouth twitched. His eyes went to the sleeping boy who would be in harm's way. "What do you propose?" he asked, cursing his reversal of fortune.

"I propose we put our heads together and think of something, that's what!" Ildric exclaimed, "You are not a killer, as you said. But you also know your people, and how to handle them best. As for me, I think best while I'm working." The wizard turned his attention to the body on the table and felt a wave of dread run up his spine that made him shudder.

They killed a god.

Ildric pulled more of the tattered wrappings aside. His unfortunate use of the body as a battering ram had caused the arms to uncross from his chest and hang free, exposing the dark brown stain on the green silk jacket. The face was gaunt and sallow, yet peaceful and strangely preserved for being interred for so long. *Perhaps a god rots more slowly,* he thought.

A scrabbling, scratching sound came from below, and two rats climbed up the table legs, peering at the wizard with beady, black eyes. They crawled to the side of the body as Ildric drew back, ready to cast another vermin warding spell. Then he noticed that both of them carried something in their mouths. One bore an acorn, and the other, a gold coin.

"Well well, what is this?" he asked, leaning to get a better look. Emen blinked, shaken out of his doom-filled thoughts.

The rats didn't move as the wizard slowly extended his metal fingers towards them. The rat with the acorn placed a tiny hand on the silver talon and dropped the item into his waiting palm. He moved to the other rat which paused for a moment longer, and dropped the coin.

"Are they friends of yours?" asked the dwarf.

"No," Ildric said, "I think they are his." He nodded to the little god. "Remember how they did not defile his body? Perhaps they were guarding him."

"What were they carrying?" Emen asked.

"One item I have seen before, the other I have not," Ildric replied. He examined the acorn, and it seemed smaller somehow. *Was it a different acorn?* The coin was not local currency; instead, it was stamped with a relief of Obamir, god of wealth, luck, and charity. *Perhaps it is a medallion or talisman, sold by the priesthood?* he thought, *Or perhaps it was not minted in the realm of mortals.*

Emen did not like being left out; it was his desk after all. "But what's special about them?"

The Eye of Omithys glowed, bathing the items in a soft green light. "It's an acorn that fell from no tree, and a gold coin that never knew a counting house or coin purse. They have no history I can see, which means they likely have no history in the mortal world."

"Oh," Emen said, wondering what else could surprise him this evening, "That's novel. What are they then?"

"Favors, I think," Ildric said, and placed the items on the little god's chest, hoping something would happen. Nothing did. "My theory is that Obamir and Eyorona gave him favors to aid him in his quest, since his own power would be greatly diminished."

"Those are divine favors? Well, they did him little good," Emen said. Then an idea occurred to him. "What does your magic eye say about that?" He pointed to one of his fallen comrades.

Ildric turned to look, saw nothing special, and turned back to find that the dwarf had pulled a weapon from under the desk. *Witch piss,* he thought, *The oldest trick in the book.*

Emen held something like a metal fork with a wooden handle. It had long, silver tongs with a white crystal bound between them. The dwarf was pointing it at him menacingly.

Ildric knew the device could be triggered with a word. Trinkets like that were made for the unlearned, and were generally frowned upon, for some were quite dangerous. "A lightning rod," the wizard said, "That's rather illegal."

"Thieves' guild," Emen said, tersely. "We don't care. Drop the staff."

Ildric weighed his options. He had one spell that was still active, and it would last for a few minutes more. To make this work, he would have to force Emen to use the device at a moment of his choosing, bluffing him into discharging the lightning rod. It was a most dangerous game.

"Drop it now!" Emen said.

Ildric took a breath and let it out slowly. "No."

"I mean it!" Emen said, pointing the lightning rod at Ildric's chest. His lips were pursed, his eyes wide.

Would he kill me? Ildric wondered, *Yes, he is that desperate, but he does not wish to.*

Emen took a breath through his flared nostrils, and his jaw twitched. The wizard brought his staff up quickly, making the dwarf panic. *Now! Do it now!* he thought.

"*S'hathas!*" Emen cried. The metal tongs crackled and a small bolt of lightning flashed from the device, illuminating the room in dazzling white light. The bolt did not strike the wizard, however, for Ildric had used his active spell to lift the body of Tavenji between them. Sparks flew and the corpse twitched for a moment, then dropped to the table with a thud, smoke rising from a burn on its chest. The two rats scattered, shrieking in alarm. The favors clattered to the floor.

"*S'hathas!*" Emen said again, waving the lightning rod at the wizard.

Ildric stood, unmoving. He knew the wizard who created the wretched thing, and had been present at its demonstration. He recalled it needed about eight seconds between discharges.

"Do you know why I use a staff instead of a wand or talisman?" he asked the dwarf.

"*S'hathas...*" Emen whimpered, backing away.

"For this," Ildric said, and deftly swung his staff, knocking the rod away, then clubbed the hapless dwarf on the head.

"Count yourself lucky I didn't cast the striking spell I used on your two lackeys," the wizard said, "I didn't want to break your neck."

Emen blinked away the stars dancing in his vision. The top of his head throbbed, and his scalp was bleeding. Worse, the wizard was standing over him, examining him with the glowing dragon eye stone.

"If you plan to curse me, there's not much you can do that nature hasn't done already," Emen said.

"Don't be so sure. But I am only searching you for more hidden surprises. Where did you come by this?" He twirled the rod in his other hand like a child's toy.

"My... my predecessor had a passion for magical trinkets." Emen said, struggling to his feet, "That was one of his favorites."

"Not a very practical assassin's weapon." He removed the crystal and disabled the device.

"He used it for punishment. He liked the way the burning smell lingered as a reminder."

"So it is not powerful enough to kill?"

"As I understand, it takes a few jolts for a grown man, but I've never used it myself... before now."

"Good to know," the wizard glowered, "I am honored."

Emen offered a weak smile, and took out a kerchief to staunch his bleeding scalp.

"Whu-a-a..." The noise took them both by surprise. Ildric held his staff defensively, thinking one of his sleeping assailants was waking up too early.

Yet they were not moving.

"Whu-u-u... whaaa..." The voice was hoarse and dry, like one who is dying of thirst.

The corpse on the table moved.

Emen jerked back, crying, "He's a vemlok! He's turned!"

Ildric prepared a spell to burn the body where it lay, even though it might fill the room with choking smoke.

"Whaaat... isss... thaaat... *smell?*" Tavenji croaked. He sniffed the air, making a long and rattling sound. "Uggh... it's me." He sat up slowly, his eyes bulging at the effort. They were clouded and pale, but were quickly becoming bloodshot.

Emen slid along the wall and out from behind his desk, moving to hide behind Ildric. The wizard did not care; he trusted Emen not to try anything stupid now.

The little god's waxy pallor was fading, turning from gray to pale, and finally to pink. His sunken cheeks filled out before their eyes, and his limbs grew more toned and muscled, like that of a dancer. The dark burn on his chest remained, and he fingered it gingerly.

"Ow," he husked, "I think I've been rather... dead."

Whatever state the little fellow was in, Ildric did not think he was possessed by a thirsting spirit. The wizard relaxed slightly, letting the inferno spell dissolve in his mind. "I believe you have been dead for at least three months, possibly more," he said, his voice shaking. He had tried to imagine what he would say at this moment, but all words seemed to lack the proper awe. "My lord Tavenji, I presume?"

"Yes?" Tavenji said, seeming to just now notice them.

Ildric got to his knees and genuflected, though with a little difficulty.

Emen stood dumbfounded, mouth dropping open. "Ta-Tavenji?" he squeaked. He looked at the wizard's bowed head for a moment, and fell to his knees a moment later, just in case the wizard was right.

The little god looked up, blinked several times, and his bloodshot eyes became a clear, bright emerald. "Is that the magic man with the silver hand? It is! And my little dwarf friend! This must be my lucky day."

The rats had returned, scampering up to his side with the acorn and coin in their mouths. They pawed at his thigh, little black eyes staring up at him.

"Oh, hello! You brought my things. What good fellows you are!" He held out his hand and the rats dropped the items in his palm, then began making almost imperceptible squeaks.

The men looked up in confusion. They were being ignored in favor of a pair of rats.

Tavenji nodded as they squeaked, emotions playing across his face like a child listening to a story. He asked questions in a high whisper, punctuated with little squeaks of his own. Finally, he sat up, let out a sigh, and addressed the rats, "I thank you with all my heart, my little friends. And I thank you for keeping me safe, and not eating any of my soft, tasty bits. Go tell your family that I am well pleased."

The two men just knelt there in dumbfounded silence.

Tavenji got off the table slowly, testing his legs, and stretched. His joints cracked and popped noisily. "Ow!" he gasped, "Everything is sore!" He glared at Ildric. "Did you *really* swing me around like a sack of grain? I have *bones*, you know!"

Ildric was at a loss for words.

Emen whispered, "I think the dirty rats informed on you."

"Yes," Tavenji said, "They squealed and told me everything."

"I, uh, well," Ildric raised his head to look up at the god, "I am sorry, but you were *dead*."

"Of course, but didn't you think I'd notice the damage once you brought me back?" Tavenji asked, cricking his neck, "What if you broke something?"

Emen and Ildric looked at each other, and the wizard had to admit, "We hadn't really planned to 'bring you back.' To be honest, I am not sure how you are alive. Although..."

"This burn, how did I get it?" Tavenji asked, pointing to the scorch mark on his chest.

Emen said, "I'm afraid that was partially my fault, milord. You see, I was aiming the lightning rod at Master Ildric here-"

"Lightning!" Tavenji exclaimed, "Well, that might have done the trick. The important thing is that I am no longer tempting the worms. For that, I thank you both, whether you intended it or not." A thought occurred to him and he examined his coin and acorn. "Wait, you didn't use up a favor, did you? It seems a little *too* lucky."

The men just looked at each other and shrugged. "I don't think so," Ildric said.

"How would we know?" asked Emen.

"Well, it would shrink a bit, for starters," Tavenji said. The coin didn't look smaller, though it was hard to tell for sure. "Hmmm," he hummed, frowning at the gold face of Obamir. "I guess if a favor was used, it was for a worthy cause." He only then seemed to notice they were on their knees. "Oh, do get up! No need to bow and scrape. My neck is sore enough without staring down at you."

"Pardon, lord, but what is the last thing you remember?" Ildric asked as he struggled to his feet.

Tavenji took a shaking breath and stared at the ceiling for a moment. Then his eyes dropped to his stained tunic and he said, "A dagger going into my heart." The little god's face was somber and drawn, quite unlike it had been while under duress as a prisoner of the Order.

Ildric pressed him, "Do you remember who did the deed?"

Emen was not sure he wanted them to delve into this line of questioning, but he was not going to step on a conversation between a wizard and a god, if a god he truly was. Emen kept silent and stared at the floor. The rats stared back at him.

Tavenji rubbed his eyes and said, "I think it was a mad man who had been attending my brother."

"Your brother?" Ildric exclaimed, "Is there *another* deity walking in the world of mortals?"

The little god nodded, a sad pout forming on his elfin face. "Yes," he said, "but not anymore. He had been suffering a very long time." Then he swiftly changed the subject. "Why is everyone sleeping?"

Ildric scratched his chin and said, "I'm afraid I had to get a little rough in my escape effort. It was the easiest option."

"Oh!" Tavenji perked up, suddenly interested, "Have we not escaped yet?"

"Er, well, not as such," Ildric said, glancing at Emen.

"Don't look at me," Emen said, "In my opinion you've escaped very handily. Congratulations." He gave a sweeping bow, showing him the door.

"Well that's no fun," Tavenji said.

"The problem that we had a moment ago," Ildric explained, "is what to do in the aftermath of my escape. I don't want the Circle of Gold coming after me, nor do I want a bloodbath in the streets. We are at an impasse, Emen and I."

"It's worse than you think," Tavenji said, "The leader of this little crime syndicate is a Llomaakitte high priest and a face-changer. He also has the Dark Heart in his possession, though I imagine it's been given to the scion by now."

Ildric gasped, his worst fears confirmed.

Emen was incredulous. "The Boss? A Llomaakitte high priest?"

Tavenji nodded, looking miserable.

Emen spat, "It's said they used to kidnap dwarf children for their wicked rituals,"

"Oh, that's not true," Tavenji said, "I mean yes, they would kidnap dwarf children, but not for some nasty ritual. They were considered good luck, you see; favored by the god that twisted nature. Dwarfs were held in high regard among the ancient cults of Chaos. Some were even raised as priests."

Emen did not like the implications. If it was true, the Boss might have elevated him in status because of some silly superstition; or worse, some actual connection to Llomaak that he was unaware of. *Good luck, indeed!* he thought, *Maybe Boss DuChat will live to regret that.*

Ildric collected his wits as best he could, and sat in Emen's chair, lest his shaking knees fail him. "So it was true," he said, swallowing in a dry throat, "The Dark Heart was in Portshia, and so was the scion. What can you tell me about him? Is it too late to stop this?"

Tavenji paced back and forth, feeling his chest for the place the dagger pierced him. He said, "The scion is a 'he,' that much was revealed. But as for his identity, I can't be sure. He's from an ancient and important blood line."

"A human bloodline?" Ildric asked, "Or some other race? Elven, perhaps?"

Tavenji shrugged.

"Wait," Emen said, getting flustered, "what is the Dark Heart? What is this scion supposed to do? What in the name of Vina's sweet tits is going on?"

The little god's eyes flashed at him, a big grin on his face.

"Blasphemy, Emen!" Ildric hissed, "That's his sister!"

"Apologies, lord!" Emen sniveled, falling to his knees, "I did not think-"

Tavenji laughed and said, "Oh, do stop it! I was never one to make mortals snivel at my feet, and I don't go in for all of this 'lord' business. Just call me Uncle Tweak if you like, or Wryley. I used to go by Wryley long ago in these parts. As for blasphemy, they say it was one of my gifts to humanity. Doesn't sound like me, though."

Neither man was quick to try on the nicknames, much less engage in more blasphemy.

Tavenji shrugged and meandered about the room, taking on a lecturing air. "To bring you up to speed, dear dwarf, the Dark Heart is a cursed drop of

Llomaak's blood that has wreaked havoc in the mortal realm for millennia. It is said that it will cause three great cataclysms, the last being the worst. The second one was known as the Time of Chaos, when the gods went silent and the portals to this world were closed.

"However, it's said that the third and last time will be the undoing of all creation, including most of the gods and their realms. It will happen after the Dark Heart is joined with the scion of an ancient bloodline. My brother knew who it was," Tavenji's voice became sad, "He was cast out, you see? Father stripped him of his role and powers, and banished him from the realms of the gods. He has been wandering, deathless, ever since. That is, until I offered him a final mercy. I had a favor from sister Lelonetha, and I used it to bring him peace."

"Epoch," Ildric said, "The lost god of destiny. *He* was the one known as the Mad Wizard?"

"Yes," Tavenji nodded, seemingly close to tears, "It's like it happened only moments ago. I gave him Mother Mercy's ring, and he slipped away. Then... then I was stabbed and woke up here. No sense of time, no memory, it wasn't even boring. It was *nothing*." He shivered.

"And that," Emen asked, "is what awaits us all? This final cataclysm will wipe out everything, even the souls of the dead?"

Tavenji sniffed back his tears, swallowing a massive lump of guilt that threatened to choke him. "Yes," he said, "If the scion has the Dark Heart, the End has already begun."

"Can we stop it?" asked the dwarf, truly frightened now.

"Anything is possible," the little god said, not entirely believing it.

The three of them stared at the floor for a full minute, unspeaking. Only the snores of the sleeping thieves and the crackling of the fire could be heard.

Then Emen straightened himself. "Well," he said, "that answers one question."

Ildric looked up, puzzled. "What question?"

"What to do about our original problem. Now please remove the ward from my door; I'm going to call a meeting of the Silver Gang."

When Daymi, Cricket, Garreth, and the others woke up, they were surrounded by the urchins and pickpockets of the Warren. Gossiping voices echoed off the ceiling, and the smell of unwashed children was strong. Struggling to their feet, their eyes found Emen Silverboss, who was standing on his desk, arms folded. Beside him stood the wizard they had captured and the body they had brought from the catacombs, looking rather alive and cheerful.

"Good evening," Emen said to the men, "As you can see, the situation has changed."

Garreth, apparently a senior thief, spoke up, "What's all this, Silverboss? Did the wizard spell you?"

"No," Emen said, pointing at them, "He spelled *you*. We just talked, albeit after a rather tense standoff and a shock or two."

"Literally and figuratively," Tavenji said, rubbing his chest.

"They's allies now," said one of the boys.

"Gotta be somethin' big going on!" said another boy.

More tongues began to wag, and Emen raised his hands to silence them. "There is something big going on, but it's bigger than we ever imagined." They quieted down as the older lads realized they'd been disarmed in their sleep. "As I am sure you know by now, there was a bit of a misunderstanding. The Talon did not mean to tread on the Circle's secrets, but he did."

That name again, Ildric thought, leaning on his staff, *Common folk and thieves love a catchy alias.*

"Words were had, threats were made, and some spells were flung about," Emen continued, "But the important thing is we found the body of the man he sought; this body, to be exact." He gestured to Tavenji, who smiled and waved. "As you can see, our new guest is not an ordinary corpse. He goes by the name of Wryley, and has some rather grim news for us. Please pay attention." He yielded the floor, rather the desktop, to Tavenji.

"Hello!" Tavenji said, hopping on the desk. "It's a pleasure to see all of your glowing faces. It's a pleasure to see anything, really." He grinned ear to ear. "As Emen Silverboss told you, I was dead, dead as a dormouse. Or is it a doornail? Whatever, the point is that I had croaked." This got some smiles from the children. Tavenji knew how to work a room.

"Why was you croaked?" asked a young child.

"I was stabbed through the heart," Tavenji replied, "Quite skillfully too. Right through the ribs in one stroke! Bravo."

"Why's you alive then?" asked one boy.

"That's a very good question!" he said, "Show of hands, who has heard of the gods?"

All hands went up, except for the lads involved in the fight, who were sulking.

"Good!" Tavenji said, "Most of you. Hooray for the clergy. Well, I am what you'd call an agent of the gods; a sort of helper, come to aid the world in its time of need."

"Balkon's balls," said Daymi.

Tavenji flinched at the name of his brother, the war god who tried to kill him, but continued unperturbed. "So while I *can* die, it's not very permanent, nor is it very fun. I don't really recommend it."

"How come you're not all rotten and bony?" a young girl asked.

"Are the gods really real?" asked another child.

"Why didn't the rats eat you?" asked a third.

"What's it like when you die?" called someone from the back.

Tavenji pointed at each as he answered, "Divine magic, I'm afraid so, mostly out of respect, and boring."

"How can you expect us to believe you're sent from the gods?" asked Garreth.

"The ears don't give it away?" Tavenji squeaked, "Well then, how about this: if you believe in the gods at all these days, it's because you have faith. People didn't need faith in the old days, because the gods were a pain in everyone's ass. Sorry, rump. Butt. Behind. Don't curse, children."

Ildric cleared his throat impatiently.

"Anyway," Tavenji continued, "you saw me yourself. The rats told me. You carried me in here from the crypts. Have you ever heard of magic that can raise the dead like this?"

Garreth folded his arms. "Might have only looked dead because of some spell," he said, casting an accusing look at Ildric.

"A skeptic!" Tavenji cried, "Using your divine gift, I see. Good for you! Gullible people are so easy to fool that after a while it's not fun anymore."

Daymi motioned to the motley tights and silk jacket, "You look like a cheap mummer playing at being Tavenji," he said. Cricket chirped his distinctive laugh.

"Oh, I only *wish* I could be Tavenji!" Tavenji wailed, "He is so much more handsome and impressive... I can only *dream* of being compared to that lovable scamp."

A little girl asked, "You know him, mister Wryley?"

"Do I?" Tavenji said, "Of course! He sent me. He needed someone clever and sneaky and articulate, but all he could find was me!" More giggles rewarded him.

"I think," Ildric interrupted, "that it would be best to tell them the grim news."

"Quite," the little god said, straightening his tunic, "The world as we know it is in grave danger. Terrible, terrible people are working to destroy not only this city, not only this land, but the world itself. That means no more you and no more me." He took no pleasure in telling this to children, but it was for the benefit of the young men as well. "There is a god of law and order, as I'm sure you know. But there is also a god of chaos. His name is Llomaak, and he wants nothing less than the end of all things."

Ildric watched the faces of the crowd for reactions, especially the older lads. No one showed any signs of guilt or panic, but he wished he could use the Eye to sense the emotions in the room. Unfortunately, he couldn't do so without upsetting people. *I should have stood at the back,* he thought.

"Why does he wanna end everything?" asked a boy who was missing an eye.

"Because he wants to win," Tavenji said, "The world is a tug-o-war between Order and Chaos, and neither are happy with a balance. But Arathus knows that the only way to have order is to have stuff around; stuff like stars, oceans, people, fish, handkerchiefs, bananas, mountains, and jam."

"Wha's bananas?" asked the boy.

"Oh, I could go *on* about bananas," Tavenji said, "but the point is that Llomaak can have total chaos only if everything gets destroyed; people, gods, bananas and all."

Cricket asked in his pinched voice, "Why would he destroy himself?"

"Only three gods would survive this destruction," Tavenji said, "Arathus, Llomaak, and Jayda the World Mother. All the others, including that dashing rogue Tavenji, would cease to exist."

He let that sink in, and then he offered hope.

"But I am here to help," he said, "I was sent into the world of mortals to keep this from happening." He sat on the edge of the desk, kicking his legs. "The really bad news is that your Boss, the Big Boss of the Circle of Gold, is a high priest of Llomaak, and he's working to destroy the world for his god."

The room began to burble over with mutterings, like a boiling pot. The older children and the young men especially gave frowning looks at Emen and his fellow conspirators. The younger children looked frightened.

"Silverboss?" Garreth called over the din, "What're we talkin' about? You trying for a split from the Circle, or is this some kind of a takeover?"

"No," Emen said, "No I'm not. I wouldn't do anything to endanger the Silver Gang, that's why we're having this meeting."

"Here," Daymi said, "You say the Boss is some mad god-monger? We supposed to believe he wants *himself* dead along with everyone else? Where's the proof?"

"Mad god-monger," Tavenji said, "I like that! As for the why of it, Llomaakittes know the afterlife is all about judgment, and they want to live their lives and avoid that judgment. So *poof!* No more afterlife."

Emen said, "As for evidence, we have none, only the word of Wryley here, who was captured by him." Heads shook at this. "But there is more to tell," he said quickly, "The council held a meeting three months ago. In that meeting, the Boss revealed another face to us. We all saw it. At first, I thought it was some spell he used, but Wryley says he is a duplict, a face-changing man from the Time of Chaos."

"A *half*-duplict," Tavenji corrected, "He's not as good as a true one, and I'd know him no matter what face he wore."

"Duplicts are faerie stories," Garreth said.

"I used to think the same thing about vemloks," Emen said, "until one tried to eat me. Wryley saved my life, and the Boss repaid him with a dagger in the heart."

"Still it's just his word," Daymi said, gesturing at the little god, "What're we supposed to do on his word?"

"Nothing," Ildric said, stepping forward, "We are telling you this so you know what is at stake. What you must do is tell no one what happened here tonight. If the Boss gets word that I was here, or Wryley is alive, or Emen let us go, then there will be terrible consequences for us all. We will try our best to foil his plans, but it depends on your silence."

Emen said, "Trust no one outside of this room; not those who weren't in the Warren tonight, not the other gangs, not even old Nanny." He walked among his gang, most of whom could look him in the eye. "This night never happened. Leave the Boss and his schemes to us. If we need your help, we will ask. Remember, eyes open..." he held up a finger, awaiting an answer.

"Mouths closed!" replied a chorus of children.

Ildric couldn't help but smile. He had judged Emen well indeed.

Chapter Six

Guilty Consciences

Ildric and Emen had exited the catacombs the way they came in, waving to the guards in the cemetery. Tavenji had been led by a boy to one of the Warren's many paths to the streets. They met at the Tower of Sight, and were now enjoying a merry fire and mulled wine. The mood, however, was sullen.

"I still don't know what to do," the little god sighed, sitting on the arm of one of Ildric's upholstered chairs. His feet were on the seat, his elbows on his knees, and his chin in his hands.

Emen, who was still getting used to being in the presence of Uncle Tweak himself, had to agree. "There are few good options," he said, "If you go after the Boss, the Circle will be out for blood. Word will get out that I betrayed him. For all I know, my lieutenants are informing on me as we speak."

Ildric nodded. Their meeting with the Silver Gang had bought time, but not a solution. He said to Emen, "I know your loyalties are in conflict here, but perhaps if we knew more about the situation in the thieves' guild?"

"Loyalties," Emen smirked, "Fear is what keeps me loyal. I have no love for the Circle."

"Then why make you a leader?" Ildric asked.

"You might ask the Boss, if or when you meet him; just don't ask me who he is, I'm not feeling suicidal," Emen said, "I only joined the Circle of Gold out of necessity."

"A story!" Tavenji exclaimed, "I hope it's a good one."

Emen looked nervously at the little god and was obliged to continue, like it or not. "My father was a gambler and got himself in debt. To work his way out of it, he offered the services of his pigeons and a certain skill at code writing. They owned him after that, you see. Even when he paid off his debts, he would never be allowed to walk away. He was trapped by his own usefulness.

"Anyway, as his health failed, he feared that the Circle would take the house and everything he owned. Mother and I would be out on the street, or worse, given 'shelter' by the Circle. That meant the Warren for me and the whorehouse for her; she was still young and very pretty, curse that it was," he sighed, "No. Father wouldn't have it; so instead, he taught me the craft and made me indispensable to them. Mother was protected after he died, and I took over as their bird man. I'm not sure if she ever knew what he- what *we* did, or for whom. All she knew was that her husband and son were good providers. She was proud of me till the end; if she ever had misgivings, she never voiced them."

He sniffed and took a sip of wine.

Tavenji wiped at a tear. He never had a mother, and often wished he had.

Emen said, "Well, there it is. Now they own me too. Making me a district boss was not so much a promotion as a tightening of the noose. Now I can't even feign ignorance."

"It also means you are privy to their plans," Ildric said, "What does this Boss have in mind?"

Emen stared into the fire. "It's a complex scheme, brilliant and absurd in scale, bold in scope; madness, really. But perhaps it doesn't need to succeed, just sound like it might?"

"Do tell," Tavenji said, dropping onto the seat of the chair and leaning forward eagerly.

The dwarf cleared his throat, scratched nervously, and revealed the Grand Plan, "It's about gaining real and legal power, making us the new rulers of the province in all but name. Maybe even that eventually."

"Oh?" Ildric exclaimed, "Bold indeed!"

Emen nodded. "His plan was to pool our resources to become moneylenders, while driving other lenders out of business. We would become the Bank of Casselvane, essentially. He plans to bring trade guilds into the fold as well; masons, carpenters, smiths, carters, clothiers, you name it. The plan is to weaken the noble houses, create a disaster during the war, then finance the rebuilding effort."

"Gods!" Ildric gasped.

Tavenji looked at him. "Hmm? Oh right, figure of speech. Gods! Quite a plan."

"The thieves' guild is going along with this?" Ildric asked, "Burning one's house down in hopes of collecting insurance is a foolish risk."

"Not when you're the bank," Emen said, "There is no financial risk for them in the aftermath; the real risk is in the maneuvering required to gain real power and influence. Most of them must depend entirely on the Boss to pull it off."

"They must think he is capable of such a thing, and trust he will not betray them," Ildric said.

"He is," Emen said, "if anyone is. As for betrayal, well, you don't cross the Circle. Besides, we all know his identity."

They waited. Emen just avoided their gaze and sipped his wine.

"Well?" Ildric demanded.

Emen wagged a finger, "Not now. There are bigger problems to deal with, if I understand things correctly."

"The Dark Heart," Tavenji nodded.

Ildric growled, "I'm thinking that the Boss, this Llomaakitte high priest, might know where to look for it. We might ask him."

"He'd likely die before he told us," Tavenji said.

Emen nodded, "Exactly. Or we would."

Ildric huffed at the god, "Well, what about your favors, the acorn and coin? One is for wisdom, I presume, and the other is for luck?"

Tavenji nodded. "It's tricky, that luck coin. You never know how it's going to answer your need. I was lucky meeting Emen here, but I didn't ask for it, and I certainly didn't recognize it when it happened." He recalled his panic as the coin had slipped his grasp and tumbled down a sewer grate.

"And the acorn?" Ildric asked.

"That is a little more reasonable," Tavenji said, "I used it to grant your little dwagon friend the knowledge of traveling along a lightning bolt. It's an old trick, but a damned fun ride. That's how we got out of the tower where you held me prisoner." Tavenji made a disapproving face, letting the old man squirm.

Emen's eyes went wide, and he looked in shock at the wizard, who could only blush.

"You..." Emen grasped for words, "you kept a god *prisoner* in your tower?"

Ildric set his jaw, trying to look contrite. "We did not *know* he was a god, and it's not as if he came out and said so. He appeared in the Tower of the Silver Moon, not *this* tower. When we asked his name, he spent days giving us riddles and songs in dead languages. "

"Days?" Tavenji remarked, "It was a week as I recall; a week tied up like a Bythian bridegroom." The little god tried to look disgusted and disapproving, the way his father Arathus managed so effortlessly. Instead, he came off as petulant and constipated.

Ildric bowed his head, saying, "Once again, I ask your forgiveness, my lord. We did not know." *But I did set you loose,* he thought.

"Well, you *did* set me loose," Tavenji said, "The dwagon said you believed me and gave me back my acorn. I owe you for that, I suppose." He waved his hand in a magnanimous way, mimicking so many monarchs he had witnessed through history. He had always wanted to wave at someone magnanimously; it was so empowering.

Emen, for his part, felt a little less guilty in the whole affair, but he supposed that would change soon. They sat in silence for a time, sipping wine and watching the fire.

Ildric spoke first, "Well, if we cannot interrogate this high priest, how are we supposed to find the Heart and the scion? We have nothing to go on but a useless prophecy that tells us little."

Tavenji intoned,

"In latter half of Dragon's Age,
the Mad One brings the world's fate.
In payment for the timeless rage,
the Tyrant's blood will blend with hate.

The scion of the sacred line
shall willingly embrace his doom,
to rend asunder all design
and place creation in its tomb."

"What?" Ildric stared at the little god, flabbergasted.

Tavenji gave him a curious look. "That was the prophesy about the Dark Heart and the scion. Why, what were *you* talking about?"

The wizard got to his feet, spilling some of his wine and staining his robes. "There was *another* prophecy? I meant the Prophecy of Kraal's Return!"

"Oh, I don't think he'll be returning, not in the shape he was in," Tavenji said.

Emen was completely lost. "Excuse me, but what is this all about?"

Ildric started pacing the room, "There was a prophecy we were debating in the Order, one about the scion of an ancient line. It has traditionally been called Kraal's Return..."

Tavenji piped up again in his sing-song voice,

"The Blood Divine returns from distant lands
and deathless ruler once again shall hold
the providence of life in mighty hands
as dark events will thrice again unfold.

The scion then must into danger leap
and take the shard of heaven to contend
with seed of bedlam in creation deep,
sending one or both to meet its end.

"Is that the one you mean?" Tavenji asked.

Ildric nodded, in a daze. "I have never heard the first one you recited."

"Well, I don't imagine so," Tavenji said, "The 'Prophecy of the Mad One' was meant for the cult of Llomaak alone."

"How do you know of it?" Ildric asked.

"God," Emen said, pointing to the god.

Tavenji shrugged, "I heard my brother speak it through the Veil. I was waiting to receive Kraal's body and take it to Arathus."

"You- *you* took Kraal's body?" he asked, amazed. Here was a god answering some of the most debated questions in history and theology, and Ildric wasn't even writing it down.

The little god nodded, kicking his leg over the arm of the chair. "He passed through a thinning in the Veil; likely at some holy site built on a spirit well. I received him, and with him came the Dark Heart inside his chest. His divine blood kept the dark power in check until he died. I delivered him to father Arathus, and I guess he took him to the abandoned realm of brother Epoch. He was laid to rest there, and the power of Llomaak's blood leeched into the eternal sands."

"How did it come back?" Emen asked.

Ildric made a guess, "Epoch somehow retrieved it from his realm and returned to Jayde. He was the Mad One, fulfilling his own prophecy."

Tavenji nodded glumly. He didn't feel the need to tell them his part in that affair. Now was not the time to be pointing fingers, especially at him

Emen swirled the wine in his glass, enjoying the heady bouquet. He intoned, "In latter half of Dragon's Age... what does that mean, exactly?"

Ildric said, "The Celvestrian calendar uses a count of days, months, years, and centuries, with each century being an 'age' named for a constellation. The starting point is the founding of the city of Celvestria in the Age of Vestra. There have since been 61 uniquely named centuries; Kraal was born in the Age of Aminus the eagle, which followed the Age of Kymboth the lion. The current century is the Age of Zhómai the dragon."

Emen chuckled, "You reminded me of my mother just then, always at lessons," he said, "What is this fetish with prophecies that rhyme? Is that some sort of rule?"

"All the true ones rhyme," Tavenji said, waving his hand.

Emen couldn't tell if he was joking or not.

Ildric pressed Tavenji for answers. "The Tyrant's blood? The sacred line? What does it mean?"

"Llomaakittes call my Royal Father the Tyrant. Presumably the 'sacred line' refers to one of his children." The little god sat up in thought. "Actually," he said, scratching his chin, "it could have been 'secret line,' not 'sacred line.' I'm not sure."

"But his children are either gods, or Kraal himself," Ildric exclaimed, "And you said Kraal is long dead, never to return, despite the other prophecy!"

"That, I did..." Tavenji nodded with a wink.

"I wonder," Emen said, "did Kraal die a virgin, do you think?"

Ildric stopped his pacing, staring at the dwarf. "Oh, gods!" he exclaimed.

"Demigods!" Tavenji corrected him, "Demi-demigods! Demi-demi-demi-demigods!"

"A sacred line," Emen muttered, furrowing his thick brow, "Kept secret, no doubt."

"The line of Kraal," the wizard said, "the heirs of Arathus..." His mind reeled. "Not Kraal himself, but one of his descendants has taken the Dark Heart, and willingly, if the prophecy is true."

Emen pointed out, "It rhymes. Must be true."

Tavenji grinned, despite the mood in the room. He liked this dwarf.

Ildric pleaded, "Do you know the meaning of the other prophecy? The one that speaks of the Dark Heart's destruction?"

"As far as I can tell," Tavenji said sagely, "it speaks of the Dark Heart's *possible* destruction." Seeing Ildric become even more flustered, he grinned and shrugged, "I've spent centuries pondering those prophecies, as have we all in the Divine Court. I think the 'Divine Blood' is probably the Dark Heart. The 'deathless ruler' is someone who once held the 'providence of life in mighty hands,' so that's a tough one." He hopped out of the chair and let his feet lead him about the floor.

"Might it be the Shadow Lord?" Ildric asked.

Tavenji shook his head. "Don't think so. He was never a ruler, not in any real sense. His sister was the eldest and queen of their people, but she died..." His face fell and his voice trailed off. Clearly he had known her and was saddened by the memory. Sighing, he said, "The Shadow Lord abdicated his claim and took the descendants of the first human tribe with him across the sea, settling here. Now he lives in the 'Sulkwood,' feeling sorry for himself."

Emen asked, "This 'shard of heaven,' is that the Dark Heart too?"

Tavenji pointed to him saying, "*That* is a good question. I don't think it is. I think it refers to a fragment of the blade that drew the blood of Llomaak in the first place."

Ildric was amazed yet again. "Someone *cut* the god and made him bleed?"

"Of course," Tavenji said, "You don't think we go bleeding all over the place for fun, do you? It means losing some of our power."

"But what manner of blade could do such a thing?" he asked.

"That," Tavenji said, "is a long story. I might have played a part in it; a rather large part, actually." His shoulders slumped and he shuffled his feet. To Ildric, he looked like a guilty schoolboy. "To make a long story *extremely* short, a blade was forged that could wound or kill a god, and it was used to try to end a great war. Instead, it set the world on a path to ultimate destruction." He took a shaking breath, and it seemed to the mortal men that the little god was on the verge of tears.

"Is that going to happen?" Emen asked, solemnly, "Is the world truly going to end?"

Tavenji replied softly, "Only if you believe the god of destiny who knew the future."

Ildric pointed out, "But men are free to forge their own destinies now. Besides, your brother's two prophecies seem to be competing with each other."

Tavenji had nothing to say to that. He had been acting on hope since he arrived in the material world, stripped of power and naked as a plucked goose.

"So," the dwarf said, "all we have to do is find the secret descendant of the King God, take the heart from him, and destroy it somehow?"

"Essentially, yes," Tavenji said, "Only, when the Dark Heart takes him, it will replace his own heart within his chest, giving him terrible power. Oh, and also I have no idea how to truly destroy it; the prophecy doesn't mention that, nor does it say the attempt will succeed."

"Lovely," Emen muttered.

Ildric added, "And I cannot seek for it using my divination. Finding it might drive me mad."

"Is there any good news?" the dwarf asked, pouring himself some more wine.

"We are all alive and working together," Ildric said, "That's a start."

Emen snorted. "For now," he said.

"So!" Tavenji clapped his hands and grinned, instantly changing his mood, "What did I miss while I was dead? Is there still a plague and an army in the city? What day is it anyway?"

Ildric sunk into his chair, reaching for the wine and finding it getting low. He offered what was left to Emen and said, "By this hour it's the 5th of Selvimoth, Hwessday. The plague has abated, but the army remains. They will march soon, so they may reach the Dissenter lands by the spring thaw."

"There's to be a war, then?" Tavenji asked.

"Likely," Ildric said, "Though the king may have a means of leverage that will forestall it."

Emen coughed on his wine, choking softly.

"Some kind of new weapon?" asked the god.

"A hostage," Ildric said, "the son of the Baron DeKenric. He has been in the king's custody for many months."

"Er," Emen coughed, "about that..."

"What?" Ildric asked.

"Um, well... that might not be quite accurate," Emen said; it was his turn to look like a guilt schoolboy, "The more I tell you, the more I guarantee that I'll swing from a rope, you realize that?"

"What do you know, Emen?" Ildric demanded, "What about DeKenric?"

Tavenji perked up, sensing something interesting. He loved moments like these, even if it meant mortal peril. He'd caused more such moments than he could recall.

Clearing his throat, Emen said, "I might have had a part in planning his escape."

"Escape?" the wizard scoffed, "If he had escaped, I would be the first person called to locate him!"

"Not if they didn't *know* he had escaped," Emen said carefully, "He was replaced-"

Tavenji snapped his fingers, an excited glee on his face. "Duplict! Another duplict!"

"Another face-changer?" Ildric gasped, "This creature is in the palace with the *king?*"

Emen nodded glumly. *Gods, I hadn't thought of that,* he realized, *I'll be lucky if they only hang me.* "He is a man named Twist. The Boss had used him for special missions before, but no one knew anything about him. He is a strange fellow with mismatched features, but he can look like anyone he chooses to. The plan was to get him in to deliver some goods to the DeKenric boy, take his place, and have the lad slip out wearing his clothes."

Ildric glared, leaning forward; his words were measured and threatening, "How long has he been gone?"

Emen shrank a bit into the chair and said, "Since the first of the year at least."

"Gods above and below!" the wizard bellowed.

"And in between!" Tavenji added.

"Almost five weeks!" Ildric raged, stamping about the floor, "They could have made it to his father by now!"

"Oh, but this is a stroke of luck!" Tavenji said, hopping on his chair and clapping, "Don't you see?"

Ildric and Emen could not.

"A duplict!" the god said, "Duplicts are creatures of chaos! Children of Llomaak from the Time of Chaos! It makes sense!"

"What makes sense?" Ildric demanded.

"Who else would a duplict high priest of Chaos trust to deliver the Dark Heart?" Tavenji asked.

Emen sputtered, "A-are you saying the scion is the DeKenric boy?" He felt a little sick at the thought.

Tavenji shrugged, "Maybe! It's a place to start!"

"But if it *were* Grigor DeKenric," Ildric said, "why risk him going off alone over the mountains?"

"He's not alone," Emen said, "He is in the company of a Maanok warlock working for Manon Wolvert."

"Oh! Say that ten times fast!" Tavenji said, "Try it! MaanokwarlockworkingforManonWolvert!"

Ildric said a silent prayer that the god would stop at one. Then he said, "So Manon Wolvert has one of the *Baedoch Khoom* working for him! That's enlightening. And Duke Wolvert is in league with the Circle of Gold as well?" Ildric raised an eyebrow at the dwarf.

"Not directly. His Maanok was the one to initiate that," said the dwarf, gesturing with his goblet, "It'sss how I became involved in all this... mess. The Maanok came to me because I was the bird man of Portshia, the only contact he knew of. I can thank the bird man of Ahrnok for that, I suppose."

"What does the Circle get in return for helping the Dissenters?" Ildric asked.

"Power," Emen said, "The Boss's grand plan. Duke Wolvert encouraged the dream, though I sssuppose it doesn't matter; the Boss doesn' plan for the worl' to be around long."

He's starting to slur his speech.

Ildric said, "Perhaps if this Boss were removed from power, his threat would diminish?" He leaned towards Emen, his face full of concern and benevolence, "Tell us, who is this evil, twisted man you call the Boss?"

Emen looked defensive for a moment, but he took a last gulp of wine and sighed. Shoulders slumping, he said, "Kobus DuChat."

Ildric sat back slowly, as though the words were a force unto themselves, widening the space between them.

"Strong wine," Tavenji remarked, flashing Emen a knowing smile, "An old trick."

Emen looked at his goblet accusingly, then to Ildric. He was going to complain, but the look of shock and betrayal on the wizard's face was more than adequate payment for such a dirty trick.

Chapter Seven

Into the Shadows

The morning after the boys' rainy night encounter was a special one. Cindra put aside her riding dresses, and after making sure the boys had turned their backs, pulled on the tight-fitting hose and quilted linen arming doublet. Then Padison unlocked the arming chest and handed them the pieces from the cart, and Adric, for the first time, helped her don her armor. It was challenging for them both, not sharing the intimacy that she and Jaron had shared, but soon the discomfort gave way to focusing on the task at hand. Cindra had been well-instructed by the armorer who fitted her for the suit, and now she directed Adric in how to equip her head to toe, or rather, toe to head.

First came the flexible armored shoes and shin guards, then thigh armor that was secured to leather ties, or arming points, on the bottom of her doublet. Next came the breastplate, then the segmented steel skirt and mail draping that covered her midsection. Then her arms and elbows were encased in jointed plate. Mail links sewn to the doublet provided protection for the gaps where her arms needed to move. Then came the shoulder pieces with their raised neck guards, the throat guard, and the 'demi-gauntlets,' which protected her hands from wrist to knuckles, leaving her leather gloves to cover her fingers. Finally, Adric placed a coif and the visored helm over her head and latched it shut. The process had taken roughly three-quarters of an hour, though she was sure it would decrease with practice.

"How do I look?" she asked, her voice muffled by the visor. The party gave her appraising looks and appreciative smiles.

Nixy cheered, "You look like my hero!" and he clapped, grinning ear to ear.

Deliah said, "You look every bit the knight you are, Lady Cindra."

Cindra smiled behind the visor, accepting the praise from both the expected and unexpected sources.

She marched about on the roadway, noticing how little visibility she had to guide her steps. *This won't do at all in the deep forest*, she thought. She raised the visor, trying to contain her proud smile as she did.

"Don't forget your weapons!" Padison called, and handed the sword belt to Adric, who hurried over to tie it about her waist. It was a beautiful belt of black leather embossed with ivy vines, and bore silver buckles and clasps; a thoughtful birthday gift from Wenyssaya. Cindra adjusted *Vyzeroth* and her Minozhian *Kos* knife into the most suitable positions.

Wenyssaya beamed and said, "I feel safer already." Cindra was not sure if she was joking or not, but the elf maid seemed sincere. She would not have taken the remark from Deliah as such.

Drahn said, "I believe everyone has eaten, and the gear is packed. Do you want me to fly ahead and scout?" he asked.

"That's a fine idea, Drahn," Cindra said.

"Also," Drahn said, "you might want to wear that pwesent from Master Ildwic." He then leaped into the air and flew off down the road, clearing the treetops.

The present from Master Ildric, Cindra thought, remembering now, *I put it in my pack and forgot about it.* Ildric Finnael had given her yet another magical trinket for her last birthday. It was a stud earring that he claimed would allow him to send her a single message. It could serve as a summons or a warning, but whatever the message would be, it likely wouldn't be good news.

That's probably why I've avoided putting it on, she thought, *that, and my piercing holes have closed long ago. Maybe there is someone in Breega who can do it?*

Mounting T'ózha was a bit of a challenge; she needed Adric's help to keep her steady as she swung herself up onto his back. T'ózha shifted his footing, feeling the new weight as Cindra adjusted herself in the saddle. Her riding trainer had told her in his boorish manner, that her armored weight shouldn't be a problem for a horse as small as T'ózha as long as she remained balanced, and wasn't constantly "squirming about like a fat whore with an itchy sausage purse."

The memory made her smile. She missed Sir Gerard; he was obnoxious to the point of absurdity, but always entertaining. Cindra never found out whose idea it was to have him train her. *Maybe it had been a punishment for him? Or me? Or both of us?*

"Let's move out," she called to the party, and they mounted their steeds and left their first camping spot behind.

Cindra's party was in good spirits that afternoon, having recovered from the wet and eerie evening of the night before. The weather had become clear and crisp, and the sun shone with mild warmth on their shoulders. Aside from the moist pickings for firewood, the journey had become far more pleasant. They had passed a scattering of farmsteads, but the pale smoke rising from the chimneys was the only sign of human habitation. No traffic met them or followed them. No other nightly visitors had been seen, spectral or otherwise.

Cindra breathed in the fresh, clean air, enjoying the play of light and shadow on the road under the gathering trees. Adric rode just behind her, followed by Nixy, then Padison and Drahn in the cart, and Deliah and Wenyssaya bringing up the rear.

The women were engaged in a conversation Cindra could not hear, but she thought it odd that the two were getting on so well. She had no interest in getting to know Deliah, that was for certain, but Wenyssaya had always been a puzzle to Cindra. It was hard to take in her age and experience by the look of her, and harder still to grasp the undeniable power that dwelt within.

Maybe I'm just intimidated by her, Cindra thought; *maybe I'm intimidated by them both?*

Bare but numerous trees grew into thick copses along the perimeter of the forest proper. Beech, oak, chestnut, and even a few wayward willow trees attempted to establish the look of a 'normal' woodland, but the Shadowood Forest, once a dark green mass on the horizon, was now looming before them in all of its dreary glory. Flocks of birds scattered from treetop to treetop, creating little storms of screeching frenzy, making the horses' ears flick to and fro. The gray trunks twisted and merged together beneath the canopy of gray-green leaves, making one tree look like many, or many look like one. Because Shadowood trees kept much of their velvety leaves year-round, not even the noonday sun could cheer the forest floor. It was unsettling and uncanny.

The road ahead was partially cleared of overhanging trees however, so the path through the forest was open to the sky. For this the party was grateful.

"I don't think I could stand more than a few days in a forest like that," Padison said.

Drahn, who was seated beside him on the wagon bench, nodded in agreement.

Adric said over his shoulder, "You might have mentioned that before we left."

"That was before I saw it!" Padison retorted, "But it's not like I'm going to turn back now."

Cindra was glad to hear this; assuming they had to enter the deep woods on foot, as Deliah said they would, someone had to stay behind with the horses and baggage, and Padison was the best with the animals. Besides, Adric was the better, more experienced, and even-tempered fighter. She gave her squire an appraising eye, wondering if he was up to it. *Am I up to it?* she mused.

Cindra called to the group, "If anyone has second thoughts about spending a week or two in a dark, creepy forest, now is the time to say so."

"I said I'd stay," Padison whined, "I just might lose my mind, that's all."

"Wouldn't be much of a loss," Adric cracked.

"That's big talk for now, *knave*," Padison said, trying out his new vocabulary, "but we'll see how you look when you come out of the deep woods. *If* you come out!"

Cindra rebuked him. "There'll be none of that, Paddy. We're *all* coming out. We are guests of the Shadow Lord, and we're bringing his son to him." She smiled at Nixy, who smiled back.

"Yeah," Paddy said, "But it's a long way to wherever he is."

Cindra had to agree, though she wouldn't let anyone see it. It *would* be a long way, and they really didn't know where they were going. Instead, she said, "Have some faith, Paddy. We're not exactly defenseless. We have steel, magic, and experience going for us."

"But what does the forest have going for *it?*" Padison muttered.

"Shut up, Paddy." Cindra said, getting annoyed.

"You're demolarizing us," Nixy said.

"Demoralizing," Drahn corrected.

As they rode under the branches of the first dark tree, Drahn shivered nervously, his purple scales turning slightly red. "Do you think there are dweedwagons in the Shadowood?" he asked no one in particular.

"Might be," Nixy said, "Wenyssaya says they live in the Blackwood Forest, at the foot of the Gartethan Mountains."

"But those mountains are so vewy far away," Drahn said, "like the land I came fwom. I have never seen a hint of dweedwagons in this fowest."

"Have ya looked?" Nixy asked.

Drahn nodded, "A little. I have flown over the woods along Casselvane Pwovince many times, but have never seen one."

"But it's a really big forest," Nixy replied, hoping to encourage him, "Ya never know. They might be hiding."

Drahn looked as deep into the dark woods as he could, trying to imagine what dweedragon in its right mind would want to live here. Then the thought occurred to him: "What if there are things in this fowest that... *eat* dweedwagons?"

Nixy thought about it and said, "Well, if there are things living here that eat dweedragons, then there must be dweedragons to eat, right? Then they'd have reason to hide."

The little creature just snorted and wrapped his tail around his legs.

Deliah spoke up, "I have never seen a dweedragon in these woods, but there are other dangers here, and they are bad enough to make a dweedragon clan think twice before moving in."

Not helping, Cindra thought.

"What kind of dangers?" asked Wenyssaya, "Do you mean humans?"

But Deliah did not elaborate.

The first night in the woods came more quickly than they were prepared for. Deliah had described a camping area that people had used for centuries, about half a day's ride into the forest. Cindra, wanting to stay ahead of Deliah's advice giving, had told Adric to collect whatever firewood he could find along the roadside. As it turned out, this was a very good idea, because it was nearly pitch black by the time they reached their destination; Cindra had to use her sword to light the way.

They were getting more efficient at least. Wenyssaya would draw any needed water from the nearby streams and use her magic to make it safe to drink. Deliah would built the fire while Adric helped Cindra out of her armor. Padison and Nixy tended to the horses as they chatted away, sharing their love of the big animals. Drahn would perch on the wagon bench and supervise, gnawing on his salted mutton jerky.

Tonight's campsite was an ancient ruin that had been consumed by the forest long ago. It lay on either side of the road, which still bore paving stones that peeked through the dirt and grass. The road bisected a circular courtyard, which was partially enclosed by a crumbling, moss-covered stone wall. The feet of a life-sized statue stood atop the central perimeter pillar of each wall; the bodies had likely been toppled and buried in the underbrush, or carried off as souvenirs. Some pillars had been toppled and their sections arranged to make seats around the ash stained fire pits.

Camp was set up by the light of Nixy's glowstone and Wenyssaya's floating faerie-lights; little globes of soft, fuzzy radiance that shone like moonlight as they bobbed above their heads. Adric soon had a modest flame growing with the aid of his tinderbox, and Padison began tying up and unsaddling the horses.

"We should make a habit of gathering firewood after midday," Cindra said, feeling the chill of night creep across her skin, "Also, we should leave some here so the next people don't have to search themselves."

"Very generous," Deliah said, "You sound like a regular camper in the wilderness."

"I am," she said with a touch of pride, "I spent almost two years with a Galindri caravan." She looked up at the stars overhead, her thoughts flying back to that frightening, wonderful time. "We would sleep under the stars most nights, except for in the dead of winter in the north lands. I've been looking forward to another chance to travel like this."

"At least we aren't camping with a large army," Wenyssaya said, "I imagine the companionship and the smells would not be nearly as pleasant."

Cindra's mind went immediately to Jaron, and she stared into the fire, keeping her feelings to herself. She thought of him every day, but had tried to avoid imagining him going to war while she rode in the other direction.

"You are not wrong," Deliah said, "This is more pleasant by far."

"I guess that means we smell nice and are pleasant company," Adric called to Padison, who chuckled.

"I didn't say *that*," Deliah said. She gave the boys a sly grin.

Adric snorted a laugh.

Nixy had helped Drahn down from the cart and they sat next to Cindra on one of the pillar sections. "Who built this place, do you think?" Nixy asked her.

Cindra looked around at the ruins in the firelight. Her friend was trying to lift her spirits, she knew. Nixy had a knack for knowing when she was getting gloomy.

"I'm not sure," she said, "but it was probably the Celvestrian Empire. They built the Joshian Way, the Red Coast Road, and most other paved roadways in Calilon."

"I wonder what it was for?" Wenyssaya said.

Deliah said, "It was a shrine to Arathus and Obamir, who bless travelers. It was also a shrine to Arahn, the Golden Sun. It's built in a circle and open to the sky, like all of his temples."

Wenyssaya said, "I remember seeing ruined temples like that near my home, and on lonely hilltops along my way to Portshia. I did not know what they were." She looked up at Navithwi the raven, who was perched on one of the broken feet.

Cindra stared at Deliah, who was looking into the fire. Her blue-gray eyes caught the light, reflecting it back like a torch in the fog; they were both beautiful and eerie. "How do you know what this place was?" Cindra asked.

Deliah fixed those eyes on her and said, "People die, buildings crumble, but lore lives on."

Dramatic, she thought.

"So this is holy ground?" Adric asked.

Deliah nodded. "Offerings used to be left along the walls for safe travel through the dark woods, and to give thanks upon coming out."

"Should we do something?" Padison asked, "Like, I dunno, say a little prayer, maybe?"

Deliah said, flatly, "If you think it will help."

Her tone caught Cindra's attention. "You are not a religious person, Deliah?" she asked.

The woman gave her a penetrating look. "That's a rather personal question, milady knight. But no, I'm not. It's not that I don't believe in the gods, for I do indeed. I just see no point in prayer."

"Because the gods fell silent?" she asked.

"Because drawing their attentions is never a wise idea," Deliah replied, "Trust me; we are better off without them."

"How can you say that?" Cindra said, "We've never known the gods as they used to be, so who's to say we are better off?" She had no idea why she was arguing religion with Deliah, other than because it was Deliah. Regardless, the woman spoke with such surety and authority that Cindra could not help but challenge it.

"Lore, milady knight," she answered, "Look to your histories. They made nations rise and fall, sanctioned countless wars, became patrons of empires, rent the heavens asunder, and bent every man, woman and child to their will. You cannot imagine what it might be like to have them with us once again." Her eyes flicked to Cindra's wrists and forearms, to the scars she kept hidden by long sleeves and leather wristbands. "Or perhaps you can imagine it. Do you recall your last night on the mountain? The storm that struck the city, and the clouds twisting over it like a hungry-"

"Yes, I do remember," Cindra broke in, "I remember it well, thank you." She rubbed her arms reflexively and then told herself it was because of the cold.

"I have twouble wemembering that night," Drahn said from Nixy's lap, "Wather, I wemember being tewwibly afwaid and wet, before the lightning stwike. It was a howwible, dweadful night."

Nixy gave him a little pat to comfort him. Even without seeing the little creature's scales turn a deeper purple, Nixy knew that Drahn's speech impediment became more distinct when he was upset.

"But that's the night you found your powers," Nixy said.

"Twue," Drahn nodded.

"*That,*" Deliah said, "is a taste of the gods in their wrath. The ancient stories are full of such tantrums, and every boon comes at a cost. Closing themselves off was the best thing they could have done."

"What was that storm about, anyway?" Padison asked, having finished with the horses, "If it wasn't the gods, what was it?"

Cindra, Nixy, Drahn and Wenyssaya looked at each other, and then back into the fire. Adric and Padison, sensing the change in their companions, exchanged quizzical looks. Deliah watched them all, her eyes flicking to their faces, reading their unease.

"You know something," she said. It was not a question.

The guilty quartet raised their eyes to meet Deliah's gaze, and then Cindra found her companions all looking to her. *Well,* she thought, *I am the leader. That makes it my decision.* She cleared her throat and sat up, saying, "It is believed by many, including Arch

Mage Finnael, that the storm was caused by an ancient artifact called the Dark Heart."

Deliah stared at her with an intensity that made Cindra flinch. The woman's eyes were disturbing on a sunny day, but became chips of gray steel in the fire-lit gloom.

"What's the Dark Heart?" Padison asked in a hushed awe, leaning forward to listen.

As if I was going to leave it at that, Cindra thought, *but maybe you're supposed to ask when you're listening to ghost stories in a creepy forest.* "It's supposedly a drop of blood from the god Llomaak himself, hardened into a large gemstone, like a ruby or something. No one has seen it in centuries, but the last time it surfaced, it corrupted the gods' chosen king, Orthicus."

"Orthicus the Great," Adric said, "Later called Orthicus the Terrible."

Cindra continued, "The Dark Heart is said to have caused the Time of Chaos. Before that, there is a legend that it destroyed an empire in ancient Hibland, when Celvestria was just a cluster of huts."

Deliah's mouth twitched as if she wanted to speak, but instead she cast her gaze into the flames, though her eyes lost none of their intensity.

"Jaron and I were out riding our horses last summer, when a strange dust storm fell over the city," Cindra said, "We took shelter in a tavern, and there was this odd old man, a wizard maybe, who had... unnatural powers. It turned out that people had reported bizarre events following a mad wizard all the way from the north. After he came to town... well, that was when the rats invaded. Then the sickness, the dying... and the vemloks."

"What?" Adric cried, "This mad wizard was responsible for that thing that killed Halvoy Quenlorden?"

"The Dark Heart was responsible," Wenyssaya said, "It is a seed of Chaos, and its very presence seems to break down the barriers between *Alsuvath* and *Rath-Mavath*.*

Cindra heard the elven words and understood them intuitively. *Alsuvath, the world of elements. Rath-Mavath, the realm of chaos.* She still could not get used to understanding words she had never heard before.

Drahn, however, had a different reaction. "Mavath is elven for chaos? Intewesting," he said.

"Yes," Wenyssaya said, "What of it?"

"I've heard *'Mash'* used as a pwoper name for Llomaak, but I didn't realize the elven word for 'chaos' was so similar. *Mash* must be a vewy old name."

This shook Deliah out of her reverie. "Where did you hear that? Who called him that?" she demanded. Her voice made the dweedragon flinch.

He said, "The first time was in the shell. Men came to destwoy our nest, and they used that name. The second time was about a week after that tewwible storm you mentioned. We were questioning a stwange little man who claimed to be a denizen of the Void. Appawently he had appeared out of thin air in the Tower of the Silver Moon. He told us his name in many, many languages, most of them no longer spoken. I identified one as First Dynasty Bythian, and one as Kin Dwon."

"What's Kin Dron?" Nixy asked.

Drahn blinked at him. "Kin *Dwon*. It is called Kin Dwon," he huffed, "It's in Ghozia."

"Oh," Nixy said, "Sorry."

Deliah asked, "What name did he give in Bythian?"

Drahn thought a moment and said, "Ama-B'shelot."

Cindra frowned and asked, "Wait, someone just *appeared* in the wizard tower? From the *Void?*"

"So he claimed," Drahn said, "He was vewy odd, and somehow he taught me a power I didn't know I had. It was like I suddenly knew how to do it. He called it 'riding the lightning,' and-"

"Why did Ildric not mention this before?" she asked.

Drahn could only shrug. Then a thought occurred to him and his head drooped. "Perhaps because I helped the man escape, and they don't know where he is now," he said meekly.

Cindra growled, "Damned wizards and their secrets..."

Padison asked Adric, "Did you know about this Dark Heart stuff?"

Adric only shook his head.

Wenyssaya turned to Deliah and asked, "Is it important that someone used the name *Mash?* You reacted strangely to this."

The woman's mind seemed far, far away. When she answered, her voice was distant and distracted. "The only people who use that name today are his priests."

*And how does she know **that**?* Cindra wondered. But instead, she asked, "Do you think this stranger in the tower was a priest of Llomaak?"

"No," Deliah said, "I think he would have us believe he was a god."

There were blank, unbelieving stares and a moment of silence, broken only by the crackling of the fire and the creaking of the branches in the breeze. Then Drahn clapped his paws together and chirped, "I knew it! Master Ildwic and I suspected it, but we never told anyone because it was so widiculous!"

"It's impossible," Cindra declared, "The gods are shut off from the world. They don't just pop in for a visit."

"Impossible?" Deliah scoffed, "The Dark Heart is in Portshia. The veil between our world and the Abyss of Chaos grows thin. Spirits are coming through to infest the dead! What is impossible now?"

Cindra couldn't answer that. She had seen creatures of legend and nightmare with her own eyes. "But a god?" she said, "What god? For what reason?"

Deliah answered, "Tavenji, and 'reason' is not his province."

Drahn nodded excitedly, happy that another shared his mad theory.

Adric sat in awe of her, now more than ever before. He asked, "How do you know these things?" It was a question everyone suddenly needed an answer for.

"My husband had an extensive library, and I had lots of spare time," Deliah replied.

Drahn looked doubtful and said, "That must be an impressive librawy."

Deliah nodded and sat in silence as the party digested these revelations. Finally, a squealing grumble could be heard over the fire.

Padison asked, "Who else is hungry?"

Shadowood, as it turned out, made for excellent campfires; it was quick to catch, and burned slow and hot. Perhaps it ignited so easily due to the strange velvety fuzz present on the bark and leaves, or maybe it was just magical.

"The stars are so clear" Nixy said, stepping away from the fire to gaze up, "I haven't seen them like this for a long time."

Cindra nodded, "The city lights and smoke make them hard to see. I missed the night skies since returning home."

Wenyssaya looked up, and a frown creased her brow. Her troubled expression did not go unnoticed, for the firelight and night shadows made her face more dramatic.

"What is it?" Cindra asked, turning to follow her gaze, "Is your bird up there?" She hadn't seen much of the black raven lately.

"No," the elf maid said. She pointed to a spot in the night sky; a red spark that hung in the inky blackness, like a small ember that had risen up from the fire and gotten stuck.

"What, that star?" Cindra asked. She knew the pole star, called *shaz g'ályo* by the Galindri, but she had never see it so bright before.

Deliah looked up and narrowed her eyes, but said nothing.

Adric said, "That's part of Vestra the Hunter, right? The arrow's tip?"

"Spear's tip," Drahn said.

Wenyssaya nodded. "It is called *Iluvdim*, the Blood Star, among my people; it grows brighter in times of strife and bloodshed."

"An ill omen; all the experts agwee," Drahn said, "It was one of the few things they could agwee on."

"Never heard of it," Padison said.

Nixy returned to the fire and sat by Wenyssaya. "Was that the elf?" he asked, "The first murderer?"

She nodded, "You remember the story. It is not one I like to tell."

But Cindra and the others were curious now. "What story?" she asked.

It was Deliah that answered, "The first elf to kill his own kind did so out of jealousy and rage," she said, "As punishment, he was placed in the sky to watch people murder each other, and serve as a warning of great violence to come."

Again, Cindra was impressed and put off by the woman's knowledge of lore, but she didn't feel like commenting on it. She couldn't argue that they were heading for evil times and bloodshed.

She gave the red speck one last look, wondering just how bright it would get.

As everyone settled in to sleep, Cindra took the first watch. As she looked at the stars, pondering every one of the evening's revelations, there was one question that kept resurfacing: *How does Deliah know so much?* She did not believe for a moment that this woman had read all of it in her husband's personal collection. Master Wyngaard was a ward master and a wealthy man, but guild wizards focused mostly on their chosen profession. Drahn said that the Order of Astrellaris had tried for a week to figure out their strange intruder and his riddles, but even with all their resources, they had been at a loss.

Yet this woman, who read her husband's books in her 'spare time,' seemed to know the ancient name of a god in a dead language, knew details about Llomaak's priesthood, knew about the Dark Heart and what it was capable of, and even knew about the ruined temple they now camped in. *Is she a priestess of some kind? Possibly a witch?*

Cindra had always suspected Deliah might be a witch. Many years ago, when her role in the festival scandal was revealed, Deliah claimed to have deciphered her husband's notes, allowing her to open the magic lock that secured the Selvinian temple's hothouse. She had stolen two roses for Sir Earnold Greenfellow, who had them enchanted by an 'unknown wizard.' But what if *she* was the one who enchanted the roses?

Witches were mistrusted, and for good reason; their knowledge was forbidden to women, and they could not be members of casting guilds, so they had to work their magic in secret. People who did that could get up to anything, and no one would be the wiser.

As she thought on it more, Cindra felt a pang of guilt for condemning her. If she *was* a witch, the crime was no different than her own. Both women had trained in disciplines forbidden to them, but Cindra had gotten caught, bringing shame to the men who helped her. *Yes, I lied, but it was to save my life from assassins,* she thought, *For the most part.*

But what is Deliah's story? Might it be similar?

She looked at the woman's back as she slept. She knew Deliah was a manipulative liar, that was certain. She had betrayed Greenfellow for Jaron, betrayed Jaron for Greenfellow, and betrayed her husband to do it. Now, the woman had left her husband and gone off into the Shadowood for mysterious reasons. *Did she even love her husband? Had she loved any of her men?*

Had she loved Jaron?

It was not something she wanted to dwell on. Yes or no, the answer would not improve Cindra's relationship with her fellow traveler.

The moon shone through the treetops as Cindra woke Adric to take the next watch in the late evening. The young man stretched, yawned, and belted his sword. Cindra did not immediately go to bed, so they sat and talked a while, tending the fire.

"Cold," Adric said.

Cindra nodded in agreement. "I'm thinking about who we might meet on the road, now that most of the region's fighting men have gone off to war."

"Bandits," he said, poking the burning logs with a stick. They popped and flared in response, casting little embers aloft. "We'd make a tempting target."

"We would indeed." Cindra had no illusions about scaring off hungry, desperate men with only her armor and sword. Once they realized she was a young woman, that would only make them bolder. Of course, underestimating their little band would be a dangerous mistake, but she hoped to avoid confrontation all together.

"Do you think the Greenfellow men will be a problem?" A nervous tremor shook his voice, or maybe it was the cold.

"I hope not. I doubt they would offer us the same welcome they did to Sir Jaron. Besides, if word of mistreatment reached my father, he'd raze the town to get at old Waliss Greenfellow." *If word reached him,* she thought.

"It's Rejick Ratham I'm worried about," he said, "If he's still there, he'd find a reason to call you out. You can bet on it."

Cindra said nothing. Her mind turned back to their match at school, which had been her crowning moment of glory. She had been bloodied by Ratham, but had given as good as she got. Indeed, she had both won the match and gotten revenge for her cousin Gaius, who had been badly hurt by Ratham in a previous contest. She had turned his taunting against him, and made him look a fool. It didn't help matters when he later learned he had been beaten by a girl. He left the school in fury and disgrace.

"But you've been training with the Su'Kraal master," he said, trying to be encouraging. "I'm sure you can take Ratham again."

"I'm not so sure." She rolled up her sleeves and showed him her scars. "My hands lost much of their strength on Tirgrim's Bluff, and the lightning strike was the final blow."

Adric leaned to look and winced, his handsome face drawing into a worried frown. "I'd heard something about your scars, but I thought it was just a rumor. Are they... painful?" His gaze followed the branching patterns along the length of her forearms, lingering on the pale scars in the shape of Valdak's blind eye.

"Not so much," she said, "Gavadaire made me train every day with cannonbells to get my strength back." She flexed her sword hand, making the muscles of her arm stand out impressively in the flattering light. Her wrist made a popping sound when she extended it; something it hadn't done before the ordeal. "I think I'm as strong as I should be," she said, "but I still worry."

"Well, I'll have your back, Paddy too."

She smiled; once again she was glad he had volunteered to serve as her squire. "I know you will," she said, patting his shoulder as she rose, "Good night."

"Good night, milady."

The second day in the woods gave the party a new appreciation for sunlight. There were mile-long stretches where the road was overshadowed, and the gloom was palpable. When the trees thinned and the sunlight warmed their skin, it was remarkably uplifting. Sighs of relief could be heard, as if they had collectively set down a heavy burden. The horses seemed more at ease as well.

Then they would plunge back into the shade, holding their hands out to feel the thin beams of light piercing the dark, as a person might feel for the rain.

Yet for all the gloom and oppression of the forest, there was life to be seen, albeit fleetingly. Creatures that usually came out at night could be spotted earlier in the day under the dark boughs. Cassel boars rooted for plentiful mushrooms, their little piglets following close. Moon hares darted between the trees, showing flashes of pale hindquarters; the little beasts were named for the way their fur seasonally changed from black to white and back again, always nose to tail. Gray and black squirrels caught the eye with their sudden, intense movements.

They were even lucky enough to see blue deer, animals with coats of bluish-gray fur that shimmered faintly in the sparse light. Five of them crossed the road behind the party, led by a majestic ten-point hart. He watched them warily as his harem of does bounded into the woods, and then he turned his crowned head and followed. Cindra thought it would have made a fine trophy for the lord callous enough to kill it. She wondered, *Did lords dare to hunt in the Shadowood? Does anyone?*

The road became clear and sun-dappled, yet to either side were the dark, twisted trees that drank the light. Even at high morning they could see no farther than a hundred feet beneath the canopy. The road was paved by flat stones laid down by the old empire long ago, for which the travelers were thankful; the rains of the last few days would have turned an unpaved road to grasping mud.

Drahn circled back every quarter hour, reporting a clear way ahead. At midday, he advised them of travelers, which was a welcomed break in their boredom.

"There is a caravan stopped a quarter mile ahead," Drahn said, a little out of breath, "They seem to be making camp."

"This early? It's only a few more hours till we reach Breega." Cindra said, "What do they look like?"

Drahn said, "There is a man and two women, and one woman is vewy old. The caravan looks Galindwi, but the people are not."

"Interesting," Cindra said, "Maybe they will appreciate the company?"

Drahn shrugged and climbed into his knapsack.

The party arrived at the campsite with Cindra riding at its head, her visor up and arm raised in greeting. The couple seemed wary, and stood as they approached. The elderly woman sitting by the fire tilted her head towards the noise as the firelight played on her deep wrinkles.

The man was in his late middle years, with dark hair graying at the temples, lanky limbs, and a weathered face with no beard. The woman was of like age, with a full figure and blond hair, which was caught in a long braid. They wore simple traveling clothes of green and brown, which showed signs of frequent mending. The old woman was wrapped in a blanket against the cold; her wispy, white hair framed her face like the head of a dandelion. Her eyes were closed, perhaps permanently, for the flesh appeared sunken and puckered.

"Hail," Cindra called, "Would you like some company?"

Upon hearing her voice, the couple looked at each other in confusion. Deliah and Wenyssaya rode into view and the couple relaxed visibly. The man said, "Please be our guests... milady?"

Cindra dismounted and strode to meet them face-to-face, hoping to reassure them that they meant no harm. Removing her helmet, she smiled and said, "Greetings. I am Lady Cindra, and these are my companions," she gestured to the others. "We are traveling north into the far Shadowood. Where might you be heading?"

"A woman in armor!" said the old woman, "Well, bless me. What's next?"

The man said, "Well met, milady. My name is Bardon, and this is my wife, Glenawyn, and her grandmother, Maewyn. We are heading north as well, though perhaps at a slower pace than yourselves. We are taking Maewyn home."

The old woman said in a quavering but hale voice, "Home to die."

Her granddaughter tsked at her, "Oh, gran. Don't speak of such things."

"Where is home?" Cindra asked.

Glenawyn said, "A small hamlet many leagues from here, called Gloamshire."

Cindra said, "That sounds like a gloomy place."

"Indeed it is," she said, "For it is deep in the north, where the power of the wood is strong."

"I am sure gran could be persuaded to tell you all about it," Bardon smiled.

Maewyn just cackled and nodded.

Glenawyn said, "Sit with us around our fire, and gran might share a story. It is what she does best."

The party stopped across the road from the travelers and saw to their horses before joining them. Once that was finished, Adric went to help Cindra doff her armor. It came off faster than it went on, so she was soon free of it, sorted and stored on the wagon. She slipped on the dark tabard of the king's service and buckled her weapon belt with the *Kos* knife at her back. Her sword was left on the wagon. It seemed bad manners to bring it to lunch.

Food was prepared swiftly, and soon they were seated about their neighbor's fire. Cindra had a thrill of nostalgia, remembering days like this with her Galindri family, when the clans came together to share stories and food by the fire. Her longing to see Majii and his family struck her now, and not for the first time on this journey.

"So, how did you come by a Galindri caravan?" she asked.

Bardon replied, "We purchased it from a family in the town of Ghat. They were in great need of coin, and we were in need of a sheltered wagon to travel north with gran."

"Their need must have been great to sell their home," Cindra said.

Bardon shrugged, "I didn't ask their business, and they didn't share it, but I know that they'd sold off most of their wares before deciding to sell the caravan. I could see their need, and though others advised against it, I gave them their asking price."

Glenawyn chuckled, "Soft of heart and head, that's my husband."

"Now, now," he chided, "no abusing me in front of our guests, if you please."

The meal was soon finished, sparse as it was, and soon mouths were free for talking. The couple had been making eyes at their strange guests, and now their questions could be held back no longer.

"If I may," Glenawyn said to Cindra, "is this a dweedragon?" She nodded towards Drahn, who was licking his little dinnerware clean.

"I am," Drahn replied for himself, giving them a little surprise. "Do you know of dweedwagons?"

"Oh!" she exclaimed, "only from gran's stories. But she never mentioned they spoke."

Maewyn, who was gumming at a softened piece of bread, only smiled.

"Well, we do," Drahn said, "Although I have never met another of my kind myself, I assume it is one of our natural talents."

"I suppose introductions are in order," Cindra said, "Forgive my rudeness. This is Drahn the Dweedragon, and this is Wenyssaya, an elf of the Blackwood Forest."

"An ilv!" exclaimed Maewyn, "I thought I felt an Ilvaya nearby. Bless me!"

"Pleased to make your acquaintance," the elf maid said, looking curiously at the blind old human.

Cindra continued around the circle, "This is Deliah, a lady of Portshia, and this young man next to Drahn is Nixyalderthor. Then there's Adric, my squire, and Padison." The boys nodded.

"Well, you're an odd company, that's for sure," Bardon said, "I've never heard of a lady-at-arms before, much less one traveling with an elf and a dweedragon. But where are you bound for in the far Shadowood?"

Cindra admitted, "We don't rightly know. We are on a quest of sorts, and we must seek out signs of the lord of the forest."

The couple shared a curious glance. Glenawyn said, "There are no true lords of the forest, unless you mean the Shadow Lord. But he is rumored to be an ancient elf." She then looked at Wenyssaya, wondering.

"I do, and he is," Cindra said, "We have reason to venture into the woods to find him, but we are not sure where to start."

Maewyn began to speak, saying, "Gloamshire is a fine place to start. It's fraught with paths, natural and unnatural, all leading into the deep wood. Many strange things are seen and heard by the woodsmen; brave hearts and stout souls they have, to go there seeking fuel for the fires. I was born there, and lived much of my life among the shadows of the trees. Those shadows creep into your bones, even if you've no eyes to know light from dark."

Cindra and the others found themselves enthralled by the old woman's words. It was as if the hunched figure had suddenly come alive, invigorated by the presence of an audience. Her voice carried a cadence and inflection of a master storyteller, rising and falling with the mood she wove.

Nixy couldn't restrain himself anymore and asked, "How did you lose them? Your eyes, I mean."

The old woman turned towards his voice and seemed to examine him with her sunken eyelids. She spoke softly at first, "You are the one called Nix-yalder-thor, 'faerie-elder's gift' in the old tongue. You wish to know how I lost my eyes?" Then, she cackled, "First, I shall tell you how I found my sight!" Reaching into her robe, she flung a pinch of powder into the campfire, and the flame leaped up with a green flash, making her guests jump. Then she continued in a light, airy voice.

"Long, long ago, I was but a little girl, living safe within the walls of Gloamshire. The little hamlet on the road had stood long against the dark wood, and its people were stout and hardy. My mother had died bringing me into the world, and it's said that her dying wish was for her child to be blessed by the Lord of the Wood. My father, gods keep him, was a blacksmith; much admired was he, and his neighbors tolerated his wont to indulge his daughter in her silly adventures.

"I was an explorer as a girl, running and leaping rather than walking, and peeking under rocks and up the branches of trees, looking for new friends among the critters of the forest. I would find worms, bugs, field mice and bird nests, and take them home to show my father. He would laugh and pat my head with his calloused hand, calling me a scamp and a ninnyhammer, and so I was! Yet he loved me dearly, and would tell me stories about each little critter I brought home. Of course, this encouraged me to find ever more little friends."

The old woman's voice dropped ominously. "So it was that I found a lovely glade deep in the forest, in a place where folk knew not to tread. The sun shone warmly there, and little wildflowers grew all about. There were ruins there as well; old stones put upon stones, the folly of some long-forgotten people. I gathered flowers for my father, picking here and there..." She pantomimed plucking and smelling flowers, "But the prettiest buds grew within an elf circle." She paused, passing a blind gaze at the faces of her audience. "Know you what that is?" she asked.

Wenyssaya said, "It is what humans call a ring of mushrooms that grow about a spirit well. But my people do not-"

"Just so!" Maewyn interrupted, pointing in the elf maid's direction, "A circle of mushrooms, growing about a magical place. I was a fool to enter it, but the young are nothing if not fools. Enter it I did, and I picked the gold and violet flowers, and danced about as the sun sank and the lightning bugs came out to talk to the stars." She made little flicking motions with her fingers, mimicking the flash of fireflies. "Alas, I fell asleep within the circle, bewitched by its power. When I awoke, it was the next morning, or so I thought. Returning home with my flowers, I met a search party led by my poor frantic father, who ran to me and snatched me up, almost crushing me, he held me so tight!

"I had been gone many days, though to me it seemed but a brief time. The whole hamlet had turned out to seek for me, and all rejoiced as father brought me home, sounding his horn to signal the others. So glad was he that he forgot to punish me, and he cried when I gave him the flowers. I was happy to make him so cheerful, but terribly sorry that I had worried everyone so."

She sighed, turning her face up to the sky. "But there had been a change wrought about me, one that no one suspected. It was as if my mother's last wish had been granted. Blessed by the Lord of the Wood, or cursed? To this day, I know not which."

Her audience waited in anticipation as she prepared the rest of her tale. Drahn's scales had shifted to red.

"Later the next day, as I walked about the walls, I spied something... odd." She pointed off into the distance. "There, upon the top of the gate, I saw what seemed to be a bird." She tilted her head to and fro, as if examining the vision before her. "But it wasn't a bird. Nor was it a bug. No, this was a new critter, one I'd never seen before. It had a face like a child, and two big eyes that looked out at the hamlet. It had arms and legs, hands and feet, and a gossamer mane of hair. And wings! Bless me; the critter had wings like a bat that sprouted from its shoulders!

"He did not notice my attentions until I was standing beneath the gate, staring dumbly. When he noticed my gaze, he seemed... puzzled. He moved to the left, and my eyes followed. He moved to the right, and my eyes followed." She extended her arm, making her fingers into tiny legs that hopped back and forth. "When he was sure I could see him, he became all aflutter, and flapped off into the woods.

"I ran to tell my father all about this strange little critter, but alas, he did not believe me. Perhaps he didn't want to encourage me any longer, since I'd not learned the forest-sense I needed. Perhaps my tale was simply too wild to be believed. I did not know it at the time, but none had seen those critters in living memory, and they were only known in the old tales of the forest. *Nixominy* they were called in Old Norsican, but my people had forgotten many of the old names and stories. Ah, well." She shrugged, and fell silent, lowering her head.

The party grew restless, and Cindra wondered if she had fallen asleep. As she took a breath to speak, Maewyn raised her head and continued, "But later the next day, there was trouble. I had not known it, for children pay these things no mind, but the grownups had been sniffing out a thief among them. Someone was stealing little belongings from people's homes. For weeks it had been happening, but everyone thought the belongings had just been misplaced. No one suspected a thief, until the miller's coin purse was emptied one day, a few coins at a time.

"He could not account for it, but every time he looked within, there were a few less than before. 'Tis a thief, for certain!' he exclaimed, and demanded the culprit come forth. Others joined in, sure that their belongings had been stolen as well. We were a poor hamlet, but what few trade goods we could afford, we were right proud of. The miller and several folk roused the constable, and a search began of people's houses, looking for stolen goods." She shook her head. "Young I was, but I knew a bad thing when it happened. People were angry and afraid, and the searching became more careless and violent. I ran out of the cottage, looking for a place to hide. It was there, in the failing light, that I saw something I'll never forget for as long as I live."

She motioned about with outstretched arms and said, "The faerie critters were back in numbers. Nixominy were sitting all along the wall, and upon the rooftops, or perched in the branches of trees they were, watching and laughing with voices like chattering squirrels. They would flap about and laugh as the people tore apart their own homes, looking for a culprit. I saw a few of them fly into our cottage, carrying little sacks. I was too frightened to tell anyone what was happening around them, so I went back inside to see what they were about.

"But they were gone," she said, "and the noise of the searching got closer. My father came into the cottage to gather me up, and our neighbors began to turn out our house. Wouldn't you know it, but they found a stash of goods under my own bed! Ooooh, they were furious and cursed my father for raising a thief. He shouted back at them, saying there must be an explanation. I knew there was, of course, but no one would believe me. But I was scared and wanted the shouting to stop, so I told them all I knew!" Maewyn waved her hands to silence an imaginary crowd, crying in the tones of a child, "It was the little bat people! They're all about, laughing at us! It wasn't me, it wasn't meeee!" She trailed her words off into a pathetic wail.

"Of course, no one believed me," she sighed, "and they called me a liar as well as a thief. But it was my father they blamed, not me. Oh, the helplessness I felt, and the shame. The little creatures had decided to lay the blame at our family's feet, so we'd be banished or punished." She motioned to her missing eyes, "It was all because I could see them, I know it. They cared not as long as they were unseen, but I had threatened them with my new gift, my new curse. So my father and I were banished from the town. We gathered what belongings we could, and the next morning we set off down the northern road, leaving our home to its fate."

She let out a long sigh and stretched, arching and cracking her back and shoulders. She faced into the flames and said, "Well, that's the tale of how I gained my sight. But you asked how I lost it. That's another tale for another time; a time, I think, best spent indoors, not under the trees." She smiled and rose with some effort, and her granddaughter helped her towards the caravan. "Good afternoon," the old woman called, "Journey safely under the trees, and if you hear the chattering of squirrels... it's probably only squirrels. Probably."

She cackled again as she disappeared into the caravan, leaving her audience to chuckle nervously as they rose to leave.

Chapter Eight

Duplicitous

The morning after their exhausting evening in the catacombs and their enlightening chat by the fire, Ildric and Tavenji went under a cloudy sky to seek an audience with the count and the king. It was a desperate move, taking the little god along; Tavenji claimed he could spot a duplict, and Ildric didn't want to leave the mischief god alone in his tower. Emen, the reluctant leader of a pack of pickpockets, was more trustworthy. Ildric was able to find Tavenji a spare robe that fit, so they left his blood-stained motley behind. He even found a twin-tailed wizard cap that covered his overly-pointy ears.

"It's been ages since I met a mortal king," Tavenji said, as they waited in the palace anteroom with the other suppliants. "Is he an impressive king? Is he a figure of the noblest of mankind, lordly in stature and ancient in wisdom, with strength in one hand and fairness in the other? Or is he just a little fat little fellow on a purple cushion?"

This drew a sharp look from both Ildric and the nearest guard, but the wizard smiled and said, "My friend here is training at being a jester for the court. Pay him no mind, he means no ill," then to Tavenji he said, "Do not make me regret bringing you. This is a king at war. He will be in no mood for your foolery… my lord."

The little god mocked him behind his back, but made no more jokes. He'd been dead once already and didn't really like it.

They soon stood before the king and his war council, which included Count Casselvane and Field Marshal Valthór. Royal audiences had turned rather informal since the New Year, and Ildric felt as if he was interrupting a busy convention of scribes and cartographers. The air smelled of incense, pipe smoke, bacon, and ink.

The herald introduced them as, "Arch Mage Ildric Finnael, and his apprentice, Master Wryley."

"Ah, Arch Mage Finnael," said King Galen, "Count Corrina here tells me that I postpone an audience with you at my peril. Tell me, have you come with perilous news matching the morning's perilous weather?"

"I am afraid so, majesty," Ildric said, bowing, "And it is of a sensitive nature. I was hoping for a more discrete venue."

"You were right about his presumptions, count," the king said, "But then, he does have a reputation for being right most of the time."

"Thank you, majesty," Ildric said.

"You also have a reputation for being a meddler in the affairs of others," said the king, "Does this matter pertain to me personally, perchance?"

"It does not, majesty," Ildric said.

"Then my councilors may hear it also," he said, "Speak on."

Ildric nodded, sighed and said, "I believe your hostage, Grigor DeKenric, has in fact... escaped."

This halted the scribblings and shuffling of papers, and gained the attention of all. There were even some smiles and chuckles. Ildric ignored them.

"Has he indeed?" asked the king, "Guards," he said, "Go and check on our guest."

"That will not do, majesty," Ildric said quickly, "I believe he has been replaced by a duplict, a face-changer who can assume his identity almost perfectly. I do hope he is confined somewhere out of the way? Not roaming the grounds as we speak?"

"I do not invite him to listen in on my war plans, no," said the king, "A face-changer, you say? Like in the stories?"

"Most stories we tell children have their roots in the past, and are often more true than we dare realize," Ildric said, "I am of the mind that we make these things into children's tales to lessen the fear in our own hearts."

Valthór demanded, "Just when did this supposed escape take place?"

"My source tells me at the beginning of the year, at least."

"And we are hearing this only now?" Valthór asked.

Ildric wished he could take the man down a peg or two, but he said, "I only learned of it last night, field marshal."

"And just who," asked the king, "is this source?"

"He is a leader in the Circle of Gold, our local gang of thieves," he said, "They had a hand in it, so I hear. This face-changer is supposedly affiliated with them."

"How can we be certain this is true?" the field marshal asked, "Perhaps the Circle of Gold is having one over on you, and they want us to kill the real DeKenric boy?"

"I had thought of that," Ildric said, "and so I searched for Grigor DeKenric with the Eye of Omithys." He held up the silver hand. "I found him here, in this palace, and also caught glimpses of him somewhere in a forest, in the company of a Maanok. Both fit what I was told."

"A Maanok!" Valthór exclaimed, "Majesty, the delivery of books on the eve of the New Year!"

"The same," Ildric said, "The Maanok accompanied the duplict coming in, and Grigor DeKenric going out. The duplict took his place, and I fear for what he may try next; for though I know of his mission, I do not know his ultimate goals."

Count Casselvane leaned forward, "Arch mage, how do you advise we proceed?"

"I advise extreme caution," he said, "If he knows we suspect him, he could vanish into the nearest crowd."

Tavenji leaned in to whisper to Ildric; it seemed the little god was barely restraining himself; he was so tense, "Are you going to mention the you-know-what? The D-A-R-K-H-E-"

"Not yet," Ildric whispered, cutting him off, "We cannot be sure he has it."

"Alright... don't forget the P-L-A-N."

Ildric turned to the king and said, "My apprentice reminds me that there are a few individuals we must question first."

Grigor DeKenric was brought into the audience hall where the king and his ministers had been working. Most had been dismissed, leaving only the king, the field marshal, Count Corrina, Ildric, and Tavenji. There were guards also, several more than before, though they stood at a discreet distance.

"Ah, young Evenast," the king said, beckoning him forward, "I trust you are well?"

Grigor gave a congenial smile and said, "Well enough, majesty, by your good graces."

"Excellent," said the king, "If you don't mind, my friend Master Ildric here has a few questions for you."

"Oh?" said Grigor, eying the wizard and his apprentice.

"It is not serious," Ildric said, coming forward, "but it could be important. Tell me, young Grigor, can you think of all the people who have visited you in your tower in the past few months? Since, say, before the New Year?

As Ildric stood before him, and his strange apprentice circled about like a man studying a sculpture, Grigor said, "Let's see... there are the two guards that bring my food every day and night, there is the healer that checks in on me every few days; there is Sir Rynard DeVine, my father's envoy; there were the two manservants who come each week... I had a book delivery sent by Sir Rynard; there were two of them, a Maanok strong-back and another one, smaller, about my height, with an unfortunate facial tumor or something. Poor fellow."

Most descriptive of the part he played, Ildric thought. "And no one else?"

Grigor appeared to think for a moment, glanced at the circling apprentice, and said, "No. No one."

"What about outside on your strolls?" Ildric asked, "Anyone of note you met with?"

"Well... Oh! I ran into Dillan DePort! Or rather, as it turns out, milord count's daughter, Lady Cindra. That was in the training hall." He smiled at the count. "She's an amazing woman, my lord," he said.

The count did not return the smile.

Ildric looked at Tavenji, who gave a little nod. The wizard, in turn, nodded to the king, who motioned to his guards. They closed immediately, pole arms leveled at the young man. Ildric and Tavenji backed out of the circle.

"What is the meaning of this?" Grigor cried, "Majesty, the ransom! There are rules..."

"Rules that only apply to noble prisoners, not to spies," said the king, "Arch mage, your findings?"

Ildric leaned on his staff and proclaimed, "Lie by omission. The guards we spoke to both claim that Grigor DeKenric met with Gavadaire LuVestra on two occasions, once in the training hall with Lady Cindra, and later that night in the prisoner's tower."

"Yes!" Grigor pleaded, "Yes, that's true! Forgive me but I had forgotten master LuVestra."

"Forgotten your former instructor, whom you invited to your room on the Long Night? I think not," Ildric said.

Grigor replied, "I did not want to be indiscreet, for it was a... a private matter." He squirmed a bit, looking guilty.

Ildric scoffed, "Private matter indeed! What private matter could you have, I wonder? Should I pry with my little eye?" He raised his silver hand, leveling the Eye at Grigor. The boy seemed unfazed; a most unusual reaction.

"No need," he said, "I'll tell you. I wanted him to deliver a message for me."

Valthór surged forward, "A message! You sent a secret message?"

"Deliver it to whom?" the wizard demanded. *Could it be? Would he have given the Dark Heart to an unwitting courier?*

"I cannot say," Grigor replied defiantly, "I swore an oath of secrecy. If you want to know, you can *try* to use your divination magic to find it."

This gave Ildric pause. *He is goading me. It **must** be the Dark Heart; he knows it would drive me mad if that is indeed what LuVestra carries.*

Valthór was incensed, saying, "We don't need a wizard to get information out of you! This violates your promise, so you are no longer protected by the rules of ransom."

"Torture me if you like," Grigor said defiantly, "My father will go to war when he learns you have done so, and this will all have been for nothing!"

Ildric shouted, "You think we are fools? No, you try to lead us into the weeds, but your secret is out!" He turned to his apprentice, "Wryley?"

"Duplict," Tavenji declared, "A damned good one too. Very few tells, but they're there. I'll stake my reputation as a 'clever boots' on it."

"What in the name of the Abyss is a duplict?" Grigor cried, starting to panic, "And who is this... this *person* that condemns me so?"

Tavenji leaned in close and removed his cap, showing his overlong pointed ears and pale mane. "Just a divine messenger, passing through," he said softly.

Grigor was dumbstruck. His eyes were wide with shock, and his lips formed a silent word: *Impossible*.

"Show us your true face, lest I find a way to break your concentration," Ildric said, raising his staff menacingly.

Grigor closed his eyes, sighed heavily, and relaxed his muscles. His face shifted, his height increased, and his body mass seemed to deflate, making his clothing hang loosely. His features became a mixture of expressions, shifting from surprise in one eye to anger in the other; from a sly smile on one corner of his mouth to down-turned disappointment on the other. His eyes were even two different colors, and the end of one eyebrow tweaked upward strangely. His hair color shifted to a mused reddish tangle. His hands became animated with nervous energy, twitching about and fidgeting.

The guards gasped and the king made a muffled curse. Even Ildric had to admit the change was unsettling.

"Twist, I presume," the wizard said.

The thin man pointed and addressed Tavenji, "You cannot be here! How are you possible?"

"I ask myself that all the time," the little god quipped.

His mismatched eyes returned to the spear points surrounding him and the angry lords before him. He asked in an odd, singsong voice, "So who did you get to? Not Sir Rynard the Fool. The Maanok? No! The dwarf!" He acted like it was a guessing game at a party.

Count Casselvane, overcoming his shock at the transformation, said, "Just what did you want with my daughter and LuVestra?"

"Your daughter, the *other* shape changer? Ha! Nothing," Twist said, "I needed a favor from LuVestra, not his cross-dressing pupil."

"What favor?" the king demanded.

Twist gave them half a grin and said to the wizard, "I needed him to deliver something to the half-elf scion before he departed; something to give his deathless father..."

This gave Ildric a chill, but he saw Tavenji shake his head. "Unlikely," said the little god, "The Shadow Lord would sense it coming the moment it entered his forest."

"Sense what?" asked Valthór, confused.

"And he's assuming we don't know the *secret* prophecy," Tavenji said, poking Twist's nose to emphasize each word, *"But we do!"*

"What prophecy?" Valthór demanded.

Ildric asked, "Where is Gavadaire LuVestra now, majesty?"

"He has left for home by sea this morning, back to the Su'Kraal monastery in Aurilon."

"Su'Kraal!" Ildric cried, "Of course! It's not just a name for a monastic order, they are literally-"

"Sons of Kraal!" Tavenji said, leaping about, "Right in front of our noses!"

"The Dark Heart!" Ildric explained, "Majesty, LuVestra is the scion foretold! He has the Dark Heart! We are-"

"Too late," Twist said, "Pity, it was such a lovely world. Hate to see it go."

Ildric took a deep breath and declared, "I think we have learned all we can from this creature, majesty. Letting it live would be too great a risk."

"So be it," said the king. He motioned again.

Ildric kept his back turned to the sight.

Valthór cried, "Execute!" and the men thrust their weapons into the thin, twisting frame, skewering him with a dozen spear points. Blood spilled upon the tiles as the duplict slumped to the floor, kneeling upright until the guards withdrew their pole arms. The life went out of his mismatched eyes and his limbs were finally still.

Tavenji sang, "The scheming duplict met with woe; the seeds of doom, the spears did sow, and lo! A dozen blooms did grow!"

The men just stared at him.

"Too soon?"

"*Who is this person*, arch mage?" the king demanded.

Ildric sighed, leaning on his staff, "That is a strange tale for another day, your majesty; right now, we have a world to try and save. By the way, I have some news about a very wealthy local merchant named Kobus DuChat..."

Chapter Nine

Slipping Away

It had been nearly a month since Grigor Evenast, heir DeKenric, was rescued from the king's Winter Palace; Braeden Khrim and his charge were only now departing on what would be a journey of over 280 miles, following the road around the Cassel Range to Kenric Castle. The time spent in Portshia's Outwalls had been nerve wracking and tense, but necessary. If the face-changer Twist had been discovered, Khrim and Grigor could easily be taken alone on the road, but in a group there was some measure of safety. While Khrim could do little to disguise himself, he could make Grigor blend in with other *swierdi* merchants easily.

"We are not exactly inconspicuous," Grigor said as they walked with the last caravan leaving the city, "Tell me again why Duke Wolvert sent a Maanok to rescue me, and not one of his own spies?"

"Firstly," Khrim said, leading his laden mule, "he now styles himself King Manon I. Second, I *am* one of his own spies; third, I am his spy master, and a *Baedoch Khoom* warlock besides. If my appearance is conspicuous, then treat me as a servant. Surely that will come easily?"

"We don't have any Maanok servants in Kenric," Grigor said, "My father doesn't trust them."

"This I know," Khrim said, "What of you? Do you trust me?"

"Not sure yet," Grigor said.

"You must," Khrim said simply, "There is little other choice."

On the morning of the 31st of Aramoth, a group of forty or so merchants and mercenary guards walked or rode past the outlying soldier encampments, looking into the grim faces that would soon be off to war. It was a war the merchants wished to get ahead of, hoping to either return to their homes in the east, or make a last minute profit from their cousins in the Dissenter lands before they fell into chaos.

Braeden Khrim stood a head above the tallest of them, and his copper skin, thick graying hair, and tattooed face made him rather distinctive. He was dressed in the warm woolen clothing of his people, decorated with their patterns. Grigor wore winter clothing that was fashionable in Portshia several years ago, courtesy of the Circle of Gold, who were their hosts for the month. The lad pulled up the hood of his cloak and took a last look at the city walls and the white tower spires of the palace that had been his prison.

After three days of crowding into tea houses or barns, the company reached its first settlement with a proper inn. The Inn at Silverbottom was not large or of high quality, but this night it was full to capacity, even serving guests that had been unable to secure space on the common room floor. Khrim and Grigor were among the half of travelers forced to camp outside the establishment, waiting in line for food from the bustling kitchen.

Silverbottom was once a busy mining village, but had decayed into little more than a way station. Still, it was a notable stop on their trip. Khrim estimated another four days to reach Syngmore at this pace. It was slow going because the journey inland gained altitude from sea level at Portshia to the upper foothills of the Cassel Range. Khrim did not find it overly taxing, but Grigor and his merchant companions were weaker. *Swierdi*, he thought, *I must have patience.*

Grigor was saying, "It's just a day's hike up the Silver Pass to the gate, and on across the mountain valley to Iron Gate. Sure you don't want to make for it?"

"I am sure," Khrim said, "It will be strongly fortified now, and they may detain us or worse, arrest us as spies."

"I suppose," Grigor said. His spirits were far from lifted.

Khrim could not blame him for his mood. He was far from safe, far from home, and his freedom would mean his father's lands would be the bulwark against invasion, rather than forced into an uneasy truce. Assuming, that is, that he made it home safely.

As they ate in relative privacy, Grigor struck up conversation. "So what's your story?" he asked, "How did you come to serve Wolvert?" They had spent the month in Portshia separately to avoid capture and suspicion, so his curiosity was understandable.

Khrim replied, "I heard of troubles in the west, beyond the Gartethan Mountains that shield Calilon from my people. I came to see if I could help."

"Why would a Maanok want to help us fix our troubles?" Grigor asked skeptically.

"Fix?" was all that Khrim said.

The journey north along the Casselvane Road was not difficult, but he was surrounded by tired, complaining *swierdi*. Their weakness and misery was rubbing off on him. He had the fleeting wish that he could strangle them all in their sleep and move off without them, but he suppressed that violent fantasy. He might have been able to do it, but it would be difficult, taxing, and ultimately defeat the purpose of waiting. Reasoning calmed the beast within, and he regained his inner peace.

Khrim rubbed at the skin under his *vaynbraas*, the blood wood bracelet that served as a discrete verge; a human's key to wielding magic. He always did so after imagining unleashing his powers. The verge was impossible to remove and became irritating at times; some warlocks wore them on the ankle or upper arm, others used finger rings or ear piercings, and some even wore them around their nether-members. Not even other warlocks trusted those fools; what a magical backlash would feel like through one's privates, he could only guess at.

Grigor had been trying to get information out of him, having been away from home for so long. "What has Manon Wolvert got planned if they besiege my father's castle once I am safely home?" he asked.

"You ask me King Manon's plans?" Khrim replied, "Is it wise that you know this?"

"I want to know if he intends to raise a siege if King Galen's army marches on my home," said the young lord, "Or does he plan to let them wear themselves out while we starve?"

Khrim said, "The southeastern lords must aid Kenric. If Wolvert moves to break a siege on Kenric lands, he risks being flanked by the northern army of the Cordobal king."

"There's a northern army?" Grigor said, surprised, "How big?"

"Big enough," Khrim said, "Although they are stripped of many of their lords and commanders."

"How did that happen?" Grigor asked.

"I made it happen," Khrim said, "I sent assassins to stake out the road, taking positions along its length.

Most of the lords leading their forces were killed before they knew they were under attack."

Grigor looked stunned at the admission. "That's horrible! What happened to dying with honor on the field?"

"Death is death," Khrim said, adjusting the braided leather band coiled about his other wrist, "Let them find honor on Balkon's Field."

They arrived in Syngmore on the 6th of Selvimoth, just ahead of a late winter storm; a good five weeks after escaping the Winter Palace in Portshia. The temperature had dropped sharply at night the last two days on the road, and all were looking forward to a warm fire and a hot meal. Snow fell in large flakes, covering the ground and the tops of heads as the merchant caravan made it through the gates of the city. Khrim studied the defenses as they passed from ward to ward, his eyes lingering on the tall castle on the hilltop and the blue and gold banners flying in the flurry of white.

The smells of so many people and industry assaulted his nostrils, and he immediately found himself wishing for the open road and a lonely campfire. Khrim's people were not so barbaric as to crowd together in their own filth, but it seemed to be the way of the 'civilized' world. *They can keep their civilization*, he thought.

They eventually came to a tavern in the second ward called the Lonely Badger, where the owner, a short, stocky man called 'Badger,' welcomed them into his house, not batting an eye at the large, grim Maanok hauling a clanking sack. *It is the mark of a true host*, Khrim thought, *not showing fear*.

"Welcome, welcome, friends!" Badger said in a confident middle tone, "Take any seat you like, so long as no one is sitting there already!" he laughed and spread his arms wide.

"Thank you," Khrim said in his accented baritone. He hoped he would not have to kill this *swierdi*; he seemed a decent sort.

They took a spot in the back corner of the tavern, not close enough to the fire pit to be comfortably warm, but allowing them to see the entire room at a glance.

"What I don't like," Grigor said as the serving wench brought their drinks, "is how Wolvert went and declared himself king. My father had dreams of self-rule, not bowing to another damned king."

"Yes, he was not pleased," Khrim agreed.

"But Wolvert still wants us to fight for him," Grigor said, "Let the two kings battle it out if they like. Why should House Evenast throw in our lot with him?"

"Your father threw in his lot with the Dissenters," Khrim reminded him, "It matters little whom he backs now. King Galen will not allow any vassal to declare domain over the king's lands."

"You may be right, but- oh gods!" Grigor's voice hushed low, "It's Corrina!"

"What?" Khrim scanned the room for a lordly-looking older man. "Where?"

"There, just coming in with his friends," Grigor said, "Gaius Corrina, the next Baron Syngmore. We were team mates at the fighting school together."

Worse, Khrim thought, *Much worse.*

He moved his chair so his back faced the young men. However, the group headed for a table a bit too close to Khrim and Grigor; so close that they could hear the conversation.

"So," said one young man, "the Big Cat plans to ride with his army to Syngmore and stay here, while your father takes charge of his forces?"

"That's the plan," Gaius said, "He'll be bringing a small force to supplement our garrison, and manage the defenses."

"But he's not an old man," another lad said, "Why won't he lead his men into battle?"

"Bad back," Gaius said, and there was a bit of laughter, "No, I'm serious! He was injured in combat in Maylione way back in the elder days, back when elves rode around on dragons."

There was more laughter after that. "Elves on dragons, I love it!" said a third lad, clapping in appreciation.

Khrim motioned to Grigor to leave, and the two rose to make their way past the table. Grigor turned away so they wouldn't see his face, and Khrim swung the sack of pewter noisily to his shoulder, cranking up his accent to the barely-intelligible point.

"Hez bettah gowan jeck de mool, makeshoor iz zafe," he boomed to Grigor's back. All eyes turned to the towering muscular figure cutting through the room like a bear through the daisies, and ignored Grigor. The two left through the front and hurried to the stables.

"What do we do now?" Grigor demanded, "He knows I was arrested and held ransom!"

"He did not see," Khrim said, "So we buy a horse and ride away tonight."

"But it's snowing tonight!" Grigor said.

Khrim grimaced at him, "You think you would be warmer in the Winter Palace in Portshia? The Evenast motto is 'Veins of Iron,' is it not?"

"Even iron gets brittle in the cold," Grigor muttered, "Where do we get a horse?"

"We are in a stable," Khrim said, "Pick one."

"Steal one?" he asked.

"Pay for it," Khrim said, hefting the bag of wares, "There is gold in the bag as well, more than enough for one horse."

"Fine," Grigor said, moving towards a decent charger that could carry the both of them.

"Hey there!" came a voice from the stable door.

They spun, finding the Corrina boy and his three friends looking in on them.

"I knew they was up to no good," said one.

"That's the master's horse," said another, "Sir Gaius Corrina, next baron o' the north lands!"

"Wait," Gaius said, motioning to Grigor, "DeKenric is it? Grigor DeKenric of House Evenast? Is that you?" He smiled, "When did they let you out?"

"You know these two, Sir Gaius?" asked one lad.

"I know *him*," Gaius said, "We were 'Ice Drakes' together at school! As I live and breathe..." He strode towards Grigor, smiling and extending his hand.

Khrim extended his own hand, pointing his fingers at Gaius Corrina's throat. A length of braided leather uncoiled from his wrist and lashed around the young man's neck, tightening instantly. Gaius choked and grasped at the cord, his face turning purple.

"What? No!" shouted Grigor, but Khrim was already selecting another target. The last coil of leather leaped off his wrist towards the neck of one of the other lads, who stumbled back, gasping for air.

"What are you doing?" Grigor screamed.

Khrim moved like a flash to the two remaining lads, who were trying to help their friends. He dropped the sack and drew a knife from his thick leather belt, quickly slashing their throats. Leaving Gaius and the other lad to choke to death, he grabbed Grigor and pushed him towards the waiting horses.

"Ride!" Khrim commanded, "Ride until it drops from under you!"

Grigor did as he was told, and as he steered his stolen mount towards the stable door, he saw that young Gaius Corrina had stopped struggling.

The cold air and falling snow made for a difficult ride northeast along the Casselvane Road, but they made good time. The horses, with bodies lathering and blood mixing with mucus and saliva, began to slow and falter and no amount of whipping would goad them any further. First Khrim's horse collapsed, then when Grigor stopped to wait for him, his horse lost its feet as well.

Now on foot, Khrim led him into the woods. "Follow me and step in my path," he said. He stretched out his hand, chanted a phrase in some unknown tongue, and began walking into the snow-covered woods. Grigor looked down to follow his tracks and saw that he had left none; he was simply walking atop the snow.

"Why did you have to kill them?" Grigor asked, most of his fury beaten out by the hard ride, "He was one of the few who treated me like a comrade at that damned school!"

"What answer did you have for his question?" Khrim asked, "He asked when they let you out! Did you have an answer?"

"Any lie would have done," Grigor said, his anger building again.

Khrim snorted, "You think he would not mention this meeting to his father the baron, who would know better? If you wish to make it home, you must do what you must do. Now let me concentrate so we leave no tracks from the dead horses."

The next two days were another trial for Grigor, and his whinging was grating on Khrim's nerves. Hunger, exhaustion, and scratching for every meal were not uncommon for Khrim, but for a lord's son, it was torture. Khrim was weighing the benefits of leaving him to die in the woods against the drawback of having to tell his father. *Someone else can tell his father,* he reasoned.

Grigor, for his part, was at his limits with his rescuer. He held neither authority nor power over the towering barbarian warlock, and had not the strength or weapons to threaten him in any way. Besides, Khrim had unknown magic. All the lad had left was whinging.

Khrim was leading them across the foothills of the Cassel Range, cutting about sixty-five miles off of their journey as the crow flies. Yet, they were not crows; the shortcut would prevent an easy pursuit, but the going was rough. With luck and a bit of wilderness lore, they would come out near the Kenric Province town of Odex, and from there, a hot meal and three days ride to the city of Kenric, seat of House Evenast.

But it seemed that Grigor could not see the end of his hardships. Khrim decided he would let the boy have his last bout of complaining before explaining things to him.

"We're lost, aren't we?" he was saying as they forded a stream in a shallow gully. "Do you have any idea where we're going?"

"Of course," Khrim said, "You are going home."

"East, maybe, or east-ish, but not home," he moaned, "We could be stuck in a crevasse tomorrow, or hit a ridge and have to walk north to the road again. Didn't you think if the way was easier, they would have simply built the road through here?"

Khrim didn't answer.

"It's been two days since we rode those poor horses to death, and you can't say how much longer we'll be walking. Had we taken care of them, we might have been half-way home by now! But no, 'ride until it drops from under you,' you said."

I will have to be convincing, Khrim thought, *Perhaps a mage glamour? It impresses the common folk, but...*

"Bloody lost now, we are," Grigor said, "Wandering the wilderness like a pair of monks on a mushroom vision..."

"All that matters," Khrim said, "is that the king does not have you." *Perhaps a beast glamour*, he decided.

"All that matters to you, maybe," Grigor said, "I'd like to see my parents again, and my home, and-"

"No," Khrim said, and his voice boomed with the low rumbling of a forest predator, his eyes became yellow like a wolf's, and his countenance turned dark and savage, "You didn't hear me. *All* that matters is that the king doesn't have you. I could send you in pieces to your father, and it would still serve our cause." And with a rumbling growl, he turned, climbed the embankment, and dissolved the glamour.

Grigor did not speak for the rest of the journey.

Chapter Ten

Squaring the Circle

Emen was not sitting idle in the Tower of Sight. The morning after their revealing chat, he awoke with a hangover and memories of strange dreams. He had seen parts of his life, past, present, and perhaps even future. Whether it was because of his predicament, or some properties of the wizard's tower, he could not say. Regardless, it disturbed and motivated him.

That morning, after the wizard and the god had departed to see the king, Emen cleaned himself up and left the tower, hoping the door had the sense to lock itself after him. Clouds had covered the sky, obscuring most of the sunlight.

A gloomy day. How fitting.

He headed immediately to the Warren, for the place would be abuzz and that would be where all the gossip was. Also, the catacombs had many more places to hide for one of his stature.

The children were all glad to see him, for many had been up all night talking about the wizard and the odd man who claimed to be sent from the gods, and the Boss who had betrayed them all. Many wanted Emen to explain things further, which he was not willing to do. He had already explained too much for one night.

"What are we gonna do now, Silverboss?" was the most frequent question.

Emen had no answer yet. "I am working on it," was all he could say, which was not very reassuring.

He worried for the orphan children because of the older lads who had been in the room last night; he worried that they would take the news badly, believing it was Emen who was betraying the Boss, not the other way around. He was worried they might be planning his removal from power in the most heinous way possible.

The fact that Daymi and Cricket were not here made him worry more. The pair had always been trouble.

He went into his parlor and began writing letters. His plan was absurd and deadly dangerous, but if he was ever going to get ahead of this, he had to act fast. He made five copies, one for each district boss, and sealed them with discreet markings in the hot wax, addressing them with the Circle's courier code. He then summoned five of his best runners to deliver them.

Finally, he made arrangements for someone to care for his birds if he did not return.

He spent the next three hours above ground, strolling the busy city streets in full view of guards, soldiers, and anyone with eyes. He avoided alleys and empty courtyards, and took the opportunity to do a little breakfast shopping in the Market Square. He did anything he could to avoid getting snatched off the streets and having his throat slit in some dark alcove. He knew his amulet that protected him from magical eyes meant little, for the Circle had real eyes everywhere. He had no doubt he was being watched the whole time.

When the hour approached, Emen made for the Rolling Fates gambling house, hoping and praying to Obamir that his luck would hold out and the other district bosses had arrived. If not, he would be in the house alone with Garreth and his personal gang of enforcers, and he was pretty sure they wouldn't be entirely on his side.

Sure enough, as he passed the entrance of the closed gambling house and headed around the side, he saw people shifting and following out of the corner of his eye. When he reached the side alley entrance, he was already surrounded.

"Lost, Silverboss?" asked a rough, heavy man in his thirties. Emen knew him only as The Sapper.

"Not at all," Emen said, "Have the other bosses arrived yet?"

"You know about their little gathering?" he asked, surprised.

"I *called* it," Emen said sharply. Now was not the time to lose his authority. His own men thought the others were here to discuss *him*.

The men looked at each other for a moment, and thankfully stood aside to let him in. Emen let out a huge sigh of relief, playing it like a snort of frustration. *So they **do** all know about last night, or at least a version of it. So much for 'eyes open, mouths closed.'*

He entered the empty hall, usually bustling with the chatter of gamblers and the rolling of dice, so busy and vital and legal, so long as the government got their cut. But the underbelly was there to see if one only looked. Right now that underbelly was looking at him from a private table in the corner.

Though he had lived with the reality of this criminal gang most of his life, never did he fear it more than when he attended these little meetings. These were not the desperate, hungry, and violent offenders that ruled the streets; no, these were the people who ruled *them*.

He was one of them now, which made him deeply uncomfortable, and had from the very start. They were business people, people of business. So upright-sounding, so respectable; except their business was fear, crime, and death.

The other five district bosses were dressed for the over-world, sitting around a table with two personal bodyguards behind each chair. Even in broad daylight, there was no trust among thieves, for many of them had once been rivals before the Boss united them. *And I am here to tell them the Boss has betrayed us all*, Emen thought. He strode over and took a seat; his only protection was the back of his chair.

He looked around at the faces of his 'colleagues,' trying to gauge their moods. There was Kaplin Jeorthea, who always seemed to have a scowl for his comrades, and today was no exception. He was the oldest and roughest of the gathering, having made his way up from the bottom, and once ruling half the city as the leader of the Blood Circle gang. He had lived to see his rivals in the Golden Hammer gang become his partners, dying not of violence, but old age. His mistrust and desire to outlive all of his rivals no doubt extended to his current crime family.

Taymen Blackburn was boss of the High Court gang, formerly the Velvet Gloves, and the youngest member of their brotherhood. He had inherited his position from his father, who sold illicit and expensive goods and services to the wealthiest members of society. He was dressed elegantly, in a dyed leather jacket and silk shirt. He watched Emen approach with great interest.

Next to him sat Mag LuMorgain, a rough and hard woman that was supposed to have been a beauty in her day, though a lifetime of smoking, drinking, and shouting had done that in. She ran the Temple district, with its several discreet whorehouses and dens of intoxication. Her business was refined debauchery, and she took pride in it. Her clothing bordered on elegant and gaudy, with a bit too much gold thread and embroidery. A wreath of pungent smoke clung to her head, issuing from a thin-stemmed pipe with a tiny bowl. She peered at the dwarf with disapproving eyes.

Falnur Dunmorrow was a dockmaster by trade and roughneck by tradition. He had inherited the territories of his ancestors in the Golden Hammer gang, mainly the docks and the people who made a living from them. He looked like a poor strong-back, but was as wealthy as any of them. He was dressed in worn leather and linen, and his face was tan and weather-etched.

Lastly there was Elmir DiCassel, the Copper District boss. He was an older and thinner man with a distinguished air and a stiff beard; his face was unreadable, as usual. He was dressed in the robes of a scribe or scholar, which was his legitimate profession. It was said he had some of the Order of Astrellaris among his clients.

None of them had a kind eye for Emen.

"What is the meaning of this, Silverthumb?" Mag asked gruffly, "Why the urgent summons, and where is the Boss?"

"Aye," Falnur said, "Can't it be held in the normal place neither?"

"I've heard," said Elmir, "that you've been in contact with Talon Finnael."

"Yes, yes," Emen said, "it's true. I am sure you all heard some version of the story by now, thanks to my loose-lipped henchmen."

"Loyal henchmen," Kaplin growled, "Loyal to the Circle."

Never 'Circle of Gold' with him, Emen thought, *He still has the Blood Circle in his heart.*

"What is the Circle of Gold, hmmm?" Emen asked, "An affiliation of several gangs, each with their own interests, and each vowing to work together." He had rehearsed this bit in his head the last three hours, and hoped it sounded as good to them as it did to him. "What binds us is not only a mutual loyalty, but a respect for one another's boundaries and territory. We don't poach. My pickpockets don't work the Gates District, and Kaplin's brutes don't extort the Silver District merchants. Everyone keeps to their own little patch.

"Except we are all united by the Boss, who makes sure it all works together seamlessly," he said, "But now, now he wants us to undo it all for some grand scheme, some pipe dream that throws everything into chaos. Why?"

"We've debated this in council before, Emen," said Taymen, "We all brought up our misgivings then, and in the end we all agreed."

"Because we didn't have all the facts," Emen said, "Certain things have come to light that throws *everything* into doubt!"

Kaplin said, "None of that excuses your collaboration with the count's pet diviner. The Talon could sniff us all out, or maybe he has already!"

"Think," Emen said, "If that were true, he would not have stumbled upon me last night. We all wear these amulets that keep us safe from scying eyes. He was looking for someone *else* and it led to my door."

"Looking for whom?" Mag asked.

Emen paused, not liking this part of his prepared speech. "Looking for a *very* important individual."

"Who?" asked Kaplin.

"You wouldn't believe me if I told you," Emen said.

"*Try us*," Mag growled.

He sighed and said, "A fallen god."

"Bollocks!"

Emen shrugged. "Told you," he said, as laughter erupted around the table.

But Kaplin was not so easily amused. "And you believed this? He told you some faerie story and you bought it all?"

"It was proved to me, rather dramatically," Emen said. He related the tale of leading Ildric to the hidden body, capturing him, and having the tables turned.

Then he went on to describe Tavenji's resurrection in detail.

"Why didn't you just vanish the wizard when you had the chance?" Kaplin asked.

It was Elmir that answered, "One does not 'just vanish' an arch mage. If anyone suspected we were behind it, there would be a blood bath."

"My thoughts exactly," Emen said.

"Alright," said Mag, "so what accord did you reach with this damned wizard and the... the patron god of thieves?" She couldn't say it with a straight face.

"It involves Boss DuChat," Emen said, "Our revived divine friend told us that the Boss wasn't using some face-changing glamour; he is an actual duplict, a fiend of chaos. More, he's a high priest of Llomaak. DuChat admitted this to him."

"There are no priests of Llomaak," Elmir said, "They were all wiped out ages ago."

"The same was said of duplicts," said Taymen, "They were supposed to be ancient history too, until we learned of Twist, and now the Boss."

Mag said, "It was bad enough knowing he kept one of those creatures on a leash, but seeing his face change that day, that gave me the shivers."

"Are you listening to yerselves?" Kaplin barked, slapping the table, "This little shit went and turned on the Boss and the Circle, *admitted to it,* and we're entertaining his nonsense? True or not, there's such a thing as loyalty to the guild and punishment for betrayal. I say we vote whether or not to bleed him in the cellar right now!"

"I vote we don't!" Emen said, "Not until he's had his say!"

"Go ahead then," Elmir said, ever the scholar, "I want to hear more."

"The Llomaakittes are after only one thing," Emen said, "the end of the world. The Time of Chaos was their doing, and this time it is all or nothing. According to Tavenji and Ildric Finnael, they are very close to making it happen. I submit to you that the Boss's grand plan is nothing more than an effort to create chaos in the city. He is also interested in making this war happen. More chaos! It all fits his twisted ideology. None of what he promised us is going to come to pass!"

This gave everyone pause, and they exchanged worried looks. Even some of the bodyguards shifted uncomfortably. Thunder rumbled in the distance, shaking the high windows.

"Supposing you're right," said Falnur, "Supposing the god of thieves is actually here, working with the Talon to save the world... what're *we* supposed to do about it?"

"Do what you've always done," Emen said, "Work for your own best interests. Assume nothing the Boss says is true, and work against his grand plan. Maintain order and the status quo."

"So who rules the Circle, if not the Boss?" Kaplin asked.

Here we go, Emen thought, *Who rules...*

Taymen said, "No one rules until his power is neutralized. The Boss has enforcers that shouldn't be trifled with."

"*Had,*" said Mag, "Dexer was his main blade, and he hasn't been seen in over a year. Probably dead."

"Dexer was bad," said Elmir, "but Twist is worse. He can look like anyone."

"Twist has been gone since the New Year," said Falnur, "He's on some mission regarding the DeKenric boy, isn't he?"

Emen decided to be as honest as necessary. "Twist is impersonating Grigor DeKenric. He might return if he keeps his wits about him and doesn't get caught."

Probably dead by now, thanks to me. Oh well.

Kaplin said, "The Boss surely has more loyal men of his own."

"Spies too, no doubt. He's a wily one."

"We've got to pool our resources, raise a bunch o' head-busters to defend our interests."

"I defend my own interests!"

The conversation devolved into bickering and Emen hung his head. He knew this wasn't going to be easy, but getting these bosses to work together was like herding cats. Everyone wanted to avoid naming a new boss, but all Emen wanted was to keep his orphans out of any fighting. He sighed and let his eyes wander.

One of Kaplin's bodyguards was fidgeting with the hilt of his short sword, tapping his fingers on the pommel.

Not good when the bodyguards are getting restless, Emen thought, *Maybe I should start planning my escape. Ha! I should have done that before arriving.*

He glanced around a bit more, trying to gauge the room. There were a few doors, but the side passage was guarded inside and out by the Silver Gang; the cellar door, the closest, was blocked by Garreth and a few of his boys. They were technically Emen's men, but he trusted none of them with his life. No one had moved to watch his back, and they probably all thought of him as a traitor. He felt wretched and alone.

Thunder struck again, and the patter of rain struck the rooftop.

"What if the Boss decides to go on the offensive?" Taymen asked, "Do we really want to fight a war of assassins?"

Kaplin said, "If DuChat wants to wreck everything we worked for over some religious idiocy, I'll personally send him to his chaos god."

So Kaplin will position himself to lead after all, Emen thought, *I saw that coming.*

Then he saw another bodyguard tapping his pommel. And another.

Wait... is that some kind of code? Oh no...

Half of the bodyguards drew their swords and thrust them into the vitals of their partners, spilling gore onto the polished tiles before their victims could draw weapons.

Gods!

As half of their protectors killed the other half, the bosses panicked. Hidden daggers were pulled from sleeves and ankle sheaths, but it was too late. Their bodyguards lunged in, slicing, hacking, and stabbing their employers, painting the tabletop with sprays of crimson. One man shouted, "*Mash bah havaath!*" as he slashed Kaplin's throat down to the bone.

Emen pushed his chair back frantically, tipping and tumbling head over heels to the floor. As he gained his feet, he saw the legs of the dying bosses under the table, thrashing and kicking helplessly, trying to run even as they were impaled again and again. Someone's bowels released and the stink of shit mixed with the sickly, metallic reek of blood.

Merciful Mother!

His heart was pounding as he ran for the back hallway leading to the cellar door. One of the assassins saw him and slashed wildly, his blade biting Emen's arm below the shoulder. The pain was intense and the dwarf stumbled into the wall, recovered, and bolted down the hallway, hearing boots coming from behind. Ahead of him was Garreth and two of his men, moving towards him. Their eyes met, and Emen could tell the men were in shock. They drew their weapons.

Will he let me pass? Please let me pass!

There was shouting around the gambling hall as the Silver Gang reacted, almost in slow motion, like they were waking from a dream into a living nightmare.

Emen reached the men guarding the cellar door, half expecting to get cut down then and there. Instead, Garreth grabbed him by the hair and forced the dwarf behind him.

"Run for it, Silverboss!" he shouted. Garreth and his men closed ranks, forming a human wall between Emen and the oncoming killers.

"Gods keep you!" Emen said in a trembling voice. He fumbled with the latch, dashed inside, and locked the door behind him, panting as he leaned against the heavy wood.

He was atop the cellar stairs with little more than a lamp to see by. The sounds of fighting came muffled through the door, and something thumped into it hard, jarring his back. It seemed the space of three gulping breaths was all the rest he was going to get. Taking the lamp off its hook, he made his way into the darkness.

I wish I had a glowstone, he thought, *I can't run for long with this damned lamp.*

The door latch rattled and the wood buckled as the assassins tried to get in.

He went to the back of the room and moved a packing crate towards the shelf against the wall, climbed it, and stretched for the false pottery jug that activated the mechanism. He cursed his height, as well as the builders who designed the hidden door. *Tall bastards!*

The false wall slid open, leading to another storage room under a different building. Shutting the way behind him, he was now faced with a difficult decision. *They could be down here at any moment,* he thought, *I assume they know all the secret doors. I can go up the stairs to the house above, or make for the Warren in the tunnels.*

Warmth trickled down his arm and the pain began to throb, reminding him he was injured. His sleeve was bloodied and he winced at the gash in his flesh. It made him feel woozy, but he refused to be captured because he had fainted at the sight of his own blood.

His mind was racing, his heart was pounding, and he was gulping the stale air. *Think!* He held the lantern behind him and saw a slight blood trail on the stone floor. "Wonderful, I'm making it easy for them," he muttered.

He thought he heard a noise from behind the false wall. He could not afford to wait and see who came through the passage, so he quickly formed a plan. He climbed the stairs, dripping a red trail as he went; he used his bloodied arm to lean on the door. It was locked, but that suited him. Then raising his arm so the blood wouldn't fall, he went back down the stairs to the heavy door that led to the tunnels.

Let them look for me in the streets, he thought, *I'll be running beneath their feet.*

But something stopped him. *No, I can't return to the Warren; I have to warn them, but I can't lead the assassins there.* His heart broke for the lads who had probably just lost their lives securing his escape. He imagined what those killers might do if they reached the Warren and started questioning his children, demanding they reveal where he was hiding. *If I can't go back or warn them, what can I do?*

The answer became obvious. Steeling his nerve, he opened the door to the labyrinth of tunnels, leaving a small red hand print. Running into the dark with only the dim lantern to guide him, he came to the juncture that led to the Warren. Yet he passed it and went onward, making sure his trail was plain to see.

I'll lead them into the maze of catacombs, he decided, *If I get lost, odds are they'll be lost too. I have my amulet to block scrying eyes, so my chances are... better than average.*

To bolster his courage, he said, "The mother bird will pretend to have a broken wing to lure a predator away from her chicks."

But mother birds could fly away when danger got too close, and Emen wasn't pretending.

Chapter Eleven

DuShonmaer

The little god was beside himself with boredom.

The hall in the palace was abuzz with activity, and many voices were raised in anger and argument, but Tavenji could only stand and listen. Ildric Finnael was urging caution as he explained that much of the home of Kobus DuChat was shielded from his divination. The king was storming about, enraged that the man responsible for his father's death was right under his nose, and Amon Corrina was smoldering with hatred for the man who had shared his table and ordered his daughter murdered at sea. DuChat was going to be very popular soon.

But observing was no fun. Tavenji wanted to play tricks on people. He wanted to go in and chase down this duplict high priest and make his life very interesting. If he still had his powers, he could make things very interesting indeed.

He whispered, "Have you ever heard of the prudish Queen Ethil of Kathica? She lived about, oh... two thousand years ago."

"I have not," Ildric said.

"Hedonistic Selvina worshipers wanted to overthrow her, so I let them in and they chased her through the palace. I turned all the door handles into floppy male members! You should have seen the look on her face! Each time she grabbed one, it got hard and-"

"Please, master Wryley; now is not the time," Ildric said. The old man looked and sounded exhausted.

Tavenji sighed heavily; he really wanted his powers back.

"Majesty," said Valthór, "our man has returned and reports that DuChat is in DuShonmaer."

"Good," the king said, "assemble a hundred men. We will march on his mansion and arrest him."

"Majesty," Ildric said, "I am sure that it will not be that simple. DuChat has no doubt prepared for this day, and has many escape routes."

"Is there no way you can penetrate those wards with your power, arch mage?"

"Alas no, majesty," he replied, "However there might be a way to track him. Once, a powerful scrying ward of mine was breached by an ember swallow sent to Lady Cindra. Perhaps we can use one again?"

Tavenji said, "Did the ember swallow know the lady?"

The count replied, "Yes, it was our family firebird, and she was tasked to care for it."

"Well, that's why then," Tavenji said, "the bird knew her well. It wouldn't be able to do that for just anybody."

Ildric's shoulders slumped. That had been his best idea.

"I know one of his secret ways," Tavenji said, "but it's down in the maze of catacombs and guarded by traps. It leads under his house."

"We can send men down there with Valdakian priests to guide them," the count suggested.

"Just not the blind ones!" Tavenji exclaimed.

No one laughed.

He sighed heavily again. *Priests poking their eyes out are ridiculous,* he thought, *why doesn't anyone else find it funny?* He began to fidget and hop about.

"Please stop sighing and moving all around," Ildric chided, "you are making me nervous."

"Imagine how *I* feel," the little god whined, "I'm not used to just standing around while people do serious things."

"You will have a task when we reach the mansion. Those who are brought out must be examined, and you can spot DuChat if he wears a different face."

"Fine," Tavenji grumped, folding his arms.

Ildric whispered to him, "Please, my lord; I have vouched for you and they have not yet demanded that I explain. Do not draw their ire, I beg of you."

"Hmmph," he said, twisting his mouth into a knot. The more important the people he was around, the more he wanted to cause mischief. It was just his nature.

Maybe that's why my siblings get so annoyed, he thought.

Before long, the men were assembled in the courtyard under the gray sky, with the lords astride their horses in the lead. Faces were grim with the news that they were storming a manor house in the city; the soldiers knew that the citizens of Portshia were not glad of their extended presence, and this would not endear them further.

Ildric and Tavenji had no horses, so they were walking at a distance behind the column.

"This is going to be interesting," Tavenji said eagerly.

Ildric turned to him, saying, "I hope it's not too interesting; the last thing this city needs is a door-to-door search by armed men."

"Or a fire," Tavenji said, "or runaway horses, or a lengthy siege on the mansion, or wizards hurling spells..."

"Let us hope it ends quickly and quietly."

"Awwww, where's the fun in that?"

Ildric just scowled.

The column began marching down the Avenue of Kings, which led from the palace gates straight to the doors of the cathedral. The procession drew little attention at first, since it was Massday and the streets were not as busy. When they reached the Temple Walk and turned left to march past the temples of Eyorona, Selvina, and Lelonetha, many heads bowed to the king and the count as they rode by. Many nervous eyes watched as the soldiers passed, the distant lightning glinting off their armor and weapons.

Tavenji could feel the tension they left in their wake. People were nervous; this was a holy day, a day of worship, and the king seemed bent on some possible violence. He wondered if there would be a riot. He hadn't seen a good riot since the last one he started well over a millennium ago. *It's amazing how a well-thrown piece of fruit can touch things off,* he mused.

He began looking about for some fruit.

The troops took up a perimeter around DuShonmaer as the king and his lords looked on, surrounded by their personal guard. There were no windows on the ground floor of the mansion that were large enough to crawl out of, so the troops were set to watch the higher ones. The rest assembled before the ornate wrought iron gate, which was currently closed and locked.

"Do you think he's escaped already?" Tavenji asked.

"Probably," Ildric muttered, "the man Valthór sent might have spooked him."

"What are the odds he knows about our little meeting in the Warren last night?"

"I doubt the children said anything that would get back to him, but those older lads... they might have informed on us."

"A sense of loyalty to their guild," Tavenji said, "not an all-together bad thing. I wonder if they believed any of it?"

"No, I'm sure they thought our news about the end of the world was all a sham. When people get used to lies and lying, they lose the ability to recognize the truth."

Tavenji nodded. "That's true... I think. Speaking of the end of the world, did you have any notion of how we might catch up with this Gavadaire fellow?"

Ildric scratched his beard and said, "I have not had the time or energy to give it much thought. If I could only rest awhile..."

Just then, the king summoned them to his side.

He said, "Arch mage, the gates are barred with magic. Are you able to open them with a spell?"

"I... shall try, majesty," Ildric said. He walked towards the entryway and the troops parted for him. Raising his silver hand, he sensed that the gate had a powerful warding spell upon it, as well as being mechanically locked. Holding his staff before him, he invoked a spell of opening and ward removal, *"Avessenwa, posthe n'thom ves."*

It took a few tense moments, but the gate creaked, trembled, and swung open. Valthór shouted an order and dozens of troops poured through the gate, heading for the many doorways within the large courtyard. Ildric stood back to watch, leaning on his staff wearily.

Tavenji looked around at the crowds that were gathering from the temples and nearby streets; the faces held a mixture of fear and confusion. Incense and perfume clashed with horse droppings and the stink of the canal, blending together in a cool breeze that promised rain. *I wonder what the citizens of Portshia think about this DuChat fellow,* he thought, *is he beloved, envied, or mistrusted? Do they think of him as one of their own, or is he too rich and powerful for that?*

No one seemed to be up in arms about it, and that was good; *boring*, but good. Maybe Ildric was right after all; a riot might be fun to start and watch, but it could lead to all kinds of complications. Besides, he was mortal now, and the thought of that timeless, mindless void of oblivion that was waiting on the other side of a sword stroke gave him reason enough to behave.

Also, fruit was out of season.

Soldiers were hauling servants out into the street. They were terrified of course; their daily routines having been shattered in a crash of breaking glass, splintering doors, and shouting. As they were forced to kneel on the cobblestones, Tavenji capered over to them and looked carefully into each of their faces.

"Well?" Ildric asked.

"Nope," he replied, "no duplicts. They're all your average, garden variety humans."

"Garden variety?"

"Middle-of-the-road. Run-of-the-mill. Nothing to write home about," he shrugged.

Ildric shook his head; the little god could really be confusing sometimes.

"Oh! Can you see how the men in the tunnel are faring?" Tavenji asked.

The wizard concentrated and the Eye of Omithys glowed, sweeping the street. "They are nearing a place that is protected from my sight. Your directions served them well, I think. Let us hope they are not too careless."

"Let's hope," he echoed. The secret thieves' guild meeting room in the catacombs led to DuChat's personal torture chamber. Tavenji had visited briefly, but much preferred the mansion upstairs.

"Arch mage, a moment," called the count. Amon Corrina dismounted and joined them in the street. "I was wondering," he began, "if you might convey a message to my daughter using the magic earring you gave her?"

"What message, my lord?"

"Regarding Gavadaire LuVestra and DuChat," he said, "I think, perhaps, it might be important on her quest and rather important to her personally."

"You are right, of course, my lord. Yet I think now is not the time. Master Wryley and I plan to pursue LuVestra across the sea, and hopefully stop him. Also, we have not yet captured DuChat. Let us wait until some things are settled before burdening her with such news?"

The count was about to reply when the sound of creaking metal and a loud *clang* echoed across the street. Turning, they saw that the gates to the mansion had slammed shut, and many soldiers were still inside, searching room to room.

"What just happened?" Tavenji asked, "Is it a trap?"

"I fear it might be," Ildric said, "My lord, I ask that you return to a safe distance with the king."

Nodding, the count did so. Tavenji followed him.

Valthór ordered his soldiers to take the servants into custody for questioning, and shouted to the men inside. Some of them came to the windows on the second and third floor overlooking the street.

"Sir?"

"The gate has shut!" Valthór called, "Be on your guard!"

"Yes, sir!"

He ordered his men to try the gate, but they received a strong shock when they touched the bars.

"Arch mage!" Valthór called, "We require your services again!"

"Very well," he said, "Stand back."

Tavenji went to the far side of the street to get a better look at the structure. Something was wrong, he could feel it. There was a power building within, a power that was very familiar and potent. It was almost like...

"Divine alchemy…" Tavenji said.

Ildric raised his staff and chanted, *"Avessenwa, posthe n'thom ves."*

"Wait!"

The spell struck the gate, causing it to creak and tremble as before, but this time the iron became orange-hot, rattling on its hinges. Before anyone could move away, the spell rebounded with great force, releasing a wave of crimson energy back at the wizard. Ildric Finnael was flung back across the cobblestones, tumbling to a stop before the frightened horses.

Tavenji had been knocked on his backside, as had most of the soldiers and bystanders. Screams filled the air, along with the shouts of soldiers and the squeals of terrified horses. The power Tavenji had felt was still building up, and he turned to look at the mansion, eyes wide in excitement and horror.

It all released at once, like a snap reverberating through the little god's soul. The mansion's windows flickered with a harsh crimson light, and crashed outward to shower glass upon the people below. Shapes moved within the rooms above and the courtyard bellow, like great snakes made of ash and smoke, flickering with a sickly blood-light.

The soldiers within began to cry out and scream, the sounds rising in pitch and intensity until they fell silent. The king watched in helpless horror as he tried to steady his mount. He witnessed one of his men in the courtyard trying to escape; his armor turned to rust and crumbled, and his flesh was rendered down to bone and dust in mere seconds, consumed by the writhing mass of living smoke.

"Chaos swarm!" Tavenji cried, "Get back! Get way back!"

This was more interesting than he had dreamed, and for once he was not happy about it. This was *bad.* Very bad.

Ildric lay motionless in the street. The little god tried to drag him away, but thankfully the count and his men were on hand to aid him. Once they reached a safe distance, Tavenji said a silent prayer to his sister Lelonetha that her priests had the sense, provision, and bravery to run out and help the wounded.

Chapter Twelve

The Rat Men

Emen could not see more than ten feet in front of him as he navigated the narrow, unfamiliar passageways. His lantern was low on oil, and his shoulder was sore from holding it aloft. His other shoulder throbbed with pain as warm blood flowed from the wound, no doubt leaving a trail for his pursuers to follow. Worse, the floors were covered with enough undisturbed dirt to make his passage plain.

He could hear their voices echoing in the distance when he stopped and held his breath. They were a few minutes behind him and gaining; his short legs were no advantage in a foot race, so he needed other options, and fast.

I need a way out, he thought, *I can't stay down here for much longer, even if I lose them. I need a healer. Badly.*

His wound had to be treated, but he hadn't the time or the free hand. Open wounds meant infection, and infection meant death, unless he could get to a Lelonethan house of healing.

The passage branched ahead yet again, leading to another blind decision. He knew he was probably heading west or south, deeper into the city, but he was also heading much deeper underground. He couldn't hear the flowing of water overhead from the sewer lines, which meant he was far below street level. Somehow, it was colder down here than it was up there. How far had he come already? It might have been a hundred yards or a mile with all the twists and turns; there was no way to tell underground.

Before long, he found he was no longer moving through catacombs. There were no niches in the walls, no human remains, only rough-hewn limestone that branched off at odd angles. Old support timbers and forgotten tools gave mute testimony to the past. *I must be in the old mines, before they were converted into tombs,* he thought, *this is not good. Every route I take is likely to be a dead end.*

The ceiling was getting lower and the way ahead became obscured by twists and turns. The air was growing thin, and he smelled stagnant water, blood, and dust. *This is some plan,* he mused, *I'm going to end up squeezed into a deep, dark hole like a gopher, until I either suffocate, starve, or they find me. At least the children in the Warren are safe. Gods, I hope they are safe.*

Something caught his eye and he moved closer to the wall, holding his lantern up to see. It was a familiar pattern of markings, like the ones his father had taught him for encoding messages for the Circle. *Has the thieves' guild made use of these tunnels recently? No... no they're...*

"Of course!" he gasped, and then covered his mouth as the sound echoed down the shaft. His father hadn't invented that code; it had been passed down to him from his ancestors who had worked in the mines! It was some kind of shorthand used for leaving warnings and directions. This code told of a way up and out of the mine; something to do with a wheel and water...

He heard a noise behind him, echoing down the tunnels. *They are getting closer,* he thought, *I must hurry.* He headed down the tunnel indicated by the markings, turning left after thirty paces, right after fifteen, and...

The passage before him was flooded. "Oh gods," he moaned. The markings on the wall told him the chamber was thirty paces ahead and to the left, but he could only move ten paces before he would be waist deep in icy, contaminated mine water.

"I'm trapped," he muttered to the walls, "they'll find me and cut my throat." Defeated, he sank to his knees. Setting the lantern down, he finally clutched his shoulder to slow the bleeding. *What's the use? Why keep it in my body a few moments longer?*

Footsteps echoed in the near distance. He thought he could hear voices. *Soon. They will be here soon. Tavenji, Uncle Tweak, God of Thieves and Fools, it was nice to know you, but damn it, I wish you still answered prayers.*

Then he wondered if Tavenji *ever* answered prayers; he didn't really seem the type. He was a god who valued boldness, wits, and guile, and rewarded those who used them.

"What would Tavenji do?" he asked himself.

Something really stupid and insane, answered a little voice.

He saw a light growing in the tunnels behind him, and resolved to follow that advice.

Hanging his lantern on a nail, he waded into the icy water. As the footsteps behind him quickened and voices were raised, he sucked in a deep breath, closed his eyes, and plunged into the flooded passage.

Keep to the left wall, swim like mad, and feel for a side passage. He kicked furiously and used his left arm to paddle. He kept his right hand raised in front of him, lest he swim into the ceiling or a support beam and knock himself out. He could feel no side passage yet. *How far is thirty paces if you're swimming?*

He heard a muffled splash behind him, but he did not look. The water was too dark and would probably damage his eyes if he opened them, so he took a little comfort. *They are swimming as blind as I am.*

His lungs were aching as he let out little bubbles of breath. *Where is it, where is it?* He felt along the left-hand wall, growing desperate for a pocket of air in a new chamber, but felt only rough stone. Then, as his reserves were failing, his hand found open water to his left. He swam with panicked speed, muscles burning and chest constricting, until his head broke the surface. He heaved and sputtered, gasping and coughing in a blackened void that echoed like the inside of a vast well.

How big is this chamber? It's supposed to be a way up, but how far up? He began treading water, moving about until his hands found the wall. As his eyes got used to the dark, he could see that it was not as black as he feared; there was a dim, pulsating light coming from high above, illuminating shapes along the walls of the narrow shaft.

It was a framework of timber that seemed to line the shaft on all sides, with crisscrossing support beams and braces. On one side of the chamber was a tangled mass of metal; what appeared to be dozens of buckets on a chain hanging over one of the crossbeams.

His mind fumbled for an explanation, searching the histories he had learned as a child. *This was a... oh, what was it... a chain of buckets for lifting water out of the mineshaft. They were attached to a waterwheel on top of the shaft, but it's probably been out of use for centuries now.*

Yet the framework was still intact, and there were boards nailed into it that would serve as a ladder.

Seeing no other alternative, he began a slow, steady climb.

His wound was burning from the acidic water, turning the dull throb into a steady, radiant ache; if pain could give off light, he was sure his shoulder could have lit the chamber. His progress was slow but steady, as he tested each rung before committing his weight to it. The climb was tortuous, but it was better than rotting in a hole.

Every few moments he would stop to rest and listen. So far the pursuers had not found the chamber, and could probably not read the coded markings. Regardless, Emen would not assume they had given him up for dead just yet.

The light at the top of the shaft was shining down through a metal grating; unless the people above had reason to open it, it was probably a permanent cover. *I might be trapped after all. Well, nothing for it. I can wait until I reach the top to despair.*

When he finally found his way to the pinnacle of the framework, he hugged the timbers and wept. He was in terrible pain and was unimaginably exhausted; he had never worked so hard in his life, and he was sure he had lost half of his blood by now. He was light-headed and shivering, partly from cold and partly from his muscles protesting. He wanted to relax, but that meant letting go and falling to his doom.

He hadn't even tried lifting the grating yet, just inches above his head.

Beyond the metal bars he heard the sound of water and the growling, grinding, and squeaking of machinery. The air was quite warm, and the light was flickering as though it were passing through the spokes of a moving wheel.

The waterwheel for the buckets and chains, he thought, *it's still in use for something.*

It was time for the moment of truth; he reached overhead and pushed on the grating. It did not move. His heart sank and he started to weep again, but a tiny voice of reason told him, *you are too weak right now, so don't expect it to move. Rest and try again.*

Emen took the time to gather his strength and wits before he made another attempt. Looking around, he noticed the grate was hinged in the middle.

It must open. But is it locked?

He stretched and reached through the bars, fumbling blindly. Every muscle protested the action, but he persisted until his fingers found a sliding bolt with no lock. He gave a great sigh of relief, thanking whatever gods would listen. Taking a moment to feel it out, he readjusted himself for the best leverage and set himself to working the bolt free. It creaked and groaned with rusty complaint, before finally sliding open.

He heard a crackle, a snap, and a snarled curse. To his horror, he looked down to see one of the assassins not twenty feet below! A rung of the ladder had snapped under his foot, but he quickly recovered and resumed his climb, glaring up at the dwarf.

"Shit!" Emen cried; his voice was rough and dry, and the word sounded like a wheeze. He shoved against the grating with frantic strength, but nearly lost his grip on the framework. "Damn it! No..." he looked down again. *How did he catch up to me so fast and silent?* The answer became obvious as he watched: the man had longer legs and arms, was uninjured, and was a trained killer.

Desperate to escape, Emen climbed a little higher on the frame, braced himself, and shoved on the metal grating with his head. It was heavy and the bars bruised his scalp, but the grate lifted slowly on squeaky hinges. His legs found their limit of reach and strength, so he grabbed for the edge of the opening.

If I slip, the grate will crash down on my hand, and I'm as good as dead.

The assassin was gaining, only ten feet below him now. He could hear the man's labored breathing and the creak of every ladder rung that brought him closer to his prey. Emen screamed as he heaved his wounded arm to the edge, pulling himself through the opening with the weight of the bars pressing on his back. His feet left the wooden frame and kicked in the air helplessly.

"Got you, dwarf!" cried the assassin, "I'll make you pay for this little chase!" The words echoed ominously, as if from the mouth of a monster.

But Emen's legs were short enough to kick up to the edge of the hole, giving him just enough leverage to hoist himself out of the man's reach. He rolled out from under the grate and dropped to the floor of the building as the metal crashed shut. He leaped up and slid the bolt closed, but that would only slow the man down for a moment. Feeling a rush of elation, he looked around at his new surroundings.

He was in the basement of a stone building. The metal grating was built into a raised ring of masonry about three feet high. There were a few tools hanging on the wall beams, but the most prominent feature was a large waterwheel next to a narrow, barred window near the ceiling, which ventilated the heat from the room. Passing legs told him the window was at street level, and beyond, he heard falling rain.

Lead pipes near the ceiling delivered water from somewhere, probably the canal system, and spilled it over the top of the wheel's wide paddles, which turned the noisy contraption. A thick hawser rope was wound about the wheel shaft, which was then belted around a pulley that drove a large wooden cam wheel. The cams clacked against a paddle that operated an enormous bellows, blowing air through a hole in a thick stone wall. The water coming off the wheel fell into a channel that flowed into a small grated sewer drain.

Emen wondered, *Where am I? Somewhere in midtown, I think. This bellows must feed a blast furnace... that would mean I'm in the Hall of Smiths, near Balkon's temple.*

The assassin began reaching through the grating, feeling for the slide bolt. Emen went to the tools, grabbed a wooden mallet, and smashed the man's fingers, causing him to shout in pain. *I can't do this forever,* he thought, *I must get out.*

Emen looked around for an exit and found a narrow stair that led to a door in the ceiling. He figured in his current state, he could make it to the room above in the time it would take for the assassin to emerge from the hole. What then? How far could he get in a foot race through the streets? He didn't like his chances. *Maybe if I called for help? No, that would surely get someone killed.*

The man tried for the bolt again.

Emen smashed at the grating, keeping him at bay.

"You can't hold me back forever, dwarf!" came a cry through the bars.

Emen agreed. There was another way out however, and it was a way that the man hopefully couldn't follow. Problem was, it was the last place Emen wanted to go.

He made one last smash at the bars, ran for the sewer drain, and lifted the small cast iron grating. Water splashed around his feet as he gazed into the drain, which looked just wide enough to squeeze through. *This is suicide. Still, it's better than being murdered, isn't it?*

The assassin slid the bolt open and lifted the grating, and Emen could see him peering from the shaft. Their eyes locked and a chill ran up the dwarf's spine.

Shit. Do it, just do it!

He sat in the water and lowered his legs into the drain. It was very cold, like the mine water, but at least it was cleaner.

The grating clanged open and the assassin climbed out, his sword at his side.

Emen lowered his hips into the hole, then he fell to his chest, arms supporting his weight on the edge of the drain. It was a tight fit, and water began to back up and flood around his shoulders and chin. Sharp pain shot through his wounded arm and he cried out.

The assassin leaped to the floor and drew his sword. Fury and cruelty were in his eyes as he strode towards him.

Emen emptied his lungs, painfully raised his arms over his head, and squeezed his shoulders together as hard as he could. The water covered his mouth and nose. He could see the man was almost on him, raising his sword.

Kicking furiously, Emen wriggled and dropped through the opening, sliding down the drainpipe in a rush of water. Within moments he was in the sewer system, splashing into an effluent flow of human waste and gods-knew-what-else.

It took him several moments to fight the current and find his footing in the shallow, putrid stream. He hefted the mallet he had managed to hang on to, readying it in case the assassin was able to pursue him. But unless the man was double-jointed, he would never fit his large bodyguard-bulk through that drain.

No one came, but Emen knew he had to move. There was more than one way into a sewer; just because he had flushed himself like a turd didn't mean his pursuer couldn't find an easier way down. Luckily there was more light down here than he expected. Storm drains from the roadside cast little shafts of dim light into the gloom, but they would not last; gloaming was approaching within the hour, and the tunnels would probably become pitch black. Rainwater from the streets began pouring in, making little waterfalls in his path.

The stench was already getting to him. The few breaths he had taken already made him want to retch, and the fumes were stinging his eyes. He tried to breathe through his shirt, but the fabric was already stained with the filthy water.

"Upstream or down?" he muttered. Down would take him under the Temple District, spilling out into the canal where the currents were deep and strong. Up would take him towards the north wall, where the inlet gates from the canal supplied water for drinking, flooding the moats, and flushing the sewers. He reasoned that the flow would be shallower and less fouled that way, so he began a weary trek along one of the narrow walkways.

Hours passed and the light died. Emen was fumbling through the darkness, guiding himself with a shoulder on the curved brick wall. He had dropped his mallet some time ago, using his good hand to clamp over his wounded arm, which was throbbing and burning. He was breathing shallow and through the mouth, as if that would somehow mitigate the stench. Twice he had fallen to his knees, teetering on the edge of the walkway. Dizzy and exhausted, he had begun to think that drowning in a river of shit was the best he could hope for.

But I won't, he thought, fighting through his delirium, *I won't drown, not today. Tonight. It's nighttime, always nighttime down here.*

There were things with him in the dark. They fell in his hair, scrambled across his face, and got into his shirt. They crunched when he stepped on them, brushed off the wall by his shoulder as he slid along the surface.

There were rats too; little eyes that reflected the scant light from the wizard lamps on the street above. They would squeak when his feet stumbled on them, and nip at his boots.

Rats... rats in the sewers. Mother told me about the rats.

"You won't get me," he muttered, "You won't have this dwarf's rump for supper."

In his delirium he recalled, *There were rats that crawled up the plumbing, crawled up the outhouse and nipped little boys in the rear; boys who spent too much time sitting. That's what mother sang, her little song she'd sing with a smile, tousling my hair when I'd go off to the privy. Funny little song.*

Rats, rats, bigger than cats,
Creeping up the hole,
They come, they come, to bite your bum,
Hungry as a troll.

He smiled at the memory, hearing her voice in his head. He heard his father's voice too, and father had told him about the Rat Men.

"Most claim the Rat Men are just sewer workers, but there are other stories, my lad. Some say they were changed; they worshiped a false god and they transformed, like the bull men and the bird men and the wolf men. They live down there in the sewers, breeding and planning and stealing food from the people above. Stealing children too!"

That's what father said, but it couldn't be true. Rat Men were just a story. Weren't they?

Emen's pulse was racing; he was shivering with fever and suffocating on the miasma that he could not escape. He longed to reach one of the storm drains and take a gulp of night air and clean water, but he was too short to reach, and the water turned out to be not so clean after all. His eyes were stinging and what little he could see was becoming a blur.

I have to rest, have to sleep, but I can't in here, not in here. They'd be on me in minutes, the crawling things and the rats. I'd be eaten alive and wake up with fewer fingers and toes. I have to keep moving.

But when he tried to take one more step, he realized he was already off his feet, leaning against the curved wall like a pillow.

No... Where did my legs go? Ah, here they are, they just don't work. I can't make them work.

He shifted his feet on the walkway with pathetic effort. He choked, coughed, and heaved his empty stomach, making a terribly strained moan that echoed down the tunnels. People on the street above might have believed it was the bellow of a horrific sewer beast.

Then he was still.

When his eyes opened again, he could not tell how much time had passed. Maybe it was a minute, maybe an hour. He felt for his fingers; they were all there. He felt for his ears and nose with filthy hands; they were intact. He felt a tickle, snorted, and a bug flew out of his nose.

Nothing has eaten me yet, he thought.

But there was a glow in the tunnel, and that was new. It was coming closer from around a bend. His eyes were in such pain that he could barely keep them open, but through the blurry haze, he began to see figures and shadows moving along the wall.

"Here, I'm here!" he called, but it sounded like a wheezing bellows, more wind than words.

The figures drew nearer, hurrying their pace. They were carrying a light before them, a soft radiance like a miniature moon on a string. Hope stirred in his heart.

Until he saw their faces.

Long, pointed noses moved to and fro, sniffing him out, and above those wicked snouts were large, round eyes that glowed with mirrored malevolence. They wore deep hoods and cloaks to hide their deformity, and their heavy boots thumped louder and faster as they closed in on him. He could imagine the filthy fur under those cloaks, and the long, clawed fingers and toes hidden by their gloves and boots.

*Rat Men! They **are** real! Gods, help me!*

Emen made a cry like a frightened animal as he turned to flee on his hands and knees. He slipped and fell face-first into the horrid stream, thrashing as strong hands grabbed him and lifted him out of the effluent. The last thing he saw before passing out was a pair of huge, round eyes staring into his face. A voice emanated from the pointed snout.

"Looks like this one's had a rough day," it said.

Emen could no longer tell dreams from reality. He was either floating, or being carried, or lying on his back on a rumbling bed of straw. There was darkness, then light, then darkness again; it was as if a pale sun was whizzing across the sky from his head to his feet, over and over again; it made him feel that the world was spinning too fast, and he had to squeeze his eyes shut. But the shaking and rumbling continued beneath him.

I am on a cart, he realized in a moment of lucidity, *I am passing under wizard lamps in the back of a cart.*

With this mystery solved, he rewarded himself by passing out again.

His next experience was fleeing from a pack of rat-faced men that squeaked and chattered behind him, scratching the cobblestones with their clawed feet and dragging their thick tails behind them. He was running as fast as he could, but he was shin-deep in muck and there was a force pushing against him like a mighty wind. Hands grabbed him and moved him about, tearing at his clothes, pulling at his boots.

Then he was awoken by the touch of warm and clean water flowing over his skin. Hands were rubbing him with lye soap and sponges, washing the filth away, yet he could not focus on who owned those hands. Pain flashed as they cleaned his wound, and he became aware that he was in a poorly-lit bath house of sorts, with candles along the wall. The floor was tiled and there was a drain, and steam was coming from somewhere. Despite the soap and water, the sewer smell was stuck in his nostrils, and he retched.

Someone smeared something under his nose, like a grease or poultice. When next he breathed in, the stench of the sewer was gone, replaced by a floral, fruity scent. His sinuses opened and he gasped, taking his first deep breath in hours. Relief overwhelmed him and he began to cry. The hands finished their business and lifted him up, lowering his naked body gently into a cool bath.

Emen felt like a hot iron being quenched. His skin was burning with fever, and the water soothed him greatly. He managed the strength to splash his face and head with his good arm, but his wounded arm refused to move. He thought, *It would be nice to sleep here,* and his eyes closed...

But the arms lifted him again, wrapping him in clean linens before carrying him off in a bundle. He could see the face of one of his saviors, and it was undeniably human.

Maybe rat men can change back? he mused.

As they carried him past a particular room, Emen saw the vision that had haunted him in the sewers. There was a figure standing in the lamplight with large, round eyes over a pointed snout, hiding under a hooded cloak. But the figure threw back the hood and lifted the snout, revealing that it was only a mask to cover the face and eyes of a man. In the light the mask was not particularly rat-like, though in his delirious state, he could not tell if he was even awake or not. He distinctly heard someone say the word "priestess."

Before he knew it, he was lying in a bed surrounded by candles. There were bowls of water nearby, and clean towels, and rolls of linen bandages. A woman entered the room, dressed in an orange and white robe. She took something from her pouch and put it to his lips.

"Drink," she said.

She had a kindly face, like someone's grandmother. Emen did as he was told, and in moments he was adrift in the most peaceful sleep he had ever known.

Chapter Thirteen

Breega

A few hours' travel brought Cindra and her companions to the village of Breega in the late afternoon. The town sat on a low hill where tower sentries could survey the surrounding wood. A tall, dark palisade ran along its perimeter, and a stout wooden gate stood open to the road, which ran through the heart of the community. Two guards stood on duty, and they motioned the party to stop.

"Hail," Cindra called to the gate guards.

"Welcome, sir... knight?" His confusion was evident, and they both squinted into her raised visor. "Who are you and what is your business in Breega?"

Cindra brought T'ózha to a halt before the gate and removed her helmet. "I am Lady Cindra Corrina, a knight of His Majesty King Galen III," It rolled off the tongue and Cindra liked saying it, "and we are traveling north along the road. We wish to stop for the night."

The men just stared, mouths agape, trying to decide if it was a joke. As the other riders and the wagon of supplies came to a halt, they decided it was not. "Er, well then welcome to Breega," said one of the men, raising his pole arm.

"Thank you," she said, nodding. She urged her horse through the gate, head held high.

Adric and Padison shared a smile and Padison rolled his eyes.

Cindra called back, "Madam Wyngaard, you know this village. Where is a good place to lodge?"

Deliah trotted to ride beside her, saying, "It has been a time since I was here, but I believe the Graybough is the only lodging house of size."

"Good enough," Cindra said.

"And it's just 'Deliah,' if you please," she said.

The palisade continued almost to the edge of the river's westward meander. A small dock was built there, and though she could not see it, Cindra knew that a few hundred yards downstream was the inlet weir of the Portshia Canal system. It ran for a good 75 miles, past several locks and water mills, irrigating fields in the Cassel Basin, and finally providing water to Portshia. Like the Joshian Way and much of Portshia itself, it was a gift of the Celvestrian Empire's conquest and ingenuity.

The rest of Breega was rustic but well-kept. Dozens of wood-framed, wattle and daub buildings packed inside the walls, making most streets unsuitable for more than one cart at a time. Atop the hill was a stone building with a tall, gable roof in the style of old Norsican long houses. It looked large enough to lodge a company of soldiers; no doubt it was the hall of the Greenfellow Maurbrik School. A temple dedicated to the war god Balkon stood a little farther down the hill; the tower with its domed, spiked roof was supposed to resemble a morning star mace, but instead had the look of a nightmarish phallus.

There were only a few trees standing inside the walls, and one of them provided shade over a small lodging house with adjoining stables. There was no sign, save a large, gray-painted branch sticking out like an outgrowth over the door. Cindra led the party to the inn and dismounted.

"For what it's worth, this will be our last night with a roof over our heads," she said. She tossed her helmet to Padison and gave T'ózha's reins to Adric.

Wenyssaya sighed at this reminder, but said nothing.

A large, simple-looking young man came out of the stables to greet them, smiling and nodding as he took charge of the horses. "Milurd," he said to Adric and Cindra. He stared for a moment at the two other women, blinking and grinning.

As Nixy collected Drahn from the wagon, the little dragon asked quietly, "Is he alwight?"

Nixy shrugged and said, "When I was at Cindra's castle, the other stable boys said some people get kicked in the head and go funny. I guess it's a danger if ya work with horses."

Drahn nodded in agreement, watching the big lad lumber away.

Padison, who was collecting the luggage asked, "Should we see if the innkeeper has space for the family behind us?"

Deliah said, "If he doesn't, perhaps you lads can give up your beds for the old woman and her granddaughter?"

Padison made a little face at that, and Adric hung his head.

The inside of the inn was a bit cozier than Cindra had hoped, made more so by the heads and antlers of game animals poking out of the wall space of the common room. There was no one present except for the innkeeper, a short old man with a deeply-lined face and a pipe stem sagging his lower lip. He examined them with one wandering eye, making a little bow of welcome.

"Lodging for six of us," Cindra said, "And do you serve food?"

"Just a loaf and ale, though you'd have to share, likely," he said, "There's a tavern up the road. As for lodging, I can fit three in one bed and three in cots."

"Good enough," she said.

Deliah spoke up, "There is a family of three a short ways behind us, would you have space for them as well? One is an old woman."

Adric glared at Padison, who looked down at his boots.

"I could offer space, ma'am," replied the innkeeper, "but no more cots, I'm afraid." He looked Deliah in the face for a moment and asked, "Do I know you? Your face seems familiar."

She shook her head, "I doubt it. I passed through Breega many years back, but I come from farther north."

He worked his pipe around in his mouth, thinking. "No," he said, "I'm recalling it was overseas. But I've not been there since long ago. Maybe I met your granny?"

She looked into his face with her cloud-gray eyes, her face unreadable. "Possibly," she said.

Deliah can't help but be mysterious, Cindra thought. It was annoying. She said, "One more thing, innkeeper. Do you have a scribe in town? I want to write a letter."

"You did what?" Adric asked, stunned.

"I announced us in a formal letter," Cindra repeated. "I asked for a meeting to offer my regards, and request safe passage through the woods."

Padison, who was arranging the cots in the room, asked, "What in the deep Abyss did you do *that* for?"

Cindra said, "I want to do the proper thing and not seem like we're skulking about."

"But what if they want to start trouble instead?" Adric asked, "I hear Sir Jaron didn't get a very warm welcome last he was here."

"That was different," Cindra replied, "He had just killed the son of Sir Waliss, and was a disgraced knight. We, on the other hand, are on a quest for the king."

"A *secret* quest," Padison said, "What if he asks you what it's about?"

"I'll tell him the king sent me on errantry, escorting travelers along the road," she said.

Adric frowned, "But there's a war on! No one would waste a knight on escort duty. That's ridiculous."

"Exactly," Cindra said, "No king would send a lady knight into battle when he can send her in the opposite direction. It makes perfect sense."

"It's an insulting notion," Adric said.

"I expected to be insulted," she said, "Why not use it to our advantage?"

Padison dropped a pack on each cot, the last belonging to Cindra. "There you go; Wenyssaya's, Nixy's, and yours." He folded his arms, "I guess me and Adric will be in the third room, on the floor."

"Along with master Bardon," Adric said.

Padison sighed, "Looks to be a cold night."

Cindra said, "Before you two heroically sacrifice yourselves to the cold floor, let's have this armor off. I'd like to feel the hearth fire on my skin."

"Aye," Adric said, not sensing any sympathy, "Maybe grandma Maewyn will finish her story."

The tavern was a good-sized establishment called the Hen and Horn. It had a common room with a large central fire pit, which was unusual for a southern-style building. A pavilion roof with a vented peak let the smoke out, and there were benches and tables near the walls. Casks of ale and beer stood by one wall, tempting the thirsty throat.

Cindra was wearing her required riding skirt and bodice, though she had plans to switch to more manly and comfortable clothing once they left town. She was expecting no trouble tonight, but wore her sword and *Kos* knife just the same. *Better than to leave them unguarded,* she figured. There were many odd looks and whispers behind her back, but she was growing used to it.

Her retinue, also known as 'the boys,' wore their weapons also, but it was because they didn't trust Rejick Ratham's home town.

They accompanied Nixy and the other women into the tavern, acting as an escort of sorts. Many eyes turned to stare, as they had come to expect. Nixy was carrying Drahn in his backpack, for the little dragon did not want to be left out of any stories, funny looks or no.

Wenyssaya was wearing a dark gray hood in an attempt to be inconspicuous, but it didn't help; her painted hands, richly-dyed dress, and willowy figure drew all eyes in the room. Deliah was just Deliah, dark and mysterious and alluring. Hardly anyone glanced at Cindra and her armed retinue while the others were around.

Padison leaned towards Cindra and whispered, "Just like those Nixominy, we've gone invisible!"

She snorted a laugh.

"Ooooh come over, come over!" called blind old Maewyn. She was sitting by the fire, flanked by her family. They had arrived shortly after, and spared no time making for a warm hearth and hot food.

The party came over to join them, and Nixy asked her, "How did you know it was us?"

Maewyn tapped the side of her nose and said, "I caught your scent, like a hound! I heard the conversations falter and turn to muttering, and I sensed the magic in the air."

"And I told her," Bardon said.

"Tsk!" she clucked her tongue and elbowed him in the ribs, "That *and* what I said."

"We are waiting for food before gran finishes anymore stories," Glenawyn said, "And I thank you again for sharing space with us at the inn!"

"It was nothing," Cindra said, "The boys were happy to help. Weren't you, boys?"

"*Yes, Lady Cindra,*" They grumbled it together, like they'd practiced it.

She laughed, "I'm still training them to be chivalrous. It takes time."

Maewyn cackled and the others chuckled, even the boys.

Dinner was hearty and filling, comprised mostly of a thick stew of meat and tubers, with chopped wetland herbs, onions, carrots, and leafy vegetables. The ale was served warm, and the bread was a bit stale, having been baked in the morning. Still, it was delicious and satisfying; a last feast before the long, dark road.

"Let's have the rest of the story then," Cindra said, "If you are up to it, of course."

"Of course!" Maewyn said, happily, "Gather 'round, gather 'round, old ears and new!" Her voice had become strong and rang through the room, "Let me recount my tale for those who have not heard; the tale of the Raven Witch of the Woods!"

Raven Witch? Cindra thought, *Is this the same story?*

Maewyn listened for the moving of chairs and the settling of conversations, motioning for her family to move aside and give her a bit of room. She sat, back to the fire, and raised her hands like an ancient priestess. Her hair was a glowing, translucent aura that hovered around the outline of her skull. Her sunken, puckered eyelids gave her a deathly countenance.

"I have told before that when I was a girl in the town of Gloamshire, I once fell asleep within an elf circle, deep in the woods. When I awoke, it was days later, and I had the power to see the unseen, specifically the tiny, bat-winged Nixominy that plague these woods. Some may know them as 'war faeries' or 'vylanviis,' or other names..."

Wenyssaya's ears pricked up at the elven word. *Little demons. I wonder where she heard that?*

"But they are real, whatever you might think" she continued, "They discovered that I could see them, and they conspired to drive me and my father from our town. He was a blacksmith, a good and honest man, but his daughter was a little ninnyhammer, and an accused thief, thanks to Nixominy mischief. We left our home in shame and sorrow, heading north along the Joshian Way to find refuge in the tiny trading post of Riverskirt, where the waters of the Kelga meet the Joshian. The road was hard, for father pulled a cart behind him with all the tools he could carry, and a great, heavy anvil. We had no mule or horse, only our poor strength. I helped as I was able, being a skinny thing no heavier than his largest hammer. Each night we fell, exhausted, though I believe father slept only as long as he dared.

"The woods are home to many strange things, and always have been," she said, lowering her voice ominously, "There were tales of strangling vines that fed on blood, ashen bears that could stand twice as tall as a man, and black wolves that could skip through the shadows at will."

This made Nixy gasp. *Shadow wolves*. A cold shiver ran up his back as he recalled the night Dexer tried to kill him. The black wolves had come from shadow and returned to shadow, dragging the screaming assassin with them.

"Yet we met none of these on the road," she said, "Instead, we met someone we never expected! When the woods became darkest and the gloom closed in, a lone woman stepped out of the trees. She carried a knife in one hand, and a handful of herbs in the other. She was a beauty, but she gave me such a fright! My father was braver, but even he was put on his edge by the stranger. She had black hair, a black cloak, and a black dress, like a raven made human. Her face was pale and fair, but her eyes were cold and gray like rain clouds, or the morning fog."

Cindra flinched at this, fighting the urge to look over at Deliah. Instead, she watched the eyes around her. Some indeed flicked in the woman's direction. Whispers tickled the ears, just beyond hearing.

"Seeing our fear, the dark woman sought to put us at ease." Maewyn's voice became refined and flowed like honey as she spoke the stranger's words. 'Well met,' said she, 'Where are the two of you going alone on such a road?'"

That even sounds like Deliah's manner, Cindra thought, *or maybe I just want it to.*

The old woman's voice changed to the gruff tones of her father, "'We are going to the Riverskirt trading post to find work,' said he. The woman asked, 'Is there not work in Gloamshire?' 'There was,' quoth my father, 'but we are driven from our home by fools.' This got the woman's attention, and she came closer. 'Fools, you say? What fools would drive away a worthy blacksmith and such a lovely little girl?' I blushed at that, I did," Maewyn giggled, "for I was not always a dried old apple, and once had a pretty face... like *this* little girl here." She pointed at Padison, and people had a good laugh.

Except Padison, who stuck his tongue out at her.

Maewyn continued, "She introduced herself, this dark woman. 'I am Nasha,' said she, 'and the Shadowood is my home. Come, and I'll accompany you on the dark road.' And so she did. It was a strange comfort having her there, smelling like moss and earth and lilacs. It was peaceful, like walking... with the night itself... beside you...'"

She lowered her head and fell silent, letting the fire crackle away.

Cindra wasn't going to fall for her tricks again. Instead, she watched as the new listeners became anxious, wondering if she had fallen asleep. The nervous fidgeting began.

"When night did fall," Maewyn said, right on cue, "we found ourselves walking a dark, empty road of gray stone, seeing naught but what was in front of our noses. But the raven-black woman did not falter in her step. Instead, she reached in her robe and pulled out a wooden stick, spoke a strange word, and behold!"

Maewyn flung her hand in the air, subtly dropping something into the fire. It flashed green behind her, making everyone jump. "Fwoosh! A flaming torch was in her hand! Father and I jumped, as you did, never seeing such a thing in our poor lives. Tales we had heard of wizards in far off lands, but also tales of witches, and they were of a darker sort. Yet this raven-haired woman seemed to mean us no harm. She smiled and led on, and before long, we saw the torchlight of the trading post on the other side of the Blackgate Bridge. We were safe.

"Or so we thought," she said, "That evening, we slept in a barn, nestled in the warm hay. But come morning, as father sought for a place to set up his trade, I heard the fluttering of wings and a chattering like eager squirrels. Looking up, I saw that two Nixominy had followed us!" Maewyn shook her head. "For all I knew, they would watch me the rest of my days, or plot to kill me in this secluded outpost, far from help. Riverskirt was never large enough for more than a few families, and there was no one who would believe the wild tales of a stranger child.

"Except..." she held up a finger, "except maybe a witch. Nasha, the Raven Witch, might believe me, knowing a magical thing or two, as she must. I ran about to find her, and saw she was on the other side of the bridge, walking the Kelga River Path to the west. Oh! I ran and ran, calling her name, hoping the dreadful beasties would not follow me. 'Nasha!' I called, 'Nasha!' Finally, she heard me and turned, piercing me with those cold gray eyes. 'Yes?' she said. I was so scared and out of breath, I just stood there panting. When finally I caught my wind, I bade her bend down so I could whisper to her."

Maewyn's voice became a harsh wisp of itself, but loud enough to carry. "I said, 'There are evil things following me. They chased us from home, and they have followed us here, now!' Nasha asked me, 'What evil? There are many wicked things in the Shadowood.'

So I leaned in close and said, 'Little bat-winged faeries!'"

Maewyn straightened her back and looked around with her blind eyes. "Well!" she said, "What adult would accept such a story from a silly child? None that *I* had met; not even my dear father believed me, not truly. But *she* did. I saw it in her eyes, and my heart leapt at it." She slapped her knee, took a drink, and continued her tale. "Together we walked back to the trading post, where father was waiting."

"Nasha asked him, 'Good blacksmith, you never shared the reason you and your daughter were driven from your home.' My father looked at me with a flash of guilt as he recounted the strange happenings in Gloamshire. He told her of the little missing things, and how the miller's coin purse became lighter and lighter each hour. They suspected a small, agile thief that could creep about unseen. They searched homes until they came to ours, and found a stash of stolen things under my bed! Then I told her of how I slept in the elf circle and awoke days later, able to see the little winged people."

Maewyn sighed, "Nasha looked deeply troubled after all was recounted. She told my father that she believed my story, and that such creatures had been seen since ancient times, when the Dread King reigned for a hundred years. She wanted to help, and restore our place back home. 'Why would you, a stranger, wish to help us?' asked my father. The raven woman's eyes turned sad and she said, 'Your daughter did not seek this gift, this curse. I would not see her suffer for it; for I bear a curse of my own that I cannot remove.' And with this, she went to the master of the trading post and got a horse for our wagon, and food enough for the journey home."

Maewyn paused to drink her ale, draining it. Drahn used her respite to ask, "What was her curse? Did she tell you?"

The old woman smiled at the sound of his voice. "You're a curious lot, you little dragons of the far north by the sea," she said, "always asking the whys and wherefores, but not a lick of patience between you." She cackled to herself.

Drahn's head tilted at the mention of other dragons, and he immediately had a dozen more questions to ask. Yet he restrained himself lest he prove her right. The crowd was already muttering in wonder at his brief interruption, so he clamped his mouth shut and fiddled with the tip of his tail, head and wings drooping as he turned crimson in embarrassment.

Cindra looked down at the necklace she wore, the one Drahn had made from his missing tail scale; it was turning a deep purple. The scale reflected her own feelings, and she felt sad for him. The little orphan was always hungry for news of more of his kind.

Nixy whispered to Drahn, "She's met other dweedragons! Maybe she can tell you where to find them?"

Drahn nodded, but kept silent. He was not going to place his hopes in the words of an old storyteller.

"Now, where was I?" the old woman asked, "Oh! The journey home. Well, there we were, readying to go back the way we came. Nasha was making her own preparations with the trade master. I was looking about for the little bat-winged people, trying not to let my gaze rest on them too long. They were there, watching us, from the eaves of the trade shop."

Maewyn made little squirrel noises as she wiggled her fingers at the ceiling. "Nasty little things. They watched us the whole time, not caring that I could see them. As the sun rose higher and the light shone bright on the river, Nasha came out and placed a cage in the wagon. It was a small wooden cage of white pine, like the kind made for chickens or doves.

"Inside, she placed a little basket of blackberries," Maewyn said, "When I asked her what the cage was for, she answered, 'In case we catch a game hen or a rabbit.'

Well, that seemed a bit silly, but what did I know?" she shrugged. "Then I asked her about the berries. She just smiled and said 'They are for us, but it is best to keep them in the cage so they don't get stolen by nasty faeries.'" Maewyn shook her head. "Odd woman she was, but cleverer than I. She put the cage with the berries behind the bench, and my father lifted me up beside him. 'I will walk behind the cart,' Nasha said."

The old woman stretched and sighed, "Oh, the first day was a long one, but better for having a beast to pull the cart. I was looking forward to some of those berries, but when we stopped to camp, we found the berries were half gone! 'Oh, it was those cursed faeries!' I said, shaking my fist at the trees. Father was baffled at this, but Nasha knew better. 'I will keep watch, and I will guard the berries,' she said. And so she did.

"The next morning, we awoke to the sound of chattering, angry squirrels," Maewyn said, "Nasha was standing there with the cage in hand, and inside I saw the faeries had been trapped!" The old woman giggled excitedly, grasping the air, as if she was drawing the cage closer to look. "I saw the little blighters up close! Nasty things, they were. They had skin like a brown toad, black eyes, upturned snouts, big, pointy ears, and sharp teeth. They even had tiny daggers and swords made of thorns. 'How did you catch them?' I asked. 'Simple,' Nasha said, 'I played at sleeping and waited for the cage door to open and the berries to move.'

"My poor father could still not see them, but he could hear the chattering noises from the empty cage. I asked her, 'aren't the bars wide enough apart that they might slip through?' She smiled and said, 'I placed a spell upon the cage, and they will be trapped inside until I release them.' Well, I was not so sure of that, but they kept in the cage all the way back to Gloamshire, eating our berries out of spite.

"When we came to the hamlet, our former neighbors were not in the mood to receive us," she said, "It seemed that more things had gone a-missing, and some took our presence as a sign that I was yet to blame! 'Why have you come back?' they shouted at my father, 'Hasn't your daughter done enough?' But before my father could rebuke them, Nasha stepped forward and held up the cage. 'Good people!' said she, 'here are your thieves! Come closer and I will show you!' And come closer they did," she said.

The old woman stood with a bit of effort and held her hand aloft, like she was presenting an invisible cage for evidence. The fire had become lower. Serving wenches moved about quietly, not wanting to disturb the performance. The audience was eager and attentive.

"The towns folk gathered 'round, unsure what to make of the woman in black," Maewyn said, "They saw nothing in the cage, until the woman took her wand and cast a spell upon it. And behold! The two faeries were revealed for all to see! The townspeople stood back in fear and awe, not just at the faeries, but at the Raven Witch, whom some had known from rumor and story. Murmurings began, and there was talk of a curse upon the hamlet." She shook her head and sat back down, saying, "Well, such is the way in little communities; always afraid of what they don't understand."

A man near the wall said, "Perhaps no one told you, but you're in a little community now."

"Careful!" cried another wag, "I'm getting afraid!"

The room had a laugh at that, and the old woman blew the hecklers a raspberry. Once the laughter died down, she continued. "Well, Nasha was having none of it; she called to them in a loud voice, 'I will end this threat for you, but on one condition! I demand that you absolve this girl and her father, and welcome them back among you!' Well, most had little enough problem with that, but others had their doubts. Rather than have long and useless talk about it, she got right to work."

Maewyn became more animated than before, acting out all she described. "The first thing she did was ask me if I saw any more of them about the town. I told her I did, but just a few. 'That won't do,' she said, and shook the cage vigorously, making the little beasties shriek! This call was answered, and as people began to sense the danger, the Raven Witch carried the cage to the square, and set it on the ground. 'Back! Back into your homes!' she cried, and hid with us in a nearby cottage.

"We could see the cage jostle back and forth as the creatures called their kin, and their kin answered. There was a fluttering mass of them gathering in the square, screaming and chattering. Oh! The sight of it! The noise and activity was so great, that others began to see them too. Some shrieked in fear, and others uttered oaths and blasphemies. Some foolish souls ventured outside with knives, skillets, whatever they could find to serve as a weapon. But to our horror, they were sliced by a hundred invisible blades! Their screams and the sight of blood drove the bravery out of them, and they fled. My father held me tight in his arms, and I felt the fear in him too. But Nasha the Raven Witch strode forth, wand held before her, and began a chanting."

Maewyn held out her arms and began muttering and chanting in some made-up language, making the listeners look at each other nervously. Her chanting rose in volume and intensity, until she gave a great shout. The fire behind her flashed and crackled, startling the cooks and the audience alike. Cindra had seen Glenawyn covertly toss some more of Maewyn's special powder into the flames. *An accomplice*, she thought with a smile.

The old woman cried, "A fire! A storm of fire rose in the square, burning all the shrieking, frantic faeries. The Raven Witch guided the flame, tracing it through the air to catch all that might escape! Oh, the smell and the sound of it!" she said, her voice shaking, "When the fire died out, the ground was littered with a hundred dead faeries, all blackened and crispy. The people came out to witness the carnage, now finally convinced of my innocence. I felt such a relief, but then I noticed that the two Nixominy in the cage were still alive, unburnt."

Maewyn hung her head and sat down. "The threat had not passed. Nasha took me aside and told me the horrible news. 'Nixominy have a queen, and she must be hunted down,' said she, 'I will need your help to find her, if you are brave enough.' Well, what could I do?" the old woman asked the crowd, "I was a child! But I could see them, and that was all Nasha needed to track them. 'I must ask my father,' I told her. 'There is no time,' said she. 'Let us leave now, while we still have daylight. I shall protect you.' Well, I think you all remember me saying what a ninnyhammer I was, so without much more thought, I agreed."

The old woman shook her head, making her flimsy mane sway in the air. "Nasha and I slipped out of the hamlet and she let the little blighters loose. They fled in fear, chattering curses at us, to be sure. Off they went, deep into the woods, and I led the Raven Witch after them. Eventually, we came to a hollowed out tree. Big and dark it was, a granddaddy of a Shadowood, with most of its leaves gone. The boughs were aflutter with angry faeries, starting to swarm about the trunk. I looked closer, and there in the hollow, I spied something I shall never forget!"

The crowd was now in rapt attention, and Cindra could feel the hairs on her arms raise in suspense.

Maewyn said, "It was reddish-brown, like a river toad, with bumpy, shiny skin. At first I thought it was a malformed child, but its belly was bloated horribly, and its face, oh its face! It was a horror to gaze upon; big black eyes that bulged, and a maw full of fangs. I shrieked, and Nasha bid me run home and don't look back. 'I can see her, child' said she, 'This fight is yours no longer.'

Her voice became frantic, "Well, run I did. I ran and ran like the terrors of the Abyss were on my heels. Noises of pain and anger I heard behind me, and before long I was too far away, hearing nothing but my own heart pounding in my ears. Eventually I returned to Gloamshire, and fell into the arms of my furious father. Oh he was not furious at me, but at the Raven Witch who had led his daughter into the woods, telling no one. I was so exhausted that I could tell him nothing of her deeds until the next morning. By then, it all seemed a bad dream, but tell him I did."

Maewyn let out a sigh. "A few days passed, and I wondered if I would ever see the Raven Witch again. I would sit at the edge of the wall and watch for her in the woods, hoping she would appear out of the shadows. But alas, she never did. At least, not that I saw..."

Then her voice became measured and truly creepy. "For one day, as I watched the woods, I heard a noise in the branches above me. I lifted my head to look... and what did I see but the two Nixominy we had caged, glaring down at me. They had survived, and they had fashioned what looked like little bows and arrows. As I drew breath to scream, they drew back the bows, evil grins spreading on their fanged faces... They loosed their arrows..."

She turned her puckered eye sockets to Nixy, "...and *that* is how I lost my sight."

The audience sat in silence for a moment, and Cindra knew they were all picturing the same horrible vision she was: that of a little girl, screaming in pain, with tiny arrows in her eyes. Then Maewyn stood and gave a little curtsy. The crowd began to shrug off the horror and clapped appreciatively.

"That was dweadful," Drahn said to no one in particular, "Do you think it's twue?"

Nixy took a deep breath and shuddered, "I hope not," he said, "But if she made it all up just to scare me for asking, it's a lot o' trouble to go through."

Drahn nodded, his scales changing back to purple from frightened blue.

Later at the inn, Cindra checked on her companions as they settled for the night. Deliah, Glenawyn, and Maewyn were sharing the large bed in the first room, which was also the most expensive room at the inn. Besides the bed, it had a dresser and a stone fireplace.

Sacrifices, she thought, recalling old comforts.

"We shall be leaving early," she said to the woman and her grandmother, "My retinue and I must first pay our respects to the master of the town."

"Fair enough," Glenawyn said, tucked in between the two extremes of womanhood, "We are not so quick to rise and make ready anyway, and we may yet stay another day."

Maewyn was already asleep.

"I shall go with you to see Sir Waliss," Deliah said, "It is part of my business on the road."

Cindra raised an eyebrow at that, but decided now was not the time to start an inquisition. "Suit yourself," she said, and looked at the three women one last time before leaving.

The maid, the mother, and the crone, she thought, remembering old tales of witches, and how they worshiped Jayda in those three aspects. Was it heresy, as she was taught, or did they know something the Jaydecean church didn't?

"Goodnight," she said, and closed the door behind her.

Next, she checked in on the boys and Glenawyn's husband, Bardon. Their room, like Cindra's, had a central fire pit which was currently crackling merrily against the cold. The three were lying on sleeping mats around the pit, but Adric had his head propped up on an elbow.

"All is well here?" Cindra asked, "Do you need anything? Mulled wine? A down quilt? Foot massage?"

"Then get it yourself!" Padison groaned, stealing her oft-used punch line.

She grinned. It was an old joke from their school days, but she still liked it.

"Adric?" she asked, "You look troubled."

"I was thinking one of us should keep watch, just in case," he said.

She shook her head. "They won't try anything. They know we are coming to see them tomorrow morning. Why go through the trouble of an ambush in town, when they can do it in their training hall?"

He made an exasperated sound and laid his head down. "Goodnight then," he said, "I hope the family known for holding grudges won't hold a grudge."

"Goodnight," she said, hoping so too.

Her own room was shared with Wenyssaya and Nixy, and they all had the luxury of cots. Drahn was already asleep in his bag under Nixy's cot, snoring gently. Wenyssaya's raven, Navithwi, was sleeping on the windowsill, its beak pointing to the floor.

It was a bit odd sharing a room with Nixy, Cindra realized. He wasn't a little boy anymore, and though he looked younger than his fourteen years, he surely had all the feelings of a normal teenager. She remembered herself at that age, and that made things more uncomfortable.

Nixy, who had been staring into the fire, looked up and smiled as she came in. "Hullo, Lady Cindra," he said. The formality sounded odd coming from his mouth.

"Evening, Your Highness," she replied. It made him squirm a bit.

"I guess you two ladies wanna change into nightclothes," he said, "It's time I found what passes for a jakes around here anyway." He smiled sheepishly, tried to smooth out his cowlick, and left the room.

Cindra began rummaging through her baggage for a nightshirt, happy for the rare opportunity to wear one to bed. Wenyssaya had hers prepared, and she began to disrobe.

"May I ask you something?" Cindra said, "It's a rather...delicate subject."

"Of course," Wenyssaya said, though her eyes were wary.

"I worry about Nixy; I mean I *have* worried about him since we met on the streets, but well, he's older now. He's becoming a young man."

"Yes," she agreed, unfastening her bodice.

She's not going to anticipate my thoughts this time, Cindra realized, and it annoyed her a bit. Sighing, she said, "I was wondering if he has... feelings for you. I mean, you two spend so much time together, he can't help but get, well, distracted."

Wenyssaya turned her violet eyes to meet Cindra's hazel ones, raising her eyebrows ever so slightly. She loosened her dress and pulled it over her head, folding it expertly as she stood naked in the cold room. Her pale, golden skin glowed in the warm light, showing goose pimples. Cindra's eyes couldn't help but move over her elegant, lithe figure, noticing the finely traced tattoos around her wrists and hands, and finding new ones on her hips, calves, and stomach. She was like a sculpture by a master artisan, embodying gentle spring in human form. *No,* Cindra reminded herself, *elven form.*

Cindra had not realized she had been entranced until the elf maid pulled her nightgown over her head and let it drop, shrouding her body in linen drapery. It was like the curtain falling on the climax of a play, and it made Cindra flinch. She felt a blush rising, and also more than a little envy.

As Wenyssaya preened and teased her golden curls out of her collar, she turned and said, "He is a sweet child, and I doubt he will have such urges for many years to come. As for myself," she added coldly, "I have never acted inappropriately towards him, nor would I."

Her change in tone caught Cindra off guard, and a cold little quiver twisted her stomach. "N-no, I, I didn't mean to imply that you- it's just that boys of his age are-"

"He is not a human boy," Wenyssaya interrupted, "He is half-elven, and of a very old elf at that; the world has not seen his kind for many, many centuries. But among my people, young boys do not begin to seek after a mate until they are close to fifty years old."

"*Fifty years?*" Cindra gaped, "That seems like a long, peaceful time for elven girls."

The elf maid shrugged, "If you like. It all depends on your sense of time." She smiled, and her normally pleasant mood returned. "It must be very difficult for you, trying to understand him."

"I thought I did, once upon a time," Cindra admitted, "But now..." Her concern for her friend returned in full, but for a different reason. "What... what do you think will happen to him when he meets his father? Will he be asked to stay?" *And for how long?* she wondered to herself.

Wenyssaya placed her folded clothes on the baggage and sat on the cot, arranging her blanket. She considered a long while before she answered. "I do not know. I like to think he will be inducted into his inheritance, perhaps trained and educated, perhaps merely protected. I really cannot say." Her voice was sad, and Cindra realized Wenyssaya worried about him at least as much as she did.

The elf woman made herself comfortable, and Cindra proceeded to remove her bodice and split skirt. *From here on out, it's breeches,* she thought. As she pulled one of Jaron's old nightshirts over her head, she remarked, "You know, I was expecting you to have a shimmering gossamer nightgown, wrapped around you by hummingbirds."

She said around a yawn, "That one is at home, and so are the birds."

Morning came slowly, its blue light seeping through the window slats with feeble progress. Cindra watched it illuminate the rafters as best it could, and thought about her upcoming meeting with Sir Waliss. She had awakened in the late watches of the night, placing a few sticks on the fire to keep it alive, but it was out now. Her decision to meet the old man seemed right at the time, but now she began to wonder. *What has he heard? Will there be lies and accusations to untangle? Will Ratham be there to call me out?*

It was all she could do to get out of bed. Once her feet hit that cold floor, she was committed. Until then, she could float in her personal Void, pondering her decisions while still in between realms of action.

Finally, she came to a conclusion: *It was stupid, but necessary.* She could live with that.

She got out of bed, trying to slip on her boots without making the cot squeak too much. She rose and arranged her clothing, making extra sure that Nixy was asleep before getting dressed. Even if he wouldn't be too aroused by a woman's body for many more years, it still made her feel weird.

Not until fifty. Imagine. I wonder if it's the same for half-elves?

To her dismay, she found that her monthly flow had begun. It was not very heavy, but was ill-timed as usual. *Just when I want to start wearing breeches*, she thought, grimacing, *Figures.*

She tended to herself discreetly, pulled on her breeches and undershirt, and then the quilted arming doublet. Her armor was currently in the boy's room, in a specially-made chest that could be carried on the back of a sturdy man. Padison was sturdy but short, and Cindra insisted that Adric always help him take it off the wagon lest he tip over.

She left her sleeping roommates and headed for the boys' room.

Bardon and Padison were groggy and sitting up when she knocked, but Adric was fast asleep.

"Kept watch for hours, I think," Paddy said, thumbing at his sleeping friend.

"He's a good squire," Cindra said.

"Too good for his own good, more like," Padison said, yawning.

"A moment, lady knight," Bardon said, scratching his chest, "and I'll be out of your way."

After Bardon dressed and gave them the room, Padison nudged Adric awake with his foot. "Wake up, Hywahl. There's a lady that needs tending to."

"Deliaaah?" Adric croaked, coming out of a dream.

Cindra snorted a laugh and knelt over his face. "You should be so lucky," she said, "It's only your knight and commander! Get up, squire."

"Oh," Adric said, groaning to sit up, "Sorry, milady."

———

Breega had awakened by the time of their appointment. The cold air bit their skin and smelled of chimney smoke and fresh bread. As they made their way up the hill, Cindra's clanking steps drew the attention of the townsfolk. Some even paused to watch them march up the steps of the school, wondering what was going to happen.

"Are you sure you want to do this?" Adric said.

They stood before the great wooden doors of the Greenfellow Maurbrik Fighting School, a long, tall and imposing structure with a tiled roof and heavy timbers. Massive shadowood carvings of mighty bears, rearing up on their hind legs, flanked the doors. The Greenfellow coat of arms hung under the eaves: a field of yellow with a green bend sinister, and three Jaydecean wheels above. Smaller dwellings had been added on to the back of the old structure in later years, probably the private quarters of the master of the hall.

"We're doing this," Cindra said, as much to herself as the others.

Adric and Padison were with her, both armed with swords. Deliah was there as well, for she insisted she had business with the old patriarch, but would not elaborate. Cindra was in full armor, sans helmet, and had her honor sword at her hip, as well as the *Kos* knife on her belt. She figured her shield would be a bit much; besides, it bore the Corrina coat of arms. She chose instead to wear the king's tabard, letting that make its own statement.

Wenyssaya, Nixy and Drahn had no reason to come, and their presence would only make things more complicated.

She used the brass knocker, shaped like bear claws, and made a resounding clapping noise that echoed down the streets of the village.

Thunk-k-k, thunk-k-k, thunk-k-k-k.

"No one home," Paddy said, "Let's go."

"Stop it," Adric scolded, though he probably shared the sentiment.

After a few tense moments, the door was opened. A woman peeked out; she was in her mid-forties, with braided, dark blond hair. She was not unattractive, but her face was careworn and troubled, with a sharp nose and thin lips. Looking over the newcomers, her gaze settled on Cindra and the black eagle on her breast.

"Are you the knight who sent the announcement?" she asked. By her tone, she might have been asking if it was some kind of poor joke.

"I am," she said, "Does Sir Waliss grant us an audience?"

The woman looked her up and down, perhaps still trying to decide if she was serious. Finally, she nodded and said, "Wait here a moment. The master doesn't get many visitors."

They waited for a good quarter of an hour, shifting from foot to foot to keep warm and commenting on the chill. Deliah did not complain nor shiver, seemingly comfortable in her woolen cloak.

When they were finally admitted, Cindra couldn't help but be impressed. The building was an older Norsican style, but was far from rustic. The pillars that lined the hall were made from dark, polished Shadowood, and carved to make twisting, intertwining patterns that rose to the ceiling. The pillars supported a second story, where the students slept. The walls of the hall were stone that was paneled with wood, and the rafters were made from fir timber. Beneath the honey colored second story were elaborate tapestries that depicted hand-to-hand battles, and between the tapestries were mounted heads of hunting trophies. The building smelled of aged lumber, smoke, and mildew.

At the far end of the hall was a large fireplace, currently blazing and filling the cold hall with merry warmth. The figure seated before the fire was not merry, however. Sir Waliss Greenfellow sat in a high-backed chair topped with a row of bear claws. He wore a thick fur cloak over his woolen robes, which were embroidered with angular designs and sported rich embellishments. By his side was the woman who had answered the door and two younger men in their teens, both stocky and tall. Neither was Rejick Ratham, but they could be his brothers, so closely did they resemble him.

Cindra bowed to the old knight, and her companions knelt. He motioned them forward. They crossed the polished wooden training floor, their footsteps echoing down its length. As they approached, they noticed that the head mounted above the fireplace was the Minozhian bull-man that Ratham had boasted about at school. It was large and mean-looking, with broad, curved horns, and the forward-facing eyes of a predator. It was unmistakable; definitely not a cow as Padison had once joked. The head hung eight feet off the floor, supposedly the same height it had stood in life. Cindra had remembered Ratham saying his uncle had kept it in his study. She wondered why and when had he moved it into his training hall. Surely not to impress *her*.

The woman spoke for Sir Waliss as they approached, calling, "We greet you, Lady Cindra Corrina, and welcome you and your companions to Breega." She sounded formal and cold, though not hostile.

Cindra replied in a clear voice, "Greetings from His Majesty, King Galen III, and His Lordship, Amon Corrina, Count Casselvane." They stopped five paces from the chair, and Cindra bowed again, noticing an old bloodstain on the floor. *Jaron's?* she wondered. Looking up, she got her first good look at the infamous Sir Waliss Greenfellow.

He had been tall once, but his frame had shrunk and bent as he approached three quarters of a century. He had a long, serious face, and a high forehead from which silvered hair was gathered back into the tipok knot of a knight. His deep-set, gray eyes studied her with an alert shrewdness, and a permanent frown creased his overhanging brow. He drew himself up in the chair with some effort, intent on looking the part of a lord in his castle.

His mouth was a disapproving line in his face. When he spoke, Cindra saw his teeth were long and crooked, and his voice was a series of raspy little air bellows. "You are the first Corrina to stand in this hall since Falon, your great-grandfather. To what do we owe the honor, *lady knight?*" The last two words were given a scornful emphasis. Jaron had described Sir Waliss as 'a man who can no longer slay with his hands, so he uses his voice.' But Cindra did not come to duel.

She said, "I have only come to offer my well wishes, and ask for safe passage through your territory, Sir Waliss."

"Safe passage?" he said, "Is it mine to give? I am not the lord of these lands."

"I know your lord is Elburd Mamfett, the Baron Waynwell," she said, "but your men patrol both the Joshian Way and the Waynwell road."

"And which are you taking?" he asked.

She knew it was a reasonable question, but she had hoped he wouldn't ask. "We are taking the Joshian Way far into the Shadowood."

"Ah, well..." he held his palms up, "I am afraid my men are marching east with the *king* in the *spring*." He made the rhyme sound playful. "The roads are... unsafe at the best of times. Are these your *fighting men?*" Again with the unsavory emphasis.

"This is my squire, Adric Hywahl, and my man-at-arms, Padison Pemwreth," she said, ignoring his tone.

But Sir Waliss just stared at them.

The woman beside him spoke. "These are schoolmates of yours?" she asked.

"They were," Cindra said to her, "I am sorry, we were not introduced?"

Waliss gestured to her, "My half-sister, Emlyn. Her son Rejick was one of your fellow students, until he was ejected for questioning the judgment of the Freekirk School."

Emlyn looked down her nose at Cindra, summoning all of her motherly glowering powers.

"That's putting it lightly," Padison said, then as Cindra glared, he added, "begging your pardon."

"Oh?" Waliss rasped, "You have something to add, stripling?"

Adric placed his hand on his friend's shoulder and said, "Paddy and I were present when it happened, Sir Waliss. With respect, it wasn't questioning Master Cord's judgment; it was outright mockery of the school, the training we received, and the instructors themselves. Ratham chose to leave, and Master Cord obliged him."

Waliss considered this as his sister huffed through her nose and shifted to and fro. Finally he said, "My nephew has his mother's temper, as she has our father's. Believe it or not, but I have always been the more reasonable one."

Cindra dared not smile in front of the woman, but said, "May I ask how Rejick fares?"

Adric and Padison knew this meant, 'Is your nephew lurking about, waiting to ambush us?' They watched and listened closely.

"Last I heard, he is well," Waliss said, "He answered our lord's call to arms and marched to Portshia a month ago. Perhaps he did not pop in on his old school chums?"

Emlyn said icily, "He will inherit the Greenfellow School, assuming he returns from the war."

"If not," Sir Waliss said, gesturing to the two young men beside her, "you have two more sons."

She stiffened, but shut her thin lips tightly until they all but disappeared.

He turned his vulture-like gaze back to Cindra and gave her a hard stare with his gray eyes. "Lady Cindra, I have heard all about your escapades, misadventures, and tall tales. I dare say they are becoming legendary among the lesser folk." He gripped the arms of the chair, and leaned forward, "I once thought that giving a knighthood to a turnip farmer and making him his champion marked your grandfather Armon as the most foolhardy and embarrassing Corrina. Perhaps this mockery of tradition skips a generation."

Adric nudged Padison when he heard the boy draw a sharp breath.

Cindra was not going to rise to the bait. She had decided to put aside her pride and take whatever the bitter old man dished out, short of violence. "Perhaps you are right," she said, "The same king that made me a knight also chained me to a mountainside. I've paid for my misdeeds, and survival breeds its own acceptance."

"Indeed it does," Waliss said, reflecting, "I hear you are useful with a bow, and used one to protect the king during that Minozhian raid... but what did you do to earn the right to bear *Vyzeroth*?" He pointed to the Honor Sword at her hip. "Was it for mighty deeds in service to your lord father?" His voice turned to syrup, "Or did daddy simply give his daughter a glowy sword to take into the dark wood?"

Cindra flinched. He was good at this. She felt his scorn rake across her like bear claws. She replied, "*Vyzeroth* is kept for ceremonial duties, and my mission is ceremonial. The champion's sword is borne by Sir Jaron Dunlorden."

He sneered at the name. "And what manner of mission deserves *your ladyship's* prowess and gravitas?" he asked, "What warrants such a retinue of fighting men?"

She raised her head slightly, saying, "The kind of mission that is none of the *school master's* damned business."

Waliss's bent frame rocked with a silent chuckle, even as his sister and nephews stiffened. "There it is," he said, pointing a bony finger, "The cat's claws come out! I was wondering if you had that fire in you." He shook his head, "Say what you will about the Corrinas, and I *have...* but they come from hardy Norsican stock. There were battle maidens in the old sagas, and more than a few warrior queens."

She inclined her head slightly. *Is he paying me a compliment?*

Waliss turned and seemed to notice Deliah for the first time. "Is this your lady in waiting?" he asked, flicking his wrist at her, "Someone to lace your bodice when you're not playing at being a knight?"

Cindra's mouth twisted. "My lady in waiting was murdered at sea by Minozhian pirates," she said, glancing up at the mounted head, "This is Deliah Wyngaard, a woman of Portshia, who asked to travel with us as far as Breega. She claims to have business with you." Then she added, "She was betrothed to your son."

This caused an uncomfortable, confused silence. That suited Cindra just fine.

Waliss peered at her, motioning her closer. "Was she, now? Come, girl. Let me get a look at you."

She stepped forward, closer but out of reach. Their gray eyes locked, her piercing storm clouds meeting his fading, watery orbs. Sir Waliss flicked his gaze over her figure, but fixated on her face.

"You are the girl my son wrote about, the one whom he caught in the embrace of that farm animal, Jaron Dunlorden."

Cindra colored at that. She was annoyed that one of his insults finally broke her cool demeanor. Worse, Waliss had noticed. The side of his mouth curled in amusement.

"And they fought over you," he continued, "yet you spurned him when it was over. Did he truly give his troth to such a fickle woman?"

Deliah said calmly, "Our betrothal was a sham, sir. He never meant to marry me, nor I him."

This caught Cindra completely by surprise. She stared at the back of Deliah's head as if expecting to find horns sprouting. Was this a lie?

Sir Waliss was not completely shocked. "I admit I was surprised when I read his letter. I never knew him to moon over a girl. Explain yourself."

"I used to live in these woods," she said, "Sir Earnold came upon me as I was fleeing from a pair of bandits. In return for his kindness, I owed him a favor." She turned and glanced at Cindra. "He wanted me to come to Portshia with him, where he would train at the Freekirk School. He played me off as his betrothed, but bade me to flirt with Jaron Dunlorden."

Cindra found she was holding her breath. She started to sweat in her armor despite the cold, and her neck muscles felt like taut cables.

"The plan was to find us together so that he might challenge Jaron to a duel," she said, staring straight into the old man's eyes, "It did not go well for him."

"You deceitful *bitch!*" Cindra hissed. She had not intended to say it out loud; at least she told herself that.

Deliah turned calmly, "What I did for Jaron's reputation was nothing compared to your exploits, dear lady knight."

Cindra wanted to draw her sword; her left hand was already on the scabbard. Adric took her wrist, gently restraining her.

Waliss sat back in his chair and laughed; it was a dry, wheezing sound, like a dying bird. He had to gasp and catch his breath, then fell into a fit of coughing. Finally, as his sister rubbed his back, he recovered enough to speak. "It- it would seem the two of you have much to discuss! Is this the business you had with me, madam? To tell me my son was a vengeful, devious knave? Why do you think I sent him off to the Freekirk School in the first place? If he didn't get that brooding idiocy drummed out of him, then at least he'd know the fighting style of his sworn enemy."

Cindra's face was red now, and she was shaking with rage. She truly wanted to kill one or both of them, and it showed. The young men shifted their stance, hands on daggers. Adric and Padison had stepped forward at her side, feet apart and hands at the ready. Adric whispered, *"This is not why we came."*

Deliah remained infuriatingly calm and replied, "No, Sir Waliss. My business involves your shame and dismissal."

Waliss lost his mirth quickly, but before he could retort, she started speaking, "I said I lived here, in the Shadowood, as did my family, back to the days of my great-grandmother, Nasha."

"What?" Cindra gasped. *She didn't mean...?*

"Nasha died three years ago at the age of one hundred and seven," she said, "Before she passed, she shared a story with me."

"Don't tell me," Cindra said, "killer faeries?"

Deliah nodded, "That story was true. She was known as the Raven Witch, and she indeed had learned magic."

The listeners exchanged looks, but said nothing more. In elder days, Deliah would have been punished for her ancestor's crime. Female descendants of witches were not trusted either.

"After that event, she crossed the Emerald Bay to Aurilon, settling in the province of Kravore, near the river border with Maylione," she said, "She sought an employer that would value her powers and not betray her. She found Mordain LuKravore, the Baron DuKort."

Sir Waliss sat up, his eyebrows arched and his eyes widened.

"She remained in his household for many years, serving the baron in his schemes, even sharing his bed. Then came the wars with Calilon, and she found a Corrina army at her doorstep."

Cindra stood transfixed. She knew this history. Her grandfather, Count Armon, led that army; leaving his wife, Julith, and their sons, Amon and Aren. That was when...

"The Battle of DuKort," Sir Waliss muttered, "I was only twenty-two, but I was the count's champion."

Deliah continued, "When the castle's defenses fell, Baron DuKort sent his women and children to the catacombs and waited in ambush for the count, but he kept Nasha by his side."

"What is this?" Waliss demanded; a deep frown creased his brow and his hands trembled.

"A confession," Deliah said, "Nasha used her magic to send the count's protector fleeing in terror. It was swift and unavoidable. No man could have stood against her spell without magical aid."

Waliss had tears in his eyes. He drew a ragged breath.

"It was not cowardice," she said, "It was treachery, and it was unfair."

The room was silent as all eyes turned to the bent old man. He placed his face in his hand and wept openly; decades of bitterness that twisted his insides began to unknot, until his grief turned to anger. He bellowed at her, "Why do you come here? Why do you open old wounds? No one believed me then, and none will believe it now!"

"They will," Deliah said, "Before I left Portshia, I sent a letter of confession to Count Casselvane, stating my great-grandmother's last wish that you be exonerated. She took the guilt of it to her grave, and it was her one regret."

This was news to Cindra. If such a letter had been delivered, surely she would have heard about it? Unless it had been delivered the day she left, or remained unread... Regardless, was it true? If not, why would she travel all this way to lie?

"I... I..." Sir Waliss could not form words, and mouthed them silently for a long moment.

Cindra felt a swell of pity for him and relief also. His story was a stain on his house, and the thought that it might be lifted gave her a glimmer of hope. It was Jaron's father's story and Jaron's as well. If Sir Waliss had not fled, a footman named Fedrick Dunlorden might not have rushed to the aid of his count. Much would have been different. She and Jaron would have never met.

Waliss stretched out his hands to the raven-haired woman, and she stepped forward to take them, kneeling before his chair. His eyes were gray on red, and his face was wet from his tears, but it was alight with peace and hope, a look he had probably not worn in over fifty years.

Cindra thought it was almost worth standing there through his abuse and Deliah's outrageous admissions.

Almost.

Chapter Fourteen

Dissonance

Cindra led the party away from Breega, keeping her eyes on the road ahead. She would not look back, lest her anger get the better of her. She would not give the woman the satisfaction of seeing her flash and fume, if she was there at all. Surely Deliah Wyngaard fed upon people's anger and jealousy. *Jealousy? Yes,* Cindra thought, *that too.*

The story of Nasha's treason and confession was still fresh in her mind, but so too was the admission that Deliah had lured Jaron into her arms for no other reason than to have Earnold Greenfellow call him out.

"Is she going to follow at a distance the whole way?" Adric asked.

Cindra sighed. Her nosy squire was not under the same obligation to sulk and ignore Deliah. "I hope she does," Cindra said, "I hope she gets eaten by a bear."

"Aww," Adric said, clicking his tongue at her, "Don't be like that. If anyone is to blame, it's that Sir Earnold. She was just repaying a life debt."

"It doesn't work like that, Adric; I hope you know that," she said, "Just because someone saves you doesn't mean you're obligated to help them kill someone else for their petty reasons."

"Yeah, I suppose..." he trailed off.

Cindra hoped he would drop the matter. The young man was too accommodating of Deliah, and wanted them all to be friends. Well, specifically him and Deliah. They rode together in silence for a time.

"What are you going to do if she keeps following us?" Adric asked.

"I don't know," Cindra snapped, "maybe give her what she deserves."

Adric shifted in his saddle, taken aback. "And what might that be?" he asked.

Cindra had no ready answer that she cared to voice.

They reached a lonely teahouse by midday and took the time to refresh themselves; there would be little else for twenty leagues. As they departed, they saw Deliah coming on in the distance. Cindra increased their pace.

Nightfall came more swiftly than the group had anticipated, and there was a scramble to gather scant firewood. Wenyssaya used her faerie lights to help, and she and Padison could be tracked through the trees only by the bobbing orbs of captured moonlight that danced above her hand.

At least Padison's infatuation hasn't been shooed away, Cindra thought, watching as Adric glumly went about his duties.

She had not consulted Nixy or Wenyssaya about dismissing Deliah from their company, and she didn't really need to; the elf maid seemed to sense the strong feelings between them, and Nixy just accepted Cindra's judgment. It was comforting to not be questioned.

Besides, she knew the other two witnesses would disseminate the story through the magic of gossip. Perhaps that was what Paddy was talking to the elf maid about now?

"She's got a fire going already," Nixy said, pointing to a distant glow in the dark, "She was stopping to gather wood along the way."

Cindra hefted her lit sword, glad for it, but wishing for a real fire. "She knows how dark it gets here, and how soon," she said, trying to stroke down his cowlick.

"She still might be useful, you know, as a guide."

"I don't trust her Nixy, and neither should you. She has too many secrets, and each time I learn one, it raises alarms. She's devious, manipulative, and doesn't..."

"...Doesn't what?"

Cindra wasn't sure how she wanted to say it. "She doesn't have the proper fear and respect of... her situation." *Fear and respect of me*, she had wanted to say.

"What do you mean?" Nixy was never good at subtext.

Cindra took a deep breath, looking at the dark boughs above them. Then she said, "Do you remember our carriage ride in the city long ago? Remember how we laughed at the pigeons on the street that would only move just enough to not get run over? Deliah's like that. She knows the danger of goading me, but she only budges just enough to avoid getting hit."

"You tried to *hit* her?"

"No, but I want to; I want to strangle her sometimes," she said, "But it wouldn't change anything. I know it's a knight's code to protect the weak and honor women, but I'm a woman too. What does the code say about that?"

He shrugged, "Dunno," he said, "I don' think they was expecting you." He gave her a mischievous smile that she had not seen in forever.

She almost preferred him this way, like he was before. *They grow up so fast,* she thought.

Then she remembered what he was.

Drahn, who was eavesdropping from the wagon, popped his head up and said, "If you want, I can go spy on her and see if she's up to no good!"

Cindra turned to him and said, "You do that if you like. Just don't go forgetting yourself and talk to her. Spies don't reveal themselves."

"What if she sees me?" he asked.

"Good spies don't get seen," Nixy replied.

The little dragon nodded and flapped into the dark canopy.

Wenyssaya grew impatient with Adric's flint and tinder, and used her magic to start burning the dense wood. Before long, she had a merry fire going to stave off the cold gloom; she helped Padison prepare the food as Adric helped Cindra out of her armor. Nixy was unsaddling the horses as he liked to do, to the elf woman's disapproval.

"Where is Drahn?" Wenyssaya asked.

"Spying on Deliah," Cindra said, "His idea."

"We would be able to keep a better eye on her if she were here," the elf maid said.

"Hmmph," Cindra grunted, not trusting herself to be nice to anyone tonight.

"I understand her association with your Sir Jaron was a ruse?" Wenyssaya said.

Cindra nodded. "Word does get around..." She glared at Adric and Padison, who avoided her gaze.

"And," the elf continued, "her great-grandmother was what your people call a witch; specifically Nasha, the Raven Witch."

"Rumor has it," Cindra said, willing the food to be done so mouths would be too busy eating.

Wenyssaya began, "I don't mean to be contrary, but-"

"Then don't," Cindra interrupted, "I don't want her with us. I can't stop her from following, but I don't want to hear her voice, see her face, or hear her name. The anger is still too fresh."

"I understand," the elf maid said, "I did not mean to be offensive. But like it or not, we might end up needing her, and she is safer with us."

Cindra snapped, "Is she?" but she regretted it at once; Wenyssaya's disappointed look was quite potent. "Consider the subject dropped" she said.

Adric doffed her armor in record time so that he might put some distance between them. The others concentrated on their tasks until the meal was ready. Her foul moods could be palpable, she knew; Jaron had said so. Hoping to hide her face in her baggage, she started sorting through her pack.

Her mind went back to some of their more memorable fights and smoldering silences. Her time at the Freekirk School had been a trial in many ways, but the worst was dealing with hurt feelings and bickering with the one she loved.

She had not meant to think about Jaron in this way; she had hoped to keep her thoughts of him happy, such as their last meeting. Her fingers happened upon the vial containing the Oil of Nim, the Selvinian contraceptive she had used before their last afternoon together. Why she had brought it, she was not sure; a reminder, perhaps, or maybe it was so her parents wouldn't snoop through her things and find it.

Next, she came across the Essence of Elder, a more practical bit of divine alchemy; it could clear the skin, heal abrasions, mask putrid odors, and improve breathing. One thing it could not do is clear the air between Cindra and her party. They now spoke in low tones, hoping not to disturb her.

Eventually, she found the ear stud Ildric Finnael had given for her birthday. It was enchanted, meant to convey a single, important message to her, should the wizard ever deem to send one. It was better than an ember swallow that could take many hours and leave a fiery arrow pointing to their location. But the thought that he might need to use such a gift had always filled her with great unease. Well, there was nothing for it. Ignoring the wizard's last gift had almost killed her.

"Wenyssaya?" she asked, "I don't suppose you could help me with this? Do elves pierce their ears?"

Dawn came too soon and stayed too long; a dull blue glow that crept under the eyelids and didn't have the decency to turn warm and bright. Cindra had the late watch, so she got to see it affect the others; she had been tending the meager fire, imagining the sun in its flickering tongues.

A noise snapped her head up; the sound of hoof-beats coming up the road. She saw Deliah emerge out of the fog, leading her black horse and carrying a bundle. Cindra got to her feet, unhappy that her limbs did not share her will to rise.

"What do you want?" she called, hand resting on her sword hilt.

The others came alert to the noise and looked towards the intrusion.

"I was returning your dweedragon," she said in a neighborly tone, "He snores a bit." She led her horse into their camp, past Cindra, and placed the sleeping Drahn on his knapsack on the wagon bench. Then she mounted and cantered north up the road. "Try and keep up," she called, and vanished into the fog.

Drahn was rather ashamed when he awoke to the shaking of the wagon and was told how he came to be there. "I don't think I was sleepy," he said, "At least, I don't wemember being sleepy."

"That's okay," Padison said, driving beside him. He said, "I fell asleep on my first watch... and my second."

"Weassuring," Drahn said, his scales shimmering to crimson.

"I said I'd slap him silly if he did it again," Adric called over his shoulder.

Drahn felt he deserved to be slapped silly himself. He had *never* failed so dramatically at a task before.

"I remember that time Drahn tried to spy on me," Nixy said with a chuckle, "He landed on the roof of the castle's aviary, slipped off the tiles, and fell right into my arms. Then he bit my nose."

So maybe I have failed dramatically before, Drahn thought with a sigh. His scales shimmered from crimson embarrassment to deep purple displeasure.

"Did you at least learn anything useful before you pulled a Padison?" Cindra asked.

"Not much," Drahn said, "She ate a meal and bathed in the wiver, then..."

"I'll go next time," Adric said eagerly.

There was laughter all around. Even Cindra had to smirk in amusement at that.

"I'm surprised we haven't seen her yet," he said.

"Maybe a bear ate her," Cindra replied, hopeful.

The woods grew darker as they went on, even as the sun rose overhead. Its radiance could be seen through the thickest canopy like embers dancing in the shadows, a feeble orange light fighting to be seen amid the gray dreariness. Happiness was found in those places where the trees thinned or cleared entirely, exposing blue sky and the yellow face of Arahn, boon to travelers. Cindra finally understood why the ancients had built sun shrines on the road into the woods. But the lifting of their spirits was short-lived, and back into the woods they went, looking behind at the dwindling light with longing.

The road began to show signs of neglect this far north, as grasses and weeds divided the paving stones with more frequency. An occasional tree root would extend too far beyond the drainage ditch and encroach upon the road, causing the stones to buckle or crack. On a well-traveled road, such growth would be hacked down regularly, but not here. Or perhaps they had been, and the forest had grown defiant.

Patches of white could be seen under the trees and along the road. At first, they seemed like eerie, pale creatures crouching in the dark; dread things that did not care that they were so visible. As it turned out, they were patches of snow that had fallen perhaps a month ago, frozen hard and hidden from the sun; ghosts of winter, unable to move on.

The search for firewood began early in the afternoon. Before long, they had a good supply on the wagon and Cindra was confident that they had enough to leave for the next travelers. One night in a comfortable inn had dulled their camping-sense, and she intended to learn from every mistake.

A few hours later, when rumps were sore and backs tired, Cindra called, "Let's stop at that clearing." She saw no sign of Deliah, which was a relief, but a fear and doubt lingered in the back of her mind. *What if a bear **had** eaten her?*

They made camp and Cindra's armor was removed. She was quite happy to be wearing trousers now; they were so comfortable and freeing, though not really meant for her hips. She wondered idly if they might find someone willing to make her a pair or two; some middle-of-the-forest tailor waiting for strange requests from eccentric travelers.

"How far is it to the next settlement... Gloamshire is it?" she asked.

"Two more days up some winding roads," Adric said, "assuming that Bardon fellow was right. There's not but a few river stations between here and there."

"Hmmm," Cindra said. Her hopes of getting well-fitting trousers anytime soon were dashed.

"I wish we could get a barge to go upriver," Padison said, "Not so many bumps at least."

"Just the occasional white water and shallows," Cindra said, "Besides, water oxen don't do well pulling loads upriver by themselves. You still need a mule or two on the river path to tow the barge. You'd be in charge of that," she said with a wink.

"Thanks," Paddy said.

"And it doesn't go all the way up," Adric added, "There's more than a few waterfalls below the confluence."

"The what now?" Padison asked.

"Confluence," Drahn explained, "a junction of two wivers; in this case, the Joshian and the Kelga."

"Is that where we're headed?" Padison asked.

"You saw the maps!" Adric said.

"I don't get maps!" Paddy whined.

"Yes, it's where we're going," Cindra said, getting out her dinner bowl, "Supposedly the Shadow Lord lives above the confluence in a place called the Fortress of Thorns."

"Where did you hear that?" Padison asked.

"Wenyssaya dreamed it last night," Cindra said.

The boys looked at the elf maid curiously.

Drahn did too. "Dweamed it?" he asked.

She nodded, "I told Lady Cindra of my dream early in her watch. They have been getting stranger of late, though they have always been strange. Last night I saw a place and heard names: *Navidundwi,* the Dark Vale, and *Thiiwa-thamanhuan,* the Fortress of Thorns. It is our destination, though I know little else, other than it lies north of the confluence in the deep woods."

"Do you trust these dreams?" Adric asked.

"Are they pwophecies?" Drahn asked.

"Yes, and no," she replied, "I trust them, but I believe they are messages, not prophecies."

"Messages from the Shadow Lord?" Nixy asked.

She replied, "I can assume so. There is a strange power that guides me, though I cannot tell if it is the Shadow Lord or not."

"Who else, or what else?" Adric asked.

"Perhaps the forest itself," she replied, "or this gift that has always been with me."

"I never asked before," Cindra said, "but from the stories of modern elves that I have heard, you seem a bit different; more powerful somehow."

"I do not know what stories you have heard," she replied, "but you are correct. There have been none like me in many generations."

"It's the blood," Nixy said, "Elven blood gets demolished with each generation."

"Diminished," she corrected.

"Yeah, that," he said, "The really old ones, like my-my father, they were amazing. But each generation gets weaker and lesser, until they are just kind of ordinary-like. Well, elf-ordinary."

"But I am different," Wenyssaya said, "I have a gift; my power is like the elder ones, like few who remain in the world today. I am not as great as the first generations, but my gifts were unmatched in my home in Du-Velthathwe."

Cindra wondered what her Hidden Grove was like, if there were buildings of wood or stone, or tree houses like in the faerie stories. She had never thought to ask Wen about her home; she hadn't thought to ask her about anything personal at all, really. Maybe it was her private nature that prevented others being nosy. Maybe Cindra was just too intimidated?

"What sort of dweams do you have that are so stwange?" Drahn asked. Apparently, some sort of permission to be curious had been implied.

Wenyssaya looked into the flames for a few moments and said, "I am in a frightening place, facing terrible sights, yet I am brave. Sometimes I am dressed in silk clothing, sometimes I wear armor. I carry a long-bladed spear, and I dance with the flames, for they are my friend. I see others, like shades in the mists, but they have an inner light. There is a storm, a living cloud of wings. There is a forge, hot and glowing like the sun. There is a dark light and a swirling vortex of power. There is blood, always much blood; yet I am brave." She finished her recitation, casting her eyes down away from the campfire. The others sat in silence, trying to imagine what played behind her eyelids at night.

Finally, Padison said, "I have dreams I'm at the fighting school during morning exercises, but I've got no pants and no one notices. Then the waitress at the Red Eagle walks by and calls out, 'Hey! He's got no pants!' Then everyone laughs."

The others looked at him like he was a fool, then they all began to laugh, even Padison.

After their meal and a good discussion about dreams, they began to settle in for the night. Adric went to sleep, for he had the late watch, and the others sat up talking quietly for a while into the gloaming. Wenyssaya wandered off alone to 'attend to her elven nature' as she called it, and Padison went to tend the horses. As the woods got truly dark, Cindra noticed an orange glow around the bend ahead of them.

Deliah, she supposed, *At least I hope it's Deliah. We don't need to run into strangers out here.*

Seeing where her gaze was fixed, Padison said, "Another camp. Think we should check it out?"

"Maybe," Cindra said, "If it's Deliah, at least we know she's not dead."

"Should I go check?" Drahn asked.

"Like last time?" Cindra smirked.

The corners of the little dragon's mouth turned down in a pout. "I don't know what happened then," he said, "I am sure I don't snore, anyways."

Cindra didn't want to tell him that he did a little. It was a distinctive whiffle, and his nose whistled sometimes. She found no need to chide him any further though.

"I'll go and see," Cindra said, "If it's her, I'll tell her she can camp with us to keep safe. If it's not, well... I'll come back and let you know."

"Want me t' go with you?" Adric asked in a muzzy voice.

"Go to sleep, Adric," Cindra said sternly. She stood up, stretched, and reached for her weapon belt.

"You're taking your sword?" Nixy asked.

She looked at the rig, wondering if she had meant to. "No," she said, "I'll leave it here. I don't want to seem too threatening." She unhooked the scabbard and handed the weapon to Nixy to hold. "Keep it safe for me," she said, and fastened the belt to her waist, adjusting the *Kos* knife at her back. "I'm not going into that black totally unarmed though. Not even to pee."

"Fair enough," Nixy said.

She strode into the darkness without a torch, not wanting to warn whoever it was if they were unfriendly. She was halfway there when she began to wish she had taken the light-giving sword with her. Twice she almost lost the road, stepping off the path and into a bush or ditch. Memories of a dark forest and a prowling predator returned with full force, and she had a thrill of fear. Yet the glow was growing nearer and brighter despite the forest's best efforts to swallow the light.

She rounded the bend enough to see a tethered black horse and a lone figure sitting by a fire, tending it with a stick. It was indeed Deliah, camping in the dark wood as if she had been doing so for much of her life, which according to her, she had. The woman's gaze lifted to the road at Cindra's approach, and she called her over. "Welcome," she said, "It was getting a bit lonely, and I was hearing noises. Pull up a log and sit."

Cindra was not feeling cordial or neighborly, so she chose to stand for the time being. "I was just checking to be sure you weren't a stranger or a pack of bandits," she said, "Also, if you wish, you can camp closer to us to be safer; if you wish."

"Generous," Deliah remarked, "To what do I owe this change of heart?"

"It's not a change of heart," Cindra said, "I still don't want you traveling with us. I just don't want your death on my conscience."

"My death?" Deliah chuckled, "That's sweet of you. I don't think you will have to worry about that."

"Because you're such an experienced camper?" Cindra asked, "Because your ancestor was some wood witch? What would you do if a group of men came out of the dark, looking for trouble?"

"Scream?" she answered.

"That's it?" Cindra asked, "Do you even know how to defend yourself?"

"Do you, lady knight?" she replied, "Have you ever been in a life or death battle against men?"

"I've fought Minozhians," she said with pride, "I've killed several, my first when I was fourteen." She wanted to take out the Kos knife, her *Lok-shíneh* war token, to show her, but thought it might seem too threatening.

"And what was that like?" Deliah asked, "Satisfying? Empowering?"

Cindra remembered feeling sick and guilty at the deed, once she had time to think about it. It was a bit worse after the Battle of Cordoshome; she had gotten the shakes badly and wanted to heave. "No," she said, "No it wasn't."

"Well then," Deliah said, "imagine killing something with a face like your own, a life like your own. Minozhians, for all their culture and traditions, are monsters; children of things that were once men long ago. Killing other humans... now, that's different."

"Like you would know?" Cindra demanded, making it more of a challenge than a question, "Killed any lately?"

Deliah just looked at her across the fire with those haunting, ice-chip eyes. Then she smiled. "What do the men call this? A pissing contest?"

"You talk and talk, Deliah," Cindra said, "you drop innuendo and snide comments wrapped in honey, but you've shown me nothing to prove that you're a woodswoman, a useful guide, or anything more than a manipulative and amoral seductress!"

"There it is!" Deliah said, sitting up, "the core of the matter. You hated me once because Jaron made a play for me, and you hate me more because it was *my* play, and it was a lie. What a petty child you are."

Cindra fumed, feeling her head grow hot. If she had taken a seat earlier, she would have risen to her feet at the words. Her hands rested on the weapon belt at her hips.

"Amoral," Deliah continued, "There's a fine choice of a word. When you have had to survive long enough, morality becomes a matter of convenience. Tell me that you lived for two years in exile, and two more dressed as a boy, and never played loose with morality."

Cindra just breathed through her hatred, unable to answer or move. She didn't trust herself to do either.

Deliah shook her head and rose, gathering some items from her pack. "How little we understand one another," she said, "Come with me if you want to truly know the depths of my amorality." She beckoned Cindra to follow as she turned and strode into the woods away from the road.

Cindra did not know what to make of that, but something in the woman's voice made her intensely curious. Taking a deep breath and looking into the darkness around her, she followed Deliah's path. The woods were instantly consuming and the darkness pressed close, and she felt like she had walked into the open maw of a beast. Yet Deliah was walking just ahead of her, apparently unafraid. Cindra steeled herself, not trusting the woman. What if she fled ahead, or led her into a trap? She felt behind her back for her *Kos* knife, just in case. Its steel-tipped horn handle, once a revolting sight, was a comfort now. The mossy smells of the forest almost covered the woman's constant scent of lilacs as she padded ahead of Cindra.

Deliah emerged into a moonlit clearing near the sound of running water. A cool radiance bathed the tall grass and reflected off the shallow meandering stream, creating little silver flashes like wiggling fish on the surface. As Cindra took in the beauty around her, Deliah began to disrobe, unfastening her travel dress and slipping free of it. Soon her pale skin was exposed to the cold night air and the soft moonlight, naked but for the wooden ring on her left hand.

She wants me to stand guard while she has a bath, Cindra thought. She was tricked indeed, just not as she had expected. She let out an annoyed sigh, feeling a bit of envy at the sight of her. Deliah was a great beauty, and what most men considered the standard of femininity. Cindra, with her broad shoulders, fighter's muscles, and slimmer hips, felt that she would never measure up to this woman's gifts. She was good enough for Jaron, of course, but then, so had Deliah been.

Men, she thought, angry at him now, though he was miles away.

"Do you know the first time we met?" Deliah asked, "It was not at the little inn at Wellgate. It was near a tea house by the bridge, some four years ago; the 'Bridge House,' I believe it's called."

"What?" Cindra asked, "I'm sure I'd remember."

"No, you wouldn't," she replied, sinking to her knees to splash water on her shoulders and arms, "You and Jaron were asleep under a tree. You'd raced your horses ahead, leaving Sir Earnold and your handmaid behind."

Cindra just stared at her back, wondering how in the Abyss this woman had known that. *She saw us sleeping?*

"I put you to sleep, actually. It was a darling sight, but I needed a lock of hair from both of you, so I had to be brief."

"You put- you needed- what in the name of the gods do you mean?" Cindra demanded. A sinking feeling began in the pit of her stomach and a chill rose up her spine with realization.

"For the spell, you see?" Deliah said cheerfully, "I'd stolen the roses from the temple hothouse, and I needed a bit of hair for your love charm."

"You- you're a witch!" Cindra gasped, "Your great-grandmother taught you magic!"

"That's jumping to conclusions," Deliah said, "It might have been my grandmother, or mother…"

"A witch! You're the damned 'mysterious wizard' who went unpunished!" she said, "You should have been hanged for it!"

"Yes, that would have been unpleasant, I am sure," Deliah said, "Did you know I even gave the roses to you and Sir Jaron? I was in disguise, of course. I do rather good 'old woman' glamour."

"You-" Cindra stammered, taking a few angry steps forward, feeling her boots sink into wet earth.

Deliah lowered her hair into the river to wet it, and then flipped it over her back, spraying Cindra with cold water. The shock struck her like a slap to the face and she recoiled.

"In six days it will be the 14th of Selvimoth, when you and Jaron first kissed at the Festival of Devotion. Shall I wish you a happy anniversary?"

Cindra growled, "You almost got him *killed*."

"Oh, I wasn't going to let poor Jaron die if I could help it," Deliah said, "Earnold had gone too far and threatened to expose my secret, so I went along with his little plan. I knew he wouldn't kill Dunlorden when he got the chance. No, Earnold was a gloater. He had to rub his enemy's face in the dirt. That's when I released the spell and gave Jaron a clear head."

She looked Cindra square in the eyes. "*No one* threatens me. I had found a decent life as the wife of a decent man, and I was content. He threatened to take that all away, so I set him up for a nice public death at the hands of his old nemesis. No one would suspect me, but I underestimated Sir Cord Freekirk; that little revelation soured my marriage. Ah, well…"

Cindra was beyond rage now; she was in shock. This woman had committed a capital crime not only by using charms on members of the nobility, but also in being the witch who made the charms. If their mission were not so important, she would march her back to Portshia in the morning to stand trial. She balled her fists with unchecked aggression, her breathing was deep through flared nostrils, and her eyes strained to see the woman in the pale light as her vision reddened with fury.

"Did it ever occur to you, I wonder," Deliah asked, "if your feelings for Jaron, or his for you, were not fanned unnaturally by the love charm? Do you really love each other as you think you do?"

Before Cindra knew it, the *Kos* knife was drawn and at her side, its metal length cold, broad and cruel. "How dare you," she hissed.

"Just a thought," Deliah said as she twisted the water from her ink-black hair, "Love magic is such a tricky thing. One can never be sure."

She took a step into the stream, but Deliah raised her hand and something caught on Cindra's boot. She fell forward to her knees as her foot tangled in a web of grass, and another runner ensnared her knife and hand.

"Now now, nothing hasty, dear," Deliah said.

Her wooden ring, Cindra thought, *it's a verge. It must have a core of silver.*

"Silly child," Deliah said, "you really have no idea what you are in the middle of, do you? The boy, the Shadow Lord, the Dark Heart... it's all coming together, and I must be a part of it. I *need* to go with you, I *will* go with you, whether you like it or not. I have waited too long to let your petty jealousy and wounded pride stop me."

Cindra cut herself free in two strokes and rose into a fighting stance, saying, "You think I will let a treacherous witch like you anywhere near Nixy? And you speak of the Dark Heart; do you have it now? Did the mad wizard give it to you? Maybe you're not just a witch, but a Llomaakitte priestess?"

"Why don't you cut open my chest and find out?" Deliah asked as she opened her arms. Seeing Cindra's eyes widen, she said, "Yes, it burrows into the breast of the bearer, replacing his heart; did you not know? That's how it got its name. But strike it with an ordinary blade, and it will strike back, and with such fury that nothing would survive it."

The words were churning in Cindra's head, bizarre but somehow true; they spoke of a deep knowledge that this woman should not know unless she was connected with it. *Gods, the danger I had let so close! What would happen if she had the Dark Heart, if she was the scion they spoke of, or worse, if she sought to give it to Nixy?* She had to stop her. 'Depths of her amorality' indeed! Deliah was a demnox in human form, a monster from the Abyss, in spirit if not in truth.

Deliah's icy gaze held her in place, daring her to act. Cindra's body trembled, partly because of the damp cold, but mostly due to the rush of battle frenzy that washed over her, the need to strike. Her fingers tightened on the handle of the knife...

Chapter Fifteen

Concurrence

Nixy watched Cindra stride into the darkness without a torch, heading for the dim glow of a distant fire. He wanted to go with, or maybe spy on them like Drahn had, though he knew he would be a much better spy. They wouldn't see him at all unless he wanted them to.

"I don't know about Lady Cindwa," Drahn said, watching her leave, "Something is deeply twoubling her."

Nixy had to agree. "She's been different since yesterday morning, when they met the Green guy."

"Gweenfellow," Drahn said, "Yes, you are wight. She has been vewy testy. My master would get like that sometimes, and it would last for days, but he is wather old."

"Do old people get grumpy like that a lot?" Nixy asked.

"Fwom what I can tell, they do," Drahn said, "I have watched my master and other wizards for over forty years, and they get fwustwated more easily as they age."

"Wow, forty years," Nixy said, "You don't look that old."

"Thank you," Drahn said, perking up, "I am forty-five, but age depends on species. You will get vewy old yourself, I imagine, being half an elf."

"Yeah," Nixy said, casting his eyes down, "Wenyssaya says I may live a few centuries. But that means…"

"Losing people you care about," Drahn said, "Yes, I know. The man who waised me is vewy old himself. I should probably go and see him soon."

Nixy looked back to see if Cindra was still visible; she was halfway down the road, slipping out of view and stumbling into a bush. Nixy had excellent night vision; he could see things that would make other people stumble and fall and he could see them yards away.

"I wonder," Drahn began, "I wonder if I should go and spy again, just to see what Lady Cindwa will say."

"I guess we're all curious," Nixy admitted.

"Vewy well," Drahn said, taking it as permission, "I shall not fail this time. No one will see me or hear me, and I will not fall asleep!" He leaped over the back of the wagon bench and flapped off into the gloom, landing on a tree branch every ten yards.

"Where is Drahn off to?" Wenyssaya asked. She had just returned from the woods herself, 'answering the call of her elven nature,' which was a very pretty-sounding term for the most indelicate of activities.

"He's going to go spy," Nixy said.

"On whom?"

Nixy motioned down the road, "Cindra. She went to spy on whoever is down there, probably Deliah."

"Everyone is spying on each other, and no one minds their own business," she said, "Typical dwivayiin behavior."

"*I'm* not spying on anybody," Padison said in defense of his species.

"Are you not?" she retorted.

His mouth turned down and he skulked away to check on the luggage. She had caught him staring at her too many times.

Nixy noticed Wenyssaya was grumpier lately. It didn't help that they would be camping outdoors for the foreseeable future; she preferred a bed and a roof, or at least a tent. Sleeping in the open rubbed her the wrong way. Nixy didn't think it was so bad, but the elf maid was used to her comforts.

"Everyone's grumpy today," Nixy said.

"It's this forest," she said, "It is so very old and cross. There is a malevolence that moves through the trees, and I don't think it is the will of your father."

"Huh? What's that mean?" he asked.

"I think the forest is haunted," she said.

"Like ghosts?" Nixy asked quietly.

"Like beings of spirit from the Time of Chaos," she said, "When that ended, many things stayed behind, feeding on what they could. Some feed on fear or sadness, some on joy or sorrow... some on flesh and blood, or the very light itself."

"You're scaring me," Nixy said, "Are you making this up?"

"No," she said, "I am just voicing my suspicions. Something is not right."

Nixy could smell the fear in his own sweat, sour and sharp over the reek of the campfire. He felt chills and goose pimples creep up his arms, and the hair on the back of his neck stood up. "I'm going to check on Cindra," he said, making sure his dagger was in place, "If there's something out there, she needs to be warned."

"Stay by the fire, Nixy?" Wenyssaya pleaded, "I am very worried."

"I'll be back sooner than you think," he said, and with that, he stepped out of the firelight and was swallowed by the shadows, vanishing even from elven eyes.

The dark was like a thick smoke, like a fluid all around him, caressing him as he moved down the road. All was visible now in the shadow world; every leaf on every tree appeared in gray detail, shining with a dark light that only he could see. The air resisted him as he moved, but time ran faster in this realm than it did in the normal world. He didn't understand why, but the deeper he went, the slower those around him seemed to move. When he went really deep, so that the air burned his skin like a dust storm and his eyes ached trying to see, it was like time was almost standing still.

He strode down the road towards the campfire at an easy pace, his footsteps on the stones sending silent vibrations through the dark. As he turned the bend, he saw a black horse tied up, and Cindra and Deliah heading into the woods away from the fire.

There was also a tall, dark figure lurking on the edges of the light; a broad-brimmed hat hid its features, and its cloak billowed slowly as it moved. The form was black as night, black as Deliah's horse, and its limbs were long and thin.

As Nixy crept closer, a pair of eyes like red stars darted around the figure's head, followed shortly by the face, as if they had noticed him at different times. When those points of light locked on him, they flashed angrily and the thing turned to advance, coming faster than Nixy was prepared for. It took him precious seconds to realize that the creature was in the shadows too, moving deeper through the dark world than he was. Panic took him and he turned to run, and like a man swimming desperately for the surface, he pushed his way out of the shadow world and into the gloomy, normal woods. He knew that the thing would be able to move much faster than him this way, but he got the sense that whatever it was could only hurt him there, if he joined it in the deep dark.

"Ilda!" he cried, lighting the glowstone around his neck. It gave off a steady light that banished the gloom a little. He ran back into camp and into Wenyssaya's arms. "You were right," he cried, "It's haunted!"

Adric awakened with a start as Padison drew his sword and got his shield, and Wenyssaya began to chant a spell through clenched teeth.

Yet nothing came.

It was over a quarter of an hour later when Drahn returned, looking rather shaken. Nixy was going to ask him what was wrong, but he saw Cindra and Deliah coming up the road together; Cindra carried a torch and Deliah led her horse. Nixy wanted to rush to meet her, but a part of him dreaded stepping away from the light of the fire.

"Cindra!" he called, waving. She waved in return. Everyone was on edge and deeply troubled; as they gathered around the fire, Deliah tied off her horse and made herself comfortable.

"What's everyone all tense about?" Cindra asked in a quiet voice. She was trembling slightly, and this made Nixy worry more.

"I saw someone in the shadows!" he said, 'the deep shadows, where only I can go."

"What was it?" Drahn squeaked.

"I dunno," he said, reverting to a frightened street urchin, "Was black n' tall n' thin, with a hat n' cloak and... and spooky lights fer eyes."

"Like you saw four days ago?" Cindra asked. She had believed him of course, since everyone in his tent saw it too, but there had been nothing there to deal with.

He nodded vigorously, "Same thing, it has to be. It came at me, but... but I don't think it can leave the Shadow. I don't think it can hurt me in the light."

"So what if the light goes out?" Cindra asked.

He didn't know. He didn't think he wanted to know. He knew he could dip into the Shadow to see if the thing was still out there, but he was afraid to see how close it might be. Not knowing was better.

Cindra sighed and sat across the fire from Deliah, shivering. She looked rather wet and was missing one of her wrist wraps, showing her lightning scars. Her boots were muddy, and so were her knees.

"Did ya have a swim?" Nixy asked, but Cindra only glanced at Deliah and said nothing.

"I- I think," Drahn began, "I think Lady Cindwa should get some west. I will take her watch."

"I will watch with you," Deliah said, "It's the least I can do to repay the lady for tonight."

Cindra looked up at her again, and Nixy saw a hint of fear in her eyes. She hid them immediately, looking down to pretend to clean her boots.

"What happened?" Nixy asked, sensing the shift. He knew they hadn't seen the figure by the distant fire, but maybe it had done something to them.

Deliah answered, "We had words, exchanged a few barbs, and finally came to an understanding. You need me with you; I have convinced her of it, and I hope we can... put the past behind us."

Drahn flapped down to Cindra's side and put his fore claws on her leg. He said something, soft and hissing, that Nixy could not make out. She nodded. Adric and Padison knelt beside her to ask what had happened, but she waved them off. Wenyssaya grew concerned about Cindra's state, but was more concerned about what she couldn't see; her magic faerie lights danced above her head, defying the shadows.

This is really weird, Nixy thought, *Everyone is acting different, everyone but Deliah.*

Deliah said, "I think it would help pass the night if each of us told a story around the fire. All of us must have some stories to share."

"Good idea," Adric said, "I claim the Battle of Cordoshome!"

"Does it have to be a real story?" Padison asked.

"No," Deliah said, "Feel free to make one up."

Cindra would have had a smart comment for that earlier, Nixy thought, *but not now.*

Deliah rose and said, "Before we begin, let me see to Nasha's baggage."

"You named your horse after your great-grandmother?" Adric asked.

Deliah looked at him slyly. "Maybe it *is* my great-grandmother," she said, her eyes wide.

Nervous chuckles followed.

Nixy wondered what story he would tell. He had some good ones to scare people; trouble was they scared him too. All of his stories had monsters. He thought of how he met Cindra, stealing her purse, but then Black Will attacked him. That was no good. He thought about his adventure breaking into Clavemont Manor, but then Black Will showed up again, and a troll too, and Lord Clavemont turned out to be a monster himself. That story was *especially* no good, since he felt compelled to never share it. He had only told Cindra, and she had told no one that he knew of.

"Anyone hear of the story of Bella of Blackwood?" Padison asked.

"I have not, and I live in the Blackwood," Wenyssaya said, "Is it a human story?"

"Yeah," Padison said, "It's got this girl, Bella, and a wolf, and these three bears... or pigs... or is it goats? Anyway, there's a troll under a bridge-"

"Sounds like you've almost heard the story yourself," Adric said.

"It's a classic!" Padison said, "My mom used to tell us the tales as children."

Padison's story was all over the place, going from cottages, to woods, to castles; it involved witches and ovens, and trolls, and poison apples, and talking cutlery. It was a mess, but it was entertaining listening to him tell it. Nixy understood why they called him 'Chatty Paddy.'

The next story was Adric's, and he told of the harrowing Minozhian attack on Cordoshome, and how Cindra saved the king, and became a knight. That one was thrilling and made Nixy's throat close up with pride for his friend. Cindra played her part down a bit, mentioning the heroism of those that held the line until death.

Wenyssaya's story was an ancient legend about how one of the elder elves helped rescue a dweedragon's eggs from a *vylas*. Troll, guadim, whatever you called them, they made his skin crawl. It was a good story, but a bit long and flowery, with a song or two thrown in. Only Drahn seemed totally entranced by it, and he had clapped when she finished. He even asked that she tell it again, but was voted down.

Nixy especially liked Deliah's story, because it involved a Sorcerer King.

"This tale is very old, at least by human standards," she said, "In fact it has been so long since I heard it told that I have forgotten the names. But it comes from the time of the ancient Bythian Empire, which flourished when the city of Celvestria was just a collection of huts.

"There was once a mighty sorcerer king who ruled over the land with a steady hand and a just heart," she began, "He was well-loved by his people, but had no one to call his own, for he wished to marry for love, not politics. He prayed to the goddess Selvina to grant him this, his greatest wish: to send him someone to love forever and always. So Selvina heard him and sent her servants to find a woman that was worthy of the king.

"They found a noble maiden of great beauty and grace, with a faithful and kind heart, and brought her to the king. He fell for her immediately and took her for his queen, but the maiden was unsure, fearing his power, for it was terrible and marvelous." She paused a moment, staring into the fire. "The sorcerer king felt her reluctance to love him, and it worried him greatly.

He had his servants go forth and seek for some magic that could secure her love, making his greatest wish come true. One of his servants brought him a gemstone which he claimed would give him a power irresistible; he only need wear it next to his heart."

"The Dark Heart!" Drahn said, "I'll bet this is the-"

"Shhh!" Nixy shushed.

"Sowwy," Drahn said.

"Indeed it was the Dark Heart," Deliah said, "but its power and origins were then known only to the faithful of Mash, who is called Llomaak today. The king took the heart, and wore it next to his breast at all times, until eventually it crept within him and replaced the heart within his chest. Now the blood of Llomaak coursed through his veins, and the power also.

"Taking a lock of hair from his beloved, he used this new power to weave an unbreakable spell, a charm that he asked Selvina herself to bless. With her divine aid, he gave his beloved everlasting youth and beauty, and everlasting love for him." She shook her head, saying, "His queen became consumed with the sight of him, with his scent, with the sound of his voice. She knew something was amiss, she knew her feelings were unnatural, but she could not help herself. When she was with him, she was fulfilled; when they were apart, there was naught but longing. It became a torture for her, and she begged him to tell her what had caused this pain.

"But he had changed," she said grimly, "He was no longer the kind and just ruler; he had become cruel as his power grew stronger. His lands began to suffer, and his advisers and priests were put to death if they questioned his commands. His queen, not knowing where to turn, begged the goddess Selvina for aid. Selvina told her the terrible truth of what her king had done, and for the first time in the history of the gods, admitted a mistake."

This raised eyebrows, at least among those with eyebrows. Drahn said, "Imagine that, a god apologizing to a mortal."

Deliah nodded, "It was not their first mistake, nor their last, and the queen was no longer mortal. The queen began to despair, but a plan grew in her mind. If she could free her king from his mortality, if she could end his terrible reign, perhaps she would end the curse as well. It took her years to work up the courage and willpower to do it, but one night, as they made love, she drew a dagger from under a pillow, and kneeling above him, plunged it into his chest."

She closed her eyes for a long moment, and the others began to wonder if the story was finished. But she raised her head and said, "She told herself she did this out of love for him, to release him from his folly. It was the most painful and difficult thing she had ever done." She sighed, "Her blade found his heart, but it was not a heart of flesh. As it struck true, there was such a terrible flash of power and fury that the palace was shaken and brought low. The temples shook and their pillars cracked, the land was rent asunder and all that was living was turned to dust. Where the capital of the Bythian Empire once stood, there is now a wasteland, a terrible place where no water exists and no one dares tread to this day."

"That's twue," Drahn said to Nixy, "It is called the Bythian Wastes."

Deliah nodded. "Only one person walked out of that wasteland; the queen herself was the sole survivor of the Sundering of Bythia. They say she wanders the world to this day, still searching for a way to end her undying love for a king long dead."

It was a good story, but it made Nixy feel sad. He wondered, *is that what it's like to live too long?*

Chapter Sixteen

The Scion

Gavadaire LuVestra had no love of the sea. He was born in a pleasant, land-locked village, and raised in a monastery that sat upon a cliff top. He loved the feel of grass and firm ground beneath his feet, and he enjoyed a good, long walk.

Instead, the week would be spent on a creaking, heaving deck, with the Emerald Sea lapping at the hull of his chartered ship. He gripped the railing, still uncertain if he felt more secure above deck or below. At least above decks, the smell of his own sick would be less noticeable as it went over the side. But then there was the wind...

"She is gentle today, no?"

Gavadaire turned. Captain Velnallen, the good-natured master of the *Gweelong*, was climbing the foredeck to join him.

"If you say so," Gavadaire muttered, happy at least to be speaking his native language again.

Velnallen and most of his crew were Aurilonian traders, conveniently bound for port in Madeless, in Gavadaire's home province of Aurleona. Their ship, called the *Monkfish* in Calilesh, earned its name; it was about the most unlovely caravel ship Gavadaire had ever seen. Its hull was tarred and stained with green algae, and the deck hadn't been scrubbed properly in who knew how long. The sails were once white, but now looked gray or tan depending on the light. It was not his first choice to travel home, but it was his only choice.

"Will you live under the sun and sky today, my friend?" the captain asked.

"I think so," Gavadaire said, "the swaying of the lantern below deck was making me nauseous."

The captain slapped him on the shoulder, saying, "Feel the wind in your face, it will help."

The western wind was steady in their sails, and would be so for most of their voyage. Once they neared the coast however, Aurilon's portion of the Gartethan mountain range would drop land breezes in their path, but only at night. The voyage looked to be 'smooth sailing,' but Gavadaire could not consider any of it smooth.

He did not remember the voyage to Portshia affecting him so, and wondered at it. That trip had been twice as long, and required them to make long tacks against the wind. Why was he so out of sorts this time? Was it his charge that made him nervous? He felt for the lump under his shirt, making sure it was secure.

"Do you return to an estate, master Gavadaire?" the captain asked, "You have lands in Aurleona?"

"No, I am not nobility. Just a man of Vestra," Gavadaire replied. He understood the assumption; Aurilonian nobles took the names of their land holdings, but so did some of the lower classes who descended from farmers who worked those lands.

Gavadaire couldn't even claim such lineage. His monastic brothers gave him the name because his mother, whom he barely remembered, came from that region. He didn't even know which village or town.

"Well, three more days at sea, Obesh willing, and you can kiss your home soil." The captain gave him an assuring smile and left him to his thoughts.

Later that evening the crew spotted dark clouds in the west, and the setting sun cast an angry red aura about their edges. They began to mutter and curse, and say hasty prayers to Obesh. Gavadaire did not worship the god of the oceans, but he wondered if now might not be a good time to start.

"What does it mean?" he asked the captain, indicating the clouds, "Foul weather?"

"Perhaps more than that," Velnallen said, "I don't like the look of the stars either. Did you notice?" He pointed to a red one that rose high in the north.

Gavadaire had seen that star before, but never so bright. "Is that one of the wandering stars?" he asked, "The brightest ones often are."

"No," Velnallen said, "That one is the tip of Vestra's Spear, and it's fixed among the constellations. But never, in all my years at sea, have I seen it shine as it has these last few days."

"What does it mean?" he asked.

"Calamity," answered the boatswain. He was trying to keep the men busy and stop their muttering, but he allowed himself a little muttering of his own. "It's an ill omen, a sign of evil times ahead."

"Does it pertain to this voyage?" Gavadaire asked.

"It pertains to the world, so it's said," the man replied.

Gavadaire had a healthy skepticism for things 'that are said' or things 'that are written,' but he didn't like the look of it, omen or not.

The next morning brought the crew's fears to light. A gray wall of clouds was forming behind them, and the wind had picked up considerably. Gavadaire tried to stay out of the way as the crew went about rigging for a gale.

"We will try and run ahead of the storm," the captain explained, "We have plenty of sea; no leeward shoreline to worry about. The water here is deep and wide."

This did not make Gavadaire feel comfortable. *They know their business*, he thought, trying to calm himself.

The ships of Aurilon most often ran 'lateen rigged,' with triangular sails that allowed for greater maneuverability. From a distance, they looked like enormous shark fins breaking the water. Now, the large sail yards had been dropped to the deck and secured, leaving only a square fore-sail to catch the strong winds. That was counter-intuitive to a landlubber like himself, until he felt the ship stabilize after the sails came down.

Yet the waters became rougher, and the ship was constantly struck with waves astern, making steering difficult. He took a firm grip on the railing, steadying himself as the deck pitched under him.

"Ho! To starboard! Shark!"

He turned to see who had called out, and found one of the sailors pointing off the right side of the ship. Through the choppy seas he could see a white fin breaking the water, perhaps fifty to eighty yards distant. It was big, perhaps a full three feet above the surface.

"White fin!" cried the boatswain.

The effect it had on the superstitious sailors was profound. Many of them took a knee, as best they could, and said prayers to Obesh. He heard the names 'Masha and Mektha.'

"What is the matter?" Gavadaire called to the captain.

Velnallen, whose face was grim, replied, "Masha and Mektha are two of the Eight Storms; white sharks that antagonize Obesh and cause him to chase them about. All sailors fear them, and any pale shark is taken as a bad omen."

"White fin to port!" cried another sailor, his voice near hysterical. All eyes turned to look for the other fin, finding it about the same distance off the left side of the ship. The faces of the men were just as white, fear showing in their darting eyes and gaping mouths.

"Two of them!" someone cried, "It *must* be the Storms!"

Gavadaire didn't believe in immortal god sharks, but he didn't like the implications of sharks keeping pace with a ship in a storm. If they went down...

"Back to work! Secure the ship!" called the captain, snapping at his fearful men.

Gavadaire's limbs were wind-battered and cold despite his winter jacket, and his cheeks and ears stung, but his chest was warm. He put his hand there, feeling to make sure that the treasure he bore was safe and secure. Months ago, he had promised to carry a family heirloom of House Evenast back to the lands of Vestra, lest it be lost or stolen. He wore it always around his neck, next to his skin; a large gemstone of amethyst or ruby. Now it pulsed with a warmth that surprised him.

The gemstone had kept him awake at night, disturbing him with strange sensations. Sometimes he had felt it move, creeping across his chest. Sometimes it seemed to echo his heartbeat. Sometimes it made him doubt his sanity. More than once he had the impulse to fling it away, but he had a duty to carry out. Once he was in Vestra, he could deliver it to the head of the noble LuVestra family, ancestors of the current Evenast line, to hold for the next Baron DeKenric; if there *was* a next Baron DeKenric.

As he clutched the warm stone to his chest, he felt a wave of dizziness pass over him, and his stomach roiled. He leaned over the edge, feeling bad for whoever might be downwind, but before he could think about heaving, he noticed the white fin.

It was *rising,* getting taller and wider moment by moment. Below it the dark sea began to lighten, as an enormous, pale mass neared the surface. Stunned, Gavadaire turned to look at the men; they had seen it too. The other distant fin also rose out of the water, looming over the waves. The terror struck the crew like thunder, pulling shouts and curses from their constricted throats as they recoiled from the railing. Men slipped and slid, knocking others down. Some held their arms before their faces, while others dashed below, or closed their eyes and began to pray desperately.

The fins had grown so high that they looked like lateen sails of ships larger than their own. The water began to swell as the massive bodies became shallow. About five ship-lengths behind them, smaller fins broke the surface, swaying back and forth, stirring the water.

Tails, Gavadaire thought. *Gods above and below!* The oath froze in his brain. He now understood what 'gods below' meant.

Impossible. This is... impossible.

His heart was pounding with helpless panic; his legs threatened to betray him if he didn't flee, but there was no place to go. His ears plugged up and he trembled. The warmth on his chest grew in intensity, but he barely noticed. He could only watch as the great white sail of a fin moved closer, cutting the waters like a knife, the noise of its progress growing louder as the smell of the depths reeked in their nostrils.

Then it fell back as the creature slowed, towering just off the starboard quarter as the head came along side. Through the churning waves, Gavadaire could see an enormous white wedge coming closer. A great black eye, bigger than a wagon wheel, beheld him from beneath the surface.

In that moment, staring into the abyss, he felt becalmed. His body was still awash with fear, but his mind had grown still. It was as if the abyss called to him, promising a home amid the waves and fathomless depths. That blackness reached into his soul and touched it, and he did not recoil. Not at first.

The head veered away as the monster submerged again; the black eye vanished into the murky darkness. Released from its spell, Gavadaire's mind was free to break. He screamed wordlessly as he flung himself away from the railing, wrapping his arms around the mizzen mast. He squeezed his eyes shut, but the terror was behind his eyelids, as clear as day. Forcing himself to look around, he saw that the other fin had descended as well, and the sharks had taken to swimming in a weaving pattern, moving near, then far, almost playfully.

He also saw that the men, if they were looking at anything but the fins, were looking at him. Their eyes were filled with madness barely held in check. Mouths quivered with ready oaths and accusations, and those closer to him moved back. Some even had weapons in hand, or tools not intended for what they had in mind.

"It's him!" someone called, "They came for *him!*"

"Throw him over!"

"He'll bring disaster upon us!"

"Great gods! The Storms want a sacrifice!"

Gavadaire did not like where this was heading; he was not convinced he could take on a crew of thirty men while unarmed, in a stormy sea. He had once faced similar odds, but he had been more than ready, and on dry land with sword in hand.

He turned to the captain, his eyes pleading. "Captain Velnallen! Please, you cannot think I am to blame for this? Tell them!"

The captain, his face awash with shock and terror, took a moment to form the words, "Never, not in all my life, have I heard a sailor tell of this. No man, neither deep in his cups, nor in a woman's arms, has told a tale as we can tell. If we live to make landfall, I'll never set sail again." He traced the symbol of the Jaydecean Wheel on his chest, making it a sacred oath. "The Storms themselves have come for something or someone, Gavadaire LuVestra. It looked you in the face. It looked you square in the face."

As if by some unspoken order, the men rushed forward to subdue him. Gavadaire found his footing and twisted out of their grasp, dodging the next few attempts. He had few places to retreat to, and nowhere to hold them off for long. His body, already in survival mode, responded with extra strength and speed. He lashed out, knocking men off their feet and turning their attacks into their fellows. *If I can make for the forward cabin, I can block the door until they come to their senses,* he thought, and kicked his way down the stairs from the quarterdeck to the main deck, fighting towards the forecastle.

Someone lashed out at him with a cargo hook, tearing his jacket and biting into his forearm. He cried out in anger, kicking at the man as he forced the hook free of his sleeve. Blood coated the tip and stained the fabric.

As if in response to the attack, there was a rush of wind and a great splash of spray upon the deck. The ship heaved as a swell of water lifted it up, and as it dropped, the massive head of the white shark was beside them. Its black eye looked down upon them before rolling back and turning white; the thing's lips drew up like a pale curtain as it bared its hellish jaws. It had row upon row of jagged teeth, each as tall as a man, and the maw was large enough to swallow the ship whole, masts and all. The stench within was like the corpse of a rotting whale; perhaps there was one inside, for there was certainly room for it.

Everyone recoiled, crying out in terror and scrambling away to the port-side railing. Gavadaire retreated into the crush of men, no longer fearing their aggression. They were all in the same boat, as it were, and there was good reason to believe that the sharks wanted him safe.

The head sank beneath the waves, and the fin retreated to join its twin behind the ship.

Gavadaire found his voice first. "I-I think they want me right where I am, thank you," he said.

The men backed away, giving him plenty of breathing room. The wind started to howl and the rain began falling as a stinging mist. As Gavadaire felt his arm to assess the damage, the captain walked down the steps with shaky legs.

"Whatever evil you bring with you," he said, "it seems Masha and Mektha themselves wish to see you safely ashore. Let us hope that Fahl and Mahl do not choose to join them, bringing the winds of Hwessa's wrath."

"I know not what they might want of me," Gavadaire said, pleading to whatever sanity might remain, "I cannot even say it is me they want, but so long as they are not attacking us, let us not attack each other?"

There was an uneasy truce as the captain agreed, and the men kissed their holy symbols, made signs to ward off evil in Gavadaire's direction and returned to their posts. Gavadaire decided to keep out of sight, retreating below decks to take his chances in the cramped, enclosed space. He opened his footlocker, removed his sword, climbed into a hammock, and waited.

He knew not when sleep took him, but his dreams were no improvement on the morning's horrors. In them, he stood upon a mountaintop, or what he thought was a mountain. It had four symmetrical sides, rising in a step pattern, and stood amid a vast plain of what looked like granite buildings of inestimable size. None of it was natural, but it was magnificent to behold; he was struck by the *order* of it all.

A searing light glowed overhead, brighter than the sun. He could not look at it; in fact he could hardly bear to turn his face upward, so harsh was its radiance. He longed for shelter, for some place to hide from that cruel illumination. His chest burned, his flesh searing.

Suddenly he was in darkness, a howling darkness that assaulted his ears. His chest no longer burned, but he felt lost in the inky black, unsure if he was still upon the mountaintop. He felt for the warmth on his chest and found the jewel, pulsing with magical life. Of course it was magic, it had to be. Why hadn't he realized that before? He drew it forth and found that it cast a bloody illumination, a reddish haze like the last rays of sunset, like candlelight through ruby glass. He held it aloft, letting it shine its faint glow around him.

He was standing on the edge of an abyss. A vast, swirling mass of dark shapes, gaping mouths, howling screams, and grasping appendages yawned at his feet. The glow managed to shine down its depths, giving unfortunate clarity to the mob. Gavadaire tried to turn away, his revulsion threatening to overcome him. His insides quivered. Empathetic pains crept across his skin as he witnessed the twisting, grinding, writhing things trying to escape the crushing mass of their own bodies. He saw misshapen faces, hideous chimeras, beasts that turned inside out, then folded in on themselves before exploding outward again in a flurry of tendrils and viscera. He saw dark, nameless things that defied description, born of malevolent madness. He saw countless eyes of all manner, shape, and size, and all of them watching him.

He trembled, nearly dropping the jewel. He covered it with his hands, willing the light to extinguish, but it remained. He clutched it to his chest, hoping to hide the light. Finally, he returned it to its place under his shirt, against his breast.

The light faded. The howling grew into an eerie music, like a chorus of rising and falling moans, grim and beautiful. His heart grew calm, and the revulsion passed. He felt at ease again.

He felt at home.

More than anything else, *this* sensation jolted him awake. There was a flash as he opened his eyes, and thunder followed. The ceiling tilted before him, and he found he still gripped the sword in his hand. He was in his hammock, swaying with the motion of the storm.

Sensing he was alone, he felt for the jewel. He wondered, *was it magic, like I dreamed? It would explain a great many things*. He drew it from under his shirt and removed it from his neck, holding it up in the lantern light.

It was dark, a deep crimson red that drank the light. There were traces of light within, as if the inner facets caught and threw off the ambient glow. They almost looked like veins of purple fire, pulsing throughout its crystalline form.

Gavadaire felt a sudden revulsion at the thing, like he was holding an ancient evil given substance. He wanted nothing more than to open a porthole and toss it overboard into the churning sea. He got out of the hammock and onto the heaving deck, stumbling towards the small hatch. It was once meant for a cannon, but now was used to empty night soil. Opening it, he squinted as the freezing mist blew into his face.

Wait a moment, he thought as realization hit, *Gemstones can hold magic spells. What if it is cursed to torment people of the wrong bloodline? What if it is only reacting because I am not of House Evenast?*

He let the hatch cover drop and latched it with his foot. His mind was reeling like the hull around him as he tried to puzzle out what was happening. *If it is cursed so, why didn't Grigor DeKenric mention that? Perhaps he did not know? But how could he not?*

He shook his head. *The sharks! What of the sharks? Did those... those **gods** show themselves because of me, because of the gemstone? Is there a connection, like the sailors said? Too many questions, too many.*

"It is only three more days at sea, assuming the giant sharks don't kill us," he said aloud, "Or if we don't sink in the storm," he added. He wanted to go on deck and see if things had changed for the better, but he was afraid they had not, and his presence would make things worse.

Instead, he took the Evenast family heirloom and buried it deep in his footlocker.

The following day was much like the last. The crew wanted to toss him overboard; he could see it in their eyes. The storm was raging farther behind them, and the white fins had submerged enough to resemble simply very large sharks trailing in the ship's wake. The weather was rough enough to make life miserable, and the food tasted slightly worse going out than it did going in.

The cut on his arm was growing warm, and he feared an infection. In the chaos of the day, he had forgotten to tend to it properly. The last thing he needed was a deadly fever.

Gavadaire avoided the men who went below deck to sleep, or see to the stores, but he was getting desperate for news. He risked poking his head above deck to try and summon the captain. The first few times, the captain simply ignored him, but the man eventually relented.

"What?" Velnallen asked, terse and cold.

"How do we fare?" Gavadaire asked.

"We fare," the captain replied, "We are ahead of the weather, but as long as the white sharks follow, so will the wrath of Obesh. Pray he doesn't catch up to them."

Gavadaire said a little silent prayer. Then he asked, "Do you have anything for a wound? One of your men gave me a nasty cut with a cargo hook."

He could see the man's mind working behind his eyes. He was wondering if the sharks would be angered if the passenger simply died of infection, rather than violence. Finally the man nodded and said, "Wait below. I have something."

Half an hour later, probably after a debate with his senior officers, the captain returned with a small ceramic jar. It was painted with fine tracery and bore the winged, golden hand of Lelonetha, Mother Mercy. He unclasped the lid and opened it, revealing a pungent, yellowish poultice.

"What is it?" Gavadaire asked, carefully removing his blood-caked shirt.

"Some kind of yarrow-based divine alchemy," he said, "It came at a pretty price, but has more than paid for itself by keeping men alive." Then he added, "I hope I am not wasting it."

"So do I," Gavadaire replied.

The gods of old had placed divine virtues in many plants, minerals, and beasts, and they had given their priests knowledge to bring out those properties with secret prayers and crafts. He had only been treated with divine alchemy once, but had been too out-of-sorts to witness it work. This time he paid attention. The captain took a clean cloth and wiped the blood away as best he could, then he dipped the unstained end in the yellow paste, saying a few words of prayer under his breath. He worked it into the wound, and he was not gentle; Gavadaire winced and sucked in his breath.

Before he was finished, the pain began to subside. As the captain secured the lid and wiped his hands clean, the wound began to tingle and itch, then actually close before Gavadaire's amazed eyes. It was slow, but certain, and he felt the flesh tighten up and ache as it healed itself.

"I'll need to bind that now," the captain said, "The rest of the healing is slower, but you should be fixed before we make port at Madeless."

"Amazing," Gavadaire said, "I learned about things like this at the monastery, but never watched it work."

"Monastery?" Velnallen asked, "What monastery?"

"The Su'Kraal monastery in Vestra," he said, "It sits on the shelf of Mount Winowyne."

"The Sons of Kraal?" he exclaimed, astonished, "You were raised as a warrior monk?"

Gavadaire nodded, said, "I did not take the monastic vows, but I learned to fight there."

"No wonder the men could not subdue you," the captain said, shaking his head, "I'll warn them not to get any more ideas."

"I thought Masha and Mektha had convinced them of that?" he said, half-joking.

The captain stared hard at him. "Whatever the gods may want, men are not above testing them; especially to save their own skins." He said nothing more, binding Gavadaire's arm before departing.

That night, the dreams returned. He found himself blind, on the edge of the Abyss once again, only this time the jewel could not help him. He felt for it desperately, but it was gone. *I locked it in my chest,* he recalled, growing frantic. The darkness was palpable; he could feel it moving against his skin, ruffling his hair. He was completely blind, but he knew what was around him. Their howling wails rang in his ears in a cacophony that threatened his sanity. He flailed and thrashed, trying to batter away the darkness.

Then he fell.

He felt his innards shift as the ground left him and he tumbled into the Abyss. His scream was lost amid the cries of the countless hordes, and their limbs clutched at him as he dropped past. He could sense them all around him, far below him. He could not see it, but he knew that the Abyss was not bottomless; it just got narrower and narrower until the bodies became a crush. They would spend eternity in a twisting, writhing struggle to reach a gasp of open air. He was heading right for it. He would be buried in it.

Gavadaire thrashed himself awake, his sword point burying into the ceiling as his legs kicked over the hammock. It took him several breaths to realize he was safe and secure below decks, on a rocking ship, on a violent sea. The memory of the Abyss was so fresh in his mind, he could smell the bodies, smell the reek of them as they rubbed themselves raw against their neighbors.

Or perhaps that was the men sleeping in their hammocks across the deck. He could not tell what was real anymore.

This, this is real, he thought, as he gripped the handle of his sword, pulling it out of the ceiling beam. He lowered himself to the deck, feeling the cold wood under his feet. *This is real,* he decided, *the ship is real, the storm is real, the sharks... Damn.* He felt his wound, recalling the fight and why it started. That meant the sharks were real; those gods of nature in chaos, white sharks that were three hundred and fifty feet long because they *wanted* to be. That too was real.

Damn.

He took deep breaths, steadying himself. *Another dream like that, and I might lose my mind altogether,* he realized. His eyes fell on his footlocker, lashed securely beneath his berth. *That cursed stone,* he thought, *it's responsible, I'm sure of it. But what to do about it...?*

He set his foot on the locker, pondering his dilemma. "I pitch you over the side, and I fail my pledge. Perhaps I anger the gods and get us all killed," he muttered at the locker lid, "But if I carry you ashore, I might wind up gibbering and insane when I meet your proper owners." He bit his lip in frustration and tasted blood.

Just then, he felt a pulse in his foot. It seemed to resonate through his locker. There it was again; a throb, a pulse, coming through the lid. *That damned stone,* he thought, *It has its own plans.*

Reluctantly, he unlocked the chest and opened the lid, half expecting the stone to be sitting on top of his things, though he had buried it deep. It was not, thankfully. He had to dig it out, but when he did, he felt a wave of relief. When he touched it, it eased his fears and calmed his heart. He trembled and his jaw quivered; he found he was near tears.

"What do you want from me?" he hissed, "What in the name of Arathus do you-"

Pain!

A flash of pain wracked his hand, making him drop the stone. So startled was he that he fell backwards, landing on his backside. The sea rocked, the deck tilted, and the lid slammed shut.

Gavadaire did not sleep anymore that night. In the morning, he decided to appear on deck, despite the accusing, murderous looks he received. Being suspect and despised was nothing new to him, but hiding in fear was. Besides, he wanted more than anything to see his homeland on the horizon. Yet it was obscured by a distant fog.

The winds were less powerful than before, and they had managed to keep ahead of the storm. *The gods were with us,* he thought. Then he wondered, *Which gods? Was it the god of the sea, or the wind, or the evil ones they pursued?*

He did not yet feel invited to climb the quarterdeck with the captain and steersman, so he peered out over the railing, searching the waters behind them.

"It would seem your guardians have either departed, or gone deep," Captain Velnallen said, "Either way, the men are more at ease. We might make it to port in one piece, all of us."

"That would be my choice as well," Gavadaire said. He also had the thought, as he was sure others had, that it might be safer to put him off the ship and take their chances.

The captain gave him a slight smile, saying, "Not all terrible voyages need end in tragedy, it seems."

"We are not ashore yet," Gavadaire said, "And there are many kinds of tragedy."

"True enough," Velnallen said, and he came down from the quarterdeck to lean on the railing beside him. They stared out at the horizon for a time, when the captain said, "You have been having rough nights. We all have of late, but you…"

It was not a question, Gavadaire knew. He had been watched. Well, he couldn't blame them. He nodded, "I have had terrible, terrible dreams. It doesn't help that we are at sea in rough waters."

"Yes, the sea affects a man's dreams, that's for certain," Velnallen said, "I myself had nightmares of those giant fins. Gods above and below, what monstrosities! To think they have been down there all along." He shuddered, "It's enough to make a man question his sanity."

Gavadaire said, "I had to remind myself it was real."

"It was," he said, "or we are a ship of madmen."

"That's a possibility too," Gavadaire said.

The captain straightened, gave the railing a pat, perhaps testing its reality, and left to make his rounds.

Gavadaire avoided sleep as much as possible that day. He was exhausted from his ordeal, but even closing his eyes sent a part of his mind back to the edge of the Abyss. So he found a place on the foredeck where he could stand, letting the pitching bow and sea spray keep him awake.

The winds had blown out enough that the captain had ordered the sail yards hoisted once again, so the ship might speed to port before the evening breezes worked against them. The ship pitched even more, but the sensation of nearly being thrown into the ocean only helped his cause.

But his body could only take so much misery. Eventually he took shelter in the forecastle space that housed the anchor winches, and allowed himself to relax. He used the meditation techniques he had learned at the monastery, breathing in the salt air through his nose, expelling through his mouth, over and over. He found peace for a time, accepting the rocking of the ship as just another step in a process. Homeward. Going homeward.

Then unbidden, sleep came to him. He felt nothing, dreamed nothing for a time. Yet when his mind began to realize its own safety, he heard the call of the Abyss and felt its clammy touch. There was no light, no comfort to be had. He was naked before the darkness, teetering on the brink. Wails assaulted his ears, and a great reek invaded his nostrils. He shook himself awake, crying out.

He was still in the forecastle, that much was certain. He felt the cold breeze, heard the familiar thumping of the bow against the waves, and felt the foremast against his back. He smelled tar, hemp rope, salt air, and the grease on the anchor winch.

But he was in complete darkness.

He strained his eyes, feeling to make sure they were open. He blinked and rubbed them, staring wildly about him like a madman, but the world remained dark. He panicked, struggling to his feet and clutching the mast, wrapping his arms about the great tree trunk and gulping air like a drowning man.

"Help me!" he called once, and then regretted it. His mind raced. *What will they do, now that I am helpless to see danger coming? Will they take their chances, so close to home? Pitch me into the sea and call it an accident?* He strained to listen as feet clomped down the stairs from the foredeck above.

"Oh, it's you," said a crewman, "What's your problem, then?" His tone was scornful, decidedly unfriendly.

"Nothing," Gavadaire said, steadying himself to stand normally, "I thought I was caught in the winch, that's all." He looked at where the man's voice came from, hoping he was making eye contact.

"Hmph," the man scoffed, then returned to his post, "Lubber," he added.

Gavadaire took several deep breaths, trying to form a plan. Could he make it below decks from here? It was hard enough with eyes, avoiding bumping into someone or teetering into the lines. He took a few steps towards the open deck, sliding his feet forward. He had trained in the dark for a time, but had not once had the need to use it.

The wind howled and caressed his hair and skin, and his mind was suddenly back in the Abyss, standing on the edge of that horrid drop, encased in tangible night. His heart began to hammer as anxiety took control of his body, making him sweat despite the cold. He lost his balance and hit the railing, feeling the brief sensation of a drop. He grabbed the wood and held fast, glad to have something, anything to steady himself.

"What's with the good luck charm?" someone asked.

"Drunk, by the looks of it," another replied.

The first speaker muttered, "Maybe he'll fall overboard on his own."

I will not fall! Gavadaire swore, *Never! Not again.* He felt his way along the railing towards the aft stairway.

The spray hit him in the face, and he imagined the spittle of frantic mouths, gasping, crying, and defiling him for not being among them. He felt the deck heave and teetered toward the Abyss, even as he tightened his grip. His balance failed and his head spun, like a man reeling home after a bender, and he kept his feet only by the grace of the wooden rail. Leaning on it heavily, he heard it creak, felt the wood give way. A shock of fear made him fling his body away from the edge. It appeared that he had been pushed back by an unseen force, but it was his Su-Kraal training in action. He fell into some crewmen, drawing curses and shoves.

Falling! Grasping hands! The sensations aroused a violent reaction in the fighting man. He lashed out at his assailants, breaking a man's wrist before his remaining sanity told him he was not in the clutches of abominations, but of his countrymen.

The scream of pain brought the captain to the deck, as the men pulled their companion away from the madman, balling their fists and gazing over the waves to look for white dorsal fins.

"What is this?" he demanded, 'I ordered no one was to harm him!"

"What about him harming us?" asked a friend of the screaming man, "All he did was push the lubber off him!" Loud agreements followed. Gavadaire stood legs apart, chest heaving and eyes wild and bulging.

"Is this true?" the captain asked, approaching, "LuVestra! What has gotten into you?"

Gotten into me, he thought, and he felt tentacles creep in his ears and up his nose, felt cold, clammy feelers violating him where he stood. Ants moved under his skin. Centipedes crept up his back. *Not real, not real,* he insisted. But it felt very real, so long as he stood still.

"I... I cannot see," he gasped, shifting and fidgeting, "I have gone blind."

"Blind?" the captain repeated, "How?"

"I don't know!" Gavadaire shouted, then composed himself. Even *he* thought he sounded mad. "I drifted off to sleep beneath the foredeck, and when I awoke..." He waved his hand before his face.

"He's cursed, make no mistake!" That was the boatswain speaking. Many voices agreed.

"Then he can be cursed on *land!*" the captain replied, "We should make port in seven hours, gods willing."

"And if they are not?" someone asked.

"Then I am sure they will appear and let us know," the captain grumbled. He stepped closer to the big warrior. "LuVestra. I am going to help you, yes? I will help you. Where do you wish to be?"

"My berth," he replied immediately, "I, I need something in my locker."

"Very well, do you want me to get it for you?"

"No!" he barked, "No, I must get it myself. Please, just take me there."

"Alright, relax. I am going to take your wrist. I just want to help you." Velnallen reached out and took his arm gently, not wanting to provoke him further.

Gavadaire flinched at the touch, but even as the mutterings of sailors became the voices of the damned in his ears, he forced himself to be led.

"We are going down," Velnallen said, "Steady now, the way is narrow."

They were finally out of the howling wind, and the sensation of the Abyss diminished, but not nearly enough. It took all his will power to trust his guide and not tear his arm away from the man. To do so would probably mean a stumble or fall, and the thought of that sensation was worse than the man's touch.

"Almost there," the captain said, placing his hand on Gavadaire's back to steady him. Gavadaire jumped at the touch, twisting and cocking his fist to strike. "Easy!" Velnallen cried, "It's just a few steps more."

It took several deep breaths before he let himself be led again. The captain was a man of his word; five steps more, and he was next to his hammock.

"Here we are," the captain said, taking a few steps back, "Your footlocker is beneath. Do you need help opening it?"

Gavadaire felt for the key in his pocket. "No," he said, "I can manage. Please, I must have privacy."

He sank to the deck, feeling for the lid. Then he added, "Thank you, my friend."

The captain nodded, then realized the blind man could not see that. "Take care of yourself, and stay in your hammock, if you please?"

Gavadaire nodded, then listened to make sure the man walked away. He fumbled with the key even as the creeping sensation began again, testing his resolve. Minutes stretched into years as he tried to get the key in the keyhole the right way, and panic threatened to overtake him. The darkness wrapped itself around his throat, his chest, his wrists, squeezing, resisting.

Not real, not real... he insisted.

He unlocked the chest and scrambled to find what he was after. He felt all about the surface of the pile. It was not there! Surely the stone had dropped onto his clothing before the lid slammed shut. Frantic, he clawed through his belongings like a pilfering thief, desperate for something valuable. Finally, as a whine of helplessness grew in his throat, he laid hands on the leather thong that held the jewel. He pulled it greedily, unsure of why he felt he needed it so. It was just a feeling, but it was the only hopeful feeling he had.

In a second, the large jewel was in his hands. Sanity returned. His body began to relax, then tremble, exhausted. He sighed, almost laughed, almost sobbed. Clutching the stone with both hands, he held it close, feeling its pulse, its warmth. He squeezed his eyes shut as tears flowed, yet he smiled. When he opened his eyes, watery light greeted his senses, and it soon manifested into the crew space, his berth, and the two crewmen watching silently from the far end of the deck.

His face became hard, but he said nothing. He need explain nothing to them; indeed, he had no explanations. He just had a feeling that the jewel had the power to tame the darkness that it had stained him with. Not remove it, but make him at peace in it. This was the first time anyone had seen the large gemstone however, so now he would have to keep it on his person at all times, like it or not. The dreams may come, but the stone would keep the horror at bay, keep it manageable.

He placed the thong over his head and tucked the jewel into his shirt, against his breast. Safe. Then he stood, gave the sailors a baleful look, then climbed into his hammock. He commenced to stare at the ceiling as if it was the most interesting thing in the world.

He awoke hours later to the tolling of the ship's bell, and a distant call from a larger one, deeper and more distant. "We are home," he said aloud, breathing deeply. He felt at peace and strangely well-rested. He had dreamed of the dark, but the jewel had been there to light his way and drive back the panic. He had teetered on the edge of the Abyss, but the power of the stone made him its master, and he had laughed as the abominations cursed him and spat at him. He drank their suffering and it made him stronger.

"Fearful dream," he whispered. He stretched his arms towards the ceiling beams, yawning. Then he felt for the stone.

It was gone.

Angered beyond reason, he leaped out of his hammock and felt for the leather thong. It was there, right where it should be. *They cut it while I slept!*

He cursed and tried to pull the thong off his neck. It resisted. Worse yet, he felt a tugging sensation. *What in the name of all the gods?* With trembling hands, he began to unlace his shirt. A mounting horror twisted like ice worms in the pit of his stomach as the laces came loose and he pulled at the fabric. His breath seized in his throat as he looked down, seeing the impossible with unbelieving eyes.

The stone and leather thong had sunk into his very flesh, into his bone, into the place where his heart had been. He felt a pulse in his chest, and a warmth that spread into his veins.

A wordless moan wrenched itself from his aching ribs as he sank to the deck, collapsing under the weight of black revelation.

Chapter Seventeen

Haunted

As she rode upon T'ózha, listening to the clop of his hooves, Cindra did not know whether to feel fear, anger, guilt, or shame. The time since the incident had been torturous to her troubled mind, filling every quiet moment with memories of what had transpired. Her stomach twisted and her hands trembled. Yet she could speak to no one about what had happened.

No one that is, except Drahn. The nosy little creature had witnessed everything from his hiding place in the trees, and had been made to promise to keep it to himself. He would place a clawed hand on her knee to offer his support, or give her a knowing look when he sensed she was drowning in her black thoughts.

Deliah, for her part, was frighteningly nonchalant about it; if there was anything to ever traumatize a person, that night would surely qualify. Yet she acted so nerveless about it, one would assume she had forgotten.

But how could anyone forget what happened? Cindra thought, as the swirl of guilt and anger and fear conspired to make her sick again.

The sunlight made the day more bearable at least. The forest on this stretch of road was closer to the river and opened to present glades of low shrubs and flowers. Some of it had been cleared by woodsmen, and the stumps still stood testament to the former occupants. On the other side of the river the trees were closer, and overhung the rushing waters. The flow was shallow, wide, and brown here, and the opposite shore was too far to reach with a thrown stone. They had not seen traffic on the waters or the road since Breega.

Almost everyone had told a story last night except Cindra; she really didn't feel like participating, but it was her duty, in a way. Morale had improved because of story time, and as the party's leader, she ought to contribute. She certainly had a great many stories to share, but wanted to avoid the ones involving grave danger or killing. *Maybe Nixy or Drahn will want to go first*, she thought.

Nixy rode up next to her, interrupting her moody introspection. "Hey," he said, "Whatcha thinking about?"

She forced herself to smile at him and said, "I'm trying to decide what story to tell."

"Oh!" he exclaimed, "you can tell about how we met! That's a good one."

"In that case," she said, "I'll leave it for you to tell. I was thinking of something lighter and less frightening."

"Oh, good idea," he said, "The nights are dark enough I suppose."

She had to agree. "Have you had anymore sightings of our visitor?"

Nixy's face scrunched into a frown. "No," he said, "I haven't really looked into the Shadow to see if it's still out there."

"What do you think it might be?" she asked, "It seems to have been following us since before we entered the forest."

He shrugged. "I wish I knew. I'm pretty sure it's not friendly though."

Cindra looked up towards the sky, gaining some strength from the sunlight. She said, "What if we confront it? Is that possible?"

"W-what do you mean?" he asked warily.

"I mean you can take others into the Shadow with you," she said, "why not try to meet it on its terms? Show it we're not afraid."

"But I *am* afraid," he said, "Aren't you?"

She gave him a weak smile and had to admit to herself that the idea scared her a bit. "Well, whether we are or aren't, it's best to show it a united front."

"I guess," he said, unconvinced.

"Anyway, what's the worst that can happen?" she asked, "If things get too ugly, you can just take us out of the Shadow. You said it couldn't follow, right?"

"I don't *think* it can," he replied, "I don't know for sure."

"Well, if it could leave the shadow world, it probably would have already," she reasoned, "If it's some kind of shadow creature, maybe your father knows about it."

"Too bad we can't ask him," he said, "Maybe Wenyssaya will have a dream about it."

"I don't envy her that dream," Cindra said, "From what you described, it sounds terrifying; like a ghost made of darkness itself." She shivered despite the daylight, and her memory flew back to her fourteenth year, when she rescued Nixy from Black Will. He had been a living man, but he had a dark spirit inside of him that appeared as a skeleton made of smoke. Yet Black Will was dead; Nixy himself witnessed him dying a grisly death atop the cathedral.

"I wonder if we could even hurt it," Nixy said, "Things work differently there; solid stuff isn't as solid, and magic has a weird... flavor. I can't explain it right."

"Well," Cindra said, trying to sound confident, "I have my magic sword, you have your magic knife, and we have a magic dragon and a magic elf. I am sure that's worth something."

She didn't mention Deliah was a witch, and would not yet list her among their assets.

She tried to mention Deliah as little as possible.

"Unwise," Deliah said.

The party had stopped for the night and Cindra had proposed her idea. The looks on their faces showed that most of them agreed with the raven-haired woman.

"I think if it can't hurt us, we should leave it alone," Wenyssaya said.

Drahn offered, "We don't know it can't hurt us, it just hasn't *yet*." He sounded brave, but his reddening scales betrayed his nervousness.

"If this is just to get out of telling your story..." Adric joked; Cindra smirked at him but remained serious.

"I say we do it!" Padison said, "I don't like the idea of some skulker following us around as it pleases. If we can scare it away-"

"We don't know how dangerous it is," Deliah said, "There are things you don't confront if you can avoid it, especially in these woods."

Wenyssaya said, "I think the Shadow Lord can best deal with it, whatever it is. We should leave it be until we reach his fortress."

Cindra said, "What if it *wants* to find his fortress? I can't help but think that it threatens our mission somehow, and we are better rid of it."

"How do you fight a shadow creature?" Adric asked, "Will our swords even touch it?"

Nixy only shrugged, though he was arguably the best qualified to answer.

Wenyssaya attempted to work it through. "I think," she said, "that the deeper we go into the Shadow, the more ethereal everything becomes. So it might be more dangerous to enter the shallow waters, rather than take the plunge, so to speak."

"Or the opposite might be true," Deliah said, folding her arms, "Fighting a creature on its own terms is foolish."

Cindra was resolute, saying, "We won't know until we at least try. Nixy thinks this thing is a threat, and I agree with him."

"But I don't wanna challenge it," he squeaked.

Cindra gave him a little frown. "You will be in charge of how long we stay exposed, Nixy," she said, "If it gets too risky, you can bring us back to reality." She was going to have her way on this, whether they liked it or not. Once she set her mind to something, she was maddeningly stubborn; Jaron could attest to that.

Adric decided it was his duty to support her, so he asked, "Alright, what do you want us to do?"

She said, "I think we should surround Nixy in a protective circle. Then we move together until we see the thing."

"And then?" Wenyssaya asked.

"We have words," Cindra said, "If that doesn't work, we try spells and steel."

The group stood in a circle a few yards away from the campfire and the tethered horses. The orange light gave no warmth at this distance, whereas the caress of night chilled the skin and bones. Nixy stood in the middle of the huddle with Drahn clinging to his back, and the warriors had swords drawn and shields ready. Wenyssaya and Deliah stood within the ring also, keeping Nixy safe between their skirts.

"Whenever you're ready, Nixy," Cindra said, bolstering her courage, "We'll see if it will face us all together."

Nixy gulped, took a deep breath, and said, "Here we go..."

He concentrated briefly, and the world shifted. Light seemed to become dark, and dark became light. The black night of the forest turned to shades of gray and pale fog, as if the shadows radiated their own feeble luminescence, straining to be seen by human eyes.

Cindra thought, *Is this what cats see when they hunt in the dark? I must be a mother cat, and protect my kittens.*

The air became colder, closer, and slightly stifling. The faint sound of horses squealing and snorting in alarm penetrated the gloom, and Cindra felt she needed to pop her ears to better hear. It had no effect. Figures in the dark took on a ghostly aspect; the trees were like a phantom forest, moving in eerie ways. The campfire gave off a dark light that was difficult to look at.

Cindra illuminated her family honor sword, *Vyzeroth,* but the blade was far too dim, as if the shadows ate the light. This was not encouraging. She had hoped her magic sword would appear more impressive in the gloom.

"Do you see it?" Drahn asked to no one in particular.

"No, not yet," Adric answered, "Paddy?"

"Nothing," Padison whispered, having lost his former bravado.

All their voices sounded weak and muffled, like they were talking into a pillow. They heard a strange breeze blowing, but felt nothing.

Wenyssaya cast a spell and her floating faerie lights appeared above her head, but they were as dim as starlight and gave no comfort.

It was Deliah who finally looked up.

"*There!*" she hissed, and pointed to the tree above them.

Hanging from one of the high boughs some twenty feet above the ground was the thing they sought, leering at them through the leaves. It was black and thin, with long fingers that clung leisurely to a thick branch. Clad all in darkness, it wore a wide-brimmed hat and a long cloak that billowed unnaturally in the soft breeze. The face under the hat was pale and indistinct, save for the lights in the eyes. They were like red coals flickering through a coat of ash, dancing back and forth as he cast his gaze on each of them.

The eyes kept going back to Nixy, it seemed.

"You there!" Cindra cried, her voice squeaking as her throat tightened, "What do you want with us?" She pointed her sword at it, noticing how the blade trembled ever so slightly.

The thing made something like a smirk and swung behind the tree, appearing on the other side to get a better look at her. It was as nimble as a squirrel, and moved with the languid grace of a forest cat.

The pale face caught the light of the fire, and Nixy gasped. The craggy, narrow features looked familiar.

"Answer me, if you can!" Cindra called, wishing she had chosen her bow instead of her sword, "We're not afraid of you," she said, all evidence to the contrary.

"*You should be,*" it rasped in a low, throaty voice that echoed strangely in the palpable gloom. The sound chilled them.

Nixy drew *Cutter*, his magic knife, and held it against his chest, feeling his heart pound. With his other hand, he gripped Wenyssaya's sleeve, making her jump a little. She looked down at the boy and saw her terror reflected in his face.

Drahn flapped off of Nixy's back and scampered out of the circle a little ways, making room to use his breath weapon if needed. The color of his scales could not be judged, but his eyes were wide and his slit pupils were large and black. His tail swished back and forth with anxiety.

Cindra did not know what to say next. The thing did not run or seem intimidated, and her plan had not gone much beyond frightening it away. Maybe Deliah had been right.

Adric hissed, "What now, Cindra?"

She took several deep breaths before answering, smelling the fear in her own sweat. She decided she greatly disliked the supernatural. "If you won't leave us alone," she called, "we will make you sorry for it!" Then she said under her breath to her female companions, "I hope you have something up your sleeves that will make it sorry."

"We might all be sorry," Deliah said, but she began to mutter a spell.

Wenyssaya already had one prepared, and wove her hands towards the tree. The bark exploded in rapid growth, entangling the figure in a snarl of twisting branches. The creature tried to pull away, but the green bonds were supple and strong.

Deliah was not taking any chances. She chanted in a harsh whisper and thrust her hands towards the shadow man. The side of the tree burst into flames, although the fire was muted and dim like the campfire. The creature howled in anger and pain and began to rapidly fade, becoming like a dark ghost. Suddenly he was out of the twisting branches and leaping away from the flames in a black flash, moving impossibly fast.

"He's gone deep!" Nixy cried in alarm.

In the time it took him to say it, the shadow figure had bounced off a nearby tree, darted to the ground, and rushed at their flank.

Drahn had to spring backwards to avoid the terrible specter, moving with cat-like reflexes. He landed several paces away with his tail and wings in the air, claws scratching the road to halt his momentum. He took a sharp breath and felt the lightning element stirring within him.

But he was too late. The thing had knocked away Padison's shield, spinning him and ripping its claws across his back, tearing through his padded gambeson. The boy screamed and fell on his face, exposing Deliah to attack. She held up a warding hand, possibly attempting another spell, but the monster lashed out at her neck.

Cindra felt hot blood strike her face as Deliah fell at her feet.

But Nixy was not idle; he focused his terror on matching the creature's tactic. He sank as deep into the Shadow as he could, taking his friends with him. The lightning-quick movements of the black specter became slower, until he was moving no faster than they. As Nixy looked into the face of the shadow man, its dark features lightened and became clear.

It's Dexer, he thought, *Somehow, it's Dexer!*

Cindra felt the shifting change like a shock, like a plunge into an icy lake; the air grew very terribly frigid and became even thicker and harsher than she imagined possible. The sound of the breeze became a roar like a mighty storm as the tension between darkness and light grew violent. Her limbs moved as if through water, her muscles protested, and her lungs heaved to draw a single breath, but she brought her sword to bear on the creature. Moving generated heat on her skin as she imposed herself between the thing and Nixy, and she thrust the glowing blade into the monster's chest, piercing the black fabric and biting flesh.

The shadow man grunted in surprise, a look of pain and annoyance creasing his features. He grabbed the glowing steel, pulled it slowly out of his rib cage, and to Cindra's shock, ripped it from her hand. His eyes flashed like candle light, and a deeper shadow seemed to move within him. For a brief moment, a fiery scar appeared on his cheek.

"Girl has a pretty sword," he said in a rumbling, echoing voice. He threw the sword away as its glow went out. *"We owe you for this,"* it said, pointing to the blazing gash under its eye.

She stiffened as the fury of battle turned to a cold wash of terror. *The voice. The eyes. The scar. Black Will.*

Drahn let out a rumble, and with a loud bark and a crack of thunder, he unleashed fury of his own. The bright, hot fork of electricity cut through the gloom; a flash of light so intense that the Shadow reality seemed to flicker. It struck the gaunt man, racing across his limbs and down to the ground. His body convulsed and flung itself across the road, passing right through their wagon and tumbling into the forest.

"Nixy, get us out!" Cindra cried, her eyes going to her fallen friend and the woman at her feet.

Nixy took a deep breath, willing himself and his friends to the 'surface' of the Shadow, returning to the normal world. Silence and warmth returned like a slap to the face, and the campfire hit them with a welcome blaze of light. Dexer was nowhere to be seen; there was a small fire burning in the tree, and the horses were the only other noise they could hear besides their own heavy breathing. The animals were quite unnerved, and the woods were eerily silent. The smells of smoke, sweat, and blood came sharply to their noses as they sucked in the natural air.

"Paddy!" cried Adric, rushing to his friend. He rolled him over enough to see the boy's face.

Padison groaned, "Easy, easy!" His throat was tight with pain and his face was contorted. Blood covered his back, oozing from four deep gashes. "Why is it always me who gets hurt?" he whined.

"You should have worn your mail," his friend chided as he tried to staunch the bleeding with the remains of the boy's gambeson.

Wenyssaya looked from Deliah to Padison and made a quick decision. "Remove his shirt! Fetch some water!" She knelt beside him and began preparing herself for powerful healing magic.

Cindra and Nixy exchanged a look. As if reading each other's thoughts, they said together, "He's back."

She pointed to Padison, saying, "Help Wen with Paddy. I'll see to Deliah." She bent over the woman, lifting up her head as she examined what must have been a mortal wound.

Drahn came over to Cindra's side and looked up into her eyes. His scales and her scale necklace were both the same color of mauve, showing their stress and exertion. He said, "Should we tell them?"

Cindra shook her head, using a kerchief to wipe the blood away from the woman's neck. The skin was smooth and flawless. Trembling, Cindra used the remaining clean cloth to wipe the blood from her own face.

Deliah opened her eyes and looked up at Cindra. "I told you it was unwise," she said quietly.

"I think it's time Nixy and I told our stories," Cindra said.

The group was huddled around the fire, trying to shake the chill from their bodies and souls. Padison had been bandaged and healed as well as Wenyssaya could manage, but he was still in pain. Everyone was trembling as the excitement and fear wore off and hearts stopped pounding so frantically.

They looked up at Cindra expectantly.

"Some of you may have heard this story, in part or in full, but you need to hear it all now." She took a breath to calm her voice and began, "Over four years ago, on my birthday, I dressed as a servant and sneaked out of the castle to explore the city. I met a little thief who cut my purse and ran."

"That was me," Nixy said, raising his hand.

"I ran him down and caught him in a deserted courtyard, but we weren't alone," she said, "Something was after him, something that knew about his parentage. It was a killer called Black Will."

"I heard of him!" Padison said, "I thought he was just a story."

"No," she said, "he was worse than the stories. He had a demnox inside of him."

The word made an impression. Worried glances were exchanged. A log in the fire popped and sparked, and everyone flinched.

"This thing that possessed him, it made him more than a man. He moved like a beast, and spoke with two voices. He took Nixy and dragged him away to kill him, but I had Nixy's knife. What I didn't know was that it was very old and very magical."

"It belonged to my mother," Nixy said, "given to her by my father; my real father."

"I used it," Cindra said, "I stabbed him in the back and slashed his cheek," she motioned under her eye. "The blade didn't just cut the man; it cut the demnox inside of him. It was enough to scare him away, at least for a while." She looked at Nixy and nodded.

Nixy gulped and said, "He came back for me again while Cindra was away and I was back with the Circle of Gold. I was breakin' a house, a big house, when he stole me right out the window; dragged me up to the top of the cathedral where a troll was waiting."

Adric was skeptical. "A troll? On the cathedral roof? Is this part of the story actually true?"

"It *is!*" Nixy exclaimed, "The troll had sent Black Will to kill me, to use my blood against my father somehow. But I was saved by... by..."

"Go ahead, Nixy," Cindra said, squeezing his hand.

"By a vemlok," he said quietly.

The others raised their eyebrows, even Wenyssaya. She thought the boy had told her everything about his misadventures.

Cindra took over the story to spare him the barrage of questions. "There is- *was* a vemlok in Portshia," she said, "He was different from the others, like a normal person, and lived under our very noses."

"Who?" Adric asked, incredulous.

"Lord Arton Clavemont," Cindra said, hardly believing it herself. He had attended her birthday feast, sitting at table with her. She suddenly wondered what had become of the woman he had brought that night.

"The albino?" Padison blurted, "I saw him on the street once! I *knew* there was something weird about him!"

"My father made shoes for him," Adric muttered, "He went to his mansion for the fittings."

Wenyssaya and Drahn were unfamiliar with the man, but were shocked nonetheless. Only Deliah seemed unsurprised.

"Clavemont killed Black Will and drove the troll out of the city," Cindra said, "but it seems the demnox didn't die, just the man it possessed."

They sat in silence for a while, absorbing this.

Then Nixy spoke up again. "That's not all of it," he said, "When I was back at the castle last year, the Circle of Gold sent Dexer to kill me. He was the Silver District boss and taught me everything I know, but he was scary and mean too. Even so, he was a better dad than the one I grew up with."

Wenyssaya placed an arm around his shoulders, rubbing warmth into them.

"Dexer found a way to get me alone, and he was going to kill me because of my real father; I'm not sure why." The boy sniffed and wiped his nose, and his voice began to tremble, "But then something happened. A swirly hole opened up in the dark, and two black wolves jumped out and pulled him in. The hole disappeared, and that was the last anyone saw of him... until tonight." Tears filled his eyes and he leaned against the elf maid, sobbing gently.

Cindra patted his knee, feeling terrible for him. She said, "In short, Black Will's demnox has returned in the body of Nixy's old mentor, and they are both out to finish the job. We have to stop them."

The weight of this news left them all sullen and weary as they stared into the fire. Finally Padison said, "Well, that would have been a great ghost story if it wasn't true."

Adric replied, "Everything will be fine," and he motioned to slap his friend on the back.

"Don't you dare," Paddy said, flinching away. Adric only grinned.

Wenyssaya told him, "You should get some rest, Padison. Your wounds will open if you move around too much."

He nodded and gingerly got to his feet, helped by Adric, who made his bedroll for him.

Wenyssaya looked across the fire to Deliah and said, "I was not aware you could use magic."

Deliah smiled and said, "I don't make it known. Witches are treated... harshly."

The boys threw her a look at the mention of witches, but quickly hid their eyes.

The elf maid nodded, having encountered that prejudice before. She said, "Are you sure you are unharmed? I could have sworn you were grievously wounded. The blood..."

Deliah shook her head, saying, "It was nothing. The blood was the boy's. I just fell and passed out, nothing more."

Cindra and Drahn shared a look, then she sniffed and looked away as the dweedragon fiddled with the tip of his tail. If Wenyssaya noticed the exchange, she pretended not to.

"If I understand it right," the elf maid said, "the black wolves were Nixy's protectors, sent by his father. The Shadow Lord was likely responsible for the portal that swallowed this Dexer person."

"Seems so," Cindra agreed, "I suppose we should call him 'Black Dexer' now."

"I wonder if that is why he is confined to the deep Shadow," the elf said, "Perhaps neither the man nor the monster has the power to leave on their own; they might need a portal to reach our world."

"A happy accident," Deliah said, "Can the boy create one?"

Nixy answered for himself, annoyed that they were talking like he wasn't there. "No I can't," he said, "At least, I've never tried."

"I suggest you don't," Deliah said, "Not until we devise a way to destroy him."

"Fine by me," he sniffed, rubbing his eyes dry.

"Who has first watch?" Adric asked.

Cindra scoffed, "You think any of us will be able to sleep?"

The young man had to agree, staring at the spot where Black Dexer had fallen, just a few yards away.

The next morning could not come fast enough. Cindra had taken first watch, and could tell that her companions were trying and failing to relax and rest. Every nightly noise made someone twitch or open their eyes and check to see that Cindra was still watching over them. She would give them a thin, non-committal smile that gave no comfort, only the reassurance that they were not about to be murdered.

Her own attempt at sleep was a bit more successful; it was more accurate to say that she passed out from exhaustion. Her dreams were disturbing and bloody, and when her heart began to race, she would awaken. This happened several times through the late watches.

Adric had let the fire die down, and Cindra woke up in the cold blue of early morning. Breakfast would be nothing better than wine or water and hardtack, as they had eaten the last of the fresh supplies the day before. It had also been several days since she had given herself a proper wash, so she decided to head down to the river and remove a layer or two of sweat and grime as best she could.

"I shall come with you," Wenyssaya said.

Cindra grudgingly accepted her company, fearing otherwise the elf woman would pout and make her feel like a horse's ass. "Suit yourself," she said.

They trekked through the trees at the river's edge and removed their boots to wade into the waters. The scent of algae and water plants greeted them as the Joshian's currents filled their ears. Cindra was planning a towel bath, so she only loosened her shirt and trousers. Wenyssaya daintily washed her legs and arms, keeping her clothes on as well. This suited Cindra, who would have otherwise felt the need to act as lookout for spying eyes. She could depend on her boys to behave themselves, but who knew who else was out there?

"You have been very different since the night before last," the elf maid said, her voice full of concern.

Here we go, Cindra thought. "This trip has changed us all, I imagine," she replied.

"No," Wenyssaya said, "you have been different since that night in particular. What happened between you and Deliah?"

Cindra bristled and wiped with her towel a bit more vigorously. "What do you think happened?" she asked.

"I imagine you had words, and perhaps more," she replied, "You knew last night that she could use magic. Did she use it when you were alone with her?"

"Good guess," Cindra said. *Damned elf,* she thought, scrubbing her scarred arms.

Wen asked hesitantly, "Was it for attack... or in defense?"

Cindra stopped scrubbing. The feelings of guilt and shame washed over her again, and she took a heaving breath. Turning to face the elf maid, she looked into her violet eyes and said, "You are the nosiest person I have ever met, do you know that?"

The woman just blinked and said, "I am observant and curious, and I sense that things have greatly changed between you. You are almost... fearful. It is most unlike you."

"Is it?" she said flatly.

"Yes," the elf replied, "You are often very brave, and dare I say, willful. That has changed. What happened between you two?"

"What does it matter to you, Wenyssaya?" she asked, getting angry now.

"You are the leader of our expedition, but I sense that has... shifted," she replied.

The babbling of the water matched the rushing of her temper, and Cindra planted her hands on her hips, her face reddening. "I am still in charge!" she said, affirming it as much to herself as to the elf.

"As you say," said the maiden, lowering her eyes, "But there is more to it." She went back to washing the length of her legs, drawing out the silence. Then she said, "Drahn knows something, I am sure. I could ask him, but that would be unfair; dweedragons are terrible liars and cannot keep a secret very long."

"Leave Drahn alone," Cindra said, returning to her scrubbing, "You don't have the right to everyone's secrets."

"I just want to help if I can," she said, "and I cannot help if I am in the dark."

Cindra snapped at her, "Is that how this usually works? You pry into people's business with your... your *elven wiles* and sympathy, and they just pour out their hearts to you?"

"Usually," she admitted.

"Well, learn to be disappointed!"

"Don't be afraid."

"I'm not afraid," Cindra retorted.

"Your necklace says otherwise," she said softly.

Cindra glanced down at the necklace Drahn had given her, seeing the scale turn from fearful blue to crimson embarrassment. She shoved it inside her shirt.

With the utmost concern, Wenyssaya asked, "What did she do to you?"

The elf's voice was so full of sincerity and worry that Cindra couldn't bring herself to be mean to her anymore. She dragged in a ragged breath, feeling it catch in her throat. Unwanted emotion welled up inside her, threatening to burst out. *No, no, no, damn it all*, she thought, fighting to keep it under control. But her burning guilt overwhelmed her, and tears ran down her cheeks. Squeezing them shut, she felt a convulsing sob taking over.

Wenyssaya rushed to take her in her arms, stroking her hair. Cindra was helpless to resist, and felt the first real release of her pain, as if the woman exuded comfort from her fingertips. Perhaps she did. They stood in the river as Cindra cried, her feet going numb from the cold.

"Come," Wenyssaya said, finally drawing her to the river bank. Sitting her down on a patch of clover, she rubbed Cindra's back until she could compose herself.

When she was finally able to speak, Cindra stared at her bare feet and said, "It's not what *she* did that is destroying me." She sniffed and wiped her nose. "Deliah said some horrible things, and I got so afraid and angry, I was sure she was dangerous to all of us. And what she said about me and Jaron..." She couldn't bring herself to repeat it; it was too cruel.

"Did she use magic on you?"

"Just to trip me up, as a warning," Cindra answered, "It was unexpected, but nothing serious."

The woman did not press her for answers, but kept rubbing her back.

"I was... I was so angry and afraid that I-" she choked on the words, "I didn't know what else to do!" She burst into tears anew.

Wenyssaya could only stare at the river, waiting patiently.

Cindra muttered with her head hung low, hair obscuring her face, "She was standing there, naked in the stream, mocking me and saying there was nothing that could keep her from following us. I was so angry... I don't know what I was thinking, or *if* I was."

Wenyssaya let peace and serenity flow through her fingers and into the girl, hoping to ease her suffering and aid her focus. It seemed to have the desired effect as Cindra's breathing became more regular and her sobbing ebbed.

Yet something had come over Cindra; a darkness that made her relive that moment with terrible clarity. She felt an icy worm twist in her guts as she experienced the rage and fear from a distance, like an observer to a tragic play.

"I had my knife," she said in a low voice, detached and cold, "My *Kos* knife. I pulled it from its sheath..."

Cindra moved her hand into view, and in it was the large knife of a Minozhian bull man, its horn handle almost too big for her to grip.

Wenyssaya stiffened.

"I think she saw the metal glint in the moonlight," Cindra said airy, "but she only smiled. Taunting... and taunting..."

The elf maid kept her hand moving in comforting circles between the young woman's strong shoulders, growing aware that she might have placed herself in real danger. She did not like the coldness in her voice; perhaps Cindra was more troubled than she imagined. Wenyssaya's eyes did not leave the shining blade, curved and wicked and as long as her forearm.

"I knew... I knew we were too deep in the woods to be seen or heard from the road..."

As we are now, the elf realized.

"I grabbed her by the back of the neck and... I..."

Wenyssaya held her breath, not wanting the warrior woman to move a muscle. The flowing of the river was like a roaring flood in her ears, and her voice squeaked a little when she spoke, guessing what had happened next. "You held the knife to her throat? You threatened her life?"

"No," Cindra said, barely audible, "I *took* her life."

The elf woman wondered if Cindra had lost her sanity. Her own breathing grew shallow and her hand twitched, ceasing its rubbing.

"I know, it's impossible," Cindra said flatly, beginning to tremble, "I felt the knife go in..."

The blade moved slowly in an upthrusting motion as she spoke, and the elf's eyes followed it with apprehension.

"Gods, it made me sick as I did it. I felt it scrape the bone and pierce her heart." Cindra gulped for air as she rasped, her voice low and tortured, "I murdered an unarmed woman! I feel like a Minozhian monster, like the one who killed Mineth."

"But... Deliah is not dead," Wenyssaya said. She had no experience with insanity, but felt that stating the obvious was important right now.

"No," Cindra droned from beneath her hair, "No she's not." The weapon slipped from her fingers as she covered her face with her hands and wept.

The elf woman did not relax until she lifted the weapon by its ring guard and moved it out of reach. They sat in silence for a while as the sun rose over the far trees across the river, and Wenyssaya pondered what to do with their clearly damaged leader.

Yet the cold shadow over Cindra's mind had passed, and her composure returned. "There was blood," she said, raising her head to the light, "Blood on the knife, blood on my hand, running down my arm. It was flowing out of her into the river as she lay in the stream, and then..." she shuddered, "then it stopped, and she just sat up."

Her hazel eyes lifted to meet the elf's violet gaze, and Wenyssaya saw they were haunted and rimmed with red, yet not the eyes of a madwoman.

"The way she looked at me... her murderer..."

Wenyssaya could not absolve her, could not even imagine how, assuming any of this were true. Then her brow furled as a new thought occurred to her. "Last night, my eyes did not deceive me; she really *was* fatally wounded, wasn't she?"

"Yes," Cindra said, "He opened her throat. But in a moment the wound had healed."

Wenyssaya felt an entirely new sense of dread. "Did she say how this is possible?"

Cindra nodded, "I think she told us; I think her campfire story was... *her* story."

"The immortal queen?" the elf exclaimed, "But that would make her over four thousand years old!"

"Four thousand six hundred, give or take," Cindra said, "I asked Drahn."

"But... but she is human... isn't she?"

"Annoyingly so," Cindra said.

"I cannot believe one of your kind could endure so long!"

Cindra rubbed her eyes and gave her a rueful little smile. "Not used to meeting women older than yourself, are you?"

"Rude," Wenyssaya said, relieved that Cindra's humor was returning at least, "I do not know anyone so old, even among the elders of my land."

"There's more," Cindra sniffled, "She told me about her and Sir Earnold Greenfellow."

"I have heard the story," the elf woman said.

"No, it was about how they met," Cindra said, "She was pursued through the forest near Breega by two men who assaulted her and... and murdered her. Sir Earnold caught them in the act and killed them. As he was kneeling over her body, she... revived. He learned her secret that day and used it against her, threatening to expose her if she didn't help him." She shivered and asked, "Can you imagine what they would do to a witch that can't die? How many different ways they would try to put her to death?"

Wenyssaya did not want to image that. What she had already seen of humanity's brutality was bad enough.

"*She* was Nasha the Raven Witch," Cindra said, "and she was responsible for Waliss Greenfellow's shame, and the chance opportunity that made Jaron's father a knight. She's the reason I know him." *But **not** the reason I love him,* she thought. "She made Drahn and I promise not to tell anyone, so if she asks, you dragged it out of me with your elven wiles."

"Fair enough," the elf said, "But one thing puzzles me. Why was she naked? Was she bathing?"

Cindra nodded, crossing her legs to rub warmth into her feet. "That's the worst part of it. After it was over, she told me she chose to have our 'little chat' naked in the stream, lest I ruin her good dress. It's like she knew she could goad me into doing something horrible." The pang of guilt struck her again hard, and she drew a deep, haggard breath.

"You mean to say that she *wanted* you to try and kill her?"

Cindra shook her head, "I think it was some kind of sick test. She wanted me to know that I couldn't make her leave if I tried, and she wanted to see how far I would go to stop her."

"Did you pass or fail, I wonder?" Wenyssaya asked.

Cindra had no answer for that. She only knew she had failed herself.

Chapter Eighteen

Remains

After Cindra's grim confession, Wenyssaya was still trying to process all that she had learned. She kept her silence through the meager breakfast and packing her bedroll, and only spoke in soft elven words to her horse and raven. If the others noticed the change in her, they said nothing.

Cindra seemed to be in better spirits, lighter of mood and more talkative with her friends. She offered some words of encouragement before saddling up and moving on, which had not happened since that night. The elf maid was glad of it, but saw that it was but a thin veneer of leadership covering a deep well of doubt and misery. The girl's healing would take time, perhaps more time than they had.

The day wore on and the road turned dark once again under the oppressive trees. Wenyssaya's mind had wandered and soon she found herself taking up the rear of their column, just ahead of Deliah. Her reverie was shattered completely as the woman spoke to her.

"Are you still with us?" the raven-haired woman asked as she rode up beside, "You seem very far away."

Wenyssaya felt a deep unease being alone with the woman, given all she knew. Yet, she gave Deliah a warm smile and said, "I was just deep in my thoughts. It is not uncommon with my people to let the mind wander."

"Yes, you live through so much history, I imagine you have a lot to think about," the woman said.

"I suppose that is true," the elf replied, "yet I was thinking less of history and more of our current situation."

"And what situation is that?"

Her tone took Wenyssaya aback, but she managed to answer casually, "Who or what we will meet on the road, and how we shall deal with it, of course."

"Sometimes," the woman said, "it is more challenging to deal with one's own traveling companions, don't you think?"

"I suppose..."

"I mean, it's not as if you can just stick a knife in them," she said airily, "That's not how civilized people solve their problems."

Wenyssaya blanched at that. She met the woman's ice chip eyes and saw a measuring stare looking back at her.

"She told you, didn't she?" Deliah asked.

"I- I don't know what you mean," she said, trying her best to sound innocent.

"You and Cindra had a long talk at the river yesterday. Tears were shed and secrets were told. She seems to be in better spirits, while you seem more pensive and wary. Shall I go on?"

"Were you spying on us?" the elf asked.

"Did I need to be?" Deliah asked, "I am a woman. I can read a face."

Wenyssaya did not answer.

"If she betrayed my trust, I shall be very cross with her," Deliah said coldly.

"It- it was my fault," Wenyssaya said, "Do not blame the girl. I was very concerned for her and only wanted to ease her burdens." She added, "She is only a child."

"A deadly child," Deliah said.

Wenyssaya felt a great blush rise in her fair face, and lowered her gaze, staring at her horse's neck.

"So," Deliah said, "she *did* tell you everything."

They rode in silence for a while. Deliah's eyes were straight ahead, cold and unreadable, and Wenyssaya reprimanded herself for being read so easily. Perhaps dweedragons were not the only ones that could not keep a secret?

"I suppose it had to come out eventually," Deliah said, "After all, Cindra is so emotionally fragile, and Drahn... well, he's a dweedragon. I'm surprised he didn't tell you first."

"They were under the impression there would be terrible consequences if they did," Wenyssaya said.

"There might yet be," Deliah said, "Such knowledge always carries a price. But do not worry yourself; the last person I killed for learning my secret deserved what he got."

The admission shocked her. "You speak of it so lightly," the elf said with distaste, "Has life become so... so cheap to you?"

Deliah laughed, "That answer would either be too short or too long for your liking." Then her voice and face turned serious. "Have you any idea how long I have endured?"

Wenyssaya nodded, saying quietly, "If you are who they think you are, the immortal queen of your story, then about four thousand and six hundred years."

"I'll take your word for it, I've lost track myself," she said, "During all that time, I learned that there are many, *many* things worse than death. My primary goal has been to avoid those things at all costs. Sometimes that means leaving a life I have grown comfortable in, and sometimes it means arranging for people to die.”

Wenyssaya could see the cold logic in that, though the lack of morality shocked her. Life was life, and it was all sacred to an elf. *Are humans so different? So callous?*

“You are thinking that all life is sacred, and elves must be morally superior,” Deliah said.

The elf maid gasped. *Does she also read minds?*

“No, I do not read minds,” Deliah said, smiling, “I just know elves better than they know themselves.” Seeing the doubt in Wenyssaya’s eyes, she said, “Did you know that an elf’s reverence for life is in inverse proportion to how long they have endured?”

“Nonsense,” Wenyssaya said.

“Perhaps it is not so for each individual, but as a people and a culture, it is true.” Deliah said, “I have known elves for most of my life, and I have seen their power diminish. I have seen the eldest of them leave the world after growing weary of it, and have seen the younger generations strive to protect it with increasing care.”

“You claim the eldest of my kind did not care for life? I do not believe you.”

“Oh, they cared in their own way,” Deliah said, “but they lived in a world where the only living things that endured were themselves. Not even the trees were as long-lived as they, and as for *my* kind,” she laughed, “they would not even bother to learn our names most of the time. Would you trouble yourself to study each leaf of a tree in spring, knowing they would wither and die in autumn?”

“I have some understanding of living with mortal races,” Wenyssaya said, feeling she was being patronized.

“No offense,” Deliah said, “but you are still a child among your people. How old are you, a century and a half? Two?”

“Two and a half.”

"The elf lord we are going to meet is more than twice *my* age; it is said he was a young child when my kind saw their first sunrise. How much care do you think he has for individual humans? How much care has he for the son he sired and has never met?"

It was a question Wenyssaya had pondered long, and she did not like the implications. Wanting to give him the benefit of the doubt, she said, "He has called for him now. Perhaps he simply wanted Nixy to come of age first?"

"From what I hear, the boy has lived a life of cruel poverty, up until he robbed the right girl. Either the Shadow Lord watched and did nothing, or he did not bother to watch. Neither are characteristics of a praiseworthy parent."

Wenyssaya found her deepest worries given voice by another, and it troubled her greatly. Was she delivering the boy to a caring father that would raise him as he ought, or did the Shadow Lord require him for another reason?

"I believe," Deliah said, "from what I have recently learned, the boy is the Shadow Lord's greatest weakness. That guadim tried to use the boy for blood magic against the father. It makes sense that the lord would want to keep him close. I see no other good reason for this venture. He is *certainly* not going to help a human king with his little civil war."

The elf maid stiffened, "How did you know that?"

"It was a guess until just now." Deliah laughed, "Really, you are *too* easy. Have you never lied in your life?"

Wenyssaya fumed at being tricked once again into revealing information, and began to understand why Cindra hated this woman enough to stab her. Not that it excused that horrific action, but she understood the urge.

Deliah softened. "I'm sorry," she said, "I don't mean to offend. It's not in the nature of the Ilvayiin to lie and dissemble. You say what you mean and mean what you say. Forgive me."

Wenyssaya pouted for a moment, then said, "*Am leviia yom.*"

"Thank you," Deliah said.

She did indeed forgive her, but she wondered if Deliah's apology was sincere. Who could tell with this woman?

They rode in silence for a time.

Once Wenyssaya had cooled enough to speak again, she decided she would be the one asking the questions. "I was wondering, since I am apparently young enough to bother learning human names, might you tell me yours? Or is Deliah your true name?"

The woman's eyes grew troubled and she replied, "When I told the story of the sorcerer king and his immortal queen, I spoke truly; it has been so long that I don't remember the names."

"You have forgotten even your own name?"

"I only used it for a century or so," she said, "After the destruction of Bythia, the names of the king and his loving queen were cursed. Even as I spread the tale and it became legend, the names were omitted. I chose a new name for myself, and another, and another... After several centuries, I struggled to recall my original name."

The elf maid considered this, and found it deeply sad. "Then you do not remember your love either?"

Deliah sighed heavily and Wenyssaya perceived that this was a naked nerve, the gap in her icy armor. But before she could apologize for asking, Deliah said, "I cannot forget. Ever. I can't recall his name, or his voice, or even his face. Time has erased his image like the wind-driven sands erase carvings in stone. Yet my love for him festers like an open wound that never heals, eating my soul and stealing every momentary joy.

"I have what everyone wants: eternal youth and beauty. Yet I cannot love whom I choose, I cannot stop loving one who hurt me. It is not the love of passion, but the love of needing and longing. It is a curse I would wish on no one." She lowered her head and took several deep breaths. No tears fell. Perhaps none were left.

Wenyssaya tried to imagine what the woman must have lived through. She realized there was a reason she used the word 'endured' rather than 'lived.' Deliah's life was a trial of endurance, and it was one she was forced to face, like it or not.

Though Wenyssaya's people were called immortal, she knew it had not been so for a very long time. Modern elves could die of old age or violence, though they lived much longer than humans and barely withered with age. Some could even choose to return to Alhanna, forsaking the world for a time, or so it was said. But to never die, even when it was preferred, that was unimaginable.

"How much of your life *do* you remember?"

The raven-haired woman raised her face to the grim canopy blocking the sun. "I remember fragments of lifetimes; bits of language and history, fashions and customs and beliefs, and the upheaval as they inevitably changed. Moving through my memory is like riding through this forest, searching for the sun. Some of it comes in flickers, some in brief and glorious radiance, and most in utter darkness. I do not know if I envy the minds of elves and dweedragons. There is so much to remember, yet I know that there is much that I should be glad to forget."

The elf maid could not argue with that.

Cindra's spirits were lifted as the day wore on. Tonight or early tomorrow they would reach Gloamshire, the first real settlement they had seen in about seventeen leagues. She was looking forward to a teahouse, an inn, a tavern, or even a barn. She wanted to see people and buildings and safe walls. She feared the darkness of the forest was seeping into her bones, taking away her inner light. It was unthinkable that people actually lived their lives in this shadow, but where there was such life, there was hope, surely.

She had been toying with the notion that it was this forest, and not her fear and temper that had led her to strike Deliah down. Yet as much as she would have wished it to be so, she could not relinquish her guilt. Perhaps she did not truly want to. It was so easy to claim another's agency over her own; to blame a demnox, or an evil spell, or a haunted wood. But she was no puppet; she had a will of her own, and a strong one at that.

And yet, perhaps this pervasive gloom played its part. At no time had the woods held any beauty in her eyes; its constant encroachment on her senses promised nothing but a growing threat and menace. The others had felt it too, that was for certain. Perhaps, had Deliah challenged her in any other setting, Cindra's better nature would have won out. She truly wished for that to be true.

"Strange," said Adric, riding behind her, "I thought we'd have seen some other travelers by now."

Cindra said, "It's not the season for trade caravans, and most of the traffic is probably between Gloamshire and Kelgerton, the provincial seat to the west. It's many days farther than Breega, but it's a proper city, and the road must be well-patrolled and maintained."

"Are we in Kelgar Province already?" Padison asked.

"We *have* been since Breega, Paddy," Cindra answered, sighing in exasperation.

"He doesn't bother with maps," Adric said.

"I don't," Padison pouted, "Besides, you'd think there'd be a sign or something."

"There *were* signs," Nixy said, piping up from beside the wagon, "Deliah pointed out rock markers in the forest that you can see from the road."

"There you go," Adric said to Paddy, "Deliah knows everything."

"Maybe she knows if there's an inn ahead," Cindra said, not that she wanted to ask her.

"I bet you're looking forward to a feather bed and a roof," Adric said.

"Don't tease us," Padison groaned, "We'd be lucky to get a flea-bitten blanket on a dirt floor in a no-temple hamlet like Gloamshire."

"I've had worse," Cindra sighed.

"By now, we all have," Adric replied.

"Well," said Drahn, "I shall be happy to curl up in my pack just about anywhere, so long as it's under an open sky and not these gloomy twees."

Nixy nodded in agreement. Drahn was currently in his pack, which was strapped on Nixy's back. The little dragon found it better than trying to nap in the bumping wagon, and Nixy liked the company.

The overgrown road continued for many miles before the terrain dropped to either side. A moss-covered stone bridge crossed the gap created by a narrow stream, which flowed southeast to the river. The sound of babbling water was pleasant, and a soft breeze tickled their skin.

"This must be Fellbrook Bridge, if I read the map right," Cindra said, "I think I see a wide spot on the other side. We'll stop for a rest and some food."

"Fellbrook," Padison muttered, peering into the shallow stream as they crossed the bridge, "Sounds lovely."

"What did you expect they'd call it?" Adric asked, "Happy Sunshine Brook?"

They stopped and unpacked with practiced efficiency. Adric helped Cindra out of most of her armor, Nixy tended the cart horses as Padison unhitched them from the wagon as best he could, wincing a lot but refusing help. The boy's wounds required attention each time they stopped, but he would not shirk his duties unless the cuts were bleeding. Cindra had to admire his pluck. Indeed, it was his best quality in moderation.

Deliah and Wenyssaya prepared their food and ate in silence. It seemed they had done most of their talking on the road. Cindra had no idea what it was all about, but the two women had ridden side-by-side for many miles, at a distance behind the rest of them. She hoped it had been a pleasant discussion, and not too specific.

The horses were restless. Cindra noticed T'ózha's head was held high and his tail was tucked. There was something wrong.

"Everyone, quiet for a moment," she said. The others looked at her in worry as they stopped what they were doing and strained their ears. All they heard was running water, the wind in the leaves, and the call of distant birds.

"What is it?" Nixy whispered.

"I'm not sure," she said, "The horses are acting strange."

"A predator?" Adric asked.

"Probably," she said, "Hopefully a normal one."

They listened to the silence around them for a time, hearing nothing unusual. The horses snorted and stamped a bit more, but eventually the tension passed.

"Could it be that... Black Will creature?" Wenyssaya asked.

"I don't think the horses can sense him," Nixy said, "They only got upset that night when I shifted us into the Shadow."

Cindra said, "Well, if anyone has to leave the camp, they don't go alone."

No one argued with that.

Their lunch was light and unsatisfying; nothing more than hardtack, dried apples, and what little water remained in their skins. Wenyssaya offered to collect some more water and purify it for drinking.

"Water, bleah," Padison said, making a face, "I miss good wine and ale. I don't suppose you know a spell that'll turn water into wine or ale, do you?"

Her expression said she didn't.

Padison looked over at Nixy feeding Nibbler. "I wonder how those horse biscuits taste?"

"Ask the horses," Cindra said, "because that food is only for them."

"But they can live on grass," he whined, "I can't."

"You'd be surprised what you can live on," Deliah said.

The banks of the brook were too steep to lead the horses down, so Nixy had to use a bucket to water the beasts. Even though the stream was within a stone's throw of the campsite, Cindra rose to go with him. She still felt something was off; it was something in the air.

"What kind of predators do you think live around here?" Nixy asked as they picked their way down the embankment.

"Bears, wolves, the usual I imagine," she said, "Hopefully nothing worse."

"Yeah," he agreed. "I mean, bears are bad enough."

He filled the bucket and together they walked back to camp, though watering seven horses required many trips to the brook. A cold breeze blew through the underbrush from the direction of the river, wafting the scents of water plants, river scum, and wet earth to their nostrils. There was another smell also, something both sickly-sweet and rancid, like a dead animal.

"Smell that?" Cindra asked, breathing deep, "We should check it out."

"Why?" Nixy sniffed, his nose wrinkling, "If it's a dead animal, we should let it lie."

She said, "If it's this close to the road, it might attract a bear. I've heard of carcasses attracting bears from as far as a league away."

"What if the bear is already there?" he whispered.

She didn't have an answer to that, but it wasn't going to stop her from satisfying her curiosity. Holding her sword before her, she led the reluctant boy downstream.

It wasn't long before they came upon the source of the smell; it was a pink shape in the middle of the brook, partially concealed by the shin-deep water.

"Cindra..." Nixy whimpered, his voice filled with dread, "It's not an animal, Cindra."

She approached the water's edge and stepped into the brook, careful of slippery rocks. Holding her breath against the unpleasant odor, she beheld a human body lying in the waters. It was the most gruesome sight she had ever seen, and she had seen a few.

Above the waterline, the body had been stripped of flesh down to the raw, pink bone. Bits of gore and linen still clung to the joints and the spaces between ribs, and patches of scalp sprouted dark hair. An empty eye socket gaped like a red tunnel, and an exposed jaw showed pearly teeth within; yet the worst was below the surface.

Whatever had done this had only worked in the open air. Below the flowing stream, the corpse was untouched and unspoiled. Half a pale face could be seen, with a blind eye staring wide, and a mouth open in a scream. The body was dressed in a tunic, trousers, and leather shoes, which were still intact under the water; also intact were the organs and viscera. Biting flies hovered over the body, taking what they could, and little fish nibbled below.

Cindra wanted to gag, and held her breath until her chest ached, fighting the impulse. Nixy had no such control, and his coughing and retching only made it harder for her to keep her own food down. Finally, she tore her eyes away from the ghastly sight, and taking Nixy's arm, led him quickly back to camp.

As they stumbled back, the others saw the shock and horror on their pale faces and rose in alarm.

"What is it?" Adric said.

"There's a body in the water," Cindra said, "It's like nothing I've ever seen."

Cindra, Adric, and Deliah went down to examine the grisly find while the others stayed in camp, content to watch the horses. Cindra had remembered to dig in her pack for the Essence of Elder, offering it to the others to dab under their noses to mask the smell. Together they followed the stream to the body.

The second viewing was not much easier than the first, and Cindra again felt her stomach roil at the sight. Adric had to turn away for a moment. Only Deliah seemed unperturbed as she walked around the corpse midstream, holding up her skirt.

"Have you seen anything like this before?" Cindra asked her.

"No," she replied.

Cindra took a moment to consider the implications of that single word, spoken by one who had seen so much. It did not bode well.

"It's not like any predator I can think of," Cindra said, taking comfort from the sound of her own voice, "A wolf or bear would have dragged it to the bank to feed on."

"Maybe," Deliah said, "A big cat could lick the flesh from the bones like this, but it's too intact. Nothing broken, no limbs missing; everything is so clean and neat."

"Acid, maybe?" Cindra asked.

"Well aren't you the educated one!" Deliah quipped, "Acid might burn flesh down to the waterline like this, but there are no acid-spitters on this continent."

Cindra wasn't sure she wanted to know what 'acid-spitters' she was referring to.

"What should we do with him?" Adric asked in a shaking voice.

"Do?" Deliah replied.

"Should we bury him? Burn him? We can't just leave him; he's a human being."

Cindra had to agree, even though moving the body out of the water would be revolting. "We have to do something with him," she said.

"I would have thought there were more pressing matters," Deliah said.

"Like what?"

"Like what if whatever did this comes back?" she replied.

Just then, a rustling in the tall grass behind them made them spin, weapons at the ready.

"Wait!" chirped a little voice, "It's only me!" Drahn bounded down the slope to the water's edge and froze as he saw the corpse. His purple scales shifted to shades of blue and red, and his reptilian eyes grew wide in fear and amazement.

"Drahn, I swear I'm going to put a bell on you if you do that again!" Cindra said as she relaxed, "What are you doing here?"

"I was curious," he said meekly, "It sounded like a mystewy, so I thought I would help if I could."

"Well, take a look if you must. What do you make of it?"

The little dweedragon stood on his hind legs in the shallows of the stream, stretching his neck to get a better look. His nose wrinkled as he snuffled the air, and his tail swished nervously in the water as he studied the corpse. "I think..." he began, "I think he was eaten by something vewy small. Smaller than me, possibly."

"What makes you say that?" Adric asked.

"Little teeth marks on the bones," he said, "Whatever ate him was wavenous, but not stwong enough to move him out of the water. It had to settle for what it could get."

"But could something that small have killed him?" Cindra wondered aloud, "A swarm of rats or carrion birds, maybe?"

"Well," Drahn said, "we cannot assume that whatever ate him also killed him. He might have died of natuwal causes."

The thought gave Cindra little comfort. "Whatever the case," she said, "we should bury him. It's the least we can do. We can gather river rocks and pile them on the body."

"Once we get it out of the water," Adric added, "Ugh. We were lucky it was downstream from the campsite."

Cindra and Adric pulled the body as gingerly as they could from the brook, careful not to cause any more damage than necessary. As Deliah and Drahn kept watch for monsters, the two warriors gathered stones to cover the body. It was slow work, but after an hour they had successfully buried the man. Cindra said a few words over the grave, reciting a prayer that had been given for her late brother's funeral.

"May the Gods Above and Below protect your sleep, may the World Mother reclaim what is hers, and may you be judged fairly in the world after. Be at peace."

"*D'athe Domos,*" Adric and Drahn said together.

Deliah bowed her head and said nothing.

The others were quite relieved to see them when they returned. They had only gone about fifty yards downstream, but in this forest it felt like a mile.

"Did you find anything else?" Nixy asked.

"No," Cindra said, "I think I might go look for tracks or something."

"You can track?" Padison asked.

"I learned a thing or two from my time with the Galindri," Cindra replied, "Teya took me on many hunts, and I got to recognize the basic signs. I'm nowhere near as good as her, but I can 'find a footprint in the mud,' as they say."

She could almost remember the saying in *l'nók-da Gatéth-sho'a*, the speech of the Galindri, but it had been so long since she had anyone to speak it with, she had fallen out of practice. Her failure to recall the words made her rather sad.

Cindra didn't return to the brook until she had been fed and armored. If anything had disturbed the body, she might have to defend herself. The others got ready to leave as Adric accompanied her downstream.

Reaching the spot where the body had been found, she began searching the edge of the brook. There were many tracks in the grass and mud, no doubt some were her own, but soon she found a trail that led farther into the wood.

"As I thought," she said, "He must have come from the north; the hamlet is only half a day away."

"See any other tracks?" Adric asked.

She said nothing but continued moving through the brush, reading the signs as best she could. The man had made a frantic trail on his way to his final resting place, stomping and slipping, crushing foliage beneath him. It began to look less and less like he had died of natural causes.

Farther along, she found a piece of clothing among the trees; it was a shapeless cap made of striped linen. It looked poor and threadbare.

"A hat?"

"Yes," she said, "The trail is getting faint, or at least it is to me, but I think it's leading back to the road." She handed him the hat for safekeeping. "We may need it to help identify him later."

They had traveled perhaps fifty yards or more into the woods, curving to their left, when they came upon a new set of tracks, and a lot of flattened and disturbed undergrowth. She walked about in a circle, trying her best to reconstruct what lay before her. Even Adric could tell what had happened.

"A horse," he said, "There are shod hoof prints leading from the road."

"And leading again into the wood," she said, pointing, "He was at a gallop, maybe, fleeing from the road. His horse fell or maybe threw him, then galloped away farther into the woods. Instead of running after it, our man ran for the brook and died there."

"But what was he running from?" Adric asked.

Cindra just shook her head. "Maybe we should look for the horse?"

"I'm going to signal the others first so they can get up here," Adric said. He climbed a slight embankment and was soon on the road, waving and calling.

Cindra followed the trail of hooves for a short way until the ground began to slope upward. The hoof prints ran to the right of the rise, circling it for many yards, until they became mingled with a second set of tracks, big and broad and clawed. She could easily fit both of her feet into one such footprint, with room to spare. There was blood on the ground, spattered on tree trunks and trailing away in smears. There was a strong musk in the air, mingled with the coppery scent of blood and the reek of innards. The other tracks had come from the opposite direction, meaning the horse likely ran right into the path of whatever killed it.

Against her better judgment and against all the sense she had learned from the Galindri, she followed the trail for another fifteen steps around an outcropping of mossy rock.

She stiffened and froze. Seeing all she needed to see, she turned and walked back the way she came, as quickly and quietly as she could.

There was a huge bear feasting on the remains of the horse. Not just any bear, but what the locals called a great gray bear, a charcoal gray mass of fur and muscle and murder. She had only caught a glimpse, but could tell that its hunched shoulders were perhaps as high as her head, dwarfing the horse it fed on. Worse, it had turned to look at her the moment she withdrew.

Even as she hurried away, trying not to run and make a racket in her armor, she could only see those black eyes and red muzzle in her mind. Her thoughts flew back to her time with Majii's family, learning about meeting animals in the wild. *"Smaller bears can be wary or shy, but great bears are to be avoided, always,"* Teya had said, *"They fear little, and if they are defending food or cubs, they fear nothing. Do not look them in the eye. Do not run, for they will catch you. Stand your ground. If they attack, tuck yourself like a woodlouse and play dead. If they are hungry and hunting... you will likely die."*

As she made for the road, she heard a resonant, huffing snort behind her and turned to look. The gray mass was coming around the rock, investigating the intrusion, clacking its teeth in the blood-soaked muzzle.

She froze and turned slowly to face it. She had to force herself to look at its paws, or the trees beside it, or the rocks; anything but its eyes. She walked backward, one step, then another, then another.

The bear slapped the ground with its monstrous claw, blowing a blast of air from its wet nostrils.

A spark of panic flickered inside her, breaking into a cold sweat within her steel shell. *I can't run,* she thought, *but I can curl up in my armor. It should protect me.* At least, she hoped it would. Her helmet was in the wagon, so she would have to cover her head with her arms. Measuring the beast's absurd size, she reconsidered. *If it wanted to, it could crush me like a kitten in a tin cup.*

She kept walking backwards, wanting to run, wanting to call out for help. Instead, she spoke softly and firmly, like she had been taught.

"Listen, master bear," she said, her voice shaking, "I'm not here to steal your breakfast. Just let me go on my way and you can get back to your tasty horse meat."

The creature snuffled the air, took a few more steps toward her, and stood upright. Cindra drew in a sharp breath, going stiff with terror. The thing was bigger than she thought. The massive carved bears decorating the Greenfellow Maurbrik School were smaller than this monster. She estimated that her five feet and seven inches would just reach above this giant's hips. At its current distance, about ten yards away, it could catch her in a single bound.

She took another step back.

"Cindra?" called a distant voice. It was Adric calling through the trees.

"Shit," Cindra hissed.

The bear's ears pricked up and it moved its head towards the noise, taking a few steps forward on its hind legs. It seemed to grow in her eyes, and she moved with a little more speed. Her body received a jolt as she backed into a tree, and the clash of metal turned the bear's attention back to her.

"Cindra!" Adric barked.

Adric has seen me, but has he seen the bear? How could he miss it?

"Cindra, the others are coming up the-"

Silence.

Yes, she thought, *you see it now. It's not a tree standing there; it's a bear, a freakishly huge bear. Now be a good boy and keep quiet.*

"Cindra!" he shouted, and she heard him crashing through the brush.

She whipped her head around and held out her arm to stop him, but it was too late. The bear decided there were too many intruders in the woods today; it spread its arms, flashing wicked, hooked claws longer than Cindra's fingers, then let out a couple of deep huffs and roared once, it's mouth gaping as it bared its teeth.

The lady knight could feel her breastplate vibrate as her knees went weak. Every instinct told her to flee, but she knew it would mean her death. Another instinct kicked in, and her hand went to the hilt of her sword.

"Help!" Adric called, and she could hear him stumbling back towards the road, "Bear! There's a bear! Help!"

He's running! The bear will-

The creature lurched forward, going on all fours to chase down the running boy. Cindra drew her honor sword and lit the blade with a thought, waving it before the charging monster's face. The bear stopped, flinching at the light but turning its massive head to face her.

I'm looking it in the eyes!

She couldn't help it. The beast was only a few feet away, face-to-face. She hadn't meant to challenge it, only distract it. *Look away, look away!* But she couldn't. Not now.

Those black eyes bored into her and she could feel the hot, rancid breath stroking her face as it huffed. Its rumbling growl rattled her bones, but her training was kicking in, giving her clarity and focus. She saw it shift its weight and knew an attack was coming.

A giant claw swiped at her. She ducked under it and rolled back beside the tree. Shredded bark showered down upon her, yet somehow her sword was still in her hand. She held it before her now, waving it like a novice fencer who had only read about sword fighting. She had no intention of using it to block a blow from those giant claws; the force of the impact would disarm her as surely as if her wrists had never healed. Instead, she hoped the light would confuse it enough to give her time to...

Another lunge and swipe from the bear made her leap back and shift to the side, putting the tree between them. It rushed and slashed again, but she was able to keep out of its reach. The tree was not large, perhaps as thick as her torso and twice as tall as the bear, but the dark wood was dense and strong.

She kept her feet moving, looking now at the forest floor to avoid roots and other obstacles that might trip her up. Her armor was fitted perfectly, allowing her to move with grace and nimbleness. This was its first combat test, and it was against a giant bear. *Damn.*

The bear made a bounding pounce around the tree, startling her with its speed and agility. A swipe struck her breastplate, tossing her through the air onto her back. *Vyzeroth* fell from her hand. Quickly, she rolled and got to her feet, darting behind the tree again, but the bear was now standing over the bright blade, pawing it even as its light went out. She drew her *Kos* knife, wondering if she could muster the strength to penetrate the creature's fur and hide.

I'd rather not get that close, she thought. She had only used it in battle once against a Minozhian warrior, and that hairy beast was only a fraction of this thing's size. *It has to have a weakness,* she thought, *maybe its eyes or nose, maybe the pads of its claws...*

The bear quickly grew tired of playing chase around the tree. It stood again, planted its claws against the trunk, and began pushing. The wood cracked, the bark split, and leaves rained down with each mighty shove. Cindra realized that it was going to bring the tree down on top of her if she didn't move. The nearest thicker tree was tens of feet away. The roots were now ripping out of the earth. If she ran to either side, it would have her in seconds.

So she did the cleverest, stupidest thing she could do. She waited for the tree to begin falling and ran away in the direction of the fall, hoping she could clear the area in the next few moments. She heard the bear snort and huff, heard the timber crack and crash as branches struck each other on the way down. Looking over her shoulder, she saw the beast coming for her. A hard branch whipped her head and scraped down her back, several more struck her arms and legs and scalp. She dived and rolled, tucking herself and covering her head as best she could.

The upper limbs of the tree crashed down on her body, slapping her hard but doing no real damage. As the dust and debris settled, she raised her head to look for the bear. It was pinned under the tree trunk, but even as she got to her feet, the monster heaved its great bulk and began shrugging off the heavy timber, snapping branches as thick as her arm with a shove of its powerful claws.

"Cindra! Run!"

It was Adric. He had returned and was moving down to help her. She saw the others on the road, looking on in horror from horseback. Deliah held the reins of Adric's horse, Smoke. The wagon was there also, with Padison watching helplessly. She saw Nixy on Nibbler, holding her own horse's reins. If she could make it to T'ózha, if the others could ride off at a gallop, maybe they could escape, but not the wagon. The bear might catch a horse at full gallop, but destroying a two-horse wagon with an injured driver would be easy. If they ran, Padison would surely die.

She could not let that happen. She ran to Adric, who had grabbed her bow and arrows. Taking them and turning, she strung the bow as quickly as she could, using her knee for leverage. The bear shook itself free of the fallen tree, tossing gray leaves and twigs left and right. It gaped its mouth at the intruders and began to charge.

Cindra pulled three arrows from the quiver, griping them in her draw hand for rapid shooting. As she nocked a black shaft to the string, she heard hoof beats coming down the embankment.

"Wait!" Wenyssaya was suddenly beside her on her white mare Thasimé, holding forth a delicate arm. "*Cimnan-diis!*" she cried, and a zone of soft blue light sprung up between them and the bear. The creature charged into it, then let out a throaty bawl, and charged away again. It stopped many yards from the edge of the field, which was now fading into transparency. Snuffling and bellowing at the forbidden ground, it paced back and forth.

Cindra felt the magic tickle her skin ever-so-slightly, recognizing the sensation. Wen had done something like this before, only the spell had been stored in a jewel carried by Navithwi. The bird had croaked those same words, and then found itself driven away from the area, along with the rest of the crows that were trying to peck Cindra to death on Tirgrim's Bluff.

"A spell to ward off beasts," Wenyssaya explained, "I was not sure it would keep one so mighty from passing, but it has for now."

"Good work," Cindra said, "Now let's get out of here before it finds a way around or through it."

"Agreed," the elf said, dismounting her horse, "But first, I must try and make peace." She walked into the field of warding, heading straight for the giant bear.

"Wait, what?" Cindra said, "Are you mad?"

"No," she said, "but the bear might be. I want to make sure he does not track us and seek revenge."

"Oh. You can do that?"

"I do not know," Wen said, glaring at her, "I've never tried it on an animal that's had a *tree* dropped on it."

"*He* dropped the tree on *me*," Cindra whined.

Drahn flapped down beside her, asking, "Lady Cindwa, where is your sword?"

She pointed. "I lost it by the felled tree."

"I shall get it for you!" he said, and flapped off around the magic field.

"Wait..." she called, but it was too late; he had given himself a mission. As she watched him fly off, her weapons hung limp and useless in her hands.

"You think you could have killed it with that little Gali bow?" Adric asked.

"Not really," she admitted, "I just didn't know what else to do."

"Spoken like a true warrior," Deliah said from the road, "Next time, try avoiding the bear altogether."

Cindra wanted to flash her a mean look, wanted to say something biting, but knew she hadn't the right. She kept her back to her instead.

Wenyssaya spoke soft elven words to the bear as Drahn retrieved *Vyzeroth*, flapping back with the tip of the blade trailing in the dirt. Shortly, the bear departed, lumbering back to its meal. The elf maid returned and mounted her horse, and before long, they were on their way again.

"Did the bear agree not to come after us?" Cindra asked.

"I don't know," Wen replied, "I do not speak bear."

"But, but you said..."

"All creatures understand Ilvasawa," she explained, "but it takes great skill and learning to understand the languages of animals."

"How do you know they all understand you if you can't understand them?" Cindra asked.

"Because once we could," she said, "I understand many animals, but I am... unusual."

Cindra thought about that for a moment, thinking that such an incredible gift was a heavy loss. Then she noticed Padison smiling at her.

"What?" she asked.

"Couldn't you find something bigger?"

"Shut up, Paddy," she said, but she had to smile too.

The remainder of the day was spent discussing the strange corpse and what might have killed him. She was no great tracker, but the signs all told of a frantic flight from the road and a mad dash through the woods. Yet no tracks followed.

"How eaten was the horse?" Padison had asked.

"It looked torn up but pretty fresh," Cindra said, "I didn't stick around to study it."

"Do you suppose it happened earlier today?" Nixy said, "What if whatever killed him is still around?"

No one had a comforting answer.

Drahn had bravely volunteered to scout ahead, flapping down the overgrown road for a quarter of a mile ahead of the party. He would wait for them to catch up, then go flapping off again. This continued for several hours until the forest turned darker and more grim, shaping the path into a gray-green tunnel that left little room to maneuver on either side. A few miles within that dense enclosure, Drahn came flapping back early with news.

"There is a twee bwanch in the woad ahead," he panted, landing on the wagon, "It looks wather heavy."

Cindra sighed, "I suppose we'll have to move it then."

"Be on your guard," Deliah said, "It may be a trap."

Cindra grew embarrassed that the thought had not occurred to her. *Of course it could be a trap,* she realized, *it's the perfect place for one. No way to turn the wagon around, no way to go forward.* She readied her bow, nocking an arrow as she peered into the gloomy woods.

They rode on until they reached the obstruction, senses alert and weapons at the ready. The limb was indeed large and heavy-looking, full of shaggy branches of gray-green leaves.

Wenyssaya rode protectively closer to Nixy's horse and closed her eyes, spreading out her hands and saying, *"Duwediis nosundave."*

Her raven croaked from the back of her horse, flapping its dark wings.

The others turned to look at her.

She opened her eyes and said, "I do not sense any ill intent in the woods."

"That just means there's not someone waiting to ambush us," Deliah said, "There might still be a mechanical device or snare."

"Master Ildwic can detect mechanical twaps," Drahn said with a hint of pride in his voice, "but of course, the Eye of Omithys is a dweedwagon artifact."

"Which we don't have with us," Cindra said, "So if there is no one around, I think we can take our chances with snares and the like. Adric? Come help me drag this thing."

Adric hopped from his horse and together they attempted to drag the limb to the roadside. It was much heavier than it looked.

"Shadowood is very dense," Deliah said, as she sat and watched them struggle, "It doesn't even float. You should put the horses to work."

Cindra grunted with effort for a few more tugs, making a few more inches of progress. Then she straightened in her armor and declared, "I think we'll use the horses."

Deliah just gave a little smile and went to examine the broken end of the tree limb.

It took about five minutes to rig the ropes and horses. They used a nearby tree as an anchor for the block and tackle pulleys, which they kept handy for wagon repair. Once the horses began pulling, it was over and done in moments.

Deliah motioned Cindra over to the base of the tree from which the branch had fallen. "What do you see here?" she asked.

Cindra had to wipe the sweat away from her eyes before she could examine it properly. She looked up at the broken stump about fourteen feet overhead. "Looks like a clean break... except..."

"A little too clean, don't you think?"

"Maybe," Cindra said, "I mean, the top of the stump looks like..." she squinted in puzzlement, "...it looks like beavers."

"*Flying* beavers?" Nixy asked, "Is this place *that* weird?"

"Weirder," Deliah said, "There are tiny wood chips on the ground. The wood was definitely gnawed."

"Wouldn't ax-work look like that too?" Nixy said.

"There are no ax marks," Deliah replied, "no uneven cuts, no long flakes. These were made by constant, even chewing."

"By what?" Cindra asked.

Deliah had no answer, and this made Cindra worry. The unknown got people killed.

"Well, let's mount up and move out of here," she said, "We can make Gloamshire by nightfall if we set a good pace. And Adric? Fetch me my helmet."

The long dark tunnel of woods continued for many more leagues, finally thinning and opening up enough to let the waning daylight peek between the gaps of the canopy. There were signs that the trees had been cleared on their left, opening the land for farming and grazing. A white stone marker could be seen in the low light, and upon it was carved the name of 'Gloamshire.'

Beyond, a gray wall of timber rose out of the gloom, encircling the hamlet. A wide turnoff led from the road to a tall wooden gate, and as the party turned onto the path, Cindra felt a sense of relief wash over her. They had made it to their second major stop with only minor injuries.

No, she recalled, *Deliah died twice, once by my hand.* She squirmed in her armor.

Navithwi the raven flapped off to roost for the night in a high treetop, croaking as it went. As the nightly chill fell upon the forest, the veil of gloaming draped the wall in a charcoal shadow under the darkening sky. The way was shut, with no sign of a watch or gate warden.

Maybe there are dangers in the night that warrant it, Cindra thought, *maybe they are just being careful.*

"Hello?" she called, "Travelers at the gate! Hello?"

There was no reply.

"Adric, try the gate," she said.

He dismounted and approached the large doors. He slipped his fingers between them and pulled, and the gate groaned open with minor effort. "Huh," he said, "Not barred." He opened the other side to make room for the wagon.

Cindra rode through the gates alone, signaling the others to wait. As she surveyed the dark buildings and empty street, her nose took in the scents of the little hamlet. She detected the faint odor of manure, of turned soil and sweet herbs, of grass and hay in an adjacent barn. One thing was notably absent, and it made her wonder.

There was no smell of smoke.

No cook fires, no warmth against the late winter chill. No smoke from the chimneys.

She removed her helmet to listen. There were no roosting birds, no chirping insects; only the faint chatter of squirrels in the trees.

The place seemed deserted.

Chapter Nineteen

Gloamshire

The little hamlet of Gloamshire was a collection of sixteen Norsican-style log cabins of differing sizes, surrounded by a dirt path and a palisade. Another path ran up the center of the cabins, ending in a village square and a large stone well. At the far end was the largest structure, a long hall made of stone and timber, similar to the Greenfellow Maurbrik School. The strong building was quite out of place for so small a hamlet.

"This doesn't look like shadowood," Adric said, looking at the houses and palisade.

"No," Deliah said, "the structures are made of pine or spruce sent down the river from the eastern or western forests. Shadowood is expensive."

"But it's all around us!"

She replied, "It's expensive partly because it's dangerous to fell trees in this forest. The army that built the Joshian Way suffered losses similar to a war."

Cindra pondered that. Her father's castle had a grand staircase made of shadowood, but she had never considered how dangerous it had been to collect all that lumber from this dreadful forest. What forces rose up to punish those who dared to fell a tree? She did not wish to find out.

"Kind of a big expense to send wood down the river just for this little place," Adric said.

Deliah replied, "Gloamshire is special; it was built a long time ago to provide a safe haven halfway through the forest. The people pay no rent for the land, but must keep supplies for travelers."

Cindra imagined that was the best explanation for the palisade; they would be easy pickings for brigands without it.

"I wonder where everyone is?" Padison asked.

As Nixy put on the backpack for Drahn to climb in, he said, "Maybe they all go to bed early?"

"No smoke, no fires," Cindra said, "Makes no sense."

The veil of night fell over the hamlet, enshrouding the party in an unsettling darkness. Cindra lit her sword and Wenyssaya summoned her faerie lights, and the soft radiance banished the gloom, throwing long shadows across the walls. The light must have startled some nearby squirrels, who chattered angrily.

Navithwi flapped down on his black wings, croaking at Wenyssaya, who held forth and arm for him to land upon. She turned to the others and said, "There is something in the trees that he does not like."

"I see someone! They're coming this way!" Nixy said, pointing off towards the village square.

Everyone else saw only a shape in the dark.

"What is it, Nixy?" Cindra asked. Her voice was pitched higher than usual, and she realized she was griping her sword too tight.

"It's just a man," he said.

They heard running footsteps and a hushed voice calling, "Out! Put them out!" Moments later, a middle aged man with a thin beard and balding head materialized out of the dark. "Put them out, please!" he cried, waving his hands, "They are drawn to the light!"

Cindra extinguished her blade as goosebumps raced up her neck. The elf maid only took a few seconds longer.

The squirrel chatter stopped.

"*They?*" she asked, "What are 'they?'"

Panting and stooping, the man whispered, "They are the reason we only move about at night. If you value your lives, you should flee here, now."

"Tonight?" asked Wenyssaya, "You mean travel the road in the dark?"

The man nodded at her, "With as little light as you dare, and no campfires. Mind, I've no idea how far away is safe."

"Perhaps," Deliah said as she dismounted, "you had better tell us what has happened. We might be of help."

"Help?" he exclaimed, "But you're just women and boys!"

With that, Cindra made up her mind to help them out of spite.

She sheathed her sword and commanded, "Just see to our horses and take us to whomever is in charge."

They stood within the long house that the man had called the 'great hall,' surrounded by sixty or more men, women and children. Smoldering embers were being stoked in the fire pit as men opened the gable vents near the roof, which were barred with iron. Many wooden pillars lined either side of the central hearth, supporting the rafters from which meat was hung and cured. Windows were glass-less, shuttered, and barred, and there were many blankets and personal belongings lining the walls. It looked like the hamlet's residents had all slept here for several days; it smelled like it too, since there was hardly any ventilation.

Cindra had announced herself and introduced her companions, which had met with many a dubious stare or comment. Taking it in stride, she was now standing before Constable Narven, a tall, thick-chested man with many scratches and cuts on his face and arms.

"What has happened here?" she asked.

"The curse of Gloamshire," he said, "It's been many generations since the nixominy last plagued us, but they are back and worse than before."

"Nixominy!" exclaimed Padison, "Like in the old blind woman's story!"

"You have met Blind Maewyn? When was this?"

"About ten days ago in Breega," Cindra replied, "She is coming here with her granddaughter Glenawyn, and Bardon, Glenawyn's husband. They're probably a day or two behind us."

A chorus of voices broke out at the news, each growing more frantic.

"They're coming here now?"

"Do you think she...?"

"It must be! She has brought the curse back to us!"

"We should send them back before we're all devoured!"

"But maybe it's her they want?"

"Quiet, all of you!" cried Constable Narven, stamping his feet. This led to a sudden hushed silence as all eyes looked to the windows and rafters, searching for something unseen.

"Don't make such a commotion, Narven," said the man who had met them outside. His name was Farn, and he was a goatherd.

"See to your own commotion, Farn!" the constable said, "Now is not the time to become a gobbling flock of snood hens."

A woman came forward from the back, trailing a five year old child behind her. She approached Cindra and asked, "Milady, were you summoned to help us? There were two men who rode out two nights ago, one north and the other south..."

Cindra's gaze went from the woman's eyes, full of hope and dread, to those of the child hiding behind his mother's skirt. "We were not summoned," she said carefully, "but we... we did find a horse and rider about a day south of here... They were... I'm sorry."

There were gasps all around and many faces fell into despair.

"Adric, do you have the hat?" she asked.

Adric produced the shapeless, threadbare hat and presented it to Cindra, who held it forth for the woman to see. Her eyes filled with tears as she took it, clutching it to her breast. She knelt down to hold her child, sobbing and trembling as others closed in to lay reassuring hands upon her. The child, confused and frightened, began to cry.

Cindra fought back tears of her own. There was no reason to describe the condition of the remains, but she did say, "I'm so sorry. We gave him a proper burial."

Deliah stepped forward and said, "Please constable, tell us exactly what has happened here."

As the people ushered the grieving woman back to a table, the constable said, "It was a week ago that they descended on us out of the deep woods. Some folk were out preparing the fields for plowing when they attacked. The beasties chased them through the west gate, but they killed and... and *ate* the last man. It was horrible; stripped him to the bone. There was nothing anyone could do, believe me, we tried." He pointed to his many injuries.

"That answers the mystewy of the body," Drahn muttered into Nixy's ear.

"They just attacked for no reason?" Deliah asked, "You could see them?"

He nodded, "It wasn't like the old stories. If they can vanish, they haven't bothered to."

Wenyssaya asked softly, "How many are there?"

Narven scratched his head and said, "Hard to tell. They were a swarm, to be sure. Hundreds, maybe more."

The elf maid blanched at the words, but hid her reaction from her companions.

Cindra leaned towards Deliah and asked, "Your 'great-grandmother' didn't experience anything like this?"

Deliah shook her head.

Adric said, "In the story, Nasha the Raven Witch burned them all in a spellfire. Have you tried fighting them with torches?"

The constable shook his head. "Torches are no use," he said, "The things move too fast, and they don't seem to mind the fire. At night they are drawn to it, but most of them sleep. In the day however..."

"They're all kinds of active in the day," said a short, burly man, "I run the horse mill across the way; name is Larren, by the by." He gave a nod to the ladies. "We hide indoors by day, but the blighters try to gnaw their way in. That's why most of us are holed up in here; it's all stone walls and a hard, shingled roof, not log and thatch like the rest."

The constable said, "They got into a few cabins through the smoke holes; damned things either forced the lid, or chewed through the wooden smoke cap. We lost the blacksmith and his son the second day, and our midwife and her husband on the third; after that, we all moved in here. We figured out that they sleep at night and don't bother us unless they're roused or angry."

"We got them angry on the fifth night," the miller said, somberly, "We caught one and beat it to death, and they retaliated." He shivered at the memory. "Killed Yax, my assistant. Poor lad."

"That's six people in a week," Cindra said with horror, "and I assume the rider we found makes seven?"

"It would seem so," said Narven, "Daven was his name. No one knows if Stev made it north on his old mare; not that there's much help to be found for many leagues."

"I think we know what blocked the road," Padison said, "They don't want no one to leave."

"This is most peculiar," Wenyssaya said, "They could have concentrated their efforts and done far more damage by now, but they seem content to keep the people contained."

"I hope our horses are safe in the barn," Nixy said. Drahn nodded in agreement from his backpack.

"They don't seem to bother with the animals," said Farn, "We have a few work horses, several goats, chickens, and a dog or two. None have been attacked that we've seen."

"Maybe we could all dress up like goats?" Nixy muttered.

Drahn said, "I assume you are kidding. Oh! I think I made a pun!"

Cindra said, "Nixy, why don't you and the jester-dragon go and do some scouting. See if you can find where these things are hiding."

"Wait!" Wenyssaya said, "Do you really think that is wise?"

"Who better?" Cindra asked, "Nixy and Drahn can see in the dark so they don't need torches. If they get into trouble, Nixy can take them into the Shadow."

"Black Will or Dexer or whoever he is lives in the Shadow," she said, "These things might have that power as well."

"Drahn handled 'Black Dexer' pretty well last time," Cindra shrugged, "We need to know what we're dealing with."

"I don't see why they need to go alone," she huffed.

"Then go with them," Cindra said.

Wenyssaya blinked several times and made as if to answer, but said nothing.

"It's alright," Nixy said, "Me and Drahn will be fine." He gave Wen's hand a squeeze and together the boy and dweedragon opened the door and disappeared into the dark.

Cindra said, "Adric and Paddy, see about getting some food and rest. Wen, please look to Paddy's bandages. I need to talk with Deliah." She took the raven-haired woman by the arm and led her to a quiet corner. "Okay Deliah, or Nasha, or whoever you are, I need to know how you beat these things last time."

"Obviously I didn't," she said, "But Maewyn's story was mostly correct. I used an inferno spell to conjure flames, killing many faeries. We tracked the others to the queen, and I did... something similar."

"Go on," Cindra said, "Now is no time to be vague."

"I got close and let them attack me so the next inferno would catch them all. It burned off my clothes, my hair, and most of my skin; the hair and skin grew back, the clothes didn't. I passed out from the pain, and awoke later in the ashes."

Cindra was shocked. "Then... you aren't immune to your own fire spell?"

"No," she replied, "Whether you amplify a natural fire, or conjure it from an elemental source, it is still fire."

"But Narven said these faeries don't mind the fire, that they're drawn to it," Cindra said, "Any ideas why?"

"None. My fire killed all of them," Deliah said, "all except the two that blinded poor Maewyn."

"You think those two could have... mated or something? Maybe they created another queen?"

Deliah shrugged. "I don't know the nature of these unnatural creatures. I doubt anyone has made a true study of them. Your guess is as good as mine."

The next hour was spent resting and listening to the talk of the villagers, and eating what spare food they could provide. Cindra had Adric remove her armor for now, and it was arranged on a table. Deliah was sleeping in a corner, somehow unfazed by the danger they were in. Wenyssaya fretted near the door, but would not open it to look outside. She paced to and fro, wringing her hands and whimpering admonitions to herself. Her raven watched her from the rafters.

"What's wrong with Wen?" Adric asked.

Cindra said, "She's worried sick about Nixy, but didn't want to go with. I said she could."

Padison scoffed, "Nice of you to offer. Are you surprised she turned it down?"

"Well if she's that worried…"

"Look at her," Paddy said, "She's scared stiff. I wouldn't want to go out there again with those faerie things lurking around."

"Everyone says they aren't active at night," Cindra said, "Several people have gone and returned since Nixy left."

"Yeah, but Nixy is the whole reason she's here," Paddy said, "He's the reason we're *all* here. If something were to happen, she'd never forgive herself."

"Neither would I," Cindra said, "But it's not like he and Drahn are helpless."

"No, I'm the most helpless one here," Paddy said, "But Wen gets really scared, or haven't you noticed?"

Cindra had not. Wenyssaya had her quirks, but she had witnessed her walk up to a giant bear to have a chat; she didn't think there was much that scared the woman.

"Paddy watches her a lot more than you do," Adric explained.

"Not in a creepy way," he said defensively, "Not really. I mean, I like her a lot, but it's more like… you know, like the statues of Selvina on her temple. You just stare at them and kind of… worship them."

"You're in awe of her," Cindra said with a smile, "I understand. She's awe-inspiring."

"Cindra's seen her naked," Adric said, ribbing his friend.

"Shut up, we're being respectful," Paddy pouted, "Anyway, you're the same with Deliah."

"That's different," Adric said, "Deliah's a normal human woman close to my age. There's actual hope that I can win her heart someday."

Cindra hadn't the heart to tell him that the exact opposite was true. Instead she said, "You know she's a witch, right?"

Adric shrugged, "Well, one of my best friends turned out to be a girl, and I didn't hold it against her."

She bowed her head to hide her big smile. She loved Adric for these little moments.

"Anyway," Paddy said, "Wenyssaya gets scared a lot. She spooks easy in the forest at night, and gets all wound up when someone leaves the campsite in the dark, like they might not come back. When they do, she relaxes with a big sigh. I try not to take too long when I go to crap so I don't worry her."

Cindra smiled and said, "That's very big of you, Paddy. Maybe you should just crap with the horses where she can see you."

"Don't be disgusting," he said, "I'm opening up my heart here."

"Sorry," she giggled, trying to be serious, "I don't mean to make jokes. I've just never seen this side of you before."

"Yeah, well, me neither," he said.

The people of the hamlet were all busy now, taking care of jobs normally done in daylight; they were too occupied to speak to their guests, but they could gossip among themselves. Many whispered about the boy in the rich clothes with the little dragon, and the dark-haired woman who looked so much like the Raven Witch of their stories; they also whispered about the elf maid and the lady knight, and how their hands and arms were marked, but none considered their presence an answer to their prayers. At worst, they were more mouths to feed in a siege; at best, they were future victims that no one in town would miss much.

The door finally opened again and Nixy and Drahn came through, much to the relief of poor Wenyssaya.

"Nixyalderthor!" she said, "Are you hurt? Is everything alright?" She went to embrace him, but it turned into a pat-down searching for injuries.

"I'm fine, we both are," he said, removing his pack and letting Drahn onto the floor.

Cindra motioned them over and they all sat together in a circle, keeping their voices low.

"They're out there now," Nixy said, "Asleep mostly, but some are on watch. They couldn't see me even though I wasn't hiding."

"How many are there?" Cindra asked.

"Too many to tell," Drahn replied, "We counted about fifty within the walls, but there are surely more in the twees beyond. They sleep on the wooftops and bwanches, hanging like bats."

"What do they look like?" Padison asked.

"About what the old lady described," Nixy said, "They's got bat wings and black little eyes and pointy ears and piggy snouts."

Drahn added, "They wesemble bats in many ways, but they are hairless except for their heads, and have human-like arms and legs."

"Are they naked, or do they wear little clothes?" Adric asked.

Cindra scoffed, "That sounds like a Padison question."

"Hey!" Paddy cried. The others chuckled.

"I was asking because if they make clothes for themselves, they might be more than just beasts. They might be intelligent."

Paddy said, "I had the same thought."

"No you didn't," Adric replied, smacking his arm.

"Well, wegardless," Drahn said in a huff, "they were *not* wearing little clothes. But *I* don't wear clothing, and I dare say I am more intelligent than *some* of us here."

"Don't be so modest," Deliah said, as she walked up and scratched his scaled head, "Mind if I join the party?"

"We thought you were asleep," Wenyssaya said.

"Things have gotten too active in here," she said, "I can understand no one wanting to be alone during a siege, but this building was never meant to house the whole population."

"Be happy there are no animals inside," Cindra said, "So, we know there are probably hundreds of faeries out there, and they can't see very well in the dark. Does that help us?"

Adric said, "It might be better to try and fight them at night. Maybe set traps for them?"

"It would have to be a big trap," Wenyssaya said, "There may be hundreds we can't see."

"Traps need bait," Deliah said, looking to Cindra, "I'd rather not volunteer."

"Cindra's got the best armor," Paddy said.

"Thanks, Paddy," she said, "You get to do my laundry for the rest of the journey."

"Might be a short journey," he said. Adric smacked his arm again.

"I was considering it anyway," Cindra said, "Paddy is right for once."

"Hah!" he exclaimed, smacking Adric's arm for a change.

"Why do we have to use a *person* as bait?" Wenyssaya asked. Her voice carried more than a hint of anxiety.

Deliah replied, "These creatures are here for the people, make no mistake. They weren't driven here by hunger or migration. They came to spread fear and exact vengeance on this hamlet."

Nixy asked, "For what the Raven Witch did? How is that the people's fault?"

"They may believe the people enlisted her help," she said, "They know two villagers left and returned again with the Raven Witch, who wiped them out. If they cannot find the witch, who then shall they take revenge upon?"

*What if they **could** find the witch?* Cindra thought, then dismissed it as her guilt returned. *That is not who I wish to be.*

"But that was ages ago!" Adric said, "Nasha is dead and old Maewyn was a little girl at the time. No one is left here who had anything to do with it."

"Since when has that ever stopped revenge?" she replied, "Perhaps they sensed Maewyn returning home, or maybe they knew Nasha's descendant was coming?"

"Well, they aren't getting *you*," Adric said fiercely; he added, "Not any of us!" when he saw Cindra and Paddy grinning at him.

The plotting began in earnest as the people of the hamlet went about preparing meals, comforting children, and making supply runs to their abandoned homes. Cindra invited the constable and the miller to sit in on their little war council, since they were the two most influential men in the community. Farn was liked and respected too, but he declined to be a part of what he called 'female folly.'

"We need to begin by counting our assets," Cindra said, "anything that can be used in a fight or in setting a trap. We have some wood axes in the wagon; I have my plate armor, a shield, my sword, and my bow and arrows. The armor is my best asset right now."

"What about the sword?" Nixy asked, "It's magical."

"Not that magical," Cindra said, "All it does is light up when I want it to. It's not as fine as your knife."

"Oh yeah, my knife, that's an asset," Nixy said, "Plus I can do the shadow thing..." He trailed off, unsure how much to tell in front of the strangers.

Wenyssaya said, "I am proficient with elemental magic, but I have an affinity for nature and healing magic. I also know several wards and a few curses, but..."

"Oh, I know plenty of those!" Padison said, "Shouting curses is about all I'm good for, unless you want me to start bleeding all over the place."

There were a few chuckles, but the men exchanged looks and Narven said, "You're an elf witch? It's said that the Raven Witch might have been an elf; do you know anything about that?"

"She was not an elf," Deliah said, "She was my great-grandmother Nasha, and she taught me a thing or two before passing on."

The men's eyes grew wide in wonder, but Larren said, "You might want to keep that to yourself for now. People tend to get riled when they're scared, and no telling what they'd be up to."

"I am well aware," she said, "As for my skills, I focus on fire and air magic, and charm spells which affect the emotions and perceptions."

Cindra pursed her lips at that; Deliah seemed to want to say more, but fell silent. She was sure the "Raven Witch" had more up her sleeve than what she let on, but nothing else was brought up, especially not her 'curse.'

Adric said, "I've got mail armor and a shield, as well as a sword and mace. Not sure which would be better."

Larren said, "They have damned tough hide for such little beasts. I fancy they'd make good armor if you skinned enough of them. We killed one by knocking it down and stepping on its wing to keep it from flying off. Then we smashed it with a hammer. Took a fair amount of blows, let me tell ya."

Wenyssaya was visibly uncomfortable and said, "That's horrible." She folded her arms and seemed to withdraw into herself.

"Not as bad as what a swarm of them can do to us," Larren said.

Cindra asked, "Wen, are you going to be able to help us fight them?"

"That depends on what you ask of me," she said, "I am not going to smash little faeries with a hammer, or be foolish enough to go outside."

Cindra said gently, "We may need you outside if that's what it takes." Padison's observations now tempered her words to the elf maid. What Cindra once saw as Wen's aloof petulance was revealed to be a cover for a wellspring of fears. *If I am going to lead people,*

Cindra thought, *I have to learn how to read them better.*

"You said yourself that you are special, even among your people," Cindra said, "That means you are our greatest asset. I wouldn't ask you to do anything I wouldn't do myself."

"I know the kinds of things you do yourself," Wenyssaya said, "and I wouldn't wish to do them."

Cindra snorted a laugh; the woman had a point.

Nixy said, "Well, I'll do whatever you need me to do."

Wenyssaya gave him a pained look, perhaps with a hint of shame.

"So will I," Drahn said, "As for my assets, I know a fair amount of human wizard spells, and I have my lightning bweath, of course." He said it like it was common knowledge that little purple dragons breathed lightning, though he had only learned it half a year ago and completely by accident.

"You know I'm with you," Adric said, "Just don't order us to do anything stupid."

"I can't promise that," Cindra said.

Deliah asked the men, "Do you still have the body of the nixominy you killed?"

Narven looked uncomfortable but said, "I do. Half a moment." He rose and went to find his belongings, returning with a bundle of soft leather. He laid it on the table and opened it, revealing the broken body of a nixominy. It was the first time most had seen one up close. Even Deliah seemed fascinated.

The little creature was engrossingly horrible; a twisted mixture of human, bat, and reptile features that combined to form a thing of nightmares. Its broken body was about eight inches tall with a wingspan over twice as long. Its wings were fleshy membranes stretched between three long digits, like those of a bat or a dweedragon, and sprouted from bulky muscles on the back, just below the shoulders. They were bruised and cracked in places, evidence of a traumatic demise.

It had glossy, reddish-brown skin covered in a mottled pattern of flattened scales, like a snake. The limbs were long and thin, and the hands and grasping feet bore wicked black claws. The belly was slightly distended, possibly because of someone it ate.

Worst of all was the face; it had an almost child-like face with large black eyes. The nose was more of a snout, set above a wide mouth full of fangs and broad, sharp incisors, perfect for gnawing and tearing. The ears were large and pointed, and the head was topped with a mane of baby-fine red hair. It looked as if it might screech and come alive at any moment, but thankfully it was quite dead.

Deliah was the one to handle it and turn it about, examining it as a collector would inspect a strange new doll. When she produced an herb gathering knife from her belt, Wenyssaya got up from the table abruptly. "What on earth are you going to do?" she asked, "It is already dead enough!"

Cindra said, "We need to know what we are dealing with, Wen. We can't afford to be surprised going into battle."

"But... but..." was all she could manage.

"Have you never killed anything before?" Deliah asked, without looking up from her work.

"No," Wenyssaya said, "No I have not, and I do not wish to start now."

"Never hunted or defended yourself?" Cindra asked.

She replied, "I don't have to kill to defend myself, and if I want food, I buy it or pick it."

Cindra sighed. *Oh dear.* Of course, five years ago she would have said the same things. She and Wenyssaya were both raised in sheltered, privileged environments, but Cindra had to learn survival skills during her time with the Galindri nomads; Wen's biggest hardship was probably traveling safe roads from the Blackwood to Portshia, eating at cheap taverns, and fending off enthralled suitors.

Cindra rose and put an arm around Wen's shoulder, leading her away a little. She said, "Wenyssaya, we may be in a fight for our lives soon. Believe it or not, I understand you not wanting to kill. Every time I've done it, it's made me feel sick. Jaron once suggested that I shouldn't want that sick feeling to go away; I agree with him."

"I just wish there was another way," the elf said, "Perhaps if the Shadow Lord-"

"If the Shadow Lord could help, he would have by now," Cindra said, "I've been thinking about that a lot; the old stories say he protects the forest, but from whom? Humans and monsters can't share the woods, so who is being protected?"

"He protects the woods from the forces of Mavathram!" she said, "He is no friend to the things that came from the Time of Chaos."

"And yet here they are," Cindra said, "His own son is trapped with us. If he knew, wouldn't he help? Maybe his power isn't what it used to be?"

Wenyssaya had no answer to that, but tears welled up in her eyes.

Cindra hugged her close and said, "We are on our own, like it or not. If we are going to finish our quest, we may have to do things we never wanted to do. We may have to be braver than we imagined."

The elf maid said nothing, but nodded her golden head and sniffled.

Deliah was gathering an audience of the morbidly curious as she attempted to cut the little corpse with her knife. She began drawing the blade across the wing membrane, making quick strokes to slice the skin. It took several tries and a harder stroke before succeeding, but the result was not impressive.

Next, she tried the same thing on the wing forearm and fingers, testing their strength. Then she tried the legs and arms, slicing as if she were chopping vegetables with a vengeance. The limbs were intact, and though they showed many indentations, the skin had not broken once.

She moved on to the chest and belly, trying to slice the creature in half. Some turned away in disgust, but as before, the herb gathering knife made no cuts, only indentations in the scaly skin as the thing's mouth discharged a red slurry of its last meal.

"This does not look good," she said to the crowd.

Adric asked, "Hey Cindra, let me borrow your knife."

She was still dealing with Wenyssaya, so she unsheathed it and handed it over without turning.

Adric took the hefty *Kos* knife in a loose grip and went over to the table. "Let's try *this* blade," he said.

Deliah sat back as Adric stretched out a wing and hacked at it with the big curved knife. People flinched, making distressed little moans as it went *thunk* into the wood. It broke the wing bone but left the skin notched and intact.

"Balkon's balls," he muttered, "That would have cleaved a pork rib ten times as thick." He then struck the creature's arm with an earnest attack; the knife's edge embedded itself in the wood as the arm bones made an audible *crack*, but the skin only showed a deep dent. It was like trying to butcher a cow with a butter knife.

"Cindra, I think we have a big problem," he said.

"A bunch of little big problems," Paddy added.

Cindra returned to the table, leaving Wenyssaya to wrestle with her misgivings.

Adric handed her back the knife and said, "Care to try that glowy sword of yours?"

She drew *Vyzeroth* and lit the blade just to make a show of it. "Alright, let's try to cut it in half," she said. People stood back as she raised the bright blade in a high, one-handed over-cut, bringing it down with all her might. She stepped into the cut, arm extended, utilizing her strong shoulder in perfect form.

The end of the sword dug into flesh and tabletop with a solid *thunk!* There were gasps all around as the creature folded under the blow, spewing fluid, but as she pried the sword free of the wood, the nixominy came up with it. The blade had bitten a fraction of an inch, and the bent corpse was now stuck on the sword. A dark green ichor oozed out and ran down the edge as Cindra held it before her, feeling truly shaken. Her strike could have severed the arm of a grown man, but it only nicked this little monster. She shook the sword, trying to dislodge the oozing corpse.

"Gods above and below," she whispered. She finally gripped the thing and pulled it off the blade, tossing it back to the table as she sought for a rag to clean off the tarnished steel.

"Let me try mine," Nixy said, drawing his little knife. It was a fine weapon with a white steel blade, a sharp trailing point, and an ornate handle made of polished shadowood in the shape of a raven's head. He called it 'Cutter,' a name he had bestowed as an eight-year-old boy who had little imagination for such things.

Nixy approached the table, knife in hand, and proceeded to make a timid little cut across the thing's leg, as one trying to slice a pie evenly while people watched and judged.

The leg was removed in one stroke.

Loud gasps and exclamations arose from the onlookers, and his companions closed in around him to get a better look. Cindra had been cleaning her sword and had missed the event.

"What... *Rath's blood, Nixy!* What did you do?" she cried, nearly dropping her under-performing sword.

"I just gave it a little slice," he squeaked, quite amazed himself. He held up the blade and saw that the metal shed the ichor immediately, leaving it clean and white. The corpse oozed more green fluid, staining the poor table which had received so much abuse this night.

"A magic blade indeed!" Deliah exclaimed. Her eyes fixated on the knife with a strange intensity, which had anyone noticed, would have given them the shivers. As it was, everyone was admiring either the knife or the dismembered faerie, seeing a ray of hope in their darkest hour.

Adric laughed and said, "Perfect! Our one faerie-killing weapon has a five-inch reach! Nothing like a challenge, eh, milady?"

She nodded, tapped Nixy on the shoulder and said, "Trade you?"

But Deliah had one more test to perform. She took the little body to the hearth, and taking a pair of wrought iron tongs, placed the nixominy on the flaming logs. People started to protest, fearing a rotten stench would fill the hall. Instead, the body of the creature remained unburnt; even the hair was barely affected. Muttering and swearing spread through the crowd as people closed in to watch.

"Stand back," Deliah said, and she raised her hand to the fire. The flames grew in height and intensity, shedding uncomfortable heat into the room as they filled the hearth, licking the edges of the stonework. Logs popped and threw sparks onto the floor, and the onlookers stepped back in fear and wonder.

As she lowered her hand, the flames died down to a normal level. She grimly approached the hearth, withdrew the body with the tongs, and laid it on the table.

Aside from a little discoloration, it was unburnt.

Nixy thought it was a pretty good plan, especially since he played such a big part in it, and because it was his idea.

He would get to keep his knife and Cindra would do the dangerous work, which suited him fine. She had that thick armor after all, and he only had his skin and pretty clothes, although they were grimy and needed a wash. He gave a reassuring smile to Cindra as Adric finished buckling on her armor and she donned her helmet.

For the plan to work, they had to know if *Cutter* would cut from the deep Shadow. With the others shielding him from view in a corner, he had descended as deep as he could go, and slashed at the body of the faerie that Cindra held up for him. The miraculous weapon severed the creature's wing with ease, making it part from the body with no visible cause. The others gasped and grinned at each other as Nixy came out of the Shadow before the common folk noticed he was gone.

"Excellent," Cindra said, "I think this plan will work. Ready, Nixy?"

"Ready, but don't give me time to think about it," he said, "Let's do this." It gave Nixy a thrill to have such an important job, even if it was kind of disgusting. But like Cindra said, he was the best suited for it.

Cindra took up her shield and borrowed mace, and they both headed outside. It was going to be an interesting evening.

"Be careful!" Wenyssaya said to them. She had hated this plan, but had to agree it seemed to have the best chance of success.

The evening had been spent building a bonfire in the dark, stacking wood and kindling near the big well in the village square. Now they were ready to light it up.

"Okay," Cindra said, "let's get their attention."

Deliah raised her arm and concentrated for a moment, and the bonfire lit with a flash; then she closed the door to the hall and waited with the others. Adric was keeping watch by one of the glass-less windows, opening the shutters just enough to see the action. Wenyssaya was standing by the door in case healing was needed, and Drahn was perched on Padison's shoulders so he could peek out of Adric's window.

The bonfire grew and grew until it lit the square, casting orange light all around and reflecting in the black little eyes of the nixominy surrounding them. Squirrel chatters began in a rising chorus as the creatures stirred and roused themselves to action. One flew at them, swooping near the fire; then another, and another. Soon the air was full of angry faeries screeching at them and gnashing their wicked teeth.

"Okay Nixy, go!" Cindra said.

Nixy dropped into the Shadow as Cindra readied her mace and shield.

All grew cold and gray as the roar of the deep Shadow assaulted his ears. He scanned the hamlet for signs of Dexer, but saw nothing. *So far, so good.* He saw the bonfire as a dark, shifting form, with Cindra silhouetted against it like a gray ghost. The dark light buffeted him, stirring currents and winds in the Shadow that made things more difficult; he had to drag in his breath and push his limbs to move against the cold gray curtain, but he was doing it.

Cindra and the faeries were moving in slow motion now, lazily swooping and striking at one another. He heard the dull *thwack* as they struck her armor and shield, and saw his friend swing her mace and make contact with one of the creatures. They were swarming her, swooping in to bite and strike at her armor, pull at the straps and search for weak spots; it was just as they planned.

Nixy went to work.

He drew his knife and took a swing at the nearest faerie in mid-flight. Wincing as he struck, he watched with macabre fascination as the creature was bisected by the magic blade. As far as anyone knew, his knife was the only thing capable of cutting things from this deep within the Shadow. It was a good thing, because there was lots to do. He tore his eyes away from the faerie parts tumbling slowly to the ground and sought out another target. It was like chopping through water with a frying pan, and his limbs grew warm and sore with the effort, but he made the little monsters pay for what they had done.

Maybe they paid a little too much.

Cindra swung her mace at the darting shapes, feeling a little better every time she made contact. She knew she was doing little harm, but it was satisfying nonetheless. Visibility was poor in her helmet with the visor down, but there was nothing for it. She preferred it to having faeries claw and chew at her face.

She used her shield to swat away attacks and kept her mace moving, striking at anything she could see. It was a terrible way to fight, but fighting wasn't her role. She was bait to lure them in, and Nixy was the trap snapping shut. She heard shrieks of pain and anguish from the beasts, and knew he was doing his part.

Looking down, she saw faerie corpses littering the ground. She saw one flying at her head and gasped as it split in two, splattering her armor with green ichor; a look of shock frozen on its horrid face.

"Nice work, Nixy!" She wasn't sure he could hear her, but it cheered her to say it.

One lost its head mid-flight, and another lost a wing. Cindra couldn't see the blade at all, only the gore it left in its wake.

Scary, she thought, *I'm glad the kid's on our side.*

Nixy was exhausted. He had killed a few dozen faeries in a short amount of time since they were so thick in the air, but his endurance was running out. He had never been this deep for this long, and had never put himself through such rigorous exercise in the Shadow. It was very cold, but moving fast caused the air to warm his skin. He was having a hard time breathing and his arms felt like lead; his thighs and calves were screaming with each step as he circled his friend, dodging her slow swings and removing the monsters that clung to her armor with a flick of his knife.

There seemed to be no end to them, and Nixy began to really worry. He could almost hear their shrieking as they saw their numbers fall dead, and the shrieking called more and more to the battle. The bonfire was calling them, and the noise was calling them, and his friend's safety all depended on his flashing little blade. But he was so tired...

Maybe if I don't go as deep, he thought, *I won't be as fast, but maybe I can last longer.*

He shifted himself out of the deepest Shadow and into the layer above, where the cold and noise were less and the air was easier to move through and breathe. He had to be a little faster though, because the weird difference in time was not as great; he could still slice anything that got close to Cindra without trouble, but he didn't want to get hit by her mace. He wasn't sure if it could harm him or not, but he'd rather not find out.

They were clinging to her now, trying to get under her plate and chew at the straps. Many had discovered her weak points and were going for the back of her thighs, where the only protection was partial plate and her linen breeches. He had to be very careful cutting the faeries there, since a stray cut would slash open her leg.

He got a weird sensation as something touched his back and moved through his torso. It made him feel kind of sick, and he nearly dropped his knife when he saw an angry faerie emerge from his chest and flap towards Cindra. *Ugh! They can go through me!* It made him feel queasy and unclean somehow, like he had gotten faerie residue on his soul.

Cindra spun around, dropping her shield and grabbing at a nixominy that was clawing her buttocks under the mail skirt. They were hurting her now, ignoring the metal skin and going for the back of her legs where she couldn't defend. Her boots were stomping on bloody faerie parts as she began to move frantically around the bonfire, trying to get out of the thick of the swarm. Nixy had to follow behind, darting to protect her backside as she spun and kicked in slow motion like a frightened mule.

He almost didn't see the dark shape fluttering down from above like a giant raven, its glowing eyes wide and wild with blood lust.

Dexer! He screamed a wordless cry of terror and rolled away as the gaunt man came leaping from a nearby rooftop, landing where the boy had been only seconds before. The man was darker than the gray landscape of the Shadow, meaning he was deeper than Nixy was; that meant he'd be faster and harder to avoid. Nixy only had one choice; he had to get out of the Shadow and flee before Black Dexer got him. But if he did it here, he'd be attacked by angry faeries.

He plunged as deep as he could into the Shadow to even the odds as he turned to run for the hall. He could hear the snarls of his pursuer over the roar of the gray phantom world around him, a world that pushed against him as he fled, dragging on his body like hot mud. His eyes began to sting and his vision blurred; every muscle ached. Something was going to give out, and soon.

A thought struck him like a lightning bolt. *My knife cuts from the Shadow into the real world... so what if it cuts from the real world into the Shadow?* Praying for luck, he took a tumble, ended up on his back, and waited for Dexer to pounce.

The monster man leaped on him, pinning him down with one clawed hand on his chest and the other poised to strike. He could see Dexer's pale face clearly now; the hairless brow, the cruel sunken eyes, the grimace he made before killing someone. He was so close.

Close enough to slash with a knife.

Cindra was panicking. The damned things were all over her, but they were focusing on her unprotected rear and thighs. A knight had to sit on a horse, so there was no armor there but a short mail skirt and a little padding. She knew she was bleeding now, but she had to resist the urge to sit down. While it would cover her vulnerable areas, it would make her immobile. They would swarm her and crawl inside her armor from all angles.

"Nixy, help!" she cried. No more faeries were dying around her, and that worried her on many levels. *Where was he? Was he alright? Gods, I hope nothing went wrong.*

As if in answer to her thoughts, she saw him suddenly appear next to the large well. He was on his back, slashing the air furiously with his little knife. He sat up, still slashing, and got to his feet, holding the blade before him against an invisible enemy.

His eyes fell upon her and he saw the peril she was in, a peril which he now shared.

"Run, Nixy!" she shouted, "Get inside!"

He hesitated for a moment as the faeries found a new target, probably guessing he was the one responsible for the deaths of their fellows. He turned and dashed for the door of the hall, which opened for him in the nick of time. Adric barred the window shutters as Deliah bolted the door behind the boy.

Now Cindra was alone with a swarm of angry nixominy, and her heart sank. There was no plan of retreat that would work now. They had hoped the creatures would be terrorized by the invisible knife-work and flee, but the monsters' morale only seemed to be heightened.

They had her and she knew it; soon they would have revenge as she was chewed to the bone just yards from safety. She could feel tiny claws scratching through the mail links at her joints, see strong little hands trying to pry up her visor; she could feel the back of her breeches torn to shreds as wicked talons and teeth ripped into her flesh.

There was only one place she could escape to, one place that did not endanger the people in the hall. The problem was that it was a place she would likely die in.

Screaming in pain and frustration, she jumped into the well.

"It was Black Dexer!" Nixy was saying as he sank on all fours, panting like an asthmatic dog, "He... came at me. I think I cut him up... but I can't be sure unless I go back..."

"No!" Wenyssaya said, "no going back! You have done enough."

"What about Cindra?" cried Adric, "Those things were all over her!"

That was when they heard the scream and the splash. Adric dared to open the shutters and look outside.

"I can't see her!" he said, "Wait, the faeries are circling the well! Gods, she fell in!"

Nixy lifted his head with effort, wanting to dash out and help, but he was utterly spent.

Adric and Padison went for the door, shoving Deliah aside as she tried to bar their way. Drahn clung to Paddy's shoulders as they rushed into the thick of the nixominy, swatting at them like mosquitoes. Adric wasted no time jumping in feet first, grabbing the bucket and rope as he fell into darkness with a loud splash.

"I can't see them!" Paddy cried. Nixominy raked at his arms and face as Drahn snapped and flapped, trying to shield him. He let out a roar, swinging his head back and forth as bolts of lightning arced from his maw. Several faeries were stunned and dropped to the ground, twitching violently.

Nixy staggered to his feet. "Help them," he croaked, "Help them!" He went for the door as Wenyssaya held him back; her eyes were full of tears and she was trembling.

He glared at Deliah, who held the door shut against the terror outside. His blue eyes met her gray ice-chip gaze, and her face seemed indifferent to his pleas. Then something melted within; her gaze softened and she took a deep breath, opened the door and strode purposefully to the well.

"Wenyssaya, come!" she called over her shoulder.

"No..." the elf maid whimpered.

Deliah muttered words and swished her arms to the side, and a strong blast of wind blew the faeries away.

Some tumbled into the bonfire while others fell amid the severed limbs of their kin, shrieking in anger.

Padison called into the well, "Adric! Cindra!" but there was no reply. The pulley wheel squeaked as the rope went slack. "I can't see them!"

Nixy finally summoned the strength to break free from the elf woman's grasp and he stumbled outside. Removing his glowstone necklace, he said, "*Ilda!*" and tossed it down the well. The crystal flashed like a white candle, falling eight feet to the murky water below where it sank with a tiny splash. They saw Adric underwater, gripping the rope with one hand and Cindra's metal gauntlet with the other. She was three feet below the surface, thrashing, trying to launch herself up, but her armor was dragging them both down. They could see her frantic face through the open visor; bodies of faeries swirled about them as she desperately groped for air. Then the light sank to the bottom, illuminating only her legs as they kicked and struggled in vain.

"The pulley!" Padison cried, and he began cranking furiously on the wheel, reeling up the bucket and his friends. He could only do so much though, for they were both very heavy. Blood began to seep through the back of his shirt as his wounds tore open.

Drahn was now on the edge of the well, peering down helplessly; he had never been good at levitation spells, not like his master. If Ildric were here, he could have saved them, or at the very least, lend his strength to cranking the wheel. Drahn whimpered in distress as he watched Adric try to raise Cindra's bulk to the surface through sheer determination. She was grasping and climbing his body as he clung to the rope, and poor Padison was struggling more with each turn of the wheel.

Deliah swept her arms about, scattering the nixominy with another gust of wind, but it was only delaying them.

Nixy tried to help with the wheel, but he was so weak that he could barely hang on as it turned.

Cindra's head finally broke the surface and she gulped for air, choking and sputtering. Dead faeries still clung to her armor in places, having wedged themselves under the plates.

Wenyssaya watched helplessly from the doorway as Deliah cast one more spell, summoning a mighty wind to blast the nixominy away. The elf knew that humans used magic at great risk when away from a spirit well; an imbalance in the energies or a break in concentration could lead to disaster. So it was no great surprise when Deliah's last spell caused her to swoon and fall at Padison's feet.

The nixominy descended on them now that there was nothing to hold them back. Soon all of Wenyssaya's companions were obscured in a cloud of bat wings and sharp talons. Nixy turned to look at her one last time.

"No!" she shouted, lurching into the night, "Get away! *Cimnan vylanviis!*" She flung her arms wide against the swarm.

A white radiance erupted from her body, expanding and flinging the creatures away. For a moment she was bathed in light, as radiant as the moon goddess Lieutrella when she danced upon the face of Jayde. Wenyssaya's hair and skirt blew in an unnatural wind that stirred up from another world; then it fell and her light went dim, and she was once again a simple elf maid, anxious and afraid to be left alone in the dark.

Chapter Twenty

Under Siege

Cindra awoke in the hall, face down on a table. There was a pale white radiance somewhere above, and Wenyssaya was beside her. Turning her head, she saw that Deliah was on the other side, and Adric and Padison were standing with their backs turned, holding up a blanket between them. The women were busy at something.

Most of her armor had been removed, and her hair and clothes were damp. Also, her legs were spread apart and felt as heavy as lead.

I jumped into the well, she remembered, *I was drowning.*

"Welcome back," Deliah said, "You have been in and out of consciousness for over an hour."

There was a dull pain along the back of her legs, and she reached to feel.

"No," Wenyssaya said, "Do not touch, please. There are healing poultices in place that must be bandaged first."

"Is it bad?" Cindra asked in a weak voice.

"It is not good, but it will get better very soon if you lie still," the elf maid said.

Cindra assessed the pain and sensations, looked again at the shielding blanket and the boys acting like blind sentries, and came to a conclusion.

"My ass is hanging out, isn't it?"

"Yes."

"Perfect," she sighed.

Wenyssaya explained, "We had to remove your armor and cut open your breeches; they were quite shredded and bloody. You suffered many deep scratches and a number of bites, but they are not beyond my skill to mend."

"That's good," Cindra said, "Is everyone else alright?"

"We are well," Deliah said, "thanks to Wenyssaya."

The elf maid blushed a little, but said nothing.

"What does that mean?" Cindra asked. The last thing she remembered was being pulled out of the well by many strong hands.

"She was able to summon a ward that protected your rescue," Deliah explained, "Some of the men from the hall helped pull you up, but it was young Adric and Padison that saved you from drowning."

She said, "I thank you all; I was sure I was going to die tonight."

"Not if we're around, milady," said Adric, though he respected her privacy and didn't turn his head.

Padison just smiled and said, "It'll take more than indestructible man-eating faeries to stop us."

"Not so indestructible," Deliah said, "We learned a thing or two, did we not?"

"Nixy killed so many, but is he alright?" Cindra asked, "He left the Shadow."

"Yes, it seems that dark stalker made another attempt on his life, so he won't be shadow-hopping anymore if he can help it," Deliah said, "He is fast asleep."

"He did wonderfully," Cindra said, "I hoped we would make the little monsters think twice about attacking us."

Deliah replied, "I believe if Wenyssaya's spell wasn't keeping them out, they would be attacking us right now."

Cindra turned to face the elf maid and asked, "So your ward is protecting the entire hall? I didn't know you could do such a thing."

"Neither did I," she said meekly, "Warding magic works on creatures that are ruled by instinct, but thinking creatures can usually overcome them."

"Unless," Deliah said, "breaking the ward releases a curse, or the ward is securing a physical object, like a door."

Deliah would know all about ward magic, Cindra thought, *She was married to Portshia's ward master. Or maybe she was an expert long before meeting him?*

"Well, I never learned things like that," Wen said, "I was taught more practical uses, like keeping dry in the rain, or protecting my bed from bugs."

Deliah said, "Not even the best human wizards could have done that so quickly and thoroughly. It would seem that you have a great gift."

"So I have been told," Wen said.

Padison piped up, "Tell her about the bodies!"

"Bodies?" Cindra asked, "The ones Nixy killed?"

"No," Deliah said, "the ones that you drowned in the well. The nixominy have a weakness."

"Drowning?"

"Water," Deliah replied, "I should have guessed; when magical creatures have a strong affinity for one element, they usually have a weakness for another. They are immune to fire, so water can harm them. Think of it as a kind of supernatural balance."

"So we have to drown them all?"

"Not necessarily," Deliah said, "the bodies we removed from your armor were far less resilient, so long as they were wet."

"I crushed one with my boot," Padison said, "It went *splat* like a bug; it was disgusting."

"Interesting, I wish I hadn't had to sacrifice my rear end for that information."

Deliah said quietly, "Remember the body in the stream; it had been eaten down to the water's surface."

"Aaah, of course," Cindra said.

Drahn's voice came from somewhere behind her, "I have a few thoughts on how we might use this weakness to our advantage. I found some intewesting seeds in the herbalist's house..."

Cindra looked around for him and asked, "Where are you?"

"Between your knees," he replied.

"Draaaahn!" she cried, "Get out of there, you little purple pervert!"

Drahn was incensed. "*Pervert?!*" he huffed, "I have been *assisting* Wenyssaya and observing her *healing techniques!* I understand you have been twaumatized, but believe me when I say that human haunches do not stwike my fancy."

She groaned, "Fine. I'm sorry."

"In fact, I find your *horse* more attwactive than you."

"I said I'm sorry!"

"Pervert indeed," he muttered.

Deliah smiled and said, "If you want to be embarrassed about someone, Adric was the one helping to remove your armor."

"Hey!" he protested, "that's my job!"

Padison giggled mercilessly at him.

Cindra could do nothing but relax and suffer the indignities.

It took several minutes more to finish binding her wounds, during which time she received a full account of what happened after she jumped into the well. The heroism of her friends touched her deeply, and she thanked them yet again; even Deliah deserved praise for stepping out to help, since the threat of being eaten alive was perhaps even more horrible if one would live to remember it.

After she had been treated, she was given a blanket to drape over her legs; then it was Padison's turn. His back was all bloody from his exertion and he had many new scratches, but Wen said he would heal much faster now with the medicines they had found in the dead midwife's house. Wenyssaya, Deliah and Drahn had gone into the deserted house after the bonfire was extinguished and the faeries had been warded off. It was a treasure trove of herbs, seeds, medicines, and simple but ingenious devices to extract the healing properties from plants.

These resources, combined with Wenyssaya's already impressive magic, made it possible for the wounds to be healed in days instead of weeks. But this meant that they would have to rest and allow time for the medicine to do its work; they could not aid in defending the hamlet.

With nothing to do but lie around on her stomach, Cindra received many visits from grateful residents who thanked her for striking back at the nixominy menace. They were amazed at her bravery, and were very curious about her family, her story, and the lightning scars on her forearms. She had little else to do, so she told the tale in short form.

What she didn't elaborate on was Nixy's role in things. His fight in the Shadow had been seen by no one, and for all the people of the hamlet knew, he had been outside with her in plain view, slicing faeries with his magic knife. Cindra made sure to leave the details of their quest secret, since there was no telling how they would treat him if they knew. Few people here spoke openly about the Shadow Lord, and fewer still gave an opinion when asked.

As for Nixy himself, he was still sleeping by the hearth fire, oblivious to everything. The night's work had completely exhausted him, and he slept until the early hours of morning.

Cindra awoke on her table with sore ribs and tingling, itching sensations from her rump down to the back of her knees. She had enough experience with healing magic to know that this was normal, but she still sorely wished she could scratch everywhere. Someone had laid a folded pair of breeches on the tabletop, presumably for her use once recovered. She had no idea who to thank for them.

Taking a look around, she saw that the villagers were all sleeping soundly, huddled together for warmth across the floor of the hall. Her friends were asleep as well, except for Adric, who was standing by an open window keeping watch.

She hissed at him to get his attention. He looked over, closed the window and barred it, then sat at her table to talk quietly.

"What did I miss?" Cindra asked.

"Not much," Adric said, "The girls and Drahn stayed up talking for a while, but I don't know if they formed a plan. Wen said she was unsure how long her ward would last, but she did something with a little necklace she was wearing; I think she cast a spell on it."

Cindra said, "She did that before when I was chained on Tirgrim's Bluff; she sent her raven with the amulet to protect me."

"How does it work?" he asked.

"The raven just spoke the magic words, I guess. I was out of my head at the time."

He was silent for a moment and said, "What do you think of our chances?"

Cindra wondered if she should give her true thoughts, or be a good leader and lie. She decided that Adric deserved the truth as she saw it.

"Not good," she said quietly, "They outnumber us, even counting every man, woman, and child. We don't have a way to take advantage of their weakness unless it starts raining, and even then it's a furious battle with few weapons. I'm out of the fight, and no one else will fit in my armor."

He nodded, saying, "Your armor took a beating; they chewed up the leather straps, so they'll need replacing. I hoped since Deliah was the Raven Witch's heir or whatever, she might have more tricks up her sleeve, but so far it hasn't amounted to much."

Cindra almost told him about Deliah's true nature, but she thought the better of it. *What good would it do him to know such a freakish story? It might ease his ardor, but it would probably do more harm than good.*

Instead, she said, "Deliah is very secretive, and I doubt we've seen all of her tricks."

He shook his head. "Drahn was going on about preserved berries and seeds or something; I couldn't tell why he was so excited," he said, "The girls were humoring him, I guess."

"I think we all need a distraction," she said, "Come dawn, things are going to get very interesting around here."

"Yeah," he said, "I'm going back to the window to see how interesting."

The sun arose, spilling the filtered light of morning across the hamlet and in through the open window. The hearth fire had died down low and people were beginning to awaken, expecting the worst. Voices were hushed as those with children saw to their needs, and many took advantage of the ward spell to go out and relieve themselves nearby; such opportunities had only been taken before in total darkness.

The nixominy were everywhere. Hundreds could be seen in the trees, on the rooftops, and hopping about the perimeter of the ward, testing its boundaries. Most of them were chattering and staring at the faerie body parts littering the ground.

Cindra slowly got off the table and stood, wrapping her blanket around her as she pulled on the breeches. The bandages made her walk stiffly; the pain wasn't bad, but the itching intensified. She shuffled over to the window where Adric was still on watch.

"Anything yet?" she asked.

"Maybe," he said, "I can't tell, but I think the spell is fading."

Cindra looked and noticed that the dim glow of the ward spell had lessened somewhat. "Maybe it's just harder to see in the light?" she said.

"No, I think they're inching closer," he said, "Once it fails, we're going to be in for it."

She nodded in agreement. "I don't think they're going to hold back this time," she said.

Wenyssaya's voice came from behind, sleepy and concerned, "Cindra, you should be lying down."

"We are worried about the ward spell," Cindra said, "Can you renew it?"

The elf woman shrugged, "I don't even know how I managed it the first time. It took quite an effort."

"Well, now might be a good time to figure it out," Adric said, "because I think it's failing." He pointed to the edge of the square where the bonfire had been.

Several nixominy were moving forward, unhindered by the edge of the ward. At first they were wary, but they pushed on with growing confidence and aggression. Finally a pack of them scampered to the ashes of the bonfire and began to feast on the remains of their fallen. Others saw this and swooped in to join, and before long the ground had been picked clean.

Cindra was both fascinated and horrified. "They're cannibals!" she said.

They must have heard her, because they all looked at the open window.

"Adric..?" She put a hand on his shoulder and squeezed.

"Got it," he replied, slamming the shutters closed and barring them.

"Everyone up," Cindra called, "they're coming!"

People began to cluster in protective groups and put their backs to the rock walls. Men climbed the ladders to the rafters, shutting and latching the doors that covered the smoke vents. Iron grates or no, there was no point of entry that would be taken for granted.

Constable Narven took charge of directing people as best he could, but there was very little anyone could do. The only precaution they had taken since the bonfire incident was to fill as many containers with water as possible, hoping to use them to weaken the intruders.

Moments later, the chatter of the faeries increased to a maddening cacophony as every wooden surface of the hall was assaulted by the claws and teeth of the swarm. Children began to cry and their parents hugged them close. Everyone was awake and alert, but utterly helpless.

"What can we do?" someone cried.

"Pray for rain!" Deliah answered.

They knew how to do that. Soon everyone was bowing their heads, begging Pokaht to bring rain, and quickly.

"Milady woodkin!" cried the miller, "can you not protect us again?"

"I don't know..." Wenyssaya replied, "I shall try." She closed her eyes, held out her arms and searched for that power she knew was within her now. "*Cimnan vylanviis!*" she cried, and a light shone about her, pushing out to the walls.

The noise of the nixominy was interrupted for a moment, but began again with more vigor.

Wenyssaya wilted as her doubts returned, and she shook her head saying, "I'm sorry..."

The window shutters rattled and clattered, the doors trembled under the continual assault, and the roof echoed with the perpetual noise of shingles being chewed on and pried at.

"What about you?" the miller asked Deliah, "You're the Raven Witch's kin! Can't you do anything?"

She shot him a look and said, "Do you think I would be just sitting here if I could?" But as she looked around, she saw that many suspicions had been confirmed, and all eyes were on her as muttering words passed between them.

Cindra came to Wenyssaya and put her arm around her. "Wen," she said, "I know you can do this; you did it before."

"I don't know *how* I did it before," she said, "Last night the power was in me, but today..."

"What about the amulet?" Cindra asked, "Adric said you cast a spell on it."

"That was Drahn's suggestion," she replied, "in case we needed to protect the stables and our horses."

"A wise notion, but it will do no good if we are all killed in here."

"I agree," Wen said softly.

"Do you think it'll work as well as the ward you made last night?"

"It should," Wen said, "I took my time to infuse the jewel with enough power. Warding these creatures is not like warding animals; they have a strong will."

"There must be something we can do," Cindra said, "we must be close to the so-called Fortress of Thorns; could we send for help?"

"We might," Wenyssaya said, "but I know not what help the Shadow Lord could provide, and my raven would not be able to escape while they're attacking us."

Nevertheless, she called Navithwi down to her and began to speak to him in the elven tongue.

It was dark in the hall despite the morning sun; what little light they saw came from the cracks around the shutters and the door. Noisy shadows moved across the light, and everyone knew that if those cracks widened significantly, matters would be much worse. Darkness was preferred.

Yet as the morning wore on, the little slivers of light grew and grew. The roof was holding up better than the windows, but some of the shingles were being worked loose. If they pried several up, they could slip past the battens and drop into the hall with ease. Navithwi croaked from the rafters at the noise above him, shifting back and forth on his perch as he awaited a chance to deliver his message.

Deliah went from window to window, slowly casting ward spells to seal them shut against the constant assault. "This will make the shutters more difficult to destroy, but will not last forever," she said.

"Why didn't you do this before?" Cindra asked.

"I just remembered how," she said quietly, "I have forgotten more spells than you can imagine."

Cindra didn't doubt it.

By midday the noise had chipped away at people's sanity. Fingers of sunlight were creeping in from above as the monsters made steady progress. Holes in the shutters revealed that they were now working in shifts, with some resting on the rooftops while others continued the assault. Nixy was making the rounds, poking his knife at any limbs or heads that tried to wedge themselves into the chewed gaps.

The mood in the crowded hall was tense and brittle; mutterings became plaintive wails, and notions threatened to become actions. People were growing desperate as they sensed their end approaching.

"Why won't they *stop?*"

"They want to *eat* us, that's why!"

"It's because the newcomers killed so many of them last night..."

"They were trying to help!"

"Got them angry... They weren't like this before..."

"Maybe they don't want all of us?"

Farn the goatherd said, "It was the lady knight and that lad who killed so many; they want them worst of all, I'll wager!"

Cindra did not like where this was going; she and the boys took up their weapons and stood between the villagers and their companions. Nixy, seeing many eyes glaring at him, went to join his friends.

Larren the miller spoke up, "Quiet, the lot of you! This is a war we're in, can't you see?"

"But it's not our war!" cried Farn, "You said *she* was the kin of the Raven Witch! What if they only want *her?*" He pointed to Deliah, who muttered a curse under her breath.

"They were attacking us before these folk even arrived," said Narven, "They've a grudge against the hamlet and its people, that's obvious."

A woman cried out, "It's the newcomers who have riled them the most! Why keep them in here with us?"

"I say we have a show of hands!" Farn said, "Who wants to turn them out?"

Many voices were raised and many hands went up.

"The elf witch can stay, she's at least useful!"

"I told you they'd bring more trouble than they were worth," Farn said.

The crowd started to press forward.

Cindra had heard enough. She did her best to imitate Sir Cord Freekirk's manner. "QUIET!" she shouted.

The villagers went silent. Even the nixominy paused their assault.

"Listen, you lot! We could have moved on and left you to your fate, but we stayed to help! We've bled for you and nearly died for you, so I don't want to hear any talk of throwing anyone out!"

This cowed a few of them into silence, but others took umbrage.

"What good is your help?" called a man towards the back, "It was a meddling witch that drew first blood last time; now we have *two* witches and a girl playing at being a knight; look where that's got us!"

"Aye! Armor and a sword doesn't make you a hero, little lady!" said Farn, "Now we're worse off than before, thanks to you!"

Many voices were raised in agreement. Some men moved forward, as if to take matters into their own hands.

Adric and Padison bristled, and Nixy grew angry. Weapons were raised in warning; they looked to their leader for a sign, a signal, anything.

But something had snapped in Cindra's mind. Maybe it was this wretched forest, maybe it was the constant, nerve-rattling noise of the nixominy, or maybe she had just had enough of fearful, ignorant, ungrateful people.

She stepped forward into the crowd, looked them square in the eyes, and said in a frosty voice, "Listen, you damned peasants. I was knighted by the king himself, and His Majesty sent me on an important quest that has *nothing* to do with this collection of huts you call home. When we learned of your troubles, we *assumed* you wanted our help. Clearly, we assumed wrong. Since you're all so eager to see us go, we'll be leaving now. May the gods give you what you deserve."

It might have been the heartless tone of her voice that shocked them so, or possibly it was Nixy's anger deepening the shadows as Cindra spoke, but no one wanted to argue now. They all watched in dismay as she ordered her party to pack their things.

"But," the constable said, "but you can't just leave! No one can."

"Wrong," Cindra snapped, "we have an amulet with a ward spell like the one Wenyssaya used last night. It will protect us as we walk out of here, take what supplies we need, and ride away."

"You'd rob us?" asked a woman.

"No," she said, "we'll leave payment for what we take. You can claim it tonight if you live that long."

Wenyssaya whispered to her, "Cindra, are we really going to just leave them?"

"Yes," she said loudly, "we are. I won't bear anymore disrespect from the likes of these people. Adric? I'll have my armor on before we go, if you please."

"Yes, milady," he said. Cindra couldn't tell if he was angry at the villagers or her. Perhaps both.

Drahn's scales turned deep purple as he climbed into his pack; Nixy put it on and gathered his bedroll, his face a mask of bitterness.

Farn stepped forward and shouted, "They have a charm! Are we just going to let them take it? It could protect us!"

Deliah glared and raised her hand, saying, "The nixominy are immune to fire, but you are not. I could burn you where you stand." The hearth fire leaped as she twitched her fingers.

Farn flinched and took a step back, as many did.

"The beasts will follow you, you know!" Narven said desperately, "They hold a mighty grudge, and you killed dozens of them."

Deliah said, "We 'meddling witches' have a better chance than you lot. Once they know you're defenseless, they *will* come back; I can assure you." She had a smugness in her voice that stung like a winter wind. Many began weeping.

Wenyssaya could not help herself; she began to weep as well. "I am so sorry," she said to the assembly, "I wish I could have done more for you."

As for Cindra, she fanned the flames of her contempt, making her heart into stone. She fully intended to leave them to their fate; that is, unless they made serious amends. Her wounded pride would have it no other way. She had literally had her ass chewed for these people, and now they were either going to kiss it, or watch it walk out the door.

The only sounds were the shuffling of feet, the pitiful whimpers of the doomed, and the incessant scratching, rattling, and gnawing of the monsters outside. Dust rained down through a dozen tiny rays of sunlight as shingles were rocked back and forth, making the nails squeal and squeak.

Now that she was armored again, Cindra turned and gazed into their hapless, miserable faces. They would have never treated Jaron or Master Cord like this, she knew. It would have been 'Please, sir knight! Save us!' but with her it was 'Thanks for nothing, little girl.'

Damn them all anyway.

Then her eyes fell on the children, and her stony heart cracked. These poor little ones would suffer and die because of the stupidity of their parents, but was it her responsibility to fight when they were clearly not wanted? She had a vital mission after all.

As her eyes began to tear up, she turned for the door. "Deliah, remove the door ward. Wenyssaya, invoke the amulet, please."

Still weeping, she spoke the words in a quavering voice, "*Cimnan-diis.*"

The amulet flashed with a powerful white light, and for the first time in hours, there was silence outside the hall. It fell so suddenly and completely that many gasped and cried out, releasing their pent-up tension like an unstrung bow.

Cindra opened the door and daylight poured in, unsullied by the wings of faeries; only their distant chattering could be heard as they were driven back to the trees.

"Wait!" called the constable, "please, you can't just abandon us to these monsters!"

"Can't we?" she asked, "Last night you were all thanking us for what we did, but today you wanted to *sacrifice* us. If you really want us to stay, you can all get on your dirty knees and beg. What was once offered freely, now has a price."

"Wha-what price, milady?"

"Some gods-damned respect," she said.

Cindra stood in the door, waiting for the people to make up their minds. There was a painful moment when they only stared at the floor, feeling sorry for themselves. Finally, Constable Narven fell to his knees; the others soon followed, though Farn was the last.

"P-please, milady knight," Narven said, "do not abandon us. Forgive our fear and... and stupidity.

We're grateful for what you've done on our behalf, grateful to all of you."

Cindra said, "You speak well for your people, constable. But do you speak for all of them?"

"Yes!" cried a woman; Cindra recognized her as the widow of the rider they had found in the stream.

Many voices followed, saying, "Yes!" or "He does!" There were even pleas for forgiveness. She stared at Farn in particular, and he wilted under her gaze, nodding his head.

"Very well," she said, "I accept your apologies. But make no mistake, we are in this together, live or die. We will do all we can to fight them, and I will expect the same from the rest of you, agreed?"

Heads nodded all around. Her companions seemed to relax.

But as she went to shut the door, she noticed the nixominy were watching her intently. They began chattering and hopping about, and suddenly a swarm of them flew to the front gate and descended on the barn.

"Oh gods, the horses!" she cried. A panicked thought struck her, *Had the faeries heard us and understood?*

They watched as a mass of faeries pried at the barn door, flew to the gable vents, and made their way inside. Cindra imagined her dear T'ózha being eaten alive, screaming in the dirt. She raced outside to the edge of the ward, where she could hear the squeals and whinnies of the frightened animals.

The others followed, afraid for their own steeds. Drahn leaped from his pack and said to Wenyssaya, "Quickly, give me the amulet and get back inside! Hurry!"

As she did so, Drahn took the chain in his mouth and ran for the barn. He had only bounded a few steps when he summoned his inner element and vanished in a flash and crackle of lightning, arcing a path across the hamlet in an instant. He left a scorched trail on the ground and appeared at the open door of the barn in a burst of light and noise.

"Well, shag my sheep. That's a neat trick," Cindra muttered. Then she recovered her wits and said, "Wenyssaya, tell that raven of yours to get help!"

The elf maid called out, *"Navithwi, hwathe we vasthil!"* and the black bird flew out the door and into the northern sky. Several nixominy followed him, but were soon outpaced.

The last thing Cindra saw as she closed the door was a rush of faeries tumbling out of the barn and coming for the hall once again.

"Wen," she said, putting her hands on the elf's shoulders, "we need you to protect us. Whatever you felt last night, whatever drove you to find that power, you need to do it again."

"I don't know if..." she began.

"Wenyssaya, look at me," Cindra said, "I know you can do it because you did it before; the only difference is the circumstance. Remember what happened: Adric and I were stuck in the well, Padison was raising the bucket..."

The clatter of the faeries returned as they smashed against the door and shutters, rattling them violently.

Wenyssaya flinched and said, "Nixy begged us to help, but... but I was afraid. Deliah was shielding them with her wind spells..."

"Deliah passed out," Cindra said, "Nixy was out there, exposed... we all were. We were all going to die!"

The noise increased as they returned to the roof, clawing, scratching, and gnawing.

"I can't... please, I can't..."

She gave Wen's shoulders a firm shake, saying, "You could have shut the door and left us to die, but you didn't! Something within you woke up; it came alive and saved us! Find it, Wenyssaya! *Find it!*"

Someone shouted, "The window! Secure that window!"

The sound of wood splintering and screams filled the hall.

Wenyssaya shook her golden head, covering her ears.

Nixy shouted, "They're inside!"

A dozen bat-winged monsters fluttered about the hall, pulling hair, ripping clothes, tearing skin.

"*Wenyssaya!*" Cindra cried, prying her hands from her ears, "Now! Do something NOW!"

A faerie landed on the elf maid's arm and bit her savagely.

She screamed in pain, then cried, "*Cimnan vylanviis, am gimthavath yon!*"

Cindra felt a familiar pain like lightning rushing through her arms and she fell back, letting go of Wenyssaya. A dazzling flash of white light burst from the woman, expanding like a physical force. It threw the faeries against the walls and ceiling, pressing them there as the building trembled and groaned, raining dust from the rafters. The glow expanded beyond the walls, violently flinging the beasts away from the hall.

The nixominy trapped inside began to flatten and distort, squealing and popping as the elf maid's curse crushed them against the walls. Someone doused one with a mug of water, and it exploded in a splash of dark green goo. Cheers erupted from the villagers.

"Yeah," Cindra said, as she wearily struggled to her feet, "that should do it. Good work, Wen."

As Wenyssaya was surrounded and praised by the grateful crowd, Cindra limped to a corner and laid down to ease her aching backside.

Chapter Twenty One

The Battle of Gloamshire

Night fell after many hours of relative peace. Wounds were tended to, meals were prepared and eaten, and repairs were made to the hall. Drahn had returned from the barn after a harrowing ordeal of trying to treat injured horses that were now afraid of his bat-like wings.

Cindra and Padison were already tired of lying on their stomachs, but Wenyssaya insisted that they rest and heal. They spent an hour playing 'noughts and crosses' on the floor, and another playing 'guess the schoolmate.'

"I'm not too tall, but I've seen it all. I'm older and bolder. My family's drink makes it hard to think..."

"Mat Belvine!"

"Yup."

"The wine gave it away."

Eventually Padison fell asleep and Deliah came to sit by Cindra. "So," she said, "did you enjoy it?"

"Enjoy what?"

"Giving them an ultimatum."

Not sure where this was leading, she answered, "A little."

"More than a little, I think. I don't blame you, by the way; I believe it was the right thing to do."

"Yes," Cindra said, "you seemed to enjoy it as well."

"Life is full of little pleasures. But I meant what I said; I think it was the right thing to do."

"The others didn't seem to think so."

"That's because they're not leaders," Deliah said, "to be a leader is to either inspire or compel. Your acts of heroism inspired them, but people are fickle."

"They are," Cindra agreed, "but I'm not sure if I acted as a knight should."

Deliah laughed, "How many knights do you know?"

Cindra had to think about that; the knights she knew made a short list, and others had treated her like an aberration. Then there was the traitorous Sir Earnold Greenfellow... and the charming Sir Gerard Valdoy, of course.

"We are supposed to defend the weak," she said finally.

"Did they seem weak when they were threatening to take our amulet and throw us to the faeries?"

"No," Cindra said.

"Then I wouldn't worry yourself over it. No one follows a leader who can neither inspire nor compel. Remember that."

Cindra no longer felt odd taking advice from Deliah, and that in itself felt odd. *When did I come to accept her?* she wondered.

"You don't think I was out of line calling them 'damned peasants?'" she asked.

"They *are* damned peasants," Deliah replied, "You are a knight and a lady of a Great House. Both must command respect from the common folk or they are worth nothing."

"It's just that I've spent time on both sides," Cindra said, "and I don't know that there is much of a difference in worth between commoner and noble."

Deliah smiled. "Each person is different; I've met commoners with more grace, wisdom and worth than some kings I've known. The truth is that the parts we play serve the system, and if you cannot change the system, then you must play by its rules."

"The rules say I was to marry a boy I'd never met and have babies," Cindra said, "so I guess *I've* changed the system."

"It's adorable that you think so, but all you've done is broken the rules. Now you must adhere to a new set of rules if you are to survive. Rule number one of being a knight: uphold your honor, and don't suffer disrespect from peasants."

It sounded obvious and crude at the same time, but that was the way of many rules of society. Jaron had never given her this lesson, but then he was a peasant himself, trained as a knight as a favor to his peasant-knight father.

She would have thought more on the matter, but she and everyone in the hall were distracted by the distant rumble of thunder. The mood lifted instantly as people dared to hope.

"Rain!" someone cried, "It's raining!"

"Not yet," another said, "but there's a chance."

"Pokaht has heard our prayers!"

As the people of the hamlet celebrated the good omen, Cindra's party gathered on the floor to discuss their options.

"This is a lucky break," Adric said, "assuming it actually rains."

"I'm not so sure," Deliah said, "if they are vulnerable to rain, they will stay well out of reach."

"So we need to make them come to us, like before," Cindra said, "bait them so they can be attacked."

"How do we do that without getting someone killed?" Nixy asked.

Drahn said, "I've been thinking about this a gweat deal, and I have a plan. It depends on powerful nature magic and a good amount of wain, which we might be getting soon."

"Nature magic?" Wenyssaya asked suspiciously, "what kind of nature magic?"

Drahn fiddled with the tip of his tail as his scales turned a nervous red. "The kind you do out in the open," he said, "surrounded by nixominy."

"I don't like this plan," Wenyssaya said.

"There is gweat wisk," Drahn agreed, "but I think it can work."

"Great risk or not, it's all we've got so far," Cindra said, "Let's hear it, Drahn."

He began, "You might wecall that the Tower of Sight back in Portshia is lined about the base with ivy vines?"

"Not really, but go on," Cindra said.

"Well, Master Ildwic wanted enchanted cweeping vines to pwotect from intwuders and to close over the door. He wanted ivy because he thought it looked pwetty, but I suggested another shwubbewy-"

"The point, Drahn. Get to the point."

"The point *is* the point, so to speak," he said, "*He* wanted ivy, but *I* wanted barberry bushes. There are barberry seeds and preserved berries in the herbalist's house."

Wenyssaya was against the plan; not only was it terribly, terribly dangerous, but she was at the heart of it. Yet, she had no better ideas.

The elf maid summoned all of her training to make the waiting more bearable. The fear that had been her constant companion since entering the Shadowood was at its peak now, chipping away at her confidence and eroding the inner peace needed to use her powers. *Hanviith*, the spirit weave that humans called 'magic,' required control, focus, and above all, faith in one's self. Bursts of panic and pain had fueled her impressive ward spells, but wards were different from *alathanviith*, or nature magic. Manipulating living things required a more gentle flow of energies, a greater control of self.

The gray morning wore on with the promise of rain, but her ward spells were fading; either the one on the barn or the one on the hall would give out, and the faeries would attack. If either faded before the rain began, it would spell disaster. Navithwi had not returned either, and there was no sign of help coming.

She pushed her worries aside and took several deep, calming breaths, but it did little to ease her anxiety.

Adric was by the window, keeping lookout. He was not happy with the plan either, but for different reasons. When their eyes met, she saw that his anxiety reflected her own.

"Are you ready?" Deliah asked, putting a hand on her arm. Wenyssaya's sleeve was stained with blood from the nixominy bite, but it had been bandaged and mostly healed.

"I think so," she said, touching the bandage, "Actually no, I am not ready. I don't think I will ever be ready for this."

"Neither am I," Deliah said, "but we are doing it anyway. That's life."

"We have different versions of life. Mine can end."

Deliah leaned in close and whispered, "At least you don't have to remember that end in great detail."

"How do you know what I will remember? The spirits of the Ilvayiin recall their lives, so it is said."

"Then make the best of it. You don't want to exist forever as a regretful spirit, do you?"

The elf maid was going to make an answer, but the question troubled her more deeply than it should have, and she had no idea why.

Just then, the gentle drumming of raindrops began to play on the roof, and Adric confirmed, "It's starting."

The sound grew louder and steadier, and before long the sweet smell of wet earth permeated the hall. People's spirits were lifted and there were many smiles all around, until they looked at the grim faces of Wenyssaya and Deliah.

The nixominy were perched in the trees, staying out of the rain as much as possible. They chattered and spat curses at the sky, but maintained their vigil as they waited for the ward spells to fail. Suddenly the door of the hall burst open and two women stumbled out, followed by a young man with a sword.

"It's *you* they want!" Adric shouted, as he threatened Deliah and Wenyssaya, "Get out! Get out and maybe the rest of us can live!" He slammed the door shut behind him, leaving the women to huddle together in the rain.

The nixominy all stirred as one; wicked little smiles creasing their faces.

The women stood in confusion for a moment, holding on to each other for reassurance as their eyes frantically searched the trees. They found death waiting for them there, hissing and grinning. The women fled, leaving the protection of the ward and making for the palisade's back gate and the fields beyond.

Once they had gotten too far from protection to double back, the faeries launched themselves into the air and descended on the hapless women.

Wenyssaya ran for her life across the muddy grass towards the safety of a tool shed at the edge of the green. She could hear Deliah's footfalls behind her, and could now hear the shrieking laughter of the swarm following them. She dared not turn around.

A strong gust of wind blasted around her, almost making her tumble. The shrieks of the faeries ceased for a moment before rising in pitch. Deliah had clearly used a spell, but Wenyssaya was too frightened to look. She might see the woman passed out on the ground and be forced to make a choice, so she would rather not know.

"Keep running!" Deliah shouted.

The elf woman felt a wave of relief, but she needed no encouragement to keep running.

The sound of wings and the pouring rain was her entire world now; her heart was fluttering like a bird's, and she kept blinking away the rain to see ahead of her. In her terror, she had not even bothered to use a weather warding spell to stay dry.

They were almost to the shed; its open door welcomed them, and the results of last night's work looked healthy and strong.

She heard Deliah slip and fall. Turning, she saw faeries pounce on her body and tear at her clothing. Deliah screamed in anguish as one of the little monsters clawed out her eye.

No! We are so close!

Wenyssaya faltered, wanting to run to the safety of the shed, but some part of her would not allow it. Whatever power she had found within her had gotten stronger; whether it was courage or desperation, she did not know.

She stopped and felt the elements swirling around her; the power of *Alhanna* permeated them all and flowed through her blood.

"*Hwesmathal am maviiyo,*" she chanted, making circles with her arms.

A roar of wind whipped at her hair and skirt, spinning towards Deliah. The rain parted as a column of swirling air washed over her, blasting the faeries away in all directions. The little twister spun about for a moment more as Deliah struggled to her feet and staggered towards the shed, her hair and clothing fluttering and snapping in the gale. Blood flowed from her eye socket.

"Nice one," she said, as Wenyssaya took her hand.

"It's my first," she replied, and they ran together into the little building. Wenyssaya slammed the door shut and collapsed with her back to it, her chest heaving like a bellows, limbs trembling.

Deliah slumped against a plow; her dark hair hung over her face as she pressed her hand to the wound. Her tattered dress was stained with mud and blood.

"You are hurt!" Wenyssaya said, "Come, let me help you..."

"I'm fine," Deliah replied, raising her head, "Just focus on your part."

Her missing eye had restored itself in moments; the gray iris was surrounded by blood-red instead of white, but the color was fading even as Wenyssaya watched. Soon, the gore on her cheek was all that remained of the injury.

The elf maid felt the door jostle against her back as the swarm assaulted the tiny structure. All they had for self-defense was a number of farming tools, shovels, and plowshares, but self-defense was not the plan.

She closed her eyes, focused on the earth beneath her hands, and waited.

The nixominy tore and chewed at the strange little shed, ripping chunks of clay from the wattle that made up the thin walls. Some tore at the thatched roof, some chewed at the door, but there were so many faeries covering the surfaces that others had to flap about or sit on the ground, waiting for a way inside. They cheered on their siblings and screamed unintelligible threats to the troublesome witches hiding within.

The only thing getting in the way was the overgrown vegetation that covered the shed from top to bottom in a sheath of thin, leafy branches.

Wenyssaya had never wanted to kill anything out of anger or fear, but she had begun to understand just how much death was essential to life. When an animal wanted to eat her, she never took it personally; she knew that they were only hungry and trying to survive, so she simply persuaded them to look elsewhere.

But these creatures were bred for murder and revenge, having no other purpose but to inflict fear, suffering, and death on Gloamshire. They could not be placated, they could not be driven away, they could only be delayed. As such, their death was essential to the lives of everyone in the hamlet, possibly even the forest itself. They were an unnatural plague, and defeating a plague was the responsibility of any healer.

Wenyssaya could feel the creatures tearing at the plants she had grown the night before. She could feel their roots, their branches, their leaves; she could feel their pain.

It was time for them to inflict pain in return.

She let her power flow into the earth, up through the roots and stems, and into every branch and twig.

The nixominy covering the shed were suddenly engulfed in an explosion of entangling, twisting growth. Some managed to pull themselves free, but most were buried in an ever-thickening mass of leaves and branches that wrapped around and immobilized them.

Just like the ivy vines on the Tower of Sight, these were enchanted to entangle and subdue intruders. But unlike ivy, the local barberry bushes had wicked thorns.

Those thorns were growing now, piercing through impenetrable flesh that had been softened and weakened by the rain. These were not like the short, wide thorns of roses; these were long and thin, like sewing needles, and grew in three-pronged nodes. As the branches grew thicker and closer together, the barbs grew more dense and lethal. Hideous screams of dying faeries could be heard, replaced by the angry, helpless chattering of those who had been watching and waiting.

Another cry arose, this time from the hamlet's back gate. Adric was leading a charge of men armed with hammers, cooking pans, pitch forks, and whatever improvised weapon they could find. They rushed through the rain and mud to the shed, swatting at the nixominy and scattering them like frightened pigeons. While some of the men kept the flying beasts at bay, the others used their weapons to finish off the entangled faeries with brutal efficiency.

Adric called, "Deliah? Wenyssaya? Are you safe?"

"We are!" the elf maid replied. She felt relief bubble up inside of her like a fountain, threatening to spill out in a fit of hysterical laughter. But she knew they were not out of the woods yet, as the saying went.

"Several dozen got away," he yelled, "They're circling us now!"

"Damn," Deliah said, "I figured as much. This trick won't work on them again."

Lightning flashed and thunder rumbled across the sky, and a new sound was heard over the pouring rain; a cacophony of throaty caws.

"Adric?" Deliah called, "what is that?"

Adric looked past the circling faeries to the sky over the edge of the forest. Against the backdrop of gray clouds, a mass of black wings came into view; a conspiracy of ravens descended on the hamlet, swooping down over the treetops to snatch and peck at the nixominy in midair.

"It's a huge flock of ravens!" he called, "I'd say that bird of yours got help, Wen!"

Dark claws tore at each other, piecing feather and armored skin alike, but the faeries were now outnumbered and weakened. The rain persisted, forcing some of the combatants to the ground where the faeries had more mobility, but Adric and the men were quick to move in and smash any nixominy that got within reach.

The battle seemed to stretch for an hour, though it was perhaps a quarter of that, but it finally ended when the last nixominy died under a booted foot. The ground was littered with tiny corpses and several dead or injured ravens.

"All clear," Adric called to the women. Then he said to one of the men, "Go and tell the others we've won the Battle of Gloamshire!"

For the first time in a week, the people of Gloamshire walked under the daytime sky without fear. It didn't matter that the cold rain soaked them to the bone; they welcomed it with open arms as a gift from Pokaht, greeting it like children, with upturned faces and opened mouths.

Cindra and Padison had the sense to stay indoors, not wanting to soak their bandages, but Nixy and Drahn were happy to frolic and play in the puddles. Lightning flashed and cracked the sky with a boom like a hundred cannons, but the little dweedragon didn't even flinch; it was a part of him now.

The roof of the hall was leaking from the many holes gnawed in the shingles, and buckets were gathered from all over the hamlet to catch the water. Wenyssaya was sitting by the hearth fire, treating the injured ravens. The healthy ones, Navithwi included, were sitting in the rafters enjoying the rising heat. Some of the villagers had taken to calling her 'the Golden Witch,' a title she was not overly fond of, but then the 'Raven Witch' was already taken.

As for the Raven Witch herself, Deliah had to be careful. The first thing she had done was wipe the blood from her face. Then, upon leaving the overgrown shed, she immediately went to look for her missing eye, lest someone else find it and ask too many questions. Adric, of course, had been alarmed by the blood on her dress, but she assured him that Wenyssaya had seen to her injury. Upon finding her mangled organ, she palmed it and walked into the hall, tossing it into the heart of the fire. She now sat across from Wenyssaya, wondering at the enigma that was her elven companion.

The rain let up by late morning and the sun broke through the clouds in the afternoon. There were plans for a celebration underway and the saviors of the hamlet were expected to attend; it was an obligation they were more than happy to accept.

I expect we will be a part of their legends now, Cindra thought, *I wonder how it will grow in the telling?*

She was amazed at how well her wounds were healing. They still itched like mad, but had only been minor flesh wounds, and Wen said scarring would be minimal. Sitting was uncomfortable, but not impossible; still, she decided to stand.

She was still wearing her armor, sans helmet, which she had donned this morning in case things went badly and she had to join the fighting. Adric had been too busy to help her remove it, and Padison had joined him in giving the horses much needed care and attention. They had also been tasked with buying what supplies they could get for the last leg of their journey.

She decided to explore the little hamlet's perimeter and stretch her legs, which were a bit stiff and sore. Clanking about in her armor was not so bad, though it would need repair before going into battle again. The humidity was a problem, but it was still very cool outside. Spring and summer would be a completely different story, however, so she enjoyed the cold breeze in her face and hair while she could.

She fingered the magic earring Ildric had given her, wondering when the wizard might make use of it and contact her, though she was not sure she wanted him to. His news was not often good.

She wondered if Jaron was well, and wished she had a way of contacting him. There was so much to tell of her mad adventure, and it was not even over yet. Maybe her tale would give him comfort as he waited for the spring thaw and the inevitable march into the Dissenter Lands. Then again, maybe he would worry needlessly. Perhaps it was best that he didn't know all she had learned and done, at least not yet. Still, she desperately wanted to hear his voice and see his smile.

Goats and chickens greeted her as she walked past the pens and coops along the north palisade. Farn was there, making sure his animals were all accounted for. He met her eyes and nodded, turning away too quickly. Cindra felt a bit of guilty pride that she and her companions had smashed his low expectations so thoroughly.

She spent time in the barn, seeing to her horse. T'ózha had received his share of bites and scratches from the nixominy attack, but Drahn had treated them as best he could. She gave him lots of pats, strokes, and fresh oats from the hamlet's granary. She even spoke to him in the Galindri tongue, as she often did in his pony days.

"T'eméko tima, t'eméko gazh han-ámeh... My good boy, my big, strong boy," she said, patting his muscled neck. He would be turning three years old in another month or so. *They change so fast,* she thought, *He's almost fully grown.*

After visiting the barn, Cindra meandered about the southern palisade, waving and smiling to people as they returned to their normal lives. There was no sign of nixominy to be seen, assuming they couldn't turn invisible like the faeries of old. Still, she felt she had to look. One thing she had learned was that one could never be too sure of anything.

As she approached the back gate, she saw that the hamlet's children were dancing and playing around the overgrown tool shed. It seemed a bit grisly, since the crushed and punctured little bodies were still entwined within, but maybe that was the point; the children had lived in mortal terror of the tiny monsters, and now they could dance around their grave. She wondered if the villagers would want their shed returned to its functional state, or just leave it as a kind of memorial.

Looking out across the village green, past the thin, rectangular fields, Cindra saw a child standing in the shade at the edge of the woods, watching them.

Strange, but every group has a loner, she figured.

Yet as she watched the children play, her eyes kept drifting back to that lone child, standing there, as if waiting for something.

She couldn't tell if it was a boy or a girl. She couldn't even tell if it was facing the field or the trees. All she could really make out was a short, thin silhouette standing in the dappled light under the leaves. Something gnawed at her nerves, making her hand reach for her sword; she found she wasn't wearing it.

Taking several more steps toward the shed, she shielded the sun from her eyes to get a better look. The children giggled and waved at her, chanting, "Lady knight, lady knight, lady knight!" as they ran about in circles.

She motioned them to stop and asked, "Children, children, hush a moment; who is that in the woods? Can you tell?"

They all turned to look, like it was a game. No one recognized the watcher, but one of the children said, "She's got no clothes."

That was when Cindra realized what had been bothering her; the figure was either naked or wearing skin tight clothing. Neither option made any sense with today's weather, unless...

The wind blew again, making the sunlight and shadow ripple across the figure. A shock of reddish hair moved in the breeze, and Cindra saw that the thing had a slender, almost feminine shape. A pair of overlarge black eyes glared at her from a narrow face.

Cold fear stirred within her.

"I want all of you to get inside *now*," she said, "I want you to tell my friends to bring me my sword and arm themselves. Quickly! Go!"

The children were wise enough to know that a command from the lady knight was not to be ignored. They did as she instructed, but one little girl paused to ask, "Are the monsters coming back?" She looked to be on the verge of tears.

"Not if I have anything to say about it," Cindra replied, "Go and find your parents. Go, little one."

The girl nodded, took a last look at the figure in the forest, and ran.

Cindra locked eyes with the dark thing in the woods, assuming a relaxed fighting stance as she drew her only weapon, her *Kos* knife. If this creature was what she feared, she knew the knife would be of little use. Regardless, she held it at her side and stood her ground.

Her Majesty the Queen, I presume?

The thin figure tilted its head and bared its overlarge teeth; Cindra heard a chattering hiss that made her skin crawl. Her heart began racing and she focused on steady, deep breaths. Hopefully her friends would be here soon.

Hurry, she thought, *please hurry.*

The thing sprang forward out of the shadows and dashed across the field; its arms were spread like a swooping eagle's wings, and its terrible claws glinted in the sunlight. It had reddish-brown skin like polished leather, and the same terrible face as the nixominy it had spawned. The black eyes, like obsidian ovals, were wide and fixated on Cindra. When it was thirty feet away, it launched itself at her, arms and legs swinging forward like a giant, grasping claw.

But Cindra was not there when it landed. She had rolled to the side and regained her stance, knife at the ready. The creature tumbled to its feet, tearing at the grass as it scrambled to reach her. Cindra slashed at the monster's outstretched arms and felt her blade slide across the scaled skin, leaving no mark. She raised her arm to protect her face and stabbed the creature in the abdomen, but it was like trying to gut an oak tree.

It clutched at Cindra's armor and heaved, tossing her like a sack of grain; she rolled with the impact and managed to hold on to her knife. The thing leaped again, and she struck it in the eye with the spike-tipped handle. The point scratched the glossy surface of the lens, but only served to enrage the monster.

Flailing and shrieking, the nixominy queen knocked Cindra's knife away and lunged to bite her in the face.

Cindra caught the creature's thin wrists, struggling to keep the razor-sharp claws from raking her; the thick skin was slick and oily, making it difficult to grip. Its bat-faced head bent lower, jaws agape. A long, pointed tongue flicked spittle on her, and the hot, slaughterhouse breath panted inches from her face.

Cindra was rather proud of her strong fighter's muscles, but this beast made her feel like a weak trainee again. It was remarkably strong for its size; as big as a girl of twelve, about five feet tall and willowy, yet it was taking all of Cindra's strength to keep its teeth and claws at bay, and she was failing. Panic began to set in, and she thrashed about, hoping to throw it off balance.

She managed to roll on top of the creature and pin its arms as she plunged her armored knee into its gut again and again. It was like striking a bag of wet sand, but if there were any more nixominy gestating in there, Cindra wanted them born bruised at the very least.

The queen bent a limber leg and dislodged her with a kick to the head. Pain flashed like a white sun in her vision, but she was used to pain; Rejick Ratham had seen to that. She regained her feet in time to dodge two more slashes to her face, bobbing and weaving like a dancer. She was too nimble and quick to be taken so easily; Gavadaire LuVestra had seen to that.

"Cindra!"

Adric's cry was as welcome as a cavalry trumpet. Without taking her eyes from her opponent, she saw her boys running towards her, followed by Nixy, Wenyssaya, Deliah, and even Drahn. Many villagers had rushed out to see what was the matter; no one was expecting what they saw.

Except possibly Deliah.

When the nixominy queen turned and saw Deliah standing by the gate, it let loose a horrid scream of anguish and hatred, launching itself at the woman. The villagers fell back in terror, stumbling over one another. Deliah could only watch wide-eyed as the nightmare bore down on her; whatever spells she could have cast to protect herself were either washed from her mind in a moment of panic, or lost in the murky recesses of her memory.

Wenyssaya was more prepared. She clenched her fists and the grass rose to ensnare the creature's feet, tripping it up. Adric leaped upon its back and began beating the misshapen skull with his mace.

"Be careful, Adric!" Cindra shouted, "It's stronger than it looks!"

He did his best to keep the thing pinned, but it pushed itself from the ground, throwing him off its back as it tore loose from the binding grass. The queen hissed and went for Deliah once more.

Drahn let out a low growl and a bark, releasing a bolt of lightning that struck the thing in the side, sending it tumbling and twitching. In a moment, the twitching stopped and it lay still.

Cindra retrieved her sword from Padison and they all approached the body, weapons and spells at the ready. Deliah stayed back several feet.

"Is it dead?" Nixy asked. He had his knife drawn, but his knees were too wobbly to get close enough to use it.

"I don't know," Cindra said, "stay back."

"Doesn't look like it's breathing," Padison said, "we know they need to breathe 'cause they can drown."

"Is it a... female?" Adric asked.

"It's the queen, for lack of a better word," Deliah replied, "the mother of this madness. But maybe all of them are female, or none of them, or they only become female when they need to be."

Drahn got a bit closer, sniffing. He asked, "Do you think it wecognized, I mean, *mistook* Deliah for the Waven Witch?"

"My *great-grandmother* and I did look very much alike," Deliah said, glaring at the dweedragon.

He gave her a sheepish look and said, "It seems you were wight about them wanting wevenge. It's almost like fate bwought-"

His words were cut off as the queen sprang to life, grabbed him by the throat, and throttled him.

"Drahn!" Nixy cried, and he rushed forward, stabbing with his magic knife. He got close enough to pierce the monster's hip before it kicked him aside, sending him tumbling into Wenyssaya. The knife went flying.

But the damage was done. The queen flung Drahn's limp body to the side and rolled to its feet, panting and moaning as it clutched the wound. The others rushed to the dweedragon's defense, raining blows upon the queen from all sides, striking with mace and sword. The leathery skin absorbed the punishment, denting and creasing momentarily before going smooth again.

The monster raked Adric's belly, but he was wearing his mail shirt. It slashed at Padison, but the boy blocked with his shield. Cindra could now keep her distance with her arming sword. Yet all they could do was keep it occupied.

"Somebody find Nixy's knife!" Cindra called.

Nixy dashed to Drahn's side as Deliah scrambled to find his knife. Wenyssaya desperately conjured more entangling growth, but the grass here was sparse and not as effective.

The queen changed tactics, switching from claw attacks to powerful bludgeoning strikes. It hammered Adric in the gut and chest, crumpling him. When Padison intervened, it pounded furiously on his shield, bringing him to his knees. Cindra tried to kick the beast away from her friends, but the thing kicked her in return, knocking her to the ground.

Then it went for Deliah, screaming in rage. The woman shrank back as the nightmare approached, limping from its single wound. Deliah searched frantically for the knife, finding it too far away and too late. She dove for it, but the creature tackled her and they rolled in the dirt until she found herself pinned beneath it, its claws raised to strike.

"You can't kill me," Deliah rasped, "but go ahead and try."

But before it could strike, Adric rushed in and tackled the queen, grappling with it as Padison and Cindra went to his aid. They struggled furiously as the companions sought to subdue the creature, unsure of what else to do.

Just when it seemed the beast would slip free again, Larren the miller rushed in and threw a bucket of water on them.

There was a moment of shock, followed by a renewed struggle, but the queen seemed weaker. Cindra took up her sword and slashed across its belly, cutting a dark green line in the leathery skin.

"Water!" she cried, "More water!"

The people of Gloamshire were already ahead of her, taking up buckets filled from the hall's leaking roof and splashing it on the struggling queen. Padison took up his mace again and bludgeoned the creature, feeling the satisfying crack of bones. Cindra plunged her sword into its chest, careful not to impale Adric who was lying beneath it. The nixominy queen gasped as sickly green blood sputtered from its mouth. Its struggling became feeble and Adric was able to renew his grip, immobilizing its arms and legs.

But the final blow was dealt by Deliah, who had retrieved Nixy's knife. She stood over the beast, a look of anger and disgust clouding her lovely face.

"Your kind will no longer plague this world," she said, "I send you back to the Abyss."

The queen looked up at her and grinned with its toothy maw; then it spoke in a high, sibilant voice, "The warrr iss already won."

Scowling, Deliah plunged the knife into the creature's heart.

The celebration that evening was not as merry as had been planned. Though the villagers were in good spirits, the seven heroes were bruised, exhausted, and healing from their wounds.

Drahn had taken the worst of it. He was unable to speak in more than a soft, rasping voice, and he could barely swallow food or water. He spent much of the night curled in Nixy's lap while Wenyssaya soothed his throat with her healing magic.

Cindra and Padison were lying down on their stomachs to rest for the evening, their previous day's healing undone by the heavy fighting. Poultices and bandages had to be reapplied, and Wenyssaya had taught Deliah some basic healing spells that would hurry things along. The good news was that come late evening, they would have the hall to themselves as the people of the hamlet gratefully returned to their homes.

However, for now they were at the mercy of their hosts, who all wanted to thank their heroes for saving their lives and forgiving them their lack of faith. It was all very gratifying and exhausting, but at least the peasants had tapped a precious keg of ale and were keeping their mugs filled.

"I think I may lie here for a couple of days," Cindra said, nursing her drink, "I feel... tenderized."

"I agree," Padison said, as he downed his third ale, "I could use a few days' sleep and a nice back massage from Wenyssaya."

"We've all gotten quite a vanity massage tonight," Cindra said, "and I don't think it's good for us."

"Why not?" Padison asked, "We're heroes, aren't we?"

"They might think so," she said, "but I don't think we should start believing it ourselves."

"Aww, you're no fun," he said, "what's wrong with believing in ourselves?"

"Confidence is good," she said, "but pride is only good in moderation. We were doing our duty to protect the weak and defeat evil; we weren't seeking to be heroes."

"Maybe *you* weren't," he mumbled.

Their conversation was interrupted by a commotion outside. A boy came bursting into the hall, making everyone jump; he was out of breath and excited, but in a good way.

"They're here!" he cried, "they just arrived at the gate!"

Many of the villagers moved to the windows or the door, looking out into the torch-lit darkness.

"What is it, Adric?" Cindra called.

Her tall squire was looking over the heads of the men at the door. "It's a caravan," he said, "I think... I think it's old Maewyn and her family!"

Sure enough, a few moments later Blind Maewyn, Glenawyn, and Bardon came into the hall, surprised and delighted by the turnout at their arrival.

"Bless me!" the old woman said, "I've never had such a homecoming!"

Glenawyn took her arm and said, "Gran, our friends from Breega are here also!"

There were many words of greeting all around, and the old woman was led to a chair by the central hearth, which was near where Cindra and Padison were laying down. Nixy was across from them, and Wenyssaya and Deliah were seated beside him. They all gave their happy greetings to the trio in weary voices; Drahn looked up with interest from Nixy's lap and tried to croak something in the manner of a salutation, but it didn't come out well.

Bardon said, "You all look rather the worse for wear! Was the journey here that rough?"

Maewyn tsked him and said, "Have you no senses, lad? There's a great tale to be heard here! Quiet now, and let our friends tell of how seven magnificent heroes came to my childhood home, found it besieged by terrible enemies, and liberated it with magic, courage, and steel."

The companions and the people of the hamlet all stared dumbly at her, wondering how she knew so much. Cindra cracked a broad smile at the wily old woman and shook her head.

"Tell on now," Maewyn said, "I have a feeling it will be told and retold for many an age."

Chapter Twenty Two

A Fly Seeking a Spider

Maveezh was sick to death of snow. She had left Portshia in the last month of summer and traveled north as far as Rickshome-on-Joshian, setting herself up in the residence previously held by Omiras Bevek. She had sent Bevek and several other Llomaakitte priests on an ill-fated quest only a few months prior, which ended in death and madness.

Then, as a punishment perhaps, she had been ordered to head north to chase the tales of a mad man. Summer had turned to autumn, and then to a harsh winter. Now she was setting out yet again in the mounting snow. It was only the 4th of Selvimoth, and she could expect more of the same for weeks in the high country.

Curse this snow, curse this mission, and curse this world, she thought as she guided her horse down the road. These forays into the eastern Shadowood were exhausting and drained her of funds and willpower, but they were necessary. She would ride west out of the city for a few days, stop at Selvanor Crossing for her last comfortable night in an inn called the Crooked Bend, then head south onto the High Forest road. From there it was four days to the other side of the woods, where the forest road met the Casselvane Road. Somewhere in between was the Woodcliff Bridge, a creaky wooden span that was once home to her quarry.

She would not always travel the entire distance; sometimes she would linger north of the bridge, sometimes south, using the village of Thorn's Pass as a base. Sometimes she would camp out near the bridge itself, listening to the roaring of the river in the chasm below.

This time she had no real plan; she would wander about until she got sick of looking, or until her supplies grew thin. *Curse the High Priest,* she thought bitterly, *I could be comfortable at DuShonmaer, sipping his port and eating his food, growing fat while I waited for the end of the world. But no...*

She came to the Crooked Bend as the sun sank towards the low hills and plains. The lands were blanketed in snow that turned blue as the sky became a deep indigo.

"Hail there, Robi!" she called to the stable hand.

He was finishing shoveling hay into the few occupied stalls. "Hail to you, Mistress! Welcome back," he called in return, then went to see to stabling her mount.

The Crooked Bend kept a fire burning, and Maveezh gloried in its warmth as she took a chair near the fireplace, dropping her luggage beside her. Several other patrons were gathered; most were locals whom she had become familiar with, by face if not by name. As she removed her gloves and rubbed her hands, the innkeeper came to wait on her.

"Mistress Goodwater, how have you been?" he asked, taking her cold hands in his large, warm paws, "It has been more than a month, hasn't it?"

"It has, Master Dunfallow." Her smile for him was genuine. He was a good fellow, a good innkeeper, and she didn't hold the same secret loathing for him with which she regarded most.

"May I take your bags to your usual room?" he asked, "I'll have some coals in a bed warmer for you, right away."

"Thank you," she said, meaning it. She liked it when people waited on her, but she truly liked it when they seemed to want to, not need to. She missed her husband for that. She sat staring into the flames as someone brought her a mulled wine, which was a luxury since the king's northern army had passed through, taking all the food and drink they could carry.

Her new identity was Trabecka Goodwater, a traveling apothecary from Rickshome. Her expeditions into the woods were to collect rare plants and ingredients for her craft. Of course, she told no one that she hailed from Portshia, and she dared not use her old alias, Lemorea Gordon. She was a wanted woman back home after her husband died trying to assassinate that wretched Corrina girl.

Fool, she thought, *Poor, dear fool. Why did you have to go and get killed? We were supposed to see the End together.*

"Off on another expedition, are we?" Dunfallow asked, sounding concerned, "It's more than a bit cold and dangerous out there alone."

"No more than I am used to," Maveezh lied, "Besides, some of the plants I collect will only grow in the winter woods."

The truth was she hated camping outdoors almost as much as she hated the cold. Still, she had gone through great lengths to research her new identity, even learning about winter forest herbs just in case someone asked. The innkeeper didn't ask, which was another reason she liked him.

"Well, I wish you'd hire someone to go with you at least," he said, placing another log on the fire, "The roads aren't as safe as they were, what with so many soldiers gone off to war."

It was a fact, she knew. Bandits had increased as the patrols had decreased; she had to kill a few herself. It had been late Tavenmoth, when the farmers south of the woods were doing their winter sowing of wheat and rye. Four men wearing mismatched armor and leering grins had stopped her on the road, demanding her purse, her horse, and her virtue. Maveezh hated bandits, perhaps more than she hated camping outdoors, but at least she understood them.

"I will feel more at ease on my own," she said, giving him a reassuring smile, "Hired men can turn on a woman alone just as sure as any bandit."

He made a worried face, shrugged, and went to see to his other guests.

She was a Llomaakitte priestess; her cult was dedicated to living life as they wished, taking what they wanted, and vanquishing whoever got in their way. However, the ultimate goal was to avoid judgment at the end of their lives, to escape the system put in place by the Tyrant god Arathus. To that end she was ordered to squat in the woods until she found the Guadim.

She woke early and packed her belongings, had a good breakfast, and departed south towards the eastern arm of the Shadowood. She had double-checked her supplies, not trusting even the innkeeper to keep his large hands out of her business. As it turned out, someone had placed an extra loaf of fresh bread in her pack. *Dear master Dunfallow.*

She had plenty of rations, warm clothing, blankets, and most importantly, her divine alchemy.

That was why it had been more than a month since her last outing; her supply of divine alchemy had dwindled and she needed to make more. A city-born woman with little to no woodland skills, she relied heavily on her quasi-magical concoctions. Because her cult had existed in secret for centuries, much of their alchemy favored trickery and survival. She had taken inventory of the little bundles, bottles, and containers and found them all in place.

Her horse trudged through the snow, finding its footing on the paving stones that topped the raised strip of road. In time, those paving stones would end, and Maveezh would have to trust that there were no hidden dangers under the thick blanket of cold. One contingency she had not planned for was to have her horse go lame deep in the woods, and have to walk out on her own.

"I don't like this any more than you do," she said to the animal, "So let's do our best to make it back in one piece, shall we?"

The horse snorted in agreement.

The eastern Shadowood was not as fearsome as the greater forest to the west, with its large, twisted trees and sun-blocking canopy. The eastern wood was a mixture of Shadowood trees and evergreens, the latter being the more plentiful farther from the river. These were the trees that Maveezh camped under for the first two nights; tall and imposing, with their sappy wood and dry needles that made for such easy, enjoyable fires. She didn't even have to use her alchemical tricks to get a fire going. Her practice with a flint and tinderbox were enough most nights.

The challenge was keeping her clothing dry. She had needed to dismount and lead her horse past hazards on the ill-kept road, and succeeded in getting her boots, leggings, and skirts quite soaked. She used no tent, since they were a pain to pitch and strike, so she relied on a clothes line near the fire. This was susceptible to nightly snowfall, as was her head and blanket.

The third day of her travel through the forest took her into the Shadowood trees. Even in the light of a clear and crisp morning, the road seemed dark and forbidding. The blue sky could hardly be seen where the boughs stretched over the forest floor. Shadowood trees rarely shed their leaves in autumn or winter; their dark green crowns turned to black and gray, matching the color of their wood and bark. It had the effect of sucking all the color and joy from under its ashen canopy. She could not imagine the drudgery and horror of traveling through the deep Shadowood to the west. Men lost their minds on those roads, it was said.

Close to midday she heard the muted rushing of the river echoing in the ravine ahead. The bridge was nearby. *Not that it matters,* she thought numbly, *the monster hasn't been seen or heard of since last summer.* She wondered what she would do if this latest outing was another failure. *I suppose I could just disappear,* she thought, feeling the amulet pressing against her chest. The high priest had loaned it to protect her from magical detection, fearing one of the count's wizards might try to track her down. Would it not hide her from the high priest as well?

"I could be dead for all he knows," she said aloud, "He probably doesn't care either way. Why not just disappear, you and me?" She patted the horse's muscled neck. "We could start a new life and try to enjoy it, for as long as the world lasts, anyway."

The horse started to wander off the path on its own, remembering that its rider usually dismounted at the bridge. Soon there would be food and rest, it knew. They had made this trip many, many times before.

Maveezh was in no mood to argue. She hopped off and led the beast to a familiar tree, where she tied the reins through the twisted trunk. She removed the saddle, arranged her things, and began to make camp. It didn't matter that she had only been traveling for a few hours today; this was going to be her stop for a couple of days.

The clearing she settled in was a well-used campsite, at least it had been. There was a stone circle for a fire pit, and it was not uncommon for travelers to restock some firewood for the next visitors. Examining the woodpile, Maveezh recognized her own meager handiwork. *I was lazy,* she thought. *Now I'll have to root around for more wood.* She knew she had no one to blame but herself, but she still cursed the imaginary traveler who failed to come this way and make a bigger stack when he left.

She finished kicking the snow away from her campsite and poured a little vial of liquid flame onto the wood in the fire pit. The alchemical mixture ignited in mid-pour, setting the damp logs alight in no time. Warmth and cheer bloomed in the gray shadows of the trees, as the sunlight fought to compete with it.

Maveezh sat on a log near the fire, warming her hands and feet. She pulled the amulet from her bodice, and for the thrill of taking a risk, removed it from around her neck.

Nothing happened. No wizard had appeared in a puff of smoke to arrest her. She felt a little pang of disappointment as she turned it over in her hands, examining its carved surface. It bore the symbol of an eye, surrounded by magical writing, and marred by a deep slash through the center. *A blinded eye,* she thought, *so much like the holy symbol of the cursed Blind God.*

Arathus may be the Tyrant God who doomed humans to be judged, but it was Valdak who did the judging. All dreaded the day when they would stand in the presence of the Blind God and hear their sentence. Would it be pleasures or pain? Being served, or being a servant? Being the vanquisher, or the vanquished?

Followers of Llomaak feared him the most. Llomaak, or Mash as he was called in ancient times, was chaos incarnate. His gift to humanity was a questioning nature and unquenchable desire to *know*. To a god of Order, this was akin to letting the new children run wild. So Arathus countered with a gift of his own: divine judgment. Llomaakittes simply wanted to enjoy one gift without suffering the other.

Now her husband, dead for almost two years, was certainly in the realm of some accursed God of the

Divine Court, suffering for his sins. She wondered where the devout of Mash went for their torment. Did the Tyrant have torture dungeons in his perfect city of Dormos? No one knew, though many had imagined creative answers to this question. Perhaps in elder days, the gods themselves had asked humanity for ideas? Humans were oh so clever when it came to administering suffering.

Poor Ghethas, she thought, staring into the fire, *I hope your judgment is not too harsh; all the more reason for creation to end, and quickly.*

Feeling weary, she stretched out on a blanket to ease her back, gazing up at the gloomy leaves.

She awoke later that evening, as the sun had abandoned its efforts, sinking well beyond the deep forest. The gray woods and shadows had turned black, and a smattering of stars could be seen overhead through the canopy, but only enough to meet the minimum requirement for a night sky. The fire had reduced the logs to glowing embers, and small tongues of red hunger licked out over the blackened cracks to consume the last morsels of fuel.

Maveezh felt a thrill of danger shoot through her, for she had not meant to fall asleep, and had not yet placed her magical protections from beasts and intruders. She might have awoken to a wolf sniffing at her, or worse, an uninvited man. Worse still, the amulet was lying beside her. She had forgotten to put it back on. She scooped it up and placed it around her neck once more.

The horse was standing silently where she had left it, and that was a comfort. She sat up and grabbed more logs for the fire, shoving them into the glowing furnace like a blacksmith with a piece of iron. They caught quickly and the flames began to rise, pushing back the darkness with a cheerful orange light.

That was when she saw she was not alone.

It sat across the road from her campsite, hunched like a gargoyle. The skin was a mottled gray or sickly green, and was stretched taut over large bones and stringy muscles. The head was like an overlarge mask with grotesque, unnatural features. Twisted horns sprouted from a ridged brow. Large, frilled ears swept back in a mockery of delicate elven faerie points. The nose was long and hooked, with warts and large nostrils. A pointed chin jutted out below, and between them, as the thin lips parted, were rows of needle-sharp teeth.

Her pounding heart skipped a beat when the thing opened its eyes. They were like little chips of hate beneath the overhanging brow, catching and reflecting the firelight like the eyes of a cat, or a very large snake.

She felt a trickle of warmth run down her thigh as her body shook with terror. *The guadim, it found **me!***

The thing stirred, shifting and stretching, toying with her. The smell hit her then, the reek of a putrid swamp, of rotting meat. Perhaps the cold and smoke had hidden that scent from her nose, but surely the horse would have smelled it. She risked another glance at the horse and saw that it was stock still, its eyes wide with terror, but totally unmoving. There was no steaming breath coming from its nostrils.

It's under a spell, she realized, *Frozen so it couldn't warn me.*

Her mind raced as she tried to think of what to say, what words could save her. Bevek and his company of men had met the thing in broad daylight; they had been armed, mounted, and with their wits about them. She was alone... gods above and below, how long *had* she been alone with it? How long had it watched her, waiting for her to wake up?

The guadim inclined its head, cracking the spiny bones in its neck. It rose slowly, unveiling its full height as it stretched its back and arms. It looked like a thin, starved corpse, clawing the air with bony fingers long enough to enclose a human head. It dropped its arms to its sides and it hunched, observing her.

Maveezh wanted to scream, but a tiny spark of strength kept her from giving this monster what it wanted. She was a Priestess of Mash after all, and she had been seeking this very meeting. No matter what her instincts told her, she was going to take charge, or die trying.

No, she would *take charge*. To the Abyss with dying.

"*M-Mash bah havaath*," she squeezed the words through a constricted throat.

The creature's eyes narrowed and its ears twitched.

Maveezh got shakily to her feet, feeling the remaining piss move down her leg as her blankets dropped away. She gulped a breath of cold winter air. "*Mash bah havaath!*" she said, conviction edging her voice. The words were as fingers grasping a ledge, all her hopes riding on their strength.

The guadim seemed to sigh, and shaking its horned head, crossed the road in two great strides. It was before her now on the other side of the campfire. It towered over her; had she been on horseback, they might have been eye to eye. Instead it glowered down at her, a hideous parent intimidating a cowering child.

"Words," it croaked in a deep voice, "It knows words, but what else does it know?"

Maveezh felt a prickle of ire rise up in her chest. It did not question the credentials of the men she had sent! She forced a frown saying, "I am a priestess of Mash, a servant of the Countless Lord! We serve the same master." Her fingers found a bundle of divine alchemy in her sleeve. "If you doubt me, I can provide proof, though you may not like it."

The beastly thing smirked, exposing its yellowed teeth. "A priestess traveling alone; I had no idea this bridge was so popular with the mortal minions of Mash."

"I came here for you, master guadim," she said, uncertain how to address such a being, "The men I sent traveling this way last summer spoke of you, and it was decided I needed to seek you out."

"The men *you* sent?" it asked, "So... you were behind their ill-advised mission. Interesting." It squatted down by the fire, knees to its chest.

She flushed, angry now. It was bad enough the high priest wouldn't let her forget how things had gone so horribly wrong, but now this abomination was offering its opinions too.

"I did what I thought was best, but we- *I* underestimated the danger. Regardless, the Dark Heart was delivered, and the scion was revealed. No doubt it is now in the hands of the chosen one." *No doubt.* It sounded so haughty, so sure, yet High Priest DuChat had told her nothing more and it rankled her.

"No doubt," the thing croaked, "But why would you risk so much to seek me out."

I am still in great danger, she knew, *My next words could save me or doom me.*

"Master Guadim," she began, clasping her hands together like a child at prayer, "you told our brethren that you had been driven from Portshia by a vemlok, a 'tamed vemlok' were your words, I believe."

The guadim's eyes narrowed and it snorted in disgust.

Have I offended it? She went on, cautiously, "You said it kept you from doing the will of Mash. May we... assist you somehow? Is there some way the priesthood of Mash could offer its services?"

The creature stared, and Maveezh waited, counting her heartbeats. *Say something, you vile thing,* she thought. Then, *Gods, I hope guadim cannot read minds.*

"You would do whatever I require of you to carry out the will of Mash?" it asked, inclining its head.

"Anything!" she begged. She wanted to accomplish her mission, but immediately began to fear what 'anything' might entail.

"Indeed?" the word rumbled in its chest, "Very well, we shall begin with sating my hunger." It turned to look at her horse.

Maveezh found the following hour horrific, even for a stomach as strong as hers. The guadim butchered her poor mount where it stood, and took its time feasting on the flesh and entrails. She had to wander from the campsite, distancing herself from the foul stench and ghastly feeding habits of her new ally.

She walked onto the center of the bridge, looking up at the veiled stars and wondering how this night had been so... fortuitous? She accomplished her goal after all, but was it dumb luck that the creature had returned to its old haunt on the same night she happened to camp there?

The amulet, she realized, *that's the answer*. She had removed the amulet before falling asleep. The guadim must have some spell or power that lets it see when its territory is being intruded upon, and all of her previous trips into the woods had been wasted because of that one detail. *I was a fly seeking a spider, yet I completely avoided its web.*

Her glance strayed to the feeding monstrosity, lingering out of morbid fascination. *What now?* She wondered, *Without a mount, how will I make any journey?* **Will** *I make any journey?*

The stars wheeled overhead, the moon rose over the night-black leaves, and the guadim finished its meal.

Maveezh returned to collect her belongings; many were still on the saddle, which she had thankfully removed early that day. "What now?" she asked, trying to sound nonchalant amid the steaming, reeking remains of her poor horse. "I hope we do not need to travel far." Her voice carried no hint of her usual sarcasm.

The guadim, its face and claws covered in gore, smirked at her. "Do you know of a man of Portshia named Clavemont?"

"Arton Clavemont?" she asked, taken aback. She racked her brain for information. "He's an albino, a baron with lands in Aurilon; he throws grand parties at his mansion; he's one of the most influential nobles in the city; they call him the Gray Baron, because of his habit of wearing gray, I suppose. His house symbol is a wyvern."

"A 'yes' would have sufficed," the guadim said.

"Well then... yes. What of him?" she asked, as the creature scrubbed off the gore with snow.

"He is the vemlok in question, of course," it said.

That took a moment to sink in. Maveezh and her husband had dined at the same table, at the *count's* table, with Clavemont. They had been to one of his parties afterward, once their phony social standing had been established. He was odd-looking and eccentric to be sure, but a *vemlok?*

She almost questioned this, but that reflexive habit of hers, barely tolerated by the high priest, would be most unwelcome here. If the guadim said Clavemont was a vemlok, then a vemlok he was.

"I did not know they could be so... well, so cordial," she murmured.

"They cannot," the guadim said, "The thirsting spirit usurps the will and makes the vemlok act like a wild animal. But Clavemont managed to tame the hunger. It is a most rare thing."

"So, are we returning to Portshia then?" Maveezh asked. She would love to return to civilization, even to the rat-infested plague city of Portshia. Besides, DuShonmaer was protected by powerful warding spells, keeping the rodents at bay. The high priest Kobus DuChat knew how to live in style.

"We are not," it said, "Paugh was driven out, but Clavemont was too. The presence of the Dark Heart made it too difficult to stay, I think. The raw chaos must have made the thirsting spirit too strong."

Paugh? she thought, *So the creature has a name. Not that I dare use it yet.*

"Clavemont is no longer in Portshia?" she asked, "Then where is he?"

"Hiding in the forest, I warrant." Paugh said, "Or perhaps the forest does not want him. Perhaps he is sulking in a field somewhere." It snorted a laugh that sounded like a sick man's cough.

"How will we find him?" she asked, almost not wanting to know.

"Whispers and bait," Paugh said with a needly grin. It arched its back and with a sick popping, stretching sound, two giant bat-like wings unfolded from its shoulders. Before Maveezh could say another word, it grasped her in its powerful fingers and launched them into the frigid night air.

Chapter Twenty Three

Muster

Jaron's daily walk took him past the Grand Portshia Theater, which had occupied his mind for the last nine days. Something had bothered him about the whole affair, and his brief meeting with the mysterious, masked author had raised his suspicions. Why go to such lengths as to disguise one's face in a frightful mask?

That in particular bothered him, as it reminded him of Cindra's stories from her Galindri exile. Evil men in beast masks were overheard threatening the realm, and she almost became their next victim. One of those very men had been killed almost two years ago, attempting to murder Cindra in the school. But did that mean that every rich fop in a mask was an evil priest of Llomaak? Of course not. Some people were just weird.

Yet he could swear he had met the man before. He could not place those eyes, but there was something familiar about them. It kept him awake at night. It made him decide to walk past the theater every day, hoping for a flash of insight or a glimpse of the man. So far, nothing.

And that wasn't the only thing that had been bothering him; eight days ago when Gavadaire bid them farewell, the fire had gone cold during their meeting. Jaron hadn't seen something like that happen since all the fires went out in the Dancing Cow tavern seven months ago; even the flame of his magic sword had been extinguished. That mad old wizard had been to blame, he was sure of it, but where was the old fool now?

Filbert decided to follow him on his morning walks, for he had jumped at any chance to leave the overcrowded training hall. The Freekirk School had become a boarding house for sullen soldiers, plucked from their daily lives and made to march east for the king. No one grumbled about it much, but they took out their frustrations by generally being unpleasant to each other.

"It's a wonder to me," Filbert said, "that the men spend so much of their time in the vicinity of the school."

"Why is that?" Jaron asked.

"Well," he said, "they're free to wander about if they like, they only need report back at morning and night for meals and roll call. But most just huddle about the block."

Jaron replied, "Most of them have never been in a city of any size, and Portshia is rather large. It'd be easy to get lost if you stray too far, especially for a peasant farmer or country yeoman."

"I suppose so," Filbert said, "but they'd be more pleasant if they went and found some other entertainments once in a while."

Jaron used a bawdy tone and asked, "What did you have in mind?"

Filbert shook his head, "Not everything is whores. There are gambling houses, taverns, the market square, libraries..."

"Libraries!" Jaron laughed, "I think you overestimate our fellow brothers-in-arms. Most of them can't read, and those that can don't do so for leisure. Nor do they have your connections."

Filbert only shrugged. It had been some time since he had been to a library himself, and wondered if his invitation was still open. Being part of a famous wizard family had its privileges. He had to remind himself that most people couldn't just walk into a library and read what they wanted.

"Have you heard anything new about Arch Mage Finnael?" Jaron asked.

"They say he's recuperating in Casselvane Keep, under guard. One thing's certain: he won't be traveling with us to war in the shape he's in."

"Pity," Jaron said, "I hear talk, and many think *he* caused the disaster at DuChat's mansion; that a nasty spell backfired on him."

"Nonsense," Filbert scoffed, "Whatever that was, it was no spell I've ever heard of."

"But aren't the wizards of the moon tower supposed to study different magics than the Mystic College? Maybe it was something new?"

"The Order of Astrellaris isn't as structured and regulated as the college, but they still have ethics. Making a spell that kills indiscriminately like that would get a wizard shunned for life."

"Then where did it come from?" Jaron asked.

"Well, if the king is to be believed, DuChat was a high priest of Llomaak. It was probably some wicked kind of divine alchemy."

"I've never heard of alchemy like that."

"No one has," Filbert said, "but then no one thought the priesthood of Chaos still existed."

They returned to the fighting school, trading the open stink of the city streets for the close stink of the courtyard; its dozens of lounging soldiers were gathered against the eastern wall to sit in the morning shade. Dozens more waited within, occupying themselves on the training floor by tossing dice or playing at cards. Some told stories from home, and Jaron recognized a few, having heard them already.

Bradric Hyne, the big horse trader's son who was Cord's new squire, approached as they entered. "Master Dunlorden, er, Sir Jaron," he said, "Sir Cord asks that you join him in the master's hall."

Jaron sighed, "Am I in trouble again?"

Bradric gave a weak smile, "I think we all are."

Jaron gave Filbert some busywork and went to the master's hall, where Cord and his brothers were gathered. As he entered, they nodded to him with dour faces and troubled eyes.

"What is it?" Jaron asked, instantly feeling a cold dread in his stomach.

Ceven spoke, "I was delivering a report to central command last night, and I heard some troubling gossip. I didn't want to spread it, but I believe it's true." He spoke softer, even though the men were quite alone and secure, "They say that an assassin has struck up north, and that the count's nephew was murdered, along with some other young knights."

"Gaius Corrina, our former student," Cord said grimly.

Jaron was struck. He had not been close with the boy, since the lad had borne him some ill will, but that had cleared up after Cindra's revelation. They had all parted on good terms.

An assassin!

Colin stroked his large mustache saying, "Word is that the count and the king are outraged, and decided to take the initiative, rather than wait for the spring thaw."

Carstin huffed, "This enemy has already claimed several nobles with their damned assassins. Remember the ambush last year along the north road to Velloness? Eleven barons! It's a wonder they didn't have a mass desertion."

Cord said, "It has been advised that lords and commanders leading their troops display no coat of arms or banner to mark them as such. We don't want a repeat of that incident."

"Balkon's bowels," Colin spat, "They already have us cowering like turtles."

A trumpet sounded outside in the street, barely audible through the high windows.

"That's an officer's summons," said Carstin, "We'd best see to it."

Jaron and the Freekirk brothers met with a mounted messenger at the school's gates. He was dressed in a herald's finery, with a blue and gold jacket and streamers upon his sleeves, and he wore a long trumpet upon a baldric.

"What news?" Cord asked in his booming voice.

The messenger said in an official tone, "Officers of His Majesty's army, the king hereby orders the readiness of all troops, wagons, beasts and baggage, to march on the morrow. You have the day to prepare. Muster will begin at daybreak and companies will proceed to either the Trader's Gate or the Golden Gate, heading north with His Majesty's banner."

"Understood," Cord said, casting his eyes down the street. From the front gate of the school, the Trader's Gate was just a block north up the street.

"All commanders are to report readiness to the palace tonight," he said, and with a nod, he rode off to his next stop, checking his folded map.

"Well, there it is," Colin said, "It would seem the rumors are true indeed."

"Don't go spreading them yet," Cord said, "If that's the reason for the change in plans, then we'll know for sure when we reach Syngmore."

"I wonder," Carstin said, "if Baron Syngmore will be best suited to lead the Corrina forces, considering his loss."

"Who can say?" Ceven said, "At least he will be motivated to fight."

"Wrath and vengeance are not the best motivations," Jaron said.

True enough, Cord thought, glad that Jaron could see that much.

"I guess we will miss the play," Filbert said glumly.

Jaron nodded in agreement as he checked the straps on his new armor. "Our worries may have been for nothing anyway. Still, I could have used the diversion."

"Same," Filbert said, "I'm still not convinced that the play is so innocent. I don't believe the author was anonymous just because he's shy."

"Perhaps not," Jaron agreed, "but it's no longer our concern. We have a long march to look forward to. It's over 200 miles to the borders of the dissenter lands. I doubt they'll be coming to meet us there."

"What's the plan?" Filbert asked. He knew that Jaron was not privy to any war planning, but it couldn't hurt to ask.

"Well," he answered, "We've been talking, the brothers and I, and we think the best bet would be the taking of Odex just south of the border, to delay DeKenric's advance, should he choose to fight. Then we'll advance east and take the towns on the way to Ahrnok. The northern army will link up with us at some point, helping to shield our flank."

"What then?" Filbert asked.

"A long siege, I imagine," Jaron said.

"Why not take the dissenter lords first?"

Jaron considered a moment and replied, "DeKenric should be held in check because we have his son hostage, and the other lords have sworn to Wolvert, who has declared himself king of the east. Once Wolvert falls, the other lords should hopefully lose heart. At least, that's what our own private war council thinks."

"Doesn't sound very likely," he said.

Jaron was about to remind Filbert that he had no experience in strategy and warfare, but then he remembered that Filbert was the most learned young man he knew. Who could say what he had studied in his visits to the libraries? "What would you do?" Jaron asked.

Filbert answered right away, having thought on it quite a bit already. "I would take the southern lands first, starting with Wensicton on the Gayles River confluence. It's the most defensible position if you want to limit approaches from Sulund, Deltovane, and Alvavane. House LuVeness of Alvavane is likely funding much of the war effort; if the southern army can secure 'King Wolvert's' banker, and prevent enemy forces from massing behind our lines, that would serve better."

Gods, we should have invited him to our private council, Jaron thought, his cheeks coloring slightly. *I hope the king has tacticians at least as good as my squire.*

"A good strategy," Jaron said, "What about DeKenric cutting off our rear flank?"

"Well, we have his son hostage, don't we?" Filbert answered with a bit of a tone that Jaron didn't like. It reminded him that Grigor's arrest had been largely his own fault. *It was all for the best, wasn't it?*

"Assuming that keeps him out of the fight," Jaron replied, "what then? Sit on Wensicton?"

"Take half the force and march through Bakshire Province straight to Ahrnok," he said.

"Bakshire Province is neutral in this," Jaron reminded him, "They haven't declared for the separatist forces."

"Nor have they declared for their rightful king, surrounded by Dissenter Houses as they are," Filbert said, "but put a royal army on their doorstep and they might decide where their loyalties lie."

Jaron chuckled, "Who would have thought you had such a head for this business? We poor soldiers were thinking of the direct route. How did you come up with all of this?"

Filbert shrugged, "I read books and maps, and studied military strategy when I could."

Jaron shook his head, "We shall see if the king and his war council agree with your strategy once we reach the Dissenter lands. In the meantime, it is our duty to get ready for the march." He slapped the young man on the back and went off to see to his horse.

The soldiers in the fighting school were busy for much of the afternoon packing their gear, making last-minute supply runs, and drilling in the courtyard. The Freekirk brothers took turns sorting out their troops, doing inspections, and issuing orders for the morning. As the captain of the company, Sir Cord gave the order that before they would leave for war, the school would be scrubbed from top to bottom, and all would be left better than they found it. He'd be damned if he left the job to Elmore and Celia, his aging caretakers. They had been run ragged enough.

Seeing the troops standing for inspection, Jaron finally got to see them as they would present themselves on the field. Most of them had little or no armor beyond their thick, quilted gambeson jackets. A few wore shirts of mail with leather gloves, but many had no proper helmets. The common weapon was a long spear or pike, and some wore arming swords or axes. There were no archers in the company, which was not unusual for Cordo men. Archers were more expensive to train and equip than spearmen, and House Freekirk trusted more in men-at-arms on horseback to carry the day.

Jaron had to admit that it was a tradition that was fast becoming antiquated.

Lastly, he looked at their footwear. The majority wore wrapped or stitched leather shoes, suitable for a day's work, but not so good for a long march in the snow. He said a prayer to the Jaydecean nature gods that the weather would be kind. If not, there would be many a blackened toe before they reached their first battle. He looked down at his own fine riding boots and thanked the gods his father had found a better life than most farmers. He knew just how little separated him from the lowly footmen arrayed before him.

The trained fighting men were another matter. There were sixteen knights or men-at-arms, all shining, polished, and arrayed at attention. Most had full or partial plate armor, or settled for brigandine armor, which looked like a studded leather or cloth jacket on the outside, but had metal strips riveted into the lining. Each had an arming sword or mace, a metal kite shield, a dagger, and a lance or spear. Some of the men fought on horseback, while others made capable footmen. They were the wealthier men in their little province, and each had a small contingent of servants and followers that would support them.

Jaron knew this meager offering was just one company in a much larger fighting force, but it felt less than encouraging. When he and Sir Cord had fought in the Battle of Lintheid, they had a similar force of Cordo men, but luckily other lords had provided archers and crossbowmen to balance out the king's forces. Come to think of it, most of those had been mercenaries hired with gold rather than landed men owing military service to their lord. Such was the way of things. *Has it been eight years already since my first battle?*

First muster and inspection had concluded, and Jaron was given the report to speed to the palace headquarters. As the men prepared for their last day in the safety of Portshia's walls, Jaron had Filbert saddle his horse.

"I shall return late, I think," Jaron told him, "I plan to do a little reconnaissance."

"What for, sir?" Filbert asked.

"I've never seen a city-wide preparation before. I might learn something," he said.

"Have fun," Filbert said, shaking his head.

Jaron didn't know if it would be fun, but it would be better than milling about the school. "Finish cleaning my armor before nightfall, and check our rations again," he said, then he guided his chestnut stallion Vortigern out of the crowded stable and into the more crowded streets.

Riding towards the Temple Walk, Jaron could already see a large crowd of men lining up to enter the Temple of Balkon, with its domed, spiked roof and imposing relief carvings. The gray and black structure was wreathed in a haze of incense and smoke, and the deep chanting of red-haired priests could be heard over the din of the city. Jaron felt his spirit drawn to the place, with his hopes and prayers on his lips, aching for release in the presence of the gods. Yet the gods were not present, and prayers were little more than offerings of breath to the empty air. *Perhaps it is better this way,* he thought, *after all, every warrior prays to Balkon, and they can't all be victorious. Better to ask history how a battle was lost than to ask a god why.*

The other temples were doing business as well; soldiers and their families spent what little they had to purchase vials of divine alchemy to treat wounds, cure sickness or keep parasites at bay. Fleas and lice were a real problem in military camps, and the women who followed the army could use all the help they could get. Jaron hoped there would be a decent amount of camp followers, for an army that marched without women suffered more sickness and hardship, and had fewer to collect and prepare the dead for burial.

The priesthoods were preparing their own troops for battle. Lelonethan brothers and sisters would set up camp hospitals, Eyoronian scholars would act as chroniclers of the campaign; Balkonittes would bless the soldiers and fight in their own units; red hatted priests of Obamir would accompany the baggage train and act as treasurers, doling out payment for service and goods. Valdakians would oversee the burial of the dead. There would even be some priests of Arathus present to bless the king's endeavors, since the King God favored rightful monarchs and disfavored upstarts.

All representatives of the Divine Court would accompany the army except the Selvinians, and whatever Tavenji's followers called themselves. The followers of the love goddess had no place in the realm of war, and Tavenji had no priesthood; he was favored by thieves and performers.

As he approached the market square he was amazed at the number of tents erected on the cobblestones, many of them flying banners he did not recognize. There were perhaps a hundred pavilion tents in all, each capable of sleeping five or more soldiers in close company. There were a great many horses too, not stabled but hobbled together in rows where they could be easily fed. The smell of human and animal waste was intense, even with the drainage grates being used to dispose of it. There were almost no merchants to be seen, save for those that could maneuver their wares through the narrow passages between tents.

Jaron knew that most of the city's merchants had been cleaned out of food and much-needed supplies, and at purveyance prices. He had purchased some goods himself and felt guilty paying so little; the merchants had made no complaints, but then they wouldn't to his face.

He could have turned towards the palace, but he wanted to explore a little more. There were a large number of soldiers being marched over the canal bridges towards the harbor district, and he wanted to find out why. He guided his horse through the congested thoroughfare towards the North River Walk, the road that ran alongside the canal. As he approached the Sea Gate and passed into the old fishing district, he saw a remarkable sight.

The harbor was full of warships. Colorful sails were furled on tall yardarms, cannons bristled from gun ports, and hundreds of men were loading supplies aboard caravels and carracks, cramming as much as they could into the lower holds. Teams of rowboats or water oxen took on tug duty, maneuvering the ships about and managing the limited space. Beyond the inner harbor were many more tall ships, awaiting the rest of the fleet.

So there is to be an invasion by sea as well! Jaron thought, *They will sail along the coast, engage any enemy ships, and land their forces... where? Kyvon-on-Gayles? That must be it.* Kyvon-on-Gayles was the seat of Sulund Province and secured the mouth of the Gayles River, which bisected the southern Dissenter territories. With that taken, they could march into Kenric or Sulund lands and be supplied on the river. *How many are committed to this assault? Twenty or more ships, each with one hundred, maybe two hundred soldiers aboard, that's as many as four thousand, maybe more..*

Would they arrive at their objective before the army made it around the Cassel Mountains by land? He wondered how much resistance they would meet. Jaron was not familiar with the naval power of the coastal Dissenter Houses, but he assumed they must have their own fleets. War with Aurilon was in the not-so-distant past, and that had mostly been a naval incursion. *Gods, what if Aurilon supports the Dissenters by sea? Surely they'd not get directly involved.* The thought was chilling, and he prayed that those men did not meet their doom aboard sinking ships.

He watched the spectacle for a good while, noticing that the local fishermen had little else to do but watch as well. Finally he turned his mount and headed back through the Sea Gate into the Silver District, making for the palace. He passed carpenters loading large and small beams of lumber aboard long carts, which Jaron recognized as disassembled siege engines. They were old-style trebuchet and mangonel parts; still useful in this age of expensive and weighty bronze cannons, and only needing to be assembled on site. Barrels of arrows were being loaded also, so many he could not guess at their number. Fletchers and arrowsmiths must have been working night and day for many months, and Jaron hoped they had been well-compensated for it.

He rode through the palace gates, past the smaller tents in the tree-lined gardens and the larger pavilions in the inner courtyard. Hopping off his horse, he went inside to find Constable Fingelm.

Arias Fingelm was more of an administrator than a fighter, but he had martial training in his youth and was tapped to aid the count in the defense of Syngmore Castle. Jaron wondered if the man had a suit of armor that still fit, as he had gone rather soft.

"Constable!" he called, spotting the man through the bustle, near a table full of paperwork. Jaron held his report up, waving it overhead.

"Ah, Sir Jaron," Fingelm said, sounding weary. "All is well at the Freekirk School, I trust?"

"As well as can be, considering," he said, "We were expecting a few more weeks before marching."

"Yes, as were we," Fingelm said, "Thankfully most of our preparations were made in advance."

"About that," Jaron said, "what made the king decide to march before the spring thaw?"

"What have you heard?" the constable asked, looking from under his red eyebrows.

"Dark news from up north," Jaron admitted, "Regarding the count's nephew."

Fingelm sighed and hung his head, "'Tis true," he said sadly, "We received a rider two days ago from Syngmore; he told us the news that Gaius Corrina and three other lads had been killed in a stable inside the city walls. Gaius and another boy had been strangled, perhaps by some magical means. Two other boys had their throats cut." The constable rubbed his eyes. "The count flew into a rage when he heard, and the king was seething, but silent. The other lords were outraged as well. There was a motion to march immediately and avenge the murder. The king thought on it for a time, and agreed."

Jaron could not imagine what Baron Corrina of Syngmore must be going through, but he shared some of the outrage at the crime. Death on the battlefield was one thing, but a cowardly murder in one's own home was quite another. It was certainly the work of an assassin, and a magic-using one at that. Such men did not come cheap, nor were they used lightly. The Dissenters were striking at the heart of House Corrina before they even took the field.

He hoped Cindra was safe on her errantry. She would be far from the fighting, just traveling the Joshian Way through the Shadowood. How perilous could that be? He had done it himself, and alone.

"And that's not all," Fingelm said quietly, "Do not make this known, but it seems we were deceived regarding Grigor Evenast, the DeKenric heir."

This was news. Jaron said, "I will keep it to myself." *As well as I can*, he thought.

"Arch Mage Finnael revealed that Grigor DeKenric had, in fact, escaped around the New Year, and the prisoner we have been keeping was a face-shifting duplict!"

"What?"

Fingelm nodded, "The king had him killed once revealed, but it is not widely known. We do not have the leverage we had hoped for on Baron DeKenric and his forces. Things may go ill sooner than we thought."

"Good to know," Jaron said, "We may have to cross the Weness River and besiege Kenric Castle."

"Let us hope it does not come to that," the constable said, "We may have the advantage of numbers, but one man on a castle wall is worth ten men assaulting it."

Jaron had to agree. He had studied sieges, but had never participated in one. The idea was daunting to even the stout of heart. Kenric was granite and steel, and not to be underestimated. "I should get back to my company," he said, and bowing, took his leave.

Chapter Twenty Four

The Buried Lord

Maveezh had never been so miserable. The guadim had snatched her up and flown with her in its talons, claws digging into her flesh. She had managed to retrieve her rations and a change of clothing from her devoured horse's saddlebags, but nothing else. She had eaten her last ration yesterday evening, and today was a cold, hungry day. Her own smell disgusted her, but it was nothing compared to her companion, which reeked of a rotting bog. Worse, the guadim had been hopping about from clearing to clearing, following some unheard call. With little warning, it would snatch her up like baggage and fly off to a new location, adding its stench to her own and terrifying her all over again.

They were now somewhere south of Syngmore castle, high up in the foothills where no trail or path could lead.

"Are we there yet?" she asked once again.

"Stop asking," the guadim snarled, "And yes, we are." It folded its wings and circled the area with heavy footfalls, looking at something in the center of the clearing. The thin blanket of snow began to melt under its gaze, trickling away down the hillside.

"Where is he?"

The guadim pointed to the spot it had uncovered; a bare patch of undisturbed earth.

Maveezh didn't know what to make of that, but then she was not sure what to expect. How did a vemlok hide itself anyway?

"He is here," Paugh said, inclining its horned head, "The Whispers see and hear much; yes, he is here."

"So what do we do now?" she asked, "Knock?"

"Feed him," the guadim said, and rushing forward, it flicked its claw across her neck, opening a vein.

Maveezh recoiled and let out a choked cry, grasping at her slashed throat. The blood flowed between her fingers, warm and sticky, soothing her dry, icy-cold hands. She had a terrible feeling about this mission, she knew something like this could happen, but hoped her faith would protect her. It seems Llomaak had chosen her to die at this time, just before the end of the world. She wouldn't even get to see it. But would she see her husband?

The initial shock wore off and her anger flashed at the creature's betrayal, its callous disregard for her life and holy mission. She wished she could strike it dead somehow, but she had nothing at hand. What would kill a monster so ancient and vile anyway? She lashed out with the only weapon she had: her words.

"Thrice cursed monster! Fickle cowardly beast! May you die and be forced to lick the Tyrant's golden ass!" She fell to her knees and sputtered, but the guadim moved in and held her head down, forcing her to watch as her life's blood flow onto the cold ground.

As her vision became dim and narrow, she watched the blood seep away, as if the dirt was drinking it. *No,* she thought, *something under the dirt.* Suddenly the hard ground parted and two pale hands broke the surface, grabbing her arms and pulling her down. She resisted with all her remaining might, twisting and heaving against the steely grip, using her last ounces of strength to hold on to every second of life she could. *There is so much to live for!*

Yet the hands had her, skin on cold skin, and were draining her life away with every heartbeat. She sank into the earth as the soil parted for her, and in a moment there was no sign that anything had happened at all; just a bare patch of undisturbed earth, and a crouching, chuckling guadim.

The earth was freezing, and all her warmth was being stolen away; she would have been freezing in a warm bed by a fire. The dirt pressed into her nose, mouth, and ears. Her eyes were shut and she couldn't breathe. She could not move to struggle; the soil had ceased to yield for her and became solid earth once again, locking her in place like a fossil. All she felt were the hands upon her arms, powerful hands that grew warmer as she grew colder.

Have you come to die? It was a voice in her head, not her own; a man's voice, silky and raw.

No, she thought, frantically, *I want to live! I came to find you!*

Then you came to die, the voice replied, *for I am death*.

She felt like she was drifting on the water, sinking into a cloud of cool air. Then there was nothing.

Nothing but the dream.

In the dream she was not herself. She was a boy, young and strong, yet pale as a bone, with translucent skin showing blue veins beneath. White hair fell about his shoulders. She examined the unfamiliar limbs and tried to speak, but she had no voice. *Who am I?* She asked herself in her thoughts.

You are me, said the masculine voice, *Observe*.

But I am dying, she thought, ever the contrary one, *How can I be-*

That is in the past, said the voice, *You died three days ago. Now you are returning. Observe so that you may survive as I have.*

She could understand that at least, though her mind reeled at the revelation. *Survive.* She would observe and survive.

I was the lord of my lands, the Count DuClavemont, wealthy and powerful, but born cursed and different, he said. Maveezh felt herself move to stand before a small mirror of bronze; within she saw a grand hall of wood and stone, with statues of wyverns stretching their wings and roaring to the ceiling. The young boy in the mirror was Arton Clavemont, no doubt about it. The albino lord had an unmistakable countenance and complexion. White lashes like feathers fluttered as he blinked. He was dressed in fine, colored garb of an ancient make; fashions Maveezh had only seen in murals and old tapestries.

I was born in Aurilon, in the Celvestrian year 4998, in the Age of Kymboth. The Gartethan calendar had not yet been made, he said, *The world was more than halfway through the Time of Chaos, the hundred year reign of terror of the mad King Orthicus.* The scene in the mirror shifted into a blur of wonders and terrors, of lands and skies filled with flying beasts and magic, of Kyraine and Guadim fighting for the will of gods who no longer spoke to them, and of mortals trying to survive it. The years flew by until the young man in the mirror had reached maturity, achieving the angled face and gracefully delicate masculine beauty of the lord she knew. But for his complexion and ears, he could be of elven kind.

I was in my twenties when I met her, he said, *my love made flesh, Navinessia, my Winter's Kiss. She was so like myself; skin like porcelain, hair like snow, and eyes like gemstones set in alabaster. She was Ilvaya, one of the People of Light; lesser than her ancient kin, but glorious and graceful beyond mortal dreams. I fell for her, and against all odds, she fell for me, and I followed her into battle with my armies against the forces of Chaos that had swept over the land.*

Maveezh felt the love he held for this elven beauty, as though she held that love herself. It was like a sickness that crept into her soul and settled there, displacing her love for her husband. As she tried to reject it, a stronger will intervened. *Observe*, it said, *Feel.*

Moments of bliss and joy interspersed with pain and danger, but always they were together and the stronger for it. Years passed; first one decade, then another. Clavemont was now the age she had always seen him, a mature but youthful forty years.

The Dark King fell. Order triumphed for a time, and my Navinessia needed healing; not of the body, but of the soul, he said, *War had changed us both, and she could not bear the pain any longer. She told me she needed to withdraw for a time, to heal her spirit.*

I did not understand what she meant. Would she leave me and return to some distant land? Would she depart for the realm of spirit where the Ilves claim to go? Would I be alone? I feared for it, I dreaded the thought of life without her, she who was my everything.

Maveezh was awash now in the fear of loss, in the emotions she shared with Clavemont. She had no choice but to give in to it now; her own loss was like a distant memory of pain. She did not know love could be so cruel, so terrifying, so vital that the removal of it was like the removal of breath, of blood.

Was this what it was to love an immortal elf? Or was this a love she had been incapable of?

She saw the woman's face very close now, could smell her scent, like holly blossoms. Were they in a moment of bliss? Were they at a parting? She could not tell; the emotions were swirling too strong and too fast, threatening to whisk her away in a whirlpool of joy, pain, sorrow and hope.

She would leave me, and she would not, he said, *She entrusted me with a secret known to no other of our kind, a secret so dangerous that only the eldest Ilves still knew it...* His voice grew strained and choked, full of pain and hurt and regret. What came next shook her to her very core. She screamed.

The cold earth heaved and was rent apart under the pale moon as the vemlok burst from her grave. She gasped, gulping in the frigid night air, but it gave no relief. She rubbed her arms, feeling the cold upon them, but it no longer bothered her. Her needs were different now.

"What have you done to me?" she husked, spitting bits of dirt as she spoke.

Clavemont rose from the earth, head first, as though he were standing on a platform under a stage. The dirt moved aside for him, even shed itself from his clothing. It rippled and closed beneath his feet. "I fed upon you; I killed you..." he said, "Then I waited."

"Waited... for what?" she said, examining her gray, claw-like hands with pale, milky eyes.

"Waited to see if a thirsting spirit would take you," he replied, "and one did. It would seem the dark times have come again."

"Why-what..." she stammered as her body trembled, "Why do I feel this pain, this guilt? Your guilt! Why did you make me feel that?"

"It was my hope," he said, "that if you felt as I did, suffered as I did, your will would steel itself against the thirsting spirit, at least for a time. It seems I was right."

She stumbled about the clearing, feeling her body to make sure it was all there. Her skin was deathly gray, her nails were extended like talons, and her clothing was saturated with dirt. She imagined her hair was a rat's nest, and she was glad to not have a mirror. But the *hunger*, the hunger was the worst she had ever felt. It pulled at every fiber of her being.

Her eyes fell on the guadim, who was squatting and smirking nearby.

"You!" she leveled a claw at him, "You used me as bait, and now *look* at me!"

It only chuckled. "Careful what you wish for," it said, "I have waited three days to see how you turned out. To be honest, I was rather hoping for a slavering, mindless ghoul."

"I should make *you* my first meal," she snarled, fingers flexing. But a hand fell on her bare shoulder and her skin drank in the blood from it, blissful and radiant, flowing through her body like a warm summer breeze over chilled flesh. She shuddered at the sensation.

"No," Clavemont said, "Take some of mine, Lemorea. A guadim is the last thing you want to feed upon. Its black blood is a pollutant, killing even the flies that bite it, or turning them vile and grotesque. It stains the land it spills upon, and taints the magic of spirit wells. Never touch a guadim unless it's with a blade."

Paugh hissed at him.

Clavemont removed his hand and she turned to face him, a bit of color returning to her eyes and cheeks. She said, "Is it true? What you showed me about our- *your* love. Is it true?"

He nodded, sadly. "Yes, all of it."

"There is more," Paugh said in a merry sing-song, "The world is ending. The age is closing. Take what you can, and to the Abyss with old pledges of faith and love." He rubbed his hands together eagerly. "The Whispers have told me much, and I have watched and learned. I know where the secret place is, and I know how to get there."

Clavemont snarled and turned away. "I came here to escape temptation and exposure. Why would I care to follow you now? Just because you fed me?"

"I came to give you her, because she sought you out," Paugh said, "Ask her."

Maveezh nodded, falling to her knees, "It is true, Lord Clavemont. I was sent from Portshia by my high priest. He seeks your aid to prevent the elves from returning to fight in the final war! He fears such power could alter the will of Mash and undo what has been done."

He recoiled at the words, saying, "Have you learned nothing? Nothing I tried to teach you?"

"I have learned, my lord," she said, "I have learned that your love for one has held you back from many, and your guilt has shackled you. Free yourself and join in the will of Mash! Do as you will, judgment be damned-"

Her words were cut off as Clavemont struck her, sending her flying back into a tree. The wood cracked and clumps of snow showered about her; she slumped to the ground, but found she was unharmed. With her back against the tree, she rose to her feet, shaving off the bark with her shoulders.

"Coward," she said, "Afraid that you will lose control again? So what? Who is left to love, to hurt? We have lost everything we cared about, you and I. What does it matter if we indulge ourselves?"

His eyes flashed and he drew his sword, dashing at her in a motion so swift it shocked even her new senses. The blade pinned her through her voice box to the tree, rendering her mute. Her eyes were wide and bloodshot as she stared into his pale blue gaze. She remembered pain, and knew she should feel it, but it just wasn't in her tonight.

"You know nothing of loss," he said, but the words sounded hollow. It was a joke almost; such sentiment coming from a corpse that fed on others.

She smiled, seeing him falter. She was a ghastly sight to behold as her eyes went wide, and her bloodless lips parted above a pierced throat.

He withdrew the blade and Maveezh felt the wound start to close. Her body demanded more blood in exchange, but she resisted the urge to touch the lord. *Resist while you can*, she thought, *Resist and keep your mind. Resist so you may honor Mash and the memory of Ghethas as you feast on the living.*

So much to live for.

Chapter Twenty Five

Bloodlines

Gavadaire suspected he was losing his mind.

He had left the port of Madeless as fast as he was able, lest the tales of his voyage mark him as the cursed man he was. He had now been on the road through the mountains of Aurleona Province for five days.

Let's see, it's... Massday? Tomorrow is Beshday, then Rolonday and after that is... Gods, why can't I think? Hwessday! That's it, Hwessday, named for Hwessa, the goddess of the winds.

He was on foot, because his last two attempts to ride had ended terribly. He had Shired a carriage in Madeless to take him to the next town, but the wheels kept falling off every few miles. Then he had purchased a horse with what precious coin he could spare, but the beast had taken ill. It finally had to be put down after it started bleeding from the eyes and nose two days ago.

He might have chalked it up to bad luck or ill omens, were it not for the cursed jewel buried in his chest. He checked it a few times a day to make sure he was not imagining things; the leather thong just disappeared into his flesh, and when he pulled on it, he felt it in his breastbone and ribs. It made him feel sick, but he had to try something.

During his time on the road, he had stopped to rest and eat at tea houses, inns, and taverns. Now those places were all abuzz with the strange tales of his visit, and he found himself avoiding them as he traveled. Roaring fires had gone cold in moments, or new fires started mysteriously. Fresh bread went moldy, wine and ale turned sour, water became stagnant or acidic, and illness befell people and animals alike. As the locals started to talk and wonder who was to blame, they eventually settled on him. He imagined this is how witches must feel, but no one had dared to confront him yet, and for that he was grateful.

Evening was falling now, and so was the temperature. Camp fires had become unreliable, so he needed real shelter. He passed a road marker that read:

DuVestra Noávu ~ 20 mi
DuVestra L'Granmaer ~ 35 mi

"One more day to the border," he muttered, "and most of another to the castle town. Then I need to find the Baron LuVestra."

There were no villages nearby, but he did see a roadside shrine up ahead where he could take some shelter from the gathering storm clouds that tumbled over the mountains.

"At least I won't bother anyone," he said. *Why am I talking to myself? Am I expecting a conversation?*

The shrine was a small building of stone and wood dedicated to Obamir, god of wealth and trade, and protector of travelers. Within was a statue of the portly deity, with a slot cut above his belt to offer coins for safe travel. Gavadaire wondered how often the shrine keeper came to empty the belly, or if the coins magically disappeared, taken by the god.

No, he thought, *there is no divine magic involved in making coins disappear. There is always a human hand behind it.*

He rubbed the idol's belly for luck, huddled as far into the shrine as he could, and bundled his woolen cloak about him. He stayed awake long enough to see the rain begin, and then passed into a deep, troubled sleep.

Gavadaire awoke, shivering, as the rays of the morning sun broke to cleave the fog in the valley pass. Water was flowing somewhere nearby, and the birds were beginning to sing in the thickets. As he stretched his limbs and his aching back, he had the brief pleasure of witnessing a beautiful morning, one devoid of nightmares, cursed gemstones, and the dread that now hung over his existence.

Gathering his things, he turned to thank Obamir for the night's shelter. To his horror, the idol was in a ruined state, as was the shrine itself.

No! It was not like this last night, surely!

The paint had cracked and peeled, showing the wood beneath, which was now rotting and gray. The idol was pitted and spotted with mold and decay. Reaching out, he rubbed the belly of the fat god, and gritty residue was eroded by his fingertips.

"No!" he shouted into the mountain morning, "It wasn't like this!"

His voice echoed across the valley, hushing all who heard it, as though the words were obscenity that shocked the listener into stunned silence.

After a long moment, the birds erupted into squawking and frenzied flight, leaving every tree and thicket and vanishing into the fog. Then the ground itself began to move, rumbling and quaking beneath his boots. Water in a nearby stream began to slosh and spray; he felt like he was again on the deck of a ship in a turbulent sea, fighting to keep his balance as the trees swayed violently.

Then as suddenly as it had come, it subsided.

Talk of the earthquake was on the lips of everyone he met the next few days. The people were shaken visibly, as were the buildings. Cracks in plaster, broken glass, and leaning house frames told of the power of the quake. But for all the disturbance and confusion, it was still the land of his birth, and he felt a special closeness with it.

It was a great comfort to return home to his people, even as they picked up the pieces from the quake. He missed the architecture, the language, and the fashions, even among the ordinary folk. Commoners wore more colorful attire than their Calilonian neighbors; shades of red, yellows, greens, and the occasional violet added to the typical blues and earth-tones.

Gavadaire's attire was pushing the boundaries of what the sumptuary laws allowed, but no one paid him any mind, and he preferred it that way. He talked to no one, and stopped only when necessary. If his curse affected anyone in the villages he passed through, no one traced it to him. The last thing he wanted to do was to cause anyone more grief, especially himself.

There was one good thing that he noticed about his new condition, and it was something that only occurred to him as he rested under a tree. He was not really tired; he had been taking breaks and sleeping almost out of habit, but the truth was he was not very fatigued at all after the constant walking. Even his feet were in good condition, though his boots should have caused him enormous blisters by now. The thing in his chest gave him a constitution and stamina that amazed him. He felt he could run all the way to Vestra if he wanted, though he was not ready to test his limits yet.

He continued on with a quickened stride, thankful for little favors.

He reached the castle town of Vestra on the 16th of Selvimoth, eleven days after he left Portshia on his ill-fated errand. He prayed that Baron Gelvard LuVestra, Grigor DeKenric's great uncle, would know how to undo this curse and free him. However, he had a growing fear that the thing was beyond anyone's means to cure.

"I wish to see the baron on a matter of great familial urgency," he said to the guard at the castle gate. His tone was a bit more desperate than he had intended.

A quarter of an hour later he was ushered into the main hall. The Baron LuVestra sat in a simple chair, flanked by his men-at-arms. He was in his mid-sixties, with graying hair and beard, and a stern countenance. He motioned for Gavadaire to step forward.

"What brings you here?" he asked, "You speak of familial urgency; do you claim to be a relation?"

Gavadaire bowed, removing his hat, and said, "Forgive the misunderstanding, baron, but I am not of your noble lineage. My mother was from Vestra; I did not know her family name, so I bear the name of her land of birth. I was actually sent here on an errand by your grandnephew Grigor DeKenric, who is being held hostage by King Galen of Calilon."

"Hostage?" he exclaimed, "Serves his father right, rebelling against that damned king. The Cordobals are a ruthless lot. What errand, exactly?"

"He bade me return a family jewel that is an heirloom of his house. He feared that he may never lay claim to his father's lands, and he said the jewel must remain with a member of the family. He bade me return it to you."

"Oh yes?" the baron said, "I am not familiar with this heirloom you speak of. If it is an Evenast jewel, then you have come to the wrong family."

"Forgive me," Gavadaire said, "but Grigor bade me deliver it to you in Vestra. I believe he feared for the other members of his house within reach of the king's wrath." Even as he spoke, he became more frantic. *He does not know of it? If that is so, then he would not know how to remove it!*

"Very well," said the baron, "if you have a jewel to deliver, be done with it."

"My lord, there is a grave problem. I… I do not know how to say this, but I believe the jewel to be cursed, and I have become ensnared by it. I was hoping you might know how to remove it."

"I know nothing of the jewel, much less a curse," he said, "Why do you believe this to be true?"

"Because, my lord," he began, opening his shirt, "I was wearing it around my neck for safekeeping, and it has… entered my body." The words choked him as he exposed the leather thong disappearing into his flesh.

"Shu d'Vaer!" exclaimed the baron, leaning forward to see, "Is this true?"

"It is, and my need is dire," Gavadaire said, "Please, if you can help in any way-"

"No," he declared, chopping the air, "If you bear some wretched artifact that can do such a thing, I do not want it in my lands, much less my house. Begone! May the gods help you, for I cannot."

Gavadaire's face fell and his shoulders slumped. *I have come all this way for nothing,* he thought, *I am truly doomed.*

"Please, my lord. I have come a great distance already… can you not send a firebird messenger to-"

"No!" he exclaimed again; then his voice grew softer, "I don't know why my kin sent you here, stranger, but it is a fool's errand. I am sorry this fate has befallen you, but I will not risk greater ills in my land because of it. Now go."

The guards motioned with their polearms for him to leave. He had neither the will nor the need to fight, so he obeyed. If his heart indeed remained in his chest, it sank with despair. Clutching his shirt closed, he fled the castle.

There was only one place he could go to get help, only one place where he would be welcome, no matter what.

Gavadaire set off at once for the Su'Kraal Monastery, the only home he ever knew.

It was a full five-day journey to the monastery through the Aurleon Mountain Pass, but Gavadaire made it there on the morning of the third day by walking long after dark. For all his labor, he was only mildly fatigued.

I have more stamina than the strongest horse, he thought, *but why does something that can be so empowering have to bring so many other horrors?*

The Su'Kraal Monastery sat upon the Spar Shómay, a jagged shelf of pockmarked sandstone and shale jutting out from the southern face of Mount Winowyne. The structure was said to be a thousand years old, built in the days of Reconstruction after the fall of Orthicus the Terrible. In truth, it had been rebuilt and refurbished many times over; there were no old buildings in this land that could claim otherwise.

The monastery's southern walls followed the shape of the precipice, behind which were a myriad of rooms and chambers, all hidden under earthworks that came almost to the top of the wall and formed a grassy yard above. Behind this stood the temple of Arathus with the sanctuary facing east and bell tower to the west. Adjacent to that was a cloistered yard, surrounded by the library, a dormitory, and several industrial buildings. The monks made their own clothes and armor, forged their own tools and weapons, and grew their own food.

Behind the main grounds was a defensive wall with a couple of towers, and the sparse gardens and vineyards that fed the inhabitants. The approach up the mountain to the gates was well-fortified, for despite the monks' reputations, they still occasionally had to defend themselves. It was a narrow path that zigzagged up the steep eastern rise, forcing an enemy to march in an almost single-file line.

For a faster ascent, there was a lift platform attached to a large reinforced winch. The brothers used it for loading and unloading carts at the bottom of the cliff, but Gavadaire had fond memories of riding it up and down as a lad.

As he made his way up the narrow approach, he resisted the urge to rush. With his present strength, he could bound up the path like a mountain goat, but that might alarm the watchers.

"Who goes there?" called a voice from the wall high above.

He peered up, searching for a face he recognized, and shouted back, "Gavadaire LuVestra! I have returned home!"

"Hey hey, Gavadaire! Welcome back! We had not had word you were coming!"

He saw an arm wave from one of the overhanging machicolations. He waved back, feeling a little spark of hope.

He heard the ringing of the bell tower before he reached the gate, and by the time it swung open for him, the majority of the monks were assembled in the courtyard to greet him.

A cheer went up as he entered the monastery, a wide grin on his face despite his worries and fears. *I am home,* he thought.

Abbot Daethan LuPell spread his arms and said, "Gavadaire! Welcome home, my lad!" The elder monk had been his father-figure growing up, and was the closest thing to family Gavadaire knew. He clasped the man's arms and they embraced.

The emotions washed over him and he began to shake with a swirling mixture of fear, desperation, relief, love, and hope. "I... I am so happy to be back!" he cried, and tears streamed down his face.

"My boy, my boy..." LuPell looked him over, worry showing in his sparkling eyes, "Was the outside world so terrible? You look a shambles."

"I will be alright, I hope," he said, and composed himself so he might greet the others who had done him the honor of turning out to greet him.

The monks were dressed more or less identically, with tunics and trousers, or simple robes, all dyed black and brown with red belts and headbands. Their hair and beards were grown out long and braided in a variety of styles, for it was forbidden to cut it. They had tanned faces and sinewy arms, and their hands and feet were rough from constant training.

Those few novices, men and boys who were not yet monks, wore simple clothes of earth tones, and cut their hair how they wished. They were like him; foundlings, orphans, and lost souls who had been taken in by the order and given purpose.

Of the monks that greeted him, there was Brother Korba, the old librarian who had taught him his letters, Brother Nathain, the chamberlain who always smelled faintly of urine from the dye vats; Brother Tellos, the monk in charge of the infirmary; Brother Reginald, the sacrist who kept the holy relics; Brother Bertran, the endurance trainer, and Prior Wellard, the combat instructor. All were like family to him.

"Brothers, Abbot, I need to speak to you on a matter of grave importance. May we go someplace private?"

Once in the abbot's private rooms, Gavadaire took his time relating the story of how he came to be in the Winter Palace, and how the prisoner and former student Grigor DeKenric tasked him with his fateful mission. The monks listened intently, their fear and horror reaching a peak when he exposed the leather thongs disappearing into his chest.

"Can you help me? What is happening to me? I don't understand!"

"It is as we have long feared," said LuPell, "But we never dreamed it would happen in our lifetimes."

"What?" Gavadaire muttered, "What does it mean?" His voice was quavering now as the monks' faces told him they knew more than they let on.

Abbot LuPell took a deep breath and said, "You never chose to join our order, and until you did, or until your wanderlust was sated, there were certain truths kept from you."

"Tell me!" he pleaded, and he clutched his chest, forcing himself to calm down. "Please, tell me."

"I shall. Brother Tellos, will you please fetch the boy?" The infirmarian nodded and left the room.

"What boy?"

LuPell said, "You best sit down. Please." He motioned towards a chair. Gavadaire did as he was bid. LuPell began, "You know the tales of the founding of the monastery and our history, but what you were not told is that the order and this sanctuary were founded to protect one young boy."

Gavadaire blinked and frowned, wondering what in the world he was talking about.

"That boy was named Ashimar, after his paternal grandmother. He was secluded here, trained, and one day became the abbot of our order. Before his entry into the monastic life however, he had a child of his own."

"And this boy, the one you sent Tellos to go and fetch, he is a descendant of this Ashimar?"

"He is," LuPell said, "as am I... and Prior Wellard, and Brother Korba, and a few others."

"I don't understand," Gavadaire said, though he felt a tightness in his chest. There was a great truth here, just on the edge of his grasp. He feared what it might reveal, almost as much as he feared the thing in his rib cage.

"Brother Korba is my father," LuPell explained, and the old librarian nodded, "as I am Prior Wellard's... and as he is yours."

Gavadaire's gaze went from man to man, seeing the truth of it, seeing the similarities in features and build as if for the first time. He saw little bits of himself there too.

"No," he said.

"It's true," Prior Wellard said, "I am your sire, though I was not told of it for many years, until I joined the order. It is a secret that *must* be kept."

Just then, Brother Tellos returned with the boy. Gavadaire turned to see a young child of perhaps six years old, with blue eyes, red hair, and a face that was both familiar and strange. He saw himself in the boy, but also someone he had known fleetingly some seven years back.

The blood drained from Gavadaire's face as he recalled that wondrous night with that girl whose name he never learned. He had been sixteen; she had been a bit older, and experienced. Her hair was the color of flame, the same as the boy's, and her face and form were burned into his mind.

The monks had given her to him for *this* purpose, for this boy, this link in a chain.

"Who- who was this Ashimar?" Gavadaire asked, though he could guess the answer.

LuPell waved them away saying, "Thank you, Brother Tellos, he may return to his studies." After the boy left, he said, "He was the son of our lord Kraal the Great, who was himself the child of Ashimae, the Lady of Lelova, and-"

"Arathus!" Gavadaire said, and immediately there was a clenching pain in his chest, as if the dark thing there twisted and railed against the word. He clutched his breast and doubled over as the brothers gasped and moved to help him.

"Do not touch him!" cried LuPell, "I feared the worst, and this confirms it." They stood back, the terror on their faces matching Gavadaire's own.

"What does it mean?" he begged, "Why is this happening to me?"

LuPell's jaw trembled as he tried to form the words, slowly and reverently. "Kraal himself took the Dark

Heart from this world, as his divine blood was strong enough to contain that evil. But now it has returned, and time and generations have diluted the potency of his line. Now the cursed blood has infected the body of the King God's scion, and it will overpower him, to the doom of us all."

He is speaking of me as if I am not here, Gavadaire realized, *like I'm only a character in the holy books.*

"Brothers," said the Abbot, "we will aid him if we can. We will do what we must. Take him to an empty cell…"

"No!" Gavadaire barked. He knew a "cell" was only a monk's sleeping chamber, but he would not be confined to an empty room to await his fate. "I wish to see the sky," he pleaded.

"Very well," LuPell said, avoiding his grandson's eyes, "take him to the cloister and let him wait under the sun."

Gavadaire sat alone under the cloister, gazing out blankly at the training yard. He nodded to those who greeted him, and smiled to those who waved, but he said nothing. There was so much to take in, so much to understand.

I am a descendant of the King God himself, he thought, and even the thought burned him. The cursed thing inside him hated that name and punished him for speaking it, even for thinking it. *Inside me is an ancient evil, the blood of Llomaak, the God of Chaos.* A rush of soothing power and comfort washed over him, rewarding and enticing him.

I am a father.

That was almost the greatest shock. He had never imagined himself raising a child, or indeed ever having one. Those few women he had bedded always used the Oil of Nim to guard against pregnancy, or some other less expensive concoction. Only his first had been unprepared, probably by design, and he had been too young, eager, and unthinking to question it.

He wondered, *What responsibilities do I owe him? What am I to do?* Then he realized that his own father, his grim and reserved combat instructor, had paid him no fatherly duties, save to make him strong and capable. *How often had I hated him for pushing me so hard? Was it love or duty that drove him so?*

I don't even know the boy's name.

None of that really mattered now. All the familial revelations in the world would not drive this curse from him. '*Now the cursed blood has infected the body of the King God's scion, and it will overpower him, to the doom of us all.*' Was the Abbot quoting a scripture? A prophesy? He had not been speaking of what might be, but what *would* be.

"So I am truly doomed," he whispered.

Yet hope remained; the monks would help as they could. The brothers, no, his *family* would do everything in their power to aid him. They were preparing now, he knew, and would call upon him soon with an answer. Some ancient ritual or spell, some divine magic left over from the age of the gods...

Hope. A fool's hope.

Clouds gathered overhead as a storm rolled in over the mountains.

Brother Reginald brought the reliquaries the Abbot had requested, and together they laid them out with great care on the altar of the sanctuary. The other brothers stood about, gazing on them with great reverence.

"These might be our best hope for saving the world," LuPell said.

"Assuming they are all real," said Prior Wellard; the other monks gasped at his sacrilege.

"Many of them were acquired at great cost and pain by our forebearers," Reginald said.

LuPell addressed his son, "Prior Wellard, these artifacts were verified by the best seers in the land."

"That was centuries ago," Wellard said, "The best seer in this or any other land today is Ildric Finnael of Calilon, and he has never examined them. Who knows who might have passed themselves off as diviners in those days?"

"That is enough, Prior," LuPell said, "we are satisfied of their authenticity."

They held each other's gaze for a tense moment, until the old librarian Brother Korba grumbled, "Enough talk, the both of you. Brother Reginald, please tell us what we have here."

Reginald nodded and proceeded to describe each object. First, he held up a face guard of bronze that covered the forehead and cheeks. It was an odd bit of armoring that was only seen these days as safety gear in fighting schools. "This is the face guard of Kraal, worn by our lord in battle against the tyrant, King Orthicus." Next, he held up a vial of dark red fluid. "This is the blood of Kraal himself, preserved and encased in an enchanted glass vial." The monks looked on with awe.

Next, Reginald held up a small knife with a carved handle of Shadowood, "This is the elven knife known as *Sugireth* , the shard of *Hanvdálni* that cut the God of Chaos and drew his blood. It was obtained from one of Kraal's own lieutenants, Lord Aldo of Vale."

There was some muttering as the assembled brothers looked upon it; they all knew the story of the knife and wondered what the abbot might have in mind for it.

"Finally," Reginald said, "there is the mirror of the Holy Mother Ashimae, Lady of Lelova. It is said that if one meditates on his reflection, he can see the truth of his inner nature."

"Has anyone tried it before?" Wellard asked.

"Many have tried," Reginald said, "but there are few who speak openly of what they saw."

"So, this is what we have at our disposal," LuPell said, "Let us search for a ritual that might be used to weaken this thing's accursed power. In the meantime, I want

Gavadaire watched and kept away from the common spaces."

Gavadaire waited and waited, watching the rain fall and the lightning arc across the sky. The day wore on and still there was no answer from the masters.

How long did I think it would take? Did I imagine there would be a simple recipe somewhere for my plight?

He thought back on his life, wondering if there had been clues to his strange lineage. He was strong and capable, but so were many others. He had excelled at the monks' fighting style, being quick and evasive. *Is that why it seems so difficult to teach it to others?* Then he thought back to the recent attempts on his life. At the fighting school... the man with the crossbow in his room... he had reacted so fast when the man shot at him, he had amazed himself. He had seen the bolt leave the weapon, knew just how fast and how much to close the door to block it...

Then there was the woman, the vemlok. He had impaled her on his sword to no effect, but she had grabbed him by the head. He had thought of it many times, how strange it had been; he should have died. But instead of draining all his blood, she had recoiled as though it burned her.

The storm grew fiercer and the rain came down in thick curtains. Even the most devoted brother and novice chose to cease their training in the yard and come in out of the deluge. The wind was blowing so that even on his bench under the cloister, Gavadaire was in danger of getting his trousers wet.

Is this me, I wonder? Is this the Eight Storms making my stay more cheerful, like those damned giant sharks?

He tried to recall his childhood lessons on the obscure nature gods. He was never a farmer or a sailor, so they rarely came to mind; the weather was the weather. But since he had witnessed two of them up close, he was taking it far more seriously.

Masha and Mektha, the sharks who cause Obesh to churn the sea... Which are the ones that disturb Pokaht and make thunder and lightning? ...Tathae and Kethae? Noda and Nada freeze the rains to make sleet or hail, Fahl and Mahl make Hwessa stir up violent winds... I wonder what forms they take? I don't think I ever asked.

He peered into the clouds to see if any giant horrors had manifested themselves. They did not.

Not yet.

The rain continued as water roared through the gutters and saturated the yard.

So much for waiting under the sun.

As the day wore on, the rains subsided and the brothers came out to assess the damage. Buildings this old always had to be constantly maintained, and harsh weather could take its toll, but Gavadaire feared his presence might make things worse. He recalled the shrine in which he spent a night, and the terrible decay it had suffered. Before wandering off, he checked the stone bench he had been sitting on. Thankfully, it had not cracked, crumbled, or become infested with mold.

Yet there were other problems. The water in the yard gave off a rotten stench, so much that the monks called upon the infirmarian to investigate. Brother Tellos searched for the cause, but when his eyes settled on Gavadaire, he hurried off.

Rot and decay. That's what I bring. How can they help me?

He felt a bit hungry, but he dared not go into the refectory where the others were dining; he didn't want to literally spoil their meals. He asked a passing novice if he wouldn't mind bringing him some food.

He ate a bowl of porridge in the south yard overlooking the cliff, wondering if he should throw himself off.

As the evening fell, Gavadaire felt the urge to go and demand an update on the brothers' progress, but he resisted. Instead, Brother Nathain found him after a bit of frantic searching and asked after his needs.

He said, "The Abbot told me to say that the research and debates will last late into the night, and that we must put you up for the evening. Will your old rooms do?"

"They will not," Gavadaire said, "I don't wish to be close to others if possible. This curse... it has effects that I cannot predict."

"Very well," Nathain said, looking relieved, "We should be able to arrange a bed for you in one of the empty storerooms."

That night, Gavadaire was haunted by frightful dreams; not of the Abyss and its swirling madness, but of himself. He was walking through the monastery, past all the old familiar buildings and faces. It was comforting and nostalgic, and things he thought long forgotten returned to his memory, or at least his dream said so.

As he talked with the passing brothers about the weather, or the evening's meal, or some such thing, he saw them begin to age, sicken, and decay. It was gradual, and neither he nor his victims acted like they noticed, as if it would be rude to mention. But inevitably they would falter, gasp, and keel over, giving him a withering, accusatory stare as they fell.

It saddened him, but did not horrify him, and this in itself was horrifying.

The more he tried to act normally and be a friend, the more the people he cared about suffered. He was not one of them anymore. He was Other.

"*I do not want this!*" He might have cried out loud or only in his dream, he could not tell. The ground shook, the walls cracked and shifted, and the tiles rained down from the rooftops.

Accept, came the answer, *Accept and be at peace.*

"No!" he cried out, *"I reject you!"*
My blood is now your blood. Accept, and be at peace.
"NO!"

Gavadaire's eyes snapped open as the morning light poured in through the tiny window. His heart was pounding like a drum, pulsing in his ears and making his body move with each beat, but it was not really his heart anymore. This thing within him, this part of Llomaak, was pouring its malignant power through his veins. It did not sound or feel like the rush of blood now; it was like the hissing of snakes and the roar of fire being fed with a bellows.

The bed sheets were soaked, and the morning had a deathly chill in the air. The little fireplace that had meant to keep him warm had gone cold, as he feared it might; yet he was not terribly uncomfortable.

Looking around the empty storeroom, he was relieved that the walls hadn't crumbled away and the ceiling hadn't collapsed. He could never tell what changes he would awaken to as the power of the Dark Heart worked in his sleep.

Accept, and be at peace.

The words echoed in his mind. Was it a memory of the dream, or was it something more? The cursed thing had never spoken to him before, neither in dreams nor in waking. He recalled the dreams he had on the ship, the terror and the abominable violations of the Abyss, and he recalled how the stone had soothed him, making him master of the writhing, howling throng. He had found comfort in its blood light, and the jewel rewarded him with peace. His thundering heart slowed with the memory.

Must I? he wondered, *Is that what I must do to contain the chaos it creates? I do not think I can. Hopefully, I might not have to soon.*

Brother Nathain entered a short while later and brought him a bowl of broth and a loaf of fresh bread.

"I have news," he said, "The abbot has decided upon a course of action and they shall call upon you soon. Preparations are being made in the sanctuary as we speak."

"Good!" he sighed, feeling his shoulders relax, "I shall be glad to be rid of it."

Nathain gave him a strange, pitying look, nodded, and left.

It was ten in the morning on the 20th when Abbot LuPell summoned Gavadaire into the sanctuary. As he entered, the brothers began a chant, arrayed in a semi-circle around the altar. LuPell wore the sacred bronze face guard and his best vestments, and carried his staff of office topped with the three pointed crown symbol of Arathus.

"Let the supplicant come forward," he intoned.

Gavadaire approached, taking in the fog of incense obscuring the domed ceiling, and the solemn faces of the brothers as their voices echoed off the high walls. He knelt before the altar and bowed his head.

"What do you seek?" LuPell asked.

"I seek to rid myself of this accursed jewel that has violated my body," he said, "I seek the removal of the Dark Heart."

"Do you accept the risk involved?"

"I do."

"Do you accept the power of your bloodline?"

"I do."

"Do you accept the ultimate will of Arathus, to whatever end it may entail?"

Gavadaire paused before answering. It was a wide-opened question.

"I do," he said, finally.

"Approach the altar and remove your shirt."

Gavadaire did as he was bid, and two brothers helped him out of his jacket and shirt. He felt a great shame as the others looked upon the leather cord sinking into his chest, eyes wide with morbid fascination.

"Lie upon the altar."

It was a strange command, but Gavadaire did as he was bid. The stone was cold, yet he felt a burning in his chest. LuPell nodded and four brothers surrounded him, holding his arms and legs.

"This is for your safety as well as ours," he said, "we do not wish for the ritual to be disrupted."

Gavadaire looked up at the man who was his grandfather, seeing the reverent mask he wore over his emotions, instead of compassion for the blood of his blood. He trusted that the man had found a solution, but had to admit that he felt a bit like a sacrifice at the moment.

"Bring the mirror," LuPell said. He stepped aside as Prior Wellard held a hand mirror in his hands.

Father, Gavadaire thought. The man stood at his head and held the reflective surface for his son to gaze into.

"Look into the mirror, and tell us what you see," the prior said.

Gavadaire saw his face, his frightened, trusting face. He had not realized how intense was his expression, how deep the worry that creased his brow. He tried to relax and gaze into his own eyes. "I see myself," he said.

"Only yourself?"

He nodded, but as he studied his own features, he saw them shift and change. A pale red light stared back at him from his own eyes, growing brighter and more baleful with every heartbeat. His skin began to crack, and that same light shone through, like fiery embers glowing past the blackened bark of a burning log. He instinctively tried to touch his face to see if it was real, and the brothers holding his arms bucked against the effort.

His voice was quavering like a frightened child's. "It's on fire..." he said, as he squirmed on the stone platform.

"Easy, easy," said the prior, "It is the power of the mirror, not your true face. Calm your mind and try to see yourself as the man you are."

Gavadaire forced himself to relax as he fixated on that terrible visage in the mirror. He thought of the man he wanted to be, the man who had dreams and aspirations that were ordinary and worldly, not the grim promises of power and darkness that were being fed into his dreams. He briefly saw the face in the mirror lose some of its fire and become a semblance of normalcy.

"I see myself," he said, relieved.

"Good," the prior said, "Now close your eyes and focus on that face, that inner self you wish to be. Remember your blood and the power of the god that resides there."

Gavadaire did so as the prior removed the mirror and stepped back. Next, he heard the abbot once again, and felt a cold trickle of fluid pool on his chest, which turned hot and threatened to burn him.

"I anoint you with the Holy Blood of Kraal, the one who vanquished the power of the Dark Heart and shall do so again."

Gavadaire felt the hot blood run down to his neck and sides as he took deep, calming breaths. The brothers' grip tightened on his limbs and all grew silent.

"Now," LuPell said, "I free you from the torment you have so bravely endured. As it was before, so shall it be again."

The brothers chanted as one, "A-RA-THUS!"

Gavadaire opened his eyes.

He saw the abbot, his grandfather, standing at his head, his arms held above him; in his hands was a small knife with a shining blade, poised to strike.

"Forgive me," he said.

Gavadaire tried to struggle, but it was too late; the blade came down before he could throw off his captors and stop it. It pierced flesh and bone, and touched the cursed jewel within.

Pain.
Light.
Fury.
The last thing that went through Abbot LuPell's mind was the counterfeit relic he had stabbed into the Dark Heart. A hideous blast of power spread across the monastery, leveling buildings like leaves in a hurricane. The Spar Shòmay upon which it sat cracked and crumbled, and the mountain itself shook with the power of the blast. It continued out and up, pushing the clouds away in a growing dome of rushing air. The noise was ungodly, and killed those who were unfortunate enough to be within thirty miles of it.

A minute later, a powerful tremor was felt in the city of Vestra, and nine minutes after that, a sound like a massive crack of thunder roared overhead; windows shattered and buildings shook, and the banners on the castle snapped to the west. A warm blast of air washed over the town, turning the cold morning into a brief spring day. As the terrified townspeople picked themselves up and looked to the east, they saw a distant cloud of debris spreading like a massive flock of birds; tiny flecks of dark against a pale sky.

Chapter Twenty Six

The Dark Trio

Spirits of Earth and Air, that's what we are!

Maveezh reveled in her newfound powers, descending the mountainside in the manner Clavemont had shown her. Arms outstretched, she glided on the wind like a hawk, launching herself from the tops of trees that rose in her path.

The elder vemlok was gliding behind her, watching her progress. Occasionally she would turn to look at him with a mad smile on her face, like a child at play. He would study her impassively as the wind blew through his pale hair and fluttered his fine clothes.

Above them both, the dark shape of the guadim blotted out the stars, like a hole in the night. The flapping of its vile wings was the only sound that could be heard over the rush of wind and the woman's sporadic giggling.

Maveezh needed to feed, that was unavoidable. Clavemont had given her a bit of his own blood after they arose from the sleep of her first day, but she needed more. Much more. She had retained her sanity and her sense of self thus far, but to deny her needs would lead to disaster.

So much to learn!

Before Clavemont, she only knew stories of vemloks that rose from the grave and hunted the living, heedless of anything but their thirst. Mindless and fearless, they inevitably became the hunted when the living tracked them to their daytime resting places. But the pale lord was an aberration, and he had taught her so much already.

Fire is our enemy, and that means the sun.

Fire and sunlight were some of the only things that could cause her pain now, so they were to be avoided. Clavemont had told her that a vemlok exposed to the sun would burn like a roast turning on a spit. Sunlight sapped their strength and greatly diminished their powers, but could not destroy them outright, not unless they lay exposed for a very long time, unable to hide or feed. The living found it easier to simply burn them any way they could.

Water was a weakness that she had heard of in few folk stories. Immersion in fresh, running water would rob her powers and make her as weak as a child, and seawater would render her as weak as any mortal woman. Rain would limit her ability to fly, at least until she became more powerful. She could not drown, but getting water in her lungs would put her in a stupor and make her vulnerable. That was to be avoided.

Large bodies of water were impossible for them to fly over for some reason, even for one as powerful and old as Clavemont. They would have to use boats and ships to get around, just like normal people; the only problem was the sun, and a limited food supply that wouldn't get suspicious.

Beheading was also fatal, but when was it ever not?

So much to learn, so little time.

Maveezh shifted her weight and angled her arms, willing herself to drift towards the faint lights in the dark distance. The three were now over the foothills of the Cassel Range, above the river valley that fed the Joshian with dozens of little tributaries. By one such tributary, near the edge of the Shadowood Forest, was a settlement that sat a few miles southwest of the castle town of Syngmore. That was their destination.

Touching down on the outskirts of the farming community, the dark trio walked towards the flickering torches of sleeping Syngmore Village. Maveezh had lost her shoes sometime during her last dirt nap, but she cared not; the touch of the earth under her feet was like a well of strength rising through her slender limbs. It gave her a confidence that thrilled her, and her stride reflected that. She had never known herself to swagger before, but she did so now.

As they neared the closest farmhouse, Clavemont stopped. "This one is yours," he said, "Indulge yourself, but I advise you to show restraint. Take what you need but do not give in to your lust. Let the thirst control you, and you may lose yourself to it."

"Yes, *master*," she grinned, playing with the word, "I'll try to be a worthy student."

He did not comment on her tone; he only watched her with appraisal, and perhaps a touch of sadness.

Paugh loomed over the lord's shoulder and said, "Together, you could drink this whole village. Imagine the possibilities."

"The possibilities of mass death?" the lord said, "We are not a plague. We are hunters."

"Imagine leading an army again," said the guadim, "You will not breach the lair of the Shadow Lord with one fledgling vemlok and old Paugh. You need numbers."

"I am not *going* to seek the Shadow Lord," he said with an edge in his voice, "I told you, I made a vow."

"Never to drink the blood of an elf; yes, I know," the guadim sneered, "But this is *ancient* blood, power such as you have never known! What will it serve if you die with the rest of creation, staying true to your vow? Do you think there will be a prize, a reward? The Judge will be no more. All the tortures the Tyrant has prepared for you will be no more. Your spirit will be no more. Even the spirit of your beloved elf witch will cease to exist. What will it serve to resist?"

Maveezh could hear the guadim's temptations as she strode towards the little cottage, hoping the pale lord would see the futility of his vow. *An army of vemloks! A feast of elven blood! Now **that** was something to look forward too.*

She inhaled the breeze, detecting the smell of living blood from the ramshackle hovel eighty yards away. Her thirst rose and her senses sharpened as she forced herself to keep a steady pace. There was another odor, a powerful one that mingled with that sweet, coppery scent; it was the smell of too much wine seeping out of the pores of a sweating drunk. She idly wondered if drinking this peasant's blood would make her tipsy. She wanted to find out.

There was a dim light in the hovel. Her nose told her it was a single tallow candle, but she would not need light. One of the wonders of her transformation was how she could now see in the dark. Living bodies gave off a spectral radiance, a ghost-light that could be seen in total darkness. Starlight was as moonlight, and moonlight was as daylight. Patches of old snow on the ground made the night even more luminous and enchanting.

What's more, Clavemont claimed she could see *spirits*. He said Portshia had several, wandering around in a semblance of their old lives, or haunting the places where they died. Such things were rare, and no one knew why some souls lingered in the world instead of meeting the Judge. Whatever the reason, it gave her a smidgen of hope that she might see her husband one last time before it all came crashing down.

Gathering her restraint, she knocked on the cottage door.

"Who-who is it?" came a quavering male voice.

"Hello?" She called through the door in a pathetic quaver, "I'm a traveler and I lost my way. Could you help me please?"

The door partially opened and a weathered, haggard face peered out. His thin, graying hair caught the candlelight, making a halo around his head that delighted the woman's new vision. He had many days of stubble about his face, and his watery eyes were yellow with jaundice. He reeked of wine and sadness, but Maveezh found him beautiful.

My first, she thought.

"May I come in?"

The man looked her up and down with a mixture of surprise and horror, and Maveezh realized what she must look like. Her clothes were filthy, her skin was gray, her hair was thick with dirt, and wildly windblown. She looked like she had been buried alive, which of course, she had.

"Wha- what in the Abyss happened to ya?" he rasped.

"I was riding north when my horse took a tumble," she whimpered, "I woke up in a ditch, and I don't know where I am. Can I please come inside?"

Apparently, vemloks once needed permission to enter a dwelling. This was difficult for the ones who had lost their minds and could only moan and shriek at people, but when the gods left the world behind, they took those protections with them. She could have forced her way in, but unlike an ordinary vemlok, she had a sense of play.

"I don'... I don' have nothin' here for you," he said, shaking his head.

Ungenerous man, she thought, but whimpered, "Please! It's so cold and dark. I don't even have shoes. Please, good master?"

He glanced down at her filthy, bare feet, and Maveezh could see the wheels working behind his eyes, the mistrust and pain evident in his face. This man lived alone for a reason, far from the other houses. He was probably the village outcast, the one people pitied even as they gossiped about him.

"I- I suppose you kin stay a bit," he said, and he opened the door, letting her in. "I don' have much to eat."

"Anything you can give me will be just fine," she said, smiling. She stepped through the door like a cat stalking a bird.

The man's hovel was filthy even by peasant standards, and reeked of week-old stew, unwashed flesh, and wine. There was no fire in the tiny hearth, but several woolen blankets were arranged on the straw-stuffed mattress like a great nest. Her enhanced vision could see fleas leaping about on the bed.

This will be a mercy, she thought, *not that mercy matters.*

"Do you live here alone?" she asked, sounding meek and unsure. She took a stool by the low table.

The man fumbled about with a ladle in the small cook pot, checking to see if there was enough to scrape into a bowl. He paused at the question but didn't answer.

"What is your name, kind master?" she asked. It was only polite.

He turned to look at her, and his jaw quivered before he spoke, as if he were grasping for the memory. "mm-Mathen," he said.

"Mathen," she repeated, "I thank you for your hospitality, Mathen."

He nodded, then went to look for a clean bowl.

"My name is Maveezh."

"Sounds foreign," he muttered.

"It's an ancient name, from a far-off land," she said proudly, "I chose it myself. It means 'word spitter' in the language of the old empire."

"Ya chose yer own name? Why would ya do that?"

"It suited me," she said, "In my faith, you cast aside your given name."

He eyed her suspiciously as he scooped some cold stew. "What faith is that?"

"The faith of the Countless Lord."

"Never heard o' that one," he said.

He passed her the bowl of unappetizing gunk, and as he did so, she brushed her fingers across the back of his hand.

"He is a taker," she said, shivering as the man's blood leeched into her fingertips. The feeling was exquisite, ecstatic, and almost erotic. The tiniest warmth spread up her hand, and she ached for more. Every fiber in her body strained and yearned for the man, like iron filings leaning towards a magnet. Yet she resisted, sitting back on the stool with her bowl.

Mathen absently rubbed the back of his hand, dismissing the tingling sensation. "A taker?" he asked, "Taker of what?"

"Of whatever he wants," she replied, smiling a bloodless smile.

This made the poor man nervous, and he retreated a few steps.

"Do you have family, Mathen?"

He hugged himself pathetically, his eyes darting about the room and settling in a dark corner. "I had a son," he muttered.

"Had? Did he die?"

Bitterly, he said, "He's doing well for himself in Portshia, last I heard."

"Oh. I never had any myself. Children can be such ungrateful little beasts, can't they?"

The man said nothing, but flicked his eyes around the room like a cornered animal.

Soon, she thought.

She stood slowly, a bit too slowly, and locked eyes with the man. "I want to thank you for the meal, Mathen." Her voice was steel cloaked in velvet. No trace of the frail waif remained.

He frowned and grew more anxious, blinking at the bowl. "But ya haven't touched it yet," he said, "I know it's poor fare, but it's all I have ta offer."

"Oh, there is more, and I shall touch it in a moment." She took a step towards him, then another, pacing like a predator stalking through the grass. She changed her voice to a soft sing-song, "I have something to give you. It is a rare gift, something very special."

"I ask for nothing," he said, retreating from the gray lady, "I don't need no rare gift. M-maybe you should go now."

Maveezh whimpered, "Mathen, you wouldn't cast me out, would you? I am just a helpless woman, alone in the darkness!"

Then she grinned wolfishly at him; she couldn't help herself.

That was enough to send the man into a panic. He groped around for something to wield, and his hand found a small ax hanging on a wall hook. Brandishing it, his yellowed eyes wide and bold, he summoned his voice and shouted, "Stay back! Stay away from me!"

She took a step towards him, her eyes alight with hunger and lust. She took another, and another.

He swung the ax wildly, striking towards the side of her head, but the iron blade had stopped; she was gripping it tightly between her thumb and forefinger, only inches from her face. Her reaction had been so swift that she hadn't the time to even think about it.

The impact of the blow jarred the man's arm, and his eyes registered terror. He tried to pry the ax from the gray woman's pinching grip, tugging and straining with both hands.

"My dear fellow," she said, closing her delicate hand around one of his wrists with the strength of a manacle, "I cannot tell you how special this moment is, as a woman, I mean." She shuddered with delight as the man's lifeblood was drawn from his veins, through his skin, and into her ravenous, dead flesh. "We live our whole lives as prey, you see; fearing the day someone bigger and stronger will make a plaything of us."

She moved her other hand to caress his face as he heaved and struggled with all his drunken might. He was not a weak man, but her small body pressed against his, pinning him to the wall.

"Now, I am no timid mouse," she said, "but even *I* have felt that fear in dark alleys and deserted streets."

Her hands grew pink, and the color moved up her arms to her shoulders. Mathen screamed with a throat so tight, it hardly made a sound. The ax fell from his numbing hand.

"It is a rare thing indeed that we find our roles reversed," she murmured softly, her gray lips becoming a warm shade of coral. "I shall be prey no longer, and you shall be the first of many."

He lashed out with wild abandon; his fist struck her cheek, then her lip, bloodying them, but the red stains were reabsorbed and the cuts healed instantly. He struck her in the face repeatedly, and she let him do it. His blows were painless, impotent, and grew weaker with every swing. Even as he bloodied his knuckles on her skull and teeth, leaving crimson streaks on her face, he nourished her. Finally, his knees gave out and he collapsed into her arms, limp as a scarecrow.

"It's not that I think you deserve it, my dear," she explained, "though chances are, you do." She laid him on his own dinner table, slipping a hand under his shirt to feel his fading heartbeat. "It is a cruel world full of cruel people, yet I do not judge you. That is not my way."

Mathen's skin turned pale and his struggling subsided. Maveezh ran her fingers up and down his chest, leaving red welts in their wake. The power she felt was intoxicating, or maybe it was his tainted blood. Regardless, she had completely dominated this pathetic creature, taken and taken until he had nothing left to give.

So this is what it feels like, she mused.

"I believe I mentioned a rare gift," she said, lowering her lips to whisper in his ear, "I am going to bury you, my dear. I am going to lay you under the very land you till, and in a few days' time, you may rise again to serve me. Won't that be a delight? You shall be a mindless slave to my will, but your service will be rewarded, I promise. There is a feast of all feasts to be had, and you may be a party to it, if you are a good boy."

But Mathen DuQuayne could no longer hear her.

Clavemont approached the cottage as Maveezh exited, carrying her limp victim in her arms. The guadim followed behind, watching the two pale monsters closely.

"You look slightly better," the lord said to his fledgling vemlok, "Your skin has a bit of color at last."

"I feel as though I could conquer the world!" she said, "I never realized how weak I was before, how soft and fragile. Every meeting was a calculation, a risk. Now..."

"There is still a risk," Clavemont said, "The dangers are fewer, but we are not invulnerable. Do not forget that a predator may become prey if it is careless."

She bore the man's body to the edge of his field and laid him in the dirt, kneeling beside him. "I always thought that predators were safer in a pack," she said, favoring the lord with a sly smile, "Why else would you turn me as you did?"

Clavemont said nothing, but watched impassively as she went about her work.

Maveezh placed her hands on the cold earth beside Mathen's body, and relished the elemental power that flowed into her palms. The sensation was not as sweet and satisfying as drawing blood, but was more of a comfort and a source of strength. Clavemont had taught her how to bury herself in the ground, much as he had done when first he dragged her to her doom.

But this time she was doing it to another. She willed the earth to part, willed it to caress and encompass the body of her victim, and finally to pull it down into the soil. Mathen's body was swallowed by the hard, tilled earth, leaving only a slight mound to mark his grave.

Good enough for another, she thought, *Perfect concealment only matters if it's my own grave.*

Clavemont said, "You will let the thirsting spirit take him with no guidance, no control." It was not a question, and his voice carried a slight rebuke, "Do you not find it cruel?"

"Did you think I was not cruel?" she asked, "I don't wish for an equal, only a foot soldier, the first of many."

The guadim hissed to itself, amused.

Maveezh looked at her hands and saw the dirt caked into in every crease and crevasse, packed under her fingernails in dark crescents. Noticing how the lord's attire was so clean and spotless, she tried an experiment. Focusing her concentration, she willed the dirt to move, to shed itself from her skin. To her delight, it obeyed, falling in little clouds of dust that sparkled in the moonlight. Next, she passed her hands over her dress and ran them through her hair. The filth and grime fell away almost effortlessly, raining down in little curtains of fine soil.

"Ah!" she exclaimed, "I feel almost human again."

It was what she said after a good bath and grooming, but now the words lacked any pertinence, sounding almost pathetic. She examined her hands once more, clean and pale in the moonlight; so slender and delicate, yet impossibly strong.

"No, that's not right," she said, "I feel radiant, radiant and irresistible." Draining the man had set her body alight, awakening her senses as never before. She turned to look at Clavemont, and as if for the first time, beheld him with her new eyes.

He appeared radiant and irresistible too, like a statue made of marble and infused with pure spirit. The red disks in his eyes flickered, reflecting the dim illumination of the night sky. He had not fed tonight, and his skin was as pale as alabaster. She found him beautiful and majestic, like a god walking in the world after a long absence.

How had I missed it before?

"Why did you make me?" she asked.

Clavemont was taken aback for a moment. "I did not make you," he said, "The thirsting spirit either comes, or it does not."

"You could have left my body for the crows, but you pulled me under the earth where the spirit could take me; you shared your guilt and suffering to keep me sane. Why?" She had been too enraptured to question his motives until now. Feeding had brought a sense of clarity.

The lord gazed at her silently, pondering. His platinum hair was rimmed with moonlight and moved in the gentle breeze, otherwise he could be mistaken for a statue. Finally, his gaze dropped to her feet. "I... I don't know," he said.

She mocked his words, "You... don't... *know?*" Maveezh was feeling her old self again, or at least her argumentative self. "*You don't know* why you created a monster like yourself, with a mind?"

"Perhaps I was curious."

"Perhaps you were lonely. Perhaps you have grown weary of hiding yourself behind a gentile mask, a wolf living among sheep."

"You think you know me?" he asked, "I have lived for a millennium; you have been a vemlok for a day. What great insight do you think you have?"

"I have an imagination. I can imagine watching all you love pass away, watching new things take their place and then pass away as well. I imagine it's incredibly lonely." She began to walk around him in slow circles, like a patron admiring a sculpture. "You masquerade as a living man, holding parties, playing the generous benefactor. Perhaps it was once a game to you, a way to toy with your food. But I think you came to depend on it, to need the love and adoration, friendship even."

"And yet I abandoned it," he said, his tone flat and hard, "Do not presume to imagine what I need."

She shrugged, "It doesn't take much imagination to figure out that puzzle. You left home at a precarious time for you; there were not one, but *two* elves in the castle. Why, it was only a matter of time before a social event put you all in the same room. You might have been seated together at the dinner table! Now *that* would have been ironic." She allowed herself a giggle.

He rounded on her, trembling with rage. "You dare to laugh? I gave you my memories so you would understand what can be lost, so you could hold on to your humanity!"

She thought, *And this is where the knife goes in...*

Maveezh stopped circling and spoke; her voice was soft and measured, "What you gave me was your pain and regret, yes, but also your powerful addiction. I know you, Gray Baron. I know you most intimately."

A look of terrible realization washed over his features. Maveezh made sure not to smile. Now was the time for careful deconstruction, to expose him to himself.

"There was one thing that you left out of your sharing, something I think was rather important," she said, "When and how did Count DuClavemont become a vemlok?"

The question had a profound effect. His shoulders slumped and his arms went slack. The rage boiled away in a moment as his chin, held high in indignation, sank to his chest. He seemed to teeter on his feet, swaying in the breeze like a lone cattail reed.

It was Paugh who answered. "He sought it out," it said in a low croak, "The Whispers told me so. He cut his wrists and ordered his men to bury him as he bled into the dirt."

Clavemont turned towards the creature, but said nothing. He did not even make eye contact, he only scowled at the spot where Maveezh had buried her first victim.

"You *chose* this fate? Why?" she asked. Then realization struck her. "Ah! Oh, you poor man." She took several steps back, mostly for her own safety. She kept her voice full of empathy, even as she relished his folly, "You sought to wait for her, to seize immortality so you wouldn't lose her."

He barely nodded. His eyes were downcast and his face looked defeated.

Maveezh wanted to roll in the dirt and laugh, but she was an expert at hiding her true feelings. "After you arose, you went to see her. It was not pain and guilt that allowed you to keep your humanity, but love. You sought to wait for her, no matter how long it took. But then-"

"I touched her," he said, choking on the words, "I touched her perfect skin, thinking I could control the taking..." His voice broke and he squeezed his eyes shut.

"And once you felt that power, you couldn't stop. You couldn't stop until she was dead." She felt a pang of guilt and heartache, but it was not her own. Maveezh shoved them aside; she would not harbor his compulsory feelings any longer.

"I lost everything that mattered," he said, as he sank to his knees, "I was mad with power and pain. My loyal men tried to stop me, but they were no match... no match at all."

"One of you had to have a tragic parting," she said, "You were both doomed the moment you fell in love."

He nodded.

"I think she knew she would be the one to leave," Maveezh said, and her words were tinged with accusation.

Clavemont's head inclined ever so slightly.

Her tone became disapproving as she teased out the thought. "How long was she planning to wait, I wonder? A year? Ten? ...Fifty?"

His pale blue eyes were looking at her from under his brow. Red flickered within.

One more push, she thought.

"It is said that the goddess Selvina keeps her prized roses in a vase, so she can enjoy their beauty; love in full bloom. Do you think she keeps them there once they begin to fade and rot?"

Clavemont raised his hands over the soil and it became firm and fluid, racing towards Maveezh in a swath of living clay. It entrapped her bare feet and clung to her ankles, where it hardened like a kiln-fired pot.

She cried out and tried to run, but Clavemont was on her before she could break free. His hands were around her head, clutching her like a vice. He clearly meant to pop her head off like a cork, and she felt the sickening, steady pull on her vertebrae. She felt the exchange of blood between them as their flesh touched, the giving and taking all at once. He was taking more.

"She loved you!" Maveezh wailed.

The pressure continued, but faltered a little.

"She loved you *so* much, she couldn't stand to see you grow old and die!" She was pouring all of her heart into her voice, hoping it would reach him. He was almost where she needed him to be, if only she could survive so long.

He was a snake with a mouse in his coils, staring into her eyes as they bulged and grew bloodshot. "Do not presume to know her mind!" he snarled, "She was far above a deceitful grave rat like you!"

"It is how I feel... about my husband..." she whimpered, "I thought only of him... as I slept in the ground."

"You said you *lost* everything you cared about," he hissed.

"I have," she gasped, "He's been dead... almost two years. Please..."

The pressure relented, but the steely grip remained. She was going lightheaded from the loss of blood. Her next words would have to count.

"I was never able to say goodbye," she said, and she almost swooned, "But now… now I see it is better… that he died."

Disgusted, Clavemont pushed her limp form away and she crashed to the ground. "Better?" he said, "What a vile thing you are. You think to instruct me on a woman's love? Not all are as fickle as you, servant of Llomaak."

"You misunderstand, my lord," she said, picking herself up, "I loved him dearly, but as I am now, I could not bear to watch him… age." She was starving again, damn him; it was a struggle to focus on words. "If he were still alive, I wouldn't dare make him a vemlok; he had poor self-control, and he would emerge a mindless ghoul. But neither could I bear to see him age while I am unchanged. The truth is… there could be only one path to immortality for my dear husband, and that is the path he already took."

Clavemont frowned and muttered, "What nonsense."

"He left me in his prime. I will always remember him as last I saw him, strong and lusty and full of confidence." She drew what strength she could from the earth, willing herself to stand up straight. "As I am now, there could be no better future for us, not as I see it."

"And if he had lived, what then?" Clavemont sneered, "Would you have killed him to preserve your precious memories?"

"He would have to live his life without me," she said, "I could not bear it otherwise."

He stared at her for many heartbeats, as his skin colored from twice-stolen blood. Finally he said, "You think my Navinessia did not intend to return until I was long dead."

"Think, my lord; think of how you have felt this last millennium, watching things change and die, over and over again. So it must have been for her. How could it not?"

"But she *promised* me she would return," he said, as if his earnestness would make it so, "She swore to come back to me when she had healed."

"You were a child to her," Maveezh said, as though explaining to a child, "She was by far your elder, and would live long after your death. I do not begrudge you the need for company and understanding. Do not begrudge her the need for love, even one so brief."

"It was not like that... She..."

"She wanted to remember her valiant lord," Maveezh said gently, "She didn't want to bury a frail old man."

Her words were moving him, she could see; moving him in the direction she wanted. Thankfully, the guadim knew enough to stay out of it. The wicked being was still hunched in the field like a putrid scarecrow, leering at them, waiting. She imagined that waiting was a guadim art form.

Maveezh had not been completely honest about her dear Ghethas. The world wouldn't last long enough to watch him grow old, so her new immortality was irrelevant. No, the problem was a bit more selfish: how could he have joined her as a mortal man in her new existence? His petty appetites and exploits were as child's play to her now, and she feared she would grow bored of him. *Ah, if only things had been different. If only he had been stronger of will, more patient, more cunning. Like me.*

An unholy ache racked her body, screaming for blood. She felt the call of the hunger, heard the wail of the thirsting spirit inside of her. It was as if every vein, every muscle, every organ were caving in on itself. She wanted to run to the nearest building, burst through the door, and bask in the blood of every living thing inside. She fought, clenching her fists and squeezing her eyes shut, forcing that furious wail to fade into the darkness for now.

Gods above and below, I need to feed.

———

Maveezh exhumed herself, rising from her grave behind the Jaydecean temple. The previous evening had been glorious and horrific as she tore through the outlying farmhouses, draining the inhabitants like a vengeful goddess. Clavemont had joined her, making sure that no one raised the alarm. The guadim did its part, using its foul magic to dampen the screams of the dying and sap their will to fight or flee. Its presence frightened the livestock and made the dogs howl, but that only served to make curious farmers come outside where death awaited.

The town had been abuzz with activity during the day as peasants ran from house to house, calling for their missing neighbors. Maveezh had felt the vibrations under the earth, taking a little pleasure from their panic even as she fought to stay awake. They would not find them of course, not unless they dug in the fields near the forest edge. She estimated she had buried thirty men and women that first night, about a tenth of the village population.

Clavemont did not approve of her work, but he did not stop her. Instead he oversaw it, like a master guiding an apprentice. He told her where to hide the bodies, how to command their obedience when they rose, and even what to do with the children.

Young ones were a problem because as vemloks, they couldn't be governed by any means, and were more trouble than they were worth. He told her it was a mercy to behead them before burial, so they wouldn't rise. Maveezh didn't have the stomach for that, so the guadim did the job, gobbling the little bodies like the monsters of her childhood stories.

'Behave, children, or the monsters will eat you!' How wrong they were; good behavior hadn't saved them when the monsters came calling.

Now, as she took in her surroundings, she said to herself, "It seems we've made an impression."

Things had changed drastically since last night; not only did the village have torches planted around the main cluster of buildings, but there were armed fighting men patrolling in groups. She could tell that many people had gathered in the meeting halls and larger buildings, even within the temple. They were clustering together, hoping to find safety in numbers.

Spreading her arms, Maveezh rose like a kite into the cold night air, drifting up and away from the activity. In the distance she saw an even more interesting sight; many hundreds of campfires lined the road between the village and the castle. She made out the shapes of men, horses, wagons, and tents. Metal gleamed in the firelight, and the smells of an army on the march assailed her nostrils.

"So the civil war has begun!" she cried, laughing into the wind.

A presence touched her mind, like an umbrageous conscience that had long been ignored.

Maveezh. Come to me.

It was Clavemont's voice in her head. She did not know he could do that, and it nettled her.

What do you want? She replied, projecting her thoughts back at him. There was no answer. *Can I not communicate the same way, or are you just ignoring me?*

Come, he demanded.

Groaning like a teenager, she descended towards the source of the call.

Clavemont and Paugh were near the edge of the woods where Maveezh had planted her strange crops. The guadim was standing tall, keeping watch like some desiccated sentinel.

"My lord," she said with a smile.

Clavemont just stared impassively. He said, "Are you still planning on going through with this mad scheme of yours?"

"I thought my intentions were plain, my dear baron. I am doing the will of Mash *and* satisfying a craving for elven blood; thank you for that, it's quite motivating. The question is, will you be joining us in the feast?"

"My vow stands."

"Tsk, how boring."

"You have seen the army out there," he said, "Do you not think it's time to leave?"

"Before my own troops have arisen? Not at all! Maybe some of those good soldiers would like to join us."

"If you attack an army with a pack of vemloks, you will be destroyed," he said, "You could kill many before they stopped you, but they *will* stop you."

"Perhaps," she admitted, "But I think they will be gone before my lovelies see their first night. Then we shall feed, and *then* we shall go to meet the guardian of the woods."

"You are so sure your powers will be enough," he said, "Do you know the first thing about military tactics?"

"You do," she replied, "If you teach me, if you help me lead them..."

"I told you, I have no wish to enter the Shadowood."

"Then why did you bother to help me with my little project?"

"If you are going to survive, you should learn to do things properly," he said, "What you do with your new existence is none of my affair."

"Yet you care that I survive." She paced about for a few moments and asked, "Have you figured out why you made me as I am?"

"I keep wondering myself."

"Am I your child, perhaps? Your heir?"

"Heir to what? I have given you nothing."

"You have given me a means to fulfill my purpose! I had no power before, only a sharpness of wit and tongue," she said, "Now I have a chance to serve my god as never before, as you should have-"

"I did not seek to be *evil!*" he said, "I was not a minion of Chaos; I was a champion of Order and virtue, fighting against the fallen king Orthicus. Yes, I sought immortality; I thought the thirsting spirits could be tamed. That was my only folly."

"Surely not your only one," she said, "As I see it, you and I have three options. Option one, we overwhelm the Shadow Lord and reap the rewards. Option two, we use our vemloks to attack the elves when they return in force. Bad odds, that. Option three, we do nothing and let them save the world. Then we spend our remaining years living like parasites, waiting to be destroyed, judged and punished by the gods. Do you have a favorite choice? I do."

"What if we deserve to be punished?"

"Ugh! If *that's* your attitude, you chose the wrong woman to consort with," she said, "Life is hard enough without worrying about an afterlife designed by a tyrant. That's the very reason we want to tear it all down."

Clavemont shook his head, walking out of the shadows of the trees and into the moonlight. As he turned his eyes toward the heavens, his gaze settled on the bright red star in the northern sky.

Maveezh said, "You have been a prisoner to your fate for a thousand years, doing what you must to survive. Yet your judgment shall be worse than that of any mortal. How many murders have you committed in your time? I could not begin to imagine."

The pale lord heaved a sigh, but said nothing.

"How much longer do you truly want to live?" she asked, "I wouldn't want to persist for centuries. This is great fun, but even fun can get boring."

"I think that your faith has blinded you to an important fact," he said, "Most people want to live as long as they can. They want a better world for their children; they want to see another day and another age. They have hope for tomorrow."

"Most people are fools," she said, waving her hand, "One way or another, they are either devourers or the devoured; that is the way of things. I say live like there is no tomorrow, then make sure tomorrow never happens. The only thing that gives life meaning is that it ends."

Clavemont said nothing, but spent the rest of the night walking through the fields in silence. Maveezh took a cue from the guadim and stood back, watched, and waited.

Two days passed as the vemloks lay buried in their graves. Maveezh was hungry and anxious, but the cold soil comforted her and eased her pains. Through the muddled haze of her stupor, she could feel the vibrations of the king's army moving north to war, and a strange, distant tremor in the earth, followed forty minutes later by a muffled report, like thunder or a mighty cannon far, far away. Then it was quiet; only the sounds of worms and gophers disturbed her sleep.

Night fell and she arose with anticipation. The village was still lit and guarded; the sentries were even more alert and anxious now that the army had moved on. Tonight would be a living nightmare for the villagers, and she almost pitied them.

Clavemont was already waiting for her near the edge of the forest, and the guadim had found a perch in a high tree where it could watch the scene. She wondered what the creature did with itself all day and how it avoided detection. I occurred to her that she had no clue as to the extent of its powers.

"Good evening, my lord," she said, smiling, "How was your sleep?"

"Reflective."

"Oh?"

He said, "I was reflecting upon why I fled the city and hid in the mountains. I might have traveled to another city or crossed the sea, but I chose to bury myself far away from living beings. I chose to disengage."

She listened, her face impassive.

He continued, "I had no plan for the future, no goal. I only wanted to remove myself from life for a time. I knew the war was coming, yet I didn't want to take sides."

"It was not about temptation?" she asked.

"It was in part," he said, "but I think at its core, it was weariness; I am tired of justifying my existence. All my life, I have schemed and maneuvered, weaving webs of deceit and illusion, and for what? Comfort? Adulation? To be treated like I mattered?

"The truth is that I am a monster. I did not start as one, but that is what I became. It was my shame that drove me into the mountains, and I was prepared to lie in the ground with it, come what may."

Maveezh felt the thirsting spirit gnawing at her, but she pushed it aside. *He is almost there.* "I have found it most liberating to embrace what I am," she said, "To be true to my nature."

"I am cursed either way," he said.

She asked him, "Did you finally decide why you made me?"

"I think it was an act of mercy; perhaps the only kind I am capable of now. I could either have let you die, or give you a chance to exist as I do. I knew not who or what you were when I took you, but I felt you deserved a chance to survive."

She said, "I imagine it was a shock to learn that I was part of what you were running from."

"It was," he admitted, "Fate decided to play a great joke upon me. That damned guadim finding me was bad enough, but to learn he had fed me Lemorea Gordon of Portshia, and she was a priestess of Llomaak?"

Of course, she thought, *we met at the Corrina girl's birthday dinner over four years ago.* "I prefer Maveezh," she said, "But you know that; I did not think to ask how."

"I overheard you while you were playing with your food," he replied, "You have a pernicious mind."

"Thank you," she said, "My way was never brute force; I am a woman, and must rely upon my wits and wiles. Or at least, that used to be the case."

He gave her a gentle yet sad smile, and pondered for a moment. Finally, he said, "I never asked you how you lost your husband."

Maveezh was taken aback by the compassion in his voice. Whether practiced or sincere, she could not tell. "He fell victim to his impulses and poor planning," she said.

"I am sorry."

Again, she thought, *he sounded sincere. So strange.* "He had found the daughter of the count in hiding, and tried to assassinate her."

"Indeed?" he said, "She survived her voyage after all?"

Maveezh said, "She was traveling in the east with a pack of Galindri nomads, and we believe she returned in secret some two years ago. Her father's knights were hiding her in the city, but my Ghethas found her."

Clavemont said, "It would have been a shame had he succeeded; I rather liked the girl's spirit."

"Then you will love this," she said, "The little trollop was disguised as a boy and training as a knight! Can you imagine? We assumed the count planned to wed her to the little bastard son of the Shadow Lord, but-"

"So *he* was the boy's father! That makes sense. That explains everything... so much power..." His voice trailed off as his eyes grew distant.

"Last I heard, she was facing trial for her crimes of deception," she said, "I wish I knew what had come of that."

"And the boy?" he asked. He still had that distant look in his eyes.

"The little blood sausage is out of our reach for now, unless you want to storm Casselvane Keep to get him," she said.

Clavemont said nothing. No denial, no reprimand, nothing. *Excellent. He is coming around,* she thought with a touch of glee.

"It is starting," said the guadim from the tree above them. It pointed to the edge of the field.

Mounds of earth were rising like hives on the skin, pushing up and growing as the corruption within prepared to burst forth. Gray hands and heads broke the surface, clawing, gulping desperately for air that was no longer needed. A chorus of ragged moans and croaking issued forth, causing the nightly noises of forest and field to go silent.

"I think," Maveezh said, "that once we let our babies feed on the village, we can raise another crop. What do you think, dear baron?"

Arton Clavemont gave her a derisive snort and shook his head.

Then he smiled, just a little.

Chapter Twenty Seven

The Road to War

A cold wind blew from the southwest, chasing across the sloping fields and whistling through the bare bones of oak trees. It swayed the pines as it ascended the foothills, racing for the sunny peaks above. Many faces lifted to feel the breeze, for though it was still a brisk and chill 19th of Selvimoth, the constant uphill marching was hot and weary work. The grim soldiers formed a line that stretched for many miles upon the Casselvane Road, and the first men to make camp would be settled in for hours before the last men arrived.

Sir Cord's company was near the front of the army; only the king and his retinue rode before them. That might change soon however, as vile ambushers had taken the lives of many a lord in the northern army, and the king had no intention of letting that fate befall his captains or himself. But at least for now, things were as they should be. The king, the count, and their combined lieutenants would reach Syngmore Castle near the late afternoon, and the army would pitch camp along the side of the road.

Sir Jaron's backside was aching from the days of riding, but he was sure his squire had it worse. Young Filbert had no money to buy a horse, and Jaron could not afford one; besides, there were none to be had in the city, unless one wanted to purchase an old nag from a poor teamster. Therefor the lad was walking, carrying his pack, mace, shield, and spear. Filbert's lanky arms and legs had filled out considerably since he had first arrived at the fighting school, but he was still thin and his back was bent. Another little earthquake like the one five days ago would surely topple him over.

"Are we there yet?" he asked.

"Not yet," Jaron said, "but that's Syngmore Village up ahead."

"Where?"

"Just there," he said, pointing, "where the smoke is rising over that field."

"It's just a smudge," Filbert said, "how can you tell?"

"This isn't my first trip along this road," Jaron said, "That field dips down into a shallow valley, and there's a stream that runs through the village and into the woods. You'll see it once we're over this rise, and the castle too."

Dirty white patches of snow still hid in the shadows of the trees, holding out as long as they could. The snow on the mountaintop was beginning to melt and run down into the valley below, and soon the narrow creek beds and tributaries would begin to fill with ice-cold water, all of it rushing to feed the Joshian River, and eventually, Portshia.

Filbert asked, "Do you think they'll come out to meet us, or hide like the last bunch?"

Jaron shrugged. "Hopefully they'll come out to cheer on their king, but I wouldn't blame them if they hid. We'll be camping on their doorstep."

"But why hide at all?" he asked, "We aren't the enemy!"

"All armies are the enemy to the villages along the march. In warmer months, they might have come out to sell us food and ale, but all they have now is what they put up for winter. They're afraid of foragers coming and taking everything."

"But we'd pay them for it," Filbert said.

"What good is coin if you've nothing to buy? You can't eat copper."

"But the castle has food stored away, surely."

"The lord will keep his granary full in wartime," Jaron said, "If he feeds our army or his peasants, he'll have less if there's a long siege."

A thought occurred to the lad. "What happens when we enter Dissenter lands? What will become of the villages there?"

Jaron sighed, "That depends on the king's orders. They're all his subjects and I don't think he'd wish to see them suffer, but this is *war* after all. His army needs to eat."

"So we might have to... forage?"

"We will. We can only hope the Dissenter lords don't burn out their own villages to deny us supplies."

Filbert was silent the rest of the way over the hill and into Syngmore Valley.

Jaron was pleased to have his very own pavilion this time out, and stood back to admire it. It was a modest, single-post tent with enough room to sleep and don his armor; he had no furniture for it, so he and Filbert would be sleeping on mats on the ground. He purchased one with the blue and gold colors of House Corrina, rather than the green and brown of his own poor house. It was to remind others that he was a Corrina knight, and the count's champion besides. Some had found it easy to forget this in light of the scandals he and Cindra had caused. He had received many odd looks, but so far no one had confronted him openly, for which he was grateful.

"Nice, snug and private; perfect for shagging," said a voice from behind him, "It's a shame your current squire isn't as pretty as your last one, eh Dunlorden?"

Frowning, Jaron wheeled about to find Sir Gerard Valdoy looming over his shoulder. His intense eyes were creased as he flashed a yellow grin, and his usually wild hair was plastered to his head with sweat.

"Oh, it's you," Jaron said. *No point in taking offense; that only makes him worse.*

"Aye, it's me," Gerard said, "at your service. Unless, of course, that service means I disgrace myself on your account."

"Something crawl up your backside, Valdoy?"

"Aye, something has," he said, hands on hips, his wild, blue eyes meeting Jaron's blue-gray gaze.

A moment passed, then another.

"Well, out with it!"

"You," he said, pointing, "*you* recommended me to train that skirted little piece of she-cat tail, didn't you?"

"*Careful,* Gerard. That's the count's daughter you're insulting."

"I know, I said *she-cat,* didn't I?"

Jaron glared and sighed, "What of it?"

"Do you have any idea what it's like teaching a girl to fight on horseback like a man, while *actual* men are watching?"

"As a point of fact, I do."

"No," he waged his finger in Jaron's face, "no, *you* knew she was a girl, but no one else did. There's a *huge* difference."

"So what are you saying? Your honor was tarnished? Your reputation got *worse* somehow?"

"I'm saying for the first time in my life, I'm embarrassed to show my face to my peers, that's what!"

"Is that why you've been wearing your helmet all this way? Seems I've done everyone a favor."

Gerard leaned in close. "Maybe *you* can bear the shame of being a disgrace to your spurs and your vows, but I take things more seriously."

"Then you should've taken your charge more seriously. The king himself wanted her training completed, so you should have been honored."

"*Honored?*"

Jaron shrugged, "I figured you had so little honor left, that you'd appreciate being tossed a bone."

Gerard stared for a hard moment before he broke into an ugly grin, took Jaron's face in his big hands, and gave it a little shake and slap. "Ha! You little shit, I see your tongue has sharpened up, even if your brain's gone dull. Too much thinking with your *dirk*, that's your problem."

Jaron knew the man's ways, and allowed himself to relax. Sir Gerard only respected someone if they could give as good as they got. He wondered if Cindra had ever managed to earn his respect.

Probably.

Cord's voice thundered in the near distance, "Dunlorden! Valdoy! Get over here!" He was standing by his supply cart, waving them over. His brothers were nearby and there was a peasant beside him, wringing his hands.

Gerard grumbled, "Oh, what now? Is he your nanny?"

Jaron, for his part, welcomed the distraction. Filbert came out of the pavilion and followed the men, boredom and curiosity getting the better of his exhaustion.

"I've got a mission for the both of you," Cord said, "I want you to follow this man back to the village and unravel a mystery."

"Mystery?" Jaron asked, "What makes you think I'm qualified for clever work?"

Cord said, "I want your squire for the clever work; I just didn't want you to feel left out."

Gerard barked a laugh, and Filbert looked suitably embarrassed for his master.

Cord said, "Actually, you were raised on a farm, which makes you more qualified to know if something is amiss. I trust your instincts."

"Then why send me?" Gerard whined.

"You were stupid enough to be standing next to him," Cord said.

"Awww!" he cried, throwing up his hands.

"What's this about?" Jaron asked.

Cord motioned to the peasant, "This fellow claims that many families have disappeared in the night. Find out why."

Jaron, Filbert, and a reluctant Sir Gerard trudged across the fields towards one of the outlying cottages, listening to the man tell his tale.

"When they didn't show fer work, we began to worry," he was saying, "There's lots to do before the spring plowing, mind you. It's manure spreading season."

"I noticed," Filbert said, as he wrinkled his nose.

"By mid-morning, we went to check on them and they was all gone, man, woman, and child. And not just from one or two cottages, but ten!"

"What about the livestock?" Jaron asked.

"Still there, sir! None would leave without their goats or pigs, or chickens at the least. It's our wealth, if you follow me."

"I do," he said. Most peasants didn't own the land they farmed, and wages, if any, were poor. One thing had not changed in over three centuries: peasants could not just pick up and leave without at least informing their lord.

They reached the outermost cottage, which was half a mile's walk from the encampment on the road. Peasants were in the fields, removing rocks and weeds, and spreading heaps of dung out of wheelbarrows. Jaron felt a wave of nostalgia for the scene, remembering simpler, harder times. He found himself missing his father, the farmer knight, who gave his son a chance at a better life.

"Gods, what a shit hole," Gerard said as he peeked in the door, "Reeks in here."

Jaron gave the peasant an apologetic look and entered the cottage, but he had to agree with Gerard. The farmhouse was in tatters and stank of filthy clothes, stale wine, and stew that had gone off.

"No livestock about," Filbert said, holding his nose.

"This fellow has none," said the peasant, "He's a drunkard, and they used to say a murderer too. His boy vanished six years ago and we never found the body; then a *wizard* showed up two years later asking about the lad, saying he was alive! Whatever it all meant, there were strange stories about this family."

"What kind of stories?" Jaron asked, lifting a flea-ridden blanket with the tip of his sword.

"The mother died after an unnatural long pregnancy, and the boy was said to be watched by ravens and evil black wolves. Bad omens all around."

To Jaron it sounded like nonsense, but that was not unusual for these small communities. Folk stories and rumors were about the only entertainment these people could afford.

"Has anyone moved things about?" Filbert asked.

"Not that I know of, sir."

"I'm not a sir, I'm a squire."

"Ah, sorry, squire. Things are as they were left."

Jaron examined the dirt floor. "So you say there was only a man living here?" he asked.

"Aye, sir."

"These footprints in the dust, they seem small, like a woman's. Barefoot too."

"Well, I'll be..." said the man.

Filbert's foot prodded a hand ax lying on the floor and he said, "There's two sets of prints here, larger and smaller, close together."

"Here by the table as well," Jaron said.

"Sounds like the old fellow got lucky," said Valdoy, "Can we move on? I think I'm getting fleas."

The next several cottages told a similar tale. Beds were rumpled, food stores were in place, and all the meager possessions one might expect were still in view. If they left, they left in a hurry, carrying little more than the clothes on their backs.

"Where would they keep all their clothes?" Filbert asked.

"On their backs," Jaron said.

"I meant a change of clothes."

"You *might* find someone's Massday best tucked away, but I doubt these people had multiple outfits to take with them."

Valdoy said, "These are piss-poor clod kickers, boy. The wardrobes and chest o' drawers are up in the castle town, not this quaint, rustic dump. They won't have no wizard lamps or enchanted larders neither."

Jaron said, "There's too many footprints to make anything out, but obviously a family lived here," He picked up a little doll made of straw and scraps of cloth, "One might say there are signs of a struggle."

"And one might say these people lived like swine. Honestly, how can you tell?"

Jaron was getting tired of Gerard's mouth, but at least the peasant man was no longer within earshot. "Peasants are like anyone else," he said, "when they knock something over, they pick it up. They keep their bowls on a shelf, not overturned on the floor."

"I'll tell you what happened," Gerard said, as he helped himself to some cold porridge, "these cowards heard the king's army was coming, and instead of cheering us on, they scattered like rats. No mystery, just a bunch of stupid villagers who didn't want to give up the goods."

"Then why not take the goods?" Filbert asked, "If they feared we'd steal their food, then why leave it behind?"

Gerard growled around a mouthful of pilfered porridge, "Who's stealing?"

"And why are just the outer houses abandoned? Why flee in secret from their neighbors?"

Jaron nodded, saying, "Something happened to them. Someone went to each house and either took people or warned them to flee."

"The barefoot woman?" Filbert said.

"Maybe..."

"Listen to you two," Gerard said, "making a fuss out of nothing. Peasants hide all the time, *especially* when a hungry army comes marching by."

"This is more than fear," Filbert insisted, "this is foul play; I'm sure of it."

Gerard's face was incredulous, like he was staring at a dog reciting poetry. "There's no blood, no bodies, and no sign of looting. *I* say they ran off. Just what are *you* saying, boy?"

Filbert stood his ground, but avoided the man's wild gaze. "I'm saying that they had at least one visitor last night, a visitor who avoided the main village and caused isolated people to leave behind all they owned, even their shoes."

"Wha- of course!" Jaron said, "I hadn't paid them any mind. The shoes!"

"What about shoes?" Gerard asked.

"They're all here," Filbert said, pointing, "Neatly tucked under the beds, in every house we've seen. Who runs out on a winter's night with no shoes?"

Gerard had to pause and consider that.

"The ground's too hard to get useful tracks, at least to my eyes," Jaron said, "Which direction do you think they went?"

"No direction makes sense," Filbert said, "South or north, and they'd meet the army or its scouts; the closest village is Hoof's Tread, thirty-five miles up the road. To the east is the mountain foothills; I suppose they might have a refuge up there. But west..."

"...Is the Shadowood," Jaron said, "They'd never wander in there to feel safe. I spent one night away from the road in those woods, and I never want to do it again."

Gerard said, "If these maggots have a hidey-hole up in the foothills, the others will know about it. I say we ask them." Then he took off his cloak and began bundling up all the salted meat, beans, peas, and other edibles he could carry.

Filbert looked like he wanted to protest; Jaron gave him an understanding glance, put his hand on the lad's shoulder, and motioned for them to leave the abandoned cottage.

Later that evening, Jaron was sitting at a bonfire with Sir Cord, his brothers, and their squires. The sun had gone down over an hour ago, and the men had just finished their evening meal of dark rye bread, pickled fish, cheese, and wine. It was better than what most were eating, but Jaron found himself looking at Syngmore Castle and wondering what was on the royal menu this evening.

The encampment stretched for many miles along the road. The garish colors of banners and pavilions, glorious in the noonday sun, had faded into darker autumn hues in a night lit only by fire.

Turning to look towards Syngmore Village, Jaron saw that the distant community had been lit as well. Torches and bonfires burned precious fuel, as did the lamps and candles in the clustered dwellings. Guards had been set along the perimeter to keep watch in the night; whether to keep people out or in, they knew not which.

"I can't account for it, but the people are scared," Jaron said. No one had a better explanation for the mystery, but neither did anyone seem to want to dwell on it.

Cord said, "They can rest a bit easier tonight, but tomorrow we march. Try not to think about it."

"It's hard not to," Jaron said, "I can't help thinking that something terrible happened to them."

Carstin let out a belch and said, "I have to agree with that Sir Gerard character; they probably fled to the foothills or into some rabbit hole. Farmers are a skittish lot."

"Not all farmers," Jaron said.

"Aye, present company excepted, Sir Jaron," he said with a wink and a grin.

Sir Colin stroked his large mustache and said, "Whatever befell them, come tomorrow they will be our lord count's problem. In war, it's wisest to look ahead, not behind. There'll be plenty of misfortune in our wake before long."

The squires exchanged somber looks. Most of them had never been on a campaign before. Bradric Hyne chewed his lower lip, as he usually did when pensive. Filbert watched the smoke and sparks rise on a current of heat, imagining the fate of many a town and village. The squires of the Freekirk brothers were seasoned men from Cordo province, but their faces fell a little at the thought. Glorious combat was one thing, but pillage and terror was another.

Sir Ceven said, "I believe the king will use mercy with the undefended towns; it's the fortified ones that will be a challenge. I understand that Syngmore Castle will be our supply depot, so we won't have to forage much during a siege."

Bradric asked, "Will we have to scale walls, do you think? I'm not one for heights and ladders."

Cord said, "That depends. If this business is to be done by year's end, we can't afford lengthy sieges to starve them out."

"Ha! It would be a miracle if it only takes a year," Sir Carstin said, "This civil war could rage on for *many* years."

Jaron asked, "How many would stay so long? It's taken four or five months for the most distant provinces to even get here. There are crops to be raised back home and families to feed."

Colin said, "Aye, there's a fair amount of conscripts who would need to return, but aside from the lords and their men-at-arms, the rest of the king's army are free companies. Or haven't you noticed all the odd banners?"

"Heraldry was never my strength," Jaron said. *Mercenaries too? How much is this costing?*

Colin smirked, "You read too many of Ceven's word books when you should've been learning pictures. A knight should know the banners of both sides in a conflict."

Jaron pursed his lips but said nothing. Colin had always run him down as a boy, having trouble accepting a farmer's son as Cord's page and squire.

"If there was a deficiency in his training," Cord said, "it was my fault. I let him decide how to spend his leisure time."

"And I was indulgent," Ceven said, "It was a pleasure to have someone share my love of literature, unlike the lunkheads I had for brothers."

"Literature?" Carstin said, "Filling his head with romances and chivalric poppycock; you see what he went and got himself into?"

"I haven't met the lady," Ceven deadpanned.

"There's plenty of blame to go around," Colin said, "but considering what we had to work with…"

"Gods damn you all!" Jaron growled, "It's bad enough I get mocked by the likes of Sir Gerard and every other knight brother, but I don't need to hear it from you lot."

They all turned in astonishment, but their gazes lowered when they saw the pain in his eyes. The squires gasped and looked to their masters, wondering if this insolence would go unpunished. Captain's adjutant or not, Sir Jaron was speaking to his betters.

But Cord said, "No, no you don't need to hear it; not in jest or in earnest. You've proven yourself as the count's champion, follies and all. No one here questions your worthiness, lad."

"I don't need to be buttered like a biscuit, I'd just appreciate some respect for once, not a parade of my flaws and 'follies' as you call them. Everyone knows what folly you mean."

They all sat in silence for a moment, rebuked and ashamed. Then Ceven said, "That's the problem with brothers; they can have your back and whittle you like wood at the same time."

The bonfire cracked and popped as the sound of other people's laughter and conversation echoed in the dark, punctuating the sullen, introspective silence.

"You're all adopted," Cord said.

Morning came early as the trumpets sounded in the predawn darkness. Tents were struck and campfires were doused as the men made ready for another weary day of marching. In three days they would cross the border into the neutral province of Calshira, where the king hoped to raise more support from Baron Hurnwaerd at Hurn Castle. South of that lay the dissenter province of Wensic and the town of Odex on the Weness River. It would be their first objective, and hopefully their first battle of the war.

But Jaron's mind was not on the march or the coming battles. His thoughts were far away, in a dark and sinister forest.

"You miss her," Filbert said, as he helped Jaron into his armor.

Jaron was startled out of his reverie. "What?"

"Lady Cindra," he said, "you get that far away look when you think about her. They call it 'woolgathering' back in Gorshed."

"How did you know I was thinking about her?"

"Because when you get that look, you mention her name soon after. I've been paying attention."

"Have you now? I require you to serve me, not be in my head."

"Sorry, Sir Jaron, but serving well means knowing your moods and manners. I've trained under you for two years now, so I dare say I've picked up a thing or two."

Jaron grumbled, "Very well, I suppose... Yes, I do miss her. We were very close for those two years, and now it feels like I've lost a limb."

"Some of the students envied you when they learned what was up," he said matter-of-factly, "There was... impolite talk, shall we say."

Jaron sighed and said, "I hate to disappoint the wags, but it was no easy thing living with her; it wasn't some fantasy come true. Each night we were filthy, bruised, and exhausted. When we weren't out in the yard or the hall, we were in each other's way, cooped up in that little room that held all of our secrets. Our moods would clash sometimes... but what I like to remember are the things that made it all worthwhile."

Filbert considered that as he fastened the ties on Jaron's armor. "How far into the Shadowood is she going?" he asked.

"I don't know," Jaron replied, "No one knows for certain; it's hoped that the boy's father will guide them somehow." Jaron had told Filbert the general nature of her quest, if not the pertinent details.

"Do you think it's very dangerous?"

Jaron shook his head, "I doubt it's as dangerous as where we're going. The Shadowood has a bad reputation, but the Joshian Road is well-traveled. I'm sure she'll be safe enough."

He certainly hoped he was right; his heart would not beat for battle if it was worrisome or broken. Yet for all his hopes and desires, he feared that this would be his final campaign. Carstin had been right; this war could last for years, with a heavy price paid in blood on both sides.

———

It had been five days since the army had marched north, heralded by that terrible, distant rumble of thunder before noon. Count Amon Corrina was now the resident lord of Syngmore Castle in his brother's absence, organizing a supply depot for the southern army. Velloness Castle would fulfill the same role in the northeast, sending vital food and ammunition to the northern forces as they took Wenmaar, Hyton, and finally, the pretender's capital of Ahrnok. It was a tremendous gamble, but the king did not want to rely on foraging alone to feed his army.

Those five days had not been without their troubles. Amon received more reports of missing villagers outside the walls just three days after the first people had vanished. There had been broken doors, smashed furniture, and many screams, but no one saw the attackers; those who ran towards the danger never came back.

Even the sentries had disappeared.

All told, a third of the village was missing. The count had ordered the remaining peasants to retreat inside the town walls. Now there were two hundred frightened, misplaced people to care for, and limited supplies.

But there was a ray of sunshine that broke through the clouds of his dark thoughts. Gavagul, the family ember swallow, had just arrived from Portshia bearing a message from his beloved wife.

The bird was perched on a tall-backed chair in Aren Corrina's day room, which Amon had been occupying. He hoped the creature's heat would not damage his brother's furniture.

"Speak," said the count.

The bird straightened a little, ruffled its feathers, and began speaking in the soft Aurilonian accent of Zara Corrina.

"My dear husband, I hope my message finds you well. I do not wish to distract you from your new duties, but

I thought you might like to hear some good news from home.

"It has been almost three weeks since that horrible incident at DuShonmaer, and I am pleased to report that Ildric Finnael is finally recovering from his injuries. He has required healing and divine alchemy at great expense, and I am tempted to bill it to His Majesty's account. Thankfully, Ildric's assistant is a gifted jester, and has managed to keep all of our spirits lifted."

Amon had to chuckle at that; the strange little man, or elf, or whatever he was, had been a frustrating house guest during the week the count had come to know him. The rogue had been pranking the servants, and liked to play irritating word games. At least he was being of help now.

Gavagul continued, "Sadly, there is no news of Cindra. Master Finnael is too weak to seek her out, and he says that the boy Nixy has a powerful scrying ward upon him. Perhaps it is for the best; he says if we cannot see them, then enemies cannot either."

The count had expected as much, yet he could not help but worry. So much was riding on her mission, and the power in the Shadowood was a great unknown.

"In closing, I send you my love, and pray to the goddess that your stay will be brief and uneventful. Give my love and condolences to dear Vallia, Lady Syngmore. My heart breaks for her and her dear, sweet Gaius; may the Blind God judge him kindly. Farewell."

Gavagul chirped, stretched, and ruffled his feathers, shedding a wave of heat across the count's face. Amon went to his plate and cut a strip of meat for the bird, his customary payment. Gavagul took the offered food happily, eyeing more.

"Thank you, Gavagul," Amon said, "take your ease on something non-flammable."

The bird looked around the room and flapped over to nestle in an unlit brazier.

Amon would have to take some time to write a proper response to his wife. He wasn't good at expressing his feelings as he spoke, and always managed better in writing. Yet the bird didn't carry physical messages, so he would read his words to Gavagul once he got them just right.

But it would have to wait. Evening was coming on, and he needed to see to the welfare of the refugees from Syngmore Village. He trusted his brother's steward to know his business of course, and trusty Constable Fingelm was on hand also, but Amon had not traveled all this way to sit idle. He called for his house guard, put on a warm coat, and went to see what he could see.

The city of Syngmore was smaller than Portshia, but because it had land on all sides, it had to be better defended within its city walls. It had seven wards, and each ward was separated by tall walls and strong gatehouses. The walls were crenelated and manned; if an enemy breached one ward, they would have to fight their way to the next, and the next, and the next.

Once inside its outer walls, Portshia had its canals and drawbridges, but was otherwise wide open. Only the Winter Palace and the keep in the Peer District were defensible. Yet for all the defenses of Syngmore Castle, Amon did not feel as safe. It was not his home.

Nor was it the home of the masses that huddled within the walls, traumatized by the events in their village. There was no easy place to house two hundred people, so most of them were gathered in the streets, waiting for their turn to get food and shelter from the castle steward and his administrators.

Amon had asked the steward if it might be possible to find lodging within the castle itself, but the man gaped at him, as if the count had suggested herding wild boar into the chapel. He had said, "I... I must confer with the Baroness Syngmore before such a *drastic* measure be taken, milord."

And that was the end of that.

The baroness, Vallia Corrina, was in secluded mourning and was not to be disturbed. Amon had been greeted by her when the royal entourage had arrived, but had not seen her since. She took all her meals in her rooms and attended mass in her private chapel.

Amon understood. He understood *completely*.

He chose to conduct his tour on the walls of the ward, above the crowded reek below. With his bodyguard trailing behind him, he strolled along the battlements, looking down at the huddled masses. The local casting guild wizards were busy lighting lamps in the advancing gloom. Using their long, curve-ended staffs, they spoke the words and filled orbs of glass with fire that needed no air, and burned without heat until dawn. Many refugee villagers had never seen this in action before, and were amazed.

Funny what we become accustomed to, he thought.

It was then that he saw a strange and unexpected sight. A man in fine clothes was walking down the crowded avenue; he wore the thin sword of a gentleman, and had a gray doublet in the Aurilonian style, with black hose and gray shoes. Most important of all, his skin was ghostly white, and his hair was platinum blond. He made for such a sight that the people parted before him, some withdrawing in fear.

"Lord Clavemont!" Amon shouted, "Up here!"

The man looked up with pale blue eyes, smiled, and waved in return.

They now sat in the count's day room by the fire. The night air was cold and brisk, breezing in through the open window. Gavagul was still sleeping in the brazier, which had been filled with coals to make him more comfortable.

"I must thank you for the kind invitation, my lord," Clavemont said.

"Not at all!" Amon said, "I'm surprised to see you here, baron. You left Portshia without so much as a note."

"I am sorry for that, but there were personal matters I needed to resolve. I have spent some time at a private retreat in the mountains."

Amon raised an eyebrow. "Oh? I know of no such retreat. I hope you arranged to use the land?"

"No, no, it's very small and humble, little more than a cottage; it's quite secluded. I have lived there for the last eight months, free of news and company; I've been quite dead to the world."

"Eight months! Much has happened since you left, my friend. The war has begun. The king and his army left here and marched into the Dissenter lands less than a week ago."

Clavemont feigned surprise. "So it has finally come."

"Oh, and news from home that might interest you," Amon continued, "it seems that Kobus DuChat was actually a lord of thieves, and the high priest of a Llomaakitte cult! He was behind many assassinations and plots to create chaos in the realm."

"DuChat? Indeed?" This was news to the pale lord.

"It's true! Arch mage Finnael and his assistant uncovered the truth and led us to his front door, but DuShonmaer was a death trap. Alas."

Clavemont was truly interested. "What happened?"

"He escaped and left behind some Divine alchemy, a nasty bit of business. Wryley called it a 'chaos storm,' or was it 'swarm?' I can't recall."

"Wryley?"

"Finnael's odd assistant. I'm not sure if he's an elf or something else. Quite a unique fellow. But I digress; the alchemy tore through the mansion and destroyed everything, including the men sent inside to search. Ildric was thrown back and gravely injured, and there was fear that it would spread to the neighboring buildings."

"That sounds truly horrible, my lord. I trust DuChat will be found?"

"That may be more difficult than one might imagine," Amon said, "since it was discovered that DuChat is a duplict face-changer!"

"Really? I always felt there was something not quite right about the man," Clavemont said, "There is a reward, I take it?"

"Yes, the king has placed a bounty on his head of a thousand imperial crowns! But I am afraid it would take a miracle to find him." Amon shook his head and looked into the fire, remembering the terror of that day, the screams and the confusion. Clavemont sat digesting the news, his face unreadable.

"If it is not prying too much, baron" Amon said, "what could have driven you away from home for so long?"

The Gray Baron heaved a sigh and said, "I was finding myself."

"I don't understand."

He smiled. "When a man hides his nature for too long, he becomes a stranger. He needs to get away from distractions so he may know himself again."

The count smiled and shook his head, saying, "That sounds suspiciously like philosophy, my friend. I'm not sure what to make of that."

"Yes, I have suffered a great deal of introspection and meditation, I'm afraid. One can find their worst enemies in the mirror."

"So it is said," Amon agreed, "What did you learn in your solitude?"

Clavemont turned his pale blue gaze to meet the count's hazel eyes, so much like his daughter's. "I am not sure yet," he said, "A part of me wants to go back to the city and act out the lie once again; but another part of me wants to fulfill my desires and be what I have avoided for so long."

"What you desire," Amon asked carefully, "is it good or evil?"

Clavemont considered. "It is necessary. I have sipped at the goblet for so long, I have forgotten what it is to drink deeply from it. I am a good man, I'm sure, but my passions drive me against my oath. It's maddening."

"If that oath was made in good faith for good reason, then it would be wrong to dismiss it," Amon said, "that is my advice to you, my friend."

The baron nodded and looked into the fire again, his face a pale mask. Presently, he said, "I have heard a rumor; you have not spoken of it yet, so I am reluctant to ask, but did your daughter survive the attack at sea?"

The count smiled and said, "She did indeed!" and he told Clavemont the whole tale, up to the point that her deception was discovered by the king.

"There was a trial, and she was found guilty of dressing as a man, attending mass at the Balkonitte temple, and training at the Freekirk School, posing as Sir Jaron Dunlorden's squire, no less."

"Gods above and below," Clavemont muttered, "that's extraordinary! What happened to her?"

"She was sentenced to be chained to the monolith upon Tirgrim's Bluff for four days. She survived, but not unscathed. The king took it as an omen that she was to be a knight after all, and saw to it that her training was completed. I made sure she had the finest armor and weapon, of course."

Clavemont was impressed. "You seem to be a proud father, regardless."

"It took some time to admit it, but I am. She would have made a fine heir, were it not for her sex. She is brave and clever... she has the Corrina fire in her, and she's as stubborn as her mother. Yes... yes, I *am* proud of her, despite her... poor choices."

"I am not sure what to say, my lord. Should I congratulate you or not?"

"You can be happy that I did not have to mourn her a second time. That would have killed me, I am sure; her mother too. Incidentally, you were called as a judge at the trial."

"Oh dear. I'm sorry I could not help."

"Even I could not help," Amon said, "and I was a judge. Her guilt was undeniable."

"Then I am glad I had no part of it," Clavemont said, "I rather like her spirit; she reminds me of a woman I once knew."

"Her spirit managed to impress His Majesty as well; even now she is off on a quest in the king's name."

"Oh?"

The count leaned closer and said, "She is escorting a young half-elven prince to his father in the Shadowood. The king wishes her to seek the help of the elf lord in the coming conflict."

Clavemont just stared back at him in shock. His eye twitched. "Is she indeed?"

Amon nodded and said, "Things are grave, my friend. Ildric Finnael and others believe that an ancient evil relic is in the hands of its final bearer, and that the End of All Things is coming. There is hope that the power of the elder elves can prevent this fate, that is, if Cindra's mission succeeds."

"So it's true," Clavemont said, his voice sounding soft and distant, "The end is coming. There is no going back." He stared hard into the fire, as if trying to see the future in the flickering light. "You say your daughter and this half-elf prince are traveling in the Shadowood now?"

"They left Portshia on the 3rd of the month, so... this will be the twenty-second day of their journey; I imagine they reached the Shadow Lord's home many days ago, assuming they didn't wander aimlessly in the woods to find him."

"And they have no idea what's coming for them," said the baron.

"Pardon?"

"I've been thinking about the hereafter, my dear count," he said, "and I do not think Valdak will judge me kindly. Do you ever worry about that?"

Amon was confused by the change in the man; the news of Cindra's quest seemed to strike him like a physical blow. "Well, I... sometimes... I think all men do," he replied.

"Some more than others. Tell me, if this was to be your last day alive, how would you comport yourself?"

Amon thought for a moment and said, "I would wish to tell my wife and daughter that I love them dearly, and would carry that love into the Outer Realms for all the gods to see."

"That is admirable, my friend. But what if you had no one to love? What if you had no one close to you?"

"Then... then I would live my life to the fullest in the time I had. I would take whatever joy I could from the world before the end." Amon wondered, *What has gotten into the man? I have never seen him so morose.*

"Even if doing so caused others pain?"

"No... I would not wish for that, I'm sure."

"Neither would I, my dear friend," Clavemont said, "I would not wish you the pain of loss again. You have been through enough."

"I don't understand, baron," the count said, "What is this about, really?"

Clavemont extended his hand.

Amon's instincts told him something was very wrong, but seeing a hand extended in friendship, he took it.

It happened so quickly, that Amon Corrina barely knew what was wrong. He only knew he felt drained, sleepy, and weak.

Then he was gone.

Clavemont went to the brazier where Gavagul was sleeping and rousted the bird, saying "I have a message."

The bird blinked, ruffled its feathers, and said, "Who to?"

"Lady Zara Corrina, Countess Casselvane."

Gavagul's eyes glazed over for a second and he said, "Ready."

The vemlok recited, "Dearest countess, this is Arton Clavemont, speaking from Syngmore Castle. It grieves me to inform you that the lord count, your husband, has passed away in his chamber. An illness came upon him rather suddenly, but before he died, he wished to tell you and Lady Cindra that he loves you both dearly, and he will carry that love with him into the Outer Realms for all the gods to see. My deepest condolences are with you; if I could be there to ease the pain of your loss, I would do all in my power. Your servant, The Gray Baron."

Gavagul's gaze went from the baron to the count, who was slumped in his chair. A mournful warble escaped his beak before he flew off into the night with all speed, leaving a streaking trail of fire behind him.

Clavemont waited for the trail to disperse before stepping out into the air and flying towards the Shadowood Forest, silent as death itself. He had his own army to lead, and it would be on the march about now.

Chapter Twenty Eight

Staged

Emen Silverthumb awoke in a soft bed in a dark room with a single candle burning on a bedside table. He stared at that flame for some time before his mind pieced together what had happened to him.

I was pulled from the sewers and bathed. They had someone heal me; I remember having my bandages changed. How long ago was that?

"Hello?" he croaked, surprised at the sound of his rough, dry throat. He coughed, sat up, and immediately felt a wave of dizziness. "Oh dear. Let's just lie back down, shall we?"

His bandages were tied under his left armpit and up to his right shoulder, then bound around his arm. Even with his untrained eye, he could tell these were done by a skilled healer. He felt his shoulder where the assassin's blade had cut him; it was tender and ached when he moved it, but not terribly so. He remembered the pain, oh that radiant pain; he had been certain that if he survived, he would lose the arm.

Apparently not.

A thought struck him and he felt around his neck in a panic. *Ah! It's there. Thank the gods.* His medallion was still there under the bandages, protecting him from magical spying eyes. *I wonder why they didn't remove it?*

"Hello?" he called, a little clearer now. He heard the clomp of heavy boots, the door opened, and he was surprised to see the silhouette of another dwarf, a woman. Sunlight poured in behind her from a distant window.

"Well hello!" she said, "You're finally awake and lucid! We thought you'd sleep until spring, since the shaking and booming didn't wake you."

"Shaking and booming?"

"Oh aye, we had an earthquake ten days ago; shook the windows, it did. Then there was that loud boom four days ago; we heard that even in the sewers."

He blinked and looked around. "Where am I?" Emen asked. The faint, stale smell of the sewer was wafting in from the hall beyond.

"You, my dear fellow, are in the Shit House," she said, grinning, "It's what we in the waste management business like to call our humble guild hall."

She had an odd accent that Emen couldn't place. He said, "Waste management? That's a fancy name for it."

"If we don't treat ourselves with respect, who will?" she asked.

"Good point."

She came farther into the room where Emen could see her features. She had dark blond hair that was braided and covered with a kerchief. She wore a blue dress that was hemmed to mid-calf, and heavy boots. Her eyes were gray in the dim light, and her face, while not lovely, had a certain charming and honest quality about it. A large mole on her jaw drew his eye as she poured him some water.

"The official name is the Portshia Plumbers' Guildhall, Canal Side," she said, "We like to call it the 'Rat's Nest' when we're in a good mood, and the 'Shit House' when we're not."

Emen smiled. "The Rat Men. I remember now. You gave me quite a fright."

"Oh, that weren't me," she said, handing him the cup, "Some of the larger boys found you and brought you back. I was tasked with caring for you after the hospitaler did her work."

"A hospitaler? One of the Lelonethan priests?"

"Priestess," she said, "Nice woman, name of Sister Tabitha. She's an infection specialist. We use her a lot, as you might imagine. She worked on you every day for a week before you were well enough to be left alone. That was a nasty wound in nastier water."

That explains why I got to keep my arm, he thought. Then he said, "I'm sorry, I didn't get your name."

"Oh! Rude of me. The name's Belwarden, Gerty Belwarden, at your service."

"Pleased to meet you, Gerty," he said, but didn't give his own; he was a wanted man after all. "I wasn't aware there were women in the plumber's guild."

"I'm not an official member," she sighed, "but my husband is. There are few dirty jobs they won't give to a dwarf of either sex."

Emen nodded. It was a sore fact of life. "I don't recognize your face or name," he said, "Are you not from Miner Town?"

"No, my husband and I migrated here from Cantra on the Eshlin Bay, up north in Shylith-Dromah. Better climate here; not that we get to enjoy it much. Still, it's better when the sewers don't freeze."

"Shylith-Dromah!" he exclaimed, "That's a long way from here."

"Aye, it is. We took a ship from Port Kiron and sailed *all* the way around; Land's Rise Coast, Diamond Coast, Red Coast, and the Crimson Bay. Every time I got my sea legs, we'd make port and I'd lose them again. Never puked so much in my life, and that's saying something."

"Why didn't you come overland?"

"Oh deary," she said ruefully, "People our size don't travel hundreds of miles with all their belongings overland. There are too many who would see us as easy pickings; brigands, Galindri, town ruffians, wild animals... I've heard more than one cautionary tale."

"What about as part of a caravan?"

"One caravan wouldn't make the entire trip. That means putting your trust in new people each leg of the journey. That's over 600 miles of trust, and that's 550 miles too many."

Emen couldn't blame her for being careful, but he couldn't believe that such a journey was so dangerous for small people. Then again, he had never left home, so what did he really know?

"Now then, Master Silverthumb," she said, "let's get you up and walking around."

His eyes widened and he asked, "How do you know my name?"

She leaned close and answered, "Dangerous men have been looking for you; they've even stopped my husband and me once, asking a load of questions. Seems a dwarf named Emen Silverthumb went missing in the sewers."

"Did they say why?" he asked carefully.

She looked uncomfortable. "They said you were a thief and a murderer. They say there's a bounty on you."

"Well, that's to be expected. When they want you dead, they make up whatever story they like."

"Sister Tabitha recognized your medallion as a magic ward. She said to keep it on you when I changed the bandages, or whatever trouble you're in will come to us."

"A wise woman," he said. *It also means I'm wealthy, so they might be hoping for a counter-offer.*

She was watching him expectantly, waiting.

"So… why didn't you turn me in?" he asked.

"Well, some of the lads considered it, but my husband and I wouldn't have it. Also… we wanted to hear your side."

He gave her a little smile and said, "Help me up and I'll tell you the whole story."

Gerty, her husband Jarl, and a few of the other plumbers sat around the table and listened with great interest as Emen told them his tale. His harrowing escape through the underground was impressive, and he won their respect at least, but they were rather uncomfortable with having a boss of the Circle of Gold in their hall. Actually, he was the only remaining boss.

Emen was surprised to learn that he had been in and out of consciousness for nineteen days; it was apparently the 24th of the month. Jarl, a rugged-looking dwarf with a mop of curly hair and a thin beard, told of the events during Emen's long convalescence.

"The gangs are feuding now," he said, "There's been a big upheaval ever since the king declared Kobus DuChat to be their secret leader and the most wanted man in the kingdom; a thousand platinum nobles on his head, no less! Well, the same day we found you, the king's men marched on DuChat's mansion. There was a terrible fire they say, magic fire by the sound of it, and many were killed. It's said that the Arch Mage Talon Finnael cast a spell that went out of control, and it backfired on him."

"Unlikely," Emen said, "Is he alright?"

"Word is he was taken to the keep in a wagon with the king's own physician looking after him."

"These gang feuds," he asked, "how bad is it?"

"Bad. There's killings every day now, and they fight in broad daylight in the street! It's worse than Cantra or Port Kiron ever was."

Emen's thoughts were with the children in the Silver District. His orphans had looked to him for leadership and protection, and he had brought a gang war down on their heads. He needed to know how they fared, but how to get a message to them? He didn't want it to get intercepted, and he didn't want to put his benefactors at risk.

"I wonder..." he began, "I wonder if one of you might do me a great favor. I'll need someone to go strolling through the Market Square with a careless purse. I need to get a coded message to a pickpocket, and that might be the best way."

"You want one of us to *purposely* get our purse cut?" asked one of the men, "Coins and all?"

"I have some coins sewn into my clothing for emergencies," Emen said, "You can use them if you like."

"We already used a few of them to pay the healer," Jarl muttered.

"Sounds like a long shot to me," the man said, "and those coins won't come back."

"Oh go on, Reys," Gerty said, "It's a few coins, it's not the end of the world."

Emen's mouth went dry. *Not yet, it's not.*

The plan went remarkably well. Thorgan, a more willing and adventurous plumber, had come back from the market later that day, minus a purse and the coded message within. Only two days later, a package was sent by courier to the Portshia Plumbers Guildhall, Canal Side. It contained the purse, minus a few coins, and a message in the code Emen had taught to Narfi, his erstwhile valet and lookout.

Good boy, Narfi.

The message said to meet at three o'clock near the Grand Portshia Theater, a nice public place where nothing too violent was likely to happen. The theater square was only a few streets over from the hall, so Emen would not have to travel far. This was good because the gang that controlled the Gates District were known for their elaborate revenge killings. Kaplin

Jeorthea had been a vicious, spiteful man, and he instilled those traits in his followers.

It was Gerty's idea that Emen should dress in her husband's work clothes, and together they would make their way to the meet; just two little Rat Men inspecting the gutters and storm drains.

"My husband and I are a common enough sight in the neighborhood," she said, "Two dwarfs are better than one, since we're known to always work together. If you went alone, you'd be more suspicious."

Emen couldn't really argue. It was a wonderful idea, save for the smell.

Jarl's sewer clothes had been cleaned, as they were after each excursion, but it didn't help much. The stench of the effluent was deep in the thick, linseed-treated fabric, and no amount of soap and clean water would get it all out. Luckily, the mask took care of that. The pointed 'beak' of the mask was stuffed with aromatic camphor, mint, and a few other scents he could not place. In addition to that, Emen was given a dab of Essence of Elder under his nose.

"We don't use this much, since it's so expensive," Gerty was saying as she adjusted her own mask and hood, "That's divine alchemy, you know."

"I recognize the scent," Emen said, lowering his mask and peering through the little eye-windows, "This was used when they found me, wasn't it?"

"Probably," she said, "That was in the evening, after we'd gone home for the day."

Once they were both covered from head to toe in full sewer gear, they headed for the theater square. It was both liberating and frustrating to be in such a disguise. Emen felt about as safe as he could feel in broad daylight, but it was so difficult to see. He had no peripheral vision, and the beak made it hard to see where he was stepping. The lenses kept fogging up and clearing with each breath, and the treated fabric was a bit stiff and hot. Still, the clothing had the advantage of parting a crowd when they walked by, since no one wanted to brush past a sewer worker.

Gerty made a point of stopping at various storm drains and gutters, making a show of inspecting them. Emen had no idea what she was looking for and didn't ask; he just stood there and pointed at things, trying to look professional.

"Up ahead," she said, "we can cut through this passage." She led him through an arched tunnel that cut through the line of buildings making up the north part of the theater square.

They came out into the open under the shade of the western building, with the theater looming before them. The area was bustling with people as they spent the cooler part of the day browsing at the many shops that lined the square. Cobblers, tinkers, tailors, coopers, leather workers, and barbers could be found here, as well as a few ale houses that competed for the theater crowds both before and after a play.

Emen's first trip to the theater had been difficult. As a young man only able to afford a ticket for the groundling pit, he had needed to climb up and balance on a partition wall, hugging a support post as he looked over the heads of taller people. As the Circle of Gold's bird man, he had been able to pay for proper gallery seats. Since becoming Silver Boss however, he was always too busy to attend, though he could easily afford a private box if he wished.

"What's this lad look like?" Gerty asked, her voice muffled through the mask.

"He's a little taller than me, brown hair, freckles... he'll be looking for two short Rat Men, so I imagine he'll find us first."

Indeed, the sharp-eyed boy had found them, and he made his presence known by smacking a stick at each barrel, chair, and crate he came across.

"There he is!" Emen said, pointing.

Gerty lifted her mask and squinted. "What's he doing?"

"Pretending to hunt for rats," Emen said with a grin. It was a technique the orphans used to give them an excuse to loiter, blending in by standing out.

Narfi came up to them and said without looking, "That you, Silver Boss?"

"Yes, good to see you, Narfi," Emen said, "What news from the Warren?"

The boy grinned but kept his face down as he said, "Glad you're alive, boss! The Warren's in a tight spot. Most o' the enforcers been killed, including Garreth, Haydn, and the Sapper. Daymi an' Cricket ain't been seen in a week. Nanny's told us all to lay low, so the other gangs don't learn where we is. We got just a few pinchers workin' to keep us fed; that's how we got yer note. Peevy found it and he asked me to look at it, knowing you was teaching me codes."

"And you're a brilliant boy for deciphering it," Emen said, lifting his mask so Narfi could see his smile.

Narfi glanced at him and blushed. "Aww..."

"So what's become of the Circle?"

Narfi shrugged. "Ain't no Circle no more, boss; all the gangs broke up, what with their bosses all killed. Golden Hammer's fightin' both the Copper Gang and Velvet Gloves, and poaching in the Market Square; Silver Gang ain't got the muscle to stop 'em. Blood Circle and Hammers are killin' each other, and the Temple Gang is pickin' the bones; it's a mess, and make no mistake!"

Emen closed his eyes and shook his head. "What about Miner Town?"

Narfi moved around them as he spoke, pretending to look for rats, "There's been men calling, lookin' fer you. Some of the neighbors got roughed up and houses were searched. They says there's a bounty on you. They says you stole from the Circle and anyone hiding you is done for."

Emen's heart sank, horrified that his neighbors had been drawn into this disaster. Gerty made an unhappy sound under her hood.

"What's we gonna do, boss?"

"I... I don't know, Narfi. I don't know," he muttered. He slid his mask back down, wanting to hide behind it forever. *What have I done? Gods, what have I done?* He turned to face the theater, wondering if a tragedy had ever been written to match what he had wrought with his thrice-damned good intentions. *'I never pictured myself as the villain,'* he thought, recalling his words on the night he met Ildric Finnael and this whole damned mess started. *If only I could take it all back and keep my mouth shut. But what chance did I have against a wizard and a god?*

Just then, the back door to the theater opened and a sweating fat man stepped out, holding it open for two other men to join him on the steps. One of the men was in dark clothes, hooded and cloaked, and wearing a mask of his own; a snarling animal's visage that left only his eyes exposed. The other man...

"Oh gods!" Emen hissed, taking a step back, "That man, the big fellow with the sword... *he's one of the assassins!*"

"What? Where?" Gerty asked, more curious than was good for her.

"There, on the theater steps. *Don't look!*"

"Well if I can't look, then how can I see?" she lifted her mask to get a better view.

"What do we do, boss?" Narfi asked, "Should I go?"

"Yes, get back to the Warren but tell them nothing, not even Nanny. Do as she says until I contact you again. Stay safe!" he gave Narfi's arm a squeeze.

"Watch yer back, Silver Boss," he said, and went down the street, smacking for rats.

"If that fellow's one of your assassins," Gerty asked, "who's the creeper in the animal mask?"

"No idea," Emen said, "I can't tell from here."

"Well then," Gerty said, adjusting her mask, "Let's go and see, shall we?" She marched across the paving stones towards the theater.

"No!" Emen hissed, but he followed her. He had to follow; he couldn't make a scene now. He tensed as he saw the assassin put a hand on his sword as Gerty approached the steps. The fat man and the masked man continued their conversation, apparently oblivious.

Gerty stopped short of the stairs, motioning Emen over. Then she pointed up at the exotic animal heads carved in stone that were spaced along the top of the theater's round walls, just under the roof eaves. "There, you see?" she said in a muffled voice, "those are drain spouts from the domed roof. Whoever designed this thing was either a genius or an idiot; where the inner eaves and the dome meet is a terrible place for water to collect, so-"

"*Excuse me*," said the fat man, sharply, "but we are trying to have a private conversation. Do you mind?" The masked man looked over too, and Emen examined his face as best he could.

Gerty turned to them and lifted her mask. "Oh! So sorry master, but my husband and I were having a disagreement about your drainage system."

"Yes, well the spouts go around the entire building, so perhaps you could have your discussion on the *other side?*"

"Oh yes, definitely we can. Sorry, sorry to both of you. Come along, dear," and she motioned for Emen to follow.

He heard the fat man say, "Begging your pardon, master playwright... eh, where were we?"

Once they were out of sight, she asked, "Was that close enough for you?"

Emen lifted his mask and said, "I think that was Kobus DuChat! And by the way, you're a madwoman."

"Aww, my husband says the same thing. Are you sure it's him though? The lord of thieves?"

Emen was sweating profusely, and not from the warm clothes. "The hair, the eyes, those eyes..." he said,

"It's him, I'd bet my life on it. That is, if you don't do it first."

"Oh, stop complaining, you've found him! Now what?"

"I didn't *want* to find him. He's the *last* person I wanted to find."

"So what's he doing with that assassin at the theater?"

"That's a very good question," he said, and his eyes fell upon the freshly painted theater poster for *Mice at Play*.

Emen mulled over the encounter in his mind all afternoon and into the night. It *had* to be DuChat. He had seen those blue, heavy-lidded eyes up close once before; they were dead eyes, a killer's eyes, and the scar over the left eyelid... it had to be him. But why? It made no sense at all; he was a wanted man, the most wanted man in the realm.

That fellow called him "master playwright." What is DuChat doing writing plays? Why risk being seen, even in disguise?

Because he can change his face, he reminded himself.

Then why wear the DuChat face under a mask?

Because... because... He rolled over on the bed, staring at the dim light under the door. *Because the other fellow knows him only by those eyes. Maybe he doesn't know it's DuChat?*

Then he remembered a detail that eluded him before, *The poster said the author was anonymous. Of course! He wrote the play in secret!*

But why write a play? Is he larking about before the world ends?

It was an infuriating puzzle and the more he pondered it, the more his weary mind introduced other diversions to muddle his thoughts. Before long he was fast asleep, dreaming of people dressed as mice and rats that followed him everywhere, chanting, *"Rats, rats, bigger than cats, creeping up the hole..."*

He awoke late the next morning to the smell of bacon sizzling in the guild hall's little kitchen. Someone, probably Gerty, had left a fresh change of clothes folded on the little table by the bed. There was a note as well, written in an unpracticed hand.
Bought you clothes, hope they fit. You look to be Jarl's size. We used some of the coin you had sewn into your old clothes.
G.

It was just as well; he was glad that his emergency money had been put to good use. He had only a few coins left to his name unless he could get to the Silver Gang's stash, but the stash was in the Warren, and there were vengeful gangs between here and there. He wondered if the Rat Men might guide him through the sewers to the Silver District, then he quickly dismissed the idea. *No. I'll never go into the sewers again. Not if I can help it.* Thinking about it made his stomach turn.

As he washed his face in a basin, he felt the three weeks of silky growth on his jaw. *I need a shave,* he thought. Checking his wound, he was happy to see that it had scarred over and no longer needed bandages. "Thank the gods," he said. He got dressed and went to see if he could beg for some bacon.

"Good morning, Reys," he said, "Are you the only one here?"

"I am," Reys said, "my shift's over and I'm heading home after breakfast."

"So it's a day *and* night job?"

"It is. There's always something that needs doing. For example, Thorgan, Jarl, and Mikles were sent to clear out a body that got stuck in a storm drain."

"A body? Whose body?"

Reys snorted a laugh, "Probably one of your gang friends. They've been disposing of bodies left and right."

Emen said nothing to that. At least it was in the local area, meaning it was probably a Blood Circle or Temple Gang member. *I hope they finish each other off,* he thought.

"So, what's your plan for the day?" Reys asked.

"I was thinking... I was thinking of seeing a play," Emen said.

"Seeing a play?" Reys laughed, "Aren't you a wanted man?"

"Not as wanted as some," he said, "There's a mystery that needs solving, and I've nothing better to do."

Going out was a huge risk, he knew, but there was nothing for it. The questions were burning his mind and he had to have an answer. *DuChat must be planning something with this play, else why go through all the trouble? It must have to do with his ultimate goal, which is city-wide chaos,* he thought, *but how do you do that with a comedy about mice?*

He borrowed one of the spare dwarf-sized hooded cloaks and left the guild hall, heading for the theater.

It was a nice sunny day and the air was crisp and cool; there was a wonderful sea breeze that managed to creep over the wall and into the streets, and the sights and sounds of the city he loved were comforting and inviting. He smelled fresh-baked bread, and his stomach grumbled, despite the piece of bacon he'd fed it. Then he passed a large pile of horse dung in the street, but instead of the pungent smell he expected, there was only a floral, fruity scent like a whiff of spring. *The Essence of Elder,* he realized, *there's still enough to hold back the bad odors.* That was why his stroll was so pleasant; he was not under assault from the everyday stink of city life. He reminded himself not to wipe his nose, lest the expensive magical ointment become an expensive, useless stain on his sleeve.

Many people were out and about in the streets this morning, though he sensed that their moods were nervous and wary. He couldn't blame them. Most of the city's fighting men had marched away, leaving the city watch stretched thin and incapable of suppressing the flash fire of gang violence. He kept his head down and made for one of the taverns near the theater, where he could keep an eye on three of the four entrances.

He spent the next few hours at a patio table watching and nursing his mug of ale, waiting for DuChat to show himself again. It was the last Pokahtday in the month of Selvimoth, the traditional opening day for the theater's spring season. *Mice at Play* would be opening this afternoon to a public eager for some pleasant distraction, and the author was sure to be in attendance.

But he might be wearing a different face, he realized.

The day wore on and he ordered his fourth ale, wondering if this wasn't a colossal waste of time. No one had come or gone from the theater, though there were barkers advertising the show, and a few street sweepers with a guild wizard giving the square a good scrubbing. He watched the fellow take a hand full of sand from his pouch and toss it in the air, then wave his wand to create a swirling vortex, which he used to scour pigeon droppings from the high wall. *Not exactly an inspiring use for the High Art, but I guess it pays the bills.*

His eyes began to drift to other faces in the crowd as they passed his little table. Old and young, fair, average and ugly, light-skinned mostly, with a smattering of dark; a Galindri man here, a Maanok woman there, a couple who might have been from Minael, judging by the garish colors they wore.

No dwarfs.

It occurred to him that many of the eyes were looking at him, and he began to feel uneasy. There were two dwarfs that were a well-known sight in this part of town, and he was neither of them. Even though he wore the dark green, hooded cloak of a plumber, his features were not hidden under a mask this time. He gulped his ale and thought about leaving.

"Emen Silverthumb." The voice came from behind and above. Emen stiffened, but did not look.

Two men came around from either side, big and nasty-looking. Emen's heart began hammering as he glanced up at their leering faces. Thankfully, he didn't recognize either of them.

"Excuse me?" he managed to say with a tight throat.

"You're Emen Silverthumb, ain't you?" It was a question, but sounded like an accusation.

His mind raced for a way out. A flare of panic welled up in his chest, and he did the only thing he felt he could do, which was turn it into anger.

"Gods damn it!" he shouted, slapping the table, "Can't a dwarf have a pint in peace? You lot are the *fourth ones this week* asking me if I'm this... this Emen Silverthumb! I know we all look alike to you, but really!"

The men were taken aback, but answered by drawing their blades and threatening him. The other patrons took their drinks and moved away.

"Is that so? What's your name then?"

"Elbert," he said, pulling a name out of thin air, "Elbert Belwarden. My cousin is Jarl Belwarden of the plumber's guild. He got me an apprenticeship."

"I didn't ask who your cousin was or where you worked," said the man, growing suspicious.

Too much information can be worse than none; it was the first rule of lying. Still he pressed on, his anger covering his terror. The four ales helped. "I'm sorry, I thought we were in the quizzing stage of our encounter. That's usually how it goes; I say I'm not him and then we move on to twenty questions."

"Show us your arm," the other man said.

Emen sighed, made an exasperated face, rolled up his right sleeve, and displayed his arm with dramatic flair. He made sure to still cover the scar below his shoulder.

"There, you see? No wound." He rotated his shoulder about and hit it a few times for good measure. It hurt quite a bit, but he didn't show it.

The suspicious fellow put his blade under Emen's chin and said, "Who said anything about a wound? How did you know which arm to show us?"

"Because," Emen said slowly, as he eyed the blade, "You are the *fourth* ones to ask me this."

That gave them pause. The man tapped the knife under Emen's chin like a thinking man taps his fingers on a table. Luckily, this was a man to whom thinking was not a pastime.

"Suppose we take you to Miner Town and see if any of them recognize you?"

"But I don't *live* in Miner Town. I live up by the North Barracks. I can show you my apartment if you like."

The men looked at each other nervously. The barracks were where they kept the city watch.

Emen spoke more calmly now, "Look, I'm sure this Silverbottom fellow is a terrible person-"

"Silver*thumb*," said the other man.

"Thumb, whatever," Emen said, "but if you go accosting every dwarf you meet, he's never going to show his face in public again. Now may I *please* be allowed to finish my drink in peace?"

The men looked at each other, came to some kind of silent decision, and sheathed their knives. "We'll be watching you," said the suspicious one as they walked away.

"Yes, yes, thank you!" Emen waved at them and took a sip of ale. It was empty, but he pretended to drink, hiding his face behind the mug as he hyperventilated into it. *Gods above and below, that was close. How did I become such an accomplished actor?* He looked at the theater and thought, *Maybe when this is all over, they'll give me a job.*

Emen had meandered back to the guild hall after his ordeal and hid in his room until he heard Gerty and

Jarl talking with the other plumbers. It was now late afternoon and the play was going to open in an hour. He figured he had better let them in on his plan and give them a chance to talk him out of it.

"You did *what?*" Gerty cried.

"I know, I know, it was a calculated risk..."

"Calculated, my ass! Suppose they knew your face! Suppose they had a brain between them! You'd be a dead man and all my efforts would be for naught!"

"I know, it was stupid, you're right. But I've caused such a mess so far, and I just want to make it right somehow."

"How does getting picked up on the street make it right?" she fumed.

"It doesn't, but... look, DuChat wrote that play for a reason, and it's a terrible reason if I don't miss my guess. I must try to stop him if I can."

"You're not thinking of going to the play, are you? ARE YOU?" she grabbed his ear and pulled.

"Ow, stop it! You're not my mother!"

"No, I'm a sweetheart compared to your mother, if she knew you were going to do something so bird-brained and... and suicidal!"

"Gerty dear," Jarl said, "He's right; he's a grown man-"

"We left home to get away from criminals like that! After what we've both lost, I'd think you'd want to deny them another victim!"

Emen noticed she was close to tears.

"Gerty, Gerty listen," her husband said, taking her by the shoulders, "I know you want to keep him safe, but remember... he's *one* of them."

She stiffened and shot Jarl a stunned look.

"I know, I know, it's a cold truth, but he was a crime boss. He was in charge of murderers and thieves. It's the life he chose, and he must choose how to deal with it. No offense, Emen."

Gerty was about to protest, but Emen said, "No, no you're right. I was a boss, and I was in charge of thieves and killers. I never had anyone killed, but that doesn't excuse me. I have to make amends for the wrongs I've done, even if it means risking my life."

There. That sounded noble, he thought, *Never mind that I didn't choose this life; it's not worth arguing over. It doesn't change anything.*

"But, but Emen," Gerty said through her tears, "You aren't what they say you are. You tried to do the right thing."

"Yes," he said, "and many have paid for it, so I must try harder. If I can do something to foil this madman's schemes, well... I have to do it."

"But you might die," she sniffed.

"I might. Believe me, it's not my first choice. But I can either sit in my room until something terrible happens, or I can try to save my friends."

Tears streamed down Gerty's cheeks as her lip quivered. He gave them a warm smile and the three of them put their arms around each other and embraced.

"Oh gods, I might cry!" Reys wailed, "The love... can you *feel the love?*" He hugged Thorgan, who pushed him away.

"Eat a floater, Reys!" Gerty yelled.

Emen had given his noble speech, so now he had no choice but to follow through with his plan. Wrapped in his concealing cloak, for what it was worth, he stood in line with hundreds of other people to enter the Grand Portshia Theater.

It had not changed much in the years since he had last been there; perhaps a fresh coat of paint had been added. Barkers began calling for gallery seats only, so he moved ahead to the front entryway. The main portal had three directions one could go; right or left led to stairs to the upper levels where tickets were required, and straight ahead led to the groundling pit and the first-floor gallery. He dropped his ten copper kenmarks in the slotted box and took a seat in the last row, choosing one near the door in case he had to make a quick escape. *That was something that had changed,* he thought, *the prices have gone up. It used to be eight ken.*

He took a moment to admire the decor and the magic of the theater. The stage was mostly bare, but for a piece of cheese and a few household items that were all of enormous size. The domed ceiling, which was painted with a night sky, was still a marvel. He once saw a play where the house-mage had created an illusion of the moon crossing the dome at night. During summer days, around noon, the hole in the dome's crown would allow a shaft of sunlight to shine down on the stage to dramatic effect.

The ticket seats above were filling up, mostly with merchants, craftsmen, and minor nobility. He searched for the familiar face of DuChat, or even the craggy face of the Boss, his alter ego, but saw neither. *How many other faces does he have anyway?*

Eventually the groundlings were let in, and the house-mage began lighting the little wizard lamps around the stage in a solemn manner. Quiet fell upon the audience. Then with a wave of his hooked staff, he extinguished the house lights. Moments later the curtain went up, and the play began to raucous applause and cheers. Minstrels in the gallery above the stage played a jaunty tune, and mummers in silly mouse costumes poured out of a man-sized mouse hole, prancing and bowing as they took their places.

Emen almost forgot why he was there.

The play was rather delightful, actually. It was about two groups of mice that had different philosophies on how to deal with a large cat. It was funny, silly, and had an undercurrent of social commentary which Emen was insightful enough to see. He had always liked his entertainment with a message buried within, so long as it didn't beat you over the head with it. Even if he *had* missed an allegory, the man sitting in front of him felt the need to explain every damned thing to his wife, who kept shushing him. Emen wanted to kick him.

The second act had ended and the third act was soon to begin, with a brief intermission to set things up. Men were coming around with chained censers of incense to hang from the second level galleries, and the gentle smoke seeped out and gathered over the heads of the groundlings.

That's different, he thought.

Emen had not seen any sign of DuChat, but he kept his eyes peeled for anyone moving in the audience. Some got up to leave and he watched them closely, but they would return after a time, probably having relieved themselves somewhere. There were some rowdies, as usual, and some hecklers. The groundling crowd was lively and a bit inebriated, and the upper tiers were only a little less so. *Where is the threat?* He swiveled his head about, sweeping the audience like a lighthouse.

"You look around an awful lot," said the fellow next to him in a gruff voice, "lose something?"

"Just my good judgment," Emen said.

The man snorted a laugh.

The third act began on a darker note. One of the groups of mice, led by the daring Brio, attempted to fight the cat Fiorus with sewing needles and rose thorns. Their attempts got mice on both sides dragged away and eaten. Mumfo, the cautious mouse, tried to lead his group to safety in another hole and leave offerings for the cat, but it also led to deaths. The cast was dwindling, and the mood in the audience was growing restless. Shouts from the groundlings were becoming more angry, and even the people in the galleries were acting more uncivil than before.

Emen felt his head begin to swim a little, as though the bad feelings were contagious. The incense, which hung over the heads of the groundlings like a mist, was a bit overpowering. Then it gave way to a pleasant fruit and floral scent that made him feel himself again.

The Essence of Elder, he thought, *it's still under my nose, working its magic.*

The body count arose until only one mouse was left. Mumfo, the peaceful mouse, walked to the edge of the stage in a sorry, bedraggled state, and began to speak. His voice was choked with sorrow and pain, and his eyes seemed haunted by the horrors he had witnessed.

"All is lost!
Our efforts come to naught!
We neither can appease him, nor resist.
No matter which we choose, we end up caught
and toyed with underneath his padded fist.
My dearest kin were pierced with tooth and claw,
and bled until they'd nothing more to bleed;
pulled even from their home by massive paw
to fill the tyrant cat's voracious need."

Emen caught the subtext as if it had been hurled at his head. The city had endured much this last winter with the king's army descending like locusts on their food stores, then taking sons and husbands to war when it left. But calling the count a tyrant? That was a few steps too far, even for a subversive play.

Was this DuChat's plan? To make people angry with a speech?

"And thus this tyrant does his master's will
to crush the life from every wretched mouse.
Our bodies are but more grist for his mill;
our sacrifices help him clean his house."

That's the king's civil war he's talking about! How did this get past the royal censors?

The audience began to mutter and murmur, sensing the meaning behind it. Mumfo took on a lighter tone, and his expression changed to one of hope,

"And yet, it need not always be this way.
The lives of mice can once again be free,
as once they were upon a younger day,
when rodents lived in field, hole, and tree."

Mumfo spat the next words,

"But freedom from the master and his pet
means bringing down the house in which they live,
or future generations may forget
the cost we paid, and lives we had to give."

At this, many of the nobles in the upper galleries leapt to their feet and shouted at the stage, crying, "Sedition!" and "Down with the author!" The reaction from the floor was angry jeers and insults thrown at the upper levels. Things were getting ugly, and Emen even felt himself becoming aggressive and resentful. Then the smell of the Essence of Elder would kick in and cleanse his mind.

My gods, he thought, as realization struck, *the incense! It must be charm magic, and I'm the only one protected! What is this wretched smoke doing to the rest of them?*

The actor, looking a bit worried but still professional, took up a torch from the stage and held it aloft. His mood seemed a mix between concern for his own safety, and outright rage. He addressed the audience in the upper levels,

"So with this fiery brand, I set alight
the works of all the tyrants in the land.
For this mouse swears to *never* stop the fight!
The rodent revolution is at hand!"

And with that, he set the torch to the back of the stage, and fire leapt to the ceiling as he exited through the mouse hole. The audience recoiled, but soon realized there was no heat from the flames, and the house-mage was over to the side, concentrating with his staff. It was all an illusion.

Yet the smoke from the incense was real, and the anger was real, and the crowd's murmuring grew louder and louder. There was no proper ending to the play. No curtain call, no music, for the minstrels had left before the final scene; no chorus came forth to thank the audience for attending, just the illusion of a fire that didn't go out.

A silky voice said, "Quite a dramatic ending, don't you think?"

Emen turned. The man next to him was wearing the same clothes as before, but not the same face.

"Hello, Emen," he said. The man was slender and pale, with an angular face, narrow lips, a thin nose, and mismatched eyes that reminded Emen of Twist. He had a scar above his left eyelid which made it droop a little; apparently it was a feature he could not alter. His hair was auburn and straight, so different from DuChat's dark, wavy curls. He had the faintest fuzz about his jaw, no doubt waiting to spring into a beard on demand.

Emen found himself trembling. "Do I call you Boss, or High Priest, or Kobus?" he asked.

"They all apply," he said, "How did you like my little play?"

Emen looked to the crowd as some started throwing things at the spectators above. "I think if you meant for your words to stir up the audience, the incense is cheating."

"Well, what author wouldn't use it if he had it? Come, we should be going now."

"I'm not going anywhere with you," Emen said, sounding more brave than he felt.

"I don't think you want to stay here much longer, unless you want to be used as a missile." He grabbed Emen roughly by the collar and guided him to the door as fights broke out among the groundlings and those in the galleries. The patrons in the ticket seats began to stumble over each other in fear of the angry mob below.

"Clever, isn't it?" the duplict said, "The poor outnumber the rich by far, and they have reached a breaking point. Famine, disease, infestation, the hungry dead, and now occupation; this city has seen all of it the past seven months." He pushed Emen out the door as city watchmen came by, attracted by the riotous noise. Whistles were blown and commands were shouted.

"It won't work, you know," Emen said, "One little brawl isn't going to turn the city upside down."

"You underestimate the power of that incense," he said, "It's Llomaakitte divine alchemy. Incidentally, how are you not affected?"

"It's a dwarf thing," he lied.

"Hmmm. Ah well. If being the Circle's bird man taught you anything, it would have been to not put all your eggs in one basket, yes?" He steered Emen to the southeast, towards the Temple Walk. Behind them, the theater doors erupted with violence that spilled into the streets as the brawl turned into a full riot. People were being dragged around by mobs, and the hapless watchmen were borne over the heads of the throng like debris carried on the tide.

Emen wanted to run, wanted to shout for help, but he knew it would be of little use. No one would come to his rescue, not with this madness breaking out. Besides, many thought that dwarfs were troublemakers, cursed little beings that were always up to no good. He had learned this the hard way growing up, from taller children and adults.

"It's funny, you know; I always thought of you as my good luck charm," DuChat said.

Emen bristled, "And how did that work out for you?"

"Not as I had hoped, but then, you had the good graces to come and see my play. Now, the night is salvaged somewhat. Ah, it's a pity we can't climb a tower for a better view."

"Of what?"

"That," DuChat replied, pointing south towards DuShonmaer. Smoke and flame were rising from one of the windows, and soon another blaze started across the street. Men moved in the distance, carrying torches. "And there," he pointed again back the way they came, and Emen could see flames creeping up the side of the theater square, eating the clinging ivy as it made for the second and third-story windows.

"Gods, what have you done?" Emen gasped.

"Oh, this is nothing my dear dwarf; just some of my faithful getting the party started. You should see what's coming. Too bad you won't last the night. Come, let's go someplace private." He pushed, dragged, and hoisted Emen down the street as people rushed past to see the flames, screaming and shouting. No one paid them any mind.

"You don't want to kill me," he pleaded, "I know things! I can take you to the Silver Gang's stash! You can be rich again!"

"I have no need of wealth anymore," he said, "it has served its purpose. But do try again; I rather like hearing you beg."

"I know other things; I was in the council of Ildric Finnael and his companion. Do you know who it was you had killed? Did you know he came back from the dead to help us?"

This gave DuChat pause, but he pushed him on, saying, "Finnael no longer matters. Nothing can stop it now. The Dark Heart is beyond his reach, and the world is already being unmade, or didn't you notice?"

"But I have hope!" he said, "Do you know *why* I have hope? Because I *know things!*"

They passed the small, dragon-topped tower of the Mystic College, where wizards and students were pouring out of their dormitories and class rooms and taking to the streets, brandishing wands and staffs. Bells were ringing in many of the temples, and people were running about in confusion. More smoke and flame could be seen, cropping up in every district.

This can't get any worse, Emen thought.

Rough hands took them both from behind and shoved them into a narrow passageway off the street. Emen found a knife at his throat, as did his abductor. It took a moment for his eyes to adjust to the dim light, but found he knew these faces rather well. His heart sank, but he tried to sound happy.

"Daymi! Cricket! Thank the gods you're alright!"

"Quiet, you dunghill rat," Cricket said, "We'll get to you in a minute."

"He's *our* bounty," Daymi snarled to the pale man as he pressed the knife to his throat, "We'll be taking him now."

"Be my guest," he said, showing his hands, "But if you're going to kill him, can I at least watch?"

Emen sighed miserably and asked, "Who's paying?"

"Blood Circle, Hammers, you name it," Cricket chirped, "You's the only boss that wasn't murdered, so they's *all* after you. Last we heard, it's up to 100 gold crowns!" He hopped up and down with glee, giggling his signature laugh.

"But I have information," Emen said, "information vital to the Boss."

"What boss?"

"Kobus DuChat," he replied.

They laughed at that. "DuChat's dead or gone, and he's no longer the Boss no how," Daymi said.

"He's still the Boss, and he's closer than you think," Emen said. The pale man just smiled. "Take a look at what's happening around you! The Boss is behind this, and you two can still be a part of it. He needs your muscle, and he needs my knowledge."

"Pathetic groveling," DuChat said.

"It's true!" he said, glaring at the pale man, "His *big plans* can be thwarted, and I know *how* and by *whom*. If you kill me or auction me off to the other gangs, he has no chance of countering them."

Daymi sneered, "You was always all talk and no walk, Emen Silvershit. Made me sick having to listen to the likes of you, 'specially after you let the Talon and his pointy-eared friend walk away. Traitor!" He gave Emen a kick to the stomach and spat on him.

Emen staggered under the blow, but Cricket kept him upright with his knife. "We don't take orders from you no more, you Miner Town fraud; we was raised up by Dexer, and he was all that you ain't."

"Time to die, dwarf," Daymi said, "Do him, Cricket."

"Wait!" Emen squeezed his eyes shut and cried, "Are you going to kill him too?"

"Oh, he'll get his turn," Daymi said, as he pressed the knife harder to the pale man's throat, "but he said he wants to watch you die."

"But he's DuChat! *He's DuChat!* And he needs me alive!"

The boys snorted a laugh. "We know what Kobus DuChat looks like, and this ain't him," Daymi said.

"He's a duplict face-changer like Twist was, remember?" Then he said to the pale man, "If you want to live, show them. Just show them, for your own sake, please!"

DuChat gave a thin smile and said, "Oh, very well, if you insist." With a brief moment of concentration, his features shifted and altered; his hair grew dark and curly, and his baby-soft fuzz grew into a dark beard. His eyes both became blue, his face widened, and his complexion changed to the olive of a proper man of the south. He even shrank a few inches and put on some bulk.

The lads jumped back and cursed, then lowered their knives. "Rath's golden shaft!" Daymi cried, his eyes wide, "It's you!"

"It's the Boss, like he said," Cricket squeaked, "DuChat!"

They just stood there in awe as Emen took one breath, then another; DuChat had given him a ray of hope. *Now they see who you are, you slippery eel. And I'm still breathing.*

DuChat smiled his most benevolent, charming smile, the kind he used to talk princes out of their wealth, and said, "My dear fellows, Dexer spoke very highly of you. I am very glad to have you back in the fold."

Emen cringed at that smile, that voice, that smug look he gave him as he turned his would-be assassins into boot-licking toadies. He hated the man for everything he had done to his life, his family, his city, and the world. He was going to make him pay if it was the last thing he did, and it just might be.

"What do you want us to do, Boss?" Daymi asked.

"First, I think we should adjourn to a more private venue, someplace where his screams can't be heard. Do you have a place in mind?"

"We can go to the Warren!" Cricket said, "The Parlor's been waiting for a boss to return, and better you than him."

"Excellent choice. Shall we?"

Cricket grabbed Emen by the collar and pushed him ahead as DuChat led them toward the street.

"See?" Emen said, "As I told you, Kobus DuChat! Lord of thieves, high priest of Llomaak, and-"

"Shut it!" Daymi said, and he slashed him in the face.

Emen stumbled, pressing his hand to his cheek to stop the blood. Through gritted teeth, he said, "And the most wanted man in the entire kingdom."

DuChat's step faltered.

"How much is the bounty on your head?" Emen asked, "A *thousand* imperial crowns?"

DuChat turned, and his smug expression melted away. Daymi and Cricket froze in their tracks and looked at each other with wide, greedy eyes.

"A thousand platinum nobles for Kobus DuChat," Emen said, his eyes boring into the man's face, savoring every little emotion that played across it. "I'm no accountant, but that's twenty times what I'm worth.

100,000 silver calimarks in common coin; a king's ransom, just a knife's thrust away."

The lads grew tense and they shifted from foot to foot, glancing from each other to DuChat with narrowed eyes. The lord of thieves let his body grow slack and relaxed, and he managed to keep his voice even. "Now boys," he began, as he shifted back to his thin, pale form, "they won't pay any rewards for *this* face."

"They will," Emen said, "Talon Finnael's pointy-eared friend Wryley can identify him no matter what face he wears, remember?"

Emen felt Cricket's hand leave his collar, and he stepped back to give them plenty of room. "I'll leave you to it then," he said.

DuChat gave him an eerie smile and said, "Well played, my little friend." Then two daggers dropped into his hands from hidden wrist sheaths as the lads lunged towards him, one going high, the other low. DuChat's weapons flashed to parry both blows, but the lads were skilled, having learned well from Dexer. Steel rang against steel in the narrow passage, until the dull thunk of blade biting flesh made Cricket falter and drop his knife. As the boy fell, DuChat spun and slashed Daymi's knife arm, but the lad had already switched the blade to his other hand, and with a snake-like motion, he drove the point under DuChat's sternum and into his heart.

The pale man's breath came out in a huff, his body stiffened, and his eyes grew wide in shock. Daymi smirked and twisted the blade, making his former boss drop his weapons and move his lips wordlessly; his blue and green eyes became distant and unfocused, and he crumpled in a heap at Daymi's feet.

Emen could have run, but he wanted to watch, wanted to make sure the man was dead before he turned his back and fled. Now he was sure, but it was too late to move.

Daymi gave him a wicked grin, then glanced at his life-long friend. "Rotten luck, Cricket," he said, "but I know you'd want me to have your share." He cleaned off his blade on his trouser leg and swaggered towards Emen, who backed away. "Now then, there's no reason I can't make a thousand nobles *plus* a hundred crowns tonight. That's what... 105,000 silver marks? I'm no accountant, but..."

His swagger turned into a stumble, then a stagger. "What in the name of-?" He couldn't finish the words. His breath came in gasps as his knife dropped from numb fingers. His heart leaped in his chest as the beat became erratic. With great effort, he raised his arm and looked at the shallow cut bleeding into his sleeve; it was the only wound he had received.

Emen felt a great relief, but also sorrow and horror; he had never seen someone die from poison, and it was terrible to watch. He wanted to reach out to Daymi in his last moments as the boy looked at him with pleading, bloodshot eyes, but before he could summon the nerve to move, it was too late.

Emen stood there for a moment over the body, thinking on his turn of luck. He took a long, deep breath, and let it out slowly.

Then he muttered, "So what am I going to do with a thousand imperial crowns?"

The first thing he did was empty their coin pouches, then hail a cab. The few on the street tonight were thundering past, carrying their fares away from the spreading flames, but Emen managed to flag one down by almost getting himself run over. The next trick was talking the driver into helping him load the limp body into the carriage. Several pieces of silver helped with this. Then he gave him the rest of the coin to get him to Casselvane Keep. How much that was, he didn't care to count, but it was enough.

The ride was a harrowing one as they drove east around the Temple Walk, past burning buildings on either side of the street, and onto the Golden Path by the Market Square. Fire-wizards were out in force, using their spells to lower the intensity of the flames and keep them from spreading, as bucket brigades worked to douse them. As Emen tried to bandage his bleeding cheek, he saw shops being broken into and people being dragged out to the street, but the carriage rode past before he could learn their fate.

They crossed a bridge to the Harbor District, then another to the Copper District, or Lowcourt. Things here were not burning yet, but it was crammed with people fleeing across the canal from the central city. The carriage had to slow down as the streets grew thick with people, animals, and whatever belongings could be loaded onto both. The Tower of the Silver Moon could be seen high above the other buildings, with little tiny figures in the windows watching the chaos down below.

Finally they crossed into the Highcourt, but not before Emen had to persuade the guards to lower the gate. He had to name drop Ildric Finnael a few times and promise them gold on his way out. Eventually, they relented.

Emen had never been in this part of the city before, but there was no time to gawk. He needed to figure out what he was going to say when he reached the keep.

Ildric Finnael had never felt more miserable.

The last three weeks had seen a brutal recovery period as he struggled to walk again. He had several broken bones, but they had been mended by the best healers humans could train. His concussion still gave him headaches and dizzy spells, and his legs and hip were atrociously sore, but he would have gone through it all again if it meant not having to bear the pain of the last forty-eight hours.

The castle was in mourning. The news had not reached the populace yet, and would not until the tumult in the city died down. Gavagul had arrived late in the evening of the 25th, and the countess had fainted upon hearing his message; she was inconsolable thereafter.

Ildric used what strength he had to confirm the message, and his vision showed him the truth of it; Constable Fingelm was traveling with the body even now, in a coffin enchanted to stave off decay. Ildric had been too weak to see much more than that.

Tavenji knew enough to keep quiet, and for that Ildric was grateful. The little god had been a constant helper during his convalescence, making jokes only by way of encouragement. He had stopped playing pranks on the household staff, and ceased his habit of singing dirty limericks in the great hall to "test the acoustics," as he put it.

"I have news," Tavenji said, bounding into Ildric's bedchamber with his face bright and cheerful, "Our little dwarf friend Emen is alive and down stairs, and he's brought the body of Kobus DuChat! Well, what would be DuChat if he was wearing the right face."

Ildric stood up from his chair at the window where he had been watching the smoke drift across the bay. "That is good news," he said, smiling, "the best news we've had in a while. I wonder what he intends to do with the reward?"

"I asked him that very question after he stopped bleeding everywhere. He mentioned something about a bunch of orphans needing his help, and undoing his past misdeeds. I think he means to reform the kids in the Silver Gang, maybe give them a better life."

"Good! Good... good for him," Ildric nodded in approval, "I judged him well, I think."

"Sounds boring if you ask me," Tavenji said, "but whatever. Kids are fun to entertain, but raising them? Ugh."

The wizard waved him off. "I'll be down to see him presently, but I have another problem."

"Oh?"

"There has been so much that has happened, so much vital news that I have been quite beside myself with indecision."

"About what?"

"I gave Lady Cindra an enchanted earring that would let her receive a single, short message. I have been meaning to tell her first of Gavadaire and the Dark Heart, then of DuChat, Twist and Grigor DeKenric, then her poor cousin Gaius... Now I must tell her of the death of her father and the fires in the city. What am I to do?"

Tavenji thought a moment and said, "What about sending the bird?"

"No, Gavagul would lead any watching eyes directly to them, or worse, to the Shadow Lord's lair. There may even be defenses there that would prevent an ember swallow from finding or reaching them. No, their mission and location must remain as secret as possible."

"Well then," Tavenji said, "as the messenger of the gods with over 20,000 years of experience, I'd say whittle it down to only the most vital information, and tell her to come home."

"Yes... yes. I shall have to sleep on that. Tomorrow will serve. I cannot bear to do it tonight."

Chapter Twenty Nine

The Fortress of Thorns

Cindra, Padison, and Drahn rode in the back of the wagon, lying on cushions donated by the grateful citizens of Gloamshire. They had lingered two more days in the hamlet after the battle, and now had enough supplies for two weeks, allowing for a lengthy stay at the fortress if there was no food to be had otherwise. Adric drove the cart and the others rode ahead while T'ózha and Smoke walked tethered behind the wagon.

Cindra and Paddy had managed to stack the supplies into comfortable furniture, with Drahn resting on Cindra's arming chest, where her armor was stored until it could be repaired. The arrangement was far from luxurious, but it was better than reopening their healing wounds.

"So how many different kinds of dweedragons are there?" Cindra asked.

Drahn's voice was still hoarse, but getting better. "No one weally knows," he said, "but there are many bestiaries on the subject. Dozens of types have been cataloged, but some descwiptions are vewy brief."

"What's a bestiary?" Paddy asked.

"A book about beasts," Cindra said, "We have one at home, but it doesn't mention dweedragons."

"That suits me," Drahn said, "I don't like being weferred to as a 'beast' anyway. Dwagons are *not* beasts."

"What are they then?" Paddy asked.

"Dwagons," Drahn said.

"Do you know what kind you are?" Cindra asked, "I mean, I know you didn't learn from your time in the egg, but do human scholars have a name for you?"

Drahn looked a little reluctant, but he said, "A woyal bullwower."

Paddy chuckled. "A what?"

The little dragon glared at him. "It's hard to pwonounce with my injuwies," he said, but tried again, "A *royal bullroarer.*"

"Royal bullroarer? Why are you called that?"

"We are 'royal' because we are purple when at ease, and our mating call sounds like a bullroarer, appawently."

"Huh," Paddy said, "What's a bullroarer sound like? Can you do the call for us?"

Drahn looked very uncomfortable and his scales turned crimson.

Cindra chided him, "Paddy! Inappropriate!" The scale on her necklace turned the same color, as she was embarrassed for him too.

"I'm sorry! I guess that was a dumb question."

"Brilliant, Paddy," Adric said, "Why don't you perform *your* mating call for us?"

"There's no telling what might show up," Drahn said, and they all had a laugh at that. His color soon returned to normal.

"What other kinds of dweedragons are there?" Cindra asked. She loved learning new things, but didn't think there was much known on the subject.

"Well, let's see," he began, "There are arboreal fretters, lapidarian fantails, Norsi paddlers, Regal twumpeters, wusty-horned fwetters, spotted cliff-divers, vinegar phantoms..."

"What's a 'fretter?'" Cindra asked.

"It is a small kind of dwagon that moves in a wapid, wepetitive fashion, like it's constantly worried; they are supposed to be *vewy* annoying to talk to."

"What's the lapidorial fantail?" Paddy asked.

"Lapidarian," Drahn said, "They are actually the only dwagons known to make their own jewelry! They cwaft their own tools to cut and polish gemstones, and use their specialized fire bweath and magical spells to work the metals. I hope to meet one someday."

"So I'm guessing Regal trumpeters sound like trumpets?" Cindra asked.

"Actually yes," Drahn replied, "they are native to Wegal Pwovince, specifically the Cwownswood Fowest. They are violet and yellow, and their mating call mimics the fanfare played for the king."

"Oh! I think I might have heard them!" Cindra said, "Once, on the road to Highcourt, I could have sworn I heard trumpets in the Crownswood. Haani said the forest was haunted, and they were ghost horns playing for long dead kings."

"Do they breathe fire too?" Paddy asked.

"No, they spit a glob of sticky, burning goo. Nasty."

"How come the books never told you what your element was?" Cindra asked.

"Because my kind are very rare, and their breath weapon was never documented. They are even more rare now, since..." he shook his head as his scales turned a deeper shade of purple. "For all I know, I am the last one."

"I'm sorry, Drahn."

"It's alwight. You know, the foremost expert on royal bullroarers was the wizard who waised me. He went to study them and found my egg. His name is Robben Thortensban."

"Thortensban? Why does that name sound familiar?" she said.

"He is a pwofessor at the Mystic College in Aldrig, last I heard," Drahn said, "Actually, I have not heard much at all for many years."

"Oh, I think Jaron must have mentioned him from his... travels. Is he still at the college?"

"I hope so. I should weally go see him someday."

"I guess he's practically your father," Cindra said.

Drahn nodded.

Nixy, Wenyssaya, and Deliah were enjoying the sunlight while they could. The road ahead was quickly turning to deepening shadow as the gray trees grew thicker, creating yet another dark tunnel. To the east the trees were much thinner, and the river could be heard tumbling past shallow stones. The rain had brought the forest to life, and rare flowers bloomed along the road, spreading sweet scents of the coming spring. Their path grew steeper as it turned west, climbing the rise in a series of switchbacks. The people of the hamlet informed them that the next fifteen miles would be a bit of a climb, and to rest their horses more frequently.

"So what's this fortress supposed to look like?" Nixy asked.

Wenyssaya could not readily answer. "My dream did not show me the fortress, only the vale and a stream. It was very brief."

"The way you can make plants grow," Deliah said, "I wouldn't be surprised if it was a massive tangle of giant thorn bushes."

"That don't sound very nice," Nixy said.

"It's meant to be a fortress, not a welcoming sight," Deliah said, "I imagine the Shadow Lord has many secrets to protect."

"Speaking of which," Wenyssaya said, "I saw you place something in your saddlebag; something wrapped in soft leather."

Deliah smiled, "And here I thought I was being so sneaky."

"What is it?" Nixy asked, "You didn't steal nothin' did you?"

"Of the three of us, which one is the pickpocket?" she asked. He looked abashed.

"We really know nothing about you, so who's to say?" said the elf maid.

"True enough," Deliah said, "If you must know, I took something they wouldn't miss, but I don't want Lady Cindra to give me grief about it. I took three of the little corpses from the battle."

"Whatever for?" Wen exclaimed.

"For study. They could be sold for quite a lot of money, I imagine."

"Why would anyone want to study such horrors?"

"My dear, *everything* is studied by someone, especially the rare and magical," Deliah said, "How did the beasts become what they are from what they once were? How do they breed, and how many more are out there? So many questions, and now someone may find the answers. That, or they'll just charge people to gawk at it."

"How much do ya think they're worth?" Nixy asked.

"Probably several hundred gold."

"So much?" Wenyssaya said, "Then there is a great fortune in that hamlet."

"Nah," Nixy said, "The more there are, the less they're worth."

"Simple law of exchange," Deliah nodded, "Rarity increases value. That queen's corpse would have sold for a small fortune though, but I doubt the lady would let me take it with us."

"Just as well," Wen said, "I'd not want to go to sleep with that thing nearby, dead or not."

Cindra played with the enchanted earring as she stared into the distance. The day had been slow going as the road inclined, and the surroundings were growing wilder. There were nice stretches where the path leveled out, but there was always a climb after. Old Maewyn's father must have been a great strong man to have pulled a cart with their belongings all the way to the Blackgate Bridge. But Cindra's party had horses, and they would reach it in half the time. A few more hours of travel should bring them to Riverskirt and the last leg of their journey. Padison and Drahn were asleep, and Adric sounded tired.

He yawned again and stretched his back, asking her, "How are the wounds?"

"Much better. I doubt I can ride for a week or so, but I can recline well enough."

He smiled and nodded, then stared into the trees. "I've been thinking a lot about Deliah."

She sighed, "Adric..."

"No, it's not what you think," he said, "She was injured in Gloamshire, between the hall and the shed. She said she was alright, but there was blood on the front of her dress and her sleeve."

Cindra squirmed a bit. "Did she say why?"

"She said Wenyssaya healed her in the shed, but there was no time for that. I didn't see any scars either."

"Maybe it was a place you don't get to see?"

"Her dress was ripped in places, but there were no scars above her neckline or on her hands, and that's where the blood was. Nothing but perfect skin. I checked."

"I bet you did," she smiled, but she was troubled. How much should she tell him?

"That's not all," he said, "The last time she was covered in blood, she said it was Padison's, but wounds like his wouldn't have sprayed so much. There's no major arteries on that part of the back."

"Maybe it was Black Dexer's?"

"Maybe..."

"What do you think it means?" she asked, wishing he wasn't so damned observant.

"I wish I knew. Nothing about her makes sense."

"Just remember, she's a witch. Nothing may be as it seems." That was as close as she wanted to get to telling him the truth. He could get used to disappointment, but Cindra didn't want him to pity her like she did.

It was pity she felt, after all. Cindra had tried to imagine living so long, never being able to stop loving a man who was long dead. What had that done to the woman's mind? Were the glimpses of Deliah's personality her true self, or was there something deeper buried within her forgotten past?

Pity, yes. Pity and fear.

Hours later, their spirits were lifted by the straightening and leveling out of the road. The trees still drank the daylight, and the way ahead was dark, but they had grown a little accustomed to the gloom and the dreariness it brought.

By the late afternoon, the road turned more to the east and then straightened north, and the sound of the river was much closer. Then the trees cleared, and the sky opened up, and a fiery sunset ignited the clouds, setting them ablaze in billowing tufts of amber and orange. A vibrant golden light shone upon the road and undergrowth, and danced on the flowing waters like tiny flickering suns. The light spilling out before them was so at odds with the shadows of the forest that it dazzled their eyes and filled their hearts with awe and wonder.

The large break in the trees was due to two rivers meeting as one. The Kelga flowed before them, coming from distant, forested mountains to the northwest, and the Joshian was on their right, flowing from the northeastern Calione Peaks and Lake Lumiras. Ahead of them on the left was the Blackgate Bridge, a long stone span that crossed the Kelga about a hundred yards from the joining of the rivers. The waters here were not particularly wide or deep, but they were swift, cold, and loud.

"It's beautiful!" Nixy cried, and he began to laugh. It became infectious, and soon the others were laughing and smiling. Even the horses were happy, relaxing their ears, noses, and tails.

On the other side of the bridge was a large, cleared area and a small assortment of buildings that looked to be very old, but well-maintained. Fish traps and a dock could be seen on the far Joshian bank, and there was a stable, a smithy, a granary, and a couple of houses, the larger one having two stories. The Joshian Way passed through the middle of the trading post and headed northeast. On this side of the Kelga River was the Kelgerton Road heading west.

"Riverskirt," Cindra said, "This is where we part ways, Paddy."

Padison nodded and examined his temporary new home. It was decided at the start that he would stay with the horses and wagon while the others trekked beyond, but he needed the rest anyway. If the party did not return within two weeks, he was to sell most of the horses and make for home as best he could. It was a grim duty, but it had to be planned for.

As they crossed the bridge, a thin man and a round, sturdy woman came out of the big house and waved.

"They seem happy to see us," Adric said.

"Is it just the two of them?" Paddy asked.

"Constable Narven said there were a few families here, but it doesn't look big enough," Cindra replied.

"Hello there!" called the man, "Where do you hail from?"

Deliah answered, "Portshia."

"By way of... Gloamshire?" asked the woman.

"Yes," Deliah said, "we spent a few days there."

Another man came stumbling out of the large house; his clothes were poor and tattered, and his head was bandaged. He came right up to Deliah's horse and said,

"Gloamshire! Are they alright? Were there any more attacks?"

Cindra, having unloaded herself from the wagon, came up to the man and said, "You must be Stev, the rider who went north for help."

"Yes!" he said, "did someone come? Did Daven get help?"

"Uh, in a manner of speaking," Cindra replied, "We found him dead by the road. I'm sorry."

He absorbed the news and nodded.

"But the hamlet was made safe, and the people were in good spirits when we left."

"Ah! The creatures, they're gone?"

"All dead," Deliah said, "as far as we can tell; their queen is dead also, so they shouldn't be back."

Cindra thought that sounded a bit noncommittal, but she figured Deliah had learned to never say never.

As the other women dismounted, Stev came up to Adric and Padison and clasped their hands saying, "Thank you young masters! Thank you so much!"

The boys shared an uncomfortable glance as Adric pointed him to the ladies, who were standing there looking annoyed. "They did most of the work," he said, "Wenyssaya of the elves, the Raven Witch's great-granddaughter Deliah, and Lady Cindra Corrina, knight of the realm."

Stev's eyes went wide as he tried to take all of that in.

"We *all* did our parts," Cindra said, being more diplomatic than she felt.

"Oh!" the woman cried, "An elf! Bless me, but you're a sight! Like a faerie story come true."

"A lady knight?" the thin man said, "I've never heard the like."

"I'm the first," Cindra said patiently.

Nixy and Drahn stood off to the side watching the exchange, seemingly forgotten. "Typical," Drahn whispered, "No mention of us. The thorn bushes were *my* idea."

Nixy replied, "I don't want a lot of people knowing what I did; at least, not *how* I did it."

Deliah gave Stev a dismissive wave, saying, "You may ride back tomorrow if you wish; I'm sure they'll tell you the entire story."

"I can't" he said, "Brigands stole my horse the day I got here! I was hoping they were honest fighting men who'd come to our aid, but... but they were just brutes and thieves."

Cindra took pity on him regardless of his blunder. "Perhaps you can ride back with Padison tomorrow," she said, "as long as our other horses can be cared for until he returns?"

The thin man stepped forward and said, "That we can do. Welcome to Riverskirt, the lot of you. I'm Odwell, and this is my wife, Alora. Are you headed west up Kelgerton way, or northeast to Rickshome?"

"Neither," Cindra said, "We're going straight north into the deep woods."

Odwell and Alora began to laugh, but the grim faces of the party told them it was not a joke.

"You're serious?" Alora asked, "Whatever for?"

Cindra said, "We have a mission to contact the Shadow Lord. That's all I can say."

Stev made a warding gesture and wandered unsteadily back in the house.

The couple looked at each other with worry and Odwell said, "No one goes into the north woods. I'd not walk but a few hours under those trees; there's things beyond that don't want you there, and they'll try to turn you back."

"What kinds of things?" Nixy asked.

"Nightmares," he replied, "terrible nightmares, and things in the dark that cut you and jab you, and the trees, the trees are so much darker there... In my youth, I spent one night in the deep woods on a dare, and I've regretted it ever since."

Their guests were silent, but looked no less resolute.

"Regardless, we must go in," Cindra said, "but not all of us. My friend Padison here will be staying behind with the horses and wagon for two weeks, if that's alright. I can pay for his lodgings."

"Two weeks!" Alora exclaimed, "You expect to be in there that long?"

"I hope that our visit will be shorter, or perhaps we can send someone back if it's to be longer. We just don't know what to expect."

"The Shadow Lord don't like intrusions, especially north of here. He has beasts that prowl about, and he sees everything," Odwell said, "We don't even cut wood on this side of the river."

"Have you ever seen him?" Deliah asked.

"No one's ever seen him up close" he said, "but some say a dark shape walks in the woods."

"Who are the 'some' that say this?" she asked.

"My brother's wife says she saw it while picking wildflowers for tea three summers back," he said, "and my own father, rest him, claimed he saw a dark shape with great, black wings across the river one night. Scared him half to death."

"We have reason to believe he will welcome us," Wenyssaya said.

Alora nodded, "Oh, that's as may be. He might let a fellow elf pass unharmed. I imagine it gets awful lonely in there."

"How do you know he's alone?" Wenyssaya asked.

"Well, I don't know for sure milady, but there's not been an elf seen in these parts for many generations."

The elf maid raised an eyebrow, but chose not to comment on the brevity of human generations.

After seeing to their horses and supplies, they were invited into the big house. The lower floor consisted of a work shop and dry goods store, with a decent-sized sitting room, benches, and some tables. As the sun went down, Odwell lit some lamps and started a fire in the hearth while Alora prepared some food for their guests.

"About these brigands," Adric said, "where have they gone?"

"Oh, the four of them headed up the Joshian Way several days ago," said Alora, "Knocked that poor fellow down, took his horse, and made off with firewood and a fresh pot pie, the blackguards."

Cindra said, "Do you think they'll be back? I don't want our horses stolen or wagon looted while we're away."

"Don't want our Padison killed neither," Padison said.

"Oh, we can hide your things if we have to," Odwell said, "These aren't the first or the worst we've encountered. They're deserters from the army that marched through the north lands last summer. They've escorted caravans here and there to make a living, but they recently turned to thieving."

"Conscripts?" Cindra asked.

"Trained men-at-arms," Odwell said, "They've got armor and weapons like yours."

"I don't like it," Cindra said to the boys.

"What's to like?" Padison said.

Nixy, who had been exploring with Drahn, asked, "How many other people live here?"

"About twenty," Alora said, "though you'd not see the rest of Riverskirt without going a bit farther west along the bank. Our two boys and their wives went off to buy goods in Stockwyrd; that's a little village almost halfway to Kelgerton. We buy what we need to run the outpost from both there and Gloamshire, and grow or catch the rest for ourselves."

"What is the purpose of this place?" Drahn asked, "It's not pwotected with a wall like Gloamshire."

"Oh, bless me! It talks!" Alora exclaimed, "I thought he was just an exotic pet."

Drahn made a miffed little snort and turned crimson.

"Oh, and he changes colors too! How pretty."

"That color means he's upset," Cindra said.

"To say the least," Drahn said.

"Oh, I'm sorry deary," Alora said, "I apologize. I've heard tell of little dragons, but only from far-away tales. Never met one, certainly."

Drahn's color changed back to purple, though he was a bit disheartened. There were no dweedragons in these woods at all, apparently.

"Well, to answer your question, we offer services that you won't find outside of a decent-sized village. Odwell is a tanner and leather worker, our son Odwick is a carter, and our other boy Alber is a blacksmith and a farrier as well. I'm a fair hand with a needle and thread, among other things. We've even got a barber, and a fellow who can read and write! You never know what folk will need during a long journey."

Deliah said, "Riverskirt is a trading post where goods from east and west change hands, and travelers can get needed repairs and a roof for the night."

"Yes, that's right," Alora said, "We've some supplies to sell too, so people don't need to go down the hill to Gloamshire and back up again. We don't have a wall because there's little need; patrols from Kelgerton keep things safe, that is, until recently."

Cindra perked up and said, "I actually need tailoring for my new breeches, and some repairs to my armor; many of the leather straps were badly chewed and need to be replaced."

Odwell said, "I can fix the armor for you milady, though it might take some time. Were the straps chewed by..." he pointed upstairs, "Stev's little monsters?"

"They were," she said, "and so was my rump, but that's healing."

"Do you need the armor fixed before you head into the woods, milady?" he asked.

"No," she said, "I'll only take my breastplate and arming doublet; I need to be able to hike over rough ground."

"Then it shall be ready when you return," Odwell said, but his smile faltered. His unspoken doubts did not need to be given voice; everyone was thinking the same thing.

'If we return.*

Early the next morning, Cindra and her company awoke in the large room over the trading post's main building. It was mostly unfurnished, but it had walls and a roof, which was all they needed. The night had been dreadfully cold since there was no fireplace or brazier upstairs, and Cindra had recommended they sleep huddled together. Padison of course had to make a joke about who should be huddled with whom, and Cindra had to kick him.

"Everyone up," she muttered around a yawn.

"Ugh, I hope they have a cot or a bed somewhere," Paddy said, "I can't manage lying on the floor on my belly for two weeks."

"I don't imagine this 'Fortress of Thorns' has many comfy places to sleep either," Adric said, "but I'm sure the people here can find you something, even if it's a haystack."

"Oh gods, I *dream* of sleeping on a haystack!" he said.

Their breakfast was sparse and they put several days of food into their packs, hoping they could return without trouble if they needed more. Cindra left her armor and shield with Odwell, while Alora, who had taken her measurements before bed, delivered her newly-fitted breeches. She paid them for their services and then she and the others made for the edge of the northern forest as the sun began to peek over the trees.

"Farewell, Paddy," she said, hugging him, "We'll be back as soon as we can. Stay out of trouble and be safe."

He returned her hug properly this time, not as awkwardly as their first embrace back home. "Don't worry about me, Lady Cindra. I'll be fine."

Adric hugged him next, saying, "Take care of yourself, Paddy. And don't be afraid to get into a little trouble; I want to hear some stories when I get back."

"Make sure you protect all these poor, helpless ladies, ya big hero," Padison said with a grin.

"Right," he laughed.

Then Wenyssaya came to him and said, "See that they change your bandages once a day, and wash your back with clean water to keep the wounds moist. I shall check on you when we return." She kissed him on the forehead.

His face flushed and he teetered a little.

"No topping that," Adric said.

"Agreed," Deliah said, "I think that's about all the goodbyes he can handle."

The rest of them waved and called their farewells, then turned to walk into the deep woods.

Cindra was once again wearing her riding dress, but she kept the bodice nice and loose. Over that, she wore the arming doublet, and over that, her breastplate. Leather gloves and boots completed her costume. The dress was not so bad for hiking, being short enough not to step on the hem or snag easily; more importantly, it was the most formal clothing she had brought with her.

Nixy too was dressed in one of the fine outfits that had been picked for him when his status was revealed. It had been carefully packed in the wagon just for this occasion, kept clean and dry by some of Wenyssaya's little spells. It was a velvet coat of crimson with paned and vented sleeves, black hose, nice leather boots, and a black and silver weapon belt similar to Cindra's, upon which hung his little magic knife. Drahn rode on his back in his own pack, so Adric carried Nixy's supplies.

Wenyssaya wore her own special finery, consisting of a dress with vine and leaf patterns, and an odd bit of clothing that was like a jacket that only covered her arms and upper back, and was buttoned at the neck. From its paned cap sleeves hung a green velvet cloak.

Adric and Deliah were dressed practically, not overly concerned with impressing anyone.

Drahn, of course, was naked.

The first day's trek was hardly the march of terror they had been told it would be. The trees were dark and gloomy, yes, but not unbearably so. The undergrowth was low and gentle; the ground was a blanket of clover and moss, and large ferns brushed them as they passed. There were animals to be seen in the dim daylight; squirrels, birds, foxes, and the occasional undefined shape would be caught out of the corner of the eye.

Navithwi the raven would fly ahead of them acting as a guide, and cawing that all was clear. They were in high spirits, and the living smells of the deep wood set their minds at ease.

The night however, was another matter.

Darkness fell quickly as the trees drank the golden light of late afternoon, casting a pall upon their hearts. They had gathered some firewood as they walked, but it hardly seemed enough to banish the coming gloom. They found a small clearing between four large shadowood trees, and made their camp.

Wenyssaya cast her faerie lights above them as they prepared their fire, but they were dim and feeble. Nixy's glowstone, which had been fished from the well in Gloamshire, was not much better. Cindra even drew her sword and lit the blade, but the darkness seemed to take up the challenge to resist them all the more.

The fire was a cold comfort; a candle in the night. They sat around it as they listened to the nightly noises, wondering who among them could sleep in such a place. Only the raven seemed at peace, sitting in a high branch with its head bowed low.

"I can take the first watch," Cindra said.

A branch snapped in the distance, making them jump.

"Not tired," Nixy said, his voice trembling. Drahn shook his head in agreement.

"I wonder how close we are?" Adric said.

"The land has been rising," Wen said, "and beyond, there should be a vale, a dark vale. A stream runs through it and... vanishes. If we follow the stream to its source, we should find our way."

"A stream that goes nowhere?" Nixy asked, "How does that work?"

Deliah said, "Water can come out of the ground, surely going back in is part of the same journey."

"Is this another dweam you had?" Drahn asked.

"Yes," Wen said, "but in the dream, I felt not only guided, but watched. I feel the same now."

"Comforting," Cindra said, "I guess no one will sleep for a while."

When sleep did come, it overtook them all. Cindra felt her eyes grow heavy and her head begin to nod, but could not find the will or the strength to wake Adric for the next watch. Instead, she stretched herself on the soft clover and within moments was drifting away.

The noises of crickets, the call of a distant owl, the wind blowing through the high boughs of trees, and the crackling of their fire, all of it served as a lullaby to her muddled mind.

Then it stopped.

An unnatural hush fell upon them as black shapes emerged from even blacker shadows, moving among the trees and through the underbrush, coming closer to the sleeping bodies. Guttural chatter broke the silence; soft and sibilant, throaty and hissing, forming words not meant for human ears to comprehend.

Death or Dream? Do we breathe?

Neither. They are blood.

Not all. Two are blood. Three are not, but this one is familiar.

That one is known. It will be dealt with again.

Look here! There is another! What is its kind?

Zjomazhi-shink-krao-lo-vashi; from the north, by the sea.

Do we kill it or drive it off?
Neither, we wait.
What if they are the threat we saw?
If that, then we breathe.
Death?
Death.

A throaty croaking issued from a branch high above as Navithwi sounded the alarm. The black shapes hissed, turned, and vanished into the shadows.

Cindra lurched awake as the silence was broken, cursing herself for falling asleep. The others soon followed.

"Ugh, dumb bird," Adric groaned, "keep it down!"

"No!" Wenyssaya hissed, "Something was here with us. He saw it."

"What was it?" Nixy asked, drawing his knife.

Wen shook her head. "I don't know," she said, "but it was close, very close." She was trembling now; her lovely violet eyes were wide and darted from shadow to shadow.

Adric was on his feet and drawing his weapon. "What did you see, Cindra?" he asked, "Wait, were you asleep too?"

She felt a pang of guilt and nodded, "I was; I couldn't help it."

"Great. You pulled a Padison," he grumbled.

"No," Deliah said, "If something in this forest wants you to sleep, you sleep. I did the same thing to Drahn the night he spied on me as I bathed."

"Hmmph," Drahn said, "I *knew* that wasn't my fault."

Apparently, nothing wanted them to sleep again for the rest of the night, for no one did.

Morning brought a gray fog that crept through the forest, blinding them to everything but the nearest trees. There was a fog over their minds as well, for they were exhausted from a restless night of watchful readiness.

Adric yawned, "So which way do we go?"

"North," Wen said.

"Which way is that?"

"Check the trees for moss," she said, "It will mostly grow on the north side."

"Not in the Shadowood," Deliah said, "there is so much shade here that it's free to grow where it likes, if it grows at all."

"So what do we do?" Nixy asked.

Deliah said, "I placed the largest rock of our campfire in the direction we were traveling." She pointed. "It should be that way."

"Should be?" Cindra asked.

"If you want certainty, bring a compass. You don't have a compass, do you?"

Cindra had to admit she didn't; the Galindri always used the sun and stars, but neither could be seen in this place. "That... was an oversight," she said.

"If you were truly prepared, it wouldn't be an adventure," Deliah said, leading the way.

After several hours of hiking through an increasingly dense wood, they found themselves on a steady decline in the terrain. Wenyssaya's little faerie lights danced over their heads, but mostly served to illuminate the fog rather than the darkness. Still, it was a comfort to be able to see their hands in front of their faces, and the back of the person walking before them.

Wenyssaya said softly, "I believe we have entered Navidundwi, the Dark Vale; now we must find a stream that goes nowhere."

"It's certainly dark," Cindra said, "but I can't tell if it's a valley or not."

Deliah said, "It may take some time, but we will find it. Be on your guard."

Navithwi was of little help, for he was used to seeing the land from above, not below the dark canopy. Deliah led them with an air of confidence, but Cindra doubted she really knew the way. How could anyone find their way in such an unwelcoming tangle of forest?

The canopy was lower and the trees were thicker and closer together; they had to duck past low branches and step over rising roots, weaving their way forward past thick bushes, moss-covered boulders, and steep gullies. The raven croaked in the distance, but the sound was muffled and faint; it could have been a hundred yards away, or twice that for all they could tell. The fog was thinning as the day wore on, allowing them to see only a few yards farther.

Cindra was tempted to take her sword and hack at the obtrusive bushes and ferns that brushed her face or blocked her path, but she had a feeling that such an act would raise the ire of someone or something dangerous. So instead she only used the sword to light her way, taking care not to cause undue harm.

She had no idea what direction they were headed, for it seemed that Deliah was feeling her way through the trees, weaving this way and that, pausing to listen for unheard signs. She wanted to ask her if she knew where she was going, but didn't want to annoy her lest she invite Cindra to lead them instead.

"Listen!" Deliah hissed, and they all froze to pay attention. A sound like rainfall was approaching, but as it drew nearer, it became the trampling of hooves crashing through the undergrowth. Extinguishing their lights for a moment, they were able to see perhaps a hundred shapes running past. Antlers and dark fur flashed between the trees; snorting breaths issued warnings, and white tails could be seen bounding into the darkness.

"Blue deer! So many of them!" Cindra whispered.

"What's got them all riled up?" Adric asked.

Just then, there was another rush of motion as more dark shapes passed on both sides of them. Snarls were heard. One of the shapes stopped in its tracks to examine them, and they saw it was a large black wolf. Its yellow eyes seemed to glow in the faint light, and its teeth and lolling tongue were the only other features that made it appear more than just a hole in the dark.

With a huff, it took off to follow the pack, vanishing before their eyes.

"Shadow wolves," Nixy said, trembling, "I was told they protect me."

"Who told you that?" Drahn whispered.

"Monsters," he said.

Eventually, they reached a thickening of green underbrush and the sound of water flowing over rocks. Making their way through the dense vegetation, they came to a rugged creek slicing through the valley. White water rushed towards them, threatening to soak their feet, but to their astonishment the torrent simply reached a point beyond which it did not flow.

"Careful where you step," Deliah said, "you don't want to fall where that water is going."

"Most curious," Wenyssaya said, "I thought the waters in my dream could not be real, but here it is."

Cindra asked Deliah, "How... how did you find it?"

She said, "I followed the sloping of the valley. Eventually we'd come to the low point, and that's where I expected the stream to be."

Nixy tugged Cindra's sleeve and said, "See? I told you she'd be a good guide."

She smoothed his cowlick and said, "When you're right, you're right."

"Where does it all go?" Adric asked.

"Pwobably into a tunnel," Drahn said.

"And from there?"

"Who knows?"

They followed the stream for about a mile through the dark and misty vale until the woods began to give way to the daylight, thinning and opening into a vast clearing before the foothills of a distant mountain. The trees were sparser upon the slope, and the gray shadowood gave way to a pale crown of bare, slender aspens.

"In another month or so, they will be decked with green leaves amid all this gray," Deliah said, "Imagine how they will look in the fall as they turn orange and gold."

They all stood and stared for a time, basking in the noonday sun and watching the clouds drift by. The air was cold and brisk, but the sun gave them all the warmth they needed in their hearts. The journey was almost over.

Navithwi the raven cawed several times and flew up the mountain side, disappearing into the distant trees.

"Do we have to climb that?" Adric asked.

"No," Wen said, "we have to go inside."

To their dismay, she was pointing to a dark hole at the base of the mountain from which the stream flowed in a white, tumbling torrent.

"You're kidding," he said.

"I don't see any thorns," Nixy said.

"I don't see a fortwess," said Drahn.

Wenyssaya led them towards the dark maw as if in a dream; her fear seemed to have evaporated with the sunshine, and now her steps were sure and determined.

The cave was wide and tall, with a seemingly natural path arising beside the stream. It was not barred or hidden by any physical means, and while it did not look inviting, it certainly did not look foreboding either.

Yet when they approached the cave mouth, they began to feel a deep sense of dread, as though one step closer would mean their violent deaths at the hands of unknown terrors. The cave now resembled the maw of some nightmarish beast, ready to swallow them whole.

"Hey! What's wrong?" Nixy asked, as Drahn scrambled out of his backpack.

Wenyssaya turned around and saw that all of her companions, apart from Nixy, were shrinking back in fear, too unnerved even to draw their weapons. Drahn had scampered to hide behind Cindra's leg, and Deliah had actually clung to Adric for protection. Neither Cindra nor Adric had the sense to do anything but stare wild-eyed at the blackness beyond, awaiting some unthinkable doom.

"Wenyssaya, what's gotten into them?" Nixy cried.

"I think it is a ward on the entrance," she said, "I think that only those of elven blood are welcome."

Nixy stormed up to the cave entrance and shouted into the gloom, "Hey! If you want me and Wen to come inside, my friends have to come too! Otherwise we can turn right around!"

The elf maid blanched at the outburst, fearful of the response, but she was also overcome with pride in her little pupil and his loyalty to his friends.

After a long moment, the terror passed from the company, and they found they had been too scared to breathe.

"Wh- what was that?" Adric asked in a shivering voice.

Deliah extracted herself from the young man and regained her composure, saying, "That was the Shadow Lord's welcome. I think he meant for us to wait outside."

"Well that's not gonna happen," Nixy said, "It's either all of us or none of us."

Cindra came up and stroked his blond head, smiling at her little friend. Then, drawing her sword for light, and perhaps out of defiance, she led them into the cave.

The cave was wider within, being perhaps twenty feet across from wall to wall, but fifteen of that was taken up by the flowing waters; the rest consisted of a smooth, relatively even path that rose slightly over the next mile. The air was cold, and their passage disturbed little gatherings of bats that flapped about over their heads. Eventually the cavern widened and the ceiling became higher, though the only sources of light were what they carried with them.

"I see fish!" Drahn said, and Cindra held her sword over the stream. The waters were surprisingly clear and perhaps only a few feet deep, and there were indeed many pale little fish swimming about, but larger ones also; sleek, gray shapes searching in the darkness for who-knew-what.

Cindra said in amazement, "I don't think the little pink ones have eyes!"

"The larger ones do," Deliah said, "They must have come from downstream in the sunlight."

"I didn't see any large fish outside," Wenyssaya said, "The stream looked too shallow."

Cindra said, "I wonder if the little ones have always been that way, or if something magical changed them."

"Creatures can change over generations, little by little," Deliah said, "It's just something that happens; call it magic if you like."

"How do you know that?" Adric asked.

But Deliah said nothing.

The passage took a slow curve to the right, opening even more. They could see it more clearly now because a light was coming from somewhere ahead, bathing the cavern in a soft, golden glow. Farther on, the wall across the stream opened up into a deep and tall recess; an elevated gallery that was revealed by a large hole in the ceiling. Sunlight poured in and lit the turquoise waters, setting the entire space aglow.

But the most astounding sight was within the recessed wall; formations of stone, some as tall as trees, reached up from the floor and down from the ceiling. Towers and mounds of rock, seemingly melted and poured like hot wax, were built upon each other, creating thick, tapering pillars of white and red stone. About their base were hundreds of icicle-like fingers, and hanging above were massive spikes of rock that clung to the ceiling in impossible ways, some as thick as tree trunks, and others as slender as spears or arrows.

The party just stood and stared for a time, marveling at the sight. It had the feel of an ancient temple; something deserving of reverence and awe, a treasure of a bygone age hidden deep in the earth.

"Was this made by someone, or is it natural?" Adric asked.

"It's natural," Drahn said, "I have read about caves with stwange wocks like this, but never thought to see them."

"I wonder how they formed?" Wenyssaya mused.

"One drop of water at a time," Deliah said, "Water can carry the tiniest of grains, like when sea water evaporates and leaves behind salt. I imagine this took a *very* long time to form."

"It doesn't seem like there could *be* enough time to do all of this," Cindra said.

"Oh, but there was," Drahn said, "Long before humans, long before the elves, there was a gweat age of dwagons, when time was marked not by the passing of seasons, but by the gwowing of mountains and the changing of the seas."

They stared for a while longer, trying to fathom the length of such an age. Failing to do so, they carried onward.

The trail curved to the left and the cavern grew narrower. They were back in darkness for only a little while longer, perhaps another 800 feet, before the air became warmer and the feeling of moisture touched their skin. Cindra sheathed her sword, for there was light ahead, and she quickened her pace.

The roof of the passage had become a narrow vault, a tall and thin archway leading to a far greater chamber beyond. There was a mist drifting overhead, as if a cloud had strayed into the cave. Warm light beckoned them, and as they turned the last bend of the passage, they beheld a sight that would live in their hearts and minds for the rest of their days.

Before them was a vast, open chamber with a ceiling towering over a thousand feet high. At its pinnacle, surrounded by hanging spikes of rock, was an enormous hole that let in the sun. A heavy fog hung in the air near the ceiling, diffusing the light into a soft glow.

They saw that the source of the stream was a waterfall that poured out of a high cave at the far end of the cavern, and flowed around a central island like a moat. On this island, which was the size of the entire Peer District of Portshia, was a forest of moss, ferns, and trees.

At the far end of the island, upon a rising plateau, was a massive mound of stone formations, very much like the ones they had seen earlier, only many, many times larger. It had slivers of light issuing from it, and it took a moment for them to realize that they were, in fact, windows. The formation was not a formation at all, but a structure; a massive fortress of domes and spires and towers of stone, crafted to imitate the natural monuments they'd witnessed earlier.

Cindra felt a sensation build up in her chest, creep up to her throat, and escape in peals of silent, joyful laughter. Tears ran down her cheeks as her breath came in trembling gasps. *This* was what she had hoped to see all her life; an impossibly beautiful place hidden away from the mundane world, a magical faerie land untouched by the clumsy hands and inquisitive minds of man. She hugged herself and let the joy wash over her, until she felt Nixy grip her arm.

Turning, she saw a wonder in his eyes that she had not seen since the night she met him, when she had led the lean, hungry street urchin through the castle's kitchens. His eyes were wide and tearful, his mouth was agape, and all the emotions swirling within him were struggling to find expression. She took his hand and squeezed it, and they walked hand-in-hand for a while.

She saw that the others too were similarly impressed, even Deliah, whom Cindra thought had seen it all.

"I think... I think I have been here before," Deliah said.

Cindra couldn't help it; she had to laugh. "Of course you have," she said, "You just forgot to mention it for two weeks!"

"No, I think I was *made* to forget," she said.

That thought was a bit sobering.

Walking a little farther, they found a bridge leading across the stream to the island. It was either an arch of natural rock, or was crafted in a manner so cunning as to not show stonework of any kind. Crossing it, they saw that along the eastward wall of the cavern were a large number of dwellings carved into the rock. They were many stories high and tiered, so that the roof of one row was the walkway of the row above it. The facades were carved to create one giant relief mural, broken only by doorways and windows. It seemed to tell the story of a people making a long journey, leaving behind a land of turmoil for a place of peace and beauty.

"I wish Paddy could see this," Adric said.

The forest before them was lush and green, with moss covering many of the rising stone pillars that grew out of the ground like giant thorns. The entire cavern was so adorned, both above and below, with sharp thorns of menacing stone.

"Fortress of Thorns," Cindra said, "not at all what I expected."

They walked past gardens of mushrooms and tubers, and shallow pools of clear water. Flowers bloomed under the skylight, catching the brief noonday sun. Carved stone benches sat upon scenic overlooks or under whispering trees, and the songs of birds echoed cheerfully through the vast space.

Wenyssaya said, "This is the strangest, most beautiful place I have ever known."

The others could only nod in dumb agreement.

Before they ascended the plateau, Cindra decided to remove her armor and weapons, trusting they would be safe in this place. Adric did as well, but Nixy kept his little knife, since it was his precious heirloom and the only keepsake of his mother and true father. Once they had freshened up and Wenyssaya removed their dust and grime with a spell, they trekked up the carved stairs to the fortress itself. Drahn used the opportunity to stretch his wings, so he flew up before them, making circles high overhead.

The structure was about 400 feet high at its tallest tower, making it 90 feet higher than the Tower of the Silver Moon, and 190 feet taller than Ildric's Tower of Sight. Its tallest tower was strangely off-center, with tapering levels that made it look rather unstable. The main structure, being the widest, was surrounded by buildings of varying shapes and sizes that were placed in a manner best described as 'globular,' as though they had dripped from above and attached themselves. This was obviously meant to imitate the formations in the earlier cave, but it made no defensive sense that Cindra could grasp.

She said, "I don't see any arrow slits, crenellations, machicolations... How is this place defended?"

Deliah chuckled, "You have to ask that after our little scare at the entrance?"

Of course, Cindra thought, *Magic. I bet there's an arsenal of magic here that humans have never seen.*

They reached the top of the plateau and saw that the fortress's many levels had covered walkways supported by tall, thin arches, which mimicked the flowstone 'icicles' of the natural cave. One such archway framed a double door, which opened on its own before them.

"Ladies first," Adric said. Nixy and Drahn nodded in agreement.

Cindra smiled, shaking her head. "My heroes," she said.

Wenyssaya took a deep breath and walked inside. The others followed, unsure of what to expect.

They entered a vast, domed rotunda; its walls began curving almost from the floor, and it had many ribs of stone that grew thinner and closer as they reached the pinnacle. There were six doors about the circumference, including the one they entered. From the ceiling hung hundreds of crystals of differing size, suspended like stars from silver chains. They began to glow brighter as the guests entered, bathing the room in soft colors which reflected off of silver and gold inlay in the walls and floor; curving, organic shapes etched in metallic splendor greeted their eyes.

In the center of the chamber, illuminated from above by a cluster of glowing white quartz, was a fifty-foot statue of a woman. She was an elf dressed in an unknown style of armor, with her foot resting on a pile of misshapen, horned skulls. Her head was bowed and her eyes were closed, as though in defeat, and her expression was troubled and mournful. Under her left arm was a crested helmet, and in her right hand was a spear with a long, shattered blade. The entire monument was painted, giving her golden skin and fiery red hair. It looked so life-like that it seemed the giant woman might raise her head and address them.

They stood in awe for a long moment, taking it all in, unable to speak. Then Cindra whispered to Wenyssaya, "Do you know who she is?" But her voice broke the spell like a sneeze in a temple; an unbecoming noise violating a sacred peace.

Yet Wenyssaya did not answer. She only stared up at the woman's face as if her mind was far, far away in another time.

"Wen? Wen?" Cindra shook the elf maid, and it brought her back to the present. "Are you alright?"

"I... Yes, I am alright." She looked like she was waking from a dream, and her lovely violet eyes were brimming with tears.

"Hey," Nixy said, "Something's happening here..."

The air grew blurry and shimmered, and a black void appeared before them, growing to the size of a door. Through it stepped a figure, tall and elegant, and brimming with power. The portal shrank to nothing with a whoosh of air.

"Welcome to my home," he said.

None but Deliah had ever seen in person one of the Damfayen, the first children of the Ilvayiin, and no one was prepared for it. Even Wenyssaya, who had glimpsed him once in a dream, was startled now by the reality of him.

The Shadow Lord was tall and imposing, with golden skin more like metal than any human complexion, and almond-shaped eyes of brilliant amber. The lines of his face were sharp and manly, yet held a softness that age could not touch. His hair was silver-white and bound at the back, draping over his shoulders and exposing his gracefully pointed ears.

He wore a circlet of silver with a black stone on the brow, and a suit of black silk with a gray gossamer robe. About his waist was a belt of silver chain, and from it hung a curved sword with a long handle of shadowood carved in the form of a raven; a companion to Nixy's knife. Upon each hand he wore a ring; one with a black obsidian, and another with an orange fire opal flecked within by little rainbow colors.

But what was most striking was the overwhelming sense of *presence* that emanated from him; it was tangible, yet indescribable. This may have been why his guests chose to bow low before him, though no one had thought to plan so beforehand.

When he spoke, his voice was clear and strong, and in perfect Calilesh.

"I am pleased to finally meet you, Wenyssaya cua Du-Velthathwe," he said, extending his hands.

She took them and curtsied a little awkwardly, her eyes fixed on his face. Then she recovered her wits and said, "My lord, it was an honor to receive your summons. May I introduce your son, Nixyalderthor

DuQuayne of Syngmore Village." She motioned for him to step forward.

"Hello," Nixy said, "Nice to finally meet you... father." He felt as awkward and uncomfortable as he had ever felt, and he was sure he was either as pale as a ghost, or red-faced, or maybe both, like a turnip.

"My child," the Shadow Lord said, "I have watched you from afar all of your life. Welcome."

Nixy turned to his friends and said, "This is Lady Cindra Corrina, the first and only lady knight of Calilon. She's my best friend."

Cindra smiled and gave her best curtsy. "My lord," she said.

"I have seen you from afar also, Lady Cindra," he said, "I thank you for saving my son's life and being his protector. Welcome."

Cindra felt a rush of pride and satisfaction that she had not expected; not since being knighted had she felt so pleased with herself.

Wenyssaya gestured to Drahn and said, "This is Drahnizhlomazhith, of the Dwimathii S'hathas." She pronounced his name like a non-dragon would; without the deep, throaty vibrations and hissing consonants. Nevertheless, Drahn extended his wings and bowed.

"Gweetings, my lord," he said, turning a little crimson at his untimely lazy tongue.

"And this is Adric Hywahl, esquire, of Portshia, and Deliah Wyngaard... also of Portshia."

Adric bowed and Deliah curtsied, but the Shadow Lord said to Deliah, "We have met before, rava-navhwal."

"I thought as much, my lord," she said, sounding the tiniest bit resentful.

Wenyssaya flinched at the exchange, aware of the subtleties at play. Adric and Nixy just stared back and forth between them, confused.

He gave her a cold little smile before turning back to the others. "I am Thásalfen, fáldweya cua Du-Dwithian, but you may call me Navasram, if it pleases you."

It was a mouthful, and had a strange, intimate quality to it. *Snow Crown, second born of the Beginning Place.* Cindra felt like she had been given a rare jewel in the form of a name, and swore she would do her best to remember it. *Navasram* was simply 'Shadow Lord,' so it would do as a formality. As for what he called Deliah, there was something 'off' about it. She decided to ask Wenyssaya later.

"So... father," Nixy asked, "do you live here all alone?"

Navasram turned to him and smiled. "No, not alone," he said, "I have many who keep my vigil with me. They are Dwimathii Vothiivoss, and they have been watching you since before you entered the Dark Vale."

He motioned with his hand, and all around them the air began to darken and shimmer for the briefest moment; suddenly they were surrounded by two dozen sleek, black figures, each of them slightly larger than Drahn.

"Dweedragons!" Drahn cried, "There *are* other dweedragons in the fowest!" He hopped about on his hind quarters, clapping his fore-claws.

The Dweedragons of Nightmares just stared back at him.

The Shadow Lord proved to be a gracious host, and after a brief tour of the fortress, he showed the party to their private chambers above the main hall. The accommodations were beyond their wildest dreams; each of them had a sizable room with a comfortable bed and a door to the outer walkway on the second floor, which offered an incredible view no matter which direction you were facing. Each room also had a fireplace that burned with a magical fire, giving heat and light without the need for wood or a chimney. Cindra had no idea when these rooms had last been used, but they had either been dusted recently, or had some magic ward that kept them free from the ravages of time.

There was a knock at her door, and Wenyssaya came in. The elf maid had a certain glow about her since entering the fortress, and Cindra couldn't blame her.

"Hello," Wen said, "may we speak?"

"Of course, what's on your mind?"

"Deliah had a private meeting with Du-Navasram, and it did not seem very friendly."

"I was meaning to ask you about that," Cindra said, "He called her, what was it, 'raven woman?' But it sounded kind of impolite."

"You are perceptive," Wen said, "Navhwalrava would have been the kind way to say it, but rava-navhwal is a bit rude."

"She thought she'd been here before, but someone made her forget. Is that something he can do?"

"I do not know, but it would not surprise me," Wenyssaya said, "There are many ancient spells and powers that have since been lost to time."

"Well, this is a place I'd certainly not want to forget. Every few minutes I look around me and giggle at how amazing it all is! I mean, it's a genuine elven palace in a hidden forest inside of a cave! Imagine waking up every morning to this view."

"It is wonderful," she agreed, "but also very lonely."

"He has all those creepy dweedragons for company," Cindra said, "but I suppose that's not the same as his own kin."

"I wonder," Wen said, "do you think he might let us see this portal to Alhanna? I have only heard rumors and legends."

"He'd probably let you see it before the rest of us," Cindra said, "He might let you take a peek inside, or maybe even visit! You could be our emissary to the elder elves."

"I doubt I could plead the king's case very convincingly."

"Forget the king," Cindra said, "that's my worry. I'm more concerned about the Dark Heart and the end of the world."

"But what about your mission?" Wen asked, "Did he not charge you to seek the help of the elves? Is that not his main concern?"

Cindra sighed, "His, perhaps; *my* main concern here is Nixy. I want to know what's to become of him. Will this be his new home? Also, why wasn't this his home to begin with? This Navasram says he's watched him all his life, so he must know how rotten it was. Why didn't he bring him here sooner?"

"Perhaps... one should not speak ill of one's host," Wen said.

"Fine. One will shut one's mouth and keep one's thoughts to one's self," Cindra said, "I'm going to get Adric and collect the things we left in the forest. Want me to pick you a mushroom or something?"

"No thank you."

Drahn was beside himself with excitement; his dream of meeting other dweedragons had finally come true! He hadn't actually had a chance to speak with them yet, and they didn't seem too eager to do so, but it was still thrilling. He would have to stop one before it popped into the Shadow, or wherever they went, and ask all he could.

He had flown down to the forest and collected his pack, flying back up with a little difficulty. As he arranged his belongings in Nixy's room, he thought about what to ask first.

"I wonder where they nest," he thought aloud, "is it in the twees outside the cave, or inside, or in the towers? I should ask who to ask, I suppose. They must have an elder."

"Who are you talking to?"

Drahn jumped. "Oh! I didn't hear you come in!"

"I was on the balcony looking around," Nixy said.

"Are you excited for this to be your new home?"

"I guess so," he shrugged, "I'm not sure if I'm staying yet."

"But where else would you go?"

Nixy shrugged again.

"Family is vewy important, and if your family is here, then you should consider staying."

"But... he doesn't *feel* like my family," Nixy said, "I know he is, but... he could have come, you know? He could have visited me, or... or brought me here."

"Well," Drahn said, "I-I guess... maybe..." He found he was at a loss for words, and began to understand how the boy felt. For Nixy, it was not a joyous occasion, like finding members of your own kind, but an unsettling time of questions without answers. If Drahn had learned that his own mother and siblings had been avoiding him, letting him think he was alone in the world, he would be quite upset about it too.

"Perhaps the journey would have been too dangerous?" he offered.

"He could have done it!" Nixy cried, "Twice he sent those black wolves to protect me, once from the troll and once from Dexer. If he could open doorways in the Shadow like that, then he could have visited me anywhere."

"You do not know of what you speak."

The voice was high, female, and had a hissing quality. Nixy and Drahn spun around to find a black dweedragon sitting several feet away.

"Where did you come fwom?" Drahn asked.

"She's been here the whole time," Nixy said, "I *knew* I felt something in the Shadow."

"You were spying on us?" Drahn exclaimed.

"Yes," she said simply, "all of you. We do not trust you."

Drahn stammered, "But, but we are guests! And Nixy is the Shadow Lord's own son!"

"Guests can be more than what they seem... or less," she said, "We have not decided if you are a threat or not."

"We are not!" Drahn said, "Why would you think such a thing?"

"We have foreseen a threat coming; one that will take many lives, one that may seal our doom," she said, "We do not know its source, but it will come from outside... like you did."

"Foreseen...? Oh, of course! We dweedwagons must have a talent for divination! We made the Eye of Omithys after all."

She peered at Drahn as though he had only just realized something obvious. "*Must have* a talent?" she asked, "Do you not know this?"

"Well, I um..." he mumbled and fiddled with his tail.

Nixy was getting angry, and the room was getting darker. "I don't like you spying on me and my friends, and I don't like your accusations!"

She looked like she was about to say something harsh, but she relented and flattened her wings. "Apologies, little lord," she said, "but we must be cautious. Much is at stake."

Nixy forced himself to relax, and the shadows retreated.

"Forgive my intrusion. I am *Shazhokramazhah*," she said in a deep, growly voice.

"What a lovely name," Drahn said.

"Thank you," she said, "I am the lord's *thirundanii*."

Drahn did not like her title so much; there was no Calilesh equivalent as far as he knew, but the elven word amounted to 'spy master.'

Nixy asked, "Can we call you 'Shaz' for short?"

She looked at him with lidded eyes, and after a long pause, said, "If you must."

"Okay Shaz, why couldn't my father have opened a shadow door and visited me?"

"Because doing so is very taxing, especially over such a distance. He was greatly weakened the first time, and it was worse the second. If he had made the trip himself, he would have been helpless upon arrival."

"Oh," Nixy said.

"The last shadow wolves he sent never returned, so I assume the risk was great."

"That's right, I need to tell you!" Nixy exclaimed, "There's a man, well, he's kind of a possessed man named Dexer, but we call him 'Black Dexer' because he's like Black Will; anyhow he's deep in the Shadow and I don't think he can get out, but he's been following us and he attacked us a few times. Well, attacked me, really. He hurt one of Cindra's friends bad and almost got me in Gloamshire."

Drahn said, "In short, a killer possessed by a demnox has been twacking us through the Shadow."

"This is most alarming," she hissed, "perhaps he is the danger we have foreseen. We will search for him."

"Be careful," Nixy said, "I think I was able to hurt him with this." He drew his little knife.

"*Sugireth!*" she said, "Of course. That would easily harm such a creature."

"Sugireth? Is that its name?" Nixy asked, "I always called it *Cutter*."

She snorted.

"It was the best I could think of at eight years old."

"It is the Shard Blade, a fragment of Hanvdálni itself! Why the Lord trusted it to that girl child..."

"What girl...? You mean my mother?"

Shaz thought a moment and said, "These are things you must ask your father, if he is so inclined to tell you. I must see to this intruder you brought to our doorstep."

Drahn hurriedly said, "Before you go, I have so many question to ask you; may I have time to speak with you about your lives here? It would mean a gweat deal."

"Perhaps," she said, and turned and vanished in a dark shimmer.

Later that evening they were called to dinner in one of the rooms off the main rotunda. It was smaller and more intimate than that vast hall, but was still impressive, even by the standards Cindra was used to.

It had an unusual table in the shape of an incomplete triangle, so that meals could be served from within, and all the guests could face one another. The room was lit by an enormous growth of crystal suspended from the ceiling by four gilded chains. It glowed with a soft golden light, making the room seem warm and inviting.

The tables had individual chairs, and the dinnerware was beautiful kiln-fired crockery, glazed the color of jade. The utensils were elegant and ornate, made of some silver-gray alloy; the knives had shadowood handles carved like raven heads, a common theme in this place.

But most impressive was that the meal was prepared and served entirely by dweedragons. Using their nimble fore claws and prehensile tails, they managed very well, and what their bodies could not accomplish, their magic took care of; plates, trays, and bottles of dandelion wine were hovered about by their concentrated gazes.

Drahn was most impressed also, though he was a little ashamed to say that his own floating spells were not nearly as potent.

"You must teach me how to do that," he said to one of the young servers, "if you have the time."

The dweedragon looked him up and down and creased its eyes in puzzlement before bounding off.

The Shadow Lord sat at the head table, with Nixy on his right and Wenyssaya on his left. Cindra and Adric were at one flanking table, and Deliah and Drahn were opposite.

Navasram said, "I hope you enjoy this feast; it is the first we have held in many a century, and I fear we may be out of practice."

The layout was beautiful and more than they could have hoped for. There was venison and pork, fish and fowl, fresh and sautéed mushrooms, various kinds of greens, and diced and seasoned tubers. There were even flat-breads with honey and berry preserves for dessert.

"I don't think you need to fear for the skill of your cooks, my lord. It's all wonderful," Cindra said.

He gave her a nod of thanks.

As the meal progressed, Cindra said, "My lord, do we have you to thank for the intervention of the ravens in Gloamshire?"

"Only for the rain," he said, "the ravens held their own council on the matter."

"The rain?" Nixy exclaimed, "You can make it rain?"

"Only if there is a potential for it, yes. We were lucky that the weather was so inclined to be influenced."

The others stared with awe, and Drahn asked, "Is that vewy difficult?"

Navasram smiled at him and said, "You cannot imagine how difficult, my dear dwimathii. It took me many days to recover."

"We thank you deeply, as do the people of the hamlet," Wenyssaya said, "the rain changed everything."

"How were such creatures allowed to breed in the first place?" Deliah asked.

They all paused, hearing the recrimination in her voice.

Navasram said, "The forest is full of Nixominy tribes. They defend their territory and play little pranks on those who would wander too far into the woods. They are pests, but beneficial pests, for the most part."

"But they are creatures of Chaos," she said, "and the ones that murdered those villagers were not beneficial."

"The world is fraught with chaos, and one must learn how to live with it," he said, "As for the ones you encountered, I believe they were looking for revenge. They have had a very long wait."

Deliah gave him a dark look.

"For what crime were they destroyed so many years ago?" he asked, "For playing pranks and driving a child and her father away from home?"

"You know the story, my lord?" Cindra asked.

"I have heard it told by the blind woman many times," he said, "I must admit, she has a talent for it."

"That blind woman was their victim," Deliah said, "they put out her eyes as a child."

"The child threatened their secrecy and led destruction to their nest," he said, "I do not condone what they did, but I have bothered to understand it."

Nixy asked, "So have you met Deliah before? Did she really find this place and you made her forget?"

Navasram nodded. "Yes," he said, "but she has a long memory and is terribly persistent."

"Let us not speak of our past or my memory," she said, "I am sure the boy has many questions to ask his father."

A good deflection, Cindra thought, *but now may not be the time for this.*

Nixy did indeed have questions, but he could think of few that would make for comfortable dinner conversation. "When did you first meet my mother?" he asked.

"When she was perhaps half your age," he said, "as a child lost in the woods; lost, but not afraid. I had not seen a child wandering without fear in these woods for many an age, and she fascinated me.

"I peered into her future and saw that she would be a great beauty, if she survived. I also saw that my fate was bound up with hers somehow, so I gave her the knife, a precious gift that she could use to protect herself; I also used it as a divination focus, allowing me to watch her from afar. But before I could learn why she was so unafraid, I was interrupted. A wandering wizard had come to search for her, and he made quite a nuisance of himself; I guided him to her and let them depart."

"That was Master Ildwic!" Drahn said, "It was before he lost his hand."

"Yes, that artifact he now possesses has given him the power to meddle in my affairs, and I had to place powerful scrying wards upon the knife, shielding the one who carried it. I have felt his gaze wandering through my past, and have discouraged it.”

“Did you know she would be my mother?”

“No, not for many years,” he said.

They ate in silence for a time, digesting the information. Then Cindra asked, “When was the last time there were children wandering the forest unafraid?”

Navasram seemed sad as he spoke, “You saw the carvings on the eastern wall of the cavern? They were once the dwellings of a number of humans who lived here with us in peace and contentment. But contentment is not an enduring human trait.”

Fascinated, she asked, “Who were they?”

“They were the descendants of the first humans to awaken, with whom I had a special affinity. I was only a child when they met their first evening, saw their first light of the moon and stars, and their first sunrise. They awoke in a cave, and had to be coaxed out, but their descendants left this cave of their own free will, eager to travel under open skies.”

“Where did they come fwom?” Drahn asked.

“From the continent you call Hibland, west across the Emerald Sea. Many thousands followed me here.”

Adric was impressed. “The elves must have had a great many ships to carry so many people, milord!” he said.

Navasram laughed, “No, we did not. We walked across lands that now lie beneath the waves; now they are only islands.”

“What became of these humans?” Cindra asked, though she was beginning to suspect.

They lived in these lands in peace for a time. Then they grew in number and became fractured, as humans do. In time they established territories and hunting grounds. Then the Others came from over the sea, and brought the Oldest War with them.”

"The Galindri!" she exclaimed, "They were the Gatéth-sho'a! I've heard some of this story from them. You are the one they call the Forest King!"

He smiled, but said, "I am no king; I abdicated my claim to the crown of my people. I am only Navasram."

Wenyssaya asked, "My lord, who is the woman commemorated in the great hall?"

He looked at her for a long moment and said, "That was my sister, and she was our queen."

Then he spoke of it no more.

The sorrow in his voice told them that no more questions would be welcomed tonight. They enjoyed the rest of their feast, speaking only of light and pleasant things.

After dinner, Cindra and her friends went their own separate ways, some to sleep, some to explore, and some to brood. She walked down the plateau and into the forest, following the torch-lit path until she came across a quiet pool of clear water. Taking off her boots, she soaked her feet in the pool and lay back on the mossy ground. The water was surprisingly warm and soothing, and as she gazed up at the stars through the skylight, she decided to stay there until her toes were good and pruney.

She awoke some time later to a bright glare in her face. As her eyes adjusted, she found it was only the moon pouring its silver light into the cave. Holding her hand up to block the light, she saw a distant twinkling beyond. Tiny blue stars were shining on the cavern ceiling, illuminating the spikes of rock, and even clinging to them in places. She stared in wonder until her arm grew tired, then she sat up and pulled her feet from the water.

Deliah was sitting on the opposite side of the pool.

Cindra jumped and gasped before she could stop herself.

"They are glowworms," Deliah said, looking up, "the lights attract their prey, catching them in their hanging webs."

"What are you doing here?" Cindra asked.

"I have no one else to talk to. Wenyssaya has been spending time with our host, and Drahn... well, he's busy looking to make new friends."

"Adric and Nixy?"

"Hmmm, they don't know me like you do, do they?"

"No," Cindra said, "no they don't."

"Good," she said, "the fewer, the better."

"I... I never apologized for what I did," Cindra said, "and I'm sorry."

"Sorry for not apologizing, or sorry for stabbing me?"

Cindra got an ill feeling as her victim spoke her crime out loud. "For both! Especially the... stabbing part."

Deliah waited. Smiling, she said, "You're not very good at this, are you?"

"I've never had to say I'm sorry to someone I've killed."

"Well, you may have to do it again someday, so you might as well get some practice."

Cindra shot her a hurt look, which turned confused. Finally, she closed her eyes and said, "I'm sorry. I'm sorry I hurt you, I'm sorry I sought to kill you, and I'm glad you're not dead," she looked her in the eyes, "Not just because you've helped us and guided us here, but because... because I never wanted to be a murderer."

Deliah pierced Cindra with her steel-gray gaze, and Cindra felt like she was looking into her soul, judging her entire life in a moment. Finally the woman said, "Very well. Let there be peace between us then?"

"Yes," Cindra said, "I'd like that."

Deliah nodded, stood up, and slowly meandered around the pool. She stared up at the moon for a while and finally said, "I have been here six times before."

"What? So many?"

She nodded. "I find my way here every four, five, six centuries. I come to these woods looking for answers and help from the only person who might be old enough and powerful enough to give it, and each time I am turned away."

Cindra felt a great swell of pity for the woman once again. She said, "Does he refuse to help, or is it not in his power?"

"He tells me that the time is not right, and that no power in this world can undo what was done, not unless the Dark Heart itself is undone. Then perhaps..."

"But, but how can he blame you for seeking him out if he makes you forget you were ever here?"

Deliah turned to face her and Cindra saw she was crying. "Because he has only altered my memory twice," she said.

Cindra stood and approached her. "I don't understand."

Drawing a ragged breath, Deliah explained, "Twice he made me forget, but my last four visits were because... because my memory simply failed. Human minds were not meant to hold so much time. I've forgotten so much of my past that for all I know I've been repeating myself *over* and *over* again for millennia! Making the same mistakes, trying the same failed plans, following the same dead ends..."

Cindra didn't know what to say. She hadn't the words.

"Look at me, bawling like a child," Deliah sniffled, "and here I thought I had no more tears left."

In the face of such a tortured life, all of Cindra's little problems seemed to shrink to nothing, and all that was left was a burning light of empathy that sought to ease what suffering it could. She took the woman in a strong embrace, feeling her wilt in her arms. As Deliah shook with little sobs, Cindra was determined to be a rock for her to lean on.

They stood there, bathed in the moonlight, until she had no more tears to cry.

Wenyssaya awoke in her bed, feeling lost and confused. She had been dreaming of a journey she took with her parents and many others, the first journey of her early life. She was a young girl of perhaps fifty, and they were all trekking through the Everwood, past waterfalls and streams, down towards the sea. They had crossed a river, but she slipped on a stone and fell into the rushing water. Her father had saved her by causing the water to lift her onto the bank.

She felt ashamed, because she had been the only one to fall; not even her brother had fallen.

Except Wenyssaya was an only child.

Shaking off the dream, she arose, got dressed, and left the room.

She looked in on Nixy, who was still sleeping. Drahn was curled up on a cushion near the fire, like a purple cat with wings.

"Sleep all you like, little ones," she whispered, "sleep in safety while you can."

Her words troubled her as she closed the door. Was there some sense of foreboding that was warning her, or was it that the stress of the long journey had made her wary? She pondered this as she made to go downstairs.

Upstairs, came a voice in her head, *Meet me here.*

She said, "Navasram? Is that you?"

There was no answer, but she knew that he wanted her to climb, so she did.

The spiral stairs were long, and went past several floors she yet to explore, but when she reached the top, she found herself in a round room some forty feet wide and just as high, with a domed ceiling. The walls had thin, tall windows of stained glass, and sculptures of many noble and important-looking elves between them. Like the giant one below, these statues were painted in lifelike colors, making them seem almost alive. Golden-skinned immortals surrounded her, making her feel both elevated and diminished.

"Welcome," Navasram said. He had been seated on an upholstered bench in the center of the room, but arose when she entered. "I wished for you to see this place. It is a kind of temple dedicated to my family and friends, all of whom left the world long, long ago. I call it my *Suvasian*."

Place of Memory, she thought, *fitting*.

"My lord, the way you called me; are you able to read my thoughts?" she asked.

"Not unless you send them," he said, "I can teach it to you if you'd like."

"Can this really be taught to one of my generation?"

He smiled and said, "You are not exactly of your generation, are you?"

"I have a greater power within me, it is true," she said, "but I do not think I am anything like them." She gestured to the statues around her.

He held her in his amber gaze for a time and asked, "Tell me your impressions of this room."

She looked around. "It is a beautiful place; very restful and peaceful, though I feel I am being watched."

He smiled and said, "Take your time. Walk around and view the works of art, and tell me then what you feel."

She did as she was bid, starting with the tallest, most regal-looking elf. She stared into his face for a very long time; not at any particular feature, but as a whole composition. Her mind wandered, swimming through a fog of memory, until the windows caught the distant glow of the noonday sun coming in over the underground forest.

Finally she tore her gaze away from the statue and looked to the Shadow Lord; her eyes were wide, frightened, and confused.

"What is happening to me?" she begged, "What are you not telling me?"

He had been sitting like a statue himself, but he rose smoothly and went to her. "Do not be afraid," he said, "It will take time."

"*What* will take time? Since we arrived I have felt like my mind is elsewhere, and it makes no sense! Please, tell me what is wrong with me!"

"There is nothing wrong with you child. This has always been a part of you, and always will. You must come to understand that before I tell you more."

Her lip quivered and she took in a ragged breath, wanting to cry, or scream, or strike him. Instead, she bowed her head and took many deep breaths as her tears stained the floor.

"That is enough for today, Wenyssaya," he said, "Go and join your friends, or do what you wish."

She met with Nixy and Cindra later that day and joined them to do a little exploring. There were many secluded grottos across the stream, with little bridges and pathways to reach them. They stopped to rest in one of them, sitting on benches carved out of the limestone. Crystal growths stirred at their presence, shedding soft light in the chamber, and they stared in wonder at the ceiling of wavy stone that seemed to be flaked with gold foil. The pool before them was clear and blue, and fish swam lazily about.

Their previous conversation had been very light and trifling, but now the silence was weighing on them in this more intimate space, with only the echoing fall of dripping water to disturb it.

"We missed you at breakfast," Cindra said, "Nixy wanted to go look for you."

"Perhaps you should have let him," she said.

"Oh? Was something wrong?"

"I... I was called by Navasram to meet him in a high chamber. He... he is trying to..."

"Trying to what?" Cindra asked, suddenly concerned.

"Did he do something to you?" Nixy asked.

"This place has done something to me," she said, "I have not felt myself since coming here. This morning I spent hours staring at a statue. I have no idea where the time went; it's like I was caught up in a waking dream, unable to tell what was real."

"And you think it's this place that's doing it, not him?"

Wenyssaya shook her head. "He said that this has always been a part of me and always will. It's as if the dreams I've had all my life are expanding and becoming more real, more involved. I think... I think he is trying to awaken something within me, and it terrifies me."

"Then tell him to stop!" Cindra said, "If it's not what you want, then he has no right to push it."

"He is not 'pushing' anything," she said, "he is trying to help me understand it, but won't tell me what it is."

"If you need me to have a word with him, I will," Cindra offered.

"Thank you," she said, "but I'm not sure that is wise."

"Since when did that ever stop me?"

They had a rare chuckle at that, but the mirth faded within a few heartbeats.

"This place holds too many secrets," Cindra said.

"More than you know," Nixy said, "Those dweedragons have been spying on us."

"Why, those little creepers," Cindra said, "Was it on the Shadow Lord's orders?"

"I don't think so," he said, "they just don't trust anybody. They said there was a terrible threat coming, and I told them about Dexer."

"Hopefully they can take care of him. I'd hate to think he was lurking about even here."

He nodded in agreement, but something else was bothering him. He seemed sad.

"What is wrong, Nixy?" Wen asked.

He shrugged and said, "I was hoping I'd get a chance to talk about some stuff with him."

"What kind of stuff?"

"Anything," he said, "There's a lot I wanna know."

Wenyssaya could tell that he meant very personal matters. Cindra knew it too, for her face grew serious and concerned.

"I'll take it up with him tomorrow," Cindra said.

"No, I mean, you don't have to..." he began.

"We didn't come all this way to have him spend time with Wen," she said, "He's going to have a good long talk with you, and soon."

Wenyssaya was not surprised at Cindra's earnestness, but hoped when the time came, she would be more diplomatic about it. She knew Cindra the Warrior, but knew very little of Cindra the Lady. She hoped the girl would be wise enough to put her brash willfulness aside and let her noble-born manners dictate the meeting.

But then she thought, *What if she has always been brash and willful?*

––––––––––

The next morning, Cindra got up early and chose her clothing for her audience with Navasram. She decided on her split-skirt dress and bodice, but over that she would wear the king's dark gray tabard with the black eagle insignia. She was here on his behalf after all, acting as ambassador as well as bodyguard.

She ate breakfast, washed her face and hair, and got dressed. When finished, she examined herself in the long mirror, not caring for what she saw. She hated her bangs and could not wait for them to grow out. The long hair in back was meant to be bound up in a *tipok* knot, but she hadn't the time to wrestle with it herself, and Adric had never learned to tie one. She had finally just bound it up in a simple bun and wore her Galindri headband to lift her bangs, like she'd done for most of the journey.

The tabard and dress were not a flattering combination. The neckline of the dress and the bodice's pretty lacing were covered by the drab fabric, making her feel like she was wearing a sack. The weapon belt gave her the appearance of a waistline, but the drab gray material was ugly, and killed the lovely blue of her dress like a jealous hag. She hoped the Shadow Lord was unconcerned with human fashions.

He met her in a small audience chamber off the main hall; an intimate setting that was a bit too small to hold the elf lord's overwhelming presence. Perhaps that is what he intended.

Cindra gave her best curtsy and waited to be addressed.

"Welcome, Lady Cindra," he said, "I understand we have matters to discuss?"

"Yes, my lord," she said, "I come on behalf of His Royal Highness Galen SuCordobal, the third of his name; rightful King of Calilon. He has asked me to implore your lordship for aid in his time of great need. Calilon faces a terrible civil war, and it is feared that the forces of Chaos have arisen again. Portshia has suffered plagues after the coming of a mad wizard, and that darkness may spread to other lands."

"Of these things I am aware," he said, "What is it you would ask of me?"

She lowered her eyes to his shoes. "Navasram, I humbly ask that you summon those warriors who have passed into Alhanna to return and aid us in our darkest hour."

He remained silent until she grew uncomfortable and raised her eyes. He had a quizzical look that she found discouraging. "Interesting. What does your king think he knows of Alhanna?" he asked.

"I cannot say, my lord; he only knows that the elves fought with Kraal in his great need," she said, "as for myself, I know a little more, thanks to Wenyssaya."

"And what does she think she knows?"

This gave her pause, but she said, "She has told us there is said to be a portal to the World of Spirit through which the elder elves can pass, and that you are its guardian, my lord."

"The eldest elves are too strong to pass into Alsuvath again. The portals between realms were shut, and the most powerful can never return in that manner. Those younger generations may yet do so, though it would cause great pain, and perhaps further diminishment. Few have tried."

Everyone knew that Arathus had closed off the gateways between Jayde and the Outer Realms, but Cindra had not considered that it might also include the elven path. That there was some kind of power limitation was also news, but it made sense; gods could not interfere with Jayde, but lesser, malignant spirits seemed to slip through the cracks once in a while.

"So... you can never go to Alhanna yourself?" she asked.

"It is far easier to pass beyond than to come within," he said, "The spirit wants to return to its source. But my fate is to be the guardian of the vault until the end, not to take my leave as I choose."

Vault? Is that where the portal is kept? She imagined elven pilgrims making their journey to the Fortress of Thorns, and stepping through a doorway into a land of eternal spirit. How many had done so, not knowing it was a one-way trip? Would they even want to return?

"Even if it could be done," he said, "my people have no interest in your affairs. Only in the Time of Chaos did we see fit to interfere."

"But those times may be upon us again, my lord; worse, it might be the end of all things."

His face grew weary. "And where would I send an army to stop it?" he asked, gesturing about, "Where is the threat? You say the mad wizard who brought this calamity was last seen in Portshia, yet your own forces did nothing. What use would an elven host be in a human city?"

She frowned. "It is said that you have great powers of Sight; can you not seek it with divination?"

"Your silver-handed mage is my equal in that, yet he has the wisdom not to try, as many have done before. Divining the Dark Heart would curse me with a window into the Abyss, and the Abyss would have a window into me. No, I would not dare to attempt it."

Cindra had not thought of that, and she was beginning to realize that there was much she had not considered. This was an ancient problem after all, and perhaps the elves had already done all they could. There was never much hope that she would leave the Shadowood at the head of an elven army, but she had believed the Shadow Lord would be of *some* help. She began to feel a tiny sample of the frustration Deliah must have felt in all her centuries of trying.

Sounding more desperate than she intended, she asked, "If we cannot find it, then... then how are we to stop it?"

His face grew somber and he closed his eyes.

He doesn't know, she thought, *he's probably been looking for an answer for longer than I can imagine, and he doesn't know.*

In the space of a few breaths his eyes snapped open and his golden gaze bored into her. "The taint of the Dark Heart is upon you! Did you meet this mad wizard?" he asked.

"I did!" she said, "While riding outside of town, I saw him and a younger man I thought to be his son. Later, Jaron and I took shelter from a bizarre dust storm, and they were there in the tavern. He said strange things and made all the fires go out."

"What did he say?"

"He called me 'girl' even though I was dressed as a man, and he said there was blood on my hands; he said, 'blood of friend and foe, old blood from long ago.' I never forgot it."

"Fascinating," he said, leaning forward, "He saw your future, I think."

What I've always feared, she thought. "So it's a prophesy? Was he a seer?"

"The seer of seers. Tell me, did he have a carved walking stick? Pale and cracked at the bottom?"

"I believe he did. Who was he?" she demanded.

He sat back, steepling his fingers as he gauged her ability to handle great truths. Finally he said, "Do you know why it is said that people write their own destinies now?"

Cindra shook her head. "I assumed it was because the gods went silent."

"No. It is because Arathus stripped the god of fate of his power and banished him into our world, where he has wandered among us for over a thousand years. You met him."

This took a few moments to digest. *There was once a god of fate... and he's now a cackling old man in rags?* Had any other being told her this, she would have laughed it off, but the Shadow Lord's demeanor made the truth of it inescapable.

"So you mean to say that I... met a *god?* A god spoke to me?"

He nodded gravely. "What is left of him, yes. When he foresaw what the future had in store, he struck his staff in rage and sorrow, cracking its base. Upon that staff was written the entire history of the world and everything in it. The cracks are said to cut through the last age, when we shall choose our own paths."

"Did you witness this, my lord?"

"No. It happened before the assembled gods in the Halls of Dormos, home of Arathus. But our patron goddess Eyorona makes her home in Alhanna, and so word of it passed to me from... one of my departed kin."

"Your sister?"

His eyes flicked to hers and she saw a moment of pain.

"Forgive me, my lord, I meant no disrespect."

"You are insightful, for a mortal," he said, "Yes, my sister."

"Do you… get to speak to her often? I lost a brother you see, and would give anything to speak with him again."

"We have not spoken in over two and a half centuries," he said.

"I am sorry, my lord."

He waved it away, saying, "What matters is that the former god of fate and bearer of the Dark Heart made a prediction about your future. I feel this may be important."

Cindra did not like the prediction one little bit. *Friend and foe? Old blood from long ago? That might include Nixy*, she thought. Then she realized it would better apply to Deliah, in which case the worst had already happened, but she didn't share this. "What do you think it means, my lord?"

"That I cannot say. Prophesies are often spoken in riddles so as to not make their meaning plain. Having too much foreknowledge is worse than having too little."

"I'm not sure I understand."

"When you look into the future, you see probabilities; things that happen because they are most likely to happen. This is because all of the decisions and events leading to it are also most likely in their own right."

"But if I know that this 'blood on my hands' is in my future, shall I not avoid it?"

"How? By not fighting when you should? By not speaking or acting when you should? Could that not also lead to the same outcome?"

"Then what good is prophecy if it can't be acted upon?"

"It can prepare you for consequences, or guide your decisions. But to know too much is to surrender your freedom to choose. You will be forever basing your actions on the memory of the future instead of the needs of the moment. That path leads to either immense boredom or madness. Consider that the god of fate himself was driven mad by knowledge of his own destiny."

She recalled Deliah's words from two nights ago about apologizing to someone she had killed: *You may have to do it again someday, so you might as well get some practice.* "So... I am fated to kill friends and enemies both, and I should just *get used* to the idea?"

"It is unclear if it is a single person or many, by action or inaction. Old blood can mean many things, and it is perhaps the most pertinent detail."

"More pertinent than the 'friend' bit?" she asked bitterly.

"It may be, in the end. Many things can change. But we have spoken on this enough. Unless there are other matters..."

"Actually, my lord, there is one. It's about Nixyalderthor, your son. He has come a long way through many dangers, and he has a great many questions. I think perhaps the sooner you speak to him, the better."

He smiled slightly. "I have not been politely chided in a long time; I forgot what it felt like."

She blushed.

"You love him, don't you?" he asked.

"Like the little brother I lost," she said, "He has filled the void in my heart; I had forgotten how to care for another, as others had cared for me."

He nodded and said, "I am gladdened to hear it. Very well, you may inform him that I shall speak to him this evening."

"Thank you, my lord," she said as she curtsied and took her leave.

———————

Nixy and his father walked in the little forest after dinner, breathing in the cool, damp fog that hung like a cloud over the trees. They had spoken of nothing of substance yet, but Nixy was still mustering the courage to confront him.

They stopped beside a pool, the same pool where Cindra had spoken to Deliah two nights before. His father sat upon a bench of stone and Nixy sat beside him, but not too close. He fidgeted as the elf lord sat stone-still, gazing into the water, waiting.

I can do this, Nixy thought, *I survived in the Circle of Gold, I fought killer faeries with Cindra, so this is nothing.*

But it wasn't nothing. These were questions he had pondered for most of his life, but especially since learning who and what he was. He lay awake at night asking these questions to the darkness; now he might get them answered if he could only work up the courage to blurt them out.

Finally he said, "Why did you leave my mother?"

The Shadow Lord took a deep breath, staring up at the distant cave ceiling. He said, "The choice was hers. Kirana was married to a man chosen by her parents before they died, but she did not care for him. I took her to live here with me, and we were happy for a brief time, but she grew lonely for her kind, and missed the sun and stars. I knew that humans are restless by nature, and asking her to stay would only drive us apart, so I let her go her own way."

"Just like that?" Nixy asked. It wasn't sounding like the big love affair he had imagined it to be, with heartsickness and all of that weepy stuff that Cindra's mother liked to read about. His father was far too matter-of-fact for his liking.

"It was never meant to last," Navasram said, "she was mortal, after all. Yet, she desired to be with me for a time, and I was lonelier than I realized." His eyes fell to the pool once more. "But when she returned to her former life, she was early with child. If she did not go back to her husband, she would have become an outcast or possibly killed, so she pretended it was his."

Nixy knew that his mother had been the subject of many stories: her childhood adventure in the Shadowood, her great beauty, and her mysterious absence were part of village lore, but it was tales of her overlong pregnancy that had most often reached his ears.

He said, "Wenyssaya told me elves used to have babies with humans to make magic-using soldiers."

"Yes, long, long ago in desperate times."

"Were they... were they elven mothers or human mothers?"

"Both," said Navasram.

Nixy glared at him. "So you *knew* what might happen. You knew that having me could use her up and kill her."

"...I knew."

"Then why didn't you help?" he cried, "Why didn't you save her?"

The Shadow Lord's calm demeanor cracked, and his golden face registered hurt and anger, but he turned his head away; the boy did not deserve his anger.

Nixy said, "I was blamed for her death, you know. My... her husband beat me on my birthday. Other days too." Tears streamed down his cheeks, but they were not for the mother he never knew. They were bitter tears born of betrayal and neglect; they were the tears of the abandoned.

Navasram lowered his head, letting his white hair cover his face like a curtain. He said, "To help her would have exposed her lie. I swore to keep our secret, and not risk our child's future." He turned to the boy and said, "I am sorry for what you suffered. I could do little but send watchers to keep you as safe as I could."

"Ravens and scary black wolves," Nixy said, "People used to think I was cursed because of it. I had no friends and everyone whispered about me."

The lord was silent. Nixy felt his father's presence grow with his guilt, like a dark pressure pushing at his soul, but the boy wasn't going to shrink from it. All of the pain in his life was welling up now; all the fear, heartbreak and loneliness was collecting in his chest, making a knotted ball that threatened to choke him if he didn't let it out.

So he did.

"I had to run away! I lived on the streets! I stole to survive and fell in with thieves and killers! *Where were you?*" he cried, "Where have you been all my life?"

There, he had done it. He hadn't meant to be so angry; in all his imaginings of this moment he had remained cold and calm, like a nobleman sitting in judgment. But his anger had flashed through him, igniting a powder keg of resentment he hadn't realized had gotten so big.

And that wasn't all. The night reacted to his rage, growing deeper and darker, rippling the pond and shaking the leaves around him. The color leeched out of the forest, and small dark shapes were revealed in the gray gloom of the Shadow.

"Get out of here, you sneaky little spies!" he shouted, "Leave us alone!"

The dweedragons looked in alarm to their lord, who calmly waved them away. They departed reluctantly, looking over their shoulders as they went.

"Stupid things have been spying on me and my friends. I told them to stop."

"They are my servants and guardians, pledged to keep me safe. Suspicion is in their nature, but I will see that they do not intrude again."

Nixy breathed deeply, letting his rage settle a bit. The darkness retreated as light and color returned. He stared at his father, demanding an answer.

Navasram composed himself and said, "I have sired countless half-human children in my time. I have watched generations of my offspring grow old and die, but never before have I created such a child out of love; not until I met your mother.

"Yet even as you grew, I was conflicted; your mother did not wish for you to be raised all alone, apart from her people, and I did not wish for you to grow up ignorant of your birthright. I knew eventually the humans would see the differences in you. So I watched and waited."

It took Nixy a moment to realize that his father was speaking to him in Ilvasawa, using that magical language to share truths in a way his own poor human speech could not.

His father said, "In time, I planned to approach you at the forest's edge, or if you had your mother's curiosity, I thought you might wander in yourself. But I had not foreseen that you would run away. My attention was diverted elsewhere for a time, and before I knew it, you were in the human city, beyond my reach."

"Why couldn't you have come to me?" Nixy asked, "Just leave the forest and visit like a normal person?"

"I am not a normal person," he said, "I am the last of my generation, the eldest of my kind still living on Jayde. What's more, I am the guardian of the vault and keeper of its secrets. An ancient enemy of our people still lives in these parts, and were I to leave this fortress unattended, all might be lost."

"The troll," Nixy said, "I've met him."

"Yes, the vylas. I am only aware of one, but one is enough. When I discovered that you had been attacked by the demnox Black Will, I feared the worst. But by then you had found a protector."

"Cindra," he nodded.

"Yes. I was grateful for all her family had done, but I knew that you would not truly be safe, even with them. The vylas is cunning, and when I foiled its attempt to reach you in the castle, it drove you back out into the streets."

Nixy well recalled the unending sorrow and misery he had felt while living as a stable boy in the castle. That had been the troll's doing, he was sure. "So you sent Wenyssaya," he said.

"It was time for her to leave her home and meet her destiny, as it was for you. I am sorry that I could neither spare you the pain of your youth, nor the path that lies before you. All I can offer is the here and now, and my love."

Nixy wasn't sure he wanted it. His father's love was cold and distant; something you wouldn't know was there unless someone told you. He had felt more warmth and attention from Dexer, back before the man tried to kill him. He had been Dexer's prize pupil; Nixy Shadowskipper, the best pickpocket and housebreaker in the Silver Gang. He hadn't exactly felt *love* from the gaunt man; but Dexer had been proud of him, and encouraging. And scary. Always scary.

"Wait a minute," Nixy said, "What do you mean about sparing me the path that lies before me?"

"All of you are heading into great danger," he said, "I cannot see much of your futures, for they converge in a place I dare not look, but your destinies are intertwined. Beyond this forest is a path that leads to war and suffering, but also hope. You must choose whether to follow it or not."

It was hard for Nixy to imagine choosing war and suffering, but he knew Cindra might, and he would choose to go with her, and Wenyssaya would choose to go with him. But what good could they do? Where was the hope? Nixy wanted answers, not riddles.

"What's this place you mean?" he asked, "Are we going someplace that scares even you?"

Navasram turned to him and said, "It is not the place, but what might be waiting for you there. I foresee a great conflict against an unknown enemy, and I feel the Dark Heart at its center. I will look no further, lest it take my sanity."

Nixy folded his arms indignantly. "Cindra told me that you said there won't be any elves coming to help us, so if they can't or won't come, what's the use of guarding the portal?"

"There is no portal."

Nixy frowned. "But Wenyssaya said-"

"Wenyssaya is young and knows little of our secrets. Her people gave up the old ways long ago, and chose to spread the tale of a doorway to Alhanna hidden in the woods. Now, they know no different, and it is better this way."

"Then... what are you guarding?" Nixy asked.

"You are my son, so I will show you in time. But for now I offer to teach you how to best use your power. There is much you must learn if you and your friends are to survive."

That was alright with Nixy. He didn't really want the elf lord to play father and try to make up for his son's miserable life; he wanted answers. *All* the answers.

"Fine," he said, "When do we start?"

Nixy had come to bed late, and didn't wish to talk about his time with his father, so Drahn had let him sleep. Now it was noon and the dweedragon was in a chipper mood, for he had been granted some time to ask questions of Shazhokramazhah and her fellow Dweedragons of Nightmare, or so Navasram had called them. He ate his midday meal with his friends, gave his scales a good polishing in his room, and made for the balcony. Leaping into the air, he beat his wings and flapped towards the cliff dwellings where the ancient humans used to live.

He didn't see anyone waiting below, so he circled a few times and called out. "Hello? Anyone home?" No one answered.

He made for a careful landing on one of the low walls separating the levels. The stonework was beautiful but very old, and he did not want to make a scratch. From his perch, he peered into one of the carved doorways, looking for signs of life. "Hello?" He walked along the wall, going from door to door. Either no one was home, or they were hiding.

Shazhokramazhah had instructed him to meet her here, he was sure of it. He hoped he understood her correctly; he hadn't heard the speech of other dragons since before hatching, so he feared he might be a little rusty.

"Shazhokramazhah?" he called. The throaty growl echoed off the walls and ceiling.

Before he knew it, he was surrounded by sleek, black shapes; two dweedragons had appeared on the wall to either side of him, and four more were below on the walkway. They spoke to him in hissing growls.

"You intrude, *Zjomazhi-shink-krao-lo-vashi.* These are *our* lairs."

"Our matriarch is not here, horde-seeker."

"We do not tolerate thieves, even if they are guests."

Drahn flinched at their words, first turning red, then crimson. "I am *not* a thief, and I am *not* looking for your hordes! I was invited by Shazhokramazhah!"

"Strange that she has not told us as much," said one.

"If I was sneaking around, why would I be calling out her name?" he said, "That's widiculous!"

"As 'widiculous' as a dweedragon that knows nothing of his kind?" said another.

"It asked me how I floated serving trays," said a younger one, "It asked me to *teach* it."

There was a communal hissing of laughter.

"I saw it casting spells like a *human!*" said another, swishing her tail.

"I am not an 'it,' I am a 'he,' and I never learned pwoper dwagon spells," Drahn said. His speech was faltering and it only made them worse.

"Or pwoper human speech either," one of them said, and the others laughed.

He turned to fly away, but another dweedragon suddenly appeared behind him, flapping in the air. Drahn squeaked in alarm and leaped to the walkaway. He was completely surrounded now.

"Where are you going, purple one?" it said.

"It is not purple now, it is turning blue," said another, "it is afraid."

"It should be afraid," said the newcomer, "one breath from us would melt the flesh from its bones."

"Leave me alone!" Drahn cried, starting to panic, "I was asked to come! Find Shazhokramazhah and ask her!"

"Ask her!" one of them mimicked, pitching its voice to a shrill wail.

Something knocked Drahn over, though no one had touched him. He tried to get up, but another invisible force swept his legs out from under him and he fell again.

"Stop it!" he cried, "Leave me alone!" Panicking, he leaped to his feet and jumped over one of the aggressors, running down the walkway. Several of them vanished behind him and reappeared in his path a moment later, using the altered flow of time in the Shadow. He was surrounded again.

"It wants to play chase," one said, "I don't think he will be very good at it."

Drahn did not want to fight his way out, not against so many, but they were keeping him from fleeing. "Please," he whimpered, "I don't want to hurt anyone."

"As if you could," said one, "so much as bear your teeth and we will make you sorry."

"I am alweady sowwy," Drahn said, and he let his element build in his chest. As they closed in on him, he focused on the far end of the walkway. The lightning within him reached a peak charge and he let it encompass him, directing it between his assailants. His body vanished in a flash, and an arc of electricity shot past the startled dweedragons, giving two of them a nasty shock. It burned a path along the stone and Drahn reemerged at the far end of the bolt, leaping into the air and flapping away.

The miniature thunder crackled through the cave. He could hear angry snarls and the beating of wings behind him as he built up another charge. He attempted to ride a lightning bolt towards the fortress, but instead of delivering him through the air as planned, the bolt raced for the ground and shot through the trees, ejecting him in a clearing by a pool.

Cindra dropped her laundry as the dweedragon tumbled out of the crackling bolt, leaving a burnt trail on the mossy ground.

"Drahn! What's going on?" she asked, moving to pick him up. He looked frantic and his scales were a terrified pale blue.

"They are howwwible!" he said, panting, "they hate me and they are howwwible." His eyes were brimming with tears and his mouth was turned down.

Cindra's gaze went up towards the black flapping shapes that circled overhead. As she glared at them, they began to turn away and vanish into thin air.

"Tell me everything," she said to him.

Cindra sat with Drahn cradled in her lap as Adric scrubbed the clothes in a large bucket. They were both dressed in breeches and boots, but while Adric was shirtless, Cindra was wearing only her bodice with nothing underneath, arms bare to the shoulder and naught but skin and taught muscle through the laces. It was more flesh than Adric was used to seeing on a woman, and he struggled to keep his eyes on his work.

"I can't suffer these creatures any longer," she said, "Dweedragons of Nightmares indeed! They spy on us, accuse us of being a threat, and what they did to you, poor Drahn... I'm going to have harsh words for the Shadow Lord about his little monsters."

"I don't understand why Shazhokramazhah lied to me," he whimpered.

"I did not lie," she said as she appeared before them.

"You!" Cindra barked. She wanted to rush to her feet, but that would have dumped Drahn on the ground, so she kept her seat. "Do you know what your stupid little brood did to him? How dare they! He is a *guest!* You invited him to be there!"

"I am sorry for their behavior," she hissed, "but I was needed elsewhere and neglected to pass on instructions."

"They shouldn't *need* instructions to be decent and kind to him!" Cindra snarled, "He was bullied and assaulted! If they were human servants in a castle, they'd be whipped or worse."

"But they are not humans; they are dweedragons, and our ways are different. We are very... territorial." Cindra started to respond, but Shaz raised her claws and said, "Yet that is not an excuse. I shall reprimand them for their treatment of him."

"Why weren't you there?" Drahn asked. The betrayal in his voice was heartbreaking for Cindra to hear, and her mood was not abated by the scant apology.

Shaz took a few steps closer and said, "One of our brood was found dead in the outer forest this morning. I have not told the others yet, but word will soon reach them."

Drahn was shocked. "What could have done it?" he asked.

"We believe it to be the possessed man that the little prince spoke of," she said, "Our sentry was strangled and his chest was crushed. It could not have been a rogue shadow wolf, for there were no teeth marks."

"Black Dexer," Cindra said, "So he did follow us here."

"I am sowwy for the loss of your kin," Drahn said.

"Thank you," she said stiffly, "It has been many generations since we lost one of our numbers to violence."

A couple of rude remarks came instantly to Cindra's mind, but she voiced neither of them. Instead, she asked, "Is there anything we can do?"

"I can think of little," Shaz said, "You cannot enter the Shadow and this intruder cannot leave it, or so it is believed. I will ask Navasram for further instructions."

She turned to leave, but paused and said to Drahn, "Once again, I am sorry for the way my kin treated you. Do you still wish to have a discussion?"

"Not up there," Drahn said, "In my bedwoom, and not without a fwiend by my side."

She nodded and vanished in a shimmer of darkness.

"Well," Adric said, "the charm is wearing off this place right quick, isn't it?"

Cindra said nothing, but pulled Drahn close and hugged him. He allowed it, grateful for the comfort.

Just then, a deep boom was heard overhead, like the roar of a distant cannon. A cloud of bats dislodged themselves from the ceiling and flapped madly about, flying for the narrow cavern entrance.

"What was that?" Adric asked, "Thunder?"

The afternoon sun was shining down through the large hole. "I only see blue skies," she said, "It sounded like cannonry."

"I doubt there's a cannon within a hundred miles of this place," he said.

As the noise rumbled into silence, Drahn said, "I think something tewwible has happened."

Chapter Thirty

The Encroaching Dark

During the next week, Cindra saw little of Nixy or Wenyssaya. The two spent much of their time together with Navasram, doing elf things. Nixy would often stay out very late, so Drahn took to sleeping in Cindra's room. In fact, he spent most of his time with her, afraid to be alone even in their private chambers. The other dweedragons could come and go through the Shadow as they pleased, and he was not about to let his guard down.

But Cindra had gone on the offensive; she had all of the Dweedragons of Nightmare assembled for a stern lecture, informing them that Drahn was an orphan that was raised by humans, just like Prince Nixyalderthor, and if they were going to mock Drahn for not fitting in, they should try it with Nixy too and see what their master thought of that.

She saw to it that they apologized to Drahn, and promised never to belittle or harass him again. They were still grieving for their murdered kin, and so gave their contrition unwillingly, especially the two who had been electrocuted. Shaz had to hiss them into submission.

The question and answer sessions with Shaz were quite fascinating for Cindra, who was glad that Drahn insisted on Calilesh as the language of choice. Dragon speech was so unsettling to listen to, and she didn't fancy sitting next to a pair of growling, hissing, snarling lizards for hours on end.

"So how do you bond with your essence?" Drahn asked, "I bonded by accident, not even knowing what it was."

She said, "There is a ritual of infusion we use to draw the element into our bodies. It both initiates the bond and allows us more control over it."

"Oh, that sounds *much* better than what happened to me," Drahn said, "I was stwuck by lightning."

"While I was holding him," Cindra said, and held up her hands, showing the faint scale patterns on her palms.

"I think the scars on your arms are quite beautiful," Drahn said.

"I doubt it'll be the next fashion, but thank you."

Shaz appeared unimpressed, but she said, "I do not know what your proper elemental bonding must be like, but I cannot imagine it would be something so violent."

Cindra asked, "Is there a way to acquire the power of lightning without... lightning?"

"Of a certainty," Shaz said, "All elements have greater and lesser expressions."

Cindra was thoughtful. *What did lightning look like in small? Maybe Ildric Finnael knows.*

"Shadow is easy to find but tricky to bond with," Shaz said, "Because it borders the element of fire and the powers of chaos and death, there are risks involved."

"Chaos and death?" Drahn said, "I don't understand."

Shaz sighed, like she did whenever she had to explain fundamental knowledge to him. "The four primal elements can mix to make compound elements. Air and water make vapor, which is generally beneficial; water and earth make wood, which includes all green, growing things; earth and fire make lava, and fire and air make smoke, which is generally harmful. Air and earth do not mix, nor do fire and water. Simple alchemy."

Cindra figured air and earth could make dust, and fire and water could also make smoke or steam, but perhaps she was thinking too practically, and not in a weird, magical, alchemical way. Drahn nodded like he understood, so Cindra pretended to as well.

"There are also polar powers of existence that influence the primal elements," Shaz continued, "Order is the power of life and structure, and Chaos is the power of death and decay. The compound elements exist in a delicate balance between them, but order and chaos affect the primal elements to create amalgams. In the hemisphere of Order these are: radiance from fire, lightning from air, ice from water, and finally crystal, which includes metals, from earth.

"In the hemisphere of Chaos are shadow, miasma, acid, and dust. The most primitive dweedragons take their powers from the primordial elements, while the nobler of our kin draw from the compounds and amalgams."

Cindra saw that Drahn was absorbing all of this like a sponge, but she would need a diagram before she could begin to grasp it. One thing caught her attention however; Shadow came from fire mixed with Chaos, death and decay. If that somehow determined what kind of powers these dweedragons possessed, it might mean the same for Nixy as well.

"Why are you called Dweedragons of Nightmares?" she asked.

Shaz replied, "It is for one of our breath attacks; the only one people survive to remember. We can breathe a black mist upon our victims, giving them horrible nightmares they never forget. It helps discourage unwelcome guests."

That's nice, Cindra thought. "And the other power?"

"A cloud of death and decay that rots flesh from bone," Shaz said.

Lovely, they could kill us with bad breath, she thought, *maybe I should be a little more cordial in the future.*

Drahn asked, "Could you teach me how to levitate things? I could never get the wizard spell to work for me pwoperly."

"Wizard spells are for the magically crippled," Shaz said, eyeing Cindra, "Your power is born of Order and Air, so you should be better at it than we are."

"Weally?" he exclaimed, "That's wonderful! Teach me, please!"

Apparently the proper dragon spell could not be taught in the language of the 'magically crippled,' so Cindra had to endure the growling, hissing, snarling speech of lizard wizards.

———

Wenyssaya had not fared well during her week with Navasram and Nixy; the ever-encroaching presence in her mind was disturbing her waking hours as well as her dreams. She would listen as Navasram shared the secrets of Nixy's birthright, teaching the boy how to use his power more effectively. Today, they were seated in the *Suvasian,* the Place of Memory, surrounded by colored windows and statues. Navasram was speaking of the elder days and the heirlooms of his House.

"This is one of the earliest swords ever made," Navasram said, holding his sheathed blade, "Before the wicked creation of the vylas, we had no need for such weapons; our tools were knives of crystal, and spears and arrows tipped with flint. Metals were used for more peaceful craft."

He drew the blade, which made a gasping sound as it left the scabbard. The sound lingered like a dying breath as the blade was held aloft, before fading to nothing. Nixy's eyes went wide.

Wenyssaya flinched.

"This is *Navhwálreth*, the Raven Blade. It was also called *Vdomeni*, the Bleeder. Its power is tied to my own life force; it knows me and obeys me."

The sword was single-edged and slightly curved, with a trailing point like Nixy's knife. The blade was 30 inches long and made of a white metal, and flared a little towards the hilt. The grip was long enough for two hands and was fashioned out of shadowood in the form of a raven, with the curved head serving as a pommel with emeralds for eyes. The crossguard ended in raven heads as well, with a black stone at its center.

"Where was it made?" Nixy asked breathlessly.

"In Du-Dwithian," he said, "A special forge was built for its construction, and the location was kept secret."

"It's beautiful," Nixy said.

"Are there shadowood trees in Du-Dwithian also?" Wenyssaya asked.

Navasram looked at her and said in Ilvasawa, "Shadowood trees began in the Everwood of our homeland."

Wenyssaya's mind began to reel as the name 'Everwood,' *Orossylwe*, repeated in her thoughts, hearkening back to a dream. She squeezed her eyes shut, but that only brought forth visions of a dark grove spreading through a vast green woodland, like a blot of ink staining a map.

Opening her eyes again, she stared at the walls and steadied her breathing, willing herself not to panic. *I am me*, she thought, *I am Wenyssaya of Du-Velthathwe, the Hidden Grove, nan-Orossylwe, not Everwood! I am me!*

If Nixy noticed her distress, he gave no sign. The Shadow Lord let him admire the sword while he watched her silently.

Finally he said, "Your knife is akin to my sword, but my blade was only a study in the craft."

Nixy said, "Shaz told me the knife is called *Sugireth*."

"Shaz? Ah, *Shazhokramazhah*. She is correct. It was crafted from a shard of a greater weapon. It had a blade similar to *Navhwálreth,* but shorter, and it was mounted on a long haft of ash heartwood. It was the deadliest weapon ever created, for it was enchanted to grow in power with every life it took, and it took a great many. It became so powerful that it made a god bleed. *Hanvdálni* was its name."

The Enervator. Wenyssaya saw it clearly in her mind, and not just because it was held by the enormous statue in the main hall. She knew its heft, its length and feel, she knew it intimately. She resisted squeezing her eyes shut again for fear of what scene might play out behind her eyelids. She gulped for air several times until Nixy turned and said, "What's wrong?"

Her voice trembled as she replied, "I... I know it. *Why do I know it?*"

"Know what?" Nixy asked, becoming worried.

"I know the weapon. I know the woods. I know things I should not!" She stood on shaking legs, fists clenched at her sides as she glared at the Shadow Lord. "*Why do I know all of it?*" she pleaded.

He stood, replacing his sword on his belt, and took her hands in his. His presence filled the room with palpable calm, like the comfort of a warm bath. As her trembling subsided and her breathing and heartbeat returned to something resembling normal, he took her in his arms.

She rested her head on his chest, breathing in his scent and triggering a wave of alien nostalgia. The steady beat of his heart was hypnotic, and he began to sway like one comforting a child.

"Why do I know?" she asked in a tiny voice.

"You know why," he replied.

Nixy just sat there with his mouth hanging open, wondering what in the world was going on. He had never seen her like this. Her eyes were wide and vacant and full of tears, and it scared him. "What's wrong with her?" he asked.

Navasram said, "She is struggling to reconcile the duality of her spirit. She is Wenyssaya of the Hidden Grove, but there is another life, another past within her."

"No," she whimpered.

"Yes," he said, "It has been a part of you all your life; without it, you would not be who you are."

"Who am I?" she breathed.

"You are Wenyssaya, Spring's Song, most gifted of your generation. You are also Drusayava, Autumn's Lament, once-queen of the Ilvayiin, and my departed sister."

She trembled.

"How...?" Nixy asked. He was on his feet now, but his knees felt weak.

"It is the only way one of the eldest generations may return," he said, "such power can no longer enter our world unless it is reborn into it. Two and a half centuries ago, I heard my sister's voice for the last time. She had existed in Alhanna as a regretful spirit, mourning the grief she had brought to our beloved Alsuvath."

"Th-the Dark Heart?" Nixy asked.

"Yes. It was she who challenged Llomavath, Bringer of Chaos. It was she who drew his blood and created the Dark Heart. It was she who doomed the world."

"Viis-imyam?" she whispered. *Little brother?*

"Imyava," he replied.

Nixy's eyes flitted between the two elves, as confused as he'd ever been. Finally he asked, "So, do I call you 'Auntie Wen' now?"

Wenyssaya began to laugh and cry all at once.

———

When Cindra next saw Wenyssaya, it was the morning of the twelfth day at the fortress. The elf maid had been absent from the evening meals, and Nixy had been vague about what had happened to her. She had left it to Drahn to check Cindra's wounds, and had locked herself in a room in the tower, taking no visitors. But today, Cindra saw her wandering the balcony outside her private quarters, so she called to her.

"Wen! Are you alright? We haven't seen you," she said.

The elf maid looked Cindra up and down, frowning at her immodest laundry day attire, as if trying to remember who she was. "I am sorry," she said, "I have been thinking."

"Thinking? About what?"

"Destiny," she said.

"Oh. I've been thinking about that myself," Cindra said. She noticed Wen was fidgeting with a ring on her finger; it was crafted of delicate silver with an orange fire opal, and Cindra recognized it at once. "Is that ring... did the Shadow Lord give that to you?"

"Yes," she said, holding it up wistfully, "It is *Drusávines Oma*, the Ring of Autumn."

"It's lovely. Um, it isn't... an engagement ring, is it?"

Wenyssaya turned to her, eyes wide, and began to giggle; her laughter became more manic and she had to turn away, leaning over the balcony rail until she stopped.

"Wen?" Cindra said, cautious now, "Wen, what's wrong?" She put her hand on the woman's shoulder but it made her flinch. "Easy! It's okay, it's okay."

"This ring keeps me steady," she said, "It stops me from spiraling down into madness, lets me breathe."

"I don't understand," Cindra said. *What has this place done to her?*

"The dreams, the visions, the memories... it keeps them at bay until I need them. They're so strong now, so strong now that I know."

"Know what?" Cindra asked.

Wen looked utterly lost as she said, "Now that I know my life is a lie."

Cindra was about to form another string of questions when a noise arose in her ear like a tiny bell, then a chorus of bells, then a cathedral bell. She winced and cried out, putting her hand to her head to block it, but it was no use.

It took Wenyssaya a moment to register concern, but she quickly took hold of Cindra's bare shoulders as the girl dropped to her knees.

Cindra's stomach churned and her whole body shivered. *Is this how it's supposed to feel?* The enchanted earring was vibrating and clamoring for her attention, a sound only she could hear. There was a voice forming out of the cacophony, a voice Cindra had been dreading. It was Arch Mage Ildric Finnael.

Your father is dead, your city burns, please come home.

"NO!" she screamed, and tore the earring from her flesh.

The friends were gathered in the small forest, taking turns sitting with Cindra, trying to comfort her. The crying had stopped hours ago, and now there was a numbness that left her unable to think or feel. She knew that sensation all too well.

Wenyssaya had done all she could, including mending the girl's torn earlobe, but she was in no condition to offer anyone comfort now. She sat nearby and mourned with her in silence.

Nixy sat beside Cindra on the ground, holding her hand. Drahn sat in his lap, resting his head upon her wrist. They said nothing, for nothing would help.

Adric and Deliah hung the laundry on a line between two trees, grateful for something to occupy themselves. Adric had been the one to suggest taking her outside, but he could not sit idle. He dealt with grief by keeping busy.

Deliah hardly dealt with grief at all.

She asked him quietly, "Do you think we will leave tomorrow?"

Adric shrugged, shaking out a wet shirt before hanging it on the line.

"We told Padison to wait two weeks before leaving," she said, "That's in two days."

"I expect she'll want to go in the morning," he said. His voice was quiet and neutral. "If we need more time, we can send a messenger. Drahn, maybe."

"I'll help you with preparations if you like," she said.

Normally, Adric would have been thrilled to have her so close and willing to speak to him, but his passion was cooled for now. He only nodded mutely.

"I've been meaning to ask you something," she said, "If it's not too personal. You don't have to answer."

He gave her a hopeful glance as he hung another shirt. His heart beat faster. "What is it?"

"Do you love her?"

He looked shocked and confused. "What? Who?"

"Cindra. Do you love her? I don't necessarily mean in a romantic way; what I mean is, why do you follow her?"

Disappointed, he thought for a moment and said, "Dillan DePort was one of the first students I met at the Freekirk School. 'He' was small, but fierce, loyal, and ballsy... begging your pardon."

"Little did you know," Deliah smiled.

"That's for sure. Anyway, us and Paddy... the three of us stood up for each other. Me and Dillan even fought Minozhians together at Cordoshome. When it came out that he was a she, well... that didn't change what we'd been through; it made a lot of odd things make sense, actually."

"Most men would never consider doing what you and Paddy did," she said.

"That's true," he said, "but most men have never been her friend or fought beside her. When she asked for a squire, I couldn't refuse. Who else would have done it?"

"You don't feel ashamed to be squire to a woman?"

"It's weird," he admitted, "all of us get strange looks from folk, there's no denying that. But I'd only feel ashamed if I let her down."

"That sounds like love, doesn't it?" Deliah asked.

"If you like," he said, blushing, "Why do you ask?"

"It's been forever since I believed in someone," she said, "I wanted a second opinion."

It was after noon when the Shadow Lord came down to the forest island and paid his respects. His dweedragons brought food for his guests, which was much welcomed. Cindra only took what Nixy offered her and ate mechanically, savoring nothing.

Navasram said, "If there is any service I can render, please do not hesitate to ask." Then he took his leave, for his experience with mortal grief taught him that it was best to let it play out among mortals.

It was an hour before anyone spoke again.

Cindra felt utterly broken, as if the floor had collapsed out from under her and shattered her like pottery. She had followed this path to protect her family, her city, and all she loved... now what was left? Did her mother live still, or did the wizard not have the time or the heart to tell her otherwise?

She had wanted to tell her father of her quest, her deeds, her failures and accomplishments. She had wanted him to be proud of her. She had wanted to be a worthy successor in his eyes.

Now that hope was lost.

"We should go," Cindra said in a soft voice. Her eyes were focused on the ground and her jaw was set.

The others turned to her, concerned.

"Now?" Nixy asked.

"The sooner, the better," she said.

Wenyssaya reminded her, "But it is almost a two day journey to Riverskirt, and it will be dark soon."

"We have light," she said, "and the dweedragons can show us the quickest way."

Adric said, "I think it'd be better to get some sleep and set out in the morning,"

She asked flatly, "Do I lead this party or not?"

The others exchanged glances.

"Get our gear packed and assembled in the great hall," she said, "I'm going home to bury my father, assuming my city is still standing."

Adric folded his arms across his bare chest and said, "The laundry will still be wet, milady."

Cindra raised her eyes and gave him a look that said she would march them naked through the woods if need be.

He sighed, "Fine, maybe the lord can magic them dry."

While the others gathered their things, Cindra took a long walk through the recesses of the cavern. The sound of trickling water followed her as she wandered narrow trails and empty chambers. The sunlight over the forest island no longer reached her, but enchanted crystals in the walls awoke at her presence, shedding a gentle candlelight glow to illuminate her path.

The passage ended in a wide grotto of smooth limestone overlooking a small crevasse, where the stream emptied into a deeper darkness. Feeling weary beyond her years, Cindra sank down to the floor and gave in to her despair. Her life felt like the vanishing stream, all of her energies flowing into a bottomless pit that led nowhere.

She began to cry once again, silently at first, then with choked and heaving breath, until she was sobbing openly. Her ugly wails echoed cruelly off the cavern walls, assaulting her with her own misery. Finally, when she could give no more to her grief, she slipped into a fitful sleep.

Cindra did not know how much time had passed when she woke, but her limbs and back were aching from the hard ground. The chamber had gone dark again.

The others will be waiting to leave, she thought, *I ought to be there to lead them home.*

Only then did she begin to consider their objections; sleep had given her a clearer head, it seemed. "I should apologize," she said to the dark, "I was too sharp."

The darkness answered.

Lady Cindra, said a voice, *come to the fortress at once.*

"What?" She touched her tender earlobe, but the earring was gone. "Hello? Who is speaking?"

At once, it repeated.

The Shadow Lord? she wondered.

Feeling wary and alone, she reached for her knife, only to find she wasn't wearing her weapon belt. If Adric had done as she had asked, it would be with her baggage in the main hall by now, along with her armor and sword. She began to stumble her way back in the dim light, feeling the wall for support.

When she reached the main cavern, she saw that night had fallen. The small forest was lit by pale moonlight and the flickering of torches upon mossy pillars of rock. She crossed one of the bridges over the stream; the fortress looked very far away in the darkness.

As she quickened her pace, she saw a dark shape silhouetted against the white walls of the fortress. It resolved itself into a purple dweedragon flapping towards her frantically.

"Cindwa!" he called, "Lady Cindwa, we must huwwy!" He landed before her, rustling the fern leaves.

"What's wrong?" she asked, "Why did the Shadow Lord summon me?"

"Something is coming," he hissed, "The other dweedwagons sensed it, and when Navaswam twied to look, his vision was blocked!"

"Coming here? Now? Is it Black Dexer?"

"They don't think so. There were many of them, too many to hide, and they are moving fast!"

"Let's get back to the fortress," she said, and they ran along the lit path.

They had not gone more than a few tens of yards before they heard a loud splash in a distant pool up ahead. They immediately stopped to listen. A dry moaning sound broke the silence; a wordless bellowing amid the slosh of water.

"Look above!" Drahn hissed.

Cindra's eyes lifted to the skylight. There were shadows, tiny figures lining the rim, too far overhead to make out. One of them moved, then another, and their shapes could be seen tumbling over a thousand feet to the ground below, landing just up ahead. Sickly thumps and another splash broke the stillness. Leaves and branches shook, and the moans became a ghastly chorus.

Cindra motioned Drahn off the path to the right. They moved quietly through the ferns and mushrooms towards the main cavern entrance, hoping to move upstream opposite the cliff dwellings and avoid the area under the skylight. They saw dark shapes continuing to drop, though some managed to slow their descent and land with a semblance of intention.

"What are they?" Drahn whispered.

Cindra could guess; she had seen one before. She mouthed the word, *Vemloks.* Drahn's frightened eyes managed to go wider.

There was a cry from above, and responding shrieks from below, and several figures began to tear through the brush towards them.

"Run!" Cindra cried, and they fled along the bank of the stream. Clumsy feet crashed through the brush; gray shapes in ragged, filthy clothing bounded towards them. Cindra's bodice left too much of her skin exposed, and they only needed to touch her to feed upon her. She saw no hope of escape, only the moment's need to run.

The beastly things were upon them now; she could see the red points of fire in their eyes, see their gaping mouths, and see that they were peasants and farmers by their clothing. Some were fully dressed, others wore little more than nightshirts, no doubt taken by the monsters in their beds. Worse, their bodies had suffered from the fall; broken limbs dangled uselessly, smashed faces with fractured jaws wore looks of rage and hunger, and viscera dangled from split flesh.

So many! she thought, seeing more and more drop from above.

Just before the closest vemloks could touch her, a pulse of rippling air issued forth from the fortress. Suddenly, the stream beside her changed course and washed up on the shore like a liquid serpent, sweeping her attackers away. They slipped and crashed into the waters behind her, flailing helplessly. As they headed downstream towards the cavern entrance, Cindra saw more of them coming up the tunnel. Apparently the zone of mortal terror that guarded the entrance held no threat for them.

Drahn had flapped over the stream and was calling her towards a bridge that connected the island to the cliff dwellings. She raced over it as more shrieking cries rose behind her. The stone dwellings had open doors and windows; there was no place to barricade themselves.

As the monsters scrambled over the stone bridge, it crumbled to pieces in an instant, dropping them helplessly into the stream. Cindra's eyes darted about and saw a great many things happening all at once. The pulse from the fortress had made the cave come alive, unleashing all manner of defenses.

More and more vemloks were pouring in from above, but they were being assaulted by swarms of bats. Shreds of flesh and clothing rained down, but if any grievous wounds had been given, they made no sign.

Great thorns of rock fell from above, striking targets below with magical accuracy; some were impaled, others were crushed. More rocky thorns jutted up from the earth, springing like traps, sharp enough to kill. But these creatures were already dead.

Coils of blood-drinking vines unwound themselves and entangled the invaders, piecing them with nasty thorns. The monsters paid them little mind; they ripped themselves free, reclaimed their lost blood, and threw off the desiccated tendrils.

Some vemloks happened upon patches of earth that turned to hot, sticky mud and dragged them under. But even as the soil hardened again, the bodies rose through it with little effort. A death trap for the living was but a nightly fact of existence for such beings.

Dozens of vemloks had gathered across the water from Cindra and Drahn, moaning as they paced to and fro. Either they could not swim, or they had learned to keep their distance from the stream. One of them took a running leap and managed to grab the edge of the footpath, but before he could pull himself up, Drahn barked a flash of lightning at him, sending him into the rushing currents. The others hissed in frustration.

A woman's voice called from above, "Fly, you fools!" Cindra looked and saw a woman in a fluttering dress, drifting down from the ceiling with practiced ease. She chided the monsters, "What have I been trying to teach you?"

The gray figures raised their arms and began to lift off the ground like kites in an uncertain breeze. Some drifted forward over the stream, while others rose stupidly up or backwards, snarling in frustration. Cindra and Drahn backed further down the walkway; their moment of relief evaporating.

"Drahn, do you have any ideas?"

"Not weally," he squeaked.

Several of them landed awkwardly on the path, grisly smiles of victory creasing their dirty faces. Drahn inhaled deeply and let loose a massive bolt of lightning so bright it burned a blue streak in Cindra's vision; she felt the hairs on her neck and arms stand on end. The sound was incredibly loud, no doubt summoning the rest of them.

The lightning tore through the line of vemloks, throwing them twitching and flailing to the ground. Cindra cheered, but her hope wilted as the creatures struggled to their feet, some with blackened, burning holes in their clothing and flesh. They came on, albeit slower and more unstable than before.

"Run again," she said, and the two of them raced down the walkway towards a distant bridge.

"Look! Dweedwagons!" Drahn called.

Cindra saw three of the sinister Dwimathii Vothiivoss flying in a line from the fortress. Their black wings dipped and they flew over the walkway towards the pursuing vemloks. One by one, they expelled a sickly green cloud upon the advancing monsters, until they were completely engulfed.

Cindra and Drahn stopped to watch, their hopes rose once more. *If they could clear us a path to the fortress,* Cindra thought, *we might just survive this.*

The black dweedragons' breath weapon was just as horrible as they claimed. As the cloud dissipated, figures could be seen swaying to and fro on the walkway. Their flesh was festering, shriveling and falling off, exposing innards that also began to blacken and decay. Rotting faces and bare ribs met their horrified eyes, and bony fingers were raised on dwindling arms, reaching for them.

Drahn and Cindra waited for them to fall.

But they didn't fall. The thirsting spirits inhabiting these wretches were not giving up just yet, not as long as there was flesh on the bones and the hunger to motivate them. They staggered towards their prey, feeling blindly for warm, healing blood.

Cindra wanted to scream, but she couldn't spare the breath. They ran for the bridge as the corpse monsters followed what senses they had left.

Once over the bridge, they followed a path that led straight to the fortress, but the distance was great, and beyond were the crisscrossing stairs up the plateau. Vemloks were swarming across the island now, as they continued to drop from high above. The mysterious woman was suspended in the air over the forest, guiding her minions with sharp commands and a wicked tongue.

"Cut them off!" she called, "Spread out, you brainless maggots! Must I do everything?"

That one has her wits, Cindra thought, *Nixy was right, they're not all mindless beasts.*

One of the monsters leaped for her, but she dodged his grasp, rolled to her feet and kept running. Another reached for her arm, fingers brushing her flesh. Cindra felt a chill and a strange pain at the touch, but pushed the sensation aside. *Keep running!*

Drahn had no time to stop and breathe lightning, and he was not made for sprinting; Cindra was catching up to him, and the vemloks were catching up to her. More were ahead, cutting them off from the fortress.

"Cindwa, catch me!" Drahn cried, and he leaped towards her. She caught him on the run, wondering why he didn't just fly to safety. He could do more from the air, surely?

She felt fingers on her arms, scratching her skin. Another hand grabbed at her shoulder and one pulled at her waist. She nearly stumbled, veering off the path as more came from her left flank. Panic and pain were taking her. *Keep your feet, keep your feet! Run!*

Drahn's chest was expanding, tingling.

Cindra had no choice but to skirt the plateau and make for the source of the stream beyond; all other directions were cut off.

Drahn's claws clutched her, digging into her arms and waist.

As she ran for the distant water, she could hear their moans and snarls right behind her. A hand snatched her arm, pulling her off balance. She tripped and fell.

Drahn released the charge within him, expanding it to envelop them both. He and Cindra vanished in a flash of lightning that tore a path across the forest, ripped through a pack of vemloks, and streaked up the first flight of stairs on the plateau. They were disgorged from the bolt in a burst of light and noise, tumbling over each other as Drahn squeaked in pain. Cindra took a moment to gather her wits as the dweedragon whimpered, "My wing... I think I bwoke it."

"What just happened?" she gasped. Her mind was still trying to process the experience. *We came so far, so fast!* She shakily got to her feet, her entire body tingling.

"I'll tell you if we survive," Drahn said, "But I can't fly now."

Without another word, she scooped him up and ran up the next level of the path. Her body ached with a cold pain where the hands had grabbed her. She felt exhausted, drained. The incline wasn't steep, but the stairs were many, and her legs were burning with effort. She panted, "I don't suppose... you could... do that trick... again?"

"I don't think so," he said, "Not without a west."

She nodded, looking up at the switchbacks she still had yet to climb. Nothing for it but to move on.

She was part way up the next ramp when the woman landed before her, blocking the path. She wore leggings under her thick dress, but no shoes. Her dark hair was wild and free, and her brown eyes were lit with little points of red fire. Her skin was pale pink and flawless, but for a deep crease at her throat and a mole on her cheek.

"Ah, I know you!" she said, smiling, "You're the count's daughter, the little brat who refused to die at sea!"

"Have... have we met?" Cindra asked, hoping she could keep the woman talking until help arrived. *Help was coming, wasn't it?* Her legs quivered with fear and exhaustion. Drahn squirmed and whimpered under her arm.

"Why yes, at your fourteenth birthday feast," she said, "I was there with my late husband, Ghethas."

"Then you must be Lemorea Gordon," Cindra said, "but that's not your evil priest name, is it?"

She laughed, "My *evil priest* name! Oh, how adorable." She took a step closer. Below, the vemloks were scrambling up the path towards them. "But you know all about secret identities and false names, don't you my dear?" Another step. "My *true* name is Maveezh, priestess of the Countless Lord, and now the harbinger of death herself."

Cindra stepped back, looking helplessly to the fortress above. *Where are they?*

Maveezh took another step and reached out to brush her cheek.

Cindra slapped the pale hand away, feeling a cold tingle on the back of her fingers. *I just fed her anyway,* she realized.

"Finally, a bit of noble blood," Maveezh said, "Hmph, how sad. It isn't much different than peasant blood. A bit thicker, maybe. But *elven* blood, now that's another matter entirely! You must introduce me to your pointy-eared friends."

A voice called from above, masculine and powerful, "Maveezh. Stop toying with her and be done with it. She deserves a quick and painless death."

Cindra looked up and saw a man hovering in the air over the forest. He was pale of hair and skin, and wore gray clothing and a sword.

Clavemont. So he's behind this.

Maveezh said, "The Gray Baron has a soft spot in his heart for you Corrinas. He spared your poor father the news of your certain death."

Cindra froze and snarled, "What about my father?"

"Oh don't worry dear," she said, "my lord said he was quick and merciful with him. Me, I never had much use for the notion." Her arms flashed out and grabbed Cindra by the head before she could even flinch.

Cindra's nerves exploded with a freezing, burning pain, and her vision turned dark and blurry. She wanted to faint. She wanted to crumple into a ball. Neither were possible, for Maveezh held her upright and was taking her slowly, making it hurt. She released Drahn and tried to pull the woman's hands away, but her fingers turned numb and cold, drained of blood.

"This is for my Ghethas," she said, "Where he failed, I shall succeed."

Cindra knew then that she was about to die.

She wasn't ready.

Not at all.

Deep gashes suddenly appeared on the woman's arms and hot blood spurted on her dress. She shrieked and released Cindra, staggering back as she looked in horror at the sudden wounds. They were actually painful and were not closing as they should.

Cindra fell to her knees. She and Drahn cowered together, awaiting retaliation for whatever had just happened.

It never came.

Instead, the night deepened and enveloped them in a dark embrace, and they were suddenly in the luminous, gray world of the Shadow. Nixy was standing before them with his little magic knife.

"Come on!" he said in a muffled voice, "Can you walk?"

Her voice was a whisper. "I'll damned well... walk away... from *her*."

Nixy put Drahn into his backpack and secured him. He shouldered Cindra's arm and guided her up the stairs, pushing against the fluid medium. The air was colder here, and the sound of wind was everywhere, though they felt nothing.

Maveezh and the vemloks were moving slowly, like in a dream. The woman's eyes flashed about in anger as she clutched her wounded arms.

"Nixy," Cindra gasped, "can they find us?"

"No," he said, "We're in the third level of the Shadow. Even in sunlight we'd be invisible, 'course then it would be really hard to move or breathe. They can't see us or touch us; we don't even leave footprints."

"The third level?" Drahn asked, "How many are there?"

"Five," Nixy said, "I've been learning stuff."

"Good boy," Cindra said, "Edu...cation is impor-" She stumbled and fell. "So tired... cold."

"Let's rest a minute," Nixy said, "Look below." He pointed to the far edge of the forest island, and Cindra struggled to raise her head and see. About a hundred gray figures scrambled lazily towards the plateau. Little black bats swarmed about them, scratching and biting, but each sortie robbed the bats of many of their numbers; their little bodies didn't contain much blood, and they fed the vemloks more blood than their attacks could spill. The ground was littered with tiny corpses.

A great many ravens had also joined the fray, but several had met the same fate as the bats. Being far more sensible creatures, they retreated, circling above and croaking insults at the invaders.

There were other shapes racing across the island from the cavern entrance; black shapes on all fours spread out through the forest from within the Shadow, coordinating their attack. They were the enormous black wolves they had seen nearly two weeks ago in the Dark Vale.

"Here comes the cavalry," Nixy said, grinning.

But Cindra had a bad feeling.

The wolves ran at their targets and pounced, leaving the Shadow and its weird dilation of time; their movements appeared slower to Cindra now, but that just made the violence more fierce to behold. Hands and arms were torn off, legs were savaged, and throats were ripped. The vemloks rushed at their attackers, but the wolves dipped back into the Shadow before they could reach them.

"Nicely done!" Drahn said, "Hooway wolves!"

The attacks continued like this for several minutes. Maveezh was shouting too faintly to hear, motioning to her minions with sluggish gestures. The vemloks were massing now, clumping together like sheep so the wolves couldn't pick them off so easily.

When Cindra wasn't watching the carnage below, she was looking up at the gray radiance of Lord Arton Clavemont, her father's murderer. If what Maveezh said was true, he claimed to have done her father a favor by killing him quickly. She silently swore to return that favor.

"Something's not wight," Drahn said.

She looked and saw that indeed, her fears were realized. Like the bats, the wolves were attacking with their mouths and claws, making flesh-contact with the undead. Each time they touched that dead flesh, it drank from them. They were moving more slowly now, even in the Shadow, tongues lolling and tails drooping. More and more were falling prey to the moaning horde as black fur vanished under a crush of gray bodies.

"Call them off," she said, "they're all going to die."

Nixy said, "That's up to them. They pledged to protect the fortress with their lives."

Cindra struggled to her feet and said, "We should get moving." She wasn't going to watch the massacre. Nixy and Drahn agreed.

They made it to the top of the plateau and took a last look at the scene below them. They were not alone. The black dweedragons sat in the Shadow, watching the carnage with helpless anguish and misery. Never before had such an army been raised or anticipated, and none of their ancient defenses were suited for this foe. A vemlok with a will strong enough to think and lead others was an unheard-of aberration, and here there were two.

Just then, a pall of hopelessness and despair washed over them; it was a sinking, draining melancholy that made them wilt and want to curl in on themselves. The dweedragons all began to whimper and moan, and Drahn ducked into his backpack as deep as he could. Cindra had felt this dread once before, and Nixy had borne it many times.

"Guadim," he said, pointing.

Indeed, Paugh the guadim had made his entrance. He beat his wings over the scene, spreading his foul stench to mix with the smells of blood and death.

"We need to get inside," Cindra said, "all of us."

Nixy said, "We can pass the magical barrier, but the doors won't open while it covers the fortress; that's okay, 'cause we can just go through them in the fifth layer."

"Oh? Alright then..." Cindra said, trusting him.

Nixy concentrated, bringing them deeper into Shadow until the sound of the wind became a howl, and the air turned to a freezing soup that resisted their every move. Already exhausted, Cindra could barely work her legs. She put her head down because the air stung her eyes. Once they reached the door, she felt a strange violation that twisted her insides; it was like pushing through a massive spider web that clung to every surface, both inside and out.

Then it was gone.

The temperature returned to normal, the howling wind vanished, and the soft glow of the great hall warmed her eyes. The ancient queen of old was looking down upon them with sadness, as though the battle was already lost.

We actually passed through the doors, she thought, *right through solid wood and metal. How is that possible?*

The others were there as well. Adric and Deliah went to support Cindra as she collapsed, and took her to the base of the statue where she could sit. Wenyssaya gingerly examined Drahn's injured wing. The black dweedragons gathered in little groups, whispering. Nixy stood before his father, who was now armed and armored for battle.

"There's two powerful vemloks leading them, and a guadim," Nixy said, "the same one that's been hunting me. I didn't see Dexer, but I'm sure he's around."

Navasram nodded and said, "He would be a fool to show himself while the wolves are out in force."

"The wolves are losing," Nixy said, "They can't kill these things fast enough. Nothing seems to work."

Cindra rasped, "Beheading works."

"Fire also," Deliah said.

"And they don't like water," Drahn said, "but I don't know how that will help in here... ow!"

"Your wing is only sprained, not broken," Wenyssaya said, "You'll be fine."

"If we survive the night," he said.

Navasram turned to Shaz and gave her an order; she left and returned with a bottle of blue liquid in her mouth. The lord brought it to Cindra and said, "This is *nenthiimore,* a gift of Eyorona. It will restore you. Take one swallow." He lifted it to her numb lips.

She drank the blue liquid, savoring its peculiar honey mead and mint flavor. She felt her strength return; her muscles twitched and ceased to ache, and she no longer felt numb and cold where the vemloks touched her. Warmth and feeling returned to her body.

Now that's divine alchemy! she thought, *Imagine giving this to an army on a long march!*

"Thank you!" she said. She stood readily and stretched. "Adric, let's have my armor on."

"A moment," Navasram said, "I must speak to you alone."

They walked into the chamber where they had met to discuss her king's request. The space held a heavy sense of foreboding now, so the lord's words would likely be dire.

"You claimed that you love my son," he said.

"I did," she replied, "I do."

"I wish to extract an oath from you, before it is too late."

This isn't good at all, she thought. "What oath?"

He said, "I would ask you to be his champion. He will need a strong sword arm to defend him on his journey."

Sensing the fatalism in his words, she said, "I would be honored, my lord."

He drew his sword. "I will require your blood; a few drops will do."

She gulped but did as he commanded, pricking her finger on the point of the blade. *Other cultures have blood oaths, why not elves?*

He held the sword before her, point down, and bade her take the grip. She did so, feeling the carved relief of feathers under her fingers. Her blood smeared on the black wood above the elf lord's hand. The raven's head seemed to be looking at her with its emerald eyes.

He spoke in Ilvasawa, "Lady Cindra of House Corrina, do you swear to serve and protect the blood and spirit of my House with your own blood and spirit?"

"I swear," she said.

"Do you swear to guide my son and protect him as he finds his path?"

"I swear."

"Then by your blood and mine, I pass the bonding. For his sake and yours, I pass the bonding. Let my spirit give you strength until the bond is complete."

She felt the grip grow warm, and the emerald eyes shone with an inner light. Then it was over. He sheathed his sword and placed a golden hand on her shoulder. "Ready yourself for battle," he said, "Time is short."

As they returned to the others, she began to wonder what had just happened. *That was some kind of blood magic, not just a vow. What did it mean to 'pass the bonding' anyway?* It was too late to ask.

The fear was building in her now. Outside, she had no time to anticipate an attack. Now, she knew what was coming. She forced herself to breathe, pushing that fear down as far as it would go. The others were doing the same as best they could.

Adric finished donning his chain shirt and began helping her into the quilted arming doublet when the doors began to smoke and decay. A vile acid was eating the wood and metal fixtures, and within moments, the great doors collapsed inward with a cloud of rancid smoke.

Everyone fell back. Cindra grabbed her honor sword and *Kos* knife. There was no time to buckle her doublet or don her breastplate; the enemy was upon them.

Paugh stood beyond the door, flanked by Clavemont and Maveezh. Half a dozen vemloks rushed for the breach, but burst into flame and ash before they could pass the threshold. The woman shook her head in disgust and motioned the others to stay back.

"We have but a moment," Navasram said, "This shall be my battleground. The rest of you must go to the vault. My dweedragons will try to discourage pursuit."

"Don't you want us to fight with you?" Cindra asked.

He shook his head and said, "You would be quickly overwhelmed." Then he knelt before Nixy. "My son," he said, "I regret that our time was so brief." He removed his ring and placed it on the boy's finger, saying, "This is Lonávitha Oma, the Ring of Midnight. Wear this, and I will always be with you."

"You're talking like you're gonna die!" Nixy said.

"I may," he said, "we have foreseen this doom approaching, but know not how it will end. You must be prepared."

Nixy's eyes misted with conflicted tears. He did not love the man like a father, nor forgive him for his absence, but he respected him as a teacher and mentor. He nodded his head wordlessly.

The room shivered as the guadim chanted in the vile language of the Abyss. The magical barrier that safeguarded the entrance began to flicker and wane.

"Go now," Navasram said, "lead them to the vault. Know that my love goes with you and always shall, no matter what may come."

The barrier snapped. The chorus of the hungry dead filled the great hall. The guadim stepped back, leaving the fighting to the pawns.

"Go!" Navasram shouted, and the party ran for the tower door.

Vemloks flooded into the great hall by the dozens, rushing as a tidal wave towards Thásalfen, the Shadow Lord. He swept his arm and a wall of flame leaped up before him. He swept his sword, severing the heads of four burning adversaries, then vanished into the Shadow. He appeared again and severed two more before the first four hit the ground.

A pack of vemloks made for the tower, following Cindra and her friends. Shazhokramazhah had shut and barred the door, placing a warding spell upon it. They clawed and pounded in futility.

Thásalfen was dispatching vemloks by the dozen, but more were coming. His flaming barrier had died as his concentration faltered, but he had more than a few spells at his disposal. He slipped into the fifth level of Shadow, raced across the hall, and shifted to the second level so he might cast spells unseen. An inferno burst amid the crowd and he sent it spinning about like a tornado of fire, filling the hall with heat and smoke. The vemloks caught like dry leaves, flames consuming them as they scattered in confusion and fear.

The second level of Shadow was perfect for combat; it still allowed interaction with the prime reality, and time flowed twice as fast. Thásalfen's inhuman speed was doubled as he darted about the hall. His armor was not the all-enclosing shell of a human knight, but a fortified garment made for minimal encumbrance; for a warrior that fights unseen and untouched.

Navhwálreth whistled and more heads flew.

Paugh was watching.

It had spent many centuries studying the ways of its enemy, and had learned a thing or two about the Shadow and its reclusive lord. He had learned how to peer into the Shadow and see the unseen; he had also learned how to share that power.

"It is time the two of you joined the fray," it said to Clavemont and Maveezh, "If you distract him, I can open the barred door."

Maveezh didn't like that idea. "Distract him? You mean offer our heads? No thank you."

"I can grant you the sight to see him, even as he burrows deeper into the Shadow," it said, "let the baron engage him in a duel, and you take your children to find the feast you promised them."

Clavemont said, "And I suppose you will sit out here and wait?"

Paugh grinned, or perhaps it was a snarl. "The Shadow gets colder the deeper you go," it said, "If I freeze the room, the Shadow will be colder still."

Clavemont smiled and said, "That suits me. What about his spells?"

"I can foul the air so badly that he will struggle to breathe. Let him try to cast his spells."

"Do it then," Maveezh said, "I'm eager to meet his kin."

Paugh chanted the words, and the eyes of the two vemloks shone with an unholy light.

Thásalfen had dispatched nearly thirty vemloks with his blade and flames, and the floor had become slick with spilled blood. His dweedragons weaved essence of darkness to snare and bind the monsters, and harried them with minor burning spells. Their death fog would only endanger their lord, so they struck out from the Shadow as best they could.

More foes were coming. Thásalfen shifted into the third layer to get a moment's rest, letting his attackers pass through him harmlessly. They filled the room once again, searching for prey. *It might be best to retreat,* he thought, *to lead them away from the others.* But in his heart he knew that was a fool's hope. These creatures were guided by stronger wills, and those wills would have to be dealt with.

He realized, *I am weak. Had I not needed to raise a tempest over Gloamshire, I might have the strength to repel this force, but my power wanes.*

He decided where he would strike from next, and dove deeper to position himself. The Shadow roared in his ears, and the air friction against his body kept the chill at bay.

He saw the two vemlok aberrations slowly move into the room as the vylas chanted, and dark energies began to swirl about. Suddenly the Shadow grew colder as frost began to form on the walls and floor. Spilled blood turned to ice. The violent, gray turbulence had been freezing before the spell, but was now as cold as a winter wind in the uttermost north. He moved to the upper levels of Shadow to ease the chill, and found the Gray Baron coming right for him, eyes aglow.

He can see me, he realized, *and the cold does not affect the undead.*

The woman was advancing toward the tower door, snatching at dweedragons in her path. The poor creatures thought they were hidden and were caught off guard; they struggled helplessly as she drained them.

I must reach the vylas, he thought, *If I can destroy it, much of their advantage would disappear.*

But the vylas flapped its foul wings and moved out of reach, filling the hall with a horrid, choking stench.

Breath became precious, and his choices, few.

He could move deeper into the Shadow to avoid the miasma for a time, but the cold would sap his strength. He could move to the higher levels and fight, but the air would be sickening. He could leave the Shadow entirely, but the undead were all around him.

I have been outmaneuvered, he thought grimly.

He took a deep, frosty breath in the deep Shadow, then surfaced to the second level to fight. For a moment he thought he saw a black figure running through the hall, but he was too occupied to look again.

Maveezh grinned as Clavemont held his own against the ghostly figure of the elf lord. He was moving so fast, but the Gray Baron matched him; the strength and skill of a practiced vemlok warrior was a thing to behold.

She moved to the tower door and commanded her minions, "Stand aside and make room for the guadim! Form a semicircle around me. That's a half-circle, you dim-witted clods!" The vemloks shuffled to comply. "Paugh! Come and deal with this accursed door!" She felt an aggressive fire running through her veins; an ancient, primal force that made her feel unstoppable. *Dragon blood*, she thought, *not as pleasurable as elven, but potent! I must have some more.*

The guadim flew into the great hall, sneering as it flapped past the frosted statue of the elf queen, with her foot on the skulls of its kin. It landed beside Maveezh and began to chant a ward-breaking spell. Once complete, it placed its hand on the door and said, "Rot."

The wood turned pale and crackled as the grain split and decayed. Paugh leaped into the air and flew to the elf queen's shoulder to watch the duel.

Maveezh gave the door a powerful kick, shattering it into splinters and dust.

The chase was on.

Cindra and the others descended in a dizzying leftward spiral as crystal lanterns awoke to their presence. Shaz and ten of her brood followed, positioning themselves at twenty-step intervals to slow any pursuit. The party descended for two hundred steps, until the air grew cold and humid. A breeze moved up the stairs, carrying the smell of damp, musty earth.

The chamber at the bottom was dark and filled with the sound of tumbling water. Cindra lit her sword and Wenyssaya conjured her floating faerie-lights. Before them was a straight path of flat stone, and on either side were wide open spaces of dark mud under a vast ceiling. Limestone statues of elves looked down upon them, some as tall as trees. Water poured from the ceiling in the black recesses of the chamber, and fell into a distant darkness far below.

They soon came to a tunnel, perhaps fifty feet long, which ended at a large circular depression framed by a relief carving of elves and entwining trees.

"The outer door to the vault," Nixy said, "I'll need a moment to open it; there's a pass phrase and a mental picture I have to focus on, so I'll need to concentrate."

Adric asked, "Will they be able to get in?"

"Maybe this door, but not the next," Nixy said.

Drahn asked, "Is the next door the portal to Alhanna? Will the elves let us enter the spiwit world?"

"There is no portal to Alhanna," Nixy said.

The others turned to him in alarm, even Wenyssaya.

"No portal?" Cindra asked, "Then what's in this precious vault?"

He just looked at her gravely and said, "You'll see." He put his hand in the center of the circular door, closed his eyes, and began to whisper something in Ilvasawa.

A noise from the stairs made them turn; it was the echoing sounds of screams. Shaz and her dweedragons appeared before them out of the Shadow, looking out of breath.

"They are coming," she hissed, "we filled the stairs with death breath to slow them, but they are many!"

Cindra turned to Nixy, who was still focused on his task. No doubt he had heard. "How many?" she asked.

"Perhaps fifty," Shaz said, drooping her wings.

This took the wind out of the others. They turned to Cindra. "What do we do?" Adric asked.

She looked to each of them in turn, assessing their strengths like a battle commander. She also saw fear and doubt that bordered on hopelessness; she knew she had to hide her own.

She said, "The cavern outside is too wide open, so we have to bottleneck them at the entrance of this tunnel. Adric and I will hold them back as Deliah and Wen use their spells."

"That many vemloks will rip right through you," Deliah said, "What we need is a distraction, not a fight."

"I'm open to suggestions," Cindra said.

The screaming and moaning got louder as the stairway lanterns awoke across the dark cavern.

"I'll make a wall of fire at the tunnel entrance," Deliah said, "That should slow them, but I have to concentrate for it to last."

Cindra nodded and Deliah walked to the end of the tunnel.

Adric exclaimed, "She can't be expected to hold them off alone!"

"She's just stalling them," Cindra replied, "Our job is to defend Nixy until the door opens. Don't worry about her, trust me."

He shot her an angry look, then hefted his sword and shield, his face grim.

"They are upon us!" Wenyssaya cried.

A horde of rotting monsters poured out of the passage and ran down the path, filling the cavern with the cries of the damned. Clothing and flesh were in tatters from the dragon breath; faces were etched with blackened decay, and some were unrecognizable.

Maveezh was the last one down the stairs. Her face was gaunt and scarred with blackened pits, and her dress was faded and brittle. She floated above the throng and laughed.

Deliah cast her spell and a wall of flame leaped up from the floor to block the tunnel mouth. She quickly backed away, shielding her face from the wave of heat. A few vemloks stumbled through the barrier and fell, thrashing as their remaining flesh burned away.

There was a shifting sound from the door. Nixy stepped back as the stone rolled into the wall, slowly revealing a dark room beyond. "It's opening, come on!" he called.

Deliah backed down the tunnel as she tried to maintain the barrier, but something was wrong. A creeping mass of thick mud was spreading across the tunnel mouth, extinguishing the flames. Vemloks began to come through, and Deliah had no time to flee. She turned to her friends and shouted, "Go! I'll hold them off!"

As the others rushed through the door and Nixy prepared to close it, Cindra saw that Adric had not taken his eyes off Deliah.

"Come on, Adric," Cindra cried, and she pulled on his arm, "Nixy, close the door!"

The stone rolled slowly across the opening.

"NO!" Adric shouted, pulling away, ""We can't just leave her! Come and help me!"

"There's no time!" Cindra cried, "You don't understand..."

He threw off her grip and rushed to help Deliah.

"Adric, NO!" Cindra wailed, "*She can't die!*"

Vemloks leaped at Deliah, but she flung little bursts of flame in their faces. It was not enough to stop them all. She backed away, steeling herself for what was coming.

Maveezh strode through the torrent of mud with her arms wide, calling out, "Spirits of Earth and Air, that's what we are! I command the very clay itself!"

Adric reached Deliah just as they overcame her. As Cindra watched in horror, her most loyal friend and comrade-in-arms swung his blade with gallantry worthy of song. A few vemloks fell before him, but the others washed over him like a tide and came on.

"Cindra, it's too late!" Nixy called, "Cindra, the door!"

She wrenched her eyes from the horror to see that the door was half closed. Tears streaming, she ran with the vemloks at her heels. One grabbed her arming doublet as she crossed the threshold. She tossed her weapons into the room and wriggled out of it as undead fingers grazed her flesh, then she lunged through the narrowing aperture with no room to spare.

Before the door shut completely, a vemlok wedged itself in the gap. Nixy jumped back, pulling his knife as bony fingers reached for his blood. The thing was only halfway through the door when it closed with a sickly, grinding crunch, taking many other arms and hands in the process.

Nixy felt as if his heart had stopped. He stumbled back and fell, still holding his knife between himself and the struggling, rotting thing that used to be Mathen DuQuayne, the man he once called 'father.'

"Aaaadric!" Cindra wailed.

Mathen freed what was left of his ruined body and dragged his torso across the floor towards the one face he recognized; pain and hunger were in his eyes.

The dweedragons jumped back in panic, unable to breathe their mist in the confined space. Drahn tumbled out of Nixy's pack and got his first look at the broken vemlok. He was too close for a lightning blast.

Wenyssaya was in tears, frightened and mournful, but the danger to Nixy motivated her and she quickly pulled him away from the monster.

Cindra screamed, *"You killed Adric!"* She rose to her feet and kicked Mathen in the face. The half-body flipped about, spilling organs, but continued its desperate attempt at a most unpleasant family reunion. She scooped up her sword, stomped on his spine to keep him in place, and swung *Vyzeroth* in a glowing arc, severing his head.

It tumbled and landed at Nixy's feet.

He could only stare down in horror at the face that haunted his memories, but Nixy was unsure what to feel as those hollow eyes lost focus on his face. Revulsion? Hate? Misplaced hope and love? Pity?

All of those he felt, but mostly terror and relief.

Maveezh was delighted. They had found the accursed vault, and more morsels were trapped inside. With the combined efforts of her children, it was only a matter of time before it was all hers.

The vemloks had finished feeding on the woman and the brave, foolish young man, and were now clawing and scratching stupidly at the round door. She sighed, wiggling her toes in the mud she had summoned to extinguish the flames; the element of earth filled her with vigor.

The woman at her feet moved and groaned. *Oh!* Maveezh thought, *She might have a little blood in her yet.* She knelt and touched the woman's throat.

Deliah's eyes snapped open and she gasped.

"You're still alive!" Maveezh said, "I'm impressed. Don't take it personally, but I need what blood you have left. I'm afraid my beauty has suffered somewhat."

She drained her, but the woman's pulse returned. She drained more blood through her greedy fingers, and more, and more... and *more*. Her face lit up like that of a thief finding a stash of jewels. "Gods above and below!" she said, "What manner of being are you?"

Deliah whispered, "I'm the last thing you'll ever see."

Maveezh laughed, "That's my line, dear thing." Her features were already filling out as the decaying ruin of her flesh healed itself. "I wonder if you'll have enough in you to restore what those dragon-beasts did to my children?" She caressed Deliah's cheek, taking what she needed slowly, giving the woman with the haunting eyes time to recover her vitality.

"When this is over, we shall become friends, you and I. *Close* friends. You can be my pet, and I will only hunt when I want a little sport." She took Deliah's hand in her own, stroking the finger with the wooden ring. "What's this? A gift from a dirt-poor lover?" Maveezh tried to remove it but Deliah struggled, so she tore off the finger and held it up for a better look.

Deliah's cry of pain drew the hungry attention of the vemloks, and half of them shambled over to feed. Deliah glared at the woman in helpless rage; her gaze would have rattled the nerves of a battle-hardened knight.

"How fierce you look!" Maveezh said, "That's good. Breaking your spirit will make our friendship so much more enjoyable. For me, anyway." She dropped Deliah's finger on her face. "You can have it back now," she said.

"You talk too much," Deliah hissed.

"Darling, in time you will come to love the sound of my voice as I do, for it will only stop when I choose to hurt you." She dug her fingers into Deliah's ribs, drawing out another horrible scream.

The vemloks fell upon her with greedy hands.

Deliah recovered her severed finger and squeezed the verge ring, using its silver core to pull a surge of magic. Then she uttered a word in Ilvasawa, a word she only used in the most dire need.

"*S'hethsella!*"

Maveezh understood the word, though the language was strange and hurt her ears.

Inferno.

The vemlok woman's eyes went wide before they were burned away, along with her clothes, hair, and flesh. Her scream was lost in the roar of the inferno as it engulfed her children, charring them to blackened bone. Not even Adric's body was spared; only his chain shirt and sword set him apart from the ruin of his foes.

The remaining score of vemloks shrank from the flame, watching as it died down to smoke and ash. With no more threat and no will to guide them, they returned to clawing and pushing at the stone, some with nothing more than crushed stumps.

A few moments later, one of the blackened corpses twitched, moved, and dragged itself slowly towards the cool comfort of the mud pit beside the footpath.

Drahn used his new levitation spell to move Mathen's remains to a discreet corner. Wenyssaya did her best to comfort Nixy, who was shaking violently. Shaz and her dweedragons sat in a mournful circle.

Cindra had collapsed in a heap against the wall. "I killed you," she groaned, "I killed you, Adric. I'm sorry. I'm so sorry." She burst into tears; her sword lay forgotten and its light guttered out.

They sat in darkness for a moment, hearing only her sobs and the constant scratching at the door.

Then Wenyssaya reignited her faerie-lights and said, "Rise up! You may mourn the dead when the battle is won!" Her voice was so strong and forceful that everyone flinched. She blinked a few times, looking about in confusion. "I... I am sorry, I did not... I didn't mean to..." She knelt beside Cindra and tried to comfort her. "You did not kill him, Cindra. He chose his own fate."

"I never told him," she cried, "I kept my stupid word to her... I didn't speak when I should have, and now his blood is on my hands."

"What's she talking about?" Nixy asked, "Never told him what?"

Wenyssaya said, "Deliah cannot die. She is the immortal queen in her tale of the Dark Heart. She lives even now, beyond this door, though I would not wish to know in what state."

"It's twue," Drahn said. The other dweedragons nodded.

"Everyone knew this except me?" Nixy asked.

"And him," Cindra said, "I should have told him. I had so many chances, but I..."

"You could not have foreseen what would happen," Wen said.

"But the god could!" Cindra said, "The god could. He told me, *blood of friend and foe.*"

No one knew what to make of that.

The door moved a little. Moans could be heard through the tiny gap.

"Is there a way out of here?" Drahn asked, "You said there was a second door, but there's only a carved welief."

Indeed there was a relief statue carved into the wall. It was a tall, stately elven woman in a simple gown. She held up one hand, palm flat. In the other hand she held an oak leaf.

"It is *Iiyorona*, wisest of the *Niithramen*," the elf maid said, "*Yuviirava*, Beloved Lady." Again, her words carried such passion and conviction that the others looked at her curiously.

"We just call her Eyorona," Nixy said, "and she's the second door." He took a deep breath and tried to calm himself. "What's in the vault is something no one knows about, not even most elves."

Cindra regained her feet and wiped her eyes. She took her *Kos* knife and handed it to Wenyssaya.

"That is not my way," Wen said.

"There's only three of us left that can hold a weapon," Cindra said quietly, "No one goes without."

Wenyssaya took the wicked knife in her delicate hand. *This knife pierced Deliah,* she thought, *what other work will it see tonight?* She tucked it into her belt without comment.

Nixy said, "Stand back. The door won't stay open long if no one's using it, so don't stand there gawking. Once you enter, just keep moving. It'll be weird." He took out his glowstone necklace and lit it. Then he placed his palm on the palm of the goddess. "I'll go first."

Nothing happened for several seconds, but then there was a sensation like all the air and sound being pulled from the room. Suddenly, a dark, oblong portal of pure Shadow yawned open beside the statue, filling their ears with a low hum and the roar of wind through a tunnel. Everyone but Nixy jumped back.

"Stay close," he said, "and try to follow my light." He held it up over his shoulder and stepped inside. Both he and the light vanished.

Wenyssaya went next, followed a little too eagerly by Drahn and the other dweedragons. Cindra lit her sword and was the last to enter the darkness.

It was as if she'd gone blind. The only thing she could see was the white glow of *Vyzeroth* and a tiny, bobbing point of light ahead that must have been Nixy's glowstone. Neither the sword nor the glowstone illuminated anything around them. She touched the blade and only saw the black silhouette of her fingers.

The tiny light was getting farther ahead and fast, so she moved her feet. She was walking on *something*, but she couldn't tell what. Her boots made no sound; in fact the only sounds were the hum and roar of the portal. She had the terrible feeling she might get lost in this blackness with no way to find the exit. *Trust Nixy,* she reminded herself.

There was a light ahead now, and it was growing larger and brighter; actually it was growing too fast, as though the ground on which she walked was moving, carrying her to the exit. She had a brief feeling of vertigo before the portal disgorged her into a long, narrow hall; she almost tripped at the sudden stop.

All of them were looking around in wonder and dismay. Nixy was watching their reactions, as if validating *his* first impression of the vault.

As Cindra's eyes adjusted to the low light, she saw before her row upon row of stone tables, like the altar tombs in her family's catacombs. Upon the tables were effigies of bodies, carved and painted so skillfully, they seemed to be...

"Real!" she gasped, examining one up close, "They're real! What is this?"

Nixy answered, "Elven *spirits* pass into Alhanna, but their bodies stay here in the vault until they return... if they want to. This place is full of elder elves that left the world behind after the wars; there are some 'younger' ones too, if you can call them that."

Cindra reached out to touch the golden skin of a lovely elf woman with auburn hair that put hers to shame. The skin was warm and soft. She might have been sleeping, but she had no breath, no pulse.

Nixy said, "Are we all here? Why hasn't the portal closed?"

As if in answer, another figure stepped out of the black maw. He was tall and gaunt, with a wide-brimmed hat and cloak made of pure Shadow, which began to dissolve in the prime reality, revealing the torn green robes of a Eyoronian monk. His eyes burned with a fierce light; many fiery wounds smoldered on his forearms and chest, and one on his cheek.

Black Dexer spoke in a rasping, doubled voice, "Nixy. Boy. It's so good to see you..."

Thásalfen had exhausted his options in the great hall. The room was too cold, the air was too vile, and the enemies had been too many. His only option was to retreat, but to where? He was surrounded by doors that led to winding stairs and much smaller rooms. Against a living enemy, this would be an advantage, but his living enemy kept out of reach, and it was using an undead master as a sword and shield. No, his only hope would be the wide open.

The cold had only gotten worse in the hall, and his weather warding spell was his only defense. Every time he tried to banish the ice, the vylas countered him.

Then it cast a fire warding spell on the hall.

Intolerable.

Braving the chill of the deep Shadow, he rushed out of the fortress. The Gray Baron followed, only to run through a cloud of death breath. The dweedragons had been waiting outside for a chance to strike.

Thásalfen exited the Shadow and turned to see his opponent's state. The vemlok had almost no exposed skin, and had dashed through the gas so quickly that it affected him little. Still, his face and hands had turned gray and emaciated, with gangrenous patches along his jaw and ears.

As the fog cleared, he saw the dweedragons had suffered wounds from the baron's blade. Some would not survive. The Shadow Lord pushed his fury aside so he would make no fatal mistakes. With this foe, it would only take one.

Thásalfen took a drink of the *nenthiimore* and felt himself restored in body and mind, but not in spirit.

I must draw the vylas out, he thought, *it is the priority, then this creature, then his mindless minions.* He drew upon the substance of Shadow to create great raven's wings, which lifted him into the air and bore him over the forest island.

Clavemont raised his arms and followed.

Their aerial duel was a brutal ballet of turns, dives, and clashes of enchanted steel. Both bore wounds from the other, and both felt the pain, but only one was affected by blood loss. The baron was willing to suffer lesser wounds if it meant striking his opponent, so Thásalfen was forced to abandon his own attacks and parry instead.

Several times he sought to destroy the baron's weapon, for though it was enchanted, it was of lesser, human lineage. But the baron was a master fencer of inhuman skill, and would not let his blade be struck so.

The vylas had finally revealed itself; it was flapping in the air near the fortress, watching the duel. Thásalfen sent a call to his remaining dweedragons, and led the Gray Baron high over the fortress. Once the baron was upon him, Thásalfen folded his wings and fell, spinning feet-first towards the ground. The baron followed. The elf lord released an inferno in his wake that spun a vortex of flame in the baron's path. Then his wings snapped open and he dove straight for the vylas.

The creature tried to dodge, but six surviving dweedragons emerged from the Shadow and attacked, biting its arms, legs, and neck. Paugh thrashed in the air and spewed a terrible acid from its mouth, showering his attackers in liquid death, but the loyal servants held on to the last, ripping the putrid flesh as much as they could.

The Shadow Lord plunged *Navhwálreth* deep into his ancient foe, piercing its wicked heart. Then with a push of his mighty wings, the blade was pulled free and Paugh crashed upon the plateau. As the baleful light left its eyes, its body began to tremble and contort; flesh bubbled and a dreadful ichor oozed from its nose, mouth, and ears. Then the vylas exploded in a burst of filth and corruption, staining the good earth with a blight that would not wash away.

Thásalfen landed nearby, his golden features drawn in disgust. His wings faded back into the darkness, and he swept his blade to cast off the creature's tainted blood.

Clavemont landed on the plateau not thirty paces away. His gray clothing was slashed and burned, but there was not a trace of blood on the fabric. His white hair was scorched and patchy, and his white skin was marred by rot and fire. They began to circle at a distance, maneuvering for advantage.

"My compliments," said Clavemont, "You are every bit the legend I heard you to be."

"Do not seek to flatter me, *vylanmuath*. You meet your end tonight."

"Perhaps," Clavemont said, "but I would be more worried about the bodies in your precious vault. Maveezh has been yearning for elven blood since I created her."

They know!

He demanded, "How did you learn the truth of the vault?"

"I was entrusted with the secret by one of your elder kin," he said, "I kept that secret for over a thousand years."

"You lie," Thásalfen said, "None of my kin would betray that secret."

"One did for love," the baron replied.

"Name them!" he demanded.

Clavemont raised his sword, saying, "Navinessia."

Just then, the ground beneath the Shadow Lord erupted and many grasping hands took his legs. Clavemont rushed forward, flinging his sword as Thásalfen shifted into the Shadow, but it pierced his shoulder before he could sink below the second level. Then Clavemont had him pinned to the ground with one hand on his throat and the other on his sword arm.

Thásalfen could fight no longer. He left the Shadow for the last time as his blood and power were leeched away. He cast his inner eye to the vault, as only he could, and he saw what transpired there. He saw their desperate need and their likely fate. Using the last of his power, he sent word to his sister, and opened one final Shadow portal.

———————

Cindra had never seen Dexer in the flesh, and he was frightful. His head was a mass of burn scars, and his ears were two holes in his head surrounded by melted flesh. He still wore the monk's robes he had used to gain access to her father's castle. He had no weapons, but his fingers ended in thick, yellow claws.

Cindra leaped between Dexer and Nixy, as Wenyssaya shielded him further. Drahn and the dweedragons backed away, unsure of what to do.

"Bweathe on him," Drahn hissed.

"We cannot," Shaz said, "it would destroy the bodies!"

A deeper, raspier voice came from Dexer's throat. "So this is what the guadim wanted," it said, "the army of the elves! So much to rip and tear! But you two," he pointed his wicked claws at Cindra and Nixy, "I owe the two of you first."

Cindra lunged with *Vyzeroth*, thrusting and slashing, driving him back towards the portal, but it had closed. Instead, he scampered backwards up the wall to the vaulted ceiling, leering down at them.

Drahn took his chance and barked a lightning bolt at him, but the monster man had learned. He leaped over their heads and landed behind them, lunging at Nixy.

The boy dropped into the third layer of Shadow where he hoped Dexer could no longer follow. Drawing *Sugireth*, he dodged and slashed at the man's hands and arms. The Shard Blade was the only known weapon that could cut from below the second layer, so it might be the only one that would do any good.

Dexer screamed in pain as the demnox recoiled from his flesh; black bones of smoke leaped from his body as new wounds sparked and flared. The black apparition returned to the flesh and Dexer lunged at Wenyssaya, grabbing her by the throat and pulling her close. Her scream was cut off as he swung her about like a shield. "Drop your weapons or I rip her head off!" he snarled, "And Nixy boy, if you don't toss that damned knife, I'll tear her into seven pieces. Show yourself!"

Nixy appeared and tossed his knife away. "Let her go," he said, "take me if you want, but don't hurt her." Wenyssaya tried to shake her head, but Nixy said, "I meant it! Let her go."

Dexer said, "Now you, Gold Cat's Daughter! Drop the shiny sword."

She obeyed, extinguishing its light and tossing it towards him. She looked down and said, "Remember what Shaz taught you, Drahn."

Drahn nodded and grumbled something in dragon language. Shaz vanished when Dexer wasn't looking.

Wenyssaya squirmed in his grasp; her eyes became bloodshot and her face reddened. She could feel the claws digging into her neck. *Once he has Nixy in his clutches, he will kill us both,* she knew.

There was a little spark within her that kindled just then, and it grew until it was a roaring fire of bravery and action. Her hand dropped to her belt and grabbed Cindra's Minozhian knife.

Cindra edged forward and wiggled her fingers at Drahn.

Nixy took another step closer to Dexer's outstretched hand.

Drahn used his new levitation spell to lift *Vyzeroth* into Cindra's waiting grasp.

Wenyssaya pulled the knife and thrust it behind her head, piercing Dexer's right eye with the steel-tipped handle. As he howled in rage, she swung it back down and drove it into his thigh.

As Dexer pushed Wen away from him and squeezed her throat, Cindra's glowing sword flashed and severed his arm at the elbow. Nixy lunged for Wenyssaya and he took them both into the deep Shadow, where he dragged her to safety. Shaz followed him, having retrieved *Sugireth.*

Cindra fell into a guard stance as her training echoed in her brain, *Distance, timing, form, and direction. If you get one wrong, it can cost you life or limb.* She shuffled her feet forward and slashed at his neck, but he spun away. With his remaining arm he grabbed the body of an elf and flung it at her. She managed to dodge it but it cost her the next attack.

Black Dexer picked up his arm and reattached it. The muscles and tendons knitted together in moments as he laughed. "The flesh is easy to heal," he said, "and your shiny sword don't count for much." As his eye healed itself, he pulled her *Kos* knife out of his thigh as an afterthought. "Want to see how to really use a knife, little girl?" He swished it through the air like the expert he was. "Come on, dance with me."

"Alright," she said, "You want a 'fair' fight, monster man?"

Drahn charged his breath attack. The dweedragons popped in and out of sight, surrounding him. Nixy moved somewhere in the Shadow.

Cindra raised her blade. "Well, *screw* fair."

He came for her. Shaz and her dweedragons bound his feet and arms with essence of darkness, but it only served to slow him. Drahn scorched him with a blast of lightning, throwing him against a stone table, and Cindra rushed in and stabbed him in the heart. The blade sunk deep, but he grabbed it and withdrew it from his chest. She tried to pull free of him, but Dexer's eyes flashed with fire and he snapped *Vyzeroth* in half, extinguishing its light.

He rose with her *Kos* knife in one hand and the broken blade in the other. Cindra backed away, putting stone altars between her and the demnox. Her broken sword was next to useless, but it was all she had.

Dexer screamed in pain as new cuts appeared on his arms, legs, and torso. He slashed the air wildly, but his blades bit nothing.

Wenyssaya rose to her feet behind an altar where Nixy had left her. Her throat was red and bleeding, but she was not badly hurt.

"Wen! How do you kill a demnox?" Cindra called.

Wen's voice was hoarse. "I don't know if you can. The body is just a vessel."

Cindra looked around; they were surrounded by empty vessels. "Can it enter any of these?"

"I don't think so... I hope not," Wen said, coughing.

Dexer smiled, creasing his face grotesquely. He leaped over the altars and landed before Cindra, who was knocked on her back.

"Cindwa!" Drahn cried.

Dexer fell upon her, driving both blades towards her chest. She caught his arms, but he was far too strong. She pushed against him with all her might as her own blades were pressed into her skin.

Then she saw something above his head: it was a dark spot suspended in the air. It grew wider.

A Shadow portal?

Suddenly Dexer reared back in agony. He dropped the blades and scrabbled behind his head. Nixy had driven *Sugireth* into the back of Dexer's skull, and was holding it there.

Something dropped through the portal, and Cindra instinctively reached for it. It was *Navhwálreth*, and it fell into her waiting hand. The weapon almost vibrated with power; a rush of strength went down her arm and shoulders, and before she could think, she flipped the sword into a reverse grip and plunged it into Black Dexer's chest.

He shook violently as he pulled at the elven sword; he could neither free it from his body nor break it. His face contorted as the black bones of the demnox tried to pull itself from his flesh, but it was fading, growing weak. The wounds it bore, once gashes of sparking fire, were flickering like dying embers.

Dexer's body went limp, but the dark force within him still struggled. Cindra felt it tug against the Shadow Lord's sword, but she had it pinned like a bug to a wall and wasn't about to let it get away. The sword was exerting some kind of power to prevent the demnox from escaping, and something told her it was because she had willed it.

No you don't, not this time.

Nixy's little knife stayed lodged in Dexer's head until the skull face of the demnox wrenched itself free and turned its burning eyes to look at him. The boy was crying defiant tears, having just helped to kill the closest thing to a father he had known. The fire that burned within those black bones flickered and died, and the bones lost their shape, dispersing into the air like a bad dream.

Nixy pulled *Sugireth* from the body, and the metal glowed white with stolen power.

It took a while for everyone to recover their wits and calm their nerves. They all knew this horrible night was not over yet; the vemloks had probably gotten past the stone door by now, and there was no other way out of the vault.

"Where are we, exactly?" Cindra asked.

"Not sure," Nixy said, "The vault is surrounded by rock, so vemloks can't pass through the walls. I know it's not near the vault entrance, so they wouldn't even know where to start looking. The shadow tunnel could have taken us in any direction."

"They don't have to look for us," Drahn said, "There's only one way out."

"Can we walk in the Shadow to get past them?" Cindra asked, "They can't touch us, right?"

"The strong ones can see us somehow," Shaz replied, "In the stairwell, the woman saw me and pursued, only to break off before the others breathed. We were all in the Shadow, but still she saw."

"They'd just follow us until we couldn't stay under anymore," Nixy said.

"What if we wait until morning?" Cindra asked.

"It's never daytime underground," Shaz said.

One of the other dweedragons said, "Perhaps Navasram will rescue us?"

"Thásalfen is dead," Wenyssaya said flatly. They all turned to look at her in dismay. No one asked how she could be sure; her voice had that strange authority again.

"I had a feeling when his sword passed to me," Cindra said, "He had me do some kind of a ritual before the battle started. I think it was blood magic."

"So what do we do?" Nixy asked, "Do we take a look out there?"

"You mean open the portal?" Drahn asked, "I don't like that idea."

"Is there a way any of them could open it?" Cindra asked.

"No," Nixy shook his head, "It only opens for people with elven blood."

They all relaxed for a moment until Cindra said, "Shit."

"What?"

"Navasram is dead," she said, "That means vemloks killed him. Probably Clavemont himself."

"...Yeah?" Nixy said, "What are you-"

"He's *full* of elven blood right now."

They all looked at each other, scrambled to their feet, and moved far from the portal wall.

Drahn said, "I'm sure it doesn't work that way. Does it work that way?"

"If it does, what are we going to do?" Nixy said.

No one had a good answer.

Finally, Wenyssaya broke the silence. "I must give myself over to her," she said.

Cindra sounded worried. "Whaaat is she talking about?" she asked.

Nixy explained, "Well... Wen's kind of my auntie. See, um..." he scratched his head and his cowlick stood up, "she was born with the spirit of my father's sister. That's why she's been all squirrelly since coming here."

"She was born with... with the what?"

"She's the queen, the statue in the great hall. Her name was Drusayava, and she died a long, long time ago. Her spirit went to Alhanna, but she was reborn-"

"Two hundred and fifty years ago," Cindra said, as realization dawned, "That's when Navasram said he last spoke to his sister."

"Yeah."

"So she's going to... give herself over to the spirit of a dead queen?"

"I guess."

"Wen," she said, "Wen, what are you hoping she'll be able to do?"

The elf maid's voice sounded distant as she fiddled with the Ring of Autumn, "I do not know. Thásalfen sent me a name before he died. I must ask what it means."

"And she will know?"

"If the spirit lives in Alhanna, she will likely know."

Drahn said, "There's not much we can do if they get in. We can't use death bweath or fire because of the bodies, and we won't last long in a melee."

Another dweedragon whimpered, "We couldn't stop them outside with all our defenses. It's hopeless."

"Nothing is hopeless," Cindra lied, "As long as we draw breath, we have a chance."

It was what a commander was supposed to say, but she didn't believe it.

Only twenty minutes had passed since Black Dexer had been destroyed, but it felt like an hour. Wenyssaya was sitting quietly with her eyes closed, and everyone else was pacing nervously. Every strategy they came up with just delayed the inevitable.

Then Wenyssaya opened her eyes and stood. The others looked at her expectantly.

"Burn them," she said.

"What?" Nixy cried, "We can't start a fire in here!"

Shaz said, "The vault contains the future! We can't-"

"It contains the *past*," she said, "Those who could come have not, and those who cannot no longer matter."

Cindra broke in. "Wen," she said, "the room is too wide open. The vemloks will eventually rush us like before, and we can't burn them so close without burning ourselves. Besides, Deliah was the fire witch."

Wenyssaya gave her a stern look, like a mother to a heedless child. "*I* dance with the flames, for they are *my* friend," she said.

"Oookay then..." Cindra said, "What do we do when they come for us?"

"They will ignore us."

"Why?"

"Because there is plenty to feed upon between us and them," she said.

There were gasps all around.

Drahn asked, "You'd use your own people to bait a twap?"

"That's not what father would have wanted," Nixy muttered.

"Thásalfen would have wanted us to fulfill our destinies," Wen replied, "Our destiny is not to die here for the sake of these abandoned shells."

There was shocked silence.

Cindra asked, "Can we have Wenyssaya back, please?"

"No."

Just then, the portal began to open across the hall. Everyone ducked behind the nearest altar; only Wenyssaya stood in the middle of the aisle.

Or perhaps it was Drusayava.

"Wen, get down!" Cindra hissed.

The elf maid did not move.

Vemloks stumbled out of the shadow door, creating a flood of broken limbs, withered bodies, and filthy clothes. Their moans became shrieks of ecstasy as they fell upon the nearest bodies, draining them in moments. They spread from altar to altar, defiling the helpless elven flesh, which grew cold and gray.

Clavemont stepped through the door before it closed. He was whole again, save for his torn clothing. In fact, his mangled horde was becoming whole as well; flesh was restored, and crushed limbs began to heal. Hair regrew and the ravages of decay reversed themselves. They even began to show signs of awareness beyond their thirst, and that was truly terrifying.

Clavemont's eyes went to Wenyssaya, who stood defiantly across the hall. He looked like a man on a potent drug; there was an ecstatic gleam in his eyes and a smile on his lips.

"Lady Elf," he said airily, "are you one of the newly awakened?"

"In a manner of speaking," she said.

"I cannot wait to make your acquaintance," he replied, "though I don't imagine your blood will be as potent as that of the golden lord."

Wenyssaya bristled.

Cindra felt a burning desire to kill that man. She felt the strength in her limbs and the fire in her heart, and her bravery was building at a dangerous rate. She gripped the handle of *Navhwálreth*, savoring its overwhelming power. No object had ever *felt* magical to her before, not like this.

Clavemont said, "I shall attend you all presently." Then he spread his arms and threw back his head, announcing, "Welcome to the feast at the end of the world!" It echoed through the hall, and the other vemloks howled in reply.

Wenyssaya solemnly bowed her head, "*Leviiam, cuam vayiin,*" she said.

Forgive me, my people.

Then she raised her arms and cried, "*S'hethsella oros orovonith!*"

Flame erupted around the vemloks with a fury none had witnessed before. A wave of heat washed across the hall and over the crouching party, punishing their eyes and faces until they ducked behind the altars. Bodies burned, both elven and undead, and smoke filled the vaulted ceiling. Wenyssaya stood teetering in the aisle as the heat buffeted her body, a look of mad grief on her face. Finally, she let loose a ghastly scream and fell to the floor, exhausted. The roar of the flames became a crackle and a whisper.

The others came out of hiding, looking for signs of movement among the charred remains. Most of the bodies were burnt to cinders, and those elves that were not engulfed in the inferno had caught fire from the heat. Hair and clothing smoldered with little flames that would spread unless extinguished.

"Merciful gods," Cindra whispered.

Nixy went to the elf maid's side. "Wenyssaya?" he said, "Are you in there?"

The black dweedragons were beside themselves with grief, sensing it was finally over.

But it was not.

Arton Clavemont descended from the ceiling and landed before them, arms outstretched. His clothing was ruined, but his burned hair and flesh were restored even as they watched.

Cindra gripped the sword.

"Such power!" he said, "Had the Shadow Lord performed such a feat, it might have finished us all at once."

"Pity he didn't," Cindra said through clenched teeth.

"Ah, Lady Cindra," he said, "I truly hoped you would be dead by now. I did not wish to be the one to kill you."

"Like you killed my father?"

"Indeed," he replied, "I spared him the pain of mourning you a second time. He was my friend and I owed him as much."

Rage took her and she attacked, unleashing a flurry of strikes that were faster than she thought possible. Clavemont was forced to leap back, drawing his sword and parrying with mad speed.

"I see the Shadow Lord left you a gift!" he exclaimed, "I wondered where he'd sent it."

Cindra's limbs were in shock, aching from a burst of speed beyond their tolerance. Her heart pounded and she felt dizzy; even her fingernails hurt.

Nixy and the dweedragons were too shocked to help; they just stood there, agape.

"Let us see if you are worthy of its lineage," Clavemont said, and pressed a series of attacks. Cindra twisted, dodged, parried, and riposted, maneuvering between rows of bodies. The power flowing through her had increased, and for a moment she felt a rush of euphoria. But when the fighting ebbed, the agony began.

I can't do this, she thought, *I **am** doing it, but I **can't**.*

Clavemont circled an altar, stroking the arm of an elven warrior. His eyes were alight with wonder. "You can master a bonded elven weapon!" he said, "Most impressive. I always did admire your spirit. But now I'm afraid I must end our acquaintance. It has been an honor, my lady." He raised his blade and prepared another withering assault.

Cindra could barely stand. Her entire existence was a constant, throbbing ache. A part of her wanted to die.

"Navinessia," said a soft voice. It was Wenyssaya, truly Wenyssaya this time. Her violet eyes swam in tears and confusion.

Clavemont shot her a look.

"She forsook the safety of the Fortress of Thorns to rest under the watchful eye of her lover," she said.

The baron leveled his sword at the elf maid. "Do not speak of her."

"She bade him farewell and healed her spirit, but she could not return to him as promised. Why could she not return?"

Clavemont regarded her like a venomous serpent, but he could neither speak nor move.

Cindra used his distraction to edge closer. Every inch was agony.

The elf maid continued, "For a century she tried to fulfill her promise, and a century more, long beyond the span of mortal lives." Her voice choked up and she wept. "Despair took her, and she has mourned her love for a thousand years! She will bear the guilt of her broken vow until the world's ending!"

Arton Clavemont felt the rapture of the elven blood leave him. No amount of power or pleasure could overcome the veil of misery that fell over his heart. Maveezh had been wrong, so very wrong. Navinessia had not abandoned him for fear of watching him die. She had been true, and he not only destroyed her body, but crippled her spirit.

Until the world's ending.

When he turned back to Cindra, he was a changed man, a man with nothing more to live for. He raised his sword in salute.

"I made it quick and painless for him," he said.

Cindra returned that favor.

———

She awoke to the light of the morning sun. She was in her own bed in the guest quarters, staring at the vaulted ceiling with its fanning ribs of stone. For the briefest moment, she believed the previous night had been just a horrible dream.

Then she moved.

Cindra's body ached all over, and her shoulders, wrists, and back were in terrible pain. Turning her head carefully, she saw an assortment of vials and ointments on the nightstand. Shaz had raided the stores of divine alchemy last night so that Cindra could sleep and heal.

But it was when she saw the sword that many of her memories came crashing back. The Raven Blade was in its scabbard, hanging on a chair near the hearth. The raven's head pommel seemed to watch her with its emerald eyes. She remembered taking Clavemont's head before he could change his mind, cutting through not only his neck, but his blade as well. She saw both *Vyzeroth* and the Gray Baron's sword lying broken on the table; symbolic tokens of villainy and vengeance.

Then she remembered Adric; that had been a hard sight to see. The dweedragons had offered to macerate his body for travel, defleshing the bones so they might be entombed in Portshia. They could have prepared his corpse with a preservation spell, but considering the state he was in, bare bones might have been better. Cindra reluctantly agreed.

Summoning her strength, she moved her legs out of bed. It took many moments before she could rise.

The stairs up from the vault had been impossible. Drahn had needed to float her, supported by Nixy and Wen. *That* had been a most unique experience. They followed a filthy set of footprints up the winding stair until they found Deliah, clothed only in thick mud, searching through her baggage for a clean dress.

The great hall was a charnel house.

Cindra stood and found it easier to walk than she thought; her hips and legs ached of course, but the sword had not demanded nearly as much of them.

The sword...

She shuffled to the table and reached out to touch its handle, and she felt like it touched her back. Nixy had informed her that *Navhwálreth* was also known as *Vdomeni*, the Bleeder. She wanted to call it the Taskmaster.

There was a knock at the door and Deliah entered the room. "Good morning," she said, "I am here to help you dress, if you need it."

"I do. Thank you."

As she helped Cindra into her traveling clothes, she said, "I am sorry about Adric. I saw what he did... for me."

Cindra only nodded.

"I know he was... he felt, that is, he had feelings..."

"He was in love with you," Cindra said.

"Yes, well... perhaps infatuated," Deliah muttered.

Cindra snapped, "You don't rush into the jaws of death for an infatuation."

"...Perhaps not." She laced up Cindra's bodice over her dress as she carefully chose her next words. "They say you blame your vow to me for what happened," she said, "They also say you blame yourself for not breaking it."

Cindra just looked at her.

"Why did you not... Why did you let him love me when you knew I couldn't love him back?" she asked.

"No one should decide who we can love and who we can't," Cindra said, "Not a meddling goddess, or a meddling witch, or a worried friend."

Deliah nodded. "I wish I could tell you that I'll always remember his sacrifice, but I will do my best to honor it while I can." She finished dressing Cindra and said, "Trust does not come easily to me, but he deserved my trust. I should have told him myself." She sniffled and Cindra saw her wipe a tear from her eye. Deliah smiled and shrugged, "I know now he was worthy of my trust, because he was worthy of yours."

Cindra felt a lump in her throat and could not prevent the tears from falling. She wept for her friend, and Deliah held her until she wept no more.

It was late afternoon before they left the fortress for the last time. The bodies had been cleared away and burned, but the vile stain of the guadim remained. The body of Thásalfen the Shadow Lord was taken to the center of the forest island and a pyre was built. Wenyssaya spoke words of safe passage and lit the flames. Dark smoke rose through the skylight, earthy and bittersweet.

"What will you do now, Shaz?" Nixy asked.

"We will restore what we can, and rebuild the brood, young prince," she said, "We will continue the vigil in our lord's name."

Drahn asked, "Is Nixy not the Shadow Lord now?"

"Nah," Nixy said, "I don't think I'll ever be that. But I don't want to be Nixy DuQuayne either. If you want, you can call me Nixy Shadowskipper from now on."

Cindra smiled and stroked his cowlick down. Then she turned to Wenyssaya. "What should we call you?" she asked.

The elf maid said, "Drusayava died long ago, and had her time in Alhanna. All that is left of her now is part of me. Wenyssaya is my name, and it always shall be."

"Suits me," Cindra said.

"What of yourselves?" Shaz asked, "What path will you take?"

Cindra replied, "We're going back to Portshia to bury my father and safeguard my city. But where we go from there...? I don't think the *gods* even know that."

The Author

Mark Rude, also known as Markalf the Going-Gray, is a wizard from Phoenix, Arizona, deep in the land of Mordor. He studied the Arts at Northern Arizona University, in the age when painting was done with paint, not pixels, and a photo shop was a place where you worked with something called 'film.'

It was in this age that he forged the story of Cindra Corrina, intending to make the story into a graphic novel, though it was not overly graphic, and not entirely novel. The comic book he called *Passage* kindled the spirit of the story. Three issues were forged in the land of Mordor, in the fires of Phoenix, before the effort was abandoned; yet the spirit of the story endured.

Cindra's tale was of epic proportions, untellable in quarterly comics that came out only once a year. Yet there was hope. Using fewer graphics, and with more emphasis on words, Cindra's story grew like the light of dawn over a darkened land. Markalf was able to spin his yarn as never before, making a nice sweater, some hand warmers, and a scarf.

Markalf the Going-Gray lives alone in a high tower, where he plots the doom of characters great and small.

www.markrude.net
www.facebook.com/markrude.net.

www.ingramcontent.com/pod-product-compliance
Lightning Source LLC
Chambersburg PA
CBHW020536120726
47903CB00001B/3